had

res

of horror-magic stirred in'

'*Wereworld* is a brilliant ac

hooked. I can't wait for t

Shortlisted for the 2011

The designer of *Bob the Builder*, creator of *Frankenstein's Cat* and *Raa Raa the Noisy Lion*, and the author/illustrator of numerous children's books, Curtis Jobling lives with his family in Cheshire, England. Although perhaps best known for his work in TV and picture books, Curtis's other love has always been horror and fantasy for an older audience. *Wereworld: Rise of the Wolf* was shortlisted for the 2011 Waterstone's Children's Book Prize.

www.curtisjobling.com

Explore Wereworld if you dare at
www.wereworldbooks.com

Books by Curtis Jobling

The Wereworld series *(in reading order)*

Rise of the Wolf
Rage of Lions
Shadow of the Hawk

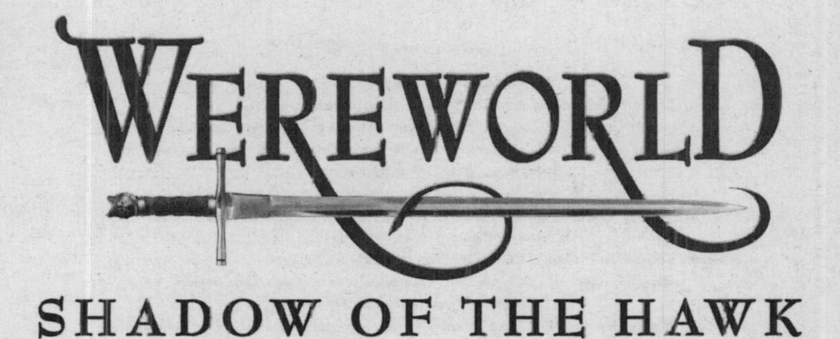

SHADOW OF THE HAWK

CURTIS JOBLING

PUFFIN

PUFFIN BOOKS

Published by the Penguin Group
Penguin Books Ltd, 80 Strand, London WC2R ORL, England
Penguin Group (USA) Inc., 375 Hudson Street, New York, New York 10014, USA
Penguin Group (Canada), 90 Eglinton Avenue East, Suite 700, Toronto, Ontario, Canada M4P 2Y3
(a division of Pearson Penguin Canada Inc.)
Penguin Ireland, 25 St Stephen's Green, Dublin 2, Ireland (a division of Penguin Books Ltd)
Penguin Group (Australia), 250 Camberwell Road, Camberwell, Victoria 3124, Australia
(a division of Pearson Australia Group Pty Ltd)
Penguin Books India Pvt Ltd, 11 Community Centre, Panchsheel Park, New Delhi – 110 017, India
Penguin Group (NZ), 67 Apollo Drive, Rosedale, Auckland 0632, New Zealand
(a division of Pearson New Zealand Ltd)
Penguin Books (South Africa) (Pty) Ltd, 24 Sturdee Avenue, Rosebank, Johannesburg 2196, South Africa

Penguin Books Ltd, Registered Offices: 80 Strand, London WC2R ORL England

British Library Cataloguing in Publication Data
A CIP catalogue record for this book is available from the British Library

ISBN: 978–0141–34049–4

www.greenpenguin.co.uk

Penguin Books is committed to a sustainable future for our business, our readers and our planet. This book is made from paper certified by the Forest Stewardship Council.

For Mum and Dad

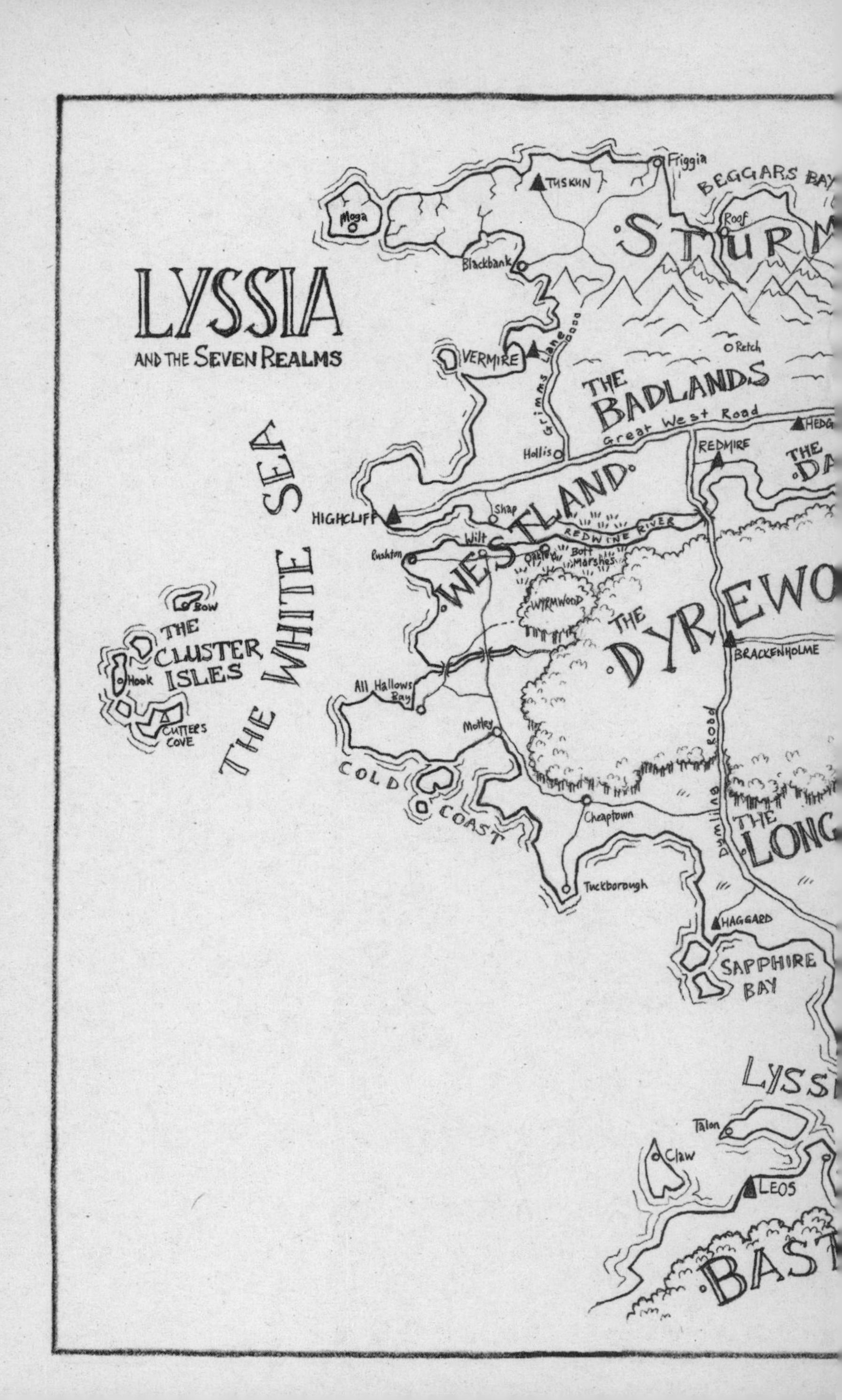

LYSSIA
AND THE SEVEN REALMS
Friggia
BEGGARS BAY
TUSKUN
Moga
Roof
Blackbank
VERMIRE
Grimms Lane
Retch
THE BADLANDS
Great West Road
Hollis
REDMIRE
HIGHCLIFF
Shap
WESTLAND
REDWINE RIVER
Wilt
Rushton
Bott Marshes
WYRMWOOD
BOW
THE CLUSTER ISLES
Hook
CUTTERS COVE
THE WHITE SEA
BRACKENHOLME
All Hallows Bay
Motley
COLD COAST
Cheaptown
Tuckborough
HAGGARD
SAPPHIRE BAY
Talon
Claw
LEOS

Rope
Shannon
SHADOWHAVEN
Roby
RIVER ROBBEN
LAKE ROBBEN
RED COAST
Bana
RIVEN
Bray
Highwater
Darke
STORMDALE
THE BARE BONES
AZRA
SILVER RIVER
Denghi
BLOOD BAY
OMIR
WINDFELL
THE SABRE SEA
Grazetown
Weatherly
Enders Point
Port Stallion
Calico
Widdershin
CAPE GALA
STRAITS
Wrecker's Reach
THE TEETH
Fort Rush
Ssotha
BRAGA
FELOS

Contents

PART I

Survivors

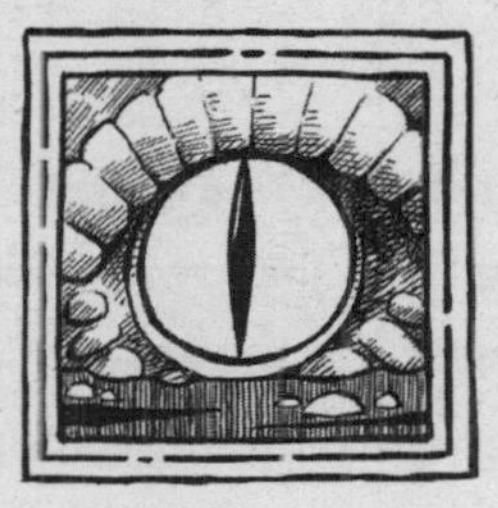

I

Savage Shores

The shrieks of strange beasts heralded his approach: a chorus of barks, booms and bellows that echoed through the jungle. Creatures dotting the riverbanks ran for cover in the dense forest, dashing out of sight at the figure's frantic approach. His legs powered through the brackish water, feet struggling for purchase on the sandy riverbed as he put distance between himself and the beach behind him at the mouth of the shallow river. Spots of sunlight broke through the emerald canopy overhead, illuminating him briefly as he passed, leaving frothing waves in his wake.

Drew Ferran looked back all the while, eyes searching the landscape for those who followed. He had to keep moving, couldn't stop for one moment. If they found him it would be back into the belly of the slave ship. The harsh cry of a nearby animal surprised him, causing him to stumble with a splash.

Indistinct shapes darted from tree to tree on either side of him, leaping through branches, shadowing his every step. Not so far away he could hear the shouts of Count Kesslar's men tracking him. Drew pushed on; he much preferred taking his chances in the wild.

He'd left chaos behind on the beach. The *Banshee* had only dropped anchor to allow the quartermaster to take men ashore to gather provisions. Those crew members remaining had made the most of the break, swimming in the bay or relaxing on deck. When the ship's cook had brought Drew his meal – foul-smelling strips of rancid meat on a heavy steel dish – the guard had casually unlocked his cell door. Drew had acted fast. Within moments both cook and guard lay unconscious, the dish having proved a surprisingly adequate improvised weapon.

Emerging on a deck loaded with slavers, Drew hadn't stopped for goodbyes. He'd instantly spied the nearby jungle-covered shore and leaped overboard. The chill ocean had been a shock to his system, but Drew was made of hardy stuff; growing up, he and his brother, Trent, had frequently swum in the White Sea. These clear waters had nothing on the Cold Coast. When he'd surfaced he'd kept his head down, swimming hard, not looking back as he headed for the beach. His newly missing hand caused him grief and made it difficult to swim, but the promise of freedom more than made up for this hindrance, granting him unexpected energy.

Manacled by the Ratlord Vanmorten in the palace of High Stable and surrounded by a horde of approaching undead, Drew had been left with little choice. By biting his own hand from his wrist, he'd lived to fight another day, but the phantom pains in the stump were a constant reminder of his loss.

Scrambling up the golden sand he'd glanced back to see rowing boats making for the shore, men-at-arms shouting to one another as they made to recapture him. Further along the beach he'd seen the quartermaster's team emerge from the trees, dropping their baskets of fruit and giving chase when they spotted Drew dashing towards the jungle's edge.

The river he was following had emerged into the sea from deep within the jungle. As the tropical forest on each bank looked impenetrable, Drew had opted to follow the river itself away from the beach. He scratched at his throat, cursing the collar Kesslar's slavers had secured around it. With the metal ring removed he would have been free to change, to embrace the Werewolf. He was amazed how quickly he'd come to rely upon his lycanthropic ability. A relatively short time ago he'd been a simple farm boy, content with his lot in life. With the discovery of his powers and the events that had followed, he'd initially resented his true identity – the last of the shapeshifting Wolflords. In time he'd learned to control the beast, call upon it in times of need, to save his friends and defeat his enemies.

Drew's feet caught against something hard on the riverbed, sending him tumbling forward, face disappearing beneath the turbulent water. Frantically, he spluttered back to the surface, struggling for air in a panic. Something large brushed against his side before hitting his legs hard. Drew's body was propelled through the air and then back beneath the water, unable to tell up from down. He opened his eyes, squinting against the storm of churning water and sand. A dark shape emerged, huge mouth opening wide to reveal rows of jagged teeth. Drew found his bearings at the last moment, kicking clear and dodging the jaws as they snapped shut.

Rising from the water, Drew gasped for breath, realizing with horror that he had been propelled into a lake. He caught a full view of the circling monster. Perhaps fifteen feet long, it bore no resemblance to anything he'd ever seen. Its skin was dark green with tough, gnarled ridges rising along the length of its body down to its great, swishing tail. Its head briefly surfaced and the beast's yellow eyes regarded him. Dozens of filthy teeth interlocked the length of its immense three-foot-long jaws, clasped together like miserly fingers. It seemed reptilian, like the rock lizards that inhabited the cliffs back home, but owed more in its terrifying appearance to the dragons from Drew's childhood storybooks.

The water erupted as the monster propelled itself at Drew, causing him to scramble backwards. Teeth took hold of his leg, threatening to pull him under as the creature began to roll. Drew disappeared beneath the foaming surface, his body spinning as the beast turned ferociously, trying to drown him. Drew felt his trousers tear, realizing with relief that the monster had only taken hold of the tattered material. With a kick he was free, propelling himself away from the chaos.

He hit the bank, scrambling against the muddy incline, struggling to find a purchase. The fingers on his remaining hand tore into the wet clay, the bank falling away around him. Exposed roots hung overhead, agonizingly out of reach. He leaped up, snatching at them before splashing pathetically back into the water. Drew staggered to his feet, working his way along the muddy slope, slipping and sliding as he searched vainly for an escape route. He caught a branch that was floating by and used it to try and hook the roots, pull them down within reach. Then the sound of surging water caused Drew to turn.

The monster's jaws had emerged from the water; the beast was launching itself at Drew. He turned the branch quickly, shoving it into the creature's open maw as it came in for the kill. The branch disappeared into its red fleshy gullet like a sword into its sheath. Instantly the monster broke away, thrashing and snapping its teeth, trying to dislodge the maddening branch. Drew didn't wait around. He kicked on, swimming once more as he headed for the lake mouth. Behind, he could hear crunching and splintering as the creature turned the branch into kindling. *Move, Drew; it'll be your bones next!*

Drew had no strength left, exhausted from fleeing his captors and then fighting the ferocious animal. He collapsed against a fallen tree that ran down from the jungle into the water, the monster racing up behind him. Drew tried to climb the trunk, crying out loud when a strip of bark came away in his hand.

But the killing blow never arrived. A rope net sailed through the air, weighted down along its edges by lead balls. The net descended over the creature, swiftly entangling the beast as it rolled. The more it struggled the tighter the net bound. More ropes flew into the lagoon, lassoing the monster and holding it fast as the crew of the *Banshee* appeared along the banks of the lake.

The fallen tree trunk shuddered as something landed overhead. Drew turned, backing away while looking up its length and squinting. The unmistakable figure of the slaver Djogo stood silhouetted in a shaft of sunlight. The leather patch over his left eye covered the empty socket Drew had left him with back in Haggard. For the first time, Drew saw an unusual scar on Djogo's bare shoulder, a triangle within a circle. *Like a brand we'd give the animals back home on the farm.*

'Nearly got yourself killed, Wolf.'

Drew looked back at the beast as the sailors subdued it, securing its limbs together, binding its jaws shut. 'What kind of monster is it?'

'A crocodile: if you think that's monstrous you'll love the Furnace!'

The crack of Djogo's whip made everyone in the water jump, as the long lash of leather snared Drew around the throat. His hand went to the noose as he struggled to breathe. Djogo tugged at the whip, the cord tightening its hold around the captive therian's throat, causing his eyes to bulge from their sockets.

'Struggle all you like, boy,' said the slaver, grinning as he yanked the lash tight, winding the whip in and hauling the choking Wolflord ever closer to him. 'It's back to the *Banshee* for you!'

2

Prisoners of War

The two captains knelt on the *Maelstrom*'s deck, each showing very different spirit. The older man kept his head bowed, although his eyes scanned the surrounding audience, weighing up the futile situation. In his twilight years, he should have been in some distant port, warming himself by a roaring fire instead of cowering on the pitching deck of a pirate ship. The fellow at his side kept his back straight, chest out, staring his enemies down, shouting and swearing all the while. Younger, cockier and with far too much to say, it looked increasingly likely he'd get them both killed.

Count Vega paced back and forth in front of them, letting the younger captain exhaust himself with his torrent of abuse. Behind Vega stood Duke Manfred, the Werestag of Stormdale, watching impassively. Queen Amelie stood beside the duke, leaning on his arm for support as the ship lurched against the waves. Bethwyn, her lady-in-waiting and constant shadow, stood at her shoulder. The Werelords were ringed by a crowd of pirates who kept a respectful distance.

Baron Hector, the young Boarlord of Redmire, stood behind the two kneeling men, watching the pacing Sharklord. Hector and his fellow therianthropes had fled Highcliff in the wake of the attack by the Doglords of Omir and the Catlords of Bast. As founding members of the Wolf's Council, he, Vega and Manfred had been instrumental in supporting Drew Ferran, the young Werewolf and rightful heir to the throne of Westland, as they defeated King Leopold, the Werelion. With the Lion trapped within Highcliff Keep, the Wolf's Council had held control of the city, laying siege to the overthrown king and waiting for his surrender. After the unexpected arrival of Leopold's allies, the group had narrowly escaped Highcliff with their lives. Their enemy had given chase, the remaining allies of the Wolf jumping on board the pirate ship, the *Maelstrom,* as the Wereshark captain tried to spirit them away from their foes.

The prisoners knew him. Vega's reputation as Pirate Prince of the Cluster Isles ensured he was known across the White Sea. When the small, ragtag fleet that had escaped Highcliff had been spotted off Vermire, three ships had come after them. Knowing that their companion vessels weren't built for battle, Vega had sent them on ahead, with the plan to regroup at the Sturmish port of Roof. The *Maelstrom* had then turned about and engaged the enemy. She'd charged into their midst, breaking their formation, leading them back towards the coast, away from the fleeing civilian ships.

'When the Kraken gets a hold of you he'll drag you down to Sosha's bed, leave you there for the crabs. You'd save Ghul a lot of time by dropping on your sword,' spat the younger captain while his companion remained silent.

'I would, dear boy, but I fear it wouldn't kill me,' sighed Vega.

He's not wrong, mused Hector. As a therianthrope the Sharklord was immune to most injuries, his accelerated healing repairing wounds that would be fatal for a mortal. There were exceptions to the rule, of course: silver and the physical attack of another werecreature could each lead directly to death.

There's always magick too, brother, hissed the Vincent-vile in Hector's ear. *Can't forget the magick now, can we?*

Hector shivered, shrugging the dark spirit away. It was unnerving to have the disembodied voice of one's dead brother following you around, especially as only Hector could hear him. The Boarlord had played his part in the death of his twin, and was paying the price each and every day. Hector rubbed the gloved palm of his left hand with the thumb of his right nervously, the leather squeaking as he circled the dark mark that stained the flesh beneath. The black spot had appeared the first time he had communed with the dead Wylderman shaman, back in the Wyrmwood. Talking with the dead was forbidden to all magisters, but desperate measures had been called for in order that he and Drew could save their friend Lady Gretchen from the wild men and their mistress, the Wereserpent. Each following occasion when he'd dabbled in communing, the dark spot had grown, the flesh corrupting with every dark act. Shivering, he clenched his gloved hands into fists and returned his gaze to the captured pirates.

'You think you're smart, Vega, but you're just lucky! It was rocks what ripped the belly out of the *Ace o' Clubs*, not any fancy move on the *Maelstrom*'s part!'

The captain was bitter that his ship had struck the submerged rocks, and understandably so. The following vessel had ploughed into the back of it, the two keeling over as men dived away from the wreckage of twisted timber and lashing ropes. That had left one ship for the *Maelstrom* to engage: the bigger, slower *Leviathan*. Pitched against the deadliest crew and craftiest captain of all the Cluster Isles, the big boat hadn't stood a chance. Vega's ship had outmanoeuvred it, dodging its catapults and sending flaming arrows, cannon fire and heavy bolts of its own into masts and deck. The battle was over and the white flag now fluttered from the mainmast – the *Leviathan*'s captain having no choice but to surrender to the count.

'Luck didn't enter into it, Fisk,' said the elderly Ransome, captain of the *Leviathan*. 'It wasn't chance that you were led into those rocks. Your enemy knew the battlefield. If you'd held back as I commanded the *Ace* might not have been reduced to driftwood. Stop whining; you were well beaten.'

Vega smiled. 'What can I say? I know these waters. Now if you're quite done, I'd like to hear about your masters.'

Captain Fisk laughed haughtily, spitting at the Sharklord. 'We won't tell you nothin', fish! The Kraken'll fillet you when he finds you!'

Hector shivered to think about what fate the Wolf's Council might face should they fall into the hands of the Squidlord

Ghul, known throughout Lyssia by his nickname the Kraken. Ghul's reputation was fearsome, built upon a lifetime of tyranny across the White Sea, showing little mercy to those poor souls he plundered. The Squidlord had been the eyes and ears of King Leopold, the Werelion, for many years, taking all that had once belonged to Count Vega in the process.

Vega nodded. 'Yes, yes, so you keep saying. The Kraken this, Ghul that, blah blah, cut me up – all very tiresome! You forget that forty-faced fool used to work for me; I know the squid *all* too well.'

'Then you know he don't take kindly to disappointment.'

'Well he should prepare himself for a world of disappointment if he thinks his army of sprats will ever catch the *Maelstrom*. Last chance, Fisk: what are Ghul's plans? What does his fleet consist of? Tell me and I'll spare your life.'

'I'd sooner embrace Sosha,' snarled Fisk defiantly, throwing the sea goddess's name in the Sharklord's face once more.

Vega's cutlass flew from its scabbard, sliding gracefully into the man's heart and out again in a fluid motion. The assembled crowd gasped, none louder than Queen Amelie. The captain of the *Ace o' Clubs* collapsed to the deck, dying eyes wide with disbelief.

He's a cold-hearted monster, whispered Vincent to Hector. The young Boarlord nodded slowly as the Sharklord flicked the blood from his blade. His chief mate Figgis stepped over Fisk's body, giving it a couple of kicks as he rolled it along the deck and hauled it over the side. Vega turned to Captain Ransome who stared back calmly.

'Been a while, Eric,' said Vega.

'Indeed, lad. You're still painting the sea red, then?'

'Only when I have to, old friend.'

'Spare the talk of friendship, Vega, if you're going to do me in like that idiot Fisk.'

'He had it coming. Parlay will only protect a pirate for so long, captain. This is war, after all.'

'You're on the wrong side, Vega,' sighed Ransome. 'You saw what sailed north from Bast. I heard what the Catlords did to your sorry fleet. There's good money to be made working for the Cats. Perhaps it's not too late. Maybe Lord Onyx can find a place for you in his navy.'

'I've burned my bridges there, Ransome. I've sided with the Wolf, if you couldn't already tell. I'm not sure the Catlords are as forgiving as you believe. A man is judged by the company he keeps, and I fear my choice of friends tells a terribly sorry tale.' He waved a hand in the direction of Hector, Manfred and Amelie.

Ransome nodded. 'Shame. You're a good captain. It would have been nice to sail alongside you once again.'

Vega crouched in front of the old pirate. His skin had taken on a grey hue, eyes darkening. Sharp white teeth glinted within the shadows of his face. 'Ghul's plans, Ransome?'

The captain of the *Leviathan* shivered, a lifetime serving the Werelords of the Sea still no preparation for the sight of one on the change. 'Half of Onyx's fleet has returned to Bast, the remainder is mooring up in Highcliff. It's unlikely they'll leave port until their cargo returns.'

'Their cargo?' asked Hector.

'Bastian warriors: thousands of 'em. Seems the Cats are making Westland their own.'

'So who patrols the White Sea?' said Vega.

'A handful of Bastian dreadnoughts are out there, but for the most part it's the pirates of the Cluster Isles. Ghul's sat on his backside for too long, growing fat on taxes he claimed in Leopold's name. Onyx has set him to work, now.'

'Doing what?' asked Manfred.

'Hunting you.'

Amelie gripped the Staglord's arm, face blanching.

'There were only three of you,' said the Sharklord. 'Where's the rest of your fleet, Ransome?'

'There's maybe twenty ships between Vermire and Blackbank, putting the word out that the *Maelstrom*'s a wanted vessel. There's a bounty too; you'll have every privateer in Lyssia hunting you before long.'

'He sees the *Maelstrom* as that much of a threat?' marvelled Vega.

'He sees the Wolf's Council as the threat. As long as the councillors live he sees Lucas's kingship as under threat.'

Hector's ears pricked up at mention of Werelion Prince Lucas potentially being king. Having served his magister's apprenticeship under the Ratlord Vankaskan, the young Boarlord had spent a great deal of time in the prince's company. He had endured the young Werelion's violent temper throughout his teenage years, and had finally been saved from the Catlord's cruelty when Drew had crashed headlong into their lives. A bully and a brat, Lucas had been spoiled by his father and his planned marriage to the Werefox,

Lady Gretchen, had been scuppered by the uprising of the Wolf's Council.

But what has happened to Leopold if his son now stands to inherit the throne? Hector thought, glancing at Queen Amelie, the Lion prince's mother.

'Lucas?' said Amelie. 'What of Leopold?'

'Dead, Your Majesty,' said Ransome respectfully. He might have been a pirate but he recognized royalty when he saw it. Manfred embraced her as she buckled at the news.

I didn't see that coming, brother, hissed the vile. *It sounds like the Werepanther has taken the Lion cub under his wing. See how the old woman sobs! Her record for keeping husbands alive is decidedly poor!*

'How did he die?' whispered the queen.

'Duke Bergan killed him, they say, although the king slayed the Bearlord in the process.'

Hector felt dizzy suddenly, the news of Bergan's demise hitting him like a hammer-blow. He glanced at Manfred who looked back pale-faced. The Stag and the Bear had been like brothers. Such news so soon after the death of his younger brother, Earl Mikkel, would wound Manfred deeply.

'What was Ghul's last command?' asked Vega, pushing past the dreadful news.

'Follow the coast. Get word to the Isle of Moga, bring the Sturmish pirates on board. If the price is right Baron Bosa might aid us.'

'He'll never join the fray,' said Vega confidently. 'He's a diehard neutral, that'll never change.'

Vega had told Hector about the Whalelord Bosa on the journey. Another old friend of his father's – the Sharklords were well known across the White Sea it appeared – Bosa would deal with any party if there were money to be made. He'd retired from piracy long ago, although there were many villains who took their booty to the old Whale. Vega had intended to visit Bosa, but Hector now wondered whether avoiding Moga altogether might not be a better idea.

Ransome shook his head, smiling grimly. 'Your old man might have been friendly with Bosa once upon a time, Vega, but that's history. Onyx is confident Bosa will sign up: it's join him or sleep with Sosha. There are only friends and enemies in the Catlords' world.'

Vega flexed his cutlass blade in his hands, sharing a look with Hector and Manfred. Ransome looked up, eyeing the sword worriedly.

'If you're going to run me through, get it done would you!'

Vega sheathed the blade, smiling at the *Leviathan's* captain. 'Fisk was an arrogant thug. He had it coming. You, on the other hand, Ransome, have my respect. I doubt you take a great deal of pleasure in hunting the *Maelstrom* and a few boat-loads of townsfolk. I give you the *Leviathan* back, your crew and the survivors of the *Ace o' Clubs* and the *Wild Fiddler*. Your lives are your own. I don't expect you to follow us; not only are you overladen with bodies, you have to replace those burnt sails before you can go anywhere.'

Ransome looked astonished. 'Thought you were going to do me in . . .'

'You thought wrong,' said Vega. 'I *do* suggest you reconsider your decision, however, and certainly think twice about rejoining the hunt. If we should encounter one another again under these circumstances I'll take great pleasure in tearing your throat from your body and feeding your guts to the gulls.'

Ransome nodded, struggling to his feet as Figgis cut his bonds. 'You won't see me again,' said the captain, but Vega was no longer listening, leading the Werelords away towards the rear of the ship.

Hector fell in behind, passing his own men, Ringlin and Ibal, once henchmen of his brother, as he followed. The two men of the Boarguard looked up, acknowledging him briefly with nods.

You seem to have straightened those two out, chimed the Vincent-vile. *Do you trust them?*

'More than some,' murmured Hector, his eyes on Vega ahead. Hector had once admired the count, the only fellow besides Drew who had ever stood up to Duke Bergan and the Wolf's Council. He'd looked out for Hector when all others had deserted him. Drew was gone and the Bearlord had turned his back on him. Vega had been there for him when Vincent had been slain, disposing of the body, tidying up loose ends and remaining silent throughout.

But as time went on, the debt he owed the count was becoming oppressive, weighing heavy on the young magister's shoulders. Vega had betrayed his 'friends' before: the Sharklord had been the one to leave Highcliff undefended when King Leopold took the throne from the old king, Wergar the Wolf. Could Hector truly trust him? What was to stop Vega from selling Hector out and revealing his dirty secret, if the price was right? The idea of owing anyone anything, especially the

Wereshark, was unbearable. He needed to pay the debt. He needed to be free of Vega.

The nobles gathered on the quarterdeck, away from the activity below. Ransome and his men were already being transferred back to the *Leviathan*, which remained lashed to the *Maelstrom* by boarding ropes. None of the ship's sails remained, the smouldering remnants hanging limply from the masts.

'It'll be days before they get her moving again,' said Vega, looking down at the sea chart that was laid out over a raised hatch.

'You realize he'll send word straight to his masters?' said Manfred.

'By the time that old girl limps back into harbour we'll be long gone.'

'Is Bergan really gone?' whispered Hector suddenly. Manfred and Vega looked at him, their faces grim as they nodded.

'So it sounds, Brenn bless his soul,' said Manfred.

Vega placed a hand on Hector's shoulder and gave him a squeeze. 'Bergan would have wanted us to continue, Hector. We need to go on to Icegarden.'

'Is that still the plan, then?' asked the Staglord.

'It has to be,' said Hector. 'We need to seek audience with Duke Henrik and find where his allegiance lies.'

'Let's hope he's feeling hospitable,' said Manfred. 'There'll be plenty of folk looking for refuge in the Whitepeaks once the Catlords march through Westland. I'd imagine half of the Dalelands are already on their way after the Omiri Dogs tore a path across Lyssia.'

'Death everywhere,' murmured Amelie, staring at the map, her eyes moist. 'It's hopeless.'

What think you, brother? Does she weep for Lyssia or her dead Lion?

Hector ignored the vile, reaching a black-gloved hand across to take hold of the queen's. She looked up at the young Boarlord.

'Your Majesty, we must stay together, stay strong. We need to show the people that they don't have to serve the Catlords – they have a choice. And Drew is out there, somewhere – he lives, I'm sure of it.'

Amelie looked warily at Vega who kept his eyes fixed on the chart. 'Do you feel no remorse, count?' she asked. 'Captain Fisk was unarmed; you could have thrown him in irons. You didn't have to kill him.'

'Please don't shed tears for Fisk, Your Majesty. He was a killer.'

'As are you, Vega.'

He looked up from the map, nodding. 'As am I, Your Majesty. Only I'm a killer who is on *your* side. We're at war. Fisk's fate helped loosen Ransome's tongue, I'm sure you'll agree. Please don't lecture me on board my ship. The kings you married were hardly shy of bloodshed.'

Amelie shuddered, releasing her hand from Hector's and turned to her lady-in-waiting. 'Come, Bethwyn,' she said. 'Let us return to our cabin. We might be stuck on board this cursed ship, but we can still choose the company we keep.'

Lady Bethwyn curtsied to the men, and followed an angry Amelie as she departed. She flashed her big, brown eyes at Hector as she passed, causing his heart to flutter.

That cow-eyed girl, Hector? And I thought you were toughening up. It seems you're still soft inside, chuckled Vincent.

'This "cursed ship" is the reason we still live,' muttered Vega. He looked across to Manfred who was watching the queen depart.

'Do you want to go with her, Manfred? Make sure she gets to her quarters all right?'

The Staglord glowered back at Vega. Hector watched the two Werelords, the air crackling with tension. Manfred's brow darkened, bumps beginning to appear beneath the skin.

The antlers, gasped the vile. *Here they come!*

'Watch your tongue, Vega,' said the duke slowly, trying to keep the beast in check. 'I don't appreciate what you're insinuating.'

'I insinuate nothing, Manfred. It's clear to me you care for her, that's all. As a friend, of course, nothing more,' said the Sharklord.

Your ridiculous little council is tearing itself apart, said the vile. *Look at them, bickering over that old widow like schoolchildren. You're doomed, Hector. All of you: doomed.*

'Shut up!' he shouted, his black-gloved fist striking the map. Manfred and Vega both looked at him in surprise. Vega smiled before returning his attention to the sea chart.

'Moga,' he said at last, poking at the island on the map. Hector avoided Manfred's gaze. His cheeks were flushed with embarrassment, but also something else. He may have spoken out of turn, but they'd listened to him; he'd silenced them. *Am I indeed their equal?*

'Moga? Really?' asked the Lord of Stormdale gruffly.

'Onyx has yet to make the Whale his offer. If we get in early, who knows? Perhaps he'll be struck by a rare moment of conscience. Maybe he'll do the right thing.'

'I would suggest we avoid Moga altogether,' said Manfred. 'Continue straight on to Sturmland. You're inviting danger by going ashore in such a dangerous port. The forces of the Werewalrus, Lady Slotha, are harboured there, are they not?'

Hector had heard all about Slotha, the Walrus of Tuskun. The tribal people of her remote region were known as the Ugri, fiercely loyal, owing more to the Wyldermen of the Dyrewood than the more civilized people of Sturmland. When Leopold overthrew the old king, Wergar the Wolf, she had sided with the Lion, gaining governance over the north-western tip of Lyssia in return for the muscle she added to the fight. In the following years she'd fortified her position in the frozen wastes, waging war on her neighbours in the Whitepeaks and striking fear into the hearts of sea traders. There was no love lost between the Walrus and the Wolf's Council.

'She has forces there, certainly, but Moga itself is still considered a free port. If anyone rules there, it's Bosa. Let me speak with him, see if I can win his aid before Onyx comes knocking.'

'We should sail on,' said Manfred. 'Hector; your thoughts?'

'We're low on supplies, Your Grace. We should stock up on fresh water and food. The few provisions we had on board when we left Highcliff are virtually all gone.'

'Besides which,' said Vega, 'our five fellow ships that fled Highcliff are ahead of us, somewhere. Chances are good that someone in Moga will have sighted them. Bosa has answers. Trust me, Manfred; we need to pay him a visit.'

The Staglord massaged his brow between thumb and forefinger, the argument lost. 'I think we're making a mistake.'

'We'll take a couple of boats ashore. Hector – can you oversee the securing of provisions? Manfred – you and I shall speak with Bosa. We keep our heads down, keep a low profile.'

Look at him, hissed Vincent. *He's enjoying this. Skulking about, piracy; he's in his element. He's pulling the strings, Hector. He's in control now.*

Vega grinned at the Boarlord and winked slyly. 'In and out. The Werewalrus Slotha won't even know we're there.'

3
The Black Staircase

The drivers cracked their whips, urging the procession of wagons and horses onwards and away from the curving cliff edge. The wagon wheels found their way into the ancient ruts worn into the dark rock road by centuries of traffic. To the people of the island the circling road was known as the Black Staircase, running all the way from the harbour below, through the city, around the mountainous island.

Drew pushed his face against the bamboo bars, looking down the cliff as the wagon he travelled in drove ever higher. There were six of them in the jail wagon, each equally miserable. No doubt Drew's fellow slaves had been picked up by Kesslar on his travels, and each bore the scars of the journey. Battered and beaten, the men were weary with exhaustion and the long time spent in the hold of the slave ship. The Goatlord Kesslar travelled at the front of the procession in a sumptuous caravan, his ill-gotten gains of blood, flesh and bone following miserably behind.

The Black Staircase rose from the docks through the strange city, past bazaars and merchants' stalls, before winding through the town houses higher up. Far below in the harbour Drew spied the *Banshee*, bobbing lazily in the crystal clear water, her cargo delivered.

At the highest point of the Black Staircase there was no sign of vegetation, the slopes of the mountain were covered with rocks and boulders as dark as jet. The road levelled out briefly as they reached the summit, turning in towards the mountain's centre. Here the wagons passed through a tall, white gatehouse. Lightly armoured guards stood to either side, inspecting the carts and their slaves as they trundled past. The people of the island reminded Drew of Djogo, Kesslar's captain, tall and rangy with dark, leathery skin. *Perhaps this is where the brute hails from?*

The wagons were moving downhill now into a bowl-shaped valley that marked the mountain's summit, a palace sitting at its centre. An outer wall curved round the grand palace structure, echoing the concentric circles of the Black Staircase. Terracotta rooftops dipped in towards its centre, the courtyard beyond not yet visible on the approach. Towers thrust up from the outer wall towards the clouds, their brickwork an ornate tapestry of black and white banded marble. The heat was oppressive; Drew felt it roll over him in waves. Occasional jets of steam broke through fissures in the ground on either side of the road, and hot gases belched violently from the earth. He held his hand to his mouth, gagging at a familiar scent in the air.

Drew's mind flew back to Hector's communing with the dead. He blanched as he thought back to his dear friend's dabbling in necromancy, speaking with the souls of the departed. The Boarlord had used a foul-smelling yellow powder, tracing out warding symbols and binding circles as part of the ritual. Despite the heat, Drew shivered. He remembered the undead playthings of Vankaskan in Cape Gala, and how it had cost him his hand. With a manacle fastened tight around his hand and a crowd of monsters hungry for his flesh, the choice between life and death had been a torturous one to make. When he closed his eyes, he could imagine the hand was still connected, could feel the flexing of ghostly fingertips. It was going to take some getting used to. Drew stared at his wrist, fully healed now, a scarred stump of flesh and bone. He sniffed at the air once again.

'Brimstone,' he said, as much to himself as to anyone who might listen.

'That's right,' said another slave, leaning against the bars on the opposite side of the wagon. 'Sulphur. What else would you expect from a volcano?'

'Welcome to Scoria!'

If the heat outdoors was stifling, inside the palace it was unbearable. Guards had led the shackled slaves into the colossal building, past crowds of onlookers into a huge, circular hall. Stone tables ringed the room, littered with food from the previous night's feasting. Flies buzzed over discarded pieces of meat, adding to the grim atmosphere. Torches burned along the wall, while a large metal grille covered the centre of the chamber, riveted in place to the polished basalt floor. A steady flow of steam emerged through the grating, turning the chamber into a sauna. A metal brazier, stacked with red-hot coals, stood beside the grille, long-handled brands buried deep within the glowing embers. Drew winced as he spied it, imagining what they might be used for.

The man who addressed the slaves rose from a tall marble chair. He was wearing no more than a loincloth, gold jewellery and a wide, slick smile. Three similarly garbed figures stood behind his throne, cloaked in shadow and steam. There wasn't a trace of hair on the speaker's body – the man didn't even have eyebrows, giving his face a permanently surprised look. His oiled skin glistened in the torchlight, reflecting different colours in the glow of the flames. Drew squinted, convinced his eyes were playing tricks on him. The man's flesh seemed to shimmer, first grey and then green, with a brief flash of blue before darkening once more.

Count Kesslar finally appeared from the rear of the group of slaves, accompanied by the Werehawk Shah, and made his way directly to the almost-naked man. Djogo stood beside Drew, his one good eye fixed upon the young Wolflord. Kesslar and the bald, barely-dressed man embraced, shaking hands heartily and laughing all the while.

'My dear Kesslar,' said the man in the loincloth. 'By the Wyrms, you've brought the enchanting Lady Shah with you, too! How is the Goat treating you, my lady?' He licked his lips, reaching a hand towards her. She backed away a step.

'Well enough,' she said pointedly. 'I trust you have kept *your* end of our bargain, Ignus?'

The bald man nodded, stroking his fingers over his smooth, oily chest. 'Like family, Shah. Like family.'

Drew didn't understand a word of what they were discussing, but paid attention nonetheless. He needed to return to Lyssia, to his friends and his people, so any information he could glean might hasten his escape. Shah was a strange one, staying close to Kesslar at all times. *Odd*, thought Drew, *considering the dark looks she always throws him*. He had his suspicions about her. The Werehawk had been the one who'd rescued him from certain death at the hands of the Catlords and carried him through the air, out of Cape Gala, bloodied and broken, only for him to wake up as Kesslar's prisoner. The notion made his head spin.

Ignus turned to Kesslar, pulling his eyes away from Shah. 'I feared you weren't returning. I was ready to send your remaining stock into the arena to celebrate your demise!'

'I wouldn't make it that easy for you, Ignus,' said the Goat-lord. 'I need every one of those souls in the Furnace, especially our brother therians. I've brought them a *true* champion to fight!'

'Really?' said Ignus, walking toward the crowd of slaves. 'Bring them forward so I may better see.'

The guards lowered their spears, jabbing at the slaves, forcing them to walk across the metal grille. Drew grimaced at the feel of hot iron against his feet, but he pushed the pain to the back of his mind. All those hours training to be a warrior under the watchful eye of Manfred back in Buck House were standing the young Wolflord in good stead.

He walked forward and stood before the man in the loincloth.

'So you're Kesslar's prize specimen, then?' said Ignus. Drew turned, looking back to the others who all struggled, stumbling, none daring to cross the hot metal floor. He stared back at Ignus, getting a good look at their oily host.

Ignus was maybe in his eighth decade. His neck looked deformed, strangely long, and he had a wide mouth with reed thin lips that seemed to stretch almost back to his ears. His eyes were bulbous, pale and honey coloured with misshapen pupils.

Ignus peered down at Drew's arm. Djogo had clapped his stump in a smaller, tighter iron, just to ensure he couldn't slip his handless arm from the manacle.

'He has only one hand, Kesslar,' Ignus said dismissively. 'Damaged goods. You really expect me to buy this one from you? This boy probably can't even wipe his own rear; he's not fit for purpose, let alone my ludus. I only take the *best* in my gladiatorial school.'

Drew's ears pricked up at mention of Ignus's ludus: *A gladiatorial school*, he wondered. *Is this connected to the Furnace that Kesslar and his cronies keep mentioning?*

'I'd be careful what you say, Ignus,' said the Goatlord, stroking his short, forked beard. 'There's more than one weapon a therian can use in battle, as well you know. This one bites!'

Ignus chortled. 'Go on then, Kesslar. Tell me what beast you've brought to Scoria, and I'll tell you what he's worth.'

'No, Ignus,' said Kesslar, wandering over to one of the tables and picking up a rotten piece of meat. He batted the flies away and collapsed into a marble chair, tearing into the rancid hunk with splintered yellow teeth. 'You guess what he is and I'll tell you what you're going to pay me.'

Ignus glanced at his companions who hovered behind his

throne. The three other men were also bald, bug-eyed and smooth-skinned, no doubt, Drew thought, relatives of the ugly fellow. Ignus returned his gaze to Drew, looking him up and down, standing back to better judge him.

'From Lyssia?'

Kesslar nodded, devouring the meat.

'The north, I'd say. A Ramlord?'

Kesslar spat on the ground. The spittle hit the metal grille, sizzling where it landed.

'The next Ram I see I'll fleece and gut. I've had all I can stomach from my pathetic cousins.'

'A Wereboar then?'

'Too much brawn,' said Kesslar. 'Look at his physique. He's built for the kill.'

'Some kind of Doglord?'

'Bigger.'

'A Bearlord!' exclaimed Ignus, clapping his hands together triumphantly. 'Have you brought me a Bearlord?'

'You were closer with dog . . .'

Ignus turned slowly, looking at Drew with a fresh, inquisitive gaze. He stepped closer, their faces inches apart. Ignus's bulbous eyes narrowed and his thin lips peeled back, his foul breath washing over Drew.

'Wolf?'

Kesslar began a slow handclap from the marble chair.

Ignus spun round. 'I don't believe you! The Wolves are dead. Wergar was the last, the Lion made sure of that!'

'He missed one of them in his eagerness to put them to the sword!'

'You're lying!'

'He's telling the truth,' snapped Shah. 'You could take the silver collar off and see for yourself, if you're so confident.'

Djogo reached into a pouch at his hip, withdrawing a short hammer and flat-headed chisel, used by the captain to remove his slaves' collars. He held them out to Ignus. The Lord of Scoria shook his head, sneering at the tall slaver.

'I see you're still making use of this beast,' he said to Kesslar.

'Djogo? Of course. One of the finest deals we ever made.'

'He's not bitten your hand yet as he did mine?'

'No, he's been dutiful to the last.'

Ignus puffed his chest out, oiled skin rippling as he suddenly grew in size. Djogo, for all his height, took a faltering step back as Ignus towered over him. He was threatening to change, intimidating Djogo, keeping the beast in check. *Interesting*, thought Drew. *Another therianthrope – but what kind?*

'I should have fed you to the volcano when I had the chance,' said Ignus. He dismissed the slaver with a shove, sending Djogo stumbling backwards.

'If you break him, you pay for him,' joked Kesslar. Shah kept her attention fixed on Drew, as Ignus rounded on him once more.

'Your master says you're a Werewolf?'

'He's not my master,' said Drew, after a long pause.

Ignus laughed. 'Very confident for one who is destined for the Furnace, aren't you?'

'If I knew what the Furnace was I might tremble for you.'

'You'll tremble soon enough,' said Ignus. He looked Drew over again like a piece of meat, licking his lips. The swollen eyes blinked quickly. He called back to Kesslar.

'How much then?'

'Remember what you paid for Stamm? Double it!'

Ignus spluttered. 'You're not serious?'

'Oh I am, Ignus. You wouldn't *believe* the lengths I've gone to, bringing this Werelord to Scoria. He's the most wanted therian in Lyssia, Bast too, no doubt, now the Catlords are after him. He's the last of the Grey Wolves – disputed heir to the throne of Westland!'

Kesslar rose and joined Ignus. He offered an open palm to the Lord of Scoria. Ignus moved to take it, snatching at thin air as Kesslar withdrew it for a moment. He stroked his short beard, nodding to himself and giving Drew a sly look.

'Twice Stamm's fee? No, I'm cheating myself.' He held out his hand once more. 'Make it *three* times, and we have a deal!'

Ignus took the Goatlord's palm and shook it firmly. 'You'll cheat me out of house and home, Kesslar, if I'm not careful.'

The slave trader grinned as one of Ignus's guards walked to the brazier of coals. Two more took hold of Drew by his shoulders, holding him in a tight grip as the guard stoked the embers.

'You'll need the silver one for the Wolf,' said Ignus, as the man withdrew a metal poker from the coals. Drew recognized the glowing silver symbol on the end of the device, a triangle within a circle; the same as the one Djogo bore on his shoulder. His rage rose, the thought of these villains scarring his flesh – the last of the Grey Wolves and rightful king of Westland – almost bringing on the change. To shapeshift now, with a collar about his throat, would prove fatal. He struggled as the guard advanced. A punch to his stomach from one of the soldiers sent him wheezing to the metal-grilled floor as the men held him still and the brand seared his flesh.

Drew's scream could be heard far below in the harbour.

4
House of the White Whale

A bitter wind blew through Moga's cobbled streets, sending shutters rattling and townsfolk scurrying for shelter. The autumnal weather was shifting across Lyssia, winter drawing ever nearer, and the north was always the first to feel the change. Inns and taverns crowded the seafront, jostling for the affections of passing sailors and fishermen, offering food, drink and company on this grim evening. The Torch of Moga, an ancient watchtower, stood proud on the town's natural stone jetty. Forty feet tall, the monolith rose from the promontory, centuries old steps carved around its perimeter leading to a timber platform. A solitary lookout stood atop, watching over the town and harbour.

The grandest tavern of all was the House of the White Whale, owing more to a castle than a drinking establishment. Three storeys high and taking up the space of four regular inns, the roof was crenellated with granite battlements, complete with turrets on each of the four corners. While providing fine food and ale to the wealthy of Moga, the White Whale was also famed for its gambling hall, where a man could bet on and with anything his heart desired, from the toss of a coin to the blood in his veins.

At the rear of the hall, beyond the gamblers and gluttons for punishment, a flight of steps rose to a mezzanine that overlooked the tables and bars, protected by a gaggle of roughnecks who looked more like pirates than guards. Here, on two huge satin cushions, sat Count Vega and Duke Manfred before the imposing figure of Baron Bosa. The Whale of Moga was busy decanting wine into three golden goblets. Manfred struggled to keep his balance – and dignity – on the cushion, while Vega sat cross-legged, looking annoyingly at ease. Bosa took a drink in each hand, rings and jewels jangling, and passed them across. Taking up the third, he raised it into the air.

'A toast,' he said, in a deep, fruity voice that belonged on a stage. 'To my dear old boating chum, Vega, and his delightful friend, Manfred!'

Manfred looked surprised by the baron's flowery language, but Vega didn't hold back.

'To the glorious health and long life of our most gracious host, the divine Bosa!'

This made the baron squeal with delight. He was the most unlikely looking pirate Lord Manfred had ever seen. Bosa was a giant, a whale in every aspect. His vast mass filled a chaise longue, his enormous belly resting on his thighs. His arms were lost within a black silk blouse that wouldn't have looked out of place on a dancing girl. Wobbling jowls linked up with a roll of double chins, his face a picture of jollity.

'It's been too long since we last shared a drink, dear Vega,' said Bosa, sinking his goblet of claret. His men stood nearby, keeping a respectful distance, but watching the two guests' every move.

'Indeed it has. I've been busy, in case you hadn't noticed. There was the small matter of Leopold stealing my islands from me.'

'Heard all about that, dear chap. Terrible business. Sounds like the Kraken's been riding roughshod over your archipelago with impunity!'

'He's a mollusc on the rear end of the Cluster Isles.'

'Is that any way to speak of a fellow Werelord?'

'Fifteen years, Bosa,' said Vega, sucking his teeth as he swilled the wine in his goblet. 'That's an awful long time for bad blood to fester.'

The Whalelord looked to Manfred and smiled. 'I must say it is a *tremendous* honour to have the Lord of Stormdale visit my little establishment. You're a long way from home, Duke Manfred. I can't imagine what drama has brought you all the way to Moga.'

Manfred could feel the colour rise in his cheeks and cleared his throat with a gruff cough. 'I'm sure you know full well what's brought us here, Baron Bosa.'

Vega raised a hand, making to apologize for his friend's straight talking, but the baron waved him away.

'They don't mince their words, these mountain men, do they, Vega?'

'I don't play these games very well either,' added Manfred. 'I'm not one for dancing round the issues.'

'You don't love dance?' gasped Bosa dramatically, before leaning over towards them, his face suddenly more serious, the fat cheeks hardening and his jaw now set. The smell of roses washed over the Werelords like a wave.

Bosa's voice was quiet when he spoke again, the playfulness gone. 'No more games, then. Tell me why you're here.'

Vega shuffled forward, trying to diffuse the tension between the Whale and the Stag. 'You'll be aware of the events in Highcliff. I'm sure word has reached every rock in the White Sea by now. The Catlords of Bast have marched to the Lion's aid; though Leopold is now dead, they're putting Lucas on the throne.'

'But *why* did they come to Lyssia?' The Whalelord jabbed his fat forefinger at the two Werelords. 'Did you not turn on the king and take the throne as yours? Is this not lawful retaliation by the Cats?'

'Not so,' said Manfred. 'Leopold had imprisoned the last surviving son of Wergar, a boy named Drew Ferran. He was rescued from the Lion's murderous rampage when he was a babe-in-arms, and had grown up as a farmer's boy on the Cold Coast. The king was about to execute the lad on the eve of his son's marriage to Lady Gretchen. We ensured that didn't happen.'

'Wergar has an heir?'

'Indeed,' said Vega. 'The rightful king of Westland. That's why Onyx came to Lyssia, to ensure a felinthrope of his choosing remains on the throne and controls the Seven Realms.'

'Where is this son of Wergar now?'

Manfred and Vega looked at one another awkwardly.

'We don't know,' said the Sharklord. 'It's complicated.'

'You've *misplaced* your king?' said Bosa, hiding a smirk.

'The boy is strong-willed,' said Manfred. 'He's his father's son, but with something else. He headed south recklessly, no army at his back, to save the life of a friend. He knows right from wrong, but has an empathy with others that's rare among the Werelords: he has the common touch.'

The three therians were quiet for a moment, each staring out over the gambling hall as the music played.

'My dear, sweet Vega,' said Bosa eventually. 'If you and your allies came here seeking sanctuary I'm afraid you came to the wrong place. I won't stand in the way of these Bastians, and I'm certainly not looking to pick a fight with Ghul. It's been many a year since my rear sat in a ship; I'm not sure it would fit any more!'

'We're not seeking your swords or support, old friend,' said Vega. 'I know what kind of hoard you sit on here, Bosa. You've the wealth of ten Werelords on this island, hidden Sosha knows where, the spoils of half a century's piracy in the Sturmish seas. You're sitting on a war chest.'

'I make no apologies for my good fortune. It's been hard earned, Vega. I'm a trader, a gambler, an opportunist; make your point.'

'The Beast of Bast will come knocking, Bosa. I merely ask you *not* to be drawn into this coming war on the side of the Catlords. I respect your decision not to fight alongside us, but please, don't assist those who'd see us dead.'

Bosa rubbed his jowls, tweaking the flesh between thumb and finger.

'Agreed, my dear Vega; I give you my word. If Ghul and the Catlords *do* come ashore, they can expect a dazzling smile, sparkling wit and a glass of the Redwine's finest, nothing more.'

Vega and Manfred rose from their cushions, each offering hands to shake on the deal. Bosa staggered to his feet, batting the hands away and embracing the Werelords, one in each arm. Manfred could just about see the count's smiling face over the Whalelord's shoulder; it appeared the Wereshark found great amusement in the Stag's embarrassment.

Below the mezzanine, towards the front of the gambling hall, Vega noticed a crowd was gathering, looking out of the huge bay windows that faced out on to the harbour street. He recognized a mob when he saw one, men and women jeering excitedly at a commotion outdoors. He pulled away from Bosa as all three Werelords turned to look.

'Moga might be my home, and a freeport aligned to no Realm, but there are other dangerous individuals on my isle. Did you bring anyone else ashore from the *Maelstrom*?' asked Bosa.

Manfred looked at Vega, answering for both of them.

'Hector.'

'Back to the *Maelstrom*!'

A dozen of Vega's men ran along the harbour front, struggling to carry barrels and sacks between them, the wind in their faces and the battle at their backs. Hector remained in the middle of them, urging them back to the landing boats. Half the goods they'd picked up lay abandoned in the market place, dropped in their hasty flight. Behind the fleeing sailors the fight continued, swords clashing as the rearguard covered their retreat. Hector cursed his ill luck.

His mission should have been straightforward. While Vega talked with Bosa, Hector was to requisition provisions for the *Maelstrom*. Vega's mate, Figgis, had accompanied him, guiding Hector to his regular supplier and leaving the Boarlord to strike the deal. It should have been uneventful; pay the man and take the goods back to the ship. Hector hadn't accounted for the distractions the port had on offer.

While he, Figgis and the more reputable crew members had got on with their job, a few of the men had slipped into a tavern for a stolen drink. One drink had led to five, and by the time they were ready to return to the *Maelstrom* an altercation had taken place. Unfortunately for Hector, his men, Ringlin and Ibal, were at the heart of the disagreement. The argument had become a fist fight, and the fists had led to knives. Two men lay dead on the stoop of the Lucky Nine tavern, cut open by the Boarguard. Chaos had erupted.

Passing beneath the Torch of Moga, the sailors ignored the shouts of the guard in the watchtower, instead concentrating on getting what goods they'd saved on to their craft. The fight drew ever closer, Hector making his way towards the battle to hasten the men along.

What fools they were to trust the Baron of Redmire with such a daring mission, rasped the Vincent-vile. *Who'd have thought a shopping errand could result in such bloodshed?*

Ringlin and Ibal were in the thick of it, three of Vega's men shoulder to shoulder with them engaged with ten Moga men, two-deep along the stone jetty, jabbing and hacking with knives and cutlasses. More appeared, rushing towards the melee, reinforcing the enemy.

'Disengage!' shouted Hector, his voice lost in the commotion. The goods were on the boats now; they had to beat a retreat and fast. There was no sign of Manfred and Vega, but they had to move – if they stayed they'd be cut down. He yelled again, but his orders fell on deaf ears. Ringlin and Ibal seemed to be enjoying the fight a little too much.

They're not listening, brother! Can you not command your own men?

Hector glanced down the jetty to where Figgis waited, beckoning him to get on the boat. The Boarlord turned back to the fight, slipping on the wet stone floor just as a cutlass ripped down across his torso. An opponent had broken the line having felled one of Vega's pirates. The man had intended to slash the magister's belly open. Hector's hapless balance might just have saved his life, his jerkin torn open as he landed on his rear.

The attacker was instantly on top of him, striking Hector's forehead with the basket handle of his cutlass. The Boarlord saw stars, throwing his arms up and clawing at the man's eyes in desperation. The man screamed as Hector's fingers found their targets, raking his face. The sound of battle was all around him, the air thick with screams and curses. A stray boot connected with Hector's temple, sending fresh shockwaves racing through his skull. He brought a knee up, connecting with the enemy's nether regions, making him release his grip with a cry.

Run, brother! Run!

Hector rolled over, crawling on all fours through puddles, vision yet to return. He could just make out Figgis ahead, calling him frantically. Then an impact in the small of his back flattened him, the knees of his foe crushing his kidneys. The man grabbed a handful of his hair, yanking Hector's head back, throat taut, exposed. He'd have unleashed the vile on the man, but all control was lost. Since the death of Vincent by his hand, Hector had been haunted by his brother's tormented spirit. However, with Hector's knowledge of dark magistry growing, he'd learned to control the vile, acquiring an ability to project the shadowy spectre forward like an attack dog. In the heat of battle, though, he now found his composure floundering. Hector felt the touch of cold steel at his neck.

No sooner had the blade touched his throat than it was gone, along with the man from his back. He heard a shrill wail and a *snap*, very possibly from his attacker. Hector rolled over. Both Vega and Manfred were in the middle of the mob, transformed into beasts. While many of the enemy leaped clear of the changed therians, some of the braver, more foolish souls, stayed for the fight.

The Werestag threw his fists into the men, dropping his antlers to catch and launch them aside. Bodies flew as he made short work of those who stood in his way. The Wereshark was more reckless, not caring how gravely he harmed his enemy. Limbs were torn free, fountains of blood erupting as Vega went into a frenzy. Within moments the pier was clear, the men from the *Maelstrom* regaining their composure, their foes defeated.

'Thanks for coming when you did, captain . . .'

Vega, still transformed, backhanded the speaker across the face, sending him sliding along the wet stone pier.

'Shut your rattle, Carney,' roared Vega. 'If I didn't need you on the *Maelstrom* I'd have left you here to be skinned alive! They'll be back shortly, and there'll be more of them. Get to the ship, we sail immediately!'

The men didn't move, staring at the transformed Sharklord fearfully.

'Are you deaf?' he screamed furiously, death-black eyes bulging, rows of razor sharp teeth bared. 'Move it!'

The men moved quickly, all but Ringlin and Ibal who had a self-satisfied swagger about them as they passed a prostrate Hector by. The short fat one patted the other on the back as they returned their weapons to their belts. Vega lunged, catching each by the throat and lifting them high. The men kicked at thin air, hands raking at the Sharklord's muscular grey forearms. Manfred stepped forward to stop him but the Pirate Prince wouldn't be halted.

'Back off, Manfred,' said Vega, focusing on the two rogues. 'This is your doing, isn't it? Pick a fight in Moga? They were Slotha's men. *Slotha's!* My boys are many things, but they're not suicidal!'

'They . . . dishonoured us . . .' gasped Ringlin.

'You have no honour!' yelled Vega. 'Why shouldn't I kill you both here and now?' He tightened his dark claws in their throats, a squeeze away from ending their lives.

'Because they're the Boarguard,' said Hector, over the mournful wail of the wind. He was back on his feet again, and Vega looked at him with disbelief. 'An attack on my men is an attack on Redmire. And on me.'

Vega let go of them, the two men crumpling to the ground in a heap. Both scrambled over one another to get away, scurrying to the end of the long pier and joining the other men on the rowboats. Only the three Werelords remained on the stone promontory, in an uneasy stand-off. They could hear Slotha's men calling for assistance, the beaten mob quickly growing into a fighting force.

'We need to return to the *Maelstrom*,' said Manfred, taking Vega by the upper arm. The Shark lord shrugged him loose, looking overhead at the Torch of Moga. The lookout had already set light to the pyre on top, the fire burning hungrily and devouring the stacked timber. Bright flames and dark smoke belched into the stormy night sky.

'Your idiot Boarguard might just have drawn Lady Slotha on to our wake. If you ever reprimand me again . . .' Vega choked on his words, furious with the young Baron of Redmire. He pointed at Hector. 'Control your dogs, magister. Or I'll control them for you.'

5
The Eighth Wonder

The spear struck Drew's temple. The skin split as his head recoiled and he crashed into the dust, ears ringing and head spinning. The weapon may have been blunt and fashioned from wood, but it was deadly enough. Drew scrambled clear as the spear stabbed into the ground where his head had been a second earlier. His attacker let the weapon glance off the floor and pirouetted, bringing it back down to Drew's new position on the baked earth of the ludus. Another roll from the young Wolf enabled him to evade the next lunge, this one destined for his bare belly. His enemy anticipated Drew's next tumble, jumping swiftly ahead of him to place a well-aimed kick at his jaw.

Just as Drew had hoped.

His hand was already coming up, snatching the foot from the air as it swung down. At the same moment he scissor-kicked his combatant's standing ankle, sweeping her legs from beneath her. She landed beside him, the wind knocked from her lungs. He reached for her, momentarily forgetting that he no longer had both hands, his left arm flailing at thin air. Cursing to himself, Drew rolled across, pinning her body while throwing his handless forearm over her throat. One of her arms was trapped beneath her, while the other was held in Drew's grasp. He needed to strike her one more time to the head. Currently, their contest stood at two strikes apiece, the next hit being the winner.

She struggled, writhing to break free, but he held her fast. She gnashed her teeth, trying to bite at his forearm, but he kept his flesh clear of her teeth. They were bright white, and sharp. Her eyes were amber, the black pupils narrowing into slits. He looked at the collar around her throat, silver like his own. *If she changes, she'll die.*

'Finish it!' shouted their gladiator master, a wiry, old fellow named Griffyn. He cracked his whip at the earth a foot from them. A cloud of dust exploded into their faces, and Drew chose the moment to release his opponent and roll away.

She was on her feet quickly, hissing at Drew while reaching for her wooden spear. Drew remained on his knees, panting heavily, looking up at the cruel sky. His skin was slick with sweat, the flesh sore from hours under the sun's burning glare.

'I won't fight her,' shouted Drew, glaring at Griffyn. The old man shook his head and readied another whiplash. The girl moved fast, leaping and landing behind Drew. He made no effort to evade her. They were both prisoners, both victims, being made to perform this foul game for the amusement of

Kesslar and Ignus. He hoped his mercy might strike a chord with the girl.

He was mistaken.

'Then you'll die,' she said, striking the wooden spear shaft hard across his head.

The clattering of plates and pots stirred Drew from his slumber, stabbing his skull like hot knives. He had a horrific headache, every noise hitting home as a hammer strikes an anvil. He'd been deposited on a trestle table in the mess, a corner of the ludus that doubled as both dining area and surgery. His presence hadn't prevented his fellow slaves and gladiators from taking their seats. They surrounded him, glowering as he tried to shuffle clear. A canopy of palm fronds overhead protected them from the worst of the midday heat, the training having halted while the gladiators ate and drank.

Drew swung his feet round from the end of the table and stood up gingerly, looking around the ludus. The other therians stood out against the rest of the slaves, together at a table of their own. While the humans wore their dull pig-iron collars, the therians wore silver chokers. Drew noticed that all gladiators and slaves bore the same mark upon their arms – the triangle within the circle – just as he'd seen upon Djogo. He looked at the scar upon his own left shoulder. His anger at Ignus and Kesslar for further disfiguring him remained undiminished. When he closed his eyes he could still feel the touch of the hot metal against his skin. The flesh was raised, the silver brand having done its damage well. *Djogo was a slave also, then? Or a gladiator?*

Shah stood nearby, in conversation with Griffyn. Both looked across when they saw him rise. Shah came over immediately, but the old man remained a distance away, watching keenly.

'Well, if it isn't the Eighth Wonder of the Furnace, a new Werelord the crowds can cheer for. You nearly got yourself killed out there this morning,' she said.

'They were wooden weapons,' said Drew, rubbing the back of his head. 'What harm could they really do?'

'Don't be arrogant, Wolf. Taboo has other weapons, remember – her claws could have removed your throat if she'd so desired.'

'Whatever therianthrope she is, she'd have risked death if she'd changed and she didn't strike me as suicidal.' He looked across the ludus to where the woman sat dining with the other therians. 'Ungrateful. But not suicidal.'

'You underestimate your opponent. Had you not considered she has more control of her therianthropy than you?'

Drew glowered at Shah. 'I didn't expect my kindness to be thrown back in my face.'

'Kindness will get you killed.'

'Excuse me,' said Drew stiffly. He didn't much like Shah, and was in no mood to be patronized by one of Kesslar's cronies. He passed by a serving table where a couple of the slaves were dishing out the gruel. Drew snatched up a pot of the anaemic looking slop and made his way to the therian table. There were seven seated in all.

'Mind if I join you?' he asked, his voice unsteady.

Each figure was fearsome looking, and none seemed especially pleased to see him. A look passed between two on the end who looked like brothers, heavy-set men with broad shoulders and massive hairy arms. One of them opened the palm of his hand and gestured towards a seat opposite. Drew smiled and sat down beside another large man who left him little room on the end of the bench. He glowered briefly at Drew, his broad nose and lips curling with contempt before turning away.

'Don't mind Krieg,' said one of the hairy brothers. 'The Rhino can be a bad-tempered beast at the best of times.'

'What's a Rhino?'

The brothers looked at one another in disbelief. Even the brute named Krieg allowed Drew a glance before shaking his head. Drew slunk low in his seat, embarrassed by his ignorance, scooping up the gruel with his fingers and shovelling it into his mouth hungrily.

'You're a Lyssian, then?' asked the other brother.

'They say he's a Wolf,' said the first. 'Is that right?'

Drew nodded, wondering where the conversation was headed.

'You're a long way from home,' said number two. 'Got a lot to learn too.'

'What do you mean?'

'Well, firstly, showing Taboc down there kindness is a surefire way of getting yourself killed.'

The young woman with the amber eyes at the opposite end of the table shot them a glare. The two brothers laughed.

'She doesn't play nice with others, poor little princess!' said the second brother.

'Shut your mouth, Balk, or I'll shut it for you!' she shouted. Balk waved her away dismissively.

'Save your boasts for the Furnace, little girl,' said Balk's brother. 'My brother and I will teach you some manners in the dust.'

Drew noticed that none of the others joined the conversation, each concentrating on their eating and ignoring the bickering.

'You're brave when you're with your brother, Arik,' the girl said. 'I'd watch your back; you can't always hide in his shadow.'

Arik grinned aggressively at the girl, baring all his teeth.

'Secondly, sleep with one eye open, Wolf,' continued Balk. 'I haven't seen you in the Furnace yet, but I suspect you can fight. Makes sense that your rivals will try to dispose of you in the night rather than risk death by tooth and claw beneath the sun.'

Drew looked at the others at the table, shivering to think that any one of them might happily murder him.

'And lastly,' said Balk, whispering the final piece of advice. Drew leaned closer to hear the words. The big man's breath was rancid. 'You'll find no friends here.'

Without warning Balk smashed Drew's face down into the bowl of gruel. His head bounced up back into the waiting fist of Arik. This time he flew back, the brother's knuckles catching him across the jaw. Drew toppled off the bench, his body slumping into the baked earth as the brothers tossed their bowls on to him, laughing and clapping as they departed. Drew lay in a heap, shaken and angry.

'Here.'

He looked up and saw the open hand of Krieg. Drew eyed it warily.

'Or stay down there like a dog. The choice is yours.'

Drew snatched at the hand, the big fingers closing around his palm. Krieg lifted him as if he were a child, plonking him back on to the bench.

'Thanks,' said Drew sheepishly.

'Don't get used to helping hands, boy,' grumbled the broad-nosed man. The Werelord opposite him chuckled. If Krieg was large, the other man was a giant – over seven feet tall, Drew guessed. He'd seen these two massive therians sparring in the ludus, hammering at one another with all their might.

'You should give the Apes a wide berth,' said the giant. 'They single out the weak. They're relentless once they get their teeth into you.'

'You sound like you speak from experience.'

'They've baited everyone here. They move on if you ignore them.' He looked down the table to the girl at the end. 'Taboo has yet to learn this lesson.'

The young woman snarled. 'They bite me, I bite back. They'll learn soon enough.'

The giant shook his head sadly. 'Seems felinthropes are incapable of turning the other cheek.'

'Felinthrope?' said Drew, shuddering. 'You're a Catlord?'

'What of it?' she asked sharply. 'You've met my kind before?'

'I've had my run-ins.'

A shaggy haired fellow the other side of Krieg leaned around the Rhino.

'You might want to put your differences aside. Once you get into the Furnace, you might depend on one another.'

Drew kept hearing mention of the Furnace. This was the arena where combat would take place, so named because of the battleground's location, Scoria's volcanic plateau.

'Depend on each other?' asked Drew. 'I thought he wanted us to fight each another?'

'That happens occasionally, if Ignus and his guests are in sadistic mood, but for the most part we therians are the main attraction,' said the shaggy man. Even in human form, the fellow's shoulders were oversized and stacked with muscles, his mass of dark brown hair framing his head like a matted thatch. His eyes were dark and heavy-lidded, his lips wide and downturned, giving his face a sombre, thoughtful appearance. 'The Lord of Scoria owns you, as he owns all of us. Our lives are over beyond the walls of the Furnace. We fight whatever they send out, be it human, beast or monster.'

'Monster?'

'You heard Stamm right,' said Krieg.

Drew had heard the roars of whatever animals Ignus kept for the arena. They were housed within the circular walls of the Furnace, out of sight of Drew and the other gladiators.

'So we look out for one another?' said Drew, struggling to make sense of the situation. The Apes, as the giant had described them, were clearly a wicked pair, and he doubted they'd spare a moment's thought for Drew if he got into trouble in the Furnace. The girl, Taboo, seemed likewise unhinged, waiting to explode.

The giant sighed, long and hard. He was around Bergan's

age, but time and the arena hadn't been kind to him. He was heavily scarred, his leathery skin dusty and grey. His dark eyes seemed sad, their lids downturned.

'You do what you must to survive. If you're looking for wise words, you've come to the wrong table. If you survive your first fight, take it from there. Live for each day, that's the only advice I have for you. Don't make plans for the future.'

The giant rose, nodding to Krieg and Stamm, before lumbering slowly away.

'The Behemoth speaks the truth,' came a voice from the far end of the table. The last of the seven Werelord gladiators was a lean, languid youth around Drew's age, lying on his back on the bench. He drummed his fingers against his stomach, the sound like the rapping of a woodpecker's beak, the flesh hard as teak.

'The Behemoth? Is that his name?'

'It's the name we know him by. I'm Drake, by the way. Just so you know . . . when I have to kill you.'

Drew chuckled, causing the others to look up. Even Drake leaned up from where he lay, twisting to stare as Drew's laughter grew in volume. The young Wolflord slapped his hand on to the table top.

'I get it,' he said, wiping a tear from his eye and rising to his feet.

'You get what?' asked Stamm, confused.

'All of this. I'm the new arrival. Some of you, like the Ape brothers, will be the cruel ones who'll taunt me. Then there'll be the one who I can't get close to for fear of losing my throat – that'd be you, Taboo.'

The woman remained seated, her face twisting angrily.

'Which brings us to the old timers: you, the Behemoth and Stamm, right, Krieg? I guess you've been here the longest? That just leaves the sarcastic, smart-mouth loose blade at the end there . . .'

Drake was already up off the bench and leaping across the table at Drew. Stamm and Krieg wrestled him back, while Taboo squealed excitedly at the conflict. Drew stood still, defiantly. He could feel the bile in his throat, thought he might vomit at any moment. His heart pounded, willing him to change, to embrace the Wolf. He couldn't show them how scared he was, couldn't let them see that they'd got to him.

'I see only one *smart-mouth* here, Wolf!' spat Drake. 'Who do you think you are? Where's your respect for your betters?'

'I was prepared to give my fellow Werelords all the respect they deserved. You each threw that back at me. It's good to know that therians are the same the world over; arrogance isn't unique to Lyssia!'

'You jumped up little turd!' grunted Stamm, letting go of Drake to reach over the table himself now. Stamm's huge mane of matted hair shook as the therian snatched at Drew, the young Wolf just dodging clear of a great dirty hand. Taboo punched the table with delight. Krieg found himself holding back both of his fellow gladiators now.

'Don't you see?' said Drew, his confidence now shifting to a heartfelt plea. 'You're *letting* Ignus treat you like animals. It doesn't have to be this way!'

'Spare your breath, child,' said Krieg wearily. 'Many have uttered similar words and all are now turned to dust.'

'Just so *you* know . . .' said Drew, staring at the therianthropes. 'I don't intend to remain here, let alone die in this sun-baked pit in the middle of the ocean. I'll be leaving Scoria as soon as the opportunity arises. It's up to you whether you'll join me or not. I lost a hand in Lyssia, was beaten, tortured and terrorized by my enemies. I need to return there, to help my people and settle some scores. You may be broken at the moment, but if you remember what it was that once made you great Werelords, come find me. I could do with some tooth and claw at my side.'

With that, Drew turned and walked away, leaving the therians staring at one another, lost for words.

On the outside Drew might have been the rightful king of Westland and the best hope for a free Lyssia, but on the inside he was still a farmer's son from the Cold Coast. *I just faced down a gang of Werelord warriors*, he thought. *They could kill me as quick as blinking*. It took every piece of will and nerve on the shepherd boy's part not to stumble as he went.

6

Blazetown

His mouth was thick with the taste of smoke. Hacking up a glob of dark spittle, he smeared it on the dirty material of his red cloak. He shuddered, thinking about the homes they had burned, the villages they had sacked, all in the name of the cause; all in the hope of finding the Wolf.

Trent Ferran looked at the burning farms around him. The sound of families sobbing mixed with the crackling of their blazing homesteads. He recognized the people, not so dissimilar from those he'd grown up around back on the Cold Coast; simple folk, for the most part, who busied themselves with tending their flocks and fields. But these people of the Longridings had aligned themselves with the enemy, siding with the Wolf and his allies. He would shed no tears for those who stood against the Lion.

Nearby, a large group of townsfolk gathered in a huddle, a

dozen Bastian warriors surrounding them. They looked pitiful, faces smeared with soot and tears, holding one another fearfully. Grazetown was one of the Longridings' largest settlements, a glorified village compared to other towns in Lyssia. They had no defensive walls, and the small militia had resisted as best they could, but, vastly inexperienced compared to the Bastians and Redcloaks, the fight had been brief and bloody. The surviving militia had been shackled. Trent didn't know what the plans were for them, but he hoped their families would be spared. He'd spilled enough blood for one night.

Trent looked at the Wolfshead blade in his hands, the sword stained dark from battle; his father's sword, found in the bloody ruins of Cape Gala, left behind by his traitorous brother, Drew. He wondered how many men Mack Ferran had killed with it in battle, fighting for the old Wolf Wergar many years ago. He thought back to the night he and his father had found his mother, murdered by Drew after he'd transformed into the beast. Trent and Mack had had no choice other than to join the Lionguard to seek revenge. The old man had spent his life trying to dissuade Trent from a military life. But with his wife so brutally taken from him, he'd had no qualms in letting Trent sign up alongside him. While Mack was fast-tracked into the Royal Guard of Highcliff, Trent found himself a new recruit for the Lionguard, his skill at horsemanship ensuring a position as an outrider for the army.

When Highcliff was taken by Drew and his allies, Mack had been killed in the initial skirmishes, apparently at the hands of the young Wolf's friends. Trent shivered to think about Drew, how he could have got somebody so wrong. They'd been as close as any brothers could be. He hadn't known what kind of monster Drew really was. When the change came and the beast took over, Trent had been helpless to stop him, as Drew betrayed his family and destroyed his world. Drew had taken both his mother and father from him. How many others would the Wolf murder? Trent had to stop him. He was no longer afraid of death. The cause was just, the Wolf his mortal enemy.

Sliding the Wolfshead blade into its sheath, he strode past the soldiers and their prisoners. Some nodded respectfully. He'd proven himself to his brother warriors now; there was no doubting his allegiance, his loyalty. Some had questioned whether he'd be able to stand up and be counted when the fight was on them; after all, he *was* the Wolf's brother. Those concerns had been quashed since their forces had left Cape Gala and begun their search of the Longridings; he was every bit the equal of his comrades.

An elderly woman broke from the huddle and rushed towards him, cradling a crying baby. She snatched at his cloak, bony knuckles clinging to the deep red material.

'Please,' she implored. 'Winter approaches and you leave us with nothing!'

The child wailed in her embrace. Its mop of curly blond hair was filthy, the face a mask of misery. The cries cut Trent to the bone. Here was one of the few innocents of Grazetown. Trent tore the woman's hand loose.

'I'm sorry,' he said regretfully, pushing the woman away. 'I can't help you.'

With that Trent strode away, the baby's screams haunting him as he departed. He walked between the torched homes towards the tall wooden building at the town's heart. This was the seat of power for Grazetown. The doors were wide open, soldiers carrying provisions and whatever else they could find from within – crates of food, barrels of wine, golden candlesticks, precious tapestries. He entered the building.

The Lord's hall had been stripped of all valuables. Bodies of slain militiamen lay about, including a few soldiers wearing the garb of the Horseguard of the Longridings. Trent stepped over the bodies as he made his way towards the soldiers gathered in front of the Lord's Table. Two figures knelt before them.

Lord Gallen and Lady Jenna, the masters of Grazetown, were broken figures. Gallen's long grey hair had been shorn off, a sign of disrespect to the Horselords. His wife sobbed quietly at his side. To the rear of the table the remaining family members stood, helpless at the hands of the Lionguard. Sorin stood directly behind the Lord and Lady, a grin as wide as the Lyssian Straits filling his broken-nosed face. The Redcloak captain remained at loggerheads with Trent, having still not forgiven the young outrider for snatching Mack Ferran's Wolfshead blade from him back in Cape Gala. Sorin made no attempt to disguise his contempt for Trent, taunting him for being the 'Wolf's brother' whenever the opportunity arose. He nodded at Trent, throwing him a filthy wink. Trent disliked the man, but he was an accomplished soldier.

'I ask you again: where's the Wolf?' said Frost.

The albino Catlord paced in front of the kneeling Horselords, every movement smooth, almost lazy. He carried his staff in his hands. Gallen lifted his gaze to Frost.

'I've told you already, we don't know his whereabouts. Since your people sacked Cape Gala my wife and I have been on the road, heading home. We were not party to the violence that took place there.'

'Come now, my lord,' said Frost. 'This isn't a difficult question, yet you insist on telling mistruths. You were seen fleeing the city with your fellow Horselords, those who had revolted against Lord Vankaskan.'

'He was no lord to us!' spat Jenna tearfully, instantly catching a look of warning from her husband.

'Now we're getting somewhere. I know he was an unpopular choice as Protector of the city in my family's absence, but he was your lord nonetheless. I do not seek a confession here; we know all we need to know from the noble Viscount Colt. He has very honourably told us *exactly* who participated in the revolt.'

Jenna sneered. 'That old nag is a traitor to the Longridings!'

'Yet he sits on the throne in Cape Gala now – imagine that!' The albino stopped pacing, swinging his staff behind his back and hooking it between his crooked elbows.

'Where – is – the – Wolf?' he said slowly.

'We don't know,' sighed Gallen. 'Brenn be my witness, we don't know.'

'You must know! You and your cohorts freed him!'

'Drew was gone when we arrived in the courtroom. All that remained were the dead and unliving, thanks to your friend the Ratlord!'

Trent trembled at the memory of the risen dead they'd encountered in Cape Gala, the handiwork of the Ratlord,

Vankaskan. The dark magister hadn't been content with killing his enemies in High Stable, instead raising them from death to torment them anew. Sorin withdrew his sword, the sound of the metal against scabbard causing the husband and wife to look warily over their shoulders. The sword shone, silver runes catching the light of the fires that burned beyond the hall's windows. Trent watched Sorin. He'd seen him question people every day since they'd left Cape Gala. It always ended the same way.

Gallen's eyes widened.

'I swear to you, we don't know where he went!'

'Wait,' said Trent, interrupting the interrogation. 'Perhaps he doesn't know the whereabouts of the Wolf. But there were others present who might.'

'Go on,' said Frost, gesturing to Trent to continue. Trent stepped forward.

'The Wolf had friends in Cape Gala, did he not? Lady Gretchen of Hedgemoor – the Werefox was close to him, wasn't she? She was with you when you left your city. Where did she head to?'

Jenna nodded at Trent, tears flowing as she looked at him imploringly.

'Wife, please –' began Gallen, but she spoke over him.

'If I tell you, how do I know you won't kill me? You have slaughtered so many of our people!'

'You have my word we shan't harm you, my lady,' promised Trent, his face grim. 'Please, answer the question and this torment shall be finished.'

'Calico,' she stammered. 'She heads to the coast.'

Trent straightened, turning to Frost. 'If she heads to Calico then the Wolf will follow.'

'You're sure of this, Ferran?'

'He chased her all the way to Cape Gala. If he lives, he'll find her, I guarantee it.'

'Good,' said Frost, spinning his staff. 'Find the Fox, find the Wolf.'

He banged the base of his staff on the floor, the metal-shod end striking the stone flags. An eight-inch spike projected from the top, the silver blade appearing in a flash. Frost turned the staff and lunged, the blade sinking deep into Gallen's heart. Frost held it there as the Horselord spluttered, his wife and family screaming in horror. The Lord of Grazetown slid from the end of the silver spear, collapsing on to the cold floor. Frost flicked off the blood before striking the base once more and the blade disappeared from whence it came. He turned, putting an arm around Trent and walked away, as Lady Jenna wailed mournfully over the body of her dead husband.

'You promised you'd spare us!' she screamed as they left.

'He said we'd spare *you*, my lady,' called Frost as he stalked out of the room, the young outrider at his side. 'Be grateful we're men of our word!'

Trent looked back at the Horselord's family grieving around their slain father.

'Well played, Ferran,' chuckled the albino. 'You're a shrewd young man. Come with me; that sword of yours is missing something.'

PART II

Red Sand, Dead Sea

I

A Beast At One's Back

For a moment he didn't recognize his own reflection. His face was tanned, beaten by the elements, while his black hair hung over his eyes, cloaking them in shadow. The water rippled as he ran his fingertips across the surface, the image fracturing with their passing, soon gone from sight.

Clasping the barrel's edge with his one hand, Drew dipped his face forward, submerging his whole head beneath the water. Although it was dusk, the water was warm after standing all day beneath the hot Scorian sun. He shook his head from side to side, the water cleansing the blood, dust and filth from his face.

When his head came up he was momentarily blinded, dragging his mutilated left arm across his eyes, blinking the water away. Slowly, he was adjusting to life without the hand, relying on his right for every little task. The phantom sensations would probably never leave him, but he could learn to tolerate them in time. As his vision returned he realized he was no longer alone. The roofless bathhouse was deserted, the human and therian gladiators had disappeared to the ludus to eat. Having spent the day surrounded by others, fighting and sparring, Drew had taken a moment for himself, disappearing into the baths of the gladiator school to reflect in solitude on his predicament. He should have known better. Privacy was a luxury he no longer enjoyed, and a lone soul separated from the pack would always be a target for predators.

Arik and Balk had appeared at the far end of the open chamber, casting long shadows in Drew's direction as they watched him, waiting for him to move. Drew could feel the adrenaline coursing through his exhausted body, preparing him for the coming fight. He wasn't ready for this. His body was battered and bruised from hours of punishing drills and contests. He eyeballed each of the brothers, baring his teeth, putting on a show of strength. But it was bravado.

The Apes had both sparred with him over the course of the day, and he'd bested each of them under the watchful eye of Griffyn, the old gladiator master. Drew had put his victories down to good luck and survival instinct. He was approaching each fight as if it were his last, each opponent in the ludus an obstacle to overcome if he was ever to see Lyssia again. Beating the Wereapes in single combat was one thing; defeating them both at once, however, was a feat that no gladiator had ever accomplished. The two brutes grinned, their huge white teeth shining within their ugly faces as they stepped forward.

Then they halted.

Their smiles transformed into sneers. Arik spat on the floor and Balk stalked away. The remaining Wereape growled, the sound deep and bassy, bouncing off the bathhouse walls and making Drew's guts quake. Then the warrior turned and lumbered after his brother. Drew remained motionless, suddenly realizing that he'd been holding his breath. Slowly he exhaled, his lips trembling as the air escaped in a steady, relieved stream. His extremities shook, his body still prepared for a fight that wasn't going to happen. *What had made them stop?*

'I can't always have your back, Wolf.'

Drew turned at the voice, surprised to see Drake standing a few feet behind him.

'I didn't see you there.'

Drake pointed after the departed Wereapes. 'They did.'

He walked past Drew towards the water barrel, grasping the wooden frame before plunging his head beneath the water's surface. For the first time, Drew got a good look at him. Drake was perhaps a year older than him, and by the look of his body he'd spent a great deal of time in the Furnace. As toned and muscular as he was, his torso was hatchmarked with old injuries, a grisly map of scars. Drew thought about his own awful injuries – the severed hand, the whipmarks on his back from Highcliff, his brand from the Furnace – and felt an empathy for another person that until that moment had been missing since he left Lyssia.

With alarm, he realized that Drake's head had been submerged for a dreadfully long time. Was Drake trying to take his own life? Drew lurched forward, grabbing the other therian by the shoulder and yanking him back out of the barrel. The two tumbled into the dirt, Drake beating Drew away with an expression of deep irritation on his face.

'What are you doing?'

'You'd been under for ages,' said Drew. 'I thought . . .'

'You thought what? I'd drowned?'

Drake got to his feet, dusting himself down, his torso and head soaking. He ran his hands through his hair, slicking it away from his face.

'You've got a lot to learn about the therians of Bast, Wolf,' chuckled Drake.

'I'm a Werecrocodile. Water is the least of my worries.'

'I fought one of those croc-creatures,' Drew gasped. 'They're like *dragons*!'

Drake laughed. 'I suppose so. My father always told me we were descended from the dragons. Perhaps he was on to something.'

Drake held his hand out to Drew, snatching his arm and helping him to his feet.

'I'm not the only Reptilelord – there are a few of us,' he said wearily, glancing towards the open archway that led from the baths back into the ludus.

'You're different when you're away from the others,' said Drew, warming to the other therian.

'I have a reputation to keep up, Wolf. I'm a killer. It'd do me no good if they all thought I was stepping into everyone else's fight. They'd think I was going soft.'

'So what was this? A rare moment of compassion?'

Drake looked hard at Drew. 'You and I aren't so different.'

'You feel that too?' said Drew. 'It's been so long since I've had a proper conversation with someone, I'd almost forgotten what it felt like. This was the last place I expected to find friendship.'

Drake arched a thin eyebrow at Drew's words. 'Friendship? You're getting ahead of yourself, Wolf. I see myself in you, back when I first arrived on Scoria.'

'When was that?'

'Nine years ago.'

'Nine years?' exclaimed Drew, unable to hide his astonishment. He tried to imagine what he was doing nine years ago. He was probably playing with the lambs on the farm, or hanging off his mother's apron strings. Drake had been in the ludus all that time, a child, just like Drew?

'I know,' replied Drake, thinking for a moment. 'I've spent half my life in this hellhole. I can hardly remember my life before the Furnace.'

Drew expected to see a change in Drake's mood, but it didn't happen. The Crocodile simply leaned back against the stone wall of the baths and stared up into the darkening sky.

'What was your story, before all this?' Drake asked.

Now it was Drew's turn to smile. 'How long do you have?'

He gave Drake a brief summary of his life, from growing up on the farm to the discovery of his lycanthropy and all that had followed.

'The last of the Grey Wolves of Lyssia, eh?' said Drake, sucking his teeth. 'You know, your old man was like a bogeyman to the people of Bast. He was the "enemy across the water", the monster who was going to sail south and attack our lands. Little did we know the real foe was closer to home.'

'Closer to home?'

'The Catlords,' muttered Drake. 'They're the reason I'm here. They conquered my people, took our land for their own and stole hundreds of children, like me. I often wonder what became of my family, whether the Cats spared my mother's life or killed her as they did my father.'

'Have you been fighting since then?'

'By the Wyrm's teeth, no! After I was brought to Scoria, I was put to work as a slave in Ignus's palace. When I began to change from child into youth they tired of me quickly – I was a liability. The last thing they needed was a Werecrocodile on the cusp of the change wandering around the palace. They sent me down here, under Griffyn's tutelage. I started in the ludus the same time as Taboo.'

'He seems strict.'

'Griffyn? I suppose he is. The old man's doing you a favour. If he cracks his whip or shoves you back into the sand to spar one more time, just remember: he's helping you stay alive. If he shows you no mercy, that's because you can expect none in the Furnace. Believe me, if anyone knows how to survive the arena, it's him.'

'Griffyn? Why?'

'He was a gladiator once himself, possibly the greatest to ever fight in the Furnace. Five years or so he fought for Ignus and his brothers. He was the crowd's favourite, a true champion. If ever a gladiator earned his freedom, it was him.'

'He doesn't look free to me.'

Drake shrugged. 'He's as free as you can ever expect to be when you're owned by Ignus. He no longer wakes each morning wondering whether the day will be his last. You and I don't have that luxury.'

Drew thought about the old man, finding it hard to imagine how he had ever been a gladiator, let alone a champion.

'How is it that Taboo is here – a prisoner, a gladiator – if she's a Felinthrope?'

'That's a question you need to ask Taboo. She'll tear my throat out if I go blabbing about her past.'

'You know her well, then?'

'Well enough, Wolf. She's the closest thing to a friend I'll ever have.'

'That's sweet.'

Drake cackled. 'Don't talk soft, Wolf. I'll still have to kill her if we come face to face in the Furnace.'

Drew shivered at the Crocodile's cold words. 'How can you say that so matter-of-factly?'

Drake turned to Drew and prodded a finger in the young Wolflord's chest. 'You need to wake up, and fast,' he said. 'This – you and me talking, shooting our mouths off – this is fun. This feels almost normal, like how folk talk to one another beyond the walls of the Furnace. Only we'll never get to experience that, will we? We're stuck here, and thinking about any other life is sheer folly. You're a gladiator, Drew, and gladiators fight and die. Don't ever forget that.'

He was about to jab Drew in the chest again with his final comment when Drew caught his finger.

'There's something you've forgotten, Drake. We may be

prisoners for now, at the mercy of Ignus and Kesslar, but we're Werelords. Think of the power each of us possesses, and what we could do if we worked together. There *is* a life for us beyond these walls. And I intend to return to it.'

Drew turned towards the ludus. 'Thanks for stepping in with the Ape brothers, Drake,' he said over his shoulder as he made for the archway from the bathhouse. 'But if you're worried about losing face in front of the other gladiators, next time feel free to leave me to fight my own battles.'

The Werecrocodile watched the Wolf go. 'You're on your own, Wolf!' he shouted after him, chuckling hollowly as Drew disappeared.

2

Deadly Waters

The *Maelstrom* remained tantalizingly out of reach of the two chasing ships' cannons, her eight white sails faintly visible in the dim light of dusk. The pursuers had been dogging the pirate ship for days now, hot on her heels since she'd fled Moga in a mist of blood. The ships represented the twin enemies of the *Maelstrom* on the high seas: the *Rainbow Serpent* of Lady Slotha and the *Quiet Death* from the Cluster Isles. Slotha had not sat idle since hearing of the bloodshed in Moga, sending the *Rainbow Serpent* out immediately. The *Quiet Death* had joined the chase not long afterwards, the lead ship in the Weresquid Ghul's fearsome fleet.

While the captain of the *Rainbow Serpent* wasn't known to the crew of the *Maelstrom*, they knew the *Quiet Death*'s commander all too well. Captain Klay was another of the Sealords, a therian of the ocean like Vega and Ghul. A pirate first and a Werelord second, the Barracuda was a butcher of men and a maker of widows. Sticking close to the *Rainbow Serpent,* Lord Klay was determined to be the Werelord to capture the elusive Count Vega and, better still, put the Shark to the sword.

Klay stood at the prow of the *Quiet Death*, as it sailed slightly ahead and to starboard of the *Rainbow Serpent*, willing his vessel to greater speeds, but his ship remained at a distance from the *Maelstrom*. Vega's ship was the fastest for sure, but the *Quiet Death* was a close second. If Klay could capture the count's ship, he might even end up with the two fastest pirate ships in the known seas. *Imagine that! And here was the* Quiet Death, *keeping apace with the Shark*. He grinned to himself. Klay had been waiting for his chance to come up against Vega. The man was a braggart and a showman, grown soft over the years on a fading reputation. His time was over. Vega didn't have the nerve to cut it as a pirate any more, better suited to flouncing around in the courts of Lyssia. *Leave the piracy to the true Sealords, Vega*.

An explosion of fire along the port side of the *Rainbow Serpent* caused Klay's head to whip round. The Sealord ran to the *Quiet Death*'s starboard to better see the destruction, the other ship only forty feet from his own. Two more eruptions along the *Rainbow Serpent's* flank sent fire racing across her frame, snaking through the cannon hatches below deck. The screams from the men within mixed with the roar of the hungry flames. Within moments the ship was careering wildly out of control as the deckhands rushed to put out fires, abandoning their posts – the Tuskun ship was lurching towards the *Quiet Death*.

'Hard to port,' screamed Klay as his own crew rushed to their posts, their pursuit of the *Maelstrom* halted by the devastation that had struck their companion vessel. Fire now covered the decks of the *Rainbow Serpent*, her crew desperately trying to tame the inferno. The *Quiet Death* was able to turn aside just in time as the other lunged across her bow, wails and flames trailing in her wake. A loud *boom* within the middle of the ship sent timbers splintering into the night sky as something exploded within the *Rainbow Serpent's* belly. Klay's crew watched in horror as burning men leaped from the other warship into the sea.

Fire and yelling on board the *Quiet Death* now caused fresh chaos, as Klay's men rushed about in a panic. The Sealord saw his mizzenmast aflame, the orange fire licking up the sails and devouring them hungrily. *How could this be happening?* He snatched hold of his first mate by the throat, shaking him like a doll.

'What's going on?'

'The fire, captain!' cried the man. 'The fire and the monster!'

Monster? Klay tossed him aside into the path of more fleeing men. They looked over their shoulders, clearly fearful of whatever awaited them there.

'Get back, you dogs!' Klay yelled, his face morphing as he began to channel the Barracuda. He whipped out his sabre as his eyes grew luminescent, teeth sharpening into long white needles. His skin took on a pale silver pallor, his mouth splitting the flesh as the jaw receded towards his ears.

'Screaming like women – I'm the only monster here! I see

you running to the foredecks and I'll cut you in two myself! Get that mast down, and quench those fires!'

To emphasize the point he took a swipe at the air in front of them, the sabre scything inches from the men's throats. They fell back as one, terrified into returning to the flames, the first mate leading the way. Buckets were hurried along lines as the crew of the *Quiet Death* were forced to clamber up the burning rigging. Flaming sails fell to the deck as the men struggled to kill the fire. Captain Klay nodded contentedly, pleased that his men were now shaping up.

He was about to return to the rest of his crew when the wet *thunk* of something hitting the deck made him halt. Klay glanced down, thinking a bucket had fallen from a sailor's grasp. The sight of a decapitated head staring back at him did not instantly register.

He looked up as a severed arm spun through the air, narrowly missing his face. Through the smoke and shadows he could see shapes moving frantically, men running, swords slashing, as a melee had broken out beneath the flaming mast. He shifted his sabre in his grip before stalking through the choking grey clouds. An arc of blood sprayed him as he emerged into the fight. His first mate's carotid artery had been opened up like a bottle of the Redwine's finest. As the body tumbled on to a pile of equally lifeless corpses, Klay squinted through the smoke, trying to spot the killer. He opened his mouth wide, teeth glistening, an armoury of shining daggers. He tried to call his men to him, rally them to his aid, but no sound came forth. With surprise and horror he felt a wet sensation washing down his chest and soaking his shirt. He reached a faltering hand up to his throat, finding a gaping hole where it used to be.

The Werefish Klay, commander of the Kraken Ghul's fleet, tumbled on to the corpses of his shipmates. As his life slipped away he stared up at the monstrous silhouette that towered over him; broad grey head, dead black eyes and razor-sharp teeth that went on forever. *So fast: never saw him coming*. The Wereshark, Count Vega, tossed the lump of torn throat and severed vocal chords on to the Barracuda's body. The last thing Klay heard was the captain of the *Maelstrom*'s voice, dark as the night.

'How's that for your *Quiet Death*, Klay?'

Hector watched the burning ships from the rear deck, the crew of the *Maelstrom* cheering all around him. The ship's rocking left him feeling constantly ill; a life at sea didn't suit the young magister's weak constitution. Hector had found it impossible to keep a meal down since boarding the *Maelstrom*, and couldn't wait until they hit land once more. Lady Bethwyn stood at his side, shivering despite her thick cloak. He wanted to put a comforting arm around her, but found his limbs unwilling.

What are you afraid of? She won't bite!

Hector snarled at the taunts of the Vincent-vile, and Bethwyn heard the noise that escaped his lips. He smiled awkwardly, embarrassment never far away. A commotion on the main deck caused a crowd to gather. Bethwyn turned and followed the men as they rushed to their returning captain. Vega was soaking, his white shirt clinging to his torso as he shook the excess water from his body. Duke Manfred passed the Sharklord his cloak.

'That was some piece of work, Vega,' said the Staglord, impressed.

'I did what had to be done. That's put their lead ships off our tail for the time being. We might be able to put some distance between ourselves and the remaining pack.'

'Klay's dead, then?' asked Hector as he approached.

Vega looked up, tousling his long dark locks dry with the cloak.

'Very much so,' said the Shark, his characteristic smile not present. 'Klay's reputation was built upon hitting hard and showing no mercy. He got what he deserved.'

Vega's plan had been as cunning as one might have expected from the Pirate Prince of the Cluster Isles. As twilight fell they'd lowered a small boat overboard, loaded up with flasks of Spyr Oil and a hooded lantern. The Shark had then clambered in and rowed silently back towards the pursuing ships, ensuring he ended up between the two.

Once in position he'd lit the flasks and launched them at the *Rainbow Serpent*, saving the last to throw at the *Quiet Death*. Diving from the boat, he'd clambered on to the pirate ship while the crew were distracted by the fires. Transformed into his therian form, he'd added to the madness, slaughtering the enemy and dispatching their captain, the terrible Lord Klay.

Vega clapped his hands, attracting the crew's attention. 'Enough lollygagging, lads! We need to make the most of Sosha's blessings. Ghul and Slotha aren't far behind. These are uncharted waters and we mean to reach Roof – let's not get complacent!'

The crew immediately dispersed back to their posts, leaving the Werelords to return to the aft deck. Queen Amelie stared at the burning ships in the west.

'Will there be survivors?'

'I should think so,' said Vega. 'I'm not a *monster*, Your Majesty. But their fate isn't our concern.'

'That's cold,' said the queen.

'That's war,' sighed Vega. 'With respect, Your Majesty, it's the business we're in.'

'Don't patronize me, Vega. You forget my people are from this part of the world. The White Wolves of Sturmland are a tough breed.'

'So tough they were chased out of Shadowhaven when the Lionguard arrived.'

Amelie slapped the Sharklord hard across the face.

'Do not mock me! The White Wolves were lucky to escape Shadowhaven with their lives. If I hadn't agreed to wed Leopold he'd have slaughtered all my people. Who knows where my brethren are now? My people are *lost*, Vega!'

See how poisonous the Sharklord is to your precious Council? I can't imagine the Wolf would be pleased to hear how the Shark speaks to his mother!

'Show some respect to the queen, Vega,' said Hector, the words out before he'd even considered them. He wished he could take them back, but it was too late.

Very good, brother!

Vega looked up, his left eyebrow threatening to lift off his head. Even Manfred was surprised to hear Hector speak to the Sharklord in such a manner. Vega bowed to Hector, smiling through a split lip he'd sustained in the melee.

'My apologies,' said the sea marshal. 'I meant no offence.'

'This quarrelling does us no good,' said Manfred. 'We need to remain unified. If we're at one another's throats then we're doomed. With my brother and Bergan gone and Drew still lost, we only have each other.'

'I'm sorry, Count Vega. I spoke out of turn,' said the queen. 'I worry about all lives in these terrible times, even those of our enemy.'

'That's understandable, Your Majesty,' said Vega, his voice now respectful. 'The beast sometimes gets the better of me.'

'The hour's late, gentlemen. We shall retire for the evening and see you at first light.'

The three male Werelords all bowed as the queen and Bethwyn departed. Hector watched Bethwyn go, the girl glancing back just once before disappearing below decks. His heart briefly skipped a beat.

'Speaking to her wouldn't hurt,' said Vega, causing Hector to start. The sea marshal didn't look up, unfurling his sketchy maps and inspecting them hopefully by lantern-light. Hector's anger flared at Vega's remark, but he remained tight-lipped.

'I'd have thought we'd have encountered one of our own ships by now,' said Manfred, casting his thumb across the waters ahead of them on the parchment. 'They're out here somewhere, Brenn help them.'

'If they're lost then they're at Sosha's mercy,' said Vega. 'Hopefully they'll all make it to Roof and we can regroup there.'

Hector looked away, back towards the door that led to the cabins.

Yes, go and speak with her, Hector. She won't be able to resist you: you're the Baron of Redmire now, remember?

Hector shivered, stepping away from the two therians as they looked back to the faded sea charts. He made his way down the staircase back to the main deck, stepping aside as sailors rushed about. The sails clapped as the wind caught them, speeding them away from the burning ships.

He spied Ringlin and Ibal, skulking in the shadows before the poop deck. Since the fight in Moga, Hector had been forced to show control over the duo, ordering them to work alongside Vega's men.

They nodded briefly as he passed them by, but didn't speak.

They don't trust you any more, brother, and who can blame them? Letting Vega take a whip to them? Flogging them in front of his crew? You're lucky they haven't slit your throat in your sleep!

'They had to be punished,' said Hector under his breath. He strode to the side of the ship, gloved hands clutching the rail. He could feel his evening meal rising in his throat, the sickness returning.

Yes, but by you, surely? Not by the Shark!

'Don't worry about me, Vincent. I know what I'm doing.'

The vile's gurgling laughter made Hector's skin crawl. He felt its cold breath rasp against his ear, while bile raced towards his mouth.

'I'll be fine,' he whispered to himself, but his words felt hollow.

3
Blood in the Dust

'You're up, Wolf!'

Drew remained seated, ignoring Griffyn's words. The din was deafening, dust falling from the ceiling into his holding pen. A grilled door barred his entrance into the Furnace, beyond which he could hear the bloodthirsty crowd's cheers. Drew had just witnessed the Wereapes, Balk and Arik, tear through ten gladiators. The brothers now stood in the centre of the arena, caked in blood and gore, roaring triumphantly at the ghoulish spectators.

'I shall not fight innocent men.'

'Then you'll die.'

Drew looked round. The old gladiator master stood behind bars at his back, there to ensure the Wolf entered the arena. He held Drew's collar in his hand, having removed the silver choker once he'd been locked into the cell. Two of Ignus's warriors stood either side of Griffyn, each carrying polearms. The foot-long blades on their ends shone brilliantly, the silver reflecting flashes of sunlight into Drew's face. He winced, raising his wrist stump to his eyes.

'Pick up your weapons, boy,' said Griffyn, insistent now. The guards began to lower their weapons towards the grilled door. 'Kesslar didn't bring you all this way to be run through in this stinking pen.'

'Then he's in for a disappointment.'

'Banish all thought of these men being innocent,' said Griffyn. 'They're killers, Wolf; gladiators. They live to fight and die.'

The Apes had now departed and the bodies of their opponents had been removed. Drew heard the grating of metal cogs as the door mechanism ground into action. The metal bars rose, hard clay falling from the spiked ends that had been buried in the baked earth. Drew choked as the hot dust blew into the cell, catching in his throat.

Griffyn reached through the bars for one of the weapons lying on the floor that had been given to the Werewolf. Drew snatched the old man's forearm, holding him fast. The two glared at one another.

'If you want to live, Wolf, pick up the weapons,' he said quietly.

'Why do you care if I live or die?'

Griffyn smiled. 'You remind me of someone I used to know.'

A guard grabbed hold of Griffyn's shoulder, trying to pull the gladiator master back.

'Pick them up and *fight*!' said Griffyn.

With that, the warriors pulled Griffyn clear and readied their polearms to strike. Drew could hear the crowd chanting and booing now, growing restless with the delay. He picked up his weapons.

The two blades were old and pitted, each caked with dried blood and rust. The first was a trident dagger with a basket handle, no doubt formerly the property of some other single-armed gladiator. Drew pulled it over his stump, using the pommel of the other weapon, a shortsword, to bang it home. The fit was tight.

Rising, Drew took a couple of deep breaths before looking back at Griffyn. The old gladiator nodded to Drew, pointing towards the exit. Saying a silent prayer to Brenn, he turned and stepped out into the Furnace.

The first thing that hit Drew was the unbearable heat. The sun glared down, while the ground felt like a bed of hot coals. The sulphurous smell was overwhelming, pockets of the noxious gas leaking from the cracked arena floor. The sand was stained crimson and brown from the day's earlier battles, the blood drying swiftly in the soaring temperature. He was walking into the heart of hell, with no turning back.

The mob filled the seating all around, a mixture of the wealthy and poor of Scoria, all united in their bloodlust. They bayed at Drew as he walked into the centre of the Furnace, screaming obscenities and howling wildly. One side of the terrace was taken up by guests from the palace of Lord Ignus, the viewing deck jutting out from the black and white marble walls. Great sails of colourful cloth kept the heat from Ignus's guests while they lounged and feasted, enjoying their sport.

On the opposite side of the arena, Drew saw a trio of figures entering the Furnace. The heat haze caused them to shimmer into focus as they approached. One carried a net and trident, a broad helmet covering his face. Another carried a spear and shield, a pot-helm hiding his head from view. The last carried a pair of shortswords, spinning them in his hands as he advanced.

'Behold!' cried Ignus from his viewing deck. He wore a long white robe, open to his midriff, baring his smooth oiled chest. His three brothers stood leaning on the balcony, similarly undressed, ugly and misshapen. Beside Ignus, Drew spied Kesslar, Shah and Djogo.

'I give you Drew of the Dyrewood, the last Grey Wolf of Lyssia!'

The crowded found new volumes, roaring their approval and chanting for blood.

'He faces Haxur of the Teeth; Obliss of Ro-Shann; and our very own Galtus, the Swords of Scoria!'

The crowd chanted the gladiators' names, each having their favourites. The one named Galtus – whom Drew had to assume carried the two swords – seemed to be popular, clearly one of Scoria's champions. They each raised their weapons to the crowd, soaking up their adulation. *They're* enjoying *this madness!*

The gladiators split formation, fanning out as they circled Drew. Each was clearly a seasoned slayer of men – better armed and armoured than the ten the Apes had slaughtered – and they moved with deadly grace. Nevertheless, Drew had no intention of killing anyone. His fight was with Ignus and Kesslar.

'I don't want to fight you . . .' began Drew, but the one with the trident moved quickly. The net flew through the air landing over Drew, the lead balls clattering about his waist as he became entangled.

'Too bad!' yelled Obliss, leaping forward to drive his pronged spear home. Drew twisted clear as the weapon ripped through the air where his stomach had been a second previously. He dived into a roll, arms pinned by the netting as he powered himself towards the spot Obliss had vacated, just as Haxur's spear struck the earth where he'd stood.

'See how he runs with his tail between his legs!' laughed Haxur.

Drew scrambled to his knees, sawing at the net with sword and parrying dagger, desperate to free himself. The crowd laughed and jeered, disappointed to see how quickly this great Wolf from the Northern continent had fallen. The gladiators laughed, clapping Galtus on the back as he stepped forward.

'You're a long way from home, Lyssian cur,' said the Scorian champion. Drew scrambled back, toppling and kicking into the dirt as he retreated. Galtus relentlessly closed in.

'Change for me, dog, and I'll have your pelt as a cloak!'

Galtus kicked Drew, sending him rolling across the hot clay. The last thing he wanted was to let the Wolf loose, but it looked increasingly like he was going to have to. Drew's shortsword arm suddenly came free from the netting, allowing him to bring it up as Galtus bore down. He parried the first sword away, but the second scored a wound across his bicep, causing the shortsword to fly from his grasp. The crowd booed, throwing stones and bits of rubbish into the Furnace.

Galtus held his swords out to either side, turning on the spot as he looked around the arena.

'This is the best Lyssia has to offer?' he bellowed. 'Let me kill him, Lord Ignus! Let me end this embarrassment before he ridicules the Furnace any further!'

Ignus stood on the platform, the subject of much of the crowd's booing. They had come to see battle, see blood. He glared across the terrace at Kesslar, then marched over to him, his face red with fury. His brothers joined him, circling the Goatlord.

'You make a mockery of my arena!' spat the outraged Lord of Scoria. 'You sell me this worthless hound for a king's ransom and have the gall to watch as I'm humiliated!'

The Scorians continued to curse and bay. Fights broke out as the mob turned on one another in anger. From where Drew lay, surrounded by killers, he could see the confrontation on the balcony, Kesslar shifting back as Ignus and his brothers began to transform. Shah and Djogo took a step away from the enraged Werelords.

Ignus's neck elongated, his jaws widening and cracking. His thin lips ripped even further back, the flesh tearing as he opened his mouth wide. His grey oily flesh rippled, shifting quickly to a sickly green, while his bulbous eyes almost popped from their sockets. He brought his hands up, now transformed into scaly claws, readying a fist to strike the Goatlord. Kesslar stood his ground, horns breaking free as the therians put on a show of their own. Even the gladiators looked up, their attention pulled away from Drew.

'You steal from me, Kesslar, and I would seek recompense!'

yelled Ignus, the Lizardlord of Scoria, his black tongue flicking over serrated teeth.

'You bought the Wolf fair and square,' brayed Kesslar, stamping a hoof angrily. 'It's not my fault if he won't fight for you!'

'I'll take what you owe me, Kesslar!' roared the Lizard. 'In blood if I have to!'

With that, the Scorian swung round with lightning speed and grabbed Djogo by his throat. In one savage motion he hurled him off the viewing deck.

'No!' shouted Shah as Kesslar's captain landed twenty feet below on the red clay floor of the Furnace. Before she could move, the three other Werelizards took hold of her, wrestling her into submission.

'Now we'll see a show!' laughed Ignus, as his warriors joined his brothers, forming a ring around Kesslar and Shah.

'He can't *do* this!' cried Shah. The Goatlord made no effort to intervene.

Djogo struggled to rise as the Lizard bellowed: 'Scoria shall have blood!'

From where he lay on the floor of the Furnace, entangled in the net, Drew watched the desperate Djogo struggling to rise. *How quickly loyalty can shift*, he thought. The slaver hobbled gingerly to his feet, scrabbling for a weapon as Obliss and Haxur advanced. *They'll kill him*, Drew mused, for a moment seized by inaction. Here was the man who had tormented him in Haggard and aboard the *Banshee*. Djogo was a monster; why should Drew care if the trio of gladiators ran the killer through? Finding only his whip, Djogo looked up to the balcony.

'Throw me a blade, I beg you!'

Ignus picked up a blunt knife from his banquet table and tossed it below, the tiny sliver of metal plinking on the hard clay. The crowd roared with laughter as Djogo ignored the insult and cracked his whip overhead, trying to ward off the gladiators.

'Been a while since you fought in the Furnace, Djogo,' sneered Obliss, avoiding the lash.

'I bet you thought you were done with the arena once the old Goat bought you!' laughed Haxur as he moved to flank the slaver. Djogo got one more whiplash away before they lunged in and brought him down, spear and trident slashing and stabbing, sending him to the dirt.

Galtus raised his swords in the air as his companions held Djogo down. The spectators suddenly went wild Too late, Galtus realized the mob were agitated not by the imminent slaughter of the slaver, but by what was happening directly behind him. He turned quickly, but not quick enough. A powerful lupine leg kicked out, connecting with Galtus's knee and breaking it at the joint. The leg buckled back at an impossible angle, sending the gladiator tumbling in a fit of wailing agony.

The transformation had taken place swiftly, Drew's body now more than accustomed to the change. He rose with the net still wrapped about his dark torso, snarling at the man and roaring in his face. Spittle hit Galtus as he slashed out with his blades, the swords tearing through net and fur as they cut into the Werewolf's flesh. The net fell away like a tattered cloak as Drew shook it loose, ignoring the fresh wounds. A mighty fist caught the man in the jaw sending him skidding along the dirt, a cloud of dust erupting in his wake.

The two other gladiators stared at the scene, shocked at the sudden and violent metamorphosis and the dramatic reversal of fortune for their fellow gladiator. Djogo winced, his body chequered with cuts as the gladiators disengaged from their fight with him to face the Wolf. They moved to flank Drew, Haxur banging his spear against his shield, calling for the Wolf to attack while Obliss readied to lunge. Drew feinted to attack Haxur, stepping forward on his left before leaping back towards Obliss. The man was already committed, throwing his weight behind his trident. Knowing what the gladiator's move would be allowed Drew to leap above the blow, high into the air as his opponent passed beneath.

Obliss looked up as the shadow descended, the Werewolf landing on him from on high. His companion having taken Drew's attack, Haxur tried to skewer the beast on his spear, a blow that would surely find its home in the therian. Instead he halted mid-thrust, the crack of Djogo's whip signalling the attack. The whip coiled around Haxur's throat, catching hard and fast. Djogo rose in the dust, pulling hard, the throttled man spinning towards him, spear flying from his grasp. Pirouetting across the Furnace floor, Haxur whirled inexorably towards Djogo to be caught in the slaver's arms.

Haxur's eyes widened as he looked down at his chest, the blunt banquet knife piercing deep through his breastplate and into his heart. Djogo let the body fall to the floor as Drew rose from the unconscious form of Obliss.

The crowd were silent for a brief, dreadful moment, before

bursting into rapturous applause. Drew stood opposite Djogo, still changed, chest heaving, as he weighed the slaver up. Djogo teetered, torso bloody, ready to collapse at any moment. He fell forward as Drew lunged, changing as he moved. Back in human form, Drew caught the slaver as they landed, the beast receding as the guards of Ignus emerged from the pens, advancing towards the combatants.

'Thank you,' panted the one-eyed warrior through bloodied teeth.

'Don't thank me yet, Djogo,' said the young therian as the guards surrounded them. 'The enemy of my enemy is still my enemy.'

4
The Bold Thunder

The crew of the *Maelstrom* had never seen anything like it. The fog that surrounded the ship was the thickest they'd ever encountered, a great bank of sea mist that swallowed everything in its path. The crew stood around every rail, squinting into the gloom. Men muttered prayers, some chanting, others whispering, the atmosphere sinister. A dread sense of foreboding filled the soul of everyone. Nobody, human or therian, was immune.

It had come on fast. The ship's lookout boy, Casper, spied it easily enough, pointing it out to Count Vega and allowing the *Maelstrom* to change course and avoid it. But somehow the fog had still intercepted them. Few ships sailed through the Sturmish Sea, its grim reputation making it a body of water to avoid whenever possible. The sails were lowered as they cut their speed, at the mercy of the mysterious fog. With

Figgis holding the wheel, Vega, Duke Manfred and Baron Hector all stood on the foredeck, looking out into the mist.

'Ship ahead!' cried out a crewman as a black shape appeared out of nowhere. Figgis turned the wheel hard, bringing the *Maelstrom* about to avoid a collision. Manfred and Hector backed away as Vega stood firm on the prow, feet apart and legs locked as the other vessel drew ever closer. The *Maelstrom* ran beside it, the distance between the ships a matter of mere feet. To their relief, the other ship wasn't in flight, simply drifting on the currents.

The ship's name painted down the side proclaimed her to be *Bold Thunder*. She was one of theirs, another escapee from Highcliff that had carried civilians when they'd fled. This was the first ship from their tiny fleet the *Maelstrom* had encountered.

'Grapples and ropes!' cried out Vega as he paced along the deck, Manfred and Hector close at his heel. Lines were hastily thrown, securing the *Bold Thunder* to the *Maelstrom* and bringing her alongside.

'Captain Crowley!' called out Vega, hailing the other ship's skipper. He waited for an answer, but none came – the ship appeared deserted. The sea marshal turned to look at his puzzled companions.

'Perhaps they're all sleeping in their cabins,' said Vega with a grim smile, unsheathing his cutlass. 'After me, lads – and stay on your toes!'

With that, Vega placed his blade between his teeth before taking hold of a mooring rope and beginning to drag himself across. Hector looked at Manfred worriedly.

'I think he means us to follow, Hector,' said the Staglord, taking hold of the rope and clambering after the count.

Hector watched him go, his insides knotting, hands sweating inside the leather gloves.

Well? Aren't you going to follow, brother? Afraid of what you'll find?

The young magister ignored the vile's taunts, stepping up on to the rails and taking a grip on the rope. It bounced in his grasp as Manfred disappeared into the fog ahead. Hector threw his legs around it, letting his body swing until he was suspended beneath it, gripping with his arms and legs. The waves lapped ten feet below him between the two ships, clapping against the hulls in anticipation of his falling.

Hector glanced back before setting off, spying Queen Amelie and Bethwyn at the edge of the rail. He'd summoned enough courage to speak to Bethwyn in the last few days – only small talk, light banter that didn't lead anywhere – but it was a start. His life felt empty without his friends: Drew, Gretchen and Whitley were lost to him, possibly forever. A blossoming friendship with Bethwyn might fill that void.

'Be careful,' whispered Bethwyn, her eyes never leaving him.

His heart beat faster now, the weight of expectation having doubled suddenly with this unexpected audience. He just needed to get across without making a fool of himself. He began to move.

At the middle point between the ships, the rope sagged, swinging wildly. Hector closed his eyes, inching his hands forward one over the other, dragging his knees onwards while gripping on for dear life. He could swear he felt the waves slapping his back, could imagine the horrors lurking in the depths waiting to take a bite. Nearing the *Bold Thunder* he found his grip slipping. Panic rising, he feared he might fall at any moment.

A firm hand took hold of his jerkin, hefting him up through the air, away from the rope, and down on to the deck of the *Bold Thunder* in one motion. His legs wobbled as he steadied himself. Vega patted his shoulder.

'Are you all right, Hector?' asked the count.

'I'm fine thank you, Vega,' he replied, trying to sound confident while his trembling voice betrayed him. He looked around as more men from the *Maelstrom* joined them.

The *Bold Thunder* was a ghost ship.

There was no sign of anyone on deck, the wheel unmanned and the sails flapping idly in the faint breeze. The men fanned out, calling to one another, remaining in earshot when the fog threatened to hide them from their shipmates. Hector unsheathed his dagger, holding it warily before him. The Lord of Stormdale pulled a lantern from its housing on the main mast, and taking out his flint and steel he set about lighting it.

'Have you seen anything like this before, Vega?' asked the Staglord as he worked on his tinderbox.

'Very rarely; sometimes piracy can be the cause of an abandoned ship, but more often than not the pirates take the ship.' He smiled at his fellow therians. 'I've done it myself!'

Hector walked towards the cabin hatch that led below decks. He flexed his left hand, the black skin of his palm rippling beneath the glove as he held it towards the handle. A hand on his shoulder caused him to jump.

'You want me to go first?'

It was Vega again; ever present, shadowing his every move.

And you thought I *was bad?* said the vile in his ear.

Hector turned to the captain as assuredly as he could. 'You're welcome to accompany me, Vega.'

The sea marshal looked impressed, gesturing to the door. 'After you, dear baron.'

Hector grasped the handle and opened the door. The dark below was impenetrable. Hector shivered, his courage deserting him. He was about to turn and suggest Vega lead when the lighted lantern was offered by Manfred.

'Here, Hector. Looks like you'll need light down there.'

Hector smiled, gratefully taking the lantern before proceeding down into the belly of the *Bold Thunder.* He heard the footsteps of the following Werelords, relieved he had them at his back. The stairs led down into a cramped corridor that ran to the officers' cabins at the rear, and forward to a cargo hold.

'The *Bold Thunder*'s a merchant ship,' said Vega, ducking as he entered the corridor behind Hector. 'Crowley's been a regular trader along the Cold Coast since I was a boy. He'd never leave his ship, not under any circumstances. This is his home, his life.'

He slapped the wall as if to emphasize the point, as Hector entered the cargo hold. Crates and barrels were lashed down against the walls, provisions that had been stowed in the hold before the violence had broken out in Highcliff. Crowley had taken as many civilians on to the *Bold Thunder* as possible, crowding them below decks as the ship had set sail. Empty bedrolls littered the floor, with not a single body occupying them.

'Where *is* everybody?' gasped Hector.

'It's like a tomb down here,' said Manfred.

'A tomb without any bodies,' added Vega quietly.

Manfred pulled his cloak tight around his chin. 'I don't like this one bit.'

Hector inspected the lashed-down goods, checking what Crowley had been shipping. Manfred followed, reading the words aloud that marked each crate and barrel.

'Grain, vegetables, wine; there's enough here to feed the *Maelstrom* for a couple of weeks. Why would they leave it behind?'

'Crowley wouldn't,' said Vega, rubbing his jaw thoughtfully. He headed towards the cabins. Manfred and Hector hurried along behind him.

The captain's quarters were well furnished. A leather-backed chair swivelled lazily behind his huge desk; ledgers, sea charts and maps remained unfurled on the table, open inkpots holding them in place. Vega skirted the desk and went over to the bunk. Rummaging beneath it he found a chest. He pulled out a knife and jammed it into the lock. With a crack the box opened, revealing gold, silver and personal artefacts; all of Crowley's worldly possessions. Vega stared up at his companions.

The three men returned above deck, where the *Maelstrom*'s away party had gathered. Vega addressed the group.

'There are goods below that we need aboard the *Maelstrom*.

Whatever happened to the crew and civilians of the *Bold Thunder*, we can't neglect the fact that we left Moga in a hurry, without anywhere near the provisions we required.'

Vega couldn't help but glance Hector's way at the mention of the disastrous encounter in Moga. Hector simmered silently.

Any opportunity to stick the knife in . . . and twist . . .

Hector looked at the gaudy dagger he always carried with him – the dagger that had ended Vincent's life. Thin wisps of black smoke materialized before his eyes as the vile's thin hand appeared to claw at its hilt.

Vega continued, aware that his men were uneasy aboard the abandoned vessel. 'I know none of you wants to be on this ship any longer than need be, so be quick about it. Peavney, you're in charge.'

One of the *Maelstrom*'s mates stepped forward as the three Werelords paced back towards the mooring ropes that held the two vessels together. Hector spied Ringlin and Ibal among them, lurking at the rear of the bunch. Both men nodded to their lord.

Seems they've found their respect again, whispered the vile. *But for how long, brother?*

Hector skidded on the deck, his legs threatening to fly from beneath him, his dagger flashing wildly as he steadied himself.

The duke and the count caught him, 'Careful, Hector,' grinned Vega. 'You could have someone's eye out.'

The vile hissed in Hector's ear. *Every barbed word the Shark says hides a meaning just for you, brother!*

'I know what I'm doing, thank you, Vega.'

Vega didn't respond to the riposte, instead crouching and

inspecting the deck. He traced his hand across the timber planks where Hector had slid, his fingers slick with brackish slime. He flicked it, the gelatinous liquid spattering on to the deck a few feet away.

'What is it?' asked Manfred, frowning.

'I have no idea,' said Vega, the mischief in his voice replaced by concern. 'I have absolutely no idea.'

5

Recrimination and Recuperation

The Lizard lounged in his stone chair, alone, staring at the open balcony that overlooked the Furnace. The last of his guests from yesterday were finally gone, having remained during the night to share in the debauched entertainment. His brothers had retired to their own quarters in the palace, nursing their heads and stomachs after their excesses.

The rap of a spear on the door, followed by it swinging open, brought the Lizardlord's attention back to the rear of the hall.

'Count Kesslar and Lady Shah, my lord,' the guard announced.

'Send them in.'

The guard stepped into the chamber, followed by the Goatlord and the raven-haired lady, and three more warriors fell in behind them. They came to a halt before the metal grate. The guards stood to the side of the pair, not retreating from the chamber. Kesslar eyed them, stroking his grey beard between bony knuckles.

'You took your time,' snapped Ignus, reaching down beside his throne to pick up a terracotta bowl. He scooped up a handful of yellow oil out of it, slapped it on to his chest and began to massage it into his skin. Shah wrinkled her nose at the sight.

'I didn't realize we were to come rushing like your lackeys, Ignus. We are still guests, are we not?'

'For the time being,' said the Lizardlord, the threat evident in his voice. 'I plan another contest in two days' time, and don't want the same debacle we witnessed yesterday. What guarantees do you give that this Wolf will cause no further chaos?'

'None, Ignus. He's troublesome, but it's not my place to break him to your will. That's *your* job. I simply supply the raw meat.'

Ignus threw the bowl at Kesslar, the pot shattering against his shoulder and sending the hot oil over his face. The Goatlord cried out, wiping the amber liquid from his eyes.

'Do not dare to enter *my* home and tell me how *I* should run my affairs, Goatlord! You made a mockery of my arena with your incompetence! I'll make a gladiator out of the Wolf, mark my words, but our business isn't finished. You still owe me for the shame you brought to the Furnace.'

'I owe you nothing,' said Kesslar.

The guards shifted at his words, spears twitching menacingly. A jet of sulphurous steam erupted from the grate, as if the volcano was adding its voice to the proceedings. Ignus pointed a clawed finger at the slave trader, his face contorting as his rage rose.

'Say that one more time, Kesslar, and you'll pay with more than blood, flesh and bone!'

The Goatlord fell silent, smearing the last of the oil's residue from his face on to his sleeve. Shah remained silent, watching the guards warily.

'Good,' said the Lizard, reclining on his throne once more. 'I think you know what I ask of you.'

'Consider it done,' muttered Kesslar.

'Speak up!'

'He's yours once more!' shouted the Goat. 'Do with him as you please!'

Shah suddenly understood and became animated. 'You can't do this, he's a free man!'

'Be quiet, Shah,' snapped Kesslar. 'Have you not yet learned? None who are in my service are truly free. What part of being a slaver do you not yet grasp?'

'But he's your friend! This is unfair!'

'This is business,' said the Goat, glaring at Ignus.

'That's the spirit, Kesslar,' said the Lizardlord. 'And I'd mind your tongue if I were you, Shah. You forget that I hold your father still. His wings may be clipped but I can do an awful lot more if I so please!'

Shah looked between them, unable to decide which she despised more.

'If you're done with me, I would like to retire to my room,' she said, her voice raw with anger.

Ignus nodded and waved a hand dismissively. Kesslar snatched at Shah's arm as she turned to depart.

'Do not do anything foolish, woman. I'd hate to lose you, too.'

Shah tugged herself free, tearing her sleeve. She took a staggering step away from Kesslar before storming from the foul hall.

Drew stared into his bowl, his stomach knotting as the grains shifted. He deftly picked out the tiny grubs from the two-day-old rice, flicking them away before proceeding to eat. His insides rumbled, hunger ensuring his search for unwanted visitors in the meal was short-lived. If there were any more of the creatures in the gloopy mush, they'd be dead soon enough once they hit his belly.

He kept his head down, not wanting to attract further attention. It had been a chaotic time since his appearance in the Furnace. Many of the human gladiators had given him a wide berth, wary of what he was capable of after defeating three of their best. Galtus and Obliss glowered at him from across the ludus, still mourning the death of Haxur and blaming the young Werewolf for his part in the gladiator's demise. Galtus's right leg was strapped in a splint, and the man never took his eyes off Drew.

The therians had been less evasive, Arik and Balk wasting no time in continuing their taunts. Drew gave them nothing, taking their insults. The remaining Werelords had kept a respectful distance, although he'd sparred in the ludus with the Rhino, Krieg and the Buffalo, Stamm. He'd trained alongside them for hours that afternoon, trading blows, parrying and wrestling, but not a word had passed between them. Presently the pair sat down at Drew's table.

'You fought well in the Furnace the other day,' said Stamm from beneath his shaggy mane. For once, the Buffalo's sombre face seemed a touch less miserable. His sad eyes twinkled as he looked at Drew with newfound respect from beneath his thick fringe.

'When you finally fought, that is,' laughed Krieg. 'I thought they were going to finish you in the pen before you got out of the gate!'

Drew wondered whether this was the precursor to more insults like the cruel games of the Ape brothers. Neither therian showed signs of aggression. Indeed, Stamm was now smiling, his thick matted hair shaking as he rocked in his seat, his laughter low and rumbling.

'I didn't know how that would play out,' Drew muttered. 'I won't take a life without just reason.'

'I could have told you the crimes those three committed in the outside world before you were led into your pen, Wolf,' said Krieg. 'That may have made your decision to fight that bit easier.'

'What do you mean?'

'All three were murderers. They were bought by Ignus to perform. None will leave alive.'

'Seems Ignus might have done something right there,' said Drew.

'Ignus serves himself when buying the lives of these killers,' said Stamm. 'His reasons are entirely selfish. He wants the very *best* killers to walk on to the red clay and do battle.'

Drew looked over his shoulder, spying the human gladiators still watching him.

'They knew Djogo. Did the slaver fight here in the past?'

'He used to be one of them, a gladiator, and a fine one for a human,' said the Wererhino, snorting as he threw his rice down his throat. 'Kesslar struck a deal with Ignus, buying the man and making him his own. Djogo's worked his way into a position of power for the Goat by all accounts. He's the exception to the rule.'

'He's a ruthless killer,' said Drew. He hadn't seen the slaver since the fight in the Furnace. He wondered what had become of him.

'The young Wolf catches on fast,' chuckled Stamm, scooping the remainder of the rice out of his own bowl. The Buffalo shoved it into his wide mouth, slurping the last grains from his thick, dirty fingertips.

Drew shook his head. 'Why did Ignus throw him into the arena?'

Krieg leaned across the table, keeping his voice low. 'Ignus and his brothers own *everything* on Scoria. Anyone who comes here is a guest of the Lizards so long as they remain in favour. It appears Kesslar displeased Ignus when his star gladiator failed to live up to expectations. That would be you, of course.'

Stamm added his voice. 'In Ignus's eyes, the Goatlord deceived him. He took Djogo as payment for Kesslar's bad business. You cost the Lizard a great deal of gold, Wolf.'

Just then the Behemoth came over, sitting down at the opposite end of the table from them. Drew felt the bench bow as he took his seat.

'Won't you join us?' asked Drew, making the most of the thaw in relations between the therians.

The Behemoth turned slowly as he was about to take his first mouthful of food. The man's eyes were spaced further apart than one might expect on a human, and his skin had a hard, hide-like quality, as if whatever beast he was remained hidden just below the surface. Without speaking, the Behemoth rose. Any fears Drew had that he'd offended the giant disappeared, as he paced further down the long table to join them, the ground trembling beneath his footsteps.

'Thank you,' said the Behemoth as he sat. 'Am I joining you to dine, or for something else?'

Stamm and Krieg looked at one another, unsure what to make of the Behemoth's question. Drew wasted no time.

'What else could you be joining us for?'

'The grand speech you made the other day – I dismissed it as sunstroke initially. But now I see you're a man of conviction. You really intend to escape the Furnace, don't you?'

'I do.'

Stamm waved his hand dismissively. 'You waste your words; talk of escape is futile.'

'How is it futile?' said Drew urgently. 'I was told the Werelords were noble; look what you've been reduced to!'

'Be quiet, boy,' said Krieg, big lips curling back to reveal teeth like blocks of granite. The therians may all have been wearing silver collars, but each was more than capable of killing Drew in human form if they put their mind to it. Nevertheless, Drew would not back down.

'You've become used to fighting alone, looking after your

own skin in the Furnace. But imagine what we could do if we were to *combine* our strength and make a stand! Do you not want to see your homelands again?'

'Our homelands are enslaved, just as we are, Wolf,' said Stamm. The laughter that had earlier been evident had disappeared, the Werebuffalo's thick mane casting shadows over his face once again, sad eyes drooping as he stared at the floor. 'Do you think Lyssia is the first of the Catlords' conquests?'

'The boy does not speak for me,' said Krieg, shaking his head.

'If we escape the arena, we can work together, Krieg. We can unite against our common enemy. You risk your life every time you enter the Furnace. Why not risk it for something noble for once?'

Krieg snatched angrily at Drew, but the young Werewolf was too quick for the Rhino, dodging out of reach. The debate was descending into a fight.

'Leave the Wolf alone, Krieg,' said the Behemoth. Krieg growled and snorted, bringing his fist back but keeping his glare on the young man.

'He's right,' the giant continued quietly. 'Each of us has been dragged to this purgatory. We all have scores to settle with Ignus and his friends, like Kesslar and the Catlords.'

'And where would your grand plan start?' asked Stamm, his voice a whisper.

The Behemoth sighed. 'Thinking was never my strength. My strength . . . would be my strength.'

Drew looked around the ludus at the other gladiators. Galtus and Obliss couldn't be trusted, but there had to be other humans present who wanted to escape. He saw Taboo eating at another table with Drake. His eyes suddenly recognized a familiar face, being led out of the small surgery tent at the rear of the ludus by master Griffyn.

'Excuse me,' said Drew, rising immediately and making his way between the tables, ignoring the jeers of Galtus and Obliss on one side and the Apes on the other.

Griffyn was in deep conversation with his man, heads close together as they spoke quietly. Drew slowed his pace. The two appeared to know one another very well. The aged gladiator had his arm around the other's shoulder in a fashion more familiar than Drew might have expected. *Almost paternal*, thought Drew. He thought back to the rare occasions as a boy when Mack Ferran would put a consoling arm around him when he was hurt. He stepped before the two men, who looked up with a mixture of surprise and shock. Griffyn seemed flustered.

'Can I help you, boy?' asked the wiry old man, his hands scratching at the silver collar that encircled his ragged throat. *So Griffyn's a therian*, thought Drew. *Yet Ignus ensures the collar remains round his neck. It seems freedom in Scoria still comes with conditions attached*. The man beside him wore a newly forged collar of iron.

'You might be able to,' said Drew, before turning to the Furnace's latest recruit. The man stared back at Drew with one good eye, the other missing from a recent fight. 'But it's Djogo I really wanted to talk to.'

6
Song of the Sirens

She swam in a lake, crystal clear waters breaking with each stroke of her arms. The shore was comfortingly close by; the silence deafening yet beautiful. She was alone, the only soul in the world, content with her solitude. Rolling over, she made a series of backstrokes, her hands cutting through the heavenly water and propelling her gently backwards. She looked up at the sun, its warm rays invigorating and caressing her from above. She let her arms trail as she kicked her feet, turning once more on to her chest, allowing a giggle to escape her lips. She dipped her head beneath the water and opened her eyes.

The darkness consumed her. If the surface world was the beautiful day, the terrible night lurked in the depths. Black shapes moved in the deep, snaking their way up, up through the black water, up towards her. Slits of light broke the shadows, opening into round globes of light. Eyes: terrible pale eyes with pinprick pupils. She struggled to return to the surface, hitting a sheet of glassy ice above.

Beyond, she could see the sunlight, tantalizingly out of reach. She hammered the ice with the balls of her fists, her lungs bursting, trying to find an escape route. She looked down once more into the darkness, as the first of the phantoms took a grip on her legs, its claws cutting deep into her flesh, and a scream burst from her mouth in a cloud of bubbles.

Bethwyn's eyes flicked open, the nightmare replaced by the cabin's darkness. She looked to the bunk opposite, the sleeping form of Queen Amelie faintly visible in the gloom. She reached a hand beneath the covers to feel her legs, the sensation of the monster's claws still evident on her skin. Finding no wounds, she relaxed once more, her head collapsing on to her pillow.

Sleeping on board the *Maelstrom* was proving difficult for the young Wildcat. Having grown up on an island in the middle of a lake, her father, Baron Mervin, the Lord of Robben, had regularly taken her boating. They were good times, happy times. But life on board the pirate ship was quite different from a lazy day on the lake.

She'd felt no split loyalties when Leopold had been overthrown. Although she shared the felinthrope heritage of the Catlords, their similarities ended there. The Wildcats were creatures of the north, native to Lyssia; they had as little in common with the Cats of Bast as with the Dogs of Omir. Mervin had wasted no time in swearing allegiance to Lord Drew, returning home to Lake Robben after the uprising, leaving his daughter behind to care for his queen.

With only Amelie and the staff of Buck House for company, Bethwyn had found herself looking forward to the visits of Baron Hector. He'd been a frequent visitor to the Staglord mansion in Highcliff, often on official business with Drew. She sensed he'd wanted to make a formal introduction to her, but the shy Boarlord had never seized the moment back in the city. Even now, on board Count Vega's ship, he struggled to find something to talk about with her.

Starting in the morning, she made a silent promise to make more effort with the magister. There was something there – it just needed coaxing out. Bethwyn's heartbeat began to slow again, as sleep promised to return.

Then she heard it.

Initially she dismissed it as the sound of the waves lapping against the *Maelstrom,* sloshing against the thick timber hull. Yet the noise was constant, a gurgling sound shifting from high to low, as water might disappear down a drain. There was something musical about the sound, an undulating rhythm that built gradually, as if in a chorus. Soon the noise was all around her, crawling through the cabin and creeping through the shadows.

Bethwyn swung her legs out of the bunk and dropped to the floor. She reached for the lamp that swung from the ceiling, unhooking it and turning up the burner. The light chased the darkness away, as the queen stirred in her cot.

'What is it?' she whispered. 'What's the matter, Bethwyn?'

'Don't you hear it, Your Majesty?'

Amelie lay still, a hand shielding the light from her face, listening intently. Her eyes widened as the gurgling sound registered. The queen pushed the covers away and climbed out of her bed, joining Bethwyn barefoot on the floorboards. She took her robe, wrapping it about herself, while her lady-in-waiting picked up her own cloak.

'That song,' said the queen. 'Where's it coming from?'

The girl opened the cabin door a crack, expecting to see crew members rushing by to investigate the strange sounds. The corridor was empty.

Bethwyn turned to the queen. 'Please, Your Majesty, remain here while I investigate.'

Amelie shook her head. 'If you think I'm going to allow you to go up there alone, you're sorely mistaken, my girl. I'm coming with you.'

The women walked along the corridor, the ship's constant creaking adding to the sinister chorus that filled the air. Bethwyn leaned against the wall as she advanced, one hand trailing along the varnished wood as she drew closer to the steps that led to the main deck. Taking hold of the rail in her free hand she rose up the staircase towards the open air. The hatch door was swinging on its hinges, left open to the night.

The men of the *Maelstrom* were gathered on the deck, standing like statues in the fog. They swayed with the motion of the ship, shifting like a field of barley. The sound was louder now, clearly coming from the sea, surrounding the ship.

'What's the matter with them?' asked the queen.

Each man stood as if under a spell, mesmerized by the gurgling drone as it came high and low through the cold night air. Bethwyn spied Hector and Manfred among them, the Boarlord and old Stag still wearing their nightshirts. She moved through the crew towards the magister, manoeuvring in front of him.

Hector's face was slack, his mouth parted slightly, eyes staring through her like she wasn't there. She waved her hand across his field of vision, but he didn't even blink, as if hypnotized. Bethwyn took his hand in hers, giving it a squeeze – nothing. She raised his wrist up and gripped harder, digging her nails in – no reaction. She glanced down at the palm, shocked to see a dark mark that filled it like an ink-stain.

'Bethwyn!' called Amelie fearfully.

Bethwyn looked for the queen, unable to see her through the bewitched crew and the unnatural fog. She kept hold of Hector's hand and began to lead him, his steps clumsy and staggering, as if sleepwalking.

'Your Majesty?'

'Bethwyn!' A scream now.

She moved fast, dragging Hector behind her like a stumbling corpse, bumping into the crew, none showing any reaction. Bethwyn burst from their midst, the magister coming to an immediate halt beside her. Queen Amelie was retreating from the railing on the port side of the *Maelstrom*. The gurgling chorus had grown louder still, rising from the depths and rolling over the decks. Bethwyn moved in front of her queen, raising the lantern to provide illumination.

A scaly green hand clung to the rails, webbing spanning the gaps between each clawed finger. Another hand lurched up beside it, this time the forearm reaching over to grasp an upright post. A dark shape followed, its head looming from the mist as its torso came over the side. Scales covered the creature's entire body, its squat skull sunk low between the shoulder blades, merging with its chest. Two enormous eyes the size of saucers blinked at the lantern light, as the beast's mouth hung open, the terrible song guttering from its throat through a maw of needle sharp teeth. Seaweed hung from the creature like an emerald shawl, clinging to its skin as it landed with a wet *thump* on the deck.

Bethwyn and Amelie screamed and clung to one another as the monster crawled towards them. From below its waist they could see the beast had a fish's body that snaked along the deck, flapping movements propelling it forward as its clawed hands dug into the decking. A long spiked dorsal fin ran along its spine to an enormous tail, the fin rattling as it advanced. Bethwyn spied pendulous breasts hanging from its chest.

'Get back!' she screamed, swinging the lantern, causing the beast to back up, its song lifting into a gurgling screech. The chorus grew from every side of the ship as Bethwyn and Amelie looked about. With rising dread the women saw more of the shapes emerging over the side. Still the crew remained motionless, oblivious to the nightmare that unfolded around them.

'What are they?' came a shout above. Bethwyn glanced up, spying the shape of the boy, Casper, straddling the spar overhead. Like the women, he seemed immune to the ghastly song of the creatures.

'Stay where you are, child!' warned Amelie.

The women moved closer to the sailors, bumping into them as the creature nearest closed in. Another joined it, this one slightly different in shape and colour, its skin a mottled red. She could hear them crawling over the decks, surrounding the crew.

'There must be nearly twenty of them, ma'am,' gasped Casper, his voice tearful. 'They're going for the lads!'

One of the sailors suddenly went down, caught in the grip of one of the sea creatures. He was quickly followed by another and in seconds, six of the men had been thinned from the crowd. None cried out. All the while the creatures sang as they tossed the sailors over the side.

The swinging hatch door slammed open suddenly as Count Vega emerged on deck. He wore his leather breeches and nothing else, having been rudely woken by the commotion and not a moment too soon. Cutlass in hand he leaped forward towards the nearest creature, which reared up on its tail. He lunged in, catching the creature across the belly, the cutlass splitting the flesh. The monster's arms shot out, grabbing the sea captain by his shoulders and pulling him towards its jaws. Vega began to transform instantly, chest and shoulders rippling and causing the beast to lose its grasp. He brought his head down, mid-change, butting it in the face, its teeth scraping furrows across his brow as its mouth crumpled. The two tumbled to the deck, Vega having badly underestimated the strength of the beast.

'Captain!' Bethwyn cried, moving to help the Wereshark, whose changed head now emerged from the violent struggle.

'Get back!' he yelled, his monstrous mouth flying down to bite at the creature's throat. Black blood fountained, spraying the count and the deck around him as the beast clawed wildly at the Shark's face.

More creatures appeared, avoiding the two women, skirting around them as they went for the men instead. Bethwyn stepped forward as the one they'd first encountered hissed, clawing at the motionless Hector beside her.

'No you don't!' she shouted, smashing the lantern over the creature's head. The Spyr Oil within erupted, sending flames over the beast and back across Hector. Monster and magister shrieked at the fire, Hector waking instantly. He swiftly patted down the flames, trying to comprehend what was happening.

'What in Brenn's name is that?' he gasped as the burning sea creature thrashed about, its face aflame.

Bethwyn noticed that the guttural singing had ceased, the creatures now distracted by their fight with the Wereshark and her fire.

'The lantern!' called Amelie. 'They're afraid of the flames!'

Bethwyn snatched up the broken lantern from the floor, sloshing the remaining oil at another beast. It roared and recoiled as the oil burst into flame, scuttling away in terror. Still it was not enough. The men continued to fall and the creatures departed with their prizes. But now the crew were being woken up by the noise and heat of the battle. They were confused and terrified but instead of being dragged over the side, limp and lifeless, they now screamed, kicking and clawing at the creatures as they tried to wrestle them overboard.

Bethwyn and Amelie moved swiftly through the men now, waking them up, the song's spell broken. The creatures were among them, bringing the men down quickly. They screeched as they attacked, huge eyes closing each time they clamped their jaws around the pirates.

'Into them, lads!' bellowed Vega as the crew of the *Maelstrom* rallied, aiding him in the fight. They picked up cudgels, knives, axes – whatever was to hand – weighing in to battle against the monstrous creatures. Duke Manfred charged into the fray, his head lowered, transformed, antlers tossing the beasts from the decks, tearing them in two in the process.

Feet thundered across the deck around Bethwyn as the crew of the *Maelstrom* fought back. A clawed hand grabbed hold of her leg, in exactly the same place where she was seized in her nightmare. She shrieked as she fell, the creature crawling up her legs and hips, over her stomach towards her face. Bethwyn raised a hand, claws springing from her fingertips as she slashed down at the monster, tearing strips from its wide face. The huge milky eyes didn't even blink, its cavernous mouth yawning open as it came to bite her. Putrid, salty breath rolled over her in a tide. She tried to scream but nothing came out, gripped as she was by fear and the beast from the deep.

Suddenly the creature halted as if on a choke-chain, huge eyes bulging. Bethwyn held it away from her, still gnashing its teeth, but instead of her it bit at the air, snatching and clawing at an invisible foe. Its hands went to its throat, Bethwyn watched as it struggled for breath. Then, with a harsh *crack* its head spun around, slime and seaweed spraying the young Wildcat as its corpse collapsed on top of her.

All around her limbs were snapped and severed as gradually Vega's men pushed the foul creatures back, forcing them off the gore-slicked deck. Through the crowd of fighting men and monsters, Bethwyn saw Hector. *Had he saved her?* The magister's left arm was raised, the black-stained palm open towards her, fingers splayed, a look of deadly concentration on his face. He was ten yards away from her. *How in the world could he have stopped the beast?*

7
Hunter's Moon

The ludus was quiet, the hour late, and the palace of Ignus asleep. Inside the labyrinth of chambers that riddled the volcano's cone, the Lizardlord's gladiators slumbered in bunks and bedrolls within the hot, carved rock. Locked away from the outside world, they were alone with one another, brother warriors who might die at each other's hand in the morning, for tomorrow Lord Ignus would bless Scoria with the blood of his finest gladiators.

One solitary figure stood in the paddock, clad in only a loincloth, his skin scarred from battle, staring at the full moon overhead. Drew took in the heavens, the moon huge and bloody in a dark sky. It reminded him of his childhood on the Cold Coast. Mack Ferran would take his boys hunting on nights like this during the autumn equinox; the 'Hunter's Moon' it was known as in Lyssia. He couldn't think of his father without thinking of the others he'd lost. He said a silent prayer to the old man, willing him to look after his mother in the afterlife. Mack Ferran had saved his life, just when it had appeared that Leopold might execute him, losing his own in the process. The little solace he took from his father's passing was that the man had absolved him of any guilt he might have felt over his mother's death. He thought of his brother, Trent, hoping he was far away from whatever war and misery the Catlords had brought upon his homeland. Most of all, he wished he could see him again.

He grimaced as he eyeballed the moon. There'd been a time when the moon had been something for Drew to fear, the beginning stages of a sickness that had transformed him into the Werewolf, setting him upon his epic path. He'd resented his destiny once, but that seemed long ago. He was the last of the Wolves of Westland, and a survivor. Now the full moon wasn't to be feared; it was his friend.

But the Hunter's Moon had its own meaning for the Scorians. When the moon was full and blood red, their volcano demanded a sacrifice. Tomorrow the fire mountain would be served a feast.

Standing with a silver collar round his throat, standing before a full moon and resisting the change, was the ultimate test of will for Drew. The Werewolf was dying to rip free. Drew was pushing his body to its limits, toughening it up for what lay ahead. His muscles flexed as he curled his hand into a fist, the stump on his other arm trembling. He could feel the moon's rays across his flesh, their touch electric. A bank of clouds passed, casting shadows over the paddock and releasing the moon's grip on Drew momentarily.

'A dangerous game you play, Wolf.'

Drew hadn't heard Djogo approach, turning suddenly to find the slaver a few yards away. Drew panted, the strain proving great, his skin slick with sweat on the humid, red night.

'Do you always creep around?' he rasped to the slaver.

Djogo didn't answer, walking closer to stand beside Drew and look up at the sky.

'Have you considered my offer?' asked Drew, dragging his forearm across his wet brow.

'I have indeed, and I still say you're a lunatic, Wolf.'

'That's not an answer. Yes or no, Djogo; I'm not looking for your opinion of my sanity.'

'Your plan is madness.'

'To a broken man, perhaps, but not to a man who has hope in his heart. Which are you, Djogo?'

The slaver sneered at Drew. 'Watch what you say. We're equals now, and wearing that silver collar means you've no beast to call upon.'

'You're right. We *are* equals. How does it feel to be an owned man?'

'It's nothing new. I was a slave and gladiator before, until Kesslar freed me from the Furnace. The Goatlord let me rise.'

'And now he's let you fall. He's discarded you. If he'd respected you he wouldn't have handed you over to Ignus!'

'He'll barter with Ignus to have me released.'

'You believe that? How long have you worked for the Goat? You know what Kesslar's capable of. Can you really afford to wait?'

'There's too much to lose . . .'

'You've nothing to lose!' cried Drew, reaching out to grab the man's arm.

'I've everything to lose,' spat Djogo, shoving Drew away angrily. 'There are more ways to wound a man than with a sword.'

Drew shook his head. 'I don't understand.'

Djogo turned his back on Drew. 'He can hurt those I care about.'

Drew considered the man's words. 'You fought here for many years, Djogo. You know the Furnace and the palace better than anybody. The old master – Griffyn – I've seen you with him. You care about him, don't you?'

Djogo said nothing.

'I don't know what your relationship is. I don't *care*, truth be told. You and I have been enemies since we first met. I don't see how the pair of us being gladiators now makes us brothers. Tomorrow I fight back, and I hope those who share my desire to be free of Scoria will stand up and be counted.'

Djogo paced back to the sleeping chambers silently. Drew watched him go, wondering if he'd angered the man further. He looked up. The sky was clear again, the moon casting her spell over the young Werewolf once more. He snarled through clenched teeth as he basked in her cold, white light.

8

A World Away

The ground was hard and uneven beneath his bedroll, promising an uncomfortable night's sleep, but Trent Ferran didn't care. He stared at the Hunter's Moon overhead. Not so long ago they'd run through fields and meadows, stalking deer under the bright night sky: Trent, his father, and his brother, Drew. He sucked his teeth, thinking of the young man who had ruined his life. He sighed, closing his eyes and willing the memories from his mind.

This had been the first day for weeks that he and his men had seen no combat. While his companions seemed indifferent, it was a relief for Trent. He'd joined the Lionguard for one reason: revenge. He hadn't signed up to burn people out of their farms and turn wives into widows. Of the hundred or so fighters he travelled with, the majority were Bastians. They were emotionless, carrying out their officer's instructions to the letter and never breaking rank. The Lionguard were sadly less disciplined than their southern counterparts, recklessly meting out their own justice in Prince Lucas's name.

It was only a matter of time before Lucas was made king: the Pantherlords from Bast, Onyx and Opal, would ensure that. While Onyx marched across Lyssia, Opal was in Highcliff watching over the prince's education while he awaited confirmation of his ascension. Trent had met Onyx briefly in the Horselords' plundered court of High Stable. The Beast of Bast cut a monstrous figure, a giant among men. It chilled Trent's heart to imagine how fearsome the transformed Werepanther might look in battle. King Leopold had been slain in the fight for Highcliff, and Queen Amelie had been kidnapped by Duke Manfred and Count Vega, two Werelords whose names now topped the kingdom's most-wanted list alongside Drew's. Lucas was now without a father or a mother. With Lyssia in such a state of flux, the vacuum was waiting to be filled. As Trent's fellow Redcloaks often said, the sooner Lucas was crowned the better.

'Asleep so soon?'

Trent opened his eyes, the Catlord Frost was standing over him. He sat up, instantly alert.

'Resting my eyes is all, sire.'

'Did your blade get blessed as I said?'

'With silver, sire.' Trent made to stand up.

Frost waved his hand, dropping on to his haunches beside the youth.

'Drop the titles, Trent. Frost will suffice. I like you, and see no need for you to jump to attention whenever I'm close by.

You're not like the other Lyssians. You're honest and true, like the best Bast has to offer.'

Trent felt his heart swell at Frost's words, recognition for his efforts warming his spirit. He felt honoured that the Catlord could be so informal in his company. He began to relax a little.

'Any word from Westland?' asked Trent.

'Onyx makes huge strides. The Great West Road is ours already, and whatever resistance the Wolf's army had provided is all but broken. Our main force marches east, through the Dalelands. I don't expect them to find much of a fight there. The real battle lies ahead with the Barebones and the Dyrewood. This war will be over once we crush the Stags and the Bears.'

Frost smiled as he stared at the moon, pink eyes glowing with an unearthly light.

'Does it have an effect on you, like the Wolf?' Trent asked.

'The moon? It affects all therians in different ways. The more passive Werelords find calm and clarity under her light. For the more aggressive, it stirs the blood, fires passion and power.' He clapped his hands. 'I could fight an army of Lyssian turncoats presently without breaking sweat,' he laughed. 'As for the Wolves? Different beasts altogether. They're connected to the lunar cycles more than any of us. I'm too young to have ever faced Wergar, but those who fought him said he was at his most ferocious while the moon was full.'

'Is Drew really the last one left?'

'The last of the Grey Wolves, most certainly. But your queen, Amelie, she's a White Wolf of the north. They were always fewer in number, so I'm informed, but fled their home of Shadowhaven when Leopold came to power. There may be some left, vagabonds. But I'd be surprised if any White Wolves still survive, to be honest. The queen and Drew may be the last of the true Werewolves.'

'We'll find him, Frost. I promise.'

The albino put an arm around the youth. 'I'm sure we will. If anyone can sniff the beast out it's you. It sickens me to think of what he did to those who raised him as their own. The Wolves of Westland are a vile breed – a blight on your land. They need to be extinguished. Utterly.'

Trent nodded. 'He won't stray far from Lady Gretchen,' he promised Frost. 'He stole her from Prince Lucas once and no doubt he'll try it again. We just need to find her, quickly.'

'That's the spirit, Trent,' said Frost, clapping his back. 'And when we do, hiding in Calico no doubt, I want you by my side. Then your blade can truly be blessed, with the Wolf's blood.'

Trent's smile was bittersweet. 'That's the greatest gift I could receive.'

Frost held his open palm out, head bowed and voice low. 'You have my word, Trent. Lead us to him and the Wolf is yours.'

Trent took Frost's hand and shook it heartily.

'Now rest, my friend. We've another march tomorrow. The Longridings is riddled with the Wolf's allies. The Werefox may be heading to Calico, but who knows where she might be hiding along the road as she makes her way there. We can leave no stone unturned.'

Trent nodded as the Catlord rose gracefully before stalking away through the tall grass towards his tent.

'So you think you're his favourite now?'

The voice was Sorin's, from his bedroll nearby.

'I wouldn't say that,' muttered Trent, relaxing on to his mat. He pulled his blanket back up, staring up at the moon once again.

'Don't get me wrong, Ferran, you're a good soldier. But a Werelord calling you his friend? That's laughable, you have to admit!'

Trent tried to block Sorin's words from his head, but he went on.

'He's plumping you up, making you feel more than you are. You're a grunt, Ferran, like the rest of us. Don't think just because his lordship says you can call him "Frost" he means anything he says.'

Sorin rustled through the grass towards him, his voice low.

'He doesn't trust you,' he said jealously. 'At the end of the day you're the Wolf's brother. When push comes to shove, Frost worries you'll betray him, betray all of us.'

Trent closed his eyes, but Sorin's words were poisonous. He heard Sorin crawl closer, his voice inches away when he next spoke.

'I think he's right.'

Trent was out of his bedroll and on top of Sorin in an instant, hunting knife at the other's throat. Sorin chuckled, his eyes wide as he looked down. Trent followed his gaze to where Sorin held his own knife to Trent's belly, ready to be driven home.

'You've got me wrong,' spat Trent angrily. 'I want the Wolf dead.'

'So you say,' snarled the broken-nosed captain of the Lionguard.

'Nobody has more reason to see Drew Ferran dead than I!'

Sorin pushed him off, the knife fight over before it had begun.

'It might be argued . . . *Ferran*,' said Sorin, slinking back towards his bedroll. 'That nobody would have more reason than you to see him live.'

Trent collapsed back on to his mat, shaking his head. *Sorin knows nothing. Drew's a monster. Monsters need to be killed.* What did Sorin know about him? Trent tried to push his captain's malignant words away, but they just kept coming back at him.

9

Bitter Blows

'Sirens?'

Duke Manfred was incredulous. He stood beside the two Wereladies in the captain's quarters.

'Some call them that,' said Vega from behind his desk. 'Others call them the Fishwives. Either way I thought they were creatures of myth before last night.'

'They were vile,' shuddered Queen Amelie, her arm around Lady Bethwyn. It was dawn, but the previous night's encounter was still all too fresh in their minds.

Hector winced at Amelie's mention of the word 'vile'.

If she only knew the true meaning of the word now, eh brother?

Hector spoke over Vincent's whispered words. 'They were like no therians I've seen before.'

'Some therians turn their back on their human form, fully embracing the beast,' said Vega. 'Legend has it the Sirens did that very thing; the once noble wives of the Fishlords swam to the seabed, accepting their bestial nature totally. Is it really so unlikely, Hector? Didn't you face and defeat the Wereserpent, Vala, in the Wyrmwood not so long ago?'

Hector nodded, his thoughts returning to the encounter with the giant Snake. He'd had Drew at his side then, his tower of strength. It seemed a distant memory.

'How was it that some were affected by their song while others weren't?' asked the magister.

'I can't explain it,' said Vega, 'although I have a theory. The Sirens of nautical mythology can only enchant males, not females. Alluring beauties, so tales tell. If these beasts are in any way connected to those of legend, that would explain why Queen Amelie and Lady Bethwyn were unaffected by their dreadful chorus.'

'But their song had no effect on you, count,' said Amelie.

'Hazarding a guess, perhaps it's because I, like them, am a beast of the sea. Maybe the Sealords are immune to their enchantments?'

'And the boy, Casper?' added Manfred, pointing out the only other member of the crew who had survived the Siren song.

Vega shrugged. 'He's still a child, not yet grown. Maybe that's why he was spared their spell.'

'The Sturmish Sea is a dreadful place,' muttered Manfred. 'The sooner we reach land the better. Where are we, Vega?'

The count looked at the map on his desk, shaking his head.

'Hard to say. These are waters I've never ventured through. My charts are old and that cursed fog has thrown out our navigation. I reckon we're somewhere north of Tuskun, but I'd wager nothing!'

'Manfred's right,' said Amelie. 'We need to find the mainland soon. Who knows what else lurks in this awful sea?'

'Your guess is as good as mine,' sighed Vega, scratching his head and running his hand through his long dark locks. He stretched in his chair, exhausted from the night's activities, as was everyone.

'The *Maelstrom* is eighteen souls light after last night. I can't decide what's best for her when we reach Roof. Do I crew up and head back out to sea? Or disembark and continue on with you, to Icegarden?'

'That's for you to decide,' said Manfred, not about to be drawn on Vega's tormented morals.

'Thank you, Your Grace. Ever helpful with your counsel,' said the Sealord sarcastically.

'Your Majesty,' said Bethwyn, turning to the queen, a tired smile across her face. 'If you could excuse me, may I head above decks?'

'You look exhausted my dear,' said Amelie.

'Here,' said Hector, seizing the moment to step forward and offer his arm. 'Let me escort you.'

Amelie smiled at the Boarlord approvingly, while Bethwyn blushed at the show of courtesy.

'Really, Baron Hector, I'm quite all right,' replied the girl. 'Please don't mistake me for a damsel in distress. I merely need to take some air.'

'Sounds like a fine idea,' said Hector. 'If you'd allow me to join you?'

'Persistent fellow, isn't he?' said Vega with a grin.

See how he can't resist making a joke at your expense, brother? hissed the Vincent-vile.

Hector ignored his brother's voice and held a gloved hand out to Bethwyn. The young woman looked at it tentatively before taking it.

'Your Majesty,' she said to Amelie, managing a clumsy curtsy before allowing herself to be led away by Hector.

The two made their way to the main deck.

She's putty in your hands, the vile persisted.

Hector shivered, trying to shake the spirit loose.

'Are you cold?' Bethwyn asked.

'A little, my lady,' he said awkwardly, hating his tormenting brother with every step.

They emerged on deck into bright daylight, the cold morning air bracing. The remaining crew were busy, rushing about their business with even greater industry than before. Figgis stood steady at the wheel, keeping the *Maelstrom*'s course steady. Casper stood beside him, watching Hector with suspicious eyes.

Even that wretched urchin distrusts you, brother.

Hector walked Bethwyn over to the rail and out of the way of the busy crew, many of whom were still scrubbing the gore and slime from the decks. The corpses of the Sirens had been tossed overboard once the battle was over, Vega waiting until they'd put some distance between themselves and the scene before burying his slain crew at sea.

'Your hand,' said Bethwyn, holding the railing. 'Is it wounded?'

'Pardon?' asked Hector, alarmed by the question.

'Your left hand: I saw it last night. You've a burn in your palm, a big one. What happened?'

'Oh, that,' said Hector, flustered. 'I burned it on a lamp. I know; I'm a fool.'

'It should be looked at.'

'Don't worry, really,' said Hector. 'I'm a magister after all. It's nothing I can't take care of.'

She nodded, seeming to accept his answer. She looked pale – exhaustion and terror having chased the warmth from her face. The crew had begun to sing a shanty, sailors chiming in as they worked to the tune's rhythm. Hector spied Ringlin and Ibal near the ship's aft, apart from their fellows, shying away from work again.

'I'd have thought we'd heard enough singing after last night,' said Bethwyn.

'They're a tough breed, aren't they? They buried their brothers only hours ago and they're finding their voices again.'

Hector rapped his gloved fingers along the rail's edge to the beat of the shanty, trying to look relaxed while his insides were in turmoil.

'You were very brave,' he finally said. 'If you and the queen hadn't acted so swiftly, who knows what might have become of us. Thank you, Bethwyn.'

'It's I who should thank you, Hector. You stopped the Siren that would have killed me, didn't you? How did you *do* that?'

Hector smiled nervously.

'I don't follow.'

'I saw you: you strangled it! You broke its neck, yet you were a great distance away. How could that be?'

She's on to us, Hector. She saw your little parlour trick, sending me out to do your dirty work. Tell her about me, brother. Tell her about your shadow hand . . .

'I wasn't so far away, my lady. Perhaps it seemed further from where you lay?'

'I could've sworn you were many yards from my struggle,' she said, raising a hand to rub her brow.

'I can't remember the night's events clearly myself. In the chaos of battle it's hard to see straight, let alone recall what happened.'

He plucked up the courage to place his hand over hers on the rail. He gave it a reassuring squeeze.

'You're safe now, my lady. That's all that matters.'

Vega, Manfred and Amelie emerged from the cabins nearby, the captain heading to the wheel while the duke and queen promenaded along the deck.

If this is courtship, brother, I was getting it wrong *all these years*, laughed the vile.

'You've been the queen's lady-in-waiting for some years now,' said Hector, his hand still on top of Bethwyn's. 'Do you not long for your own life, away from service?'

'I'm the queen's confidante,' replied the young Wildcat. 'I was appointed her companion, and that's more important than ever now.'

'How long must you remain with her for?'

She turned, puzzled, her big brown eyes narrowing. He kept his hand over hers, Bethwyn having not yet pulled away.

'For as long as she needs me. In Highcliff my responsibilities were manifold: music, languages, writing letters for the queen. Out here, however, I do whatever she asks.'

Hector nodded.

'You're most noble, Bethwyn. You do your father and Robben proud.'

'I do my duty, Hector.'

Don't make a fool out of yourself, piggy. What could she ever see in you? A sickly bookworm with a penchant for dark magistry . . .

Hector cleared his throat, taking a big lungful of sea air. His heart felt like it might leap from his chest as he squeezed her hand once more.

'I would speak with Baron Mervin once this war is over, my lady.'

'Regarding what?'

'Regarding your hand, Lady Bethwyn.'

She didn't react immediately, but when his words registered, a shocked look flew across her face as she whipped her hand away. Hector raised his black-gloved palms by way of apology.

'My lady, I'm sorry if my words cause offence!'

You clumsy oaf! Do you really think this is how one asks a Werelady for her hand in marriage? Stick to your books and scrolls, fool!

'You caught me unawares, my lord,' she gasped, bringing her hands to her bosom and clenching them together. She backed away, the colour having returned to her cheeks in a crimson blush. Her big brown eyes looked anywhere but at Hector. He took a step forward as she retreated.

'My lady . . .' he began, but he was interrupted by her flustered response.

'I must return to the queen. Thank you, again, for your kindness last night, and just now. Walking up. Thank you. The fresh air . . .'

With that she was hurrying after the queen, leaving Hector alone by the rail. He turned, grinding his fists into the timber banister, shaking his head.

That went well, I thought!

'Curse you, Vincent! Cease your incessant chatter!'

Too late, brother: I'm already cursed!

Hector opened his left hand, the black leather creaking as he splayed his fingers. His head was splitting, an ache cutting into his temple. He could feel anger rising, threatening to erupt in glorious fury: anger at their predicament, at Vega, at Bethwyn and at his own hapless attempts to charm her.

Hector clenched his hand tight, his eyes alone seeing the black smoke curling around it, the vile in his grasp, choked in his fist.

'Hold your tongue, vile. You forget the control I have over you. The Siren last night was a reminder. You're mine, Vincent, to do my bidding, as and when I please!'

Hector waited for a smart-mouthed response from the vile, but nothing came. He kept his fist closed, thumping it on to the rail as he closed his eyes, letting his head slump miserably into his chest.

Count Vega looked down from the poop deck, watching the Boarlord of Redmire rage. He winced as Hector snarled and spat, holding a heated discussion with himself. Vega worried about the magister, after all he'd been through – continued to go through. He knew Hector had a good heart and prayed the young man stayed out of the shadows.

The cabin boy, Casper, handed the sea marshal his goblet. Vega smiled as he took it, washing the day's first brandy down his throat. He'd purloined a bottle from the *Bold Thunder* for himself, while handing the rest over to Cook. He'd make sure the lads had a drink this day. They'd earned it after last night's horrors.

'Captain,' said the boy, still at the count's side.

'What is it lad?' asked Vega, giving the cabin boy his full attention.

'Last night, those Mermaids – I saw what happened.'

Vega put a hand on the boy's head, ruffling his hair.

'Saw what, lad?'

Casper looked across the deck. Vega followed his gaze as it settled upon the irate Boarlord.

'I saw what he did to that monster.'

Vega's cheery mood vanished in an instant. He crouched down beside the boy, turning him to face him. Casper looked shocked, and more than a little frightened. When Vega spoke again, his voice was a whisper.

'What did you see, Casper?'

'Wasn't natural, the way he killed it. His hand, Captain: that black hand. It was dark magick, I swear to Sosha. The magister scares me.'

'Then stay close to me, my boy,' said the Wereshark. The boy smiled nervously at Vega, the captain, his hero, his everything. The count brushed Casper's mop of dark hair out of his eyes.

'Stay close to me.'

Part III

The Fires of the Furnace

I

Battle of the Beasts

The crowd had enjoyed their fill of blood. Fifty gladiators had entered the Furnace and only twenty-five had walked away. Every appetite had been catered for. Horseback warriors had jousted, boxers had duelled with bare fists, bowmen had peppered opponents with arrows while spearmen had launched their javelins. Swords, scimitars, axes and tridents had clashed across the volcanic earth, limbs and heads severed and hoisted as trophies. The Bestiari, specialists in fighting animals, had come up against lions, bears, jackals and wolves. The cruellest contests involved two recently condemned criminals pitted against one another: one armed but blindfolded – the other unarmed but clear-sighted. The blindfold ultimately proved too great a handicap. Now the Scorians quietened as Lord Ignus appeared upon his balcony.

'People of Scoria, I give you the rarest gift. I show the fire mountain the greatest generosity – my therian warriors from across the known world. You all saw the Blood Moon last night, signalling the need for sacrifice. Those gladiators who have fallen thus far today shall have gone some way to quench the mountain's thirst, but she hungers for yet more. We must honour Scoria with the mightiest offerings in order to appease her fire. My Eight Wonders enter the Furnace. The contest is over when only five remain standing.'

He cast his hands over the arena below, oily skin glistening in the midday sun.

'Behold: the Battle of the Beasts!'

Eight iron gates were cranked open around the Furnace, each one sending clouds of dust billowing into the arena. From out of the pens the therian gladiators strode forward. Ignus clapped his hands, turning to his fellow nobles and Lizardlords who had gathered as honoured guests. He'd just witnessed his most recent acquisition from Kesslar provide the fight of his life. Djogo had triumphed against the trident-wielding Obliss of Ro-Shann. Of the Goatlord there had been no sign. Ignus suspected Kesslar was still smarting from the humiliation he'd dealt him.

Drew squinted through the dust clouds as he looked around the Furnace. He'd seen Djogo moments earlier when the gladiator had returned to the gates, the two sharing a look as they'd passed. Drew walked forward as the sand settled, taking in the combatants. The Behemoth had entered from a gate directly opposite. To his side the Wereapes, Arik and Balk, had appeared, immediately moving together into a pair. Between Drew and the brothers stood Taboo, limbering up as she prepared for the fight. To the other side of Drew stood the Rhino, Krieg, flanked by the lean figure of Drake. The Werecrocodile looked the most relaxed of all, turning to look towards the chanting crowd. Last of all, between Drake and the Behemoth, Stamm could be seen, the Buffalo shaking the dust from his shaggy mane. Drew wondered who – if any – would follow his lead.

None of the other Werelords carried weapons. In a cruel twist devised by Ignus, they were to use tooth, claw and their therian strength alone to best their opponents. Only Drew's trident dagger remained on his stumped wrist. Drew hoped to avoid the Behemoth in the coming fight. The giant had been responsive to the idea of breaking out, but that was yesterday. Here, in the heat of the arena, it might count for nought. There had to be a fight: and that fight would separate those who were with Drew and those who were against him. Arik and Balk were certain enemies, while questions remained over Drake and Taboo.

Then the battle began.

It happened so fast, triggered by the two brothers. As if reacting to Drew's thoughts, the Apelords wasted no time, rushing Taboo as their opening gambit. As they charged they changed, forearms exploding with muscles while their backs expanded, silver bristles bursting from their skin. Within seconds the brothers flanked the young woman, their mouths open to reveal huge, deadly canines.

Taboo was ready. She kicked up the dust, sending a cloud into the air to provide cover. By the time Arik brought his huge hand down at her, the girl had gone. She shot a lithe leg through the dusty air, her clawed foot striking and piercing the Ape's shoulder, sending him tumbling away. When Balk's fist flew through the air where he'd imagined she stood, Taboo rolled out of the dust, transformed, her body shimmering with dark black stripes across orange skin. The Weretiger snarled, unfazed by the brutes.

Drew turned just in time to see the bowed head of Krieg charging him. The Rhino was transformed, head down and shoulders thick with hide armour. Dodging the great horn, Drew caught the brunt of the attack from the Rhino's shoulder. The collision was colossal, the pain immense. Drew was catapulted into the air and back towards his gate and landed in the dirt. As he flew he tried to breathe, the air having been crushed from his lungs.

Drew rolled, choking and gasping as he saw Krieg skid, changing his angle of attack. The head was his primary weapon and the ground thundered as he sped back towards Drew.

'Krieg!' he yelled, his breath returned. 'What are you doing? We can fight *together*!'

'It can't work, boy!' Krieg snorted as he charged. 'Better let me finish you, end this quickly. Three of us have to die, and I won't be one of them!'

Drew hadn't wanted to fight Krieg. He had believed he'd be an ally, but he'd got it wrong. Drew let the Wolf in, and the transformation was rapid. He leaped up from the floor on to powerful, lupine legs, his clawed feet digging into the dirt for extra purchase. The specially built trident dagger sat snugly on his left arm, while his clawed right hand was open. His yellow eyes blazed with purpose as he peeled back his lips to reveal deadly teeth. He let out a deafening roar to alert Krieg.

The crowd screamed deliriously as Drew changed, but he ignored their cheers, his attention focused on the Rhino. The armour plating over Krieg's head, shoulders and back afforded him a confidence in battle that few therians would know.

Drew's trident dagger bounced off the main horn, sending his arm ringing with shock. He dropped to one side as the brute raced to the centre of the Furnace, allowing his clawed hand to rake the Rhino's flank. Drew felt the claws struggle for any purchase, scraping harmlessly over Krieg's armoured skin.

The Rhino was far bigger than the Wolf, but what Drew lacked in size he made up for in agility. He readied himself for Krieg's next attack using the same defence as before, raising the dagger again. At the last moment, with Krieg almost on top of him, Drew leaped in the air, spinning and coming down to land on the Rhino's shoulders. Krieg snorted, swinging his head, legs still pumping, momentum carrying him forwards. Drew held on tight, his arms around the Rhino's throat as Krieg charged on.

Krieg looked up suddenly as the arena wall appeared before him. He felt Drew's feet dig into the armour of his back as he sprang away to safety, the Rhino struggling vainly to slow down. He crashed into the wall with a sickening crunch, rocks and rubble coming loose and showering him as he collapsed to the Furnace floor in a heap.

Drew landed gracefully, looking around the arena as the other battles that raged. Taboo had been joined by Stamm, evening up the fight against the Apes. The Crocodile, Drake, was darting around the Behemoth, who now stood transformed. Drew was amazed by the sight.

He'd heard about mammoths as a child, giant beasts from Bast, dismissing them as being as mythical as dragons. The animals the other therians were brethren to – crocodile, rhino, ape and buffalo – he could comprehend. But the Weremammoth was beyond all his experience. He was monstrously impressive – twice Drew's height, with legs like battering rams, the Behemoth dominated everything around him. Enormous fists smashed down, narrowly missing his opponent. Huge ears flapped from the side of his boulder-sized head, while curling ivory tusks jutted from his mouth. A snaking trunk swung through the air, smacking Drake across his long, toothy snout and sending the Werecrocodile flying.

The Apes were brutal. Their silver backs rippled with muscles as their powerful arms lashed out at their enemies. While Stamm was holding his own with Arik, Taboo was faring less well with Balk, tiring under the relentless blows of the Wereape, as his fists connected with alarming frequency.

Having assessed the field, Drew chose his opponent.

With a couple of bounds he bowled into Balk, hitting him square in the back and the two of them went down.

'Dog!' snarled the Ape. 'The Cat can wait! Let's see the colour of your blood!'

Drew didn't answer, squirming out of reach of the Ape's mighty arms. He'd made a mistake, choosing to wrestle the monster. Balk bit into his shoulder. Drew roared, snapping his own jaws down the side of the Ape's face. A black ear came away with a wet rip. Wailing, Balk disengaged, lifting a hand to the wound.

'I see yours is red,' spat the Werewolf, poised for the next attack. Then suddenly an arm slid over his throat from behind, muscles flexing as Arik snatched hold. *I thought he was fighting Stamm!* Drew's head thundered as the blood struggled to find a way through his restricted arteries.

Balk was about to join the attack when his jaw cracked, a flying kick from Taboo sending his head recoiling. Teeth flew as the Tiger landed, panting hard. The Ape went for her, drawn away from his brother's fight with the Wolf.

Drew was seeing lights – fading fast. With a desperate burst he yanked his left arm free of Arik's other fist, burying the trident dagger in the Ape's forearm. The beast roared, releasing its grip, the dagger tearing a lump of flesh with it. The enraged Ape smashed his other arm down on to Drew's back, flattening him. He rolled over in time to see both Arik's arms raised, fists curled and about to strike.

Then without warning, the horns of the Buffalo, Stamm, crashed into Arik's back, the two Werelords going down beside the stunned Drew. He saw the damage the Apes had done to Stamm, one of his arms broken and limp at his side, his torso ripped and torn. Balk now returned to the fracas, while some distance away, Drew saw Taboo lying wounded and still.

Seizing Stamm's curling horns, Balk hauled the Buffalo's head up, holding the neck exposed. From beneath, Arik opened his jaws wide as his teeth connected with Stamm's throat. Drew caught a despairing look in Stamm's eyes as his neck was torn open.

Drew pounced, his heart full of rage. He had only known Stamm from their few exchanges in the ludus, but the Buffalo's valiant assistance had struck deep. Balk tried to bat Drew away, but the Wolf wouldn't be halted. He took three, four more punches as he dragged the Ape off Stamm, the butchered Buffalo landing on Arik beneath him. The fifth punch came and Drew opened his mouth, closing his jaws around Balk's fist. Bones, knuckles and tendons crunched as he ground his muzzle closed.

Balk screamed, trying to prise the Wolf's jaws apart with his other hand, but Drew's teeth snapped together, taking four fat fingers off with two quick bites. The bloodied Ape fell, kicking at the Wolf, but Drew was too swift, his clawed hand snatching hold of Balk's jaw. The monster grasped at him with broken, bloody hands, but Drew's grip was solid. He raised his powerful leg and brought his foot down hard on Balk's chest. A sickening crunch sounded above the noise of combat in the Furnace, and the Wereape lay dead in the dust.

Drew turned to see Arik struggle from beneath the slain Buffalo, letting loose a despairing wail at the sight of his brother's demise. The Ape bounded high, blotting out the sun as he came down on to Drew.

The Werewolf readied himself for the impact, but the expected blow didn't come from above, but from the side – Drew was barged clear of Arik's attack. Krieg had replaced him, taking the Ape's barrage. The two went down, Arik landing directly on top of Krieg with a wet *crack*, throwing a cloud of red dust into the air. The combat between the Ape and Rhino was over instantly. As the cloud settled, Drew could see Krieg's huge horn, standing proud from the silverback of the Wereape. Krieg pushed him back, the dead Arik sliding off his horn into the bloody dust.

'Thank you,' Drew whispered, embracing Krieg. Taboo stood nearby, battered but not beaten. The bloodthirsty crowd were wild with excitement. Ignoring the mob of onlookers, the three therians walked across the Furnace towards the two who still fought.

The Behemoth and Drake still battled, trading blows, but not dealing any true damage to one another. This combat took place beneath the viewing balcony of the palace, but all eyes had been fixed upon Drew's battle.

'Enough!' yelled Ignus. 'We have our victors!'

Drake and the Behemoth parted as Drew joined them, Krieg and Taboo following.

'The fire mountain has been appeased!' cried Ignus as the audience cheered. 'We are blessed for another year, the glorious death of these noble Werelords has sated Scoria's hunger!'

The Lizardlord was so busy performing to the crowd that he paid little attention to the five therians who stood below. Drew stepped in front of the Behemoth and nodded to him.

'You're sure?' asked the Weremammoth.

Drew smiled, grimly. The Behemoth bent his head, allowing Drew to clamber on to his tusks, crouching low.

'Today the Furnace has witnessed the greatest contest Scoria has ever seen!' continued Ignus, arms open and enjoying his oratory. 'The fire mountain has had her fill of blood, both human *and* therian!'

The Weremammoth swung his head, tossing Drew

skywards, the lycanthrope springing from his haunches to gain extra speed flew through the air, towards the balcony.

'Not quite!' he shouted, landing on the balcony with deadly grace to a chorus of frantic screams. 'Your fire mountain is still thirsty!'

2

The Upper Claw

The guests on the balcony fled as the Werewolf of Westland rose to his full height. Instantly the palace guards rushed him, sending him leaping clear on to the stone banquet table. Plates and goblets scattered beneath his clawed feet, clattering across the floor as the rich and powerful of Scoria screamed. The guards fanned out, trying to anticipate the Wolf's next move, but Drew was on the prowl, making his way closer to Lord Ignus who was already changing. The Lizardlord shook off his robe, his long neck ballooning as it stretched and twisted, mouth gaping open. His skin turned a mottled green and hooked, black claws burst from his fingers as a reptilian tail snaked out behind him. Panic increased in the room as Drake landed on the balcony to join the fray, and then Taboo followed her brother therians into the palace.

Below, the Furnace gates broke open. Scoria's human

gladiators surged through, carrying poles, ladders, anything that might help them clamber out of the arena. Deep within the walls of the coliseum, fighting had broken out as others chose different escape routes. The cage doors that had kept them imprisoned had been mysteriously unlocked, allowing them to surge over any astonished soldiers that dared stand in their way. The wild beasts were freed from their pens, running riot through the corridors that encircled the arena. Soldiers, civilians – all fell beneath their teeth and claws. The breakout had caught the Scorians by surprise.

Drake and Taboo darted between the guards' spears, striking home with ease, filling the air with a fine red spray. The guards, so used to bullying manacled slaves around, struggled to hold the therian warriors back. With the guards preoccupied, that just left Drew facing the Lizardlord.

'Where's Kesslar?' snarled Drew as Ignus stood transformed, bathed in the sulphurous steam that billowed through the floor grate. His eyes bulged, thin rubbery lips peeling back to reveal jagged teeth.

'Kesslar isn't your concern, Wolf! You'll put your collar back on if you know what's good for you!'

Ignus's three siblings emerged through the yellow mist behind him, Lizards like their brother . None looked lean or fit like Drew and his companions. The Lizards of Scoria had grown used to a life of gluttonous luxury, feeding their addictions with whatever took their fancy. One was a tall, skinny wretch, while his fat brother loped beside him. The third one was top heavy with stunted legs, and then there was Ignus, their glorious leader, too used to letting others fight his battles.

The Lizardmen rushed Drew, all four attacking in clumsy unison. *These weren't the odds I'd hoped for*, thought Drew, bounding over their heads as they dived across the stone table. He landed with a *clang* on the grille, just behind the slowest of them. He lashed out his leg, clawed feet tearing the top-heavy one's hamstring in two and putting him out of action.

Down to three.

The fattest Lizard leaped back over the table, directly on top of Drew, but the Werewolf was ready for him, catching him on his clawed feet. His knees compressed up to his chin as the monstrous mouth snapped inches from his face and scaly hands clawed at Drew's throat. The grille vent groaned and buckled beneath the impact of their combined weight. Drew snarled and kicked back, the fat Lizardlord's eyes widened as he was propelled through the air, disappearing over the balcony's edge.

Two down. Two to go.

Drew jumped away from the grille, landing before the stone throne. Ignus and his last sibling separated, the lanky one snatching a silver spear from a fallen guard.

'It's been a while since I slew another therian,' the Lizard rasped, Ignus grinning at his side.

'I'd like to say the same,' said Drew.

The Lizard lunged, but Drew parried the spear away with the trident dagger. The reptile came a second time, and Drew knocked him the other way. Snarling, the Lizard put his weight behind the spear, stabbing high at Drew's chest. The Wolf caught hold of the spear in the crux of the trident dagger, halting its progress. His foe looked shocked as Drew bit down on the wooden pole, snapping the gleaming blade off. Before he could react, Drew buried the spearhead in the Lizard's chest, the hapless therian still clutching the broken spear shaft as black blood gushed from his bosom.

And then there was one.

Ignus screamed to his men for assistance, but they were occupied by the therian gladiators. Silver weapons or not, none were seasoned warriors like Taboo and Drake. The pile of Scorian corpses grew.

Drew was about to offer Ignus a chance to surrender, to end the bloodshed, but he was spared the speech. Ignus ducked low, flicking his tail out and round, whipping Drew's legs from beneath him. The Wolf toppled backwards, crashing on to the throne. Before he could rise, Ignus had leaped, straddling him, pinning Drew to the chair.

The Wolf struggled to escape the Lizard's hold, but the hooked claws were buried in his arms, fixing him in place. He snapped his jaws at Ignus's reptilian face, the Lizard's eyes blinking as a wicked grin spread across his reed-thin lips. The Lord of Scoria's bony forehead came down like a hammer-blow, cracking Drew's muzzle and leaving the Werewolf stunned. He was aware of the Lizard's mouth gaping open, its jaws separating, but he was helpless to stop it.

Darkness enveloped him, the world hot, wet and terrible. With sick dread he realized his head was in the Lizardlord's gullet. He tried to shake it loose, open his jaws to bite the monster from the inside, but the Lizard's constrictive mouth was too powerful, too tight. He could smell Ignus's stomach acids, noxious and overwhelming, heavy with the stench of bacteria and infection. The monster meant to suffocate him, and was close to succeeding.

Drew's feet scrabbled at the base of the chair, struggling for purchase on the polished stone floor. His clawed toes found a crack in the flags. Digging in with all his might, he pushed back, straightening his legs. Slowly, the stone throne rocked. With each push the chair shifted looser off its back legs. He felt the Lizard's tongue flickering over his closed jaws inside its throat. A final shove sent the throne back hard, crashing into the wall behind before lurching forward, sending Wolf and Lizard flying from the seat.

They landed on the grilled floor, the iron grate buckling again. Drew's arms were now free and he jabbed with the trident dagger and clawed with his hand as he pounded Ignus's leathery torso. The Lizard choked and gagged, coughing the strangulated Werewolf's head from its ballooned throat. Drew shook the reptilian Werelord's saliva from his eyes, glancing up in time to see the stone throne rocking back towards them, sheering from its plinth.

The Wolf rolled clear on to the polished stone floor as the throne crashed down on to Ignus. It landed with a bone-crunching *clang*, metal screeching as the grate tore free from its housing. Lizard, throne and twisted grille all disappeared into the sulphurous hole, the screaming of iron against rock mixing with the wails of Ignus as the Lord of Scoria plummeted to his doom.

Black smoke rolled through the palace of the Lizardlords and fires raged deep within the ludus, the house of the gladiators burning out of control. The corridors that encircled the Furnace were a scene of carnage and the sounds of combat still rang from the vaulted walls. An enormous lion lay on a pile of bodies, chewing on a corpse as if relaxing with its kill in the wild. Screams echoed through the thoroughfare as the coliseum burned.

Drew and his companions emerged into the sunlight. The air was parched and dry, unlike the humid, chemical atmosphere in the throne room, and Drew could feel his sweat already drying. He looked at Taboo and Drake at his side, his fellow therians shifting back to their human forms. All three bore many wounds, but most were superficial.

They headed away from the smoking palace, the curved black and white walls cracking as the fires raged at their backs. Huge portions of the terracotta roof broke away, crumbling into the arena, as Ignus's coliseum threatened to collapse in on itself. The survivors of the battle, a crowd of gladiators and slaves, had gathered by the gatehouse at the top of the Black Staircase.

'Friends, we feared the Furnace had taken you!'

Krieg smiled as he greeted them. Beside him stood the Behemoth and a hundred or so fighters.

'That's the first time I've seen you smile,' said Drew, shaking the Rhinolord's hand. The greeting was warm and earnest. Drew looked up at the Behemoth, nodding respectfully.

'Thank you. We couldn't have done that without you.'

'We couldn't have done that without many people,' said the Behemoth, standing to one side as three other figures emerged from the crowd.

Shah stood with her arm around Griffyn, the wizened trainer weary as he leaned on her. Drew could see the family resemblance now, the same shaped nose and sharp cheekbones.

'Your grandfather?'

'Father,' corrected Shah.

Drew was shocked. He'd have put sixty years between the old man and his daughter. He could only imagine how hard the trainer's life must have been beneath the boot of Ignus.

'You risked a great deal unlocking the gates in the house of gladiators, Shah. If Ignus or Kesslar had discovered your complicity, you'd have been killed.'

'Strange how the actions of one can inspire others, Drew of the Dyrewood,' she said, smiling as she glanced up at the other man beside her. The one-eyed warrior looked down at Drew.

'Come, Wolf,' said Djogo. 'We need to get you back to Lyssia.'

3
The White Isle

It might have been missed had it not been for the keen eyesight of the cabin boy, Casper, perched atop the *Maelstrom*'s crow's nest. Count Vega extended his spyglass to better see the island – a barren stack of chalk-white rocks that erupted from the grey waters. It looked unremarkable, a pile of bleached bones floating on the Sturmish Sea, the flesh picked bare from a long-dead leviathan.

'It's land all right,' said Vega, 'but I've seen more life hanging from a gallows.'

'Can we not alight there, even if only briefly?' asked Baron Hector.

Vega stared at the Boarlord as if he'd grown another head. 'For what possible reason?'

'This life at sea is all too familiar to you and your crew, Vega. You forget that myself, Manfred and the ladies are *landlubbers*, as your crew so eloquently put it.' Hector smiled. 'Solid ground beneath our feet would make a welcome interruption to our journey.'

Vega rubbed his chin and looked at Manfred. 'You feel this way too?'

The Duke tipped his head to one side. 'To be honest I'd rather we kept going until we hit the mainland. The longer we're in these foul waters the less safe I feel. Hanging around out here we're giving Ghul and Slotha every opportunity to capture us.'

Hector turned to the Staglord, opening his gloved hands in a show of reasoning.

'Vega *did* say we needed to plot a new route, calculate where we are. Where better than a spot of dry land? Don't worry about our enemies. Anyone who follows us through that green fog will struggle to emerge on this side anywhere near us. Besides, think of Queen Amelie and Lady Bethwyn. Wouldn't this provide a pleasant, albeit brief, distraction from their journey?'

The Duke looked over his shoulder as if the queen might suddenly appear. He rubbed a hand over his stubbled jaw.

'Hector may have a point there.'

'Exactly,' said Hector, smiling as he clapped his hands together. 'Then it's agreed. We stop to take some air. Really, what harm can it do?'

There was a knock at Hector's cabin door. He hurriedly threw the blanket over the satchel on his bunk.

'Enter.'

The door swung open and the tall figure of Ringlin stepped in, ducking beneath the low door frame.

'Close it behind you,' said Hector, waiting for his man to shut the door before pulling his blanket back once again. The Boarguard rogue looked over the magister's shoulder, watching Hector as he packed his bag. Hector's ungloved hands rolled bottles and jars over the rough mattress, glass containers clinking as they collided, his fingers hurriedly sorting what was needed. There was also the narrow mahogany box containing the silver arrow that Bergan had entrusted to him in Highcliff. Hector's hands hovered over the black candlestick, fingers brushing the dark wax before stowing it in the satchel.

'You're packing a lot of gear there if you're only going to stretch your legs, my lord,' observed Ringlin slyly.

'If I were visiting the island for a constitutional, I'd hardly need you accompanying me, Ringlin.'

The tall man smiled.

'Is Ibal also ready?'

'He is, my lord. He's on deck now, making sure he gets us a spot together on the same landing boat.'

'Good,' said Hector, fastening the clasps on his bag and throwing it over his shoulder. He was about to pass Ringlin when the tall man placed a hand on his chest, stopping him. Hector's face instantly darkened.

'Your hands, my lord,' reminded the Boarguard. Hector glanced back to the bunk, spying the black leather gloves by the pillow.

Hector smiled nervously, snatching them up and pulling

them on. Ringlin watched as his master tugged the glove over the left hand, the black scar now almost filling the palm.

'On the island,' said Hector, taking hold of the door handle, 'you and Ibal are to stay close to me. You'll be my eyes and ears if need be.'

'I don't follow.'

'You will,' said the magister, opening the door.

Two longboats rowed away from the *Maelstrom* in the twilight, the ship anchored a safe distance from the White Isle. Vega was on the first, accompanying Manfred, Amelie and Bethwyn, as six of his men rowed them ever nearer the rocky outcrop. Behind came Hector's boat, Ringlin and Ibal helping with the rowing.

Very clever brother, whispered Vincent's vile. *You've got them all dancing to your tune. You're getting good at this.*

Hector sat at the rear, his knees drawn up, satchel on his lap, arms crossed over it. The men were too busy rowing to hear or notice him muttering to himself.

'Hardly. There was some truth to my suggestion. Stretching one's legs on solid ground is a good idea.'

But stretching one's legs on this *solid ground, brother? Why did you not tell them of the voice? Do you fear they'll think you mad?*

Hector had heard the voice for the last two nights, calling him across the water, teasing him as to the White Isle's whereabouts. Hector winced, thinking about the sensation. Voice wasn't the correct word, as no true words were recognizable within the call. More it was a series of images lancing through his mind, feelings and flashes of knowledge tantalizingly out of reach. The strange language was archaic, but somehow Hector recognized it. In his heart he knew the call held the answers to a world of questions, answers that he'd find in no ancient tomes or scrolls. It was connected to the communing, he was sure, the telepathy similar to his bond with Vincent's vile. But there was a great power behind this; the call promised something. Hector needed to discover what.

'Is it mad to search for the answers to one's questions?'

Perhaps if it means putting those you care for in peril, brother. But what do I know? I'm just a wicked spirit sent here to torment you. It's not my place to suffer from a guilty conscience. I'll leave that to you . . .

The launches drew closer. The rocks thrust skyward at jagged angles, reaching up like bony fingers. The island was perhaps half a mile long and maybe a hundred feet tall at its highest point, a pyramid of splintered stone, bereft of plant life. As the boats searched for a mooring point, the sailors took special care to avoid the rocks beneath the surface, faintly visible through the waves. If the *Maelstrom* had drawn nearer, such hidden dangers could have ripped a hole in her hull.

As if to prove this point, the call came up from the lead boat as the broken shell of a wrecked ship was spied. The vessel was on its side, broken masts clinging on to the rocks, a jagged wound in its belly suffering the constant pounding of the waves. Beyond the wreck, the crew could see a rocky stretch of beach, perhaps a few hundred feet long and the perfect place to get ashore.

Hector felt the call again, an alien tongue rich in old magick, luring him closer. He looked at the crewmen, checking their reactions, convinced they too heard the summons. But the sailors rowed on, oblivious, the message inaudible to all but the magister. As the lead boat hit the shore, Vega leaped off the prow, his booted feet landing on the shingle beach. At this precise moment Hector felt a stabbing pain behind his eyes, as if a blade had been slipped into his skull. He wavered at the rear of the boat, one hand grasping the seat while the other snatched at his temple.

Images flashed*: skin against rock; blood on stone; a black eye opening suddenly. A recognizable word:* Welcome.

Hector opened his eyes, snorting for breath. His throat burned as if scorched by acid. Ringlin glanced up, catching sight of his master's shocked expression.

'You all right, my lord?'

You're not all right, are you, brother? I heard it too. It's expecting you.

The second boat hit the beach, the sailors jumping out and dragging it on to the pebbles alongside the first. Amelie and Bethwyn were already ashore, their winter cloaks wrapped tightly around them. Vega stood beside Manfred, looking up and down the length of beach.

'Everybody stay close,' said the captain. 'No wandering off. Keep a shipmate at your side at all times. Last thing we need is to lose anyone on this white rock.'

Casper appeared between the count and the duke, a wooden case on his back. The captain removed it and laid it flat on the beach, opening it up.

'What's this then, Vega?' asked Manfred, watching the sea marshal at work.

'Our best bet at working out where in Sosha's big blue

we are,' said Vega, removing a sextant from the box and placing it gently to one side. The navigational artefacts were all utterly fascinating to Manfred who reached a tentative hand towards one. Vega smacked at the hand, shooing the duke away.

'An astrolabe, Your Grace,' said Vega. 'You know how to use one?'

'Um . . .' muttered Manfred sheepishly as Amelie watched, smiling.

'Might be best if you leave it to someone who does, eh, Manfred?' grinned the Sharklord.

Manfred managed a chuckle, despite the admonishment.

'This is actually the best time of day for me to take a sighting,' said Vega. 'It may only be twilight, but the sun's still up and the first stars are in the sky. I should be able to pinpoint our whereabouts. Seems Hector was paying attention after all when he recommended we stop here.'

'Talking of our Boarlord,' said Manfred, looking about. 'Where's he got to?'

Hector paced along the shore, Ringlin and Ibal at his side, the landing party left behind around the bluff. The pebbles disappeared now, replaced by sheets of seaweed slicked rock that sloped off beneath the surface of the waves. Hector slipped occasionally, but wouldn't be slowed.

'Take care, my lord,' said Ringlin as he caught a stumbling Ibal. 'It's treacherous here; you need to watch your footing.'

Oh bless him, hissed Vincent. *See how he cares? He doesn't want you breaking your neck. Not while they still need paying, anyway!*

Hector didn't answer either soul, instead keeping up his pace. He could feel the pull, close now, promising answers.

Images flashed again: *the dark; a black curtain; a mouth; a kiss*.

Hector could feel his heart quicken as he slipped over the rocky ledge, dropping into a rockpool up to his knees. He clambered up again, and his gloved hands scrabbled over the white stone as he rounded the next outcrop, revealing another smaller cove beyond. The beach was empty and gloomy, broken in its centre by a tall, thin crevice in the rock. The black crack snaked twenty feet up the stunted chalk cliff, the high-tide water washing in through its entrance and rushing out once again. Hector dropped from the ledge into the water and waded the remaining distance, the Boarguard joining him.

Hector stood ankle-deep in the water as the sea surged into the cave. Perhaps a foot across, the gap was just wide enough to allow single file entrance. As the tide sluiced back between his feet, he could have sworn he heard the word again: *Welcome*.

He turned to his henchmen. Ibal held his sickle in his hand, turning the blade nervously in his grasp while glancing at Ringlin. The tall man simply stared at the thin cave entrance, his serrated long knife still sheathed.

'You're going in there, aren't you?'

Hector nodded.

'And you won't follow, unless you hear me scream. Understand?'

Ringlin and Ibal nodded, the short man letting loose a nervous giggle before throwing a fat hand over his mouth.

'Brenn be with you,' muttered the tall man.

Don't count on it, brother, whispered Vincent as Hector squeezed through the gap. *Brenn deserted you long, long ago.*

4
New Oaths

Scoria was a changed island. It had once known law and order, albeit the bloodthirsty variety of the Lizardlords'. But now chaos reigned. The mansions of the Black Staircase had been sacked, stripped of all their worth, the merchants and nobles who lived there long gone. When the Werewolf and his allies had leaped on to Lord Ignus's balcony, the island's wealthiest had fled the coliseum with their guards and entourages in tow, grabbed what they could carry, and raced to the harbour, sailing on the first ships they found. All else was left to those who remained: the slaves, prisoners and gladiators.

With the Lizardlords gone, it had been left to Drew and the surviving therians to assume control: there were few on Scoria who would argue with their word.

Those freed slaves who could work as sailors were guaranteed passage, crewing up on the remaining ships as, one by one, they set sail from Scoria. Those with trades or families also secured transport, with the remainder forced to stay on the island.

By now, only one ship remained in the harbour, anchored beyond the cove. She was all too familiar to Drew: the *Banshee*, the commandeered slave vessel that had belonged to Count Kesslar and would now take the young Wolflord home to Lyssia. Drew stood on the harbour walls, staring at the black ship, her decks alive with activity. The boat had been his prison as the Goatlord transported him to Scoria. Now she was going to return him to his homeland.

'She's ugly,' came a voice from behind. Drew turned and found Djogo stood there, smiling grimly. 'Though I'm one to talk.'

Drew might have laughed if Djogo's words weren't so barbed. He looked at the eye patch.

'The eye, Djogo –' said Drew, trying to find the words to apologize for the wound he'd inflicted back in Haggard.'

Djogo snorted, ignoring the young therian as he stared at the *Banshee*.

'Still no sign of Kesslar,' he said. 'His face is known throughout Scoria – if he remained he'd have been spotted by now. I think we can assume he was behind the theft.'

While Drew and his companions had led their revolt against the Lizardlords, Ignus's private chambers had been burgled, the true wealth of Scoria stolen from his personal vault. The rarest jewels and gems that the Lizard had stashed away down the years, ill-gotten gains from a lifetime trading in the misfortune of others, had been kept secure in a longbox under constant watch. The four warriors who guarded the hoard were found slain, gored from throat to navel or run clean through. Drew had no doubt whatsoever that the horns of the Goat were responsible. The treasure of Scoria was gone, and so was the count.

'Why didn't he take the *Banshee*?' asked Drew.

'Dragging that loot down the Black Staircase would have slowed his escape. By the time he hit the harbour he'd have been with the other rich pigs, struggling to get away. With the *Banshee* anchored so far from the shore, he must have jumped on to another ship.'

Drew shook his head.

'The Goat has so much to answer for. How many innocent souls fought and died in the Furnace so he could make a coin?'

Djogo nodded slowly. 'He'd have happily harmed those closest to me. There can be no forgiveness.'

'Who would he have harmed?' said Drew, although he already knew the answer: the Hawklady.

'Kesslar has never tolerated any divided loyalties within his ranks. My – friendship – with Lady Shah would have enraged him if he'd ever known how deep my feelings ran for her. Once he allowed Ignus to throw me into the Furnace, she was on her own, her safety hanging in the balance. Even her own father couldn't protect her from Kesslar because he was left languishing in the ludus. I would have my revenge on the Goatlord.'

'With respect, Djogo – finding Kesslar's like searching for a needle in a haystack. Don't devote your life to hunting Kesslar down. Find a new future, with Shah.'

Djogo grimaced. 'She's a Werelady. What future would she want with a human?'

'It's clear she cares for you. You've a chance at a new beginning now.'

'She needs to choose a therian as her mate. It is her duty as a Werehawk, is it not?'

'I'm not the best person to speak to about duty – I've run away from it at every opportunity. Only now do I see what I must do. I need to return to Lyssia.'

'And I'll be at your side,' said Djogo, staring at the black ship. Drew glanced sharply at the tall warrior. *Did I hear him correctly?*

'You'd accompany me?'

Djogo turned, his face deadly serious, one good eye trained on the Wolf.

'I worked for Kesslar for many years, first as his slave, then as his soldier. I've done many things in the Goat's name that I'm not proud of, terrible things that should've seen me put to the sword. The balance needs redressing. By serving you, Drew of the Dyrewood, I can set that in motion.'

Drew was speechless. Here stood Djogo, Kesslar's own killer, offering his services. Did Drew *want* to have such a man associated with him – *serving* him? Could he stand shoulder to shoulder with the murderer who'd been his mortal enemy? Could Drew *trust* Djogo?

'I absolve you of any debt you feel you owe me, Djogo. You should go where you wish.'

Djogo smiled, the expression hitting Drew like a slap to the face. He'd grown too used to seeing the tall warrior sneering.

'I'm not alone in wanting to aid you, Wolflord; there are others who'd benefit from hearing your words.'

The Werelords had gathered aboard the *Banshee*, Djogo the only human present. The former slaver stood beside Drew, trying not to look across at where Shah stood with her father, Baron Griffyn. Taboo and Drake stood either side of a large porthole that looked out towards Scoria, while the Behemoth towered behind Krieg.

Drew faced the assembly. 'Are you certain this is what you want to do with your freedom?'

Krieg spoke up. 'We have our freedom thanks to you. If it weren't for your courage, we'd still be in the coliseum fighting for our miserable lives, or worse, dead. We'll stand by you, Drew. We're all therian brothers – and sisters – of the Furnace.'

'You didn't treat me like a brother when I arrived,' said Drew.

'Do you think we were met with open arms when we first came to Scoria, Wolf?' laughed Drake. 'You got the measure of the Ape brothers pretty quickly – they'd have killed you in your sleep if you'd sought friendship.'

'If you'd looked for friendship,' said Krieg, 'you'd be dead now. You're tough, Drew, as tough as any of us.'

'This is my fight, though,' said Drew. 'Lyssia isn't your homeland.'

A huge hand landed gently on Drew's shoulder and the Behemoth's deep voice made Drew's bones rattle. 'Our homelands are enslaved. Do you not think our people would have sailed to Scoria to free us if they could? We share the same foe. The Catlords must be stopped.'

'I don't understand,' said Drew to Taboo. 'Why would Onyx and the Catlords allow one of their own to fight in the Furnace? They're your family, aren't they?'

The Tiger looked up, baring her teeth. They all looked away, except Drew, who held her gaze.

'I have no family.'

Drew hastily moved the subject away from Taboo's story.

'If you join me, you join my mission,' Drew told the group. 'Rescue Lyssia from these vicious Cats and restore power to the Lyssians – therians and humans alike. You've all tasted the bitterness of slavery; you know how it feels to live in servitude to another. We must unite with the people, start treating them as our equals. It's time for us, the Werelords, to serve the people.' He held out his hand.

The therians looked at one another, Krieg nodding to each in turn as they bowed their heads in agreement.

Each of the therians stepped forward, placing their hands on the Wolf's single hand.

'What happens now?' said Drew, unsure of what they'd agreed to.

'You sail to Lyssia, and we go with you,' said Krieg. 'We fight at your side, Drew. Fight or die. The Furnace is behind us but the battle goes on.'

Drew smiled and nodded, looking at each of them in turn.

'You have my word, brothers and sisters. When Lyssia is won, we shall return to Bast and your homelands. We'll free your people from the reign of the Catlords.'

5

The Host

With daylight fading behind him, Hector felt he'd stepped into the dead of night. A little illumination was provided by phosphorescent lichen that pockmarked the cave walls, covering the pale rock beyond the tide-mark's reach. He'd expected to find sea creatures scuttling away in the shallow rock pools, but like the rest of the island the cave was devoid of life bar the strange lichen. At its widest the cave was ten feet across, the fissure broadening like an opening eye, before closing once more at its rearmost point.

Where's your host? teased Vincent. *All alone again . . .*

Hector shook his head, dismissing the vile's words as his hands played over the chamber's walls. He leaned close, squinting, tracing his gloved fingertips over the white stone. The pale light revealed strange markings, symbols scrawled into the chalk that resonated with Hector.

'Language,' muttered Hector to himself. He tilted his head, trying to translate the archaic shapes. To the magister, the markings read vertically, from floor to ceiling – or the other way round – and the more he stared the more they struck a chord with the images that had flashed through his mind's eye.

He sensed Vincent's vile was still listening, and half expected it to chime in, but the phantom remained unusually silent, as if it knew Hector was approaching the truth. The higher Hector looked up the cavern walls, the more markings he discovered.

'A scripture, perhaps. Or a diary. But who wrote it?'

Still no responses were forthcoming from the vile. With the greatest mass of symbols being higher up, Hector tottered on tiptoe in the shallow pools, craning his neck to better examine the ceiling. The hanging stalactites were jagged and broken, severed in places where whoever marked the walls had smashed them from the roof in order to reach bare wall. Hector marvelled at the many markings, the symbols crossing over one another, runes illegible, as if the author had gone mad over a tremendous period of time.

One long black stalactite hung in the ceiling's centre, directly above Hector's head, the rock black and gnarly as opposed to smooth and white.

'Different from the others . . .' Hector whispered to himself again, when Vincent finally responded.

You don't know the half of it, brother.

Two long, skeletal arms separated from the dark mass like a threadbare fan, foot-long fingers splaying out as a pair of hands yawned open. Hector gasped, quickly realizing the figure was suspended upside down, the arms connecting with the shoulders at the base of the body mass. A bulbous head slowly swung down from where it had been tucked away close to the chest. Hector looked straight into the creature's face, nose-to-nose, trembling chin to pale, white forehead.

The face was smooth and hairless, the skin almost translucent. Blue veins were faintly visible, like wisps of pale smoke frozen within marble flesh. It had no nose to speak of, just two angry-looking red holes puncturing the middle of its face. A pair of dark slits widened, revealing cloudy black eyes that stared soullessly at the magister. Then its mouth creaked slowly open. Long teeth, splintered like a graveyard fence emerged from behind blood-red lips, the creature's fetid breath catching Hector fully in the face. The stench of death was unmistakable, causing the Boarlord to gag, but he couldn't pull his eyes away from those of the creature.

'*Welcome.*'

Casper sat on the shingle beach, skimming pebbles into the water. He looked up the shore towards his captain and the Staglord, the two therians having finished consulting the captain's navigation equipment. The duke held a sea chart over the wooden case, the Sharklord scribbling on to the map feverishly with an inked quill. Casper looked the other way down the beach, spying the queen and her lady.

Casper had taken quite a shine to Bethwyn. The noblewoman had been happy to talk with the cabin boy, answering his many questions about the fascinating continent of Lyssia. Casper was used to the sea – the mainland was a world he couldn't wait to explore once the *Maelstrom* reached Roof.

The sun had dropped below the horizon, the sky turning a deep indigo as night came on fast. Casper was ready to return to the ship now, regretting not bringing his cloak. Winter seemed especially bitter in the Sturmish Sea. He'd hoped to catch sight of an iceberg so far north, but when Figgis had mentioned how an ice-flow could tear open the greatest warship, that had killed his interest swiftly. He reached down and grabbed at a thin, white pebble but it was rooted in the beach, resisting his attempts to pull it free. Another identical stone popped up beside it, and then another. They looked like razor shells at first glance, four of them side by side. It was only when a fifth emerged and closed tight around his hand that he realized they weren't pebbles at all.

They were fingers.

Casper's scream was heard on the *Maelstrom*.

The creature's mouth hung open, its voice as clear in Hector's head as that of his dead brother, although the vile was silent. The pale white head was connected to ragged shoulder blades by the scrawniest length of neck, giving the impression that the skull might tear loose with the slightest provocation. The black eyes remained fixed on Hector as a dark tongue emerged from between the teeth, flickering over the Boarlord's face like a serpent's kiss. Hector swayed, staring at his suspended host, moving left to right, wanting to pull away but locked into its gaze.

'*Why have you sought me out?*'

'I . . . I . . .' stammered Hector nervously, fear snatching the words from his throat. 'I heard your call.'

Again the tongue flickered, but still Hector couldn't step away. He had no trouble understanding the words now, in such close proximity. The telepathy that had drawn him to the island was now abandoned. The language was new and unnatural to Hector, yet somehow he was able to follow and respond.

'*But you are not one of my kin. What are you?*'

'I'm a Boarlord.'

'*Boarlord.*'

There was silence as the creature considered this. Hector glanced at the rest of the body. The beast's head seemed to glow compared to the rest of its form, skeletal with black skin drawn tight across the bones. The torso was an emaciated bag of bones, while the creature's feet remained clamped to the ceiling.

'*How is it you know the tongue of my kin? I have called them for many moons and they fail to come. Now you hear my call?*'

'I can't explain,' said Hector, his eyes on the creature's black pupils once more. They held him like a rabbit in a snare. Hector waved his hands towards the walls.

'This language – I recognize it, though I've never studied it. And I *know* languages. Where are you from?'

'*My home is the isle.*'

'This island?'

'*I dwell here but this is not my home. Our isle is bigger. Much bigger. Another white isle.*'

'How did you come here? You mention others, but you seem alone. Are you lost? Separated from your people?'

'*People.*'

His host made a sound, somewhere between a growl and a laugh. Hector shivered as if someone had walked over his tomb. He sensed that, fragile though the creature seemed, it was more powerful than anything he'd ever encountered, and that included the Wereserpent, Vala. This beast was born from old magicks, while somehow still being connected to therian-kind like the Boarlord.

'Perhaps I can help you get home?'

'*In return for what?*'

'I don't know. What do you offer?'

'*You have an understanding, Boarlord, that is rare beyond my kin. A magister, are you not? You are not the first of your order who has visited me seeking answers. You know some dark magick, Boarlord, but you only scratch the surface. Tell me: what do you know of the Children of the Blue Flame?*'

Hector had to think for a moment. He was about to shrug and shake his head, about to say that he knew nothing, when his left hand spasmed, involuntarily. He raised it before his face, black leather creaking as the palm and fingers clenched.

Images flashed: *The shaman of the Wyrmwood; the risen corpse of Captain Brutus in the Pits, pale, blue eyes that flashed in the night.*

'The undead,' whispered Hector.

The creature made the noise again.

'*You are no stranger to the Children of the Blue Flame. You do not fear them?*'

Hector puffed his chest out, confident he had the answers to the creature's riddles. He pulled the glove off his hand, showing the beast the black mark.

'Fear them? I command them!'

The creature's tongue snaked out, perhaps a foot in length, stroking the palm of Hector's hand. He shuddered at the touch but kept his arm up, elbow locked. He couldn't let the host see his fear.

'*You do not understand them, Blackhand. You do not see how they can help you.*'

'What is there to understand? How can they help me?'

Again, the growling laughter from the creature.

'*For one who hungers for knowledge, your appetite is easily sated.*'

'Tell me what I'm missing, then. Show me what you know!'

'*Good,*' said the host. '*We have our bargain.*'

'We do?' asked Hector. He was unsure where this was heading. Beyond the cave, Hector could hear screaming.

'*We have a bargain, Blackhand. I show you what may come to pass, what can be yours.*'

'In return for what?'

'*An embrace, magister.*'

The creature's mouth opened wider now, the splintered teeth trembling with anticipation. Again, a scream outside. Shouting from the beach. Hector had no time to waste.

'We have a deal,' he said. The host's long, skeletal arms swept down towards him, enormous fingers reaching about Hector's skull. Its touch was as cold as death itself.

'Get back on the boats!'

Vega dashed along the shore, grabbing his men and tossing them towards the sea and away from the beach. He was partly transformed, his skin darkening as his hands and teeth sharpened with every step. In the eerie twilight moans rose from the beach as the bleached and buried dead hauled themselves from the shingle. Rocks and pebbles tumbled away from hands and heads emerging from the ground, grasping hungrily at the living.

Casper held tight on to Vega's torso like a limpet. He'd been the first to encounter the corpses, but not the last. Amelie and Bethwyn had been dragged to the floor, decayed hands tugging at them. Manfred had dashed to their aid as Vega hauled the boy out of danger, but more of the *Maelstrom*'s men were falling foul of the creatures.

One of the cursed souls had risen fully, taking hold of one of Vega's less agile crewmen. Its skin was parchment thin and clung to every bone on the dead man's body, drained of all fluid. Tattered breeches hinted at the dead man's life; perhaps it had once been a sailor from the wrecked ship. Twin blue fires danced in its eyes as it brought its mouth to the screaming sailor's throat, burying its teeth in warm flesh.

'Move!' screamed Vega as more of the dead emerged from their pebbly graves. Those who got too close took a blow from his clawed fingers, but Vega had no intention of tarrying. They had to get off the devil's rock, and quick.

He waded through the water towards the boats, where the last of his men struggled to clamber aboard.

'Did anyone see Hector?'

'Went round the shore with his men, captain,' replied a sailor, pointing. 'Beyond that outcrop.'

Vega was waist high in the water now and passed Casper to Manfred.

He looked at the beach, counting around twenty of the shambling dead sailors, a clutch of them gathering around the body of his fallen shipmate and tearing hungrily into him. Their moans echoed across the island.

'Keep away from the shore, but try and get round that outcrop. I'll go ahead, see if I can find them.'

Vega dived below the surface and swam, skirting the jagged rocks around the White Isle's coastline before heading back towards the beach. As he emerged from the waves he could see Hector's henchmen standing on guard before a tall, thin cave entrance. Both looked startled to see the transformed Sharklord, each of them glancing warily around their small stretch of beach.

'Why all the screaming?' asked Ringlin nervously. 'It's enough to wake the dead!'

Ibal's giggles were cut short when Vega threw him a dark and serious look.

'Where's Hector?'

'The master said he wasn't to be interrupted,' said Ringlin cockily, sneering at Vega defiantly. 'Them's our orders.'

'Out of my way,' said Vega, making to push past them. Both men raised their hands to bar his progress, but neither was a match for an angry Sharklord. He punched each in the stomach, grabbed them by their necks and hurled them back into the water just as the first rowboat emerged into the cove.

'I don't have time for your idiotic loyalty!' he snarled. 'Get on the boats. *Now!*'

As if on cue, the first of the risen dead crawled around the outcrop, blue eyes glowing in the dark. Ringlin and Ibal needed no further prompting, running to the boat as Vega disappeared into the cave.

Beyond, in the dark, Vega could hear movements. It was the sound of glass clinking against glass. Gradually the fissure opened into a tall, bell-shaped chamber. The seawater sloshed around his ankles. Vega shook his head, trying to comprehend what he witnessed.

Hector hung in the air, held tight in the long, black arms of some creature that was suspended from the cavern's ceiling. The beast was upside down. Its long and thin fingers with bony knuckles reminded Vega of the spindly legs of a spider crab. He could see the bald, white dome of its skull against Hector's neck, its face buried in his throat, the Boarlord's head lolling to one side. The glassy clinking sound came from the magister's satchel, which still hung around his shoulder, banging against his hip as his legs and feet trembled in the air above the rushing tide.

Vega raised up his hands to grab at Hector's shoulder. Instantly the beast raised its head, still upside down, revealing its hideous visage with a hiss. Its waxy skin was stretched over its smooth skull, enlarged black eyes narrowing at the Sharklord's interruption. The lower portion of its head was dedicated to a maw of sharp, splintered teeth that ran red with the Boarlord's blood. Vega recoiled, the wound bubbling at Hector's neck.

'Hector!' cried the Sharklord, as the creature screeched something unintelligible.

'No, Vega,' said Hector, his voice weak, body trembling spasmodically in the monster's embrace.

What? He wants *this?* Vega shook his head, his mind collapsing at the notion that the young magister might have *willingly* let the creature attack him. The captain of the *Maelstrom* had seen men take leave of their minds enough times to know when they needed saving from themselves. He whipped out his cutlass, plunging it swiftly into the monster's chest.

The beast thrashed, screeching as it dropped the Boarlord. Hector landed in the swirling water below with a splash. Vega snatched at him with his free hand as he lunged in once more with his cutlass.

'No!' shouted the Boarlord in vain, but the Wereshark took no notice, standing over the stricken magister as the creature lashed out with its long arms. A thin sheet of black flesh began to appear beneath the beast's arms and between its fingers, a dark elastic membrane that connected joint to joint. Its head snapped towards Vega, blood pooling in the two sword wounds in its torso. Its movements were frantic as its body continued its change. Vega wasn't about to wait and see any further transformation – if it was anything like a therian then his cutlass would have caused it no harm at all. He brought his open hand back and swung.

The white, skeletal head ripped free from the creature's shoulders with the impact of the Wereshark's blow. The skull went flying across the cave and shattered against the scarred chalk wall. The decapitated body shook uncontrollably as Vega picked up Hector, the young man's eyes wild with madness as he stared over the Pirate Prince's shoulder.

'No,' the magister whispered as Vega carried him from the host's cave, out into the cold night.

PART IV

The Kiss of Silver

I

The Hawklord's Tale

If the survivors of Scoria had hoped for a peaceful crossing to Lyssia, they were sorely disappointed. The further the *Banshee* sailed north, the more restless the Sabre Sea became. It was a credit to the crew that they handled the conditions without complaint, content to be out from under the cruel hoof of Count Kesslar. Djogo had assumed captaincy of the vessel, a position he'd held under the Goatlord, but now the sailors were cooperative and his whip remained in his belt.

Slaves were no longer the cargo of the *Banshee*. Instead, her hold and decks were packed with warriors – former gladiators who had sworn allegiance to the Wolflord. They came from all across the world, each with his own story of enslavement and sorrow to tell. But now their spirits were high, and their loyalty to Drew seemed absolute. His small army numbered over a hundred, each man promising his blade to the cause.

Not a moment of the journey was spent idle, with the soldiers training throughout, ensuring they remained combat-ready and fighting fit. Drills and exercises were overseen by the Werelords, with Baron Griffyn pulling the strings. When he wasn't training the Wolf's army, the Hawklord was deep in conversation with Drew.

'Was my father a good man?'

Griffyn sat on one side of the enormous window that spanned the rear of the *Banshee,* with Drew at the opposite end of the sill. The spacious quarters had once been home to Kesslar, but the Goat's belongings had been stripped from the cabin and now lay on the seabed in Scoria's harbour. Practical furniture, such as the captain's desk, chairs, table and bunks had remained in place, now providing a home to Drew's Werelord companions, the seven therians sharing the cabin and making it their own. It was crowded, but still infinitely better than the labyrinth of the Furnace. While the others slept, the old Hawk and the young Wolf sat quietly, talking in whispered tones.

'I'd love to tell you a string of beautiful lies, Drew, truly I would. Wergar was a hard man. He'd never back out of a fight or argument; he was stubborn, hotheaded, and as tough as Sturmish steel. There was never a more fearsome sight than the Werewolf charging into battle, howling and roaring, scything Moonbrand through the bloody air. You couldn't imagine a more beautiful sword than your father's white blade. Wergar had friends and enemies and nothing in between.'

Griffyn took a sup from the tankard he held in his gnarled hand. 'I was honoured to be considered his friend.'

'The more I hear, the more he sounds like a brute.'

'He was a man of conviction, Drew, and he was the king.'

'King of Westland though, not the Barebones.'

'It mattered little back then, just as now; whosoever ruled in Highcliff ruled over all the Seven Realms. Consider Westland as the head of a great beast, and the remaining realms the body. It's long been acknowledged that there's only one king in Lyssia, and that's the one who sits on the throne in Highcliff. The Wolves ruled for two hundred years, Drew; nobody ever contested their place until the Lion arrived.'

Drew chewed his thumb as he stared out of the window, watching the churning waves as they flashed moonlight in the *Banshee*'s wake.

'So you knew Bergan, Manfred and Mikkel then? Were they your friends too?'

Griffyn smiled. 'They were once.'

'What changed?'

'Allegiances,' sighed the old Hawk. 'I'm sure you know all about Bergan's quandary when Leopold took power. He and the Staglords all played their parts in persuading Wergar to surrender his crown. They didn't know the Lion would go back on his word, but each of them deserted Wergar, and I hope each feels the pain of that betrayal to this day.'

'You've got them wrong, Griffyn. They're good men; they were my Wolf's Council, my advisers after we took Highcliff. It's cruel to hope they still suffer for something that happened so long ago.'

Griffyn looked surprised. 'I apologise, Lord Drew. I didn't mean to offend, but my opinion stands. I've earned it.'

'How?'

Griffyn rose stiffly, unfastening his jerkin.

'I was a loyal Kingsman, right until the last, to the moment Leopold chopped off your father's head. And I continued to remain loyal afterwards.'

Drew flinched at mention of Wergar's execution. He'd never known the man, but they were still joined by the bond of blood. The old Hawklord shook off his jerkin, popping the buttons of his shirt. Drew shifted uncomfortably.

'The Hawklords would – and did – die for your father, Drew. We were his staunchest allies and one of the fiercest weapons Wergar had in his arsenal. '*Death from above*' our enemies would scream when we soared into battle.'

Griffyn's face was wistful as he shrugged off the shirt.

'The other Werelords bowed and swore fealty to whoever sat on the throne. Not so the Hawklords, even after the Wolf and his pack were slain. We remained loyal to the dead king. This enraged the Lion, so much so that he made an example of me.'

Griffyn turned, the moonlight that streamed through the window illuminating his back. Two enormous scars ran from his shoulders down to the base of his spine, great discoloured swathes of pale, colourless skin. There was nothing neat or orderly about the old wounds, the torn flesh undulating, in and out, jagged and angry where his skin had been hacked away many years ago.

'Leopold took my wings. They held me down in the Court of Highcliff, the stench of your murdered and burned family still thick in the air, while the Bear and Stags watched. All the Werelords were there: Horses, Rams, Boars, the lot of them. The Lion took a silver blade to my beautiful wings. He carved them off.'

Drew was nauseous. He turned away, unable to look at the Hawklord's awful scars. The image was there in his mind: Leopold holding Griffyn down while he sawed the Werehawk's wings from his back. When he looked back, Griffyn was already rebuttoning his shirt.

'So, as you can imagine, I find it difficult to forgive after all these years.'

'I'm sorry, my Lord, I didn't . . .'

'You weren't to know,' said Griffyn, dismissing Drew. 'Bergan and Manfred are good men who were put in an awful situation. They escaped the Lion's wrath with their bodies intact but their pride battered. I might not have suffered this fate if I hadn't been so stubborn.'

Griffyn grimaced as he continued. 'Leopold's Lionguard dragged me back to Windfell, accompanied by the lickspittle Skeer – one of my Hawklord brothers – parading me before my people as a warning to all; if any Hawk should show their wings again, they were signing their own death warrant. Skeer was the only Hawk who sided with the Lion, happily swearing allegiance long before Wergar's murder. I was forced to deliver the message on behalf of Leopold. While the Lionguard displayed my severed wings to the Hawklords I recounted Leopold's decree, outlawing my people's falconthropy.'

'Falconthropy?'

'The therianthropy of the Hawklords, Drew. You have

your lycanthropes, felinthropes, caninthropes and the like. The Hawks are the falconthropes.'

'Leopold outlawed your transformation?'

'That's right,' said Griffyn, sitting down again on the windowsill. 'In addition, for their treasonous behaviour, the Hawklords were forbidden to return to the Barebones. We were banished, chased from our homeland, to be executed should we return. Leopold's army put Windfell under Skeer's command, and I was kept in court as a plaything for the new baron, a reminder to our people of what insubordination led to.'

'Where are the Hawklords now?'

'Dead. Gone. Forgotten. I honestly don't know. Leopold and Skeer destroyed my people. Windfell was emptied of Hawklords overnight, never to return. We were powerful and great in number, manning towers and keeps along the spine of the Barebones, acting as commanders and scouts in every army of the Seven Realms. But Leopold put us to the sword.'

'But Scoria? How did you get from Windfell to the Furnace?'

'That's where our mutual acquaintance Kesslar comes in,' said the Hawk, smacking his bony hand against the window frame.

'Kesslar and Skeer were friends from long, long ago. Opportunists, liars, thieves – they had so much in common. Kesslar was a frequent visitor to Windfell, the only place he was welcome, having taken advantage of his brother therians' kindness in the other courts of the Seven Realms. The Goat took a shine not just to me, but my daughter.'

Griffyn paused, glancing towards where Shah slept in her bunk.

'How old was she?'

'Twelve, just a child. Kesslar made Skeer an offer and the old Falcon couldn't say no. Deal done, the Goat had me shipped over to Scoria to fight in the Furnace, while he kept Shah as his own.'

Drew tried to imagine what kind of life that must have been for the young Shah. She'd been in a dark mood since he'd met her, and even with their freedom secured, a shadow still hung over Shah's head.

'She must have been terrified.'

'I don't doubt it for a moment, but we Hawklords are made of strong stuff. After four years in the Furnace, I'd earned the respect of my masters and freedom from the arena. I'd earned gold for my achievements, as well as lodging of my own away from the slaves and gladiators. While I moved into the ludus to train the Lizards' gladiators, my daughter was by then working for Kesslar, the eyes and wings that got him into places nobody else could reach.'

'How did she and Djogo come to know one another?'

'She saw him fight in the Furnace,' said the Hawklord. 'He was the greatest human gladiator I ever trained. When Kesslar bought him from Ignus, he and Shah began to spend time together, aboard this ship while Kesslar travelled, picking up slaves. A fondness grew, surrounded by the misery the Goatlord thrived upon.'

'She seems troubled,' whispered Drew, staring at her dark form in the recesses of the cabin.

'If she could get her talons into Kesslar, she'd tear his throat out.'

'Because of what he did to you?'

'No,' sighed the Hawk. 'Because of what happened to her child.'

'Child?' gasped Drew.

'Hush, lad,' said Griffyn, his voice low. He edged closer along the window seat towards Drew.

'She and Djogo have a child?'

'No, Drew, this was long before Djogo. My daughter met a fellow while she travelled with Kesslar, a charming, dangerous man who thought a little too much of himself – certainly not a marriageable prospect. She was a teenage girl and thought she was in love. Perhaps they were; we'll never know. Anyway, a child came from this union, unbeknown to Kesslar. The father was gone before my daughter even knew she was expecting. We hid the pregnancy from the Goat, Shah remaining in Scoria for the final months while Kesslar was away.

'The baby was born days before the Goat returned with the *Banshee* full of fresh slaves. Shah had no time at all with the child. I had it – him – taken away, using what coin I'd saved to have the baby taken to his father. If Kesslar had found my daughter with a child, Brenn knows what he'd have done with them. Punish her? Sell the child? I only hope the baby was delivered to the father. To this day I worry about what became of him. That child is my only regret.'

Drew put a hand on the old Hawk's crooked shoulder. 'You did what you had to, protecting your daughter and grandchild.'

'If I had that time again, I'd have killed Kesslar before surrendering one of my own. My only regret,' he repeated.

Drew wanted to comfort the old Hawklord but was unable to find the words.

'We all have regrets,' he said eventually, thinking back to Whitley and Gretchen, how he'd never had the chance to say goodbye to them. He wondered where Hector was, what had become of his dear friend, whether he'd ever see him again.

Griffyn smiled, the grin creasing his weatherbeaten face.

'You're too young for regrets, Drew. You've got time on your side. You can make changes and right your wrongs. Better still, right *others'* wrongs. And as long as I live and breathe I shall be by your side to help you do just that.'

2
The Game

Digging his feet into the loose earth, Trent scrambled the remaining distance up the hillside. He'd left the campsite behind him, his comrades' calls still echoing at his back as they searched for the escaped prisoners. They'd had forty captured men of the Longridings and Romari, all manacled and chained, and three of them had escaped. They'd been caught in the grasslands, drawing ever nearer to Calico where Lady Gretchen no doubt hid.

For one prisoner to go missing was extraordinary; for three to have escaped there must have been a traitor in the camp. Not one to let the tracks go cold, Trent was immediately up and away once the shout went out.

The footprints disappeared up the bluff to the east of the camp. Looking up, Trent could see a swaying rank of grass silhouetted against the moonlight, marking the highest point of the snaking ridge. He hauled himself to the summit, snatching at tufts of grass to stop himself from tumbling back. Breathing hard, he staggered to his feet and looked down. A huge meadow of unspoiled long grass disappeared into the darkness. The bluff was rocky on this side, a steep, treacherous bank of rough stones and loose earth filling the slope to the north and south. Trent watched his step as the rocks skittered underfoot, the scree plummeting sixty feet to the grasslands below.

He glanced along the ridge to see two figures to the north, a hundred feet or so feet away. By the clear night sky he recognized Sorin as one of them. The other was having his manacles removed, before being handed a shortsword by Sorin. With a hearty shove the prisoner was then sent tumbling down the embankment, a cloud of earth and stones erupting in his wake as he rolled and spun down into the grass.

'Wait!' called Trent, scrambling along the ridge, but by the time he'd caught up with Sorin the prisoner had disappeared from view below.

'What in Brenn's name are you doing? Are you behind this, Sorin? There's *three* of them that have escaped!'

'That's right, farmboy,' said Sorin, winking at Trent. Three pairs of unlocked manacles lay at his feet. 'Was me what freed them, wasn't it.'

Trent struck the broken-nosed captain in the face, his knuckles cracking as the two of them went down.

'Get off me you fool!' shouted Sorin, hammering the side of Trent's head with his fists as the younger man tried to pin him down.

'Traitor!' yelled Trent, finding fresh strength as he grappled with his senior officer. He couldn't hear the captain's voice; his mind and struggle was focused on Sorin the traitor. Traitor, just like Drew.

Sorin's fist caught Trent across the jaw, sending the young outrider over the ridge and down the rocky embankment. He bounced and twirled, losing all sense of up and down, his body a whirling mass of limbs. His head struck hard rock – once, twice – his temple splitting before he juddered to a halt in the grass at the base of the scree.

Trent tried to focus his eyes, stars spinning overhead. He lifted a hand, feeling the torn flesh over his eye, his fingertips coming away crimson.

'You'd call *me* a traitor, Ferran?' laughed Sorin from above, staggering back to his feet. 'I was obeying orders. Lord Pinkeye told me to have three picked out and sent down here. For the game.'

'The game?' called up Trent, dabbing at his streaming brow.

'Our lordship needs to hunt, Ferran. That's why I brought them away from the camp. He can lose control when his blood's up.'

Trent rolled on to his belly and began to crawl up the embankment, the loose earth falling down on top of him. He struggled frantically, trying to find purchase in the scree, but it was impossible. A scream from the long grass behind made him stop and turn, his eyes wide and fearful.

'You gave them swords?' he shouted to Sorin.

'Pinkeye likes his prey to have a little fight in 'em, doesn't he?' called down the captain, crouching over the incline. 'I hope you brought your pa's Wolfshead blade with you, Ferran. Best of luck, eh?'

With that, Sorin turned and disappeared from view.

'Sorin!' Trent cried in vain. 'Sorin!'

Trent looked up and down the ridge base, desperate to find a way of climbing out. He was blind to a means of escape, the long grass to his right was as high as his head and constantly swaying. Reluctantly, he unsheathed the Wolfshead blade and started to follow the stony bank northwards. He glanced up as he went, constantly searching for a route out.

Sorin had played the situation perfectly and let Trent leap to his own conclusions. Before Trent knew it, he was lying at the bottom of an impossible slope waiting for the Catlord to tear him to pieces. The captain was a sly fellow.

'Brenn, help me . . .'

A gurgling cry came from the long grass nearby. Trent recognized the wet sound in the voice; blood, pooling at the back of the man's throat. He shook his head and moved onwards. *Not your concern, Trent.*

'The beast,' a voice sobbed. 'Dear Brenn, the beast . . .'

Trent ground his teeth, ignoring the man's pleas. He had to look after his own skin, thanks to Sorin. The sobbing man's cries tugged at him as he walked past, like hooks beneath his skin. *Keep going, Trent. Don't stop now. You can't stop. The man's a traitor. His death rattle's on its way. He got what was coming.*

But with each step, the begging cries of the man snagged hold of Trent's conscience. He couldn't leave *anything* to die – that much Mack Ferran had taught him on the Cold Coast.

He cursed angrily, wiping the blood from his temple along

his sleeve as he turned and set off into the long grass. Away from the ridge he strode, cutting the grass back with his longsword, staggering hesitantly towards the cries of a scared and dying man.

Thirty or so paces from the slope, Trent found him, lying on a flattened bed of grass. The tall, feathery fronds lay bent and broken about him, his limbs spread-eagled as if he'd prepared a nest for the night. The man still held the shortsword that Sorin had given him, his right hand feebly raising it as Trent appeared. The man's head remained still against the floor, although his eyes stayed fixed on the Ferran boy as his lips trembled.

The man's mouth was awash with blood, pink spittle foaming between his teeth, his belly torn wide open. Trent gagged, the food from his evening meal racing up his throat. He turned away, trying to hold it down but only partly succeeding.

'Please . . .' begged the man, finding his words again. 'Kill . . . me . . .'

Trent turned back, his face a mask of pity and horror. He raised the Wolfshead blade and faltered, unable to put the poor man out of his misery. Before he could act decisively, the grasses split to his right as a white shape sprang from the darkness, the moonlight catching the beast's shining fur as it flew. Trent just had time to parry the monster away, before the sword flew from his grasp and the two tumbled into the bloody grass.

The Catlord's white head was huge, the width of Trent's torso. The jaws snapped at his face, teeth the size of daggers. Claws held Trent's shoulders, pinning him to the ground and preventing his escape. He raised his left forearm towards the monster, catching the Cat's bite with it before it tore at his skull. The teeth clamped down hard, cutting into the steel armoured bracer and threatening to snap his arm in two. Trent screamed as the Cat's pink eyes shone, demonic in the moonlight; Frost was possessed by the change, by the hunt, by the kill. The bracer bowed, the metal sleeve groaning, about to break. Trent jabbed at the Catlord's eyes with his free hand, hooking his thumb in and striking home.

With a roar, Frost released his grip on the Redcloak, leaping off the boy and bounding back into the grasses. The shouting of soldiers echoed down from the ridge, as Bastians and Lionguard investigated the commotion. Trent rolled over on to the body of the dying man, but the beast was gone. The light had gone from the prisoner's eyes, life's last breath steaming from his still lips.

Trent scrambled about in the bloody grass, fingers searching for his dropped blade. A low growl emanated from the shadows, the beast was still close by. Did Frost know that it was Trent he was facing? *Surely he recognizes me?* Trent's hand brushed cold steel, fingers racing along its length until they found the handle. Snatching it up he tracked back through the grass, towards the voices on the ridge.

He stumbled from the tall grass, collapsing against the pebbled hillside. Above he heard Bastians and Lyssians alike, shouting for him to climb up, to keep moving. He resheathed the Wolfshead blade and began his ascent again, hands and feet clawing at the bank, every handful of loose earth sending him sliding back again. The growling sound drew closer as his comrades shouted their support, looking on with morbid fascination as the beast closed in.

'Keep moving, Ferran!'

'It's coming, man!'

'Climb for your life!'

Trent wanted to scream, but that was wasted energy. He was fighting for survival now – the changed Catlord behind him was out of his mind with bloodlust. Trent was just one more human delivered by Sorin, a mouse for the cat to play with until it stopped twitching.

Trent's hand caught a flat rock overhead, a few feet below a larger boulder that protruded from the scree bank. He didn't have time to check its suitability, trusting it would remain in place as he hauled himself up. His muscles strained and burned as he trusted his body weight to the flat ledge. It remained in place, deeply embedded, allowing him to finally make progress.

'It's on you, Ferran!'

'I can see it in the grass!'

Trent threw his right hand forward towards the larger boulder, his fingers scrabbling for purchase as he launched himself towards the higher point. The men cheered overhead, willing him on. This would put him clear of the grasses; give him the chance to find a route out while Frost regained his senses.

The boulder ripped free as it took Trent's weight, the bank collapsing as he fell in a shower of dirt, rock and pebbles back to the base of the ridge. Trent spluttered, the dust cloud blinding and choking him as he struggled to rise from the debris. The grasses parted in front of him as a figure emerged.

Trent had expected a clawed paw to strike out; tear his throat, his stomach, put an end to his fight. Instead, a smooth, human hand was extended before him, as the lithe outline of Frost stood over him, naked in the moonlight. The albino Catlord flexed his fingers, beckoning Trent to take his offered palm. He rubbed his other hand against his injured eye, squinting and blinking as he focused on the terrified outrider.

'Got me good there, Trent,' said the felinthrope, smiling through bloodied teeth. He nodded at his hand. The Redcloak hesitantly took it as Frost hauled him to his feet.

'A word of warning, Trent: never get in the way of a Catlord when he's hunting game. Come, let's return to camp. I owe you a hundred apologies.'

3

The Bloody Bay

At a glance he looked like any other sailor on ship's watch in Denghi. A fringe of black hair poked out from the rim of his kash, the headdress popular with the men of the desert. A white scarf was wrapped around his face in the Omiri style, grey eyes peering out from the narrow slit, watching all who passed along the wharf. His bare torso was weather-beaten and tanned, three-quarter length white leggings covered his legs, leaving his bare feet exposed to the elements. His right hand rested on his hip, a shortsword lodged within the sash, while his left was missing, a basket handled trident dagger sitting on the stump in its place. He stood between the rails at the head of the *Banshee*'s gangway, apparently relaxed. There were few captains in Denghi who could boast the rightful king of Westland as their watchman.

The port was crowded with a variety of ships, greater in

number than any Drew had seen before. All Hallows Bay, Highcliff and Cape Gala had been busy, bustling harbours, but there was a manic energy to Denghi. Griffyn had explained to Drew that this port in the Bloody Bay was the only truly neutral city in Omir. Pasha to the north was under the control of Lord Canan's Doglords, while Ro-Shann to the south was home to Lady Hayfa, the Hyena. Both Canan and Hayfa were enemies of the true ruler of Omir, King Faisal of Azra, but each respected the neutrality of Denghi. It was the only place in Omir where one could find agents of all three factions rubbing shoulders with one another.

The choice of where they should land had been limited. As predicted, they'd passed patrolling Bastian warships while they slunk across the Sabre Sea. As the *Banshee* was known to the Bastians as a slaver, she was allowed on her way with little interference. Djogo and Shah had welcomed the captain of one such vessel aboard while the Werelords and small army of gladiators hid in the hold. They'd made their excuses for Kesslar's absence, telling the Bastians that the Goat was sleeping off a barrel of wine below decks. The captain had warned Djogo to steer clear of the southern waters, due to the military activity in the Lyssian Straits. The *Banshee* had no other option than to head for Denghi.

The slave vessel was moored at the end of the port's longest pier, a five-hundred-foot-long wharf that reached out into the Bloody Bay. Every inch of the pier was crowded with merchants, fishermen, sailors and ne'er-do-wells, haggling with one another over goods. The air was alive with sounds and smells: music from cantinas clashing with shouting traders, monkeys chattering, dogs barking, spices burning, meats cooking. Apart from one Bastian warship, anchored a little further round the bay, there was no sign of the military within the harbour. Lyssia may have been at war, but there seemed to be little conflict in Denghi.

Three figures approached the gangplank from the pier. Djogo came first, his face open, identity unhidden. He was known in Omir, with a fearsome reputation hard-earned. Denghi had been a regular stop-off for Kesslar down the years for buying and selling slaves. Behind came Griffyn and Krieg, their faces obscured by kashes. The trio traversed the gangway, Drew nodding as they passed. He followed them as they disappeared below, another sailor replacing him at the top of the planked walkway.

The Werelords gathered around the desk in the captain's cabin, Djogo standing by the door. A crude map of Lyssia was carved into the tabletop, which the Goat had used to plot his raids around the continent. The allies of the Wolf now used it to plan their next move.

Griffyn cast his hand across the map wearily.

'Lyssia is turbulent, more so than ever before,' said the Hawklord, pinching his sharp nose between thumb and forefinger.

'Turbulent?' asked Drew. 'Beyond that Bastian frigate, there's no sign of war in Denghi.'

'The battle rages beneath calm waters,' said Krieg 'It would appear the seaport has dodged much of Omir's fighting, but that could change at any moment.'

'You said Denghi was neutral.'

'So it is. But news is that Lord Canan is allied with the Catlords,' said the Rhino.

'Cats and Dogs, unified?' chuckled the Behemoth, the noise like a grinding millstone.

'I know,' agreed Griffyn. 'Unlikely unions have sprung up across Lyssia. There is talk that Lady Hayfa has also agreed terms with Canan. Her forces are already mobilizing, ensuring that Faisal is surrounded to the north and south by powerful enemies, allied against him. They mean to attack Azra.'

'Are they powerful enough to succeed?' asked Drake.

'If the Catlords lend their claws, this Desert King will die,' said Taboo, sneering out of the porthole towards the Bastian warship.

'Grim days indeed for the Jackal,' said Drake.

'And the rest of Lyssia?' said Drew, keen to hear news of the west.

'Broken,' said Djogo. 'Highcliff has fallen to the Catlords, your Wolf's Council chased from Westland. Lucas sits on the throne in place of his dead father.'

'Leopold, dead?' said Drew, clearly shocked.

'It's said that Duke Bergan killed him,' said the old Hawklord.

Good old Bergan. I knew he wouldn't let us down if he got the chance.

Drew noticed Griffyn was avoiding eye contact. 'What is it?'

'The duke is dead, too, Drew; killed in his battle with Leopold.'

Drew stared at Griffyn's bowed head, the old man's words not sinking in straight away.

'The whereabouts of your mother and others – Queen Amelie, Duke Manfred and Baron Hector – isn't known, though Earl Mikkel was slain by the Doglords. The remains of your Wolf's Council are being bandied about as Lyssia's 'most wanted'; there's a price on their heads – and your own.'

Drew hardly heard Griffyn. Mikkel and his dear friend and mentor, Bergan, dead. He'd always felt certain he would see the Bearlord again, didn't imagine that he would never get to make amends to the giant, bearded duke for fleeing Highcliff in secret.

Krieg tugged at the kash around Drew's face.

'It's more important than ever we keep your identity secret, my friend,' said the Rhino, before placing a consoling hand on the Wolf's shoulder. 'If Onyx offers riches in return for your head, you'll have fewer friends than ever.'

'Hector and Whitley,' said Drew, his attention still on the Hawklord. 'And Gretchen. Any news?'

'As I said, Hector fled Highcliff when Onyx took the city. I couldn't tell you if he's alive. Lady Gretchen and Lady Whitley disappeared from Cape Gala after you were taken by Kesslar. Their whereabouts are unknown, but many of the Horselords fled Cape Gala to Calico on the coast, so your friends may have joined them. Duke Brand, the Bull, reigns there, his fortress city one of the few that makes a stand against the Bastians. A fleet of the Catlord's warships gathers off the coast, blockading the Lyssian Straits.'

'Have the other realms not come to Westland's aid? What of Sturmland? The Barebones?'

Krieg raised his voice now as Griffyn shook his head. 'The Lords of Sturmland have taken no side, while the Barebones are split – the Stags of Stormdale and Highwater stand in favour of the Wolf, while the Crows of Riven supposedly remain neutral.'

'Supposedly?'

'Their contempt for the other Werelords of the Barebones is famous – they want the realm for themselves. I find it hard to believe they aren't involved in some way with the attacks on Highwater.'

'Highwater's been attacked?' asked Drew.

'The Staglord cities are without their lords, one brother dead, the other missing,' replied Griffyn, pointing a bony finger at the mountain range on the map. 'Even now Onyx moves his pieces into play, his army having taken the Dalelands and now laying siege to Highwater.'

'But surely Highwater is full of civilians?'

'Not so. Word reached the remaining Stags that a combined army of Bastians and Omiri approached. The innocents have evacuated south to the safety of Stormdale. Brenn-willing, the civilians will be spared this conflict and the battle will play out in Highwater. The men of the Barebones are a tough bunch, and Highwater is well protected: they'll be prepared for a long siege.'

'Is there *nobody* who can aid them?'

'The Stags have no allies. The Bear is gone from Brackenholme, and Windfell to the south remains deserted,' sighed Griffyn. 'My homeland is no more than a ghost town while the Lion's lackey, Skeer, rules the roost.'

Shah, at her father's side, now spoke up. 'Not for long. Skeer's time is running out. When we return to Windfell, we'll turn the traitorous old bird out of the nest and make it our own again.'

'Brave words, Hawk,' said Krieg. 'But what hope do you and your father have of defeating whatever force awaits you in Windfell? Where are your fellow Hawklords in your time of need?'

Griffyn looked up from the table, his eyes settling upon Drew again, who stared straight back, shocked at the old warrior's tide of bad news.

'Where are the Hawklords, baron?' asked Drew, his voice quiet as he struggled with his grief.

'Scattered,' replied Griffyn. 'Many took on lives as normal, mortal men – like you, Drew, before you discovered your lycanthropy. Can you imagine? Forbidden to embrace the beast? Having your gift denied you? My people were broken just as Windfell was. They're lost.'

'Is there no way of reaching them?'

Griffyn wavered, his eyes narrowing. The Hawklord sat down, looking back to the map. His finger traced a line up the Silver River from Denghi, past Azra, to the Barebones, coming to a halt. The Werelords were silent as they watched him, waiting for Griffyn to speak. He closed his eyes and spoke.

'There is a place most sacred to my people, the great mountain of Tor Raptor, ancient tomb of the Hawklords of Windfell. Only the just and rightful lord may safely enter the Screaming Peak.'

'Screaming Peak?' Drew asked.

'It's a cavern within Tor Raptor's summit. When the stones are lifted, Tor Raptor screams to her children.'

'Screams?' Krieg was fascinated, as were the others.

'It's the one way in which the true Lord of Windfell may call the Hawklords home. It's the only way.'

'Sounds like a legend to me, old timer,' sighed Drake. 'We need more than wailing mountains to best our foes.'

The Hawklord opened his eyes, settling them upon Drew. The young Wolf nodded.

'We need an army,' he said.

4

Back from the Dead

'Come in,' called Count Vega, as a series of knocks on the door took his attention away from his desk. A heavily cloaked Duke Manfred entered the cabin, stamping his feet and clapping his hands, tiny snowflakes shaking loose from his shoulders.

'Is it chilly outside, Your Grace?'

'It's as cold as Ragnor's chin!' grunted the duke miserably.

'Interesting you mention old Henrik's father. We're close to the coast of Sturmland again by my reckoning, maybe a day or two out of Friggia. That business with the Sirens and then the White Isle almost did for us – thank Sosha that I was able to get my bearings.'

The two Werelords were silent for a moment, memories of their brief visit to the lonely island all too vivid. Vega reached into a cabinet and pulled out a bottle and glass, pushing them across the table towards Manfred.

'There really was no need for you to take a watch you know. The last thing I need is a frozen Stag tumbling on to the deck, shattering into a thousand pieces. Would scare the lives out of my men.'

'It's the least I can do, mucking in with your crew,' said the old Duke, unstoppering the bottle and pouring himself a glass with shivering hands. He threw it down his throat swiftly, barking a spluttering cough at the drink.

'Friggia you say?' muttered the duke. 'Do you plan to stop there?'

'I'd hoped we could make it straight to Roof. Perhaps we still can. Stopping in Friggia would be dangerous. It's one of Slotha's ports; we want to bypass it if possible. There's no way Onyx's forces could have reached this far north yet. We should get to Icegarden through the back door, so to speak.'

'How's Amelie?'

Vega smiled, a rakish grin breaking his handsome features. The captain of the *Maelstrom* had watched the tender friendship between Manfred and the queen blossom into something else. Neither of the therians would admit to such feelings – they'd deny it instantly – but there was no fooling the Sharklord.

'I invited her into my company, but she still needs rest. It appears the encounters on the White Isle have left their scars upon her.'

Manfred nodded, staring back into the open stove, the flames warming his hands and soul.

'And Hector?' said the Staglord. 'Any news?'

Vega ran a hand through his long, black hair, wincing at the thought of the young magister.

'He still sleeps.'

'Sleep is a good thing. I thought he was dead.'

'He might have killed us all.'

'How can you say that, Vega? The poor lad was attacked by that creature, wasn't he?'

The count scratched at his scalp. 'He was and he wasn't.'

'Don't start with the cryptic talk, Vega!'

'Yes, the creature attacked him, could easily have killed him. But I think he deliberately allowed the beast to assault him.'

'How so?' The duke sounded shocked.

'We landed on the White Isle on Hector's insistence. I suspect he wanted us to go there, knew what awaited us, and put all our lives in danger.'

'How could he have possibly known what was on the island? That's preposterous, Vega!'

'I don't know. This communing he's confessed to carrying out, this necromancy – who knows what he's tapped into? You can't tell me Hector isn't a changed man. He *knew* there was something on that island. His actions led to one of my men getting killed. It has something to do with dark magistry, I'm sure of it. I don't have the answers, Manfred, but I believe Hector does.'

The duke scratched at the grey stubble on his jaw, saddened to hear Vega's accusations, but he didn't defend the Boarlord. It was plain for all to see that the sickly Hector bore little resemblance to the happy young boy he'd first met ten years ago in the court of Redmire.

'Does Lady Bethwyn still attend him?'

'She has a soft spot for our magister,' said Vega, staring at the cabin door, his thoughts distant. 'She is another therian of the Dalelands after all. She seems a lovely girl, very trusting. I hope Hector doesn't betray that trust.'

'What on earth do you mean?'

The count shook his head wearily and then smiled at the duke. 'I'm thinking aloud, that's all. He's a complex character, our Baron of Redmire, Manfred.'

'You worry too much,' said Manfred, unfastening his cloak at last as his body warmed up. 'He's not as misguided as you suggest, my friend. Just a little misunderstood.'

Vega nodded but said nothing, his mind lingering on the memory of two bickering brothers on the staircase of Bevan's tower, arguing over their father's throne for a final, fatal time.

Bethwyn clenched the cloth in her fist, her knuckles turning white as she squeezed the excess water from it. Beyond the porthole, sleet raced past, blurring streaks of white against the pitch-black night. Bethwyn moved her hand over Hector's head, gently mopping his brow with the damp cloth, the warm scented water settling across his clammy skin. For seven days and nights she'd kept vigil over the Boarlord, Queen Amelie relieving her of her other responsibilities in order to care for the magister. She wondered if his terrible fever would ever break.

By the time the rowboats had returned to the *Maelstrom* from the White Isle, many had assumed the baron was bound for a watery grave, few giving him any chance of survival.

His throat was torn and his blood loss great, the wound refusing to heal as a normal injury would for a therian. Using what medicinal knowledge she and others had, Bethwyn had patched Hector up, cleaning, staunching and dressing the bite as best she could. She'd changed the bandage frequently over the following days, but the festering smell never went away. The Boarguard, Ringlin and Ibal, always lurked nearby, making Bethwyn uncomfortable. The tall one didn't have a nice word to say about anyone, while the looks the fat giggling one gave her made her skin crawl. All the while the Boarlord had clung to the sliver of life, refusing to give up his fight.

Bethwyn brushed the matted hair from Hector's brow. He'd lost a lot of weight since she'd first met him in Highcliff, his puppy fat all gone as his skin clung tightly to his cheekbones. His skin had a deathly pallor to it, almost yellow beneath the lantern light. She shivered, throwing another piece of wood on to the stove. She closed the grille door with the poker before facing the sickly Boarlord once more.

Hector's left arm had found its way out of the covers. She picked it up at the wrist and elbow and was about to tuck it back below the blanket when she paused. She turned it over in her hands, revealing the palm. The black mark she'd seen when they'd encountered the Sirens had grown, the entire palm now blackened and the skin darkening between each finger. This wasn't the first time she'd examined the hand while Hector slept. While the rest of his body burned with a fever, the corrupted palm remained cold to the touch. *As cold as death itself*, thought Bethwyn.

Suddenly the hand snatched at her wrist, causing her to cry out in shock. It clasped hard, the chill flesh tight on her skin, fingers holding her in their grasp. Hector's eyes were open, watching her, his head motionless on the pillow.

'Gretchen.'

His voice was a whisper, cracked lips trembling as he tried to smile. Bethwyn should have been happy to see his eyes and hear his voice, but she couldn't get over the shock of his grip. *He's mistaken me for another.* She tugged back, trying to free her wrist.

'I dreamt it was you. So caring and kind,' he said slowly and quietly.

'Please, Hector; it's me, Bethwyn,' she said, but he wouldn't relinquish his hold.

'I was in such a dark place, Gretchen, so cold and alone. And you were the warmth I could cling to. It was your light that brought me back from the darkness. It was your love.'

'Hector, you're hurting,' she cried, as the magister's hand tightened its grip. *Can he not hear me?* It was as if he were unaware of his hand's action while her words simply didn't register.

'I knew you wouldn't abandon me to the dark,' he said, eyes closing as tears rolled down his face. 'I knew you'd save me from the nightmare, Gretchen . . .'

Bethwyn was crying out now, trying to prise his fingers away, but the more she struggled the tighter he held on. His words were rambling, making no sense, as if he were sleep talking. *Is he even conscious? Does he* know *he's hurting me?*

'I would speak with your father when the time comes,

Gretchen. I would seek your hand my love, for we should be together. We *belong* together.'

Bethwyn shrieked, frantically trying to shake him loose, as the door burst open. Vega was between the two of them immediately, trying to bat Hector's hand away. When he realized the Boar wouldn't relinquish his grip, he took his own fingers to Hector's, pulling them back hard. The Shark-lord was surprised by the magister's strength, the hold like a trap. Finally the fingers opened enough to allow the girl to pull her arm free, the flesh of her wrist livid with red welts.

'What are you *thinking*?' shouted Vega, shaking Hector by the shoulders in his cot.

'What?' muttered Hector, his eyes blinking as if waking from a dream. 'I didn't . . .'

'You were *hurting* her!' said the count as Manfred and Amelie appeared in the doorway. Bethwyn rushed into the queen's arms.

'Bethwyn?' gasped Hector, deeply confused.

Manfred stood to one side, escorting Amelie and Bethwyn from the room. He passed Ringlin and Ibal entering as he left, the Staglord unable to resist glowering at the Boarguard. The men watched the three leave before joining Vega in their sickly master's cabin.

'I didn't know,' whispered Hector. 'I was dreaming . . .'

'Dreaming or not, Hector, that girl has tended to you for the last seven days.'

Vega leaned over the bed and brought his face close to Hector's. 'Tell me, Hector: did you *know* what was waiting for us on that island? What kind of monster was that in the cavern? One of my men died on that beach, devoured by the dead, while you explored that cave.'

'I don't know . . . what you're talking . . .' stammered Hector, but the captain of the *Maelstrom* continued.

'I thought you and I had an understanding, Hector. I was there in Bevan's Tower, remember? I helped you with that mess. I thought it was an accident . . .'

'It *was* an accident, Vega!' cried Hector, fully awake now, his face contorting with resentment.

'That may be,' said the Sharklord. 'But our visit to the White Isle was no accident. Your encounter with that monster didn't look like a struggle to me, Hector. It looked like . . . like an *embrace* . . .'

Vega stood up, straightening his collar.

'I'm disappointed, Hector. I've looked out for you, shown you nothing but compassion and friendship, and this is how you repay me. Well, I'm watching you. You know more than you're telling us, only I'm not as foolish as the others. I know your secrets, just remember that.'

Count Vega turned, barging between the Boarguard and slamming the cabin door shut as he left. Ringlin and Ibal watched him leave, then looked back to the Lord of Redmire as he lay in his sickbed. Hector's face darkened as he lifted his blackened hand to his throat. He took hold of the bandages, yanking them loose, the stained dressing crunching as he pulled it from his wound. The scar was scabbed over, slowly on the mend. He rubbed his black hand across his neck and heaved himself upright, swaying woozily on the bed. He looked at the two men, his face full of thunder, eyes bright with fury and revenge. The stare spoke volumes to the Boarguard. Ibal giggled and Ringlin nodded.

Hector's whisper hissed from his broken lips. 'Vega must die.'

5

Overwhelming Odds

Opening into the ocean at Bloody Bay, the Silver River had earned its name on two counts. Firstly, as the main tributary from the Barebones to the Sabre Sea, it was the swiftest and most profitable trade route for moving precious metals out of the mountains. It was said that whoever controlled the Silver River controlled Omir, the stewardship of the waterway being a constant bone of contention between the Werelords of the Desert Realm.

As Drew stood on the poop deck of the *Banshee* and looked east towards the sunrise, he marvelled at the other cause for the river's name. With the sun's first rays breaking over the horizon, the mighty river threw its light back to the heavens. Drew squinted, raising his hand to shield his eyes from the metallic glare of the water.

'It's something else, isn't it?'

He blinked as his eyes slowly refocused on Lady Shah at his side.

'A jewel in the desert's crown,' agreed Drew, turning from the blinding vision.

The crew made the most of the fair weather, and unfurled the sails, grateful for the wind that spirited them westward up the river. Djogo stood at the wheel on the deck below, the former slaver enjoying his newfound freedom, even managing to share a rare joke with Drake who lounged nearby. The sun's rays were warm on Drew's back, a welcome change from the freezing night. They might have been in the land of sand, but the night reminded him of the Cold Coast. Winter had arrived across Lyssia, even flirting with Omir. The snow-capped mountains of the Barebones straddled the horizon, their ultimate destination.

'When did you last visit the mountains?'

'Fifteen years ago,' replied Shah, pausing to think about the long absence. 'I was but a girl, handed over to Kesslar by Skeer, along with my father.'

'And you've encountered no other Hawklords in your travels since then?'

'None. I hear mention of them occasionally, reported sightings, but their spirits were broken when my father's wings were taken. We were a shamed species to King Leopold, lower than humans in his eyes.'

'Do you really think your father can call them home? This Screaming Peak – it sounds like something from a storybook.'

'He was taken there as a child by his father, its secrets passed on to him. I just hope we can find it.'

The *Banshee* wasn't a huge ship but she looked out of place on the Silver River. Her big black prow cut a great wake through the water, sending the smaller fishing vessels, barges and skiffs towards the shores. The waterway was wide and deep, navigable to big ships such as the *Banshee* to where the river split at Two Rivers. This wild port town at the foot of the Barebones where mountain met desert was where the Werelords now headed. From Two Rivers they would disembark and hike on towards Tor Raptor. Drew's eyes settled on the former slaver who commanded the ship's wheel on the deck below, his thoughts returning to the private talks the two had shared.

'Djogo seems to be very fond of you,' said Drew.

'What's he told you?'

'He says you're friends – that's all you can ever be, he a human, you a therian.'

Shah shivered and smiled. 'I've loved before, Drew, and it didn't end well . . .' Her voice trailed off as she stared upriver to where a number of craft jostled against one another.

'What is it?' said Drake as he walked up to the poop deck to join them.

'A massacre,' said Shah, still looking ahead, her face impassive. 'An ambush.'

'You can see *that*?' asked Drew, suddenly anxious. They had to retain their anonymity and stay out of the fray – the last thing the group needed was a fight, especially someone else's. He strained his eyes, seeing only blurs aboard the boats ahead, plus the occasional glint of steel.

'You have your nose, Wolf. I have my sight.'

'Who's fighting?' asked Drake.

'Hard to tell, but the skiff in the middle is under attack from two others. They're badly outnumbered.'

She arched an eyebrow. 'A Doglord of some kind leads the assault.'

'Really?' said Drew, mention of a therian so similar to his own kind piquing his interest. His instinct told him they should step in. The men of the *Banshee* had noticed the commotion as well, stopping their work to watch.

Shah saw that Drew was agitated. She placed a hand on his shoulder. 'You cannot join every fight.'

'It feels wrong,' he growled as they watched the skirmish. He was about to say more when her fingers dug into his skin. He winced, noticing her nails had transformed into talons.

'What's the matter?' Drew gasped.

'A child's in danger!'

Before Drew could respond, Drake had taken a running jump, launching himself from the deck of the *Banshee*.

'Drake!' cried Shah, but the Crocodile was already gone, swimming speedily towards the fracas. The pair could see his long dark shape powering through the water in the direction of the three boats, transforming as he swam.

'He'll get himself killed!' fretted Shah.

'How many are there?' asked Drew.

'Too many.'

Shah arched her back, grey wings emerging with a flourish. Her head was changing, features growing sharper, her nose and mouth blending together into an amber beak as a frill of charcoal feathers emerged through her black hair. A large avian eye stared down at Drew as he stood in the Hawklady's shadow.

She prepared to take flight, taking to the air from the *Banshee*'s wooden deck. Drew needed no invitation, catching hold of her legs as she took off. The Werehawk looked down, surprised at the presence of a passenger.

'You've carried me once before!' he shouted, as if to persuade her not to drop him. Shah shook him loose, his one hand not strong enough to keep hold, only to snatch him up again in her powerful talons. They quickly put the *Banshee* behind them as they closed in on the battle. Drake was there already, wading into the midst of the combatants, turning the air red around him. As they neared, Drew felt the change coming, the Wolf's aspects gradually shifting through his body. By the time Shah was flying over the ambushed skiff, she was launching a changed Werewolf into a gang of shocked swordsmen.

Drew's claws flew, the lycanthrope spinning as he scattered the mob of attacking warriors along the deck. His foot crunched into a torso, ribs crumpling as the man was catapulted overboard. Drew's hand battered another, sending him colliding into his companion's blade, the two toppling in a bloody mess. A scimitar sailed down, one fighter finding a way past the claws towards the Werewolf's throat. Drew's trident dagger flashed, deflecting the blade off the basket hilt.

Drew took in the scene. The skiff's oarsmen lay dead, some floating face down in the river, butchered in the attack. Two sleeker boats were moored alongside the skiff, grapples having hauled it in so the warriors could board. The dozen or so invaders wore crimson kashes, the splash of red reminding Drew of the Lionguard. He looked to the prow. A girl no more than ten years old cowered there, two warriors in white valiantly standing between her and the enemy, their dead comrades littering the deck.

Drake tried to cut his way through the red-kashed warriors towards the girl, but the attackers were ready for him, throwing their blades up as he tore into them. Drew was drawn to the towering dog-headed warrior in the middle of the skiff. He held an enormous spear in one hand, barking orders as he faced the therians.

'You've nothing to fear!' cried the Doglord to his soldiers. 'Silver or not, they'll still bleed from your blades!'

The warriors attacked, spurred on by their master. Scimitars rained down on Drew and Shah. The Hawklady leaped off the boat to hover over the water, lashing out with her talons. Drew ducked and weaved, returning his own volley of claw, tooth and dagger at the warriors. He glanced up to see the two brave defenders at the front of the skiff tumble lifelessly to their knees, the attackers' numerous scimitars too much for them. With mighty wing beats Shah rushed to the prow, landing over the girl and snatching up a pair of swords.

'Leave the girl alone!'

The red-kashed warriors hesitated for a moment, facing the transformed Werehawk armed with twin blades. The Doglord urged them forward, Shah's swords finding the first few who got too close, before the caninthrope turned to face the Werecrocodile. Bodies, oars, scimitars and benches made the battleground uneven for all the combatants. The *Banshee* remained too far away, leaving the three therians alone in their fight against the men in red kashes. The Doglord's giant spear lanced through the air towards Drake, but the Crocodile stumbled clear and into the enemy mob. He went down beneath them as the Doglord turned his attention on Drew.

The spear splintered the deck where the Wolf had stood a moment earlier. Drew hurdled the weapon and leaped, kicking the Dog's jaw. The beast's head snapped back, the blow sending him crashing into his men. They pushed him forward once more, allowing him to take another stab at Drew. The Werehound was fast, and deadly with his spear, the blade finding Drew as he tried to dodge clear. The foot-long silver dagger tore deep into Drew's shoulder, tearing the flesh and glancing off bone. The Wolf howled in agony, dizzy with nausea from the deadly blade.

'You must be the Werewolf everyone's so keen to meet. Let's see what they make of you when I'm wearing your skin as a cloak!' the Doglord taunted.

The spear jabbed forward again, but Drew threw his head out of the way just in time, the blade missing his face by a hair's breadth. He took hold of the spear shaft as it passed, hooking it under his arm and throwing his weight behind it as he swung it hard to one side. The Doglord kept hold of the other end, unable to stop himself from being propelled into his own men. Three of them tumbled overboard and the Hound narrowly avoided joining them. But before Drew could press home his advantage the remaining red-kashed warriors leaped on him.

Drew lashed out blindly, but scimitar cuts criss-crossed his back as his attackers slashed at him and blood pumped relentlessly from his shoulder wound. He was overwhelmed, knocking one red-kashed fighter off only to see two more take his place. The longer he remained on the deck, the more chance the fight would end badly. More sword blows were finding their mark now, the Doglord's warriors proving fearless and blindly obedient under his command.

But just as it began to look hopeless, the men in red started to fall away, their blows becoming less frequent as their numbers were thinned. Drew looked up to see hands, limbs, fingers and flesh flying as Drake tore a path through the warriors towards him. The Doglord brought his spear round, striking out at the Werecrocodile, but Drake was too fast, his reptilian tail whipped out from behind. Two men went overboard, legs broken, before the tail struck the Doglord, sending him bouncing on to the deck, spear clattering down on top of him.

Two more soldiers stood over Drew, one aiming an executioner's blow to his neck. Drew knew all too well that no therian healing could replace a missing head. Drake was on them instantly, his reptilian body blocking the blows as he put himself in harm's way. The red warriors were strong, but no match for a transformed therian gladiator. The executioner suddenly found he was missing a hand, Drake spitting it back at him as he toppled. The last man let loose a wail as the Crocodile's jaws closed around his neck and snapped closed. He let the body collapse to the deck before turning to his friend.

'Quick, Drew,' gasped Drake, extending his clawed hand. 'On your feet!'

One moment the Werecrocodile stood over Drew, the epitome of the heroic warrior, lit by the rising sun. The next, a foot-long silver spearhead burst from Drake's puffing chest. The Crocodile's face froze in agony. Drake's eyes rolled down to look at the bloody blade that protruded from his sternum, as Drew watched in horror. The spearhead was savagely twisted, before the Doglord whipped it free from behind with a roar of triumph.

Drew didn't wait for Drake's body to land.

The Wolf dived across the skiff to where the Doglord lay against the gunwales in a pile of broken oars, past the spear, hitting the monster with a ferocious impact. The hull splintered open, sending the wrestling therians into the Silver River, struggling for dominance as they sank. Drew's teeth found the Dog's muzzle and nose, biting down hard.

The Dog reached up, trying desperately to prise the jaws open, but it was hopeless. The struggling slowed, Drew's own head and chest thundering as he felt his last breaths escape his body. He released his hold and kicked back towards the surface, but not before he caught sight of the Doglord, choked and drowned on blood and water, sinking towards the bottom of the cold river.

Drew resurfaced as the *Banshee* neared, the two enemy boats having disengaged from the skiff now, beating a hasty retreat to the southern bank. Drew threw his arm over the skiff's broken side, taking a great lungful of air, his body already returning to human form. He clambered aboard, spying Shah with the girl in her arms, struggling to stand upright on the gore-slicked deck. Her face was ashen as she stared aft.

Drake lay on a bed of dead warriors, clawed hands over the hole in his chest. He, too, was returning to his human form while he clung to life, his lips smacking clumsily as he tried to smile at Drew. The young Wolflord crawled to him, placing his hand over the fatal wound.

'Never doubt it, Wolf . . .' whispered the dying therian as his eyes began to close. 'I had your back . . .'

A tear rolled down Drew's cheek as he held Drake in his arms, the young Werecrocodile drifting off to sleep for the final time.

6
Straight and True

The candlelight cast long shadows over the captain's desk as Count Vega dipped his quill pen into the inkpot. The nib swept across the open page, the Sharklord's handwriting as flamboyant as one would expect from the Pirate Prince. He'd kept a journal since his first commission as a captain, thirty of the leather-bound volumes filling the bookcase in his cabin. He was aware that the crew, many of whom were illiterate, considered the habit eccentric, but it was one of the few things that kept Vega feeling civilized during his travels.

The hour was late and the night quiet. With most aboard the *Maelstrom* asleep bar the skeleton crew, it was the perfect time to write uninterrupted. The ship, of course, was more crowded than usual; Vega had to wonder if he'd ever truly have it back for himself. Although it was pleasant to spend time in the company of other Werelords, especially Manfred, his guests were beginning to overstay their welcomes. *Typical dirt-walkers*, his mother would have said. He'd get them to Roof all right, but he wasn't sure where his own path led. Perhaps he'd leave the *Maelstrom* with Figgis as he went inland with the queen and the duke – he couldn't abandon the Wolf's Council now.

Vega wondered if anyone truly considered him a changed character. He'd been described as 'the count without a court', shamed for betraying Wergar to help Leopold rise to power. There was more to the story than that, of course. Bergan and Manfred had recovered well enough after bowing before Leopold, although Vega suspected the parts they'd played in the Wolf's downfall had kept them awake at night. He hoped so, anyway – he'd be cursed if he was the only Werelord who carried a guilty conscience wherever he went.

Vega's respect for Drew was a new feeling for the Sharklord. He'd sworn an oath of loyalty to the boy's father years ago, and Leopold since, but he'd taken those vows lightly. Young and impetuous, he'd been more concerned with gold, swash-buckling his way across the White Sea. Now, older and wiser, the count took his promise to the young Wolf seriously – to aid Wergar's son as they set about righting past wrongs and making Lyssia a safe place for all. With Bergan and Mikkel gone and Drew's whereabouts unknown, he held on to the hope that the Wolf's Council still stood for something. He prayed to Sosha that the boy lived.

The ink burst from the nib suddenly, sending a small black puddle over his script. He cursed, blotting at it with a piece of paper. The stain slowly drying, Vega stared at the inkblot, and his thoughts drifted towards the last member of the Wolf's Council, the Baron of Redmire. Vega had seen Hector's palm while poor Bethwyn had nursed him. The girl had tried to keep the scarred hand hidden, possibly due to some misguided sense of loyalty, but the sea marshal had spied it all the same: a black mark. Hector's was flesh corrupted by something – but what?

Vega wasn't sure when it had happened, but things had gone very wrong for the Boarlord. The young man had been losing control long before the dreadful encounter on the White Isle. Had he started to unravel after the death of his brother? It had been an accident, of course. At least, Vega had *assumed* that was the case. He shook his head. No, Vincent was wicked; he'd have killed Hector that night if fate hadn't intervened. Perhaps Hector's ill luck had begun when he'd first communed with the dead Wylderman shaman in the Wyrmwood.

Hector's decline had really spiralled after Drew's departure. When they were all living in Highcliff, Vega had enjoyed the company of both young men, as had the entire Wolf's Council. It had been good to watch the boys' friendship blossom, each benefiting from the other's best traits. Drew had become more worldly wise with the Boarlord's help, whereas time with the Wolf had allowed Hector to become more confident, more vocal. Hector had changed further without Drew, but it was all for the worse.

The rapping of a loose rope against his cabin window pulled Vega away from his dark thoughts. He swivelled in his seat, staring back at the small panels of glass that filled the rear wall of the captain's quarters. The rope flashed faintly into view as it whipped down and struck the window. Vega grimaced: some fool hadn't tied the thing off. He hated seeing such lazy attention to detail on the *Maelstrom*, and if he did nothing about it now it'd be sure to keep him awake all night. Replacing the quill in the inkpot, Vega rose from his desk, taking his black cape and fastening it around his throat. He checked the carriage clock that was fixed to his desk, which told him it was the second hour after midnight. Leaving the cabin he made his way above deck, heading aft.

Arriving aloft, Vega caught sight of a couple of crew members working on the foredeck. Only one sailor paid attention to the captain's arrival, the chief mate Figgis who acknowledged him with a brief nod. The count glanced up the main mast, spying Casper on his way down from the midnight watch. Vega was proud of how seriously the lad took his duties as a cabin boy and lookout. He'd been up there for three hours, earning himself a warm bunk on his return. Marching up the steps to the poop deck, Vega passed the wheel, lashed down for the night, stepping through the darkness towards the stern.

Vega stopped at the railing. He'd expected the offending rope to be attached to a working part of the ship. Instead it was a relatively short length tied to the rail, serving no purpose. He looked over the side, spying the tattered end banging against his cabin windows as the water churned white below. *Who'd fasten a length of rope to the aft of the ship?* What good did it do other than annoy the count and bring him aloft? Vega looked at how the rope was tied; it wasn't a nautical knot, which meant it wasn't one of his crew. The Sharklord suddenly felt a sick, cold feeling in his stomach. He turned.

Hector stood behind him, flanked by two other figures in the shadows. His men kept an eye towards the prow of the *Maelstrom,* on the lookout for passers by, while the Boarlord's eyes were fixed on the count.

'What is this, Hector?' asked Vega, trying to keep his voice calm while his guts were in knots. *Why did he feel so anxious? How could Hector put him so on edge?*

'I needed to see you, Vega.'

'Why the rope trick? You could have come and knocked for me. Don't you know, by now? My door's always open to friends, Hector.'

Vega glanced past the trio, trying to spy anyone beyond them, but could see no one. They were alone.

'I needed you up here. On deck.'

Hector's voice was rough from disuse. He'd not ventured on to the deck since he'd awoken from his week-long coma. Clearly, the Boarlord had chosen the time of this meeting carefully.

'Well,' said Vega, opening his arms. 'You have my attention. What do you want?'

Vega smiled, but it was a mask. The poop deck seemed charged with energy, the Sharklord's ears threatening to pop as if a great pressure was in the air.

'You kept pushing, Vega.'

'What?'

'You kept poking, belittling me.'

'What are you talking about, Hector?'

'You treat me like a child, a foolish boy who can't do anything right. Is that how you see me?'

Hector took a couple of steps forward. If he'd been in awe of Vega previously, he wasn't showing it. Hector didn't seem in the least bit nervous about challenging the Wereshark.

'Hold on,' said Vega, wanting to raise his voice but sensing that, if he did, something very bad might happen. The Sharklord's hunches rarely steered him wrong.

'I don't know what you're talking about, but you're mistaken. I've stood by your side, my young friend, through every cursed thing that's happened.'

'Don't patronize me, *friend*,' spat Hector. 'As for being at my side, perhaps *you're* the cursed one. Perhaps it's *you* who brings misery and death to all you touch.'

Vega saw the young Boarlord's hands curled into fists at his side. His men were no calmer, each of them agitated as they shadowed him. Vega could see where this was heading.

'Hector,' he said calmly. 'Before you do anything stupid, just think . . .'

'*Silence!*' hissed Hector, throwing his ungloved hand up, palm open towards the captain of the *Maelstrom*.

Vega couldn't get another word out. His throat felt restricted, closed tight as if held by some invisible force. He clawed at his neck, fingers scratching the skin, trying to sever whatever constricted him, but finding nothing. The sensation was sickening, an invisible noose around his throat, tightening as he struggled. He wanted to shout, to scream, but Hector had silenced him utterly. He took a step forward, grabbing Hector by the shoulders. He tried to mouth the word '*please*', but all that came forth was spittle.

Vega's eyes widened as he felt something cold and sharp in

his guts. He felt it cut through his flesh, burying itself among his internal organs as the blood flowed out around it. Hector's face contorted with both horror and sadness, eyes red with tears.

'Getting rid of Vincent,' whispered Hector. 'Did you think you could keep me in your debt forever? You're just like the others, Vega. Worse: you're a two-faced serpent. You belong on the seabed with the other bottom-dwellers.'

Hector stepped back, as Vega, still spluttering, looked down. In his hands the Boarlord held an arrow, its beautifully crafted silver head slick with blood. *Where had Hector got it from? It doesn't matter now*, thought Vega, his fingers fumbling over his stomach as his white shirt turned crimson.

Ringlin and Ibal stepped forward, the fat one giggling quietly as he handed a hessian sack with an attached rope to the tall one. Ringlin lifted the rope over Vega's head, a noose that fitted snugly around the count's neck. He pulled it tight before releasing it. Vega instantly staggered at the weight of the sack, recognizing the unmistakable clang of the heavy balls of shot from the *Maelstrom*'s cannons.

Hector snapped his left hand shut, black hand vanishing out of sight, as Vega struggled to breathe with the sack around his throat. He didn't know whether to struggle for the noose or keep his hands over the bleeding wound. He wanted to beg Hector, ask him to stop the madness, apologize for whatever wrongs the lad imagined the count had done him. But he didn't get the chance.

Hector nodded to his henchmen, who stepped forward and grabbed Count Vega, fearsome captain of the *Maelstrom*, Pirate

Prince of the Cluster Isles and terror of the White Sea. They gave him a hearty shove, sending him flying back over the aft rail of the ship.

Hector turned away before Vega had even gone over the side. To his shock and horror he saw the cabin boy, Casper, barge past him out of nowhere, and sprint between Ringlin and Ibal as they deposited the Sharklord into the cold Sturmish Sea. Ibal was quick with his sickle, grabbing the boy by his mop of hair and whipping the curved blade to his throat.

'No!' gasped Hector, his old self returning briefly.

Kill the boy! snarled the Vincent-vile gleefully, fresh from throttling the Sharklord. *He's seen too much!*

Before Hector could issue any command, the lad bit down hard on the fat man's hand and stamped on his foot, Ibal relinquished his grip instantly and Casper didn't hesitate, leaping overboard after his captain.

Hector rushed to the rail and looked over, astonished by the boy's suicidal act of blind loyalty. All he saw was the white water disappearing behind the *Maelstrom*, the great ship leaving her dying captain to the ocean as a lonely length of rope whipped behind her in the black night.

7
The Jewel of Omir

If Highcliff's defences had once impressed Drew, the walls of Azra put them firmly in the shade. The shining city walls rose fifty feet high, encircling Omir's capital like a steel crown. Sandblasted by fierce winds, the mighty walls were polished like glass, breathtaking to the eye and intimidating to the enemy. The battlements were manned by gold-helmeted warriors, looking down at the people who crowded around the River Gate. Drew couldn't help but stare as he and his companions approached, jaw slack with awe behind his kash.

The *Banshee* remained moored in Kaza, a small port a mile south of Azra and used by the great city for access to the river. The Silver Road that ran between the two was marked by many small shops, inns and trade posts, effectively forming a ramshackle town of its own. Those who couldn't gain access to Azra had settled on the Silver Road, waiting for their chance to gain entrance, and many had put down roots, now calling the road their home.

Merchants from the river travelled up the road to queue and seek entrance into King Faisal's city. But there were others present: families with children, fearful looking people who sought refuge in Azra. Drew was shocked by the number of slaves they also encountered, shackled to one another by chain and collar. Some ferried goods up and down the Silver Road, while others carried their masters and mistresses in silk-covered chairs over the heads of the crowd. It was in the middle of this throng where Drew found himself, jostled by slave and trader as he and his companions pushed towards the gate.

'Bringing her to the Jackal's door was a mistake. We should have handed her over to the port authorities,' growled Djogo.

'I'd sooner leave her with Kesslar,' said Drew, thinking back to the unruly dockers they'd encountered in Kaza. The girl was in a state of shock after the fight on the river that morning, too traumatized to speak. The Werelords had taken the slain body of Drake to the shore, breaking the journey to bury the brave Werecrocodile. They had worked alongside one another, digging deep into the hot sand as they prepared the grave. Krieg had said a few words for their fallen brother while the rest watched in silent respect. None would forget the sacrifice Drake had made in saving the lives of both Drew and the child. The young Wolflord and his companions had decided to take the girl to the city, delivering her safely to the gate guards. They would know what to do with her.

Walking beside Drew, Lady Shah carried the girl in her arms. The girl had warmed to Shah, and the Hawklady had taken her under her wing. In addition to the slain soldiers who'd accompanied the girl, Djogo had found the body of an older, noble-looking gentleman, a silver javelin piercing his chest. Judging by the choice of weapon, Drew assumed he'd been a known Werelord, the girl perhaps a relative. Either way, Azra was the safest place for her.

'Are random attacks common on the Silver River?' Drew asked Djogo as Shah pushed on ahead through the crowd, the exhausted girl sleeping in her arms.

'Yes, but they're usually river pirates, not Doglords and Omiri warriors. That was a coordinated attack; seems the dead Werelord back there had enemies.'

Four warriors from the *Banshee* followed them, pulling a covered cart along behind. The body of the slain nobleman lay beneath the tarpaulin.

'Are there not safer ways to travel than the river?'

The tall warrior shrugged.

'In the Desert Realm? It's a balancing act. The smaller your group, the more chance you have of travelling unnoticed, but if you're attacked you're in trouble. The larger your number, the more noticeable you are to your enemies, but you'll get there in one piece. The Omiri are a secretive people – they've turned subterfuge into a fine art. Misdirection and smoke-screens have won numerous wars in the desert.'

Djogo clapped the boards of the wagon behind them. 'If war is on Omir's doorstep, then the realm's therians will be returning to their respective homes, quickly and quietly. Our friend here wasn't as well versed in subterfuge as his brethren.'

'Perhaps he was betrayed?'

'Not our problem now. Let's drop the child and corpse off and be on our way.'

'I can't believe how many slaves I'm seeing. I hadn't expected to see this outside of Scoria.'

'I'll say one thing for the Jackals,' whispered Djogo. 'They treat their slaves better than the Lizards do. But that wouldn't take much, would it?'

'Sounds like you don't want to be here.'

'You don't know the half of it, Wolf,' said the warrior as they neared the gate, pulling his kash across his face.

A dozen soldiers stood at the gate, checking the papers of anyone who sought admittance into Azra. Wearing golden helmets that rose to sharp points, some carried scimitars at their hips. Others carried the long spears that the Omiri favoured. At nine foot long they were somewhere between a pike and javelin. All the guards wore yolk-yellow capes round their shoulders. All in all, they looked both regal and lethal.

All of a sudden the crowd shuffling up towards the gate seemed to get thicker, and Drew found himself separated by the pushing throng, which drove a wedge between him and his companions.

'Djogo,' called Drew, trying to catch the tall warrior's attention, but he and the other crew members pulling the cart had fallen behind. Looking forward, Drew saw Shah had reached the guards and was trying to reason with a man who appeared to be an officer. The girl shifted in the Hawklady's grasp, beginning to wake with the din of the crowd.

Suddenly Drew found himself shoved to the front of the shouting and bickering traders, face to face with some more of the guards. One of them said something unintelligible to Drew.

'I'm sorry,' he said. 'I don't understand.'

The guard's officer overheard Drew's remark, and left Shah momentarily, stepping closer to speak with the young Westlander.

'You're not Omiri?' he asked, his voice thickly accented but understandable.

'No,' smiled Drew, awkwardly.

'I tried to explain . . .' called Shah, but the man ignored her.

'Only Omiri enter Azra!' said the man, harshly.

'I don't seek entrance!' said Drew, aware that he was shouting and struggling to be heard. Both the officer and Drew caught sight of a scuffle taking place, beyond where Djogo and the men from the *Banshee* stood with the handcart. An altercation between merchants had descended into a fist fight. The officer looked back at Drew.

'Then what do you seek?'

'If you'd let me finish . . .' yelled Shah, but the officer's attention returned to the brawl. Many in the crowd were jeering as the merchants fought, the guards standing back while the men exhausted themselves. A fat slaver watched from his silk covered sedan chair, clapping with glee. The fight was spreading as a woman carrying a tall basket of fruit was knocked into. The basket tumbled, clattering into Djogo and the *Banshee*'s men, sending an avalanche of lemons over them. More fists flew as the woman's companions joined the melee.

'Who is this man?' said the captain to Shah as he poked Drew's chest.

At that moment, the crowd barged into the fat slaver's litter and sent it over, crashing into the handcart. A wheel sheared off, clattering over on to the wailing slaver's body, while the Werelord's corpse toppled from the broken cart on to the road. Several women in the crowd screamed, spurring the guards to push forward through the panicking mob. Soldiers and civilians instantly recognized the slain therian. Acting quickly, half the guards tried to hold the crowd back while others moved towards the men from the *Banshee*.

At that moment, Djogo's kash fell loose as he was jostled by the crowd.

'*Djogo!*'

The guards' cries of recognition were not happy ones. *They know him*, realized Drew. *Curse the man and his business with Kesslar!*

The soldiers immediately lowered their long spears and unsheathed their scimitars. In response, the tall, one-eyed warrior whipped out his own weapons. The crowd parted as the fist fight suddenly escalated into sword fight. Not prepared to leave their man outnumbered, the warriors from the *Banshee* withdrew their daggers and shortswords.

'Wait!' cried Shah, making a grab at the officer. With the fight spiralling out of control, the captain mistook Shah's hand as an assault. He swung his arm back, scimitar pommel crashing into Shah's forehead, sending woman and girl to the ground, instantly lost in the crowd.

'Don't harm them!' shouted Drew, pushing past the guards to get to them.

To his horror Drew found the commander now turning on

him, taking hold and twisting Drew's forearm in his grasp. He stumbled on to one knee, surprised at the other's strength. The officer forced Drew's hand up his back, the young man bellowing as he threatened to collapse. He couldn't get into a fight, yet he couldn't allow his companions to be harmed.

'You don't understand! We just want to leave the girl with you!'

He tried to plead, but the soldier wouldn't listen. Feet stamped around him as another turbaned warrior came forward, striking Drew over his head with the flat of his blade. Drew's head rang as he collapsed on to the sand-covered flags and the officer jumped on him. Through the legs of the crowd, he could see Shah, trampled by the wild mob.

Drew had no choice.

The first notion the captain had that he was no longer wrestling with a human was when the arm he held twisted violently, throwing him one hundred and eighty degrees through the air. He landed with a crunch, his view of the world on its head as the beast rose to its full height, towering over him. The crowd screamed as the Werewolf roared.

Drew's eyes scanned the crowd around the overturned cart as they backed away. Djogo and the gladiators were being overpowered by superior numbers, and the guards had already removed Shah from the chaos. Of the child, there was no sign. Drew felt sick, having brought the girl to the gates of Azra only for her to be lost.

Reinforcements flooded out of the gate as the Omiri circled him, scimitars and spears raised. They'd clearly fought Werelords before, and were treating Drew with a healthy dose of respect. He snapped his jaws, lashing out with the trident dagger while he frantically tried to decide what to do. Overhead, bowmen lined the walls, taking aim at the Wolf.

Fools, he thought. *Can't they see we were bringing an innocent to them?* But all the guards saw was a target that needed taking down. He needed to get back to the *Banshee*, regroup with the others, and find a way of rescuing their companions. He couldn't be drawn into a fight here. These men were innocent – foolish, but innocent. He couldn't take their lives.

Dropping into a crouch he sprang backwards, high, narrowly avoiding the guards' long spears before landing behind them. A dozen arrows rained down from the walls, half of them finding their target. The Werewolf crashed to the floor, the wind taken from his sails. The arrows weren't silver, but they hurt. Drew cried with agony as he scrambled to his feet, body still aching from the river battle wounds.

Drew stumbled down the Silver Road towards the port of Kaza, onlookers screaming and moving clear as he lurched along. The long spears flew, most hitting the paved road or bouncing off Drew's thick, furred skin, but a couple punched their way home, breaking flesh and jarring bone. He howled, going down again.

Booted Omiri feet surrounded him now as, dizzied, he tried to keep moving, willing his body on.

'Wolf!'

The shout came from the captain of the guard behind. The Werewolf looked back, guards parting to reveal the captured men of the *Banshee*. The captain forced Djogo to his knees, the prisoner's hands tied behind his back. Raising his scimitar high, the blade hovered in the air above the ex-slaver's neck, ready to fly.

PART V

Dangerous Games

I

Witness

Looking back nervously, the young woman checked she wasn't being followed as she hurried along the lurching corridor. Clutching the bottle of water, Bethwyn walked past the queen's cabin and continued on, deeper into the belly of the *Maelstrom*. With a final glance to ensure she was alone, the girl from Robben opened the door to the dark cargo hold and slipped inside.

Closing the door firmly, Bethwyn weaved between the lashed-down crates and barrels, gingerly making her way towards the prow. The hold's contents were severely depleted, many weeks at sea having exhausted the *Maelstrom*'s provisions, leaving the pirates surviving on short rations and in desperate need of making land. Upon hearing the queen was thirsty, the ship's cook, a gaunt fellow named Holman, had handed over the bottle to the lady-in-waiting, telling her to make it last; fresh water was a luxury, more precious than food.

As Bethwyn neared the prow, she felt guilty for taking the bottle from Holman. He was a kind man who had always ensured she got a little extra when serving up the crew's meagre portions of food. But she'd needed the bottle, an excuse to go below decks and disappear for a while, attending her mistress. There were prying eyes aloft that might question her absence without any plausible reason. She finally arrived at the thick curved wall that marked the head of the hold and the prow of the *Maelstrom*. The others waited, gathered around a hooded lantern that gave out a tiny amount of light.

'Nobody followed you?' asked Amelie, moving up along the crate where she sat to make room. Bethwyn collapsed beside her, shaking her head.

'He doesn't suspect you?' asked Duke Manfred.

'He asked where I was going. If he follows that up, Master Holman will tell him the same thing – I'm with the queen, not to be disturbed.' Bethwyn raised the bottle as if to emphasize the ruse.

'Good,' said Manfred, rubbing his knuckles against his temple. 'What we discuss must never reach Hector's ears.'

'Murderous traitor,' said Figgis, eyes narrowing in his leathery old face.

'Steady on,' said Manfred. 'We don't know for sure he's a killer.'

'You call me a liar? I saw it with my own eyes!'

'What on earth would young Hector gain from killing

Vega? The count was his friend. I question what you saw. I have to. I owe that to Hector.'

The first mate spat at mention of the magister's name.

'Gentlemen,' said Amelie, raising her hand gently.

Figgis bowed to his queen before nodding to Manfred. The duke returned the gesture, to Bethwyn's relief. She'd watched the old pirate trying to hold his nerve over the course of the day. He'd reported what he'd seen directly to Amelie late last night, hot on the heels of the captain disappearing. A search of the boat had followed, whereupon the crew discovered that Casper was gone, too. Everyone aboard the *Maelstrom* was suspicious, none more so than Figgis who'd stared daggers at Hector and his men all day long. It was only now, the following night, that the four had the opportunity to discuss the events in detail.

'It's as I said last night,' said Figgis, his wiry arms sagging as he recounted what he'd seen. 'I was doing my rounds when the captain come aloft; disappeared up to the poop deck and never came back. The boy followed him up there too. Then the three of them – Hector and his men – came down. Asked them where the captain was, I did. They said they'd never seen him. When I got up there they was nowhere to be seen, neither the captain nor the boy.'

Bethwyn was surprised to see tears rolling down Figgis's cheeks. The old man was as hard as they came, a long life of piracy behind him and many years by Vega's side. As first mate he'd taken command of the *Maelstrom*, but the responsibility didn't sit easy on his gnarled shoulders.

'Why didn't you challenge Hector at the time?' said Amelie.

'Question the Boarlord, Your Majesty?' Figgis shook his head. 'I didn't know right away what had gone on. I went up there to find the captain gone, a bloodstain on the deck. By the time I returned your Lord of Redmire had scarpered to his cabin, along with his men.'

Manfred shook his head wearily.

'It makes no sense. *Why* would Hector harm one of us, especially one who's looked out for him these recent months?'

'May well be that the captain looked out for him,' said Figgis. 'But look at what happened in Moga. Then we had the White Isle – that was his doing too, so the captain said. That traitor let us land there when he knew it was cursed. He's a bad one, that boy.'

'How can you say that? Hector's given everything in the service of the Wolf's Council, Figgis.'

Manfred can't help himself, thought Bethwyn. *He has to defend Hector. He knows there's good in him, and can't believe there's any bad.*

The Staglord continued. 'Couldn't it be that Vega slipped? Struck his head? Fell overboard?'

Figgis laughed. 'This is a Wereshark you're talking about, my lord. The captain knew every inch of the *Maelstrom* blindfolded. I never saw him slip on this deck in all the years I've been with him. And even if he fell overboard, he's a shark. He'd have swum back to the ship, wouldn't he?'

'Unless he was injured,' said Amelie.

'Exactly, Your Majesty,' said the first mate. 'And regardless of whether the captain fell overboard or not, there's Casper going missing too. Two going overboard and not a trace of either?'

'I have to agree with Duke Manfred here,' Amelie put in. 'Captain Figgis, I believe you saw what you say, I truly do. But the notion, that this dear young man could have done something so out of character? It's simply too much.'

Figgis looked like he might scream, his face shifting from bloodless white through angry red and then furious purple.

'I believe Figgis.'

Manfred and Amelie turned to look at Bethwyn, the girl's big brown eyes wide with fright, but chin set with determination.

'You believe him?' asked Manfred, incredulously. 'But Hector's your friend!'

'I cannot let friendship stand in the way of the truth, Your Grace.'

'What makes you think this is true, my dear?' said Amelie, placing her palms over the trembling lady-in-waiting's hands. 'Is this on account of what happened when he woke from his long slumber? Surely you realized that was his fever talking?'

'That was upsetting, Your Majesty, but there were other things. His hand . . .'

'What about it?' said Manfred.

'Something . . . something *bad* has got into it. His hand is blackened, Your Grace. It's so cold to the touch, too. It reminds me of dead skin, all the life leached from it. I saw it well enough when I tended him.'

'A diseased hand doesn't make for a diseased mind,' said Amelie, but the girl from Robben continued.

'When the Sirens attacked the ship, Hector killed one that would have slain me, only from a great distance away. His left hand, the black palm – he had it open, as if controlling something. I know Hector's a magister, and I know he uses magicks and cantrips to heal, but this was something else.'

Manfred sighed. 'The communing.'

Amelie looked at the Staglord with horror. 'Hector has *communed*? When?'

'The first occasion was in the Wyrmwood, when he, Drew and Gretchen encountered Vala.'

'The *first* occasion?' gasped the queen. 'This has happened more than once?'

'Yes, regrettably. We thought we'd steered him off that course, but perhaps he has continued to commune in secret.'

The four were silent. Bethwyn tried to stifle her tears, holding them back with all her will. She felt as though she'd betrayed Hector, but he was a changed boy from the bumbling Boarlord who'd made his bashful appearances at Buck House. She feared for him.

'So,' said Amelie quietly. 'What do we do with him?'

'I've been on ships where the likes of him would've been thrown overboard like bait,' spat Figgis. 'So long as he's aboard the *Maelstrom* he's cursing us all. Who knows what he might do next?'

Amelie and Bethwyn shivered at the thought of the pirate's justice, but neither spoke up.

'No, we won't execute him,' said the Staglord. 'He'd need a trial before his peers and besides, we still have no evidence. If he *did* send Vega and the boy overboard, how did he do it? And how did he make sure the count never came back?'

'He can't stay on board,' said Figgis, his voice calm. 'The men already whisper. They won't hold back forever.'

Manfred rose, stretching. 'We need to return to our quarters, show our faces aloft before our absence alerts Hector.'

The others stood, Manfred helping Amelie to her feet. Figgis picked the lantern up, peering through the dark hold and checking the path ahead.

'Lead the way, Captain Figgis,' said Manfred, placing a hand on the old man's shoulder.

'I wish you wouldn't call me that,' muttered the old pirate. 'There's only one captain of the *Maelstrom*, the best man I ever sailed with, and he's in Sosha's arms now.'

The old pirate stopped, his free hand scratching at the thin white hair at the back of his head. He turned back to the therians, his eyes catching the lantern light and glowing like embers.

'There's one more thing I'd wanted to tell you, my lord and lady, but feared not on account of an oath.'

'An oath?'

'Aye, my lord. To Captain Vega. Only thing is, he's dead now, ain't he? So, where does that leave my oath?'

Manfred glanced to Amelie and Bethwyn, but the women had no answer.

'If there's something you need to tell us, Figgis, go ahead man.'

'The captain . . . he *did* something for your baron. He got rid of something for him.'

'What's that supposed to mean?' said Manfred.

'We thought it was an accident, y'see? Captain didn't think it was done on purpose, but the more I think about it, the more I think Hector *meant* to kill him.'

'Kill who?' said Amelie.

'Lord Vincent,' said Figgis. 'Hector killed his brother.'

Amelie gasped.

'Why would Vega help Hector cover this up?' asked Manfred, shaking with shock.

'Like I say, the captain believed it was an accident, but he could see others thinking otherwise. If word got out, Hector's life would be as good as over. I got rid of the Boarlord's body myself, Sosha forgive me. What a fool I was.'

Manfred patted Figgis on the shoulder. 'Your loyalty to Vega, even in death, is commendable, but you've done the right thing by telling us.'

The Staglord fixed each of them with a steady gaze. 'It's more important than ever before that we remain tight-lipped over what we've discussed here tonight. This is a dangerous game we play with the Boarlord. Hector appears deadlier than I could've ever imagined. He can never know our plans.'

'But what *are* our plans?' said Amelie.

'I need to inspect the count's sea charts,' said Manfred. 'Vega may yet be able to help us, from beyond the grave.'

2

In the Jaws of the Jackal

'You're a long way from home, Wolf.'

The two captives stood alongside one another, surrounded by the royal court and twenty of Azra's finest warriors. While Djogo's gaze was fixed on his feet, Drew's eyes lingered on the frescoed domed ceiling above, the centuries-old art pre-dating anything he'd seen in the galleries of Highcliff. He looked around. Majestic marble pillars and busts of ancient kings, fluttering curtains laced with gold and priceless artefacts from Lyssia and beyond – the show of opulence wasn't missed by Drew. He'd grown up under the mistaken belief that the Omiri were savages. A quick glance around the palace revealed that nothing could have been further from the truth. Here was an ancient, rich culture to rival anything in the Seven Realms.

Drew let his gaze return to the figure on the throne who had spoken: King Faisal, the Jackal of Omir.

'Not by choice. I'm sorry if my arrival has caused you any concern,' Drew said, raising his bound arms towards the seated figure. His forearms had been lashed together, knotted behind his elbows. 'If you could remove these ropes I'll be on my way.'

The crowd laughed, all except the king who rose from his throne. The audience quieted instantly as he strode gracefully down the dais steps towards Drew and his companion. By Drew's reckoning, Faisal had to be as old as Bergan if he'd fought Wergar during the Werewar. If so, he wore his years well, the Werejackal's tanned skin smooth, without scars and wrinkles, his features fine and unspoiled. He wore a simple white toga and a crown of twined golden rope. His feet were bare and paced silently across the polished marble floor. Beautiful wasn't a word Drew would ordinarily use to describe a man, but in Faisal's case no other would fit, The king came to a halt before Drew, his almond eyes inspecting the Wolf intently.

'You have your father's arrogance.' His voice was rich and honey-toned, matching his appearance. Although Western wasn't his first language, he was as fluent as any lord of Lyssia in the tongue.

'If I do, it's dumb luck,' said Drew. 'I never met Wergar.'

'Then your arrogance is your own, Wolf. Your dead, arrogant father would be proud.'

Drew prickled. He'd never known Wergar and stories of his exploits were mixed, his role ranging from hero to barbarian. Regardless, Faisal's words cut deep.

'I understand Wergar waged war with Omir, Your Majesty,' said Drew. 'But that was his war. Not mine.'

'Your father was the only Werelord ever to break the defences of Azra, and without the forces of Brackenholme and Stormdale to assist him. It cost him the lives of many. For months he campaigned in my burning deserts, his men dying of thirst and starvation. If he hadn't had the help of the Hawklords his bones would have joined those of his Wolfguard in the sand.'

There was mention of the Hawks of the Barebones again, loyal to Wergar.

'The Hawklords helped him win that war?'

'The Hawklords would side with anyone who might help feather their nest!' shouted a pale-skinned stocky man in a long black cloak. He looked out of place in the Omiri palace.

'I don't believe that,' said Drew. 'Griffyn's a good man, a noble therian, one of the last of his kind.'

'You claim to know the old Hawk?' scoffed the man in black. 'He's probably dead now, a relic of the past. There are few of them left, and the only good one sits in Windfell: Baron Skeer!'

Faisal smiled. 'You'll have to forgive my guest, Lord Rook. The Crowlords have never seen eye to eye with the Hawklords. I'd have to say I agree with him. Then again, the Crows never attacked my city, did they?

'I swore fealty to the Wolf to end the siege of Azra, but that agreement didn't last long. By the time he limped home to Westland, bloodied and battered from the fight in Omir, his therian brothers had turned on him, handing his head to the Lion on a platter. They tell me you consider those who betrayed your father as your friends and allies: the Bearlord and Staglords?'

'Bergan explained what happened long ago. He kept no secrets from me. If you're hoping to make me doubt my friends, you're barking up the wrong tree, King Faisal.'

The king sneered, disappointed. 'No doubt you now know that your precious Wolf's Council is broken? The Bearlord's dead, I hear, and the surviving Staglord lost. You'd be the last flame the Catlords need to snuff out, and then Lyssia will finally be rid of the Wolf.'

Drew hung his head, the blow hitting home. Faisal nodded, content to see the youth's heartache.

'How have I wronged you, Your Majesty?'

Faisal's laughter was musical, joined by the guffaws of his courtiers. The king shook his head and sighed.

'It's bad enough you come to my city, the son of the only therian ever to defeat me in battle. Yet look who *accompanies* you.'

The king turned to face Djogo, his hand reaching out and gently taking the tall warrior's jaw in his slender fingers. He lifted the brute's head, almond eyes widening as he stared into Djogo's one good eye.

'Djogo,' he whispered. 'Kesslar's hound, returning to the scene of the crime.'

'What crime?' asked Drew.

'Your companions didn't explain what business they'd had in Azra previously, then? Splendid: let me elaborate.'

Djogo glanced at Drew briefly, the look apologetic. *What in Brenn's name did you* do, *Djogo?*

'The Goatlord, Kesslar, lodged here for a time,' continued the king, pacing around the bound men. 'Initially, he was a generous, thoughtful guest, and we were most gracious hosts.'

'He was a slaver!' interrupted Drew.

'Look around you, Wolf. Azra is built on slaves. They're a currency like any other in Omir.

'It didn't take him long to betray our trust. He invited three of my cousins aboard his ship to dine. They took gifts, as is our tradition: gold, jewels and spices. My cousins and their entourages stayed with him aboard his vessel as guests that night.

'When the morning came, they were gone. The bodies of several guards were found in the Silver River, throats slit. Your work, Djogo?'

The ex-slaver said nothing, his eyes returning to the floor.

'Where are they now, fiend? My people, my cousins? Do they live, or did they die in some distant arena, for the amusement of Kesslar and his friends?'

Djogo spoke at last. 'All were sold into slavery, but only the strongest went to the arena. Two Jackals died in the Furnace in Scoria. The third, the youngest, was sold to a Bastian Catlord.'

'Brenn, no,' muttered Drew miserably. 'Why, Djogo?'

The tall warrior looked at Drew, his face emotionless. 'I worked for Kesslar. I was a slaver. It was the only world I knew. There was no right or wrong; it was my job.'

Drew thought Faisal might strike Djogo at any moment, the king's face shimmering with fury. He bared his teeth as he looked at each of them, speaking clearly and with deadly purpose.

'I see you each bear the mark of gladiator upon your shoulders. That pleases me greatly.'

As he spoke, the crowd backed away, while the golden helmed palace guard stepped forward, long spears and scimitars raised.

'You've got us wrong, Faisal,' said Drew. 'We're not friends of Kesslar's – we're his enemies, as are you!'

'Finding your voice now, Wolf? Do you plead for forgiveness?'

Drew growled as he answered. 'I've done you no wrong. We brought a child to your gate, a girl who'd been attacked upon the river.'

'You brought the body of Prince Fier to our gates, Wolf!' shouted the king. 'The child who accompanied him was nowhere to be seen!'

'That's not true! We had no idea who that corpse was, only that he was heading to Azra when he was attacked! Why *else* would we bring his body to you? The girl was the only survivor . . .'

'They killed Prince Fier,' interrupted Rook. 'You can't trust the Wolf – no wonder half of Lyssia hunts him. No doubt he and Kesslar's people are agents of the Doglords, sent here to cause your family further harm. Kill him now, Your Majesty. Do every realm a favour.'

'The child!' cried Drew. 'Someone must have *seen* her! We brought her here along with your slain lord!'

'There was no child,' said Faisal. 'What? You thought you could show us the body of my uncle and demand a ransom for my daughter?'

'Your daughter? We brought her back to you! Search for her; you'll find her!'

'Just words!' cried Faisal as he paced back up the marble steps to his throne. 'Even now my warriors make their way to Kaza to seize your ship. I'll find my daughter, wherever you've hidden her, so beg away, Wolf. You'll say anything now to spare your life!' He turned to his guards adding, 'And throw the cyclops a weapon; he'll need it.'

Two guards hastily untied the captives. As they stepped back, one threw a scimitar on to the floor, the blade ringing as it struck the marble. Djogo glanced at it and then back to Drew.

'We won't fight,' said the ex-slaver, standing shoulder to shoulder with the man he'd sworn his allegiance to.

Drew spoke. 'The Djogo you knew may have been a killer, Faisal, but he's a changed man now.'

'Nobody ever truly changes. Bring the woman.'

Drew and Djogo watched in alarm as the struggling figure of Lady Shah was dragged into the throne room. She kicked and fought as she was hauled before the king, her hands bound and her face bearing bruises. A white gag was looped around her face, muffling her screams.

'I never forget a face. Lady Shah, isn't it? A friend of yours and Kesslar's?' said Faisal. He aimed the question at Djogo.

Lord Rook walked over to Shah and gripped her tightly by the arms. The Crow held his cheek close to hers, as a lover might in an embrace.

'Lady Shah,' he whispered. 'Daughter of Baron Griffyn. How the Hawks fall . . .'

Rook raised a stubby, silver dagger to Shah's throat, placing the point into the hollow beneath her chin. Her eyes widened, pleading for him to stop.

'You *will* fight,' said Faisal. 'Or the woman dies.'

'Don't do this, Faisal!' yelled Drew.

His words were wasted though, and should have been directed at Djogo. The tall warrior bent down to the ground, snatching up the scimitar. His good eye blinked, as he shook his head.

'I'm so sorry, Drew,' said the ex-slaver.

The scimitar scythed through the air.

3

Duel

Drew and Djogo paced around one another across the patterned throne room floor, a black marble mosaic flecked with the bright white stars of the heavens.

'We don't have to do this,' said Drew, his feet moving, keeping the distance between them constant. The guards formed a circular wall of spears and swords around them, weapons lashing out when the combatants got too close. A transformed Drew might have bounded over them, but he didn't fancy his odds of clearing the long spears from a standing jump.

'We do,' said Djogo, shifting the scimitar in his grip.

'If either of us dies, it's for what?'

'If you die, it's so that Shah lives,' said the warrior. 'If I die, it's Brenn's wish that you go on from here.'

'And if neither of us dies?'

'If neither of us dies . . . they kill Shah.' Djogo glanced to where Rook held the Hawklady, the knife jutting into her neck. 'You heard what he said.'

Faisal watched from his throne as the other nobles gathered around him, fellow Jackals who shared his hatred for the Wolf and the Goat.

Rook suddenly shouted, jabbing Shah in the jaw, the blade breaking the surface of her flesh.

'Fight!'

Shah kicked her heels, boots squeaking as they scraped the marble, unable to writhe away from the Crow's grip.

That was enough for Djogo.

The warrior lunged at Drew, the scimitar cutting an 'X' through the air. Though still weary from their encounter at the River Gate, both men were recovered enough to fight for their lives.

Drew rolled clear as a sword blow hit the marble floor, sending sparks flying. A chunk of the ancient mosaic broke away, skittering across the court. Drew had to keep moving, evading, while he thought of a plan. *I can't kill Djogo. He's shown faith in me. What kind of man would I be if I betrayed that trust now? He might be blinded by his love for Shah, but there has to be another way!*

Of all the human foes Drew had faced in battle, Djogo was the one he feared the most. He'd been relieved when the tall warrior pledged his allegiance on Scoria, removing the threat that he'd ever fight him again. Drew had given his all, but this was different; he didn't want to see the man dead. He wanted him to live. He wanted the *three* of them to live.

Djogo brought the scimitar down lightning fast towards Drew's chest. The young Wolflord leaped back, narrowly missing having his stomach opened, only to feel the cold bite of a spearhead in his back. The guard propelled him forward towards Djogo's return swing, leaving Drew with no option but to dive at him, tackling him around the chest and wrestling him to the floor.

The two rolled, Drew's one hand his only means of holding the scimitar back.

'Please, Djogo!'

'There's no other way!' grunted the ex-slaver.

Djogo butted Drew in the face, sending him reeling away, blinded. Instincts kicked in as the Wolflord scrambled, eyes streaming as blood poured from his nose. The scimitar clanged against the floor inches from where he'd landed. The therian shook his head and prayed his vision would return. He heard the scrape of the scimitar as Djogo got to his feet, the blade dragging along the floor. Drew scrambled away from the telltale noise, foolishly forgetting the other perils that faced him in the arena. A guard's scimitar ripped across his back, felling him with a scream of pain just as his vision cleared.

Surrounded by a wall of armed warriors, he faced an opponent focused on slaying him. That's all the Omiri nobles wanted – two hated enemies fighting to the death, slaver versus Werewolf. Drew spat blood on to the marble floor, letting loose a monstrous growl that caused the guards to shift warily.

Time to give the people what they want.

The guard with the scimitar took another pot shot at Drew,

but his timing couldn't have been worse. Drew had embraced the change, and all he now saw was a room full of enemies. His clawed foot shot up from the floor, kicking the warrior hard in his chest, sending him flying back through the air. He hit a marble pillar, landing in a crumpled heap, his polished breastplate battered out of shape. By the time his scimitar fell from his unconscious grasp, Drew had fully transformed, the Werewolf crouching on the floor, ready for battle.

Djogo swung at a surprised guard, disarming him with a deft flick of his scimitar. The guard's weapon flipped through the air and into Djogo's other hand, the Werewolf now facing an even deadlier foe. The ex-slaver spun the scimitars at his sides as he closed on the therian.

Drew watched Djogo's swirling blades, searching for a way past them. They weren't silver, but Djogo was adept enough with any weapon to open him up in moments. No therian healing would help him against such serious wounds. The warriors who ringed them were ready now, should either combatant turn on them again. Spears and scimitars hovered, ready to strike out at therian or human should they stagger too close.

'You can't win this fight!' growled Drew, moving quickly around the arena.

'One of us has to,' said Djogo, his voice laden with anger and regret.

Djogo ran at Drew, preparing to leap into the air to cut down at the Wolf. At the last moment, Drew realized it was a bluff, the warrior hitting the marble floor in a diving slide aimed at taking out the Werewolf's legs. Drew hurdled the swordsman, narrowly missing his booted feet, but the scimitars left a trail of red mist in their wake as they scored the Wolf and he hit the floor with a snarl.

The Jackals cheered at the sight of the Wolf's blood. Drew looked down at his torso, his dark, clawed hand dabbing at the wounds the scimitars had left behind. *They won't be content until either Djogo or I lie dead.*

Djogo leaped back again, blades cutting downwards in deadly swipes. When Drew ducked one way the warrior followed, closing off his escape route. He'd switch to the other, only to find him waiting. Years of fighting in the Furnace and across Lyssia had honed Djogo into a formidable fighter, predicting Drew's every move.

With an imperceptible glance, Drew marked two spearmen next to one another in the wall, their long weapons poised. Quickly he manoeuvred towards them, avoiding Djogo's blows while ensuring the two were eventually at his back.

The Werewolf allowed his huge, clawed feet to strike the ground loudly, black claws scraping the marble and drawing attention. He retreated, one step after another, his head dipped at such an angle that he could still see the guards behind through the corner of his eye. One was unable to resist any longer, bringing his long spear back and stabbing at the Wolf.

The lycanthrope twisted, turning on his haunches and snatching hold of the spear. With a hard tug on the shaft Drew brought the man flying forward, the guard releasing his grip on the spear and flailing towards Djogo. The one-eyed warrior deflected the hapless spearman with his forearms as the guard struck him, the two hitting the marble together.

Drew was moving before they'd landed, whipping the long spear around and sprinting. He lowered the spear haft, praying it would find purchase. The hard, wooden end of the weapon *clunked* into a hole in the broken mosaic, halting his run instantly and sending the Werewolf into the air. To his relief, the spear buckled but didn't break, launching Drew skywards, vaulting him high over the guards. Their long spears jabbed up but in vain, the monstrous, grey Wolflord sailed above and beyond them.

And landed on the throne.

The nobles roared at the sight of the Wolf straddling King Faisal, pinning him to his seat. Canine features appeared in a wave, the Jackal-lords changing and howling for the Wolf's blood. Faisal bellowed with shock as Drew snatched him round the throat, his clawed feet digging into the king's thighs, drawing blood through the once-pristine white robes. Though the king's head expanded, transforming into the Jackal as his features distorted, his throat remained the size of a mortal man's in Drew's lupine grip. Faisal choked, his airways cut off. The Jackal's eyes bulged as Drew bared his teeth, holding his grip as the king floundered in a blind panic.

While many warriors rushed to their king's aid, others overpowered Djogo, tearing the scimitars from his grip before he was inspired to do anything foolish. He looked on with awe as the Wolf held Omir to ransom.

'Kill the Wolf!' screamed Rook from nearby, baring Shah's throat once more, a jagged red cut now visible where he'd sliced her with the blade.

'Call off your dogs!' said Drew, his lips peeled back as he growled into the Werejackal's ear.

Faisal glanced frantically from side to side, his hands out to his family, warning them to retreat. Drew allowed his grip to relax, enough to allow the Jackal to breathe. He gasped at the air, struggling to get oxygen past the Werewolf's claws.

'Tell the Crow to release Shah,' said Drew. '*Now!*'

'Let . . . her . . . go!' whispered the king through his clenched throat.

Rook watched with disbelief, shaking Shah like a rag doll. 'But, Your Majesty . . .'

'Release her!' said Faisal.

Reluctantly the Crowlord let Shah go, the Hawklady stumbling to Djogo, who pulled himself free of the guards and tore her gag away. The two held one another, as if their lives depended upon it.

'You won't get out of this palace alive, Wolf!' spat Faisal, strangled in Drew's grip.

The Werewolf tightened his hold again. 'I'll get all the way to Westland with my hand around your throat if I have to, Faisal!' snarled Drew. 'It didn't have to be like this,' he went on, the fury momentarily gone from his voice. 'I told you the truth, Faisal, and you chose to ignore me. We came here in peace, but you ensure we leave as enemies . . .'

'She's returned!'

The woman's cry echoed through the throne room as her footsteps raced through the hall towards the throne. Whoever she was, she was oblivious to the drama that played out in front of her. Her voice was cheery as she approached, more guards accompanying her into the chamber.

'See, my love! She's returned to us!'

The woman looked up at the last. Jackals' heads looked down upon her as her shocked eyes landed upon the king, helpless in the Werewolf's grip. She held the girl from the skiff in her arms, the child's big almond eyes wide as she clutched the woman's chest.

'My daughter . . .' said Faisal, the fight instantly gone from his body.

Drew looked from the king down to the child, who raised a trembling finger towards the Werewolf.

'It's him, mother,' she said, sniffing back the tears. The girl's featured softened suddenly, from fear to admiration.

'He's the one who saved me.'

4

The Port at the End of the World

There were few places in Lyssia as remote and inhospitable as Friggia. Situated on the northernmost point of Beggars' Bay, it was the one port in Sturmland that the Sturmish people avoided. Linked by road to the Rat city of Vermire and Lady Slotha's city of Tuskun, the Walrus had claimed the town for herself. While the majority of the Tuskun fleet were harboured in Blackbank on the southern coast of the Sturm Peninsula, a few of her warships considered Friggia, on the northern coast, their home, launching raids against those brave souls who dared sail the Sturmish Sea. Like their neighbours in Vermire, the Tuskuns were pirates to the core.

With a snowstorm having descended, any other harbour in Lyssia would have been deserted, but not Friggia. The hour was late and the weather grim, but the Tuskun port was in no mood to sleep, with both streets and ships busy with activity.

However, while the largest piers and docks that housed the bigger ships were bustling, the smaller jetties were quieter, all but deserted, with fishing boats moored for the night. Three figures stood on the end of one such jetty, shrouded in swirling snow. Behind them, a rowing boat was being tied up, and a handful of men clambered up from it on to the wooden walkway.

'By Brenn's whiskers,' said Manfred. 'I thought it was cold in the Barebones but this is something else!'

'You're in the north now, Your Grace,' said Hector. 'They don't do anything by half measures up here.'

The reluctant new captain of the *Maelstrom*, Figgis, had nothing to say, watching the six other men finish securing the rowboat before they came over to join them.

'Are we clear as to our tasks?' asked Manfred, looking to each of them. 'Captain Figgis is to remain here with the boat while we split into two groups.'

Manfred pointed to the ship's cook, Holman, and the grey looking fellow nodded back. 'Master Holman, I'll accompany you while you see about getting some fresh produce for the stores – meat, vegetables, whatever passes for food up here in the rear end of nowhere. Hector,' Manfred nodded at the young Boarloard, 'you'll procure drinking water for the ship, in addition to something a bit stronger as a reward for the boys. Let's keep it quiet, eh? Last thing we want to do is attract unwanted attention to our visit.'

Hector's face was stoic and humourless. 'You can count on me, Your Grace.'

Ringlin and Ibal waited for their master a short distance

away along the jetty. Both were well wrapped up against the elements, while Hector wore his cloak hood down, careless of the bitter snowstorm. The magister was about to follow his men when he stopped, turning to Manfred and placing his gloved left hand on the duke's arm.

'Is everything all right, Manfred?' asked Hector quietly and earnestly, dropping the formalities he'd used before the men.

'Whatever do you mean, Hector?' blustered the Staglord, glancing at the magister's hand on his wrist.

'You haven't seemed yourself lately, especially since that awful business with Vega and that poor boy going missing.'

Manfred sighed, wearily staring at the young Boarlord from beneath his bushy grey brow.

'Which of us *has* been ourselves since the disappearance of the count, Hector? It's a terrible thing to come to terms with. It's . . . unbelievable . . . that something so tragic could befall our friend on his own ship, no?'

'Unbelievable,' said Hector, nodding. 'Just so you know; I'm always here to talk to, should you wish to unburden yourself of anything. We friends must stick together.'

'Friends,' agreed Manfred, smiling sadly. 'Together.'

The duke shook the baron's hand before turning back to his complement of men from the *Maelstrom*. With no further word the group split up, setting off into Friggia with their own very different agendas.

'That wasn't the agreed price,' said Hector, wagging a finger at the innkeeper.

The two men stood on the frozen cobbles of the alleyway

that ran the length of the Black Gate Tavern, cellar doors open at their feet. Lantern light from below was cast skyward, illuminating the haggling pair, their men working together beneath the inn.

'That's the price now,' said the innkeeper, jutting his jowls out confidently.

'Is that how you do things up here? Renege on business deals at your whim?'

'That's how we're doing things tonight. I don't give a tinker's cuss how you do things in . . . Highcliff . . .'

The innkeeper let his sentence trail away, grinning.

So, whispered the Vincent-vile. *He knows where we're from, eh? Sounds like a threat, brother. He's a cocky one, isn't he?*

A solitary dray horse stood nearby harnessed to a cart, its head bowed, eyes fixed on the men in dispute. Ringlin and Ibal were working with the innkeeper's hulking barrel-boy in the cellar, rolling three large barrels towards the hatch-ramp. The barrel-boy was a mute giant of a man, who said nothing and did all his master commanded; a child trapped in a man's body was the expression that leaped to Hector's mind. The two rogues glanced up as Hector negotiated, paying close attention to where the conversation was heading.

'It sounds like you're getting greedy, sir,' said Hector, his gaunt cheekbones lifting slightly as he managed a sickly smile.

'I'm a businessman, that's all. Way I see it you're not just paying me for the barrels of brandy, boy.' He lowered his voice. 'You're paying for my silence.'

Hector shook his head from side to side. 'I swear, why does

it always have to end this way?' he said in a tired and irritated voice. He lifted his left hand and opened his palm.

Instantly the innkeeper was spluttering as he struggled with the invisible force tangled around his throat. Hector tightened his grip in the air, watching his brother's vile twist around the neck of the innkeeper like a deadly black noose.

'You had every chance of doing a nice bit of business with me tonight and walking away with your life. Three barrels of brandy, that's all I asked for. We had a deal; we shook on it. I distinctly recall shaking on it, don't you?'

The man collapsed to his knees, eyes bulging as his fingernails clawed at his fat throat, tearing the skin away in strips.

'Greed, sir; a terrible, ugly thing, I'm sure you'll agree. I'd love to say it was pleasant doing business with you, but . . .'

Hector clenched his fist tight, mind focused solely on the vile as he saw the phantom's attack through to its grisly end. Whereas previously, back in Highcliff, his control over the vile had been sporadic, inspired by surging emotions, since his encounter with the host on the White Isle he had a deeper understanding of his abilities. He yanked his hand back through the air, as if tugging a rope. The innkeeper's throat made a wet snapping sound, before he fell to the floor, neck broken.

Hector looked into the cellar where Ringlin, Ibal and the barrel-boy stared back. The man-child looked worried now, the realization of what had just happened suddenly dawning on him. He stared at the Boarguard who let the final barrel roll to a halt at the base of the ramp. Ibal pulled his sickle from his belt, while Ringlin gently unsheathed his long knife, twirling the blade as they advanced on the barrel-boy. From his vantage point above Hector lost sight of the trio as the giant mute retreated fearfully into the recesses of the cellar.

Done, brother.

Hector was surprised at Vincent. There was a new understanding between magister and vile, as if the spirit realized its master had unlocked a great many secrets that had previously been hidden. The Vincent-vile was showing a newfound respect to Hector, fear playing a large part in that. The host had hinted many things to Hector as it fed from his throat. It had shown him how to inflict pain, not just on the living, but the dead.

Even with a world of dark magick at his fingertips, waiting to be explored, Hector found himself wavering. He'd done what had to be done to get rid of Vega. He knew the Sharklord would have betrayed him in time; he'd already humiliated him in front of Bethwyn at every opportunity. Hector only regretted the fact that he'd allowed the sea marshal to get so close to him. He wouldn't make the same mistake again. For the first time ever, Hector felt in control of his magistry.

The innkeeper had brought it on himself. He'd been an enemy of the Wolf's Council, and Hector had to eliminate him. Who could have imagined that his knowledge of dark magicks could actually be used for *good*? Despite the freezing cold that bit at his face, Hector felt a warmth in his heart that had been missing for too long. He was helping Drew once again, helping what was left of the Wolf's Council, with his Brenn-given gift.

Stepping over the dead body, Hector made his way towards

the street, where the singing of folk inside the Black Gate Tavern spilled out of the door. It was only a matter of time before the innkeeper's clientele realized he was missing. Hector looked back over his shoulder as the first barrel emerged from the cellar, the Boarguard working it into the alley. It was time to return to the *Maelstrom*. Hurriedly, the two rogues loaded up the wagon before setting off back to the harbour.

Ibal cracked his whip over the nag's head and the dray horse picked up its pace along the slippery dock road. With their task completed quicker than expected, Hector was hopeful they'd be back at the rowboat first. It'd be good to show Manfred how capable he was, after everything that had gone on in the recent weeks. The duke's people had looked after Hector in Highcliff when he'd been taken ill, allowing him to convalesce in Buck House. After the chaos in Moga and the White Isle, and with Vega finally out of the way, Hector felt it was time to repay the Staglord for the many kindnesses he'd shown him. Arriving back at the boat, mission accomplished, was the first step towards Hector proving his trustworthiness to Manfred once more.

Three barrels of brandy and four casks of fresh water sat in the back of the cart with Hector, his men riding up front. As they pulled away, the magister couldn't help but stare back in the direction of the Black Gate Tavern. Customers were already exiting the inn as they'd left, in search of the fat oaf who had run the place after he'd failed to return to the bar. Judging by the shouting that had begun to chase them down the lane, they'd found his body, and that of the slain simpleton in the cellar. Hector glanced back nervously at the thick grooves the wagon wheels had cut into the snow-covered floor of the lane. A trail to follow: the sooner they were back aboard the *Maelstrom* the better. The last thing Hector needed was a hue and cry on his back with the miserable servants of Slotha hunting him.

Pulling up at the jetty where Figgis had moored the boat, the Boarguard jumped into the back of the dray, clambering past Hector to unload the barrels. The distant cries of angry men told the Boarlord all he needed to know. *Here's hoping old Manfred's right behind us, then*, thought Hector as he jumped down on to the frozen cobbles.

He walked up the jetty, boots slapping the frosty timber planks as he strode through the stiff gale. He slowed as he neared the remaining length of the wooden pier, coming to a staggering halt.

The rowboat was gone.

Initially Hector thought he'd come to the wrong jetty, but that was impossible; there were only a couple at this end of the harbour, and this was certainly the one. He then noticed the other vessels that had been moored along the jetty had been cut free – coracles, fishing boats and the like. A couple drifted some distance away in the choppy, black water.

Cut free.

He looked across to the next pier; again, the rowboats had been released, their only means of returning to the *Maelstrom* had been snatched away. He ran back to the dock road, finding his two companions rolling the first barrel along the planking towards him.

'Stop what you're doing,' he said. 'The boat's gone. We need to find Manfred, let him know Figgis has abandoned us.'

But even as he said it, he knew what had happened.

'What's that, my lord?' asked Ringlin, his face white with worry. Ibal gave a sickly, nervous giggle, looking back up the docks towards where torches and lanterns had begun to appear. Ringlin was shocked to see his master smile.

'So that was your game then, Manfred?' Hector said, to himself as much as anyone else.

If his men understood, they didn't respond, instead drawing their weapons.

The Stag shows his true colours, brother; the last of the Wolf's Council stabs you in the back. You can trust nobody.

'You're right for once, Vincent,' Hector said, walking past Ringlin and Ibal to stand in front of the horse and cart.

'What are you doing, my lord?' said Ringlin, his voice etched with panic as the approaching mob materialized through the swirling snowstorm, following the telltale passage of the dray through the white streets.

Hector stood calmly as the men appeared. Within moments they had surrounded the Boarlord and his henchmen. Ringlin and Ibal held their weapons at the ready; if they were to die, they'd take some of the Walrus's men with them. The locals were already shouting, calling to see the colour of the Westlanders' innards.

Hector raised his hands, palms out to the mob. 'Silence,' he said simply.

A cold unlike anything the men of Friggia had experienced before suddenly descended over the mob. To each man it felt as if Death's skeletal hand had traced a bony finger across their hearts, silencing them instantly. Hector smiled.

'Take me to the Werewalrus, Lady Slotha.'

'It is done,' said Manfred as he clambered back aboard the *Maelstrom*, the crew helping the elderly duke find his footing on the icy deck. Amelie and Bethwyn stood waiting for them, arms around one another as the frosty wind whipped around them.

'He cannot follow?' asked Amelie.

'Not unless he fancies a bracing swim,' replied Figgis, the last man to climb up from the rowboat.

'I hope to Brenn we've done the right thing,' said the queen, squeezing her lady-in-waiting in a fearful embrace.

'Don't you be worryin' about nothin',' said Figgis, before turning to the Staglord. 'Where to, Your Grace?'

'Onwards to Roof, dear captain,' said Manfred. 'And from there to Icegarden, and the protection of Duke Henrik. I pray he's in a generous mood.'

5

A Captive Audience

From the lofty balcony, Drew's view of Omir was as great as any in the Desert Realm. To the east the Sabre Sea bled across the horizon, separating sand from sky. To the west the Barebone Mountains stood tantalizingly close, their snow-capped peaks glistening like diamonds. Drew glanced down. The city sprawled below the palace, while the gleaming outer wall of Azra kept it safe. A road ran atop the wall's entire circumference, with soldiers, wagons and teams of horses moving along it, above the city. Only two gatehouses allowed entrance to the city: Copper Gate to the north, and Silver Gate to the south. These structures were as big as many castles in the west, housing garrisons of warriors who manned the defences; so long as the walls stood, Azra remained Faisal's.

The *Banshee* was still in Kaza under armed guard. Regardless of the fact that Drew's company had brought the king's daughter safely home, the Omiri took no chances. Drew wanted to be away as soon as possible, but realized that he wouldn't be able to leave now. Not while an army gathered in the north.

Tents of all sizes dotted the desert several miles from Azra, the amassed force as huge as any Drew had seen. Siege engines intermittently towered into the sky, their definition wavering in the intense heat haze. He counted at least thirty of the machines, the sole purpose of each to break down Azra's fabled walls. Drew looked down at the city's defences once more. Faisal's force was overwhelmingly outnumbered, the wall just about evening up the contest. *One wall to stop this mighty army.*

'Impressive, no?' said King Faisal as he joined Drew at the balcony.

'The walls? Or the army on your doorstep?'

'Both.'

'How long have they been there?'

'They began to gather a week ago. More arrive each day, so our scouts report. Who knows how many more shall arrive or when they intend to attack?'

'Who are they?'

'It's Lord Canan, and the Doglords. For ten years he's waged war in Omir, each year taking more of the desert from me. While fighting has intensified recently, he's never dared an assault upon Azra before. I wonder what now makes him so brazen . . .'

Faisal turned and walked back through his throne room. Drew followed, the yellow cloaked warriors of the palace guard shadowing him all the while. He wore no manacles, but he was their prisoner nonetheless. *Does Faisal know about the Dogs' alliance with the Cats? Has he heard the rumour of Hayfa joining forces with Canan?* Drew had a terrible feeling in the pit of his stomach. *Three armies against Azra? This city will fall . . .*

After yesterday's drama, the king was a changed man. Drew and his companions might have been captives, but that didn't stop Faisal from extending every courtesy to them. The three had been taken to separate quarters under armed guard, where they could bathe, dine and sleep. Drew's body cried out for rest and the time to allow his injuries to heal properly, but they needed to be moving again, and swiftly. It was mid-morning when they finally returned to Faisal's throne room. Shah now stood with Djogo, the two talking quietly while courtiers eyed them suspiciously.

'How's your daughter this morning?' asked Drew, as Faisal went to sit on his throne. A slave knelt at his feet with a tray of olives and grapes at the ready, raising them up instinctively whenever the king's hand reached out.

'Kara is better. Thank you again, for bringing her safely home. My wife is herself once more.'

'I wasn't alone,' said Drew, casting his hand towards his companions. 'It's Shah you must thank. It was her vision that allowed us to stop the Doglord's attack when we did. Without her, the outcome might not have been so joyous.'

Faisal nodded to the Werehawk, his smile forced.

'You must understand, Lady Shah, I find it . . . difficult, to express my thanks to a Hawklord, after the part your kind played in breaking Azra's walls so many years ago.'

'Understandable,' said Shah, stepping beside Drew. 'But it's alarming that your enemies might attack your own so close to home. What was your daughter *doing* on that boat in the first place?'

'Being brought home.' Faisal's face was serious as he considered how close he'd come to losing his daughter.

'The body you returned was that of my uncle, Prince Fier. He'd been schooling Kara in Denghi, where he served as my envoy. Word had reached us that Canan's forces were marching on Azra. We had no choice but to have them return.'

'How was it they came under attack?' asked Drew.

Faisal frowned. Before he could answer Lord Rook stepped forward and spoke for him.

'The king's enemies have a long and deadly reach, Wolf.'

'But it was Doglords who attacked the skiff,' said Drew. He watched the black robed man carefully, the Crow having taken far too much delight in tormenting Shah the previous day.

'We only have *your* word that it was the Dogs who attacked them,' said Rook. 'It was probably just river pirates. Either way, she's safe now.'

'It was a Doglord, all right, your daughter will vouch for that, Your Majesty,' said Drew. 'I left one at the bottom of the Silver River.'

'I would imagine poor Kara can remember little from the traumatic event. The child is still in shock. How very convenient that you left the villain's corpse on the riverbed,' said the Crowlord.

'Let's talk about convenient,' said Drew, facing Rook.

'How did the Dogs know that the king's daughter was travelling to Azra? I know maps and I understand distance: how did word reach the Doglords in the north, alerting them that the child was on her way? To get a message to the Dogs so swiftly? That sounds like something that would require *wings,* don't you agree, Lord Rook?'

'Mind what you insinuate, pup,' said Rook. 'They were simply pirates; bandits, Your Majesty.'

Drew turned to the king, fed up with the Crow's interruptions.

'Armed with silver weapons? They're wealthy bandits Rook speaks of,' said Drew. 'This sounds like a coordinated attack. Your enemies are mobilizing against you, Your Majesty, and I fear their number is far greater than you imagine, and that some are closer than you know.'

Rook took hold of Drew, turning him about so they were face to face.

'You think the king isn't *worried* about yesterday's events? You assume an awful lot, son of Wergar. Your greatest concern should be your own immediate future.'

'As I understood, this is the court of King Faisal, not the Crows of Riven,' Drew snapped. 'While your interest in my welfare is appreciated, Rook, it's the king I seek audience with. Not some visiting dignitary from a small town in the Barebones.'

'Mind your tongue, Wolf!' said Rook. 'You and your *friends* are enemies of Omir. The good people of the Desert Realm have long memories. They remember Wergar's war all too well.'

Drew ignored the man, speaking directly to Faisal.

'You have Kara back, Your Majesty, thanks to our actions. One of my companions, Drake, died saving her. A brave man and a Werelord of the first rank, he gave his life for a complete stranger, many miles from his homeland. Surely you can let us go?'

Faisal stroked his jaw as Drew spoke, pondering the young Wolflord's words.

'You're the reason there's a war in the west, boy,' said the king finally. 'The Seven Realms fight over Highcliff's throne. Some say it should be yours. I've yet to hear your thoughts on the matter.'

Drew grimaced. The Jackal realized all too well the young Werewolf's value.

'Up until recently I'd no interest in the throne of Westland. But that was before I saw the cruelty that takes place across Lyssia in the names of monsters like Leopold, Lucas and Kesslar.'

Djogo and Shah looked down, ashamed, when Drew mentioned the Goatlord.

'The people of Lyssia have made a stand; they've rallied behind the Wolf's banner, risen in my name. I'd betray them all if I didn't fight now, to free them from tyranny. Brackenholme, Westland, the Longridings and the Barebones –'

'Don't mention my homeland as your ally, Wolf,' said Rook. 'The Staglords might have made a stand at your side, but what good did it do their home?'

Drew cocked his head at mention of the Stags. 'Why? What's happened?'

The Crowlord jutted out his jaw as he relayed the news from the Barebones. 'Highwater is surrounded by Onyx's forces, and sure to fall. As for your Staglords, no doubt you're aware that one brother's dead and the other's disappeared. So please, Wolf, don't tell me you've friends in the Mountain Realm. You'll find none there.'

Shah stepped towards the Rook. 'Highwater laid siege to? Tell me, Crow, where do the black birds of Riven fit into this picture. Highwater is on your doorstep, is it not?'

Rook prickled at the Hawklady's words.

'We Crowlords remain removed from conflict. We seek nothing but peace and neutrality.'

Shah laughed out loud, but when she looked back at Rook her face was stony.

'How can you stand there and say the Crows of Riven want nothing but peace? Your father, Count Croke, has perched on that pile of slate for almost a century. In all those years he's bullied and bickered with his neighbours, trying to wrestle control of the Barebones away from the Stags of Stormdale. You expect me to believe he sits neutral while his lifelong nemeses are beaten black and blue by the Catlords? Tell me: how soon before a Crow resides in Stormdale, Rook?'

Rook lurched towards Shah, lashing out with a fist, only the swift action of the palace guards restraining him in time.

'You witch!' spat the Crowlord. 'You dare lecture me on what's best for the Barebones? Your kind don't belong in my mountains any more than a fish belongs in a tree! You're relics, Shah – you and whatever Hawklord scum remain! Skeer's the best of your bad bunch, and he did right striking a deal with

Leopold back in the day. He rules Windfell now, the last of the Hawks. Soon enough we'll see how Windfell looks with black feathers on the throne!'

His eyes bulged with fury as Shah stayed close to Djogo. Drew looked from the Crow to Faisal. He was surprised to see the Jackal staring straight at him, ignoring the shocked Shah and the raving Rook, his expression unreadable.

Drew rounded on the Crow. 'Isn't Baron Griffyn the rightful Lord of Windfell?'

'Griffyn? That wretched creature no longer has wings. Someone should wring his neck, put the poor buzzard out of his misery.'

Ignoring the Crow, Drew turned to Faisal. 'A Doglord army approaches, Your Majesty, possibly the same one that was allied to the Catlords that attacked Westland. Now they gather north of Azra, the Cats returning the favour to the Dogs. I wager you'll find Bastians fighting alongside Omiri.'

'Let them come!' cried one of Faisal's cousins. 'Their bodies will litter the base of Azra's walls!'

'We can defeat this army from the north!' shouted another.

'And the one from the south?' asked Drew, turning to the crowd. 'Talk spreads like wildfire in Denghi. Lady Hayfa has struck a bargain with Lord Canan. Her army will come to the aid of the Doglords as well. Send scouts south – I guarantee you'll find her. That's three armies, my lords, surrounding your city. They're going to carve Azra up between them!'

'Preposterous!' scoffed Rook. 'Don't listen to him, Your Majesty. He spreads mistrust and fear. You should have killed this monster and his companions when they landed here.'

'Let us continue our quest,' continued Drew. 'We head into the Barebones with Baron Griffyn's blessing. He will lead us to the ancient tomb of his forefathers, the Screaming Peak. From there, the baron shall summon the Hawklords from every corner of Lyssia.'

Drew held the king's gaze as he spoke, the room quiet but for the spluttering of Lord Rook.

'Your aid won't be forgotten, King Faisal. We'll return, in number, and help you defeat the army that approaches Azra, be they Dogs, Cats or any other kind of beast. You shall have the Hawklords as allies this time!'

Rook moved past Drew, bringing his lips closer to Faisal's ear.

'The Wolf will promise you anything to save his hide, Your Majesty. Kill him now and let all Lyssia know – you'll be a hero throughout the Seven Realms! With one thrust of your blade you can end this war!'

Slowly, the king turned to the Crowlord.

'My dear Lord Rook,' he said, smiling as he spoke. 'I think you may have just outstayed your welcome.'

'You're not serious,' said Rook, his face frozen in a shocked smile.

'I'm very serious. I shall be closing the gates of Azra tonight for the last time to all but my allies. Anyone else should leave. That would include you.'

'But I'm here on my father's behalf. We *are* your allies.'

'These are turbulent times, Lord Rook. Your father would appreciate your presence in Riven no doubt, with war threatening us all. I only want those loyal to Azra within these walls.'

Rook was furious, spittle frothing at his lips as he looked around the room snarling, his eyes settling on Drew and his companions.

'You side with your prisoners, Faisal? Is this how little you think of my kind? You take a Wolf's word over mine?'

Faisal rose and walked towards the enraged Lord of Riven.

'This has nothing to do with the Wolf and everything to do with the Crow. Many questions remain unanswered regarding the enemy at my gates and allegiances in the Barebones. You offer little to put my mind at ease.'

'Don't be fooled by the Wolf's gossip,' said Rook, but he choked on his words, struggling for conviction.

'I gave you every chance to walk away from Azra with your reputation intact. I tolerated your actions yesterday, taking such delight in holding the Hawklady hostage. I thought the Wolf and Hawk were my enemies . . .'

'They *are* your enemies!' said Rook. 'You should kill them!'

'And now you attack a guest in my palace, a lady no less.'

'She's no lady!' squawked Rook. The Crowlord was now surrounded by palace guards, the other nobles having moved clear of the volatile therian.

'What good does your presence here do me and my people, Rook? Why do you wish the Wolf dead so dearly? Whom do you truly serve?'

'If you don't kill them . . .'

'If I don't kill them, what exactly?' exclaimed the king, releasing the Jackal at last.

Faisal arched his back, letting the white robes that draped across his shoulders tumble away as his tanned torso tripled in size. His arms popped with muscles, fingers shifting into claws that pointed menacingly towards Rook. His neck and head broadened, the smooth fur of the Jackal racing through his flesh as sharp ears rose and a long, canine snout worked its way through his face.

'Hold your tongue, Crowlord, before you say something you regret,' growled the Werejackal.

Drew heard the snarls of the other therians in the court. A cloud passed in front of the sun, darkening the throne room. His cousins and fellow Jackal-lords growled in unison, the beasts all too visible in their angry faces.

'You have one hour, Crow,' said Faisal. 'The death of my dear uncle Lord Fier is shrouded by the stench of treachery, and the young Wolflord's words have allowed me to see clearly. Gather your belongings and leave my city. If you're still here after that, I shan't be responsible for my fellow Jackals' actions. A threat against their king is a threat to all.'

Rook looked quickly around the room, noticing the assembled Jackal-lords' state of agitation. He backed up warily, eyes flitting between the warriors and therians.

'You've made a grave mistake siding with these beasts, Faisal,' warned the Werecrow as he retreated through the throne room, armed guards escorting him closely. Turning on his heel, the Lord of Riven stormed from the chamber, long robe billowing as he left a shower of black feathers in his wake.

Drew kept his distance as the transformed Werejackal watched the Crow disappear. Faisal's broad shoulders heaved up and down. Gradually he returned to human form, the Jackal and temper subsiding.

Finally the king looked back at Drew. 'The black bird says I'm mistaken to trust you,' said Faisal, his narrow eyes studying the young therian carefully. The look he gave the Wolf seemed confrontational, as if he were laying down a challenge.

'Prove him wrong.'

6

Nowhere to Run

The calls of the chasing pack seemed distant, their cries carried away on the chill wind that raced across the Longridings. Their torches were visible, flaming brands held aloft by the riders as they scoured the grasslands for fugitives. Trent spurred Storm on through the long grass, keen to put distance between himself and his comrades. With their constant shouting they were making enough noise to wake the dead, and if their enemies were to be caught, stealth had to play a large part.

The tall fronds whipped at horse and youth as they sped along, Trent's eyes picking out the broken grass ahead that marked the route his quarry had taken. Once again, his mind raced back to the Cold Coast where he and his father – and brother – had hunted by night, often on foot, occasionally on horseback, but always by the light of the moon. The pale light of the heavenly body illuminated the path ahead – the sawgrass clumsily broken in his foe's desperate desire to escape. The man was injured, of that much he was sure, judging by the blood he caught sight of on the pale yellow blades of grass.

The trail came to a sudden halt as the grass fell away suddenly before him. Trent reined Storm in, the horse snorting as she skidded to an abrupt stop, her hooves kicking at the frozen earth and sending a shower of pebbles skittering off the lip of the ravine. Trent lurched forward in his saddle, patting Storm's neck as clouds of steam snorted from her nostrils. Directly below them a small gorge cut through the grasslands, rocky inclines rising steeply from either side of a rushing, bubbling brook. Storm stepped nervously as Trent surveyed the terrain, looking north and south up the length of the rocky valley.

'He went down here,' he said, as much to the horse as himself. 'And so do we.'

He gently prodded his heels into Storm's flanks, urging her over the edge of the ravine. Reluctantly, the horse proceeded, hooves gingerly picking a path down the steep, rocky slope. Occasionally they passed a bloodied rock, a red handprint smeared against a slab of stone where the fugitive had scrambled down to the gorge's bottom. Arriving at the base of the slope, Trent hopped down out of the saddle for a moment, leading Storm to the stream, his eyes wide and alert, searching the shadowy valley for a sighting of the enemy. He let Storm drink from the noisy stream momentarily, jumping across to the other side and searching the other bank. There was no bloody trail, no telltale marks left behind on the rocks. He glanced south down the ravine where the brook disappeared into the distance, back in the direction of the rest of his force.

'He won't have gone back that way, not after he witnessed what was done to his companions.'

He jumped back up into his saddle, his horse refreshed by the cold water. 'North it is. We follow the stream.'

Lord Frost's force had encountered a large band of travellers earlier that day, around dusk, making their way west through the Longridings. The group had numbered nearly two hundred, mainly civilians, such as farmers, traders and a smattering of Romari. There were also a number of Horselords within their ranks – the Werelords immediately rushing to the defence of their companions when the Lionguard had launched an unprovoked attack against the caravan. The initial offensive had left a sour taste in Trent's mouth. The fact that Romari were present had been enough for the Redcloaks to decide that the group were the enemy, the travellers' loyalty to the Wolf and their antics in Cape Gala still fresh in their minds. As it transpired, their hunch had been correct, but Trent had put that down to blind luck rather than reasoned deduction.

The initial battle had been fierce, the Romari and Horselords engaging Redcloaks and Bastians while the remaining refugees fled across the grasslands. Once the enemy had been defeated, at some cost to Frost's small army, the Catlord had questioned the surviving prisoners. With the aid of Sorin, he had prised a great deal of information from the group, including the knowledge that more Werelords had been travelling with the group, escaping with the other civilians when the battle had commenced. Putting the prisoners to the sword, the Lionguard and Bastians had given chase, gradually picking up those who had fled. The soldiers had cheered as one after another of the refugees had been rounded up and clapped in irons. Only a handful remained at large, and Trent was determined to return to the camp with a trophy of his own.

Trent pushed on along the banks of the brook, Storm picking up pace as the outrider grew in confidence. *This is the only way he could have gone. Nowhere left to run. I have you now.* The foe must have thought the stream would mask his passage, which it would have done ordinarily. However, the noise of the water rushing over the rocks would also conceal Trent's approach, the constant gurgling covering the approach of Storm's hooves. He unsheathed the Wolfshead blade as he rode, controlling his horse by his thighs and heels alone, letting the longsword trail through the air to his right. He sat up in his saddle neck straight, eyes searching the ravine ahead.

'There you are.'

The figure had collapsed ahead, leaning hard against a boulder that sat in the middle of the stream. The fugitive looked up as he caught sight of the approaching rider. The bearded man grunted, clutching his chest as if in pain. Then he was off, running along the shallow streambed. Trent kicked Storm's flanks, forcing the horse into a canter.

The fleeing man tripped and stumbled, feet splashing through the icy water. He glanced over his shoulder as Storm thundered closer, gaining on him swiftly. Trent allowed the horse to charge past, her hooves narrowly missing the man but frightening him enough to send him spreadeagled into the stream. He landed face first in the cold water, momentarily blinded as he surfaced, gasping for air. Trent turned Storm around, squeezing his thighs against her back and urging her to rear up, her hooves threatening to strike the enemy.

The fugitive began to change, heavy horns emerged from the old man's skull, twisting and curling about his head. His short grey beard began to lengthen as his ribcage cracked within his chest, a sound like hammer hitting steel. Trent showed no fear. *Here was the trophy he had sought: an enemy therian, a traitorous Werelord.* He expertly prompted Storm to lash out, the horse's hooves connecting with the shifting Werelord's horned head with a hollow *crack*.

The man went down on his side, his head bouncing off the rocks on the streambed, his face half submerged in the water. Trent could see the cold liquid rushing through his enemy's slack mouth, racing into his airways and threatening to fill his lungs. He quickly dismounted, landing beside the Werelord in the water, hooking his arms beneath the fellow's partially transformed torso. He heaved the therian on to the bank, throwing him on to his stomach and binding him swiftly with ropes.

More riders arrived, the snorting of horses mingling with the cheers and jeers of the soldiers as they looked down at the hog-tied Werelord. The horns around his head reminded Trent of the old ram they had kept on the farm, the tuft of a grey beard beneath his chin further enhancing the resemblance. *A Ramlord? There had been one in Cape Gala, at the court of High Stable. Was this the one of the Werelords they'd been searching for?*

Trent looked back at his companions, smiling proudly. The old therian snorted, rolling on to his side to view his captors.

'Well done, boys,' the aged Ramlord spluttered. 'You chased down an old man.'

'Chased down a traitor,' replied Frost, his voice rich and smooth. The Catlord jumped from his horse and landed in the stream, hardly making a splash. His pink eyes widened as he waded towards the bank where the Ram lay, coming to stand beside Trent. He patted the young outrider's back.

'Good work, Sergeant Ferran.'

'Ferran?' said the Ram incredulously, but the only reply he received was the albino's boot to the temple. Trent stared down at the bound captive as two of the Bastian warriors hauled him on to the back of one of their horses, puzzling over the prisoner's reaction to his name.

He knows my name, Trent mused as he clambered back on Storm's back. *He knows Drew.*

7

The Stars Over Azra

Alone in the heavens, with only the stars for company, the young Wolflord was transported through time and space. He was a child, back at the farmhouse on the Cold Coast, Tilly Ferran rocking him in her chair while the two of them gazed into the night sky. His mother had the gift, so old Mack always told him: she could read the stars, divine a person's fortune on a clear, cloudless night. He tried to recall the things she'd promised him, the events she predicted would come to pass, but all he could remember was the smell of her hair and the feel of her hand over his. For the first time in months, Drew felt a tear roll down his cheek.

'I'm not interrupting you, am I?'

Drew glanced up from the star chart mosaic, wiping the tear from his face with the flat of his hand, as King Faisal paced through the darkness towards him. The rest of the king's guests were still gathered at the far end of the throne room, feasting one last time before on the eve of war. Djogo and Shah were with them, the frosty relations between the two factions thawing, speeded along by fine food and drink. The Hawklady occasionally looked across the room, concerned by his dark mood. Drew had no appetite for feasting, and even less for company.

'I'm sorry, Your Majesty. I was a world away.'

Faisal walked around the mosaic, circling Drew as he remained rooted in the middle.

'They say Azra is the home of all Lyssia's knowledge. The art of magistry began here, would you believe it? The libraries beneath the palace would rival any in the Seven Realms, Drew. This city was the seat of learning for Brenn's wisest children at one time. Terrifying to think that this could all be lost if the Dogs and the Cats overrun our walls.'

'I recognize the stars,' said Drew, gesturing to the marble constellations. 'There's the Stag, the Serpent. Over there are the Twin Boars.'

'And you're standing on the Wolf,' said Faisal, smiling.

Drew took a step back.

'So I am.'

'Not in the mood for a feast? You surprise me. The morning brings danger to all of us; you, with your journey, and us, with impending war. We Jackals always dine as if it's our last meal on the eve of battle.'

'I can't stomach it,' sighed Drew. 'Have you heard back from your scouts?'

'You were right, Wolf. The Hyena's forces amass to the

south of the Silver River. You'll have to leave swiftly at first light if you're to sail out of Kaza before they take the port town.'

'Are you prepared for them?'

'Azra is always ready for war. This is the Jewel of Omir. It's been fought over for centuries. This is just one more chapter in this city's rich history.'

'You sound as if you're looking forward to war.'

'I look forward to action. It's the waiting I can't abide. My warriors are ready. Azra's ready.'

'But still . . .' said Drew, scratching the back of his head as he stared out of the archway that led to the balcony. Hundreds of fires dotted the horizon to the north, twinkling like fireflies over a pitch-black meadow.

'Don't hold your tongue now, Drew. If you truly are the king of Westland, then speak freely. It's been long years since another king has been my guest.'

Drew looked wearily at the handsome Jackal. 'There are so many of them. You're badly outnumbered.'

'You underestimate our defences. Besides, the people will man the walls should the warriors fall.'

'I fear for your people.'

'This is their home. They take pride in their land.'

'Even the slaves?'

Faisal grimaced, shaking his head at the Wolflord. 'I wouldn't bring such a matter up if I were you, Drew. We're just getting to know one another. Politics have killed the greatest friendships as sure as swords before now.'

Drew bit his lip, shaking his head. His mind went back to

the belly of the *Banshee*, to the Furnace and the cruel antics of Kesslar and the Lizardlords. 'I can't stand here silent. It goes against all I believe in. I've *been* a slave, Faisal. Walk even one step with a collar round your throat and you may change your tune. No man should be owned by another.'

'We shall have to agree to disagree, Wolf cub.'

'Don't mock me, Faisal,' said Drew, angry now. 'I haven't fought my way back to Lyssia just to sit quietly while a fool spouts barbaric beliefs at me, be he a beggar or a king.'

The Jackal snarled. If any of the palace guard had been present, they might have seized Drew for offending the king so. But the two were alone, facing one another across the ancient mosaic.

'This is my land, Wolf – my city. Your place is in the West. Keep your so-called enlightened thinking on the other side of the Barebones.'

Drew stepped forward, eyeballing the king. 'How many slaves are there in this city?'

'I've no idea, they are too many to count.'

'Estimate for me, Your Majesty.'

'Tens of thousands, I should imagine.'

'Tomorrow, your city will be overrun, even if we can call the Hawklords to our side. You haven't enough warriors to man the walls against three armies.'

'And what would you propose?'

'Free them.'

Faisal recoiled as if he'd been slapped in the face.

'Release the slaves. Grant them citizenship of Azra as free men. Free the slaves and you'll save your city.'

Faisal stared at Drew, weighing the youth up. He clearly hadn't expected Drew to speak so frankly to him. Perhaps Drew might have kept silent if he hadn't been so weary. The thought of journeying to Tor Raptor made his legs feel heavy suddenly. He stifled a yawn.

'It's been a long day, Your Majesty, and I must be away before dawn's first light. I thank you for your hospitality, and your understanding. Until I return, with the Hawklords . . .'

Drew bowed, turning to walk away, as King Faisal called after him.

'I don't understand how turning slaves into free men will save Azra.'

The Wolflord continued to walk away, calling back as he went. 'Put a roof over a man's head and you give him a home. Put a sword in his hand and pride in his heart – you give him something to fight for. You give him hope.'

The fire had burned low by the time Drew returned to his bedchamber, just a handful of coals still kicking out heat as the cold air of the desert spread through the room. The guest quarters could have housed the entire Ferran family and their neighbours, the opulence on a scale Drew had never seen before, not even in Scoria. An enormous round bed dominated the room, circular steps leading up to it like a sacrificial altar. The carvings around the marble fireplace were as intricate as anything he'd seen in the Temple of Brenn in Highcliff. Bejewelled curtains billowed round the door on to the balcony, gems flashing like the stars in the night sky beyond. The Azrans did nothing by half-measures.

Even with the thick doors closed at Drew's back, the noise from the throne room below still echoed through the walls of the palace. Faisal wasn't lying when he said the Jackals liked to feast the night before a battle. He looked around the room, a nagging sensation descending over him. *Something isn't right*. He paused, trying to figure out what irked him, but couldn't put his finger on it.

Drew shivered, striding towards the balcony, the freezing air raising goosebumps on his flesh. The room felt like a mausoleum, the cold marble only enhancing the sensation. He stared at the fires of the enemy encampments beyond the walls, spreading east to west as far as the eye could see. *Does Faisal truly understand the magnitude of what he's facing? Will he take the advice of a boy like me?*

Drew grabbed the handle and pulled the balcony door closed, stopping before he dropped the latch. He suddenly realized what was nagging him: the doors had been closed when he'd left the bedchamber. Drew turned quickly, eyes searching the room. He channelled the Wolf's senses, his vision heightening instantly as he sniffed at the air. Stepping carefully across the chamber, he reached over to the chest at the foot of the bed. A sheathed longsword rested atop it, a gift from the king and a small token of apology for the treatment Drew and his friends had endured. Drew snatched the handle, shaking the scabbard from the blade where it fell quietly on to the rug.

He snorted at the air once more, picking up the scent of the intruder. With his lupine eyes now adjusted to the dim light, he could see through the gloom as if it were day. He pulled at the jewel-encrusted curtains, tearing them clear of the windows to reveal what they hid, but found nothing. He leaped across the room towards the tall closet, flicking the door open only to find it empty. Lastly he dashed back towards the bed, dancing up the steps and pulling back the sheets from where they hung to the marble floor. Ducking down, Drew looked beneath the bed. There was nobody there. The prowler was gone.

He collapsed on to the enormous round bed, his heart beating fast, relieved to not be caught in a fight once more but disappointed to have not captured his intruder. He turned his head, the moonlight that streamed through the glass doors illuminating the clean white sheets that spread out before him. Drew's eyes widened. *There you are.*

A single long feather lay on his pillow, black as night itself. Drew shivered as he reached across and picked it up, the waxy texture sliding across his skin. He turned it between his fingertips, considering the gift's meaning. Rook was watching him. There would be no hiding from the Crowlord.

8

A Welcome in Tuskun

The dogs' paws pounded through the deep snow, hauling the sleds through the blizzard, whipcracks urging them on their way. Hector lay on his side, lashed to the sledge as a hunter might bind his kill. Goyt, an old Sturmish pelt-trader caught trapping in the queen's woods, lay strapped down before him, head tucked to his chest, the cold and exhaustion having taken their toll on him. Hector felt Ibal's fat belly at his back; the magister was grateful for the warmth of his portly Boarguard. The rogue's giggles had ceased two days ago back in Friggia, the mob having worked some of their anger out on the three southerners before throwing them in the jail for the remainder of the night. They'd departed the Sturmish port at first light, heading inland on a handful of dog sleds, heading for the City of the Walrus.

Ringlin was on one of the other sledges, bound to some

other criminals who were being transported to Tuskun. The cold was unbearable, the temperature having remained well below freezing during their entire journey. Hector's teeth chattered incessantly, his entire body struggling with the extreme conditions. Who could have imagined the warmth of Ibal's fat belly might keep him alive? There were six of them in all being taken to Slotha, each responsible for very different crimes. The queen of Tuskun was a notoriously ill-tempered, violent woman: he hoped the Walrus would allow him the chance to speak in his defence.

The driver let out a cheer, the noise echoing over the chasing sleds. Hector craned his neck, looking up ahead to where they headed. The blizzard lifted briefly, allowing the magister a clear view of Tuskun's jagged black walls as they loomed into view. To describe the outer defence as a wall was an exaggeration; giant slabs of grey slate had been driven into the ground around the entire city, dozens of tall wooden watchtowers dotted around its circumference. The sharp, splintered defences reminded Hector of Vega's teeth when the Sharklord was transformed: fearsome and deadly.

Not so deadly in the end, eh, brother? whispered the Vincentvile slyly.

Timber gates groaned open, a portcullis grinding clear out of the sleds' path as they raced past beneath it. The city within bore little resemblance to any civilized settlement Hector had ever visited. It was little more than a shantytown, a crowded slum, the locals standing aside as the dog sleds raced up the slippery, stinking streets, a steaming river of feculence steadily streaming beside the road. Hector gagged at the stench as the whip cracked overhead and the driver yelled at his hounds.

The buildings in the city were wooden for the most part, though the Boarlord spotted the occasional stone structure as they raced by. Bones of all shapes and sizes featured everywhere, the skulls of wild beasts adorning doors, giant animal ribs and femurs woven into the rooftops, walls and windows of the houses. Clearly, this was a city of hunters. These people lived to kill.

The sledge jostled up the rutted avenue, slush and filth splashing off the road surface into the faces of the prisoners. Hector thought he might vomit, smearing the sewage from his face against Goyt's shoulder at his side. The driver pulled hard at the reins, the dogs yelping and barking as they slowed, the sled grinding to a halt in the blackened slush before a great black building. Enormous whale jawbones formed an arch above the open doors of Slotha's Longhouse. Two heavy-set guards stood either side of the entrance, each carrying a long barbed harpoon. The pair didn't move as the driver jumped off the sled, waiting for the others to join him.

'Goyt. Ibal. We're here,' Hector whispered. The fat Boarguard grunted a brief acknowledgement.

Hector gave Goyt a shove with his knee. The impact was enough to jar Goyt's head, which lolled back from his chest with a *crack*. The old trapper's face was blue, his eyes wide and frozen over.

Welcome to Tuskun, brother.

The Longhouse resembled the hull of an upturned ship, the interior an arched tunnel that disappeared into darkness. An enormous firepit dominated the hall, belching clouds of black smoke to the ceiling where it struggled to escape through a single, squat chimney. Guards like those at the entrance occupied the chamber, each carrying harpoons and axes and clad in sealskins and furs. Their faces were leathery, long drooping black moustaches and beards obscuring their mouths. Each of them stared intently at the five prisoners as they were marched towards the roaring fire, manacles jangling, and forced to their knees.

Hector looked back over his shoulder. Outside, beyond the open doors, he could hear the snarling of sled dogs as they tore into Goyt's corpse, an unexpected reward for their hard run to Tuskun. Hector shivered, despite the heat, and turned back. Beyond the fire he saw a great mass advancing through the shadows. As she got closer her form was illuminated by the dancing flames. Her flesh was on show to all, between tattered leather strips pulled tight across her broad frame, the skin bulging between the straps. A bearskin robe was draped from her shoulder.

'So,' grunted Slotha, the Werewalrus, as she strode around the firepit and made her way behind her captives. 'These are the prisoners the good people of Friggia have delivered to me? This is the *fresh meat* . . .'

I don't like the sound of this, dear brother . . .

The sled drivers standing to one side bowed, their hands clasped together as if in prayer.

'Go get yourselves fed.'

The three departed, apparently happy to be away from their queen, while a man who looked like a councillor unrolled a scroll. The vicious-looking Ugri warriors stepped forward, one standing in front of each prisoner as Slotha manoeuvred behind them.

'What crimes?' asked the therian lady, as she settled behind the first man to Hector's right. The man's eyes were fearful, darting from the guard to the councillor and then back to the magister.

'Defamation of Your Majesty's character in a tavern,' said the councillor, sneering as he read the charge.

'What did you say, man?' whispered Slotha, momentarily lowering her head between the terrified man and Hector, her lips wobbling as she muttered into his ear. Hector got a whiff of the woman's breath, as foul as a bucket of rotting fish.

'I . . . I . . . but I . . .' the man couldn't speak, his whole body trembling as he began to shuffle forwards away from her. The warrior standing in front of him reached over, clasping the man's hair in his fist and holding him firmly in his place. Hector could hear Slotha grunting behind him now, her bones cracking as her body shifted. He recognized the noise of a therianthrope on the change instantly. The councillor finished the stuttering man's sentence for him.

'He called you a "fat cow", Your Majesty.'

The man's eyes widened further as the wet sound of blades tearing through flesh cut through the air beside Hector. The Boarlord took a brief glance at the man as he spluttered blood from his trembling lips before the guard released his head, allowing the body to topple forward to the floor. Two great gashes were visible in the man's back, his spine exposed where a pair of blades had sunk through his body, butchering him on the spot. With a grunt, Slotha moved behind Hector.

'Next,' she snarled, her voice deep and wet, her teeth grating.

'Murder,' said the councillor. 'He and his companions killed an innkeeper and his man.'

Hector heard the queen shift her bulk behind him, as a warrior reached forward and took hold of his scalp in a dirty hand.

'A moment, I beg of you!' said Hector quickly.

The councillor arched his eyebrows as Hector struggled in the warrior's grasp.

'The charge is quite straightforward; you apparently admitted to your crime in Friggia.'

'I believe Her Majesty would benefit from the full story!'

'Spit it out, then!' she said, smacking her lips.

'I'm Baron Hector, the Boarlord of Redmire. I'm one of the Wolf's Council.'

The councillor looked astonished as Slotha grabbed Hector by the shoulder and spun him about, his hair tearing from his scalp as he turned to face the queen of Tuskun.

'Oh, but what good fortune!' she roared, clapping her hands together. 'Sosha smiles up at me!'

Nothing had prepared Hector for the sight of the monstrous Werewalrus. The scraps of clothing that had clung to her had been ripped away, her pasty, pale skin now mottled dark brown and covered in calluses and warts, her stocky legs having transformed into huge, flat flippers. Her clawed fingers were long and webbed, her hands wide and wobbling as she clapped them together. Her long, greasy hair hung down her back, neck and lips bristling with oily whiskers. A pair of yard-long tusks protruded down from her top lip, ivory blades that dripped crimson with the dead man's blood.

'You have the look of your father,' she grunted, clawing at his face with a flippered hand. 'He was an ugly pig, too!'

You have my permission to roar at the irony, chuckled the Vincent-vile to Hector.

'Hold him still,' she gushed excitedly as her warrior grabbed his head once again. 'I want to look into this one's eyes while I run him through. Imagine Prince Lucas's joy when I deliver a spitted Boarlord to him!'

'Wait!' shouted Hector, as Slotha raised her tusks, ready to strike his chest. She paused, waiting for him to speak.

'I know there's a price on my head, but grant my sorry life a few more days, I beg of you, Your Majesty. Killing me would be too easy – the prince would prefer it if you delivered me alive, I can promise you. I know him, I served him for years. Let him do what he will with me. I guarantee he'll be doubly grateful . . .'

Slotha looked from Hector to her councillor. The man shrugged, leaving the decision entirely to her whim.

'You say I should let you live and go to Highcliff?'

'Hand me over as a gift alive rather than dead. I have information that will aid the Catlords in their war.'

'Tell *me* your information then, Piglord.'

Hector managed a thin smile.

Roll the bones, brother!

'I shall not. My information is for Prince Lucas and him

alone. Deliver me to him and your reward shall be greater than you could possibly imagine, Lady Slotha.'

'That's *Queen* Slotha,' she snorted.

'I know,' said Hector as the warrior's grip on his hair tightened. 'The queen of the North and the king of Westland; can you *imagine* what you might discuss together?'

Slotha smacked her lips as if savouring a previously unknown taste. Hector kept his eyes fixed on her.

She's taken the bait, Hector! Well done!

'I deliver you alive to Highcliff?'

'Myself and my two men.' Hector gestured to Ringlin and Ibal at his side with a quick glance.

'Very well,' said the Werewalrus, shuffling past the two rogues who breathed audible sighs of relief at their temporary pardon. She settled behind the last prisoner, who was afforded no such kindness.

'That one's a thief, Your Majesty,' said the councillor, answering her unvoiced question.

'But remember, Piglord,' she said, rearing up behind the bound man as he knelt before her. The Ugri warrior held the prisoner's head as he kicked out, trying to roll clear. She lunged down fast, the tusks puncturing the man's back and disappearing up to her gums. The blood erupted as she tore them free.

'No tricks.'

Hector bowed on his knees, his heart near exploding.

'Ready the *Myrmidon*,' said the Walrus of Tuskun. 'We sail to Highcliff to meet the prince.'

PART VI

Talons and Turncoats

I

Two Rivers

It would be hard to imagine a more unusual party of people than the one that disembarked from the *Banshee* at the border town of Two Rivers. Drew led the way, the mountainous figure of the Behemoth following, over seven feet of towering muscle behind him. The Weremammoth carried an enormous stone mallet across one shoulder, a weapon the strongest man would struggle to lift with both hands. Following him came the crooked figure of Baron Griffyn alongside the Catlady, Taboo.

Krieg awaited them at the head of the docks, his spiked mace swinging from his hip, grimacing as they approached. A chill wind blew through the ramshackle harbour, sending sand through the air like a shower of broken glass.

'Good to be off that wretched boat, isn't it?'

'It's good to be on our way again,' said Drew, the passing

townsfolk eyeing them suspiciously. 'I just hope our friends are safe in Azra. Did you find horses?'

The Rhino nodded, and set off up the street, Drew at his shoulder and the others behind.

'How's the old man?' asked Krieg, without looking back.

'He misses her, which is understandable, but she has Djogo. She'll be fine.'

Faisal had insisted the Hawklady and Djogo remain behind in Azra as his guests. Effectively, the Jackal was holding her to ransom; the guarantee that the Hawklords would return and fight for him, honouring the promise Drew made on their behalf. There had never been any doubt in Drew's mind that the Hawklords, *if* they could summon them, would aid them, but that clearly hadn't been the case for Faisal. Considering the previous visit of Wolf and Hawk to Azra years ago, the king had fair reason to feel that way.

Faisal had passed a decree that very night, granting every single slave in the city of Azra his or her freedom. While the therian lords of the city had accepted this without challenge, the merchant classes had been horrified; it would take all of Faisal's political know-how to put their minds at ease in the following days. Delighted, Drew was in no doubt that the Jackal would bring his people in line; overnight their militia had swelled by tens of thousands. Suddenly, the odds for the people of Azra against the three advancing armies didn't seem so grim.

Furthermore, the hundred gladiators who had journeyed from Scoria had joined Djogo and Shah in the desert city. The men were an elite fighting force who could be put to good use by Faisal, under Djogo's command. There was no need for Drew to drag his small army up into the Barebones. It seemed a far sounder plan to leave them in Azra to aid the Jackal in any way they could. As shows of goodwill went, it was much appreciated by Faisal, who immediately set them to work alongside his own soldiers, training and drilling the civilians and former slaves in preparation for battle. A skeleton crew had remained on the *Banshee*, transporting the remaining therians to Two Rivers.

A prospecting town, Two Rivers was the last place a ship the size of the *Banshee* could navigate up to on the Silver River. Being on the border of the Desert and Mountain Realms, it was a wild old town with little law or order. Home to gem diggers, bounty hunters, the crazed and the criminal, Drew hoped they could pass through the town quickly. A run-down avenue ran through its centre, low buildings lining the pitted road on either side. Trading posts and taverns made up the majority of businesses, jostling for the attention of passers by. The group kept their heads down as they followed Krieg, aware they were being watched, the townsfolk making no attempt to hide their interest in the travellers. Krieg led them to the end of the street, marching up to a squat looking stable block with paddocks attached. The wind stirred up dust devils, sand whipping through the air as they hurried towards the horse trader's establishment.

As they approached, Drew pulled up short, placing his hand on Krieg's shoulder.

'You're sure he can be trusted?'

'As trusted as anyone can be in a fleapit like Two Rivers. Why?'

Drew shivered as he tried to shake off the uneasy feeling. 'No matter, Krieg; lead on,' he said as the Rhino entered the building.

The stable was split down the middle by a filthy path, camels on one side and horses on the other. A bearded man in brown robes emerged down the passage, dragging a sack of grain behind him. He looked up, recognizing Krieg immediately.

'These your friends, then?' he said in a thick, Omiri accent.

The man straightened, looking past Krieg towards his companions. His eyes seemed a little too large for his features, as if his face had frozen mid-choke and refused to return to normal.

'The horses,' said Krieg, wasting no time on banter. The Rhino unstrung a pouch from his hip, jingling it in his hand. 'I have the money, as agreed.'

'Is that everything?' said the big-eyed man, watching Krieg weigh the bag of coins. Krieg tossed it, the trader catching it mid-air.

'Count them, if you distrust me,' said the Rhino, his voice serious.

Drew took a moment to look around the interior of the building while the horse trader rooted through the money pouch. It was the largest structure they'd seen in Two Rivers, with a hayloft above that ran around the entire stable. Bright though it was outdoors, it was dark in here, a couple of lanterns kept the filthy walkway illuminated, but all else was shrouded in darkness. Taboo and Griffyn held a quiet conversation at his back, while the Behemoth stood to the rear, staring back at the doors.

Drew still felt on edge. Although the atmosphere in the stable was heavy with the smell of captive animals, a gut feeling told Drew that something wasn't right. Not wanting to alarm the horse trader, Drew let a little of the Wolf in. His heightened sense of smell revealed something else beyond the stench of animal faeces. He smelled alcohol, sweat and steel. His ears pricked as he concentrated, listening beyond the snorting horses and spitting camels. Floorboards creaked in the loft above.

'Do you work here alone?' asked Drew.

The man looked up, lips smacking nervously as Drew's eyes remained fixed upon the shadowy first floor overhead.

'Indeed. Why do you ask?'

'It sounds like you've rats in your hayloft, in that case. Big ones, judging by the noise they're making up there.'

Instantly Krieg had his spiked mace out, while Taboo raised her spear. Drew kept his eyes focused upon the hayloft, catching sight of movements now as would-be-assassins darted through the darkness.

'What treachery is this?' spat Krieg. 'I make a deal with you in good faith . . .'

The trader's eyes widened further as Krieg stepped towards him, twirling the mace in his grasp, the spikes spinning menacingly.

'They . . . they saw you come!' stammered the man, his eyes looking up. 'This isn't my . . .'

The trader collapsed to the floor, unable to complete his sentence, the feathered flight of an arrow sticking out of his throat as the coins showered down on top of him. An arrow hit Griffyn's back, while Krieg crashed through the partition fence, an arrow protruding from his chest. Instantly the therians dived into the pens, camels and horses panicking at the intruders in their enclosures. Taboo had found a ladder on the rear wall, leaping halfway up in one bound. She thrust her spear up through the hatch, a foe screaming as it struck home.

Feet hammered along the walkway above, the ambushers scrambling to find better positions from which to strike. Drew stayed close to Griffyn, supporting the winded Hawklord as they dashed for cover. A horse whinnied beside him as an arrow punched into its flank with a wet snap. It kicked out, striking another animal at its side, the pen transformed into a deadly arena.

'They could have avoided this,' said Drew, the Hawklord grimacing as they ducked behind a post.

'It appears they'd rather fight,' said Griffyn. 'There must be quite a reward on your head!'

Drew pulled the arrow from the Hawklord's back, the tip embedded in the leather strapping of his breastplate. Griffyn grunted as the pair stared in shock at the shining silver arrowhead.

'These are no regular bandits, young Wolf.'

'Stay here!'

A mountain of crates lined the rear of the horse enclosure, providing Drew with a means to reach the first floor. He changed as he bounded, feet elongating into grey, clawed paws as he raced up the stacked boxes towards the hayloft. Bursting on to the dark landing, his longsword arced through the air, striking a drawn bow from an assassin's hands. The man in black reached for a scimitar on his hip, but was already flying through the air, the Werewolf catching him in the chest with a kick. The attacker disappeared over the hayloft rail, vanishing into the enclosure below.

Another black-kashed warrior lunged at Drew, his silver scimitar tearing a cut down the Werewolf's back. Drew roared, bringing his trident dagger around to disarm the man on his following blow. The scimitar flew from the man's grasp as Drew's longsword struck home.

On the opposite hayloft Drew caught a glimpse of Taboo, the Weretiger cornered, jabbing with her spear and slashing with her claws. She was outnumbered three to one, and if her enemies had silver weapons she was in terrible danger.

Glancing below Drew spied the Behemoth, dragging the wounded Krieg to safety through a crowd of alarmed camels. By Brenn's grace the silver arrow embedded in the Rhino's chest hadn't proved fatal. The Weremammoth looked up, noticing Drew as he pointed across to the other hayloft with his sword.

'Take its legs!' shouted Drew, and the giant instantly understood.

Leaning Krieg against the wall, the Weremammoth swung his enormous stone mallet around his head. The therianthrope transformed with each rotation, the weapon's speed increasing with the Mammoth's burgeoning muscles. Finally he brought it round into one of the supporting posts that held the hayloft up. The mallet's stone head shattered the pillar in two, sending the ceiling crashing down around him. Fearless, the Behemoth remained where he was, raising a huge arm over his head as beams and floorboards crashed down on top of him, along with the trio of assassins.

As the dust settled, Drew looked across the stable, searching the debris below for Taboo. There was no sign of her, only the broken limbed corpses of the black-kashed warriors.

'Up here, Wolf!'

To his relief, Drew saw the Weretiger suspended from a rafter across the way. She hauled herself over the beam, holding a hand to her bloodied side. Drew leaned on the balcony, chest heaving as he returned to human form. Below, Griffyn staggered over to Krieg, the two Werelords comparing their near-fatal wounds. The Behemoth, cloaked in sawdust and splintered wood, waved a mighty hand up towards Drew, his voice rumbling through the devastation.

'We need to go.'

By the time the people of Two Rivers had investigated why camels were roaming their miserable, dust-ridden streets, the five therians had departed. Taking the sturdiest mounts they could find, the riders took a trail through the foothills that followed the southern branch of the river, leaving the barter town behind them.

The terrain was barren and rocky, vegetation sparse, the environment utterly inhospitable. Here and there the odd gnarled tree had managed to survive against the odds, its roots gripping the rocky slopes for dear life as the cold winds battered it.

The Behemoth brought up the rear of the group, riding the stockiest workhorse any of the therians had ever seen.

Taller and uglier than the mountain ponies the others were riding, it had a broad back, thick legs and a desire to carry heavy burdens. None came heavier than the Behemoth, or less experienced at riding for that matter. After suffering the horse's attempts to buck him off, Weremammoth and mount had struck an uneasy alliance, riding in stalemated silence. His companions bit their lips, resisting the temptation to tease him over his newfound friend.

Griffyn led the way, with Drew at his back. Taboo followed the Wolf, with Krieg close behind. Taboo had declined her companions' attention, insisting the cut along her side was a mere graze. *I've never encountered a tougher woman*, thought Drew, ever amazed by both her strength and stubbornness. The Rhino had taken care of his chest wound while the others readied their horses, Griffyn staunching the bleeding with dressings from his pack. In obvious discomfort, Krieg had stifled his complaints on the uncomfortable ride.

'So who were they?' said Drew, his pony shadowing Griffyn's in front.

'I doubt we'll ever know,' replied the Hawklord. 'They carried no clues as to who was behind the ambush.'

'They could have been anyone's agents: Dog, Cat, Hyena . . . Crow!'

'Their choice of weapons is most alarming: silver. The Scorians used it to keep therian gladiators in check, but in Lyssia? It was outlawed across the entire continent, yet these assassins used it by blade and bow. Such a deadly metal doesn't come cheap; our enemies have wealthy benefactors.'

Drew thought back to the scars on his back from his time

as a prisoner in Highcliff, whipped by the silver studded whip of Captain Brutus.

'The Catlords reintroduced silver to Lyssia.'

'Another connection then, tying your enemies together, Wolf,' said Griffyn, kicking his pony's flanks to encourage her on.

The night was beginning to close in as Drew looked back. The lights of Two Rivers shone below; would anybody follow them, seeking retribution for the death of the men in the stable? Further back, across the desert, the horizon glowed: Azra. *Are those the fires of the enemy camps? Or does the city burn?* Drew looked ahead once more at the trail disappearing into the distance, following the stream that tumbled down the rocky slope towards them. Drew stared up at the mountains, their snow-capped summits glowing dully in the twilight.

'I just hope we stay well ahead of our enemies,' said Drew, urging his mount after Griffyn's.

'We must remain alert, Drew,' said Griffyn, his eyes scanning the mountains in front of them. *His mountains*.

'I fear we've been watched since we first set foot on to Omir's sands, young Wolf. The enemy follows our every move.'

2

The Wrong Answers

The soldiers of the Lionguard were in a relaxed mood, gathered around their fires, playing cards and tossing bones. Sorin led the festivities, winning more than his fair share of coin from his men. The Bastian contingent of Lord Frost's force remained removed from their comrades, polishing armour and sharpening weapons. The albino Catlord had retired to his tent, dining on the best food that his warriors had confiscated from the people of the Longridings. With the camp preoccupied, it was relatively easy for Trent to enter the prisoner's tent unnoticed. Letting the door flap swing shut behind him, he looked down upon the captive Werelord.

'Tell me,' Trent said, standing over the bound prisoner. 'What was he like?'

Baron Ewan looked up slowly. The Ramlord's face was a rich palette of bruises, a mask of purple, black and blue. Sorin had used the flat of his silver-blessed longsword on the Lord of Haggard, beating the old man about head and body, dealing him injuries that could only heal over a mortal span of time. Nobody had tended the old man's wounds.

'Who?' asked Ewan, through broken lips. His left eye was closed shut, while his bloodshot right was fixed squarely on Trent.

'The Wolf – Drew,' replied Trent, trying to sound cold and impassive.

The old Werelord studied him. 'Why so interested?'

'What kind of man is he? We hear so many things. How did you find him?'

Ewan smiled, his swollen lips tearing anew through the bruising. He winced, arching his back, catching his breath.

'What's the matter?' asked Trent, concern creeping into his voice.

'Chest,' said the Ram.

Lord Frost had ensured that his interrogators had thoroughly worked Ewan over. The Catlord had even participated himself, the Ram's greatest screams caused by the albino. Trent hadn't the stomach to witness the torturing of prisoners. He could kill a man, at the command of his superior officers, but torture wasn't why he'd signed up to the Lionguard.

Trent could see the rolls of tightly bound ropes that wound around the beaten old man, securing him to the stake in the ground. Therianthrope or not, the bonds were excessive. Sorin and his cronies had battered the baron to within an inch of his life, his hands broken by the cruel captain's zealous work. Trent crouched and loosened the ropes, letting a clutch of them fall to the ground.

Ewan relaxed a little, leaning back and straightening his bent legs, bringing his bound hands up before him to massage his chest. Trent filled a mug of water for the Werelord, holding it to his lips as Ewan drank thirstily.

'My boy,' he whispered. 'Thank you.'

'Why?'

'That was the greatest drink I've ever savoured in my long and glorious life. A barrel of the Redwine's finest couldn't compete with it.'

Trent smiled, taking the cup away. 'The Wolf,' he said again. 'What of him?'

'He came to me in Haggard, a prisoner of the Goatlord, Kesslar. He was thrown into the cells beneath my keep alongside my people and I. We got to know one another. He had no reason to lie when he recounted all he'd been through. The death of his parents at the hands of the Lion and the Rats . . .'

'*He* killed my mother!' interrupted Trent.

Ewan sighed. 'Did you want to hear my story?'

Trent grimaced, before nodding. The Ramlord continued.

'Drew was instrumental in freeing my people, helping us rise against our enemies. He then rode south, and I accompanied him as he sought to save Lady Gretchen from the claws of Prince Lucas.'

Ewan paused, expecting the young Redcloak to cut in once more. When he didn't, he carried on.

'Lucas and Vanmorten took Cape Gala from the Horselords,

stole the sovereign state from the people of the Longridings – *my people* – with the help of the Bastian invaders. While the majority sailed north to attack Highcliff, a small force was left behind in Çape Gala. Once again, Drew came to the aid of his friends, trying to rescue them from Vankaskan.'

Ewan hung his head.

'I betrayed him. I handed him over to the monster, Vankaskan. I recognize that villain, Sorin, as one of his. My boy, they turned High Stable into a monstrous circus, slaying Werelords and humans alike. Only their torment didn't end there. The Rat did such vile things . . .'

'What more of the Wolf?'

'He was gone,' whispered Ewan. 'Disappeared. At one moment, he was on the balcony; the next, gone. Vanished on the wind. I don't know what happened to him.'

Trent couldn't look at the baron. He didn't want to believe him, but much of what the old therian said made sense. Still, he'd seen what had happened back on the family farm. *Drew had turned on Ma*.

'But Drew,' said Trent. 'He's a monster! He's a Werewolf, for Brenn's sake!'

'There are monsters across Lyssia – human and therian alike. Your brother's a good man.'

'He killed our moth–' Trent stopped, biting his lip. 'How did you know he was my brother?'

'You didn't say as much, but I'd heard mention of a Sergeant Ferran,' sighed Ewan. 'They might have beaten me, but not entirely senseless. My hearing works well enough. You and Drew are brothers?'

'*Were* brothers,' corrected Trent. 'Until he killed my ma.'

Ewan shook his head sadly. 'You believe everything you're told, lad?'

'I saw it with my own *eyes,* old man! Don't think to lecture me on the Wolf's true nature. Nobody knows Drew better than I!'

'I fear you believe what you want to, Master Ferran. Could it be you're mistaken?'

'You know nothing. He's pulled the wool over your eyes, Sheeplord, clearly. My brother could charm his way into any fool's heart.'

'There you go,' said the old man. '*My brother* – the bond is strong between you. Search your heart, boy. You know I'm telling you the truth . . .'

Ewan was cut short as Trent stepped forward, his fist raised above his head, ready to strike. The Ramlord's bruised eyes went as wide as the swelling would allow, the aged therian shrinking back in anticipation of the blow. Trent wavered, snarling. He stepped behind him swiftly, binding Ewan's ropes once again. Trent knew rope mastery as well as anyone, having learned under his father back on the Ferran farm. He gave them a sharp tug, the Ramlord's battered arms creaking as he was secured once more.

Trent got up. 'Keep your poisonous words to yourself in future, you old fool,' he said.

'It was you who came to me, seeking answers,' said Ewan as Trent strode out of the tent – straight into Lord Frost, chewing on a haunch of bloody meat. Trent jumped with shock.

'It's lamb,' said the Catlord, offering it to Trent. The youth looked at the meat: any rarer and it would still be bleating.

'No thank you, my lord,' replied Trent, regaining his composure. 'My appetite is lacking.'

'Speaking with the prisoner, eh? Did he offer us anything new?'

'No, my lord.'

'It's Frost, remember. You and I are friends now, Trent, just remember that.' The Catlord took another bite of the lamb and looked at the tent door. 'You've just reminded me. Our prisoner should never be left unguarded. I'll speak with Sorin; arrange for a guard to be posted on the Ram at all times. Good man, Trent. Go get yourself some rest.'

Trent bowed nervously, his cheeks flushed with colour at having been discovered speaking with the prisoner. He strode away in the direction of the corral; his horse, Storm, needed bedding down for the night. He glanced back as he walked away. Frost watched him go, tearing another mouthful of meat from the joint of lamb. Trent turned his gaze to the ground, feeling the Catlord's eyes burning holes in his back.

Fool, Trent, he berated himself. *Giving Frost cause to distrust me. That's the last time I seek answers.*

3

Tor Raptor's Mercy

If the foothills of Omir had appeared treacherous, nothing had prepared the travellers for the perilous trail through the Barebones. Another old mountain road had led to Windfell, but the group had passed it by. The city of the Hawklords wasn't their destination; it was their tomb they sought, high up in the sky. Only Griffyn seemed at ease, the old Hawk returning home for the first time in fifteen years, while his fellow therians gripped the reins of their mounts with white knuckles. At the rear, the Behemoth was slumped in the saddle of his stocky horse. Krieg and Taboo were in front of him, the ravine drop to their right bringing on terrible bouts of vertigo. Further ahead, Drew followed Griffyn closely, his reins wrapped around his trident dagger.

Occasionally Drew glanced into the chasm, a morbid fascination with the deadly drop luring him like a moth to candlelight. With each of his horse's steps, the hooves dislodged stones that skittered away from the path, bouncing off the sloping rock and disappearing into space. Drew brought his eyes back to Griffyn ahead, smacking his lips as he breathed the cold, thin air. The wind changed direction with alarming regularity, sudden updrafts replaced by blustering downdrafts that threatened to knock the riders from their saddles. As they climbed Tor Raptor the Mighty, giant of the Barebones, wispy clouds drifted all about her and the surrounding peaks.

Griffyn twisted around, smiling at the pale-faced Wolflord. 'Breathtaking?'

'And then some,' replied Drew as another gust of wind hit him. 'But I'm struggling to breathe, here. How much further?'

'Some way yet, cub. See that?'

Griffyn pointed ahead to where the cliffs of Tor Raptor appeared to collide with those of the neighbouring mountain, as if the two giant landmasses had collapsed against one another. The path was all but invisible, with a thin sliver of vertical light the only indication that the trail emerged on the other side. The drop between the two vanished into gloomy blackness, swallowed up by the enormous ravine's dark depths.

'I see it,' shouted Drew over the wind. 'But I don't like it!'

'The Falling Road: it's not to be liked, it's to be endured! We travel to the tomb of my fathers. Look about you, Wolf – see the burial sites and barrows of my kinsmen.'

Drew looked up, scouring the cliffs for sign of human or therian touch. There they were, dotting the mountain hundreds of feet above. At first glance they appeared to be rock formations, but closer inspection revealed them to be cairns, tall spires of rocks that the Hawklords had placed to mark out the chambers of the dead.

'The tombs of the Hawklords, Baron Griffyn? Left unguarded on a mountain side?'

'You think we fear graverobbers in the Barebones, Drew? If the mountain doesn't kill you, there are other things on Tor Raptor that protect our tombs. My forefathers do not readily relinquish their worldly goods, even in death . . .'

Griffyn let this last statement hang in the air, the sinister implication not lost on Drew. *Even in death?*

The Hawklord swung in his saddle, leaning precariously out to see around Drew. The Wolflord blanched when he imagined the old man tumbling from his seat.

'Our friends look unwell,' chortled Griffyn. 'It appears the Barebones aren't for the faint-hearted!'

'You might feel like them if you weren't a Hawklord!' said Drew in their defence.

'You forget, young Wolf,' said Griffyn, gesturing at his shoulders with a hooked thumb. 'My wings were taken from me many years ago. If I fall here, I'd be as dead as anyone else. Lean forward in your saddle, respect the path, and pray the mountain remains merciful.'

The Hawklord cast his hand heavenwards, the snowcapped giant of the Barebones towering above them.

'You are in Tor Raptor's talons now!'

As fierce as the winds had been on the cliff path an hour before, nothing had prepared the therians for the gale that greeted them on the Falling Road. Dismounting when they approached the monstrous chasm, Drew had marvelled at the sheer cliffs on either side as they reached across to one another. He whispered a brief, heartfelt prayer to Brenn as he followed Griffyn into the darkness, leading his pony along behind.

The Hawklord had warned them to keep their voices low when traversing the Falling Road. Avalanches were commonplace, where massive boulders had caught between the cliffs, weighed down with packed ice, waiting for the chance to break free and plummet towards the road. As if the threat from above and raging winds weren't enough, the path was nothing more than scree. The therians' feet and ponies' hooves scrambled for purchase as they passed over the ice and gravel. Frequently, Drew found himself casting his trident dagger out, grateful for the barbed weapon as he snatched hold of the cliff wall to stop himself from falling.

While Griffyn had little trouble on the path, the same could not be said for Taboo, Krieg and the Behemoth. The Weremammoth had taken some persuading to traverse the treacherous road, and his companions shared his concerns. These people were from jungles and savannas, not freezing mountains. This world was alien to them. With words of encouragement from Drew and Griffyn they'd continued on, none wishing to break their oath to the young Wolflord. Their loyalty and courage filled Drew's heart with hope.

Ahead, Griffyn waited, cloak wrapped around his body as defence against the freezing wind. His pony hunkered against the cliff face, sheltering as best it could, as Drew slowly and carefully approached. His voice was controlled when he spoke over the howling gale.

'We need to pick up our pace, Drew. The night closes in. If we can get beyond the Falling Road we may find somewhere to pitch camp before tackling the summit tomorrow.'

Drew looked back, spying Taboo appearing around the cliff path a hundred yards or so behind. The others were behind the Weretiger, somewhere – hopefully making steady and safe progress.

He turned back to Griffyn, squinting as sleet peppered his face.

'How far to the end?'

'We're halfway through,' replied the Hawklord.

Only halfway, thought Drew. *And we've been on this murderous road for over an hour.*

His nerves were shot, his body on the brink of exhaustion, adrenaline the only thing keeping him moving. Drew noticed that Griffyn was looking up. He followed the Hawk's gaze. The black wall of rock rose at a skewed angle overhead, meeting the opposing cliff high above, boulders the size of houses buttressed and braced against one another. It looked like a monstrous cathedral ceiling, hewn crudely from the mountains. With such an awe-inspiring, religious feel to the place, it was no wonder the Hawklords had chosen Tor Raptor as the site of their oldest tombs.

As he watched, a few blocks of ice came away from the natural ceiling, falling from where they'd been packed in place. They were closely followed by a large slab. Drew leaned back against the cliff wall as the frozen debris rushed by. The sound of them crashing on to the ravine bottom bounced back up towards them from hundreds of feet below. Drew held his breath as the reverberations disturbed the ice overhead, cracking noises from the strained ceiling audible over the wind, but was relieved to see nothing else break free.

The Hawklord beckoned him frantically now, urging him to follow swiftly. Drew's booted feet scrambled along the smooth path, the rock pitched off at an angle ensuring that one false step would send the Wolflord slipping to his doom.

Then a sudden, terrible shriek echoed overhead, as if the mountain itself cried out in agony. After a couple of awful, ponderous heartbeats, the scream was joined by the sound of the monstrous ceiling cracking. The noise shook Drew's body as he pressed himself once more against the cliff, the rock at his back trembling and shuddering as stone, ice and snow high above them buckled and began to fall. He looked up in horror as the crashing cascade of black and white death hurtled towards him. Drew glanced back along the ledge as Taboo was suddenly engulfed by the icy downpour, disappearing from view in the blink of an eye. Rocks and snow rained down around him. A fist-sized block of ice hit his shoulder, narrowly missing his skull but still sending him staggering to his knees, while a great lance of granite fell like a guillotine, shearing his pony in two and dragging it over the edge. Boulders hit the path, smashing and tearing the narrow trail away all around him. Drew's scream was cut short as the deafening roar of the avalanche choked the breath from his battered body.

4
The Scene of the Crime

As the *Myrmidon* eased into Highcliff, six of Tuskun's finest Ugri warriors stood to attention on the icy foredeck. Before them, Hector took in the city, the night casting a brooding menace over the all-too-quiet port. This city had been his home for a time, a metropolis that brimmed with life from all over Lyssia. Before the curfew of the Wolf's Council, Highcliff had been a city that rarely slept. Now, with the Lord Protector and his friends gone, as well as the majority of the city's inhabitants, Highcliff was a ghost town. Hector placed his black-gloved hands on the frosted rail, manacles jangling between them, as he surveyed the results of the Lion's vengeance.

The pier that the *Myrmidon* pulled alongside had once sported tall lanterns that lit the way for sailors and fishermen alike. Now it was dotted with gibbets that contained the dead and dying. Hector stared at the rusting cages, crows and gulls squawking as they bickered over the morsels within. The unmistakable Greycloaks of the Wolfguard hung around the throats of corpses and captives alike. The moans of the unfortunate souls could be heard by the crew of the warship, but the Tuskuns ignored them. The Ugri were the toughest, most fearsome men the frozen north had spawned, each over six foot tall and seemingly as broad. During the journey, Hector couldn't so much as scratch his nose without one of them glowering or growling. They stood to one side as the heavy barefoot steps of their queen approached.

'Is it as you remember, Piglord?' laughed Slotha, the Walrus of Tuskun. While many of Lyssia's Werelords chose to keep their human appearance on most occasions, saving their shapeshifting for when the time arose, Slotha held no such discipline. Her hold over the Ugri warriors was the result of her many victories in battle combined with her intimidating presence. Easily the tallest woman Hector had ever met, and as broad as any barbarian who worked in her service, she revelled in her frightening therian image. While not completely transformed, there were enough elements of the Werewalrus on show to strike fear into the hearts of most men. Her large hands were still webbed, her fingernails sharp claws, and her wide feet slapped the deck with each step. Her muscular arms held the dark, mottled texture of the beast, while her head kept the key features of the walrus; dark whiskers sprouted from around her lips, while a suggestion of her tusks remained in evidence, sliding down around her jaw.

'It's quite . . . changed,' managed Hector, refusing to look at the monstrous woman. He'd endured days at sea in her company, and every additional moment in her presence made him fearful she'd back down on their agreement. He'd seen at first hand how vicious she could be with her prisoners. Here was a therian who enjoyed the kill.

'Changed how?'

Hector looked back at the swinging bodies in their cages. 'They've done away with the sea lanterns, I notice,' he said calmly.

Slotha snorted at Hector's dark humour.

The *Myrmidon* secured, the crew extended their gangway across to the stone pier. Two dozen torch-carrying Lionguard awaited them, alongside half as many Bastian warriors. More cavalry gathered on the docks, along with an empty carriage awaiting the visitors. The Ugri grunted, unimpressed by the southerners' show of strength.

'Take him ashore,' grunted Slotha, shifting her great mass to one side. 'We've an audience with Prince Lucas.'

As the procession climbed through the steep city towards Highcliff Keep, Hector's mind cast back to the frantic escape he'd endured, chased through the streets by Omiri warriors. That seemed like another life now, the youth who'd fled bearing little resemblance to the man who returned.

Looking out of the carriage he noticed the city was far from deserted. Lights were on in many homes and taverns, showing that Highcliff was still inhabited, but the streets were devoid of life, the curfew he'd helped set in place still standing. A veil of fear had settled over the city.

An Ugri warrior sat on either side of him, while opposite the huge frame of Slotha filled the entire padded bench.

'What's the matter, Piglord? Disappointed with what they've done to your city?' asked the Walrus.

'This isn't my city, Your Majesty. My home is far to the east of here – Redmire, capital of the Dalelands. But I'd be lying if I said Highcliff meant nothing to me. This is the city where I learned who my friends were.'

His voice was clipped, the words catching in his throat.

Slotha smiled. 'You've got a world full of regrets, boy.'

'Only one,' answered Hector, looking at his manacled hands. 'I never truly said goodbye to him.'

Since Friggia, Hector had tried not to think about Drew, but it was impossible. The Stags, Shark and Bear might have betrayed him, but Drew had been long gone by then. He'd heard the rumours about Drew falling to his death in Cape Gala. The Wolf had been the only true friend he'd ever known. But his hatred for the things done in the Wolf's name, in his absence, remained undiminished. Each of the other Werelords had betrayed him over time and each had paid the price. First the selfish Earl Mikkel had fallen, the Doglords of Omir having slain the Staglord as he'd fled to his home in the Barebones. Then Duke Bergan, the Lord Protector who had humiliated him, stripping him of power within the Wolf's Council, had been slain in Highcliff. Count Vega had held Hector to ransom, dangling the grisly truth of Vincent's death over his head like a guillotine. The Sharklord's reputation had been built upon dishonesty – Hector had done the right thing, getting rid of the count before the Shark could bite.

The last of the quartet had disappointed him most of all, Duke Manfred having left him for dead in Friggia. With dear

Drew no doubt dead and those he'd once considered friends having turned on him, what choice did Hector have but to switch his allegiance to the Catlords? They wouldn't fear the power he commanded. They would embrace his magistry. And Manfred? He would pay for his betrayal.

That's it, dear brother, whispered the Vincent-vile. *A reckoning comes . . .*

'Sounds like the Piglord was in love,' teased the Walrus.

Hector directed the conversation back at her. 'I know very little about love, Your Majesty,' he said. 'A lifetime with my head buried in books has allowed me few opportunities to enjoy the company of the fairer sex.'

'A bookworm, like your father was, then?'

'You knew him?'

'Lord Huth visited Tuskun when I was in my youth. For a while my father petitioned his to arrange marriage.'

Hector coughed suddenly, shocked at the news that his father might have once been wed to such a fearsome warrior queen as Slotha. Never could a match be more misplaced. The Werewalrus glowered at her captive Boarlord.

'And what stopped the marriage from taking place?'

'Your father's constitution, apparently,' she said, strangely wistful for the briefest moment at what might have been. 'The cold northern air played havoc with his breathing.'

'That sounds about right,' said Hector, slowly regaining his composure.

Slotha sneered at him. 'Weakling Boars: it was the best thing that could have happened. Any child of that union would have polluted the bloodlines of the Walruses. My father did right by me. He spared me the embarrassment of a marriage with your kind, and saved me for something greater.'

'You mean to impress Prince Lucas?'

'He's a Prince,' she said stiffly. 'I'm the queen in the North. Who knows what . . . *alliance* we can agree upon. This is my first visit to Highcliff. I intend to make it memorable.'

'I'm sure it'll be memorable,' said Hector, dabbing at his lips as he reclined in his seat. 'The Court of Highcliff won't forget you in a hurry.'

5

The Screaming Peak

The trident dagger remained buried within the ice, the battered old blade the only thing stopping Drew from sliding off the slope into thin air. The muscles in his left arm strained, his elbow locked as he struggled to remain motionless. The toes of his torn boots were braced against the ice, as if they might somehow stop his body from falling should the trident dagger snap. The blade was bowing, the metal bending back on itself as it threatened to break. Drew looked up, grimacing, as the old Hawklord skidded down the incline towards him, somehow keeping his balance.

The avalanche on the Falling Road had been no accident. A loud shriek had set the rock- and ice-fall in motion, timed to perfection. While Drew and Griffyn had avoided the deadly downpour, what fate had befallen their companions wasn't known. The path behind them had been cut off, choked in a cloud of dusty ice and broken stone. Drew's stomach lurched when he thought about Krieg, Taboo and the Behemoth. The trio had followed him to Lyssia to fight by his side: that the mountain might have killed them broke his heart. The two survivors had continued on alone, minus their ponies and provisions, which had been carried away by the barrage of boulders. Drew and Griffyn were left to pray that their friends had survived and could find their way back to the lower path to Windfell.

'Your hand!' called Griffyn, reaching his out, palm open.

Drew threw his body forward, the hands of the two Werelords clamping over one another's wrists. The baron deftly hauled Drew back up the slope and on to the sliver of a path they'd been following. The young Wolflord collapsed against the cliff, body trembling as he struggled to regain his composure, while the Hawklord seemed perversely relaxed.

'I can't go on!' Drew cried, gasping for breath, the air so thin his lungs ached.

Griffyn looked down, thin hair whipping across his face as he smiled. 'It appears youth counts for nothing: experience everything. Remember, these are *my* mountains, Drew. Come, we mustn't delay. We approach the summit, my friend. We must try and reach the Screaming Peak before nightfall and find shelter by the tomb. The last place one wants to be stranded at night is on Tor Raptor's back!'

Drew rubbed the strained muscles of his arms. 'Any sign of our enemy?'

'None,' said Griffyn.

'Perhaps we've lost them. You did say this path's location was guarded by the Hawklords, didn't you?'

'Yes, but that's not to say our enemy hasn't found another route to the summit.'

'Are you sure the Hawklords will hear your call?'

Griffyn stroked his grizzled jaw, glancing at the sky around them. Below, the clouds rolled like a smoky sea, the jagged peaks of Tor Raptor's sisters visible like islands through the fading light.

'They'll hear it, Drew, no matter where they are. How many still live, however, is another question entirely.'

Griffyn helped Drew to his feet, the young Wolf craning his neck to look towards the summit. Drew shook his head, trying not to linger on the dizzying sight.

'If I don't die of a broken neck the vertigo might give me a heart attack,' he murmured. 'How in Lyssia did you get your dead to the summit?'

'How do you think?' grinned the Hawklord grimly. 'We flew them.'

Their hopes of beating the sunset had long gone, the dark settling over the Barebones as the two therians struggled on. Drew caught sight of Griffyn disappearing over a ledge above. There were hand and footholds aplenty here, but they were hidden by the ice and the night. Drew waited a moment for the old man to reappear, to offer a hand to help him climb up, but Griffyn didn't appear.

Cursing, Drew hacked at the ice, forcing the trident dagger in once again, crying in pain as the cold metal rubbed against the stump of his wrist. He thought he'd got used to the feel of the basket handle against the sheared bones, but the freezing weather that crowned Tor Raptor caused a new, unknown discomfort. He reached up with his right hand, black and blue fingertips desperately trying to catch the ledge.

He could feel his will slipping, along with his grip on the mountainside. His eyes drifted down into the empty sky. Death would be swift if he fell. There were worse ways to die.

I can't stop now, I have to fight on. For my friends and my people! For Taboo and Krieg and the Behemoth!

Drew brought his head up and stared at the moon.

Her light might have been cold but the warmth he felt inside was unmistakable, and he let it flood through him. Not for the first time on the mountain, Drew let the Wolf in, just enough to feel his fingers tearing into claws, a lupine hand taking a firm grip on the overhang. With a growl he hauled himself high, ripping the dagger free as he kicked back against the rocks below.

His torso landed on the ledge, the rock digging deep into the fur that covered his stomach. Drew grunted as he scrambled and snatched at the darkness ahead, legs kicking out into space, threatening to send him toppling back into nothingness. The bent and battered trident dagger bounced off the ledge ahead, causing the sheet ice to shatter in great shards. Gradually, he inched forward, his right leg finally finding its way above the overhang, his knee finding purchase as he rolled his exhausted body on to the ledge.

'You took your time, Wolf.'

Drew turned his head, looking towards the voice as the

wind tugged at his legs where they dangled across the overhang. The ledge opened on to a rocky platform perhaps twenty feet across, receding towards a sheer wall of rock that rose the remaining fifty feet to Tor Raptor's peak. A jagged, triangular crack was visible at the wall's base, rising ten feet up to a point, a dark doorway that disappeared into the mountain. A figure stepped out of the shadows into the moonlight, Baron Griffyn held before him, head pulled back and a familiar short, silver knife pressed to his throat.

'We've been here before, Rook,' said Drew to the Crowlord, rolling over on to his stomach, inching away from the overhang. 'Only last time it was a woman you threatened as opposed to an old man. Let the Hawk go. Face me like a therian.'

'Hawk? This cripple? If he was a Hawk he'd have wings! Let's see how he flies, eh?' To emphasize the point, Rook skirted Drew and marched towards the edge, instantly causing the young Wolflord to raise his hand.

'No, wait!'

'What do you want?' gasped Griffyn, his feet struggling in vain to halt the Werecrow's progress towards the drop.

Drew looked about frantically, his hand catching hold of a long dagger of broken ice.

'Riven, Stormdale, Windfell: everything! I want the Barebones, Griffyn!' shouted Rook, propelling the old man forward.

The dagger of ice hit Rook square in the face, Drew's aim was faultless. The Crow cawed furiously, instantly releasing Griffyn, who hit the ice and slid towards the edge. Rook collapsed, screaming obscenities as his hands went to his shattered face. Drew dived for the Hawklord's arms, catching Griffyn's hand as he disappeared from the ledge. The old man hung there for a moment, the weight of his body drawing the young Wolflord ever closer to the edge. Behind, Drew heard the screams of the Crowlord as Rook began to change.

'Release me, Drew, before we both fall,' shouted Griffyn, eyes wide with fearful sincerity.

'I won't let you go,' gasped Drew, tears streaming as he struggled to keep hold of the Hawklord, his body still sliding closer to oblivion.

'Beware the dead, Drew. Open the windows; call my people to you and take what's yours by rights. I brought it here,' whispered Griffyn. 'I kept it safe.'

Drew growled, calling upon whatever lycanthropic strength remained inside, but it was no use. The Werewolf's clawed hand was gripping at the Hawklord's tearing sleeve. Griffyn glanced past Drew's shoulder, his face a mask of alarm as his eyes settled on the enemy at Drew's back.

'Brenn protect you, Drew!' he cried as he tore his arm loose and fell into the night, swallowed by the darkness below.

Drew rolled quickly, almost following Griffyn over the edge as the ice shattered beside him, a longsword crashing into the ledge. He looked up to see clouds pass over the moon above.

With a blood-curdling screech the Werecrow threw his arms out, wings erupting from his back in an explosion of feathers. The lord of Riven had fully changed – Rook's features had utterly gone to be replaced by the monstrous head, sharp black beak open and tongue rattling within. His arm came back down, the sword smashing into the ground where Drew had lain moments earlier. The Wolflord scrambled across the ice, making towards the rock face as the Werecrow followed. Rook was in no danger of slipping, his feet having shifted into long, dark talons that gripped the ice securely.

'Where do you run to?' squawked Rook, his huge chest rippling, muscles and feathers ruffling as he stalked closer. 'Wolves don't belong in the sky!'

Drew reached the rock wall. Every muscle burned, every ounce of energy having been spent climbing Tor Raptor. He tried to call on the Wolf, but there was little left. Tugging his longsword from its battered scabbard, he glanced at the dark doorway. A series of runes were carved around the triangular entrance.

Beware the dead, Drew . . .

The Werecrow leaped suddenly, closing on the Wolf with a beat of his enormous wings. Rook's sword came down, Drew raising his own in defence, the metal ringing in his grasp with the full weight of the Crowlord behind it. With the steel shattering, the weapon flew from his grip, the blade broken in two. Drew didn't wait, crawling quickly through the dark arch. As he passed over the threshold, the runes began to glow with a pale silver light, their ghostly illumination bouncing off the rock walls within.

Behind, Drew heard the Werecrow laugh, a wheezing screech of glee as it followed him into the tomb. He scrambled on, staggering briefly to his feet before tumbling down a flight of stone steps. Drew rolled to a halt in the centre of a great round chamber, the walls of which were inscribed with silver sigils like those that glowed outside. A large window was cut through the rock overhead, open to the night sky beyond. The runes seemed to beat with a rising rhythm, the thrum of which reverberated through Drew's ears, causing his teeth to chatter and his bones to ache. It was like a slow, drawn-out heartbeat, as if Tor Raptor's summit were alive, awakening with his arrival. The noise gripped his chest, as if it might crush him at any moment. Drew wearily climbed to his feet, squinting through the other-worldly light.

At first glance it looked as if a series of caves were carved within the domed walls, but then he saw the wrapped bodies set within each of the alcoves; the mummified remains of the Hawklords of old. He counted twelve such catacombs pock-marking the chamber, with chests laid at the feet and head of each mummy. He might have stared at them in wonder longer if it had not been for the dark, feathered monster that descended the steps into the room.

Rook let his wings flap once more, sending clouds of dust swirling through the air. His feet scraped against the cold, stone floor, talons grating on the smooth stone and sending shivers racing up Drew's spine. The young Wolflord retreated, soon finding the wall at his back.

'Done running, Wolf?' sneered the Werecrow. 'Griffyn will have to make do with the mountainside. You can have his bed in this dead birds' nest.'

Rook took another step into the chamber just as moonlight began to stream in through the window above. The disturbed dust glittered in the air like tiny silver stars as the light settled on the catacomb behind Drew. The alcove glowed suddenly as the moon's rays landed upon it, a shaft of pale blue light glowed dimly on the mummy's chest; it held a sword in its grasp.

'What dark magistry is this?' squawked Rook, taking another step closer to Drew, but less steadily now, looking over his mighty winged shoulders around the room.

Drew's instincts told him what to do. He reached behind, his fingers settling around the sword's handle. The mummy instantly released its grip. With his hand closing around the sword, the blade glowed brighter, its pale blue light flashing bright white in Drew's grasp.

'There's nothing dark about it,' said Drew breathlessly, his eyes fixed on the shining blade in astonishment. The young Wolflord was so entranced by the weapon that he didn't notice Rook raise his own blade.

Before the Crow could strike, a sudden, violent wind whipped through the tomb, throwing the young Wolf to the ground. He looked up, his left arm sheltering his eyes from the blinding gale. Lord Rook teetered forwards and backwards as the wind hurtled around him, buffeting him from side to side and lifting him into the air.

Drew could make out a series of dark shadows racing from each of the alcoves and joining the cyclone. The Werecrow let out a scream as the speeding winds smashed into his wings, cartilage snapping and feathers flying in a ghastly black shower. His cry increased in pitch as cuts began to appear across his body, first his arms and legs, flesh tearing and bones breaking. Next the wounds appeared across his chest and back, as shadowy talons tore into his torso. As the feathers and blood flew, the Crowlord of Riven's screams reached a deafening roar, forcing Drew to look away.

The wind dropped suddenly, as did the body of the Crowlord. Spluttering and coughing, Drew looked back into the centre of the tomb, his eyes settling on the corpse of Rook, his head back-to-front and his body slashed to ribbons. Feathers floated through the blood-misted air as the moon continued to shine into the chamber. Drew felt his heart constricting once more as the shadows that had joined the deadly whirlwind began to take a more solid form.

Twelve dark figures appeared, their form shifting all the time as they closed in around him. Drew's mouth was dry, and when he tried to breathe he felt the pressure growing in his chest. Skeletal black hands emerged from the wraiths, reaching out towards him, their taloned fingers grasping. He brought the white sword round, holding it in his trembling grasp, a hopeless attempt at warding the demons away.

As one, the phantoms retreated, and the air returned to Drew's lungs in a surging life-giving wave. His chest heaved as he watched the dozen shapes suddenly switch, from grim black wraiths into ethereal white angels. Dazzled by the stunning light, Drew looked on as the dozen figures seemed to shrink in height. The Wolf righted himself, standing gingerly as he looked over the glowing shapes. *Are they kneeling? Bowing?*

Beyond the sentinels, Drew could see twelve runes carved into the tomb wall shining as bright as the sword in his hand, forming a perfect circle. He limped over, between the ghosts, taking care to avoid touching them. The runes encircled a round stone set in the rock, similar to a small millstone, with a dimple carved into the middle. Hooking the sword beneath his left arm, he tried to prise the stone's edge, but there was nothing to take hold of. Returning the sword to his hand, he smashed the twisted end off the end of the trident dagger, sending it to the floor with a clatter. He then placed the metal-capped stump into the hollow and pushed. The stone grated, sliding back against the rock around it. With a sudden *clang* the stone fell away, revealing a tunnel that began to rip the air from the room.

Drew dropped to the floor, his tattered cloak flapping and shearing free from his shoulders, sucked away through the hole and out into the dark space beyond the mountain. One after another the white ghosts were drawn through the hole, screeching and screaming as they went, the sound deafening, their light blinding, as Drew gripped the cold stone wall for fear of being torn through the tunnel after them.

6

A Gift from the North

Hector couldn't believe the change that had taken place in the prince. Having spent a torturous time in Lucas's service under the tutelage of the wicked Vankaskan, he'd seen the young Lionlord go from strength to strength physically, changing from a boy to a man well before his years. An expert warrior with blade in hand, with total mastery of his felinthropy, he was the image of his dead father, King Leopold, a worthy successor to the Lion King's crown. But the figure that sat on the throne before him was a shadow of that bold, impetuous youth, a ghost of the Werelord he'd once known and feared. Where was the old Lucas?

He's in there, brother. Just you wait and see . . .

Prince Lucas had remained silent when the Tuskun party arrived. He'd stayed silent while Queen Slotha had announced, with much bluster, that she'd brought a gift from the north to the Lion of Westland. The Lord Chancellor, Vanmorten, had gone through the formalities with the Werewalrus, willing her to hurry to the end of her grand speech, his eyes fixed on the young Boarlord who stood manacled between her guards. The Ugri warriors propelled the magister forward, sending Hector to his knees.

'Kill him.'

Lucas's voice was clear and calm. This was new to Hector – the prince he'd served had been prone to great emotional rants and tantrums. Vanmorten turned slowly and stared at the throne. His face was hidden within his cowl, the scars from his battles with Drew having left him hideously disfigured twice over.

Lucas was sitting upright in the stone chair, spine stiff against its back. The rear of the hall was shrouded in darkness, the torches unlit in their sconces around the throne. Lucas's hands rested on the carved snakes on the chair's arms as he stared at Hector. Leopold's iron crown sat firmly upon his head, his son's blond hair lank and lifeless beneath it.

'I don't think so,' replied a voice from behind the throne. 'Let's hear what the Boarlord says before rushing to any judgement, Lucas.'

The woman who stepped into the light was the polar opposite to the queen of Tuskun. Whereas Slotha was a towering figure who cast a huge, intimidating shadow, the other was slight and slender. Hector had seen nobody like her in all of Lyssia, her skin so black it seemed to glow with a dull, purple light, while her eyes shone yellow like the sun. She came to a halt before him, looking down at the kneeling magister. Her head was shaved smooth, every bump of her skull visible in the torchlight. While others in the chamber avoided eye contact with her, Hector was unable to draw his eyes away. He'd heard the tales about her, and she was even more fascinating in the flesh: Opal, the Catlady of Bast. She arched her eyebrow in surprise as the Boarlord fixed his gaze upon her.

'I would have his head on a spike, to go with those of other traitors,' spat the young Lion, his lips peeling back to show a full set of sharp, white teeth. 'What can he possibly say that will spare my wrath?'

'It might be wise to listen to his final words, Your Highness,' said Vanmorten, trying to reason with the impatient prince. 'Think of it as an amusement!'

'If the prince wants him dead, so be it,' declared Slotha, clapping her huge hands. An Ugri stepped forward, unhitching an axe from his belt. The audience gasped as he raised it over Hector's head.

'Put that away!' shouted Vanmorten.

'He's *my* prisoner,' growled Slotha, bearing her tusks in a jutting snarl.

'He *was* your prisoner,' corrected Vanmorten. 'Up until the point you presented him as a gift to Prince Lucas.'

The Ugri warrior glanced at his queen who, with a nod of the head, commanded he step down. She glared at the Wererat as the Lord Chancellor turned back to the prince. Opal watched, smiling, enjoying the tension in the great hall.

'Hear what he says, Your Highness, then do what you will,' said the Ratlord.

Lucas nodded. He looked tired to Hector, his former vigour and energy having all but disappeared, to be replaced by pale flesh and red-ringed eyes. Something wasn't right.

'Go ahead, Piggy. Speak your mind for the last time.'

Hector struggled to his feet, the manacled hands making the task awkward. He pulled his eyes from Opal, focusing on the prince.

'Your Highness,' he said, which caused Lucas to chuckle.

'You dare call me that after your betrayal . . .'

Vanmorten and Opal looked at the prince, their glares encouraging him to quieten. Miraculously, this seemed to work.

The prince pays heed to his advisers' words, brother, whispered Vincent. *Let's hope his advisers in turn are open to suggestion . . .*

Hector cleared his throat, the interruption having thrown him. His guts were knotted, twisted around themselves with anxiety. He'd placed his throat in the Lion's jaws on an all-or-nothing roll of the bones.

'As Baron of Redmire and Lord of the Dalelands, I offer the Emerald Realm to you, Prince Lucas, as well as my services as magister and councillor.'

The room was quiet as the members of Lucas's court looked at one another in astonishment.

Finally, Vanmorten spoke. 'Is this some kind of trick, Boarlord?'

'It's no trick. I'm giving you the Dalelands, Prince Lucas: hilt, blade and scabbard. You have our allegiance and my support as you secure lordship over Lyssia. What does that give you: Westland, the Cluster Isles, the Longridings and now the Dalelands? That's four of the Seven Realms: the throne is yours, Your Highness.'

'I've already taken the Dalelands, Piggy,' said Lucas, glaring at Hector with utter contempt. 'It's no longer yours to give.'

'But it is, Your Highness,' said Hector. 'You can attack the Dales, but Brenn's law stands above all others: the Boars of Redmire rule the Dalelands, and as Baron of Redmire I speak on behalf of all my people. The support of the Emerald Realm is mine to give, and mine alone. You have our fealty.'

'Do I hear you correctly?' said the Ratlord. 'This is the same young Boar who was a founding member of the Wolf's Council, a traitor who turned against the House of Lions and all that was lawful? Why the change of heart, boy? Why the sudden allegiance to your rightful monarch? It doesn't have anything to do with your capture in the north and your friends being defeated, does it?'

The manacles jangled as Hector lifted his arms, right hand raised as he begged permission to speak.

'I wasn't *captured* in the north. Had I chosen to, I could have left Friggia at any point in time. I asked to be escorted to Slotha in . . .'

'That's *Queen* Slotha!' shouted the Walrus, backhanding him.

Hector looked up at the massive Werelady as she hulked over him. He winced, his split lip torn and streaming as he spoke through gritted, bloodied teeth.

'I asked to be escorted to *Queen* Slotha, so I could be brought here to parlay with you. I was never caught by the Tuskuns. I come here willingly. I'm worth more to you alive than dead.'

'What possible value do you have?' asked Vanmorten. 'I could have you sign a declaration right now, declaring your allegiance, before removing your head from your shoulders. You're a bumpkin, Hector – a child of the country who has wandered into a man's city. You offer nothing. You're out of your depth.'

Vanmorten stepped up to the magister, his face inches from Hector's. The young therian could smell the awful cocktail of flowers and rotten flesh, the rose water applied to mask the Ratlord's ghoulish stench. He could see inside the cowl now, one half of the Lord Chancellor's face bare skull, the other blackened flesh. The Rat spoke again through his lipless mouth.

'You're drowning.'

They don't fear you, brother. They don't respect you. They mock you. I fear you may join me, Hector, all too soon . . .

Hector could sense the mood shifting in the chamber. They'd heard enough. They'd take his signature and then his life. *Last chance to shine*. He raised his voice so all could hear.

'I'm your ally, Prince Lucas, whether you like it or not. My foes are your foes, and I've already slain one of them.'

Lucas leaned forward and guffawed, his weariness lifting for a moment before he collapsed into the stone chair once again. Vanmorten and Slotha also laughed, joined by a chorus of jeers from the Lionguard. Only Opal remained straight-faced.

'Who've you killed?' she asked.

'Vega. I killed him aboard the *Maelstrom*. The count is dead.'

'Lies!' shouted Vanmorten.

'Kill him!' laughed Slotha. 'I'll do it myself,' she added, snatching the axe from her Ugri bodyguard.

'Stay your hand, woman,' growled the Werepanther.

The Ugri and their queen stared at the woman in shock, but her command was followed. Slotha reluctantly released her hand from the axe haft, glowering at the Catlady.

'How in Brenn's name do you expect us to believe you killed Vega?' asked the prince.

'As much as I hate to admit it, Vega's the most cunning captain on the White Sea,' said Slotha. 'There's no way this wetling fool could've killed him, my dear prince.'

Oh she is *keen, isn't she?* hissed Vincent. *Perhaps there'll be a royal marriage after all, although Slotha's quite a step down from Gretchen.*

'Unlikely,' said Hector, accidentally aloud.

'What's unlikely?' said Vanmorten.

'My killing Vega,' replied Hector, covering his tracks. 'Unlikely, but not impossible: I buried a silver arrow within him, and then I had my men toss him overboard. That arrow is still in my possession, stained dark with the Sharklord's blood. That is, if Slotha hasn't taken it from my belongings. The Wolf's Council is dead to me. My future lies in your service, Your Highness.'

'You've worked for the prince before, young magister, and it didn't end . . . well,' said the Lord Chancellor. 'Even if his Highness were to allow you to live, a notion that I struggle with, what guarantee do we have that you wouldn't bite your master's hand again?'

Lucas nodded. 'I've heard enough,' he said, turning to the

Wererat. 'Get him to sign over the Dalelands, and a confession while he's at it. Cut him up into tiny pieces if he resists, Vanmorten.'

The Ratlord bowed low as Hector felt the hands of the Ugri warriors on his shoulders.

'You're making a mistake!' cried Hector, struggling to break free from the men as Slotha stepped in front of him.

'You're the same, dreadful wretch who snivelled around in my shadow, Piggy!' shouted Lucas, waving his hand dismissively. 'You haven't changed one bit!'

'I enjoyed our time together, Boarlord,' said Slotha, smiling, unable to resist one last slap. Her clawed fingernails raked across Hector's face, leaving bright red ribbons of torn flesh in their wake. The magister broke free of the Ugri's grasp, raising both his hands, gloved fingers splayed wide, the manacles taut. The prince jumped back in his throne suddenly, the old Lucas coming to the fore as he growled defensively. But if he feared Hector might attack him, he was mistaken. The Boarlord had another target.

The Vincent-vile flew from his grasp, fast as an arrow, whipping around the enormous throat of Lady Slotha. Her huge jaw hung open as the spirit coiled around her thick neck, slipping between the folds of her chin like an invisible garrotte. She stumbled towards the throne, staggering up the dais steps, hands grasping at Lucas. The prince leaped up to stand on the stone chair and lashed out, striking her hands away. He roared to try and warn her off, but she was wild beyond reasoning.

The Ugri warriors realized what was happening, the magister's hands moving as they manipulated the space before him, black leather fingers throttling thin air. They leaped, but not quickly enough; Opal was before them in a flash, her face shifting into that of the Werepanther, clawed hands ready to rip into them if they moved an inch closer. The Ugri stepped back, neutered and helpless as their mistress fell to her knees.

Her tongue lolled from her mouth now, purple and snake-like, as her bulging eyes rolled in her head. The tusks of the Walrus jutted down, ivory sabres that sawed vainly at the air. Hector yanked his hands back, as if pulling a rug from beneath a giant's feet, hauling the vile back with all his might. The neck of the Werewalrus made an awful, wet cracking sound as her huge head collapsed into her shoulders. With a wheezing death rattle, the queen of Tuskun fell to the flagged floor with a loud thud.

Brilliant, dear brother, panted Vincent, fresh from the kill.

Hector's heart shook like a rattle within his chest, his skin covered in sweat as he looked at the Lion, the Rat and the Panther.

'You're wrong, Lucas,' he said, sounding calmer than he felt. 'I've changed more than you could ever know.'

'Whatever . . . whatever he just did,' stammered Lucas. 'He could do that again. Kill him. Kill him now, before he uses his dark magick upon me!'

Opal raised her hand to the prince, demanding silence.

She's the one you need to talk to, brother. She's the one who makes the decisions around here.

'I've seen dark magistry before,' said Opal. 'In Cape Gala. Your old mentor, Vankaskan, he knew a thing or two.

But that trick you just played. That wasn't one of his, was it?'

'I heard he died,' said Hector, avoiding answering the question.

'He was slain by your friend, the Wolf,' snarled Vanmorten, stepping forward and towering over the Boarlord. If he feared Hector's power, he didn't show it.

'I would pay my respects to him,' said Hector. 'He set me on my path.'

'Then let me escort you up Grimm's Lane to Vermire, Pig. Visit his skull in my father's tomb and see how my brothers greet you!'

'Quiet, Vanmorten,' said Opal calmly. She looked at Hector, her big yellow eyes unblinking. And she smiled. 'You risk much allowing yourself to be brought to Highcliff by the Walrus, offering yourself to us. What you bring – this great power of magistry – would make our enemies quake. What do you want in return, Hector?'

All eyes were on the Boarlord.

Take the leap, brother. Leave the Wolf. Embrace your own *destiny.*

'I want a pardon,' said Hector, 'a guarantee that no harm will befall me at the hands of your forces. I need unhindered access throughout the realms, no restrictions on my movements. There's much I need to research if my magistry is to be a true weapon at your disposal. The Wolf's Council saw it as an aberration. They were feeble-minded fools.'

Good Hector, keep going.

'And I'll need a position within the royal court; Lord Magister to the king would be nice.'

'Never,' spat Lucas, while Opal raised her hand to silence him again.

'Go on,' she said.

'Duke Manfred's the only remaining member of the Wolf's Council, discounting myself. He wronged me, and I'd have his life too. He's taken your mother to Icegarden, Your Highness. I want to be there when we capture him, to play my part in bringing the Stag down. Then, finally, your enemies will all have been defeated.'

'Not all of them,' said the prince. 'The Wolf. What of him?'

Hector's bloody lips felt suddenly dry as he cleared his throat. 'They say he fell to his death. But if he yet lives, I'll help you bring him down.'

You really mean that, brother? If it came to it, you'd kill Drew?

Opal looked to Vanmorten and the prince. While Lucas sneered, Vanmorten allowed the briefest of nods. Opal turned back to Hector.

'We appear to have an agreement, Boarlord,' she said, her yellow eyes finally narrowing as she grinned. The Catlady leaped over the corpse of the Walrus and extended her hand to Hector. He reached a gloved palm out and shook it.

Vanmorten watched, his face hidden within his cowl. Hector couldn't tell whether the look he gave them was one of approval or disgust.

'So, Icegarden,' said Lucas. 'That's where they've taken my mother. We'll wipe those Sturmish scum off the map for harbouring traitors.'

Lucas stood, uneasy on his feet as if drunk. Hector watched the young Lion warily; he'd never seen him like this. He could see him by torchlight, unkempt and dishevelled. The old Lucas would never have allowed himself to be seen in such a state. The look in his eyes was wild.

'I wouldn't have just four of these realms bowing down before me. We must assemble our armies, Opal: the Lions, the Cats, the Rats and the Dogs. I'll have all of the Seven Realms kneeling before me, with my foot on their backs and my sword at their throats if that's what it takes!'

'And we'll have the Boars to assist us too,' sniggered Vanmorten.

'You shall,' said Hector, turning to the Ratlord and smiling. 'But first, I'll take you up on your offer, Lord Chancellor. Please, take me to Vermire.'

7

Return to the Pack

The Barebones loomed large over the eastern horizon, their snow-capped peaks faintly visible by the starlight. Trent Ferran found himself staring at the distant mountain range, as the wind raced through the Longridings around him. His Redcloak flapped, clapping at the air, as he gripped it tightly about his throat. He shivered as he glanced at the peaks one last time, the hairs prickling on his arms, before turning and pacing through the camp towards the prison tent.

One guard stood to attention in front of the weighted down door-flaps. Trent quickened his pace into a brisk, officious stride as he approached. He made to walk past the guard.

'Sergeant,' said the man, older than the young outrider and clearly resenting having to call him his superior. He remained barring Trent's path.

'Stand aside, Eaves,' said Trent, staring the man down.

'Can't do that, sergeant,' said the man, revealing a hint of a smug smile. Very few of Captain Sorin's friends in the camp respected the young sergeant, Trent having received the promotion at Lord Frost's insistence. The albino Catlord had his favourites, none more blessed than the youth from the Cold Coast.

'Why's that, Eaves?'

'Captain's orders.'

'Forget Sorin. I'm here on the command of Lord Frost, to question the prisoner. You want to take that up with his lordship?'

Trent eyeballed the man. He might have been twenty years his junior, but he was the same height, and equally as broad; the apple hadn't fallen far from the tree with Mack Ferran's son. Reluctantly, Eaves stood aside. Trent stepped past, glowering as he went, allowing the tent flap to swing shut behind him. The young soldier paused for a moment to tie the door cords, fastening it tight so it couldn't be opened in a hurry. Satisfied it was secured, he walked quietly into the heart of the dark tent, to the beaten figure kneeling in a slumped heap.

'One more thing,' said Trent as he stood over Baron Ewan.

The Ramlord looked up. 'You came back?' he whispered through broken lips.

'You don't believe Drew killed my mother. Then who did?'

'The Wererat Vanmorten killed your mother, lad.'

Ewan's voice was serious and hard.

'How can you *know* that, though?'

'Drew's word would have been enough for me. I wouldn't

doubt anything that lad told me. But you forget: I spent time in Cape Gala, while the Wererat Vankaskan lorded it around High Stable. That one couldn't hold a secret if his life depended upon it; his brother's murder of your mother was something they were proud of. I heard him gloat as much with my own ears.'

Trent's skin felt suddenly cold all over, a clamminess that spread from his extremities up towards his chest and throat. He felt a chill seize his heart, fearing the broken Ramlord spoke the truth.

He has *to be lying!*

'You'll say anything if it spares Sorin's beatings,' said Trent, struggling to hold back the tears. But his voice was trembling, the young outrider was assailed by doubt.

'What more can possibly be done to me?' laughed the Ramlord quietly. 'My body and heart are weak after your captain's work. I am already at Death's dark door. The long sleep would be a blessed relief after what your *friends* have done to me.'

'This can't be true,' sobbed Trent, unable to hold back his emotions any longer.

'Not a day has passed since your mother was murdered when Drew hasn't thought about the horror done to his family. And that his own father – *and brother* – should think he'd killed her? Can you imagine the torment?'

Tears rolled down Trent's cheeks, a steady stream that couldn't be stopped. He hunched double, retching, a dry heave causing his back to shudder. He dropped to his knees, choking, wanting to shout, but instead silently screaming. *What have I done?*

'I've hunted him,' he whispered. 'Hunted him for . . . for those who killed my family! What have I done? I'm damned . . .'

'All is not in vain,' urged Ewan. 'You can still help him. Lady Gretchen and Lady Whitley: your masters believe they've fled to the south, to Calico or Port Stallion.'

'They haven't?'

'No! They've gone north, to Brackenholme! Go after them, help them, boy: they're in grave danger!'

A slow handclap caused both of them to look up. The lithe figure of Lord Frost prowled into the room, the severed cords that had bound the door shut fluttering behind him. Trent looked back at Ewan, the look on his face as surprised as the Ramlord's. Ewan smiled sadly at the young man, Trent's eyes wide with horror as the full ramifications of Frost's presence dawned on him. He'd heard *everything*. The Catlord wore a pair of leather breeches and nothing else, his pale feet padding silently across the earth floor. Sorin followed at his shoulder, the broken-nosed captain grinning broadly.

'Excellent work, Trent,' said the albino. 'Excellent!'

He placed his white hand on Trent's shoulder and gave him a squeeze. Trent felt the Catlord's claws through the material of his cloak, digging into his flesh.

'You've outdone yourself, my friend. I didn't hear it all, but you unearthed the gem at the end: Brackenholme.'

Trent wearily rose to his feet, red-ringed eyes still wet with tears. Ewan looked up, his broken face trembling but forgiving. Sorin paced across and launched a vicious kick at the old therian, his booted heel hitting him square in the breast. Ewan collapsed, slumped against his ropes.

'Kill him,' said Frost, clapping Trent's back.

The young man's hand hovered over the pommel of the Wolfshead in his scabbard. *All this time, helping my enemy, hunting my brother, betraying my family* . . .

The Wolfshead blade slid out of its sheath, rising up in the air over the Ramlord in a smooth motion. It hovered there, the executioner's steel poised to fall. Every ounce of Trent's rage was unleashed as he let the sword fly in a furious swing, not down towards the Ramlord, but around him in a fluid arc.

Frost stood motionless, his pink eyes widening in wonder as he stared at the young outrider, poised to strike again. The Catlord's eyes settled on the Redcloak's sword, the edge of the blade dark with blood. He glanced down to his stomach, disbelief spreading across his face as a widening red line appeared across the toned flesh. The albino changed quickly, calling upon his felinthrope healing to try and halt the wound's progress, but it was hopeless; the Wolfshead blade was blessed with silver, at the Catlord's own command.

As Frost fell to his knees, mid-change, Sorin leaped past him, his own sword meeting Trent's as the young sergeant defended himself.

'You traitorous scum!' shouted Sorin, raining blows down on Trent as the younger man parried. 'You're as bad as the other Ferrans! A Wolf, just like your brother and father!'

Trent had heard enough insults. He could take the barrage

of sword-blows, but he wouldn't listen to Sorin besmirch the Ferran name. The next time Sorin's sword struck Trent's, the young man dived forward, catching him in the ribs with his shoulder. The air exploded from Sorin's lungs as the two crashed down to earth, both swords flying, Trent on top of the captain.

Sorin threw a wild punch upwards, but with little power, and the young man batted it away and landed a flurry of blows on Sorin's face. The captain stopped moving, his features battered, as Trent rolled away, panting and panicked.

The tent-flaps swung open as the guard entered, stumbling blindly into the scene. Trent wasted no time on Sorin's man, snatching up the Wolfshead blade and leaping up from the floor in a savage lunge. The sword disappeared through Eaves' stomach, rising up out of his back. The guard fell to the floor, dead in an instant.

Trent scrambled across to Ewan, cutting the Ramlord's bonds as he tumbled into his arms.

'Come, my lord,' said Trent. 'We need to go.'

Before Ewan could answer, another voice cut in.

'They'll find you and your kin. They'll kill you all. My brothers and sisters won't stop.'

Trent looked up and saw Lord Frost yet lived, the albino Catlord kneeling, his clawed fingers failing to hold his open stomach in place. He'd part-changed, the White Panther visible throughout, but he looked paler than ever, like a ghost, the enormous puddle of blood that he knelt in steadily growing. His pink eyes fluttered as he stared at Trent, head lolling, a sickly smile across his jagged feline mouth.

Trent rose and walked over to him, dragging the Wolfshead blade behind him.

'You strike a blow against a Catlord, you strike a blow against all my kind.'

Trent lifted the sword high before answering. 'You strike a blow against a Ferran, you strike a blow against our whole family.'

The sword sliced down, the severed head of Lord Frost rolling to a halt beside the body of Eaves. Trent looked back to Ewan in time to see Sorin at his back, risen from the floor, his face a red mask, his sword raised to strike. The captain's face was twisted, bloody skin broken by white snarling teeth and even brighter eyes. Trent began the turn, bringing the Wolfshead blade up to parry the below, but he was too slow, his poise all wrong. Sorin's sword was descending.

The killing blow never struck, the sword clattering from the captain's dying grasp. A horn burst from Sorin's chest, his ribcage splintering, as the changed Ramlord launched himself from the floor into his back. Shock, agony and horror flashed in Sorin's eyes as he and Baron Ewan collapsed. The Lionguard captain was dead before he hit the dirt. Trent skidded along the ground to catch Ewan as he rolled away from Sorin's corpse, wheezing with the strain of the transformation. The Ramlord was heavy, his head lolling against the youth's chest as his strength faded fast.

'We need to go,' cried Trent.

'No, boy,' he said. 'Go on your own.'

'I can take you with me, if we leave now!'

'Slow you down,' spluttered the wheezing old Ram.

Trent shook his head, dragging the Werelord towards the wall of the tent, but Ewan was right. Fully transformed, he was a deadweight in Trent's arms, his limbs useless.

'My time's up,' said Ewan. 'The long sleep awaits me. Go. Help your brother. His friends.'

Trent choked back the tears, nodding. Outside he could hear shouting, the commotion in the tent not having been missed by the rest of the camp.

'The girls,' whispered Ewan, his voice trailing away.

'What?' asked Trent, bending his ear closer to the Wereram's battered face.

'In danger. Gretchen, Whitley . . . Brackenholme.'

A rattling wheeze escaped Ewan's chest as his voice trailed away. His eyes stared at the tent ceiling, the light fading from them.

'They travel . . . with . . . Baba Korga . . .'

Then he was gone, his broken chest no longer moving, the fight over.

Trent didn't wait. More shouting from the camp told him he'd overstayed his welcome. He rushed over to the wall of the tent, slashing through it with a swing of the Wolfshead blade. Trent slipped out of the tent, pacing swiftly through the camp, striding between his fellow soldiers as he headed to where the horses were tethered. Bastian and Lionguard alike walked past him in the opposite direction as the cry went up from the prison tent. He was sure they were looking at him, could feel their questioning gaze as he strode by, but none stopped him.

By the time Trent found his horse, Storm, the rest of the

camp had descended upon the prison tent. By the time the Bastians and Lionguard began looking for the culprit, the outrider was already on his way, galloping across the Longridings, towards the Dyrewood.

Towards Brackenholme.

8

The Heirs and the Honest

Taloned fingers squeezed Drew's windpipe, rousing him from his fevered slumber, threatening to tear his throat out in a flash. His eyes were instantly open, feet scrambling against the freezing stone floor of the Hawklords' tomb as he struggled in vain to slip free of the deadly hold. He brought his hand up to prise his attacker's fingers loose, but the other's free hand shoved him away, the grip tightening suddenly and shutting off Drew's airway. Drew went limp in surrender, eyes fixed firmly on his foe.

The therian was unmistakably a Hawklord, although dramatically different in appearance from Shah. When Griffyn's daughter had transformed she had looked elegant, majestic, a true mistress of the sky. The falconthrope who held Drew's life in his talons was a rougher looking character. Rusty brown wings folded behind his back. The red feathers were tattered and threadbare in places, old wounds visible beneath missing plumage. A shortbow swung from his hip as he towered over Drew, his head craning in close to better inspect the young Wolflord. One long scar ran down the left side of the Hawk-lord's face, from the top of his crown, over his eye, disappearing beneath his jaw. His razor-sharp yellow beak snapped at Drew's face, and his big, black killer's eyes blinked suspiciously.

'You're well off the beaten track, boy,' croaked the Hawk. 'Thought you'd try and take from our kin, did ya?'

Drew's mouth gasped at the air like a fish out of water, no words escaping. Changing into the Wolf wasn't an option – the clawed fingers of the Hawk would puncture his neck like a knife through soft fruit. He could sense unconsciousness – and ultimately death – fast approaching. The Hawk looked across at Rook's corpse where it lay on the floor, illuminated by a shaft of morning sunlight from the window above.

'Thieves!' snapped the Werehawk, shaking Drew like a rag doll. 'The Crow promised you a fortune if you helped 'im rob our tomb, did he? Well the Crow's dead, boy, and you're about to join 'im . . .'

'Red Rufus!'

The Hawk bobbed his head, opening his beak to hiss in the direction of the staircase that led into the Screaming Peak. Another figure descended the steps, striding over towards the rust-feathered falconthrope and his prisoner.

'Let him breathe,' commanded the newcomer, a blur before Drew's cloudy vision as he was about to pass out.

Reluctantly, Red Rufus released his grip, letting Drew collapse on to the floor, snatching great lungfuls of air.

'Let me kill 'im, Carsten,' said Red Rufus, flexing his talons, ready to lash out. 'Let's see 'is gizzard, eh?'

The one called Carsten raised his hand, silencing Red Rufus. 'Let the lad speak first, Red Rufus, hear what he's got to say. Then you can open him up.'

As Drew's vision recovered, Carsten shifted into focus. In his fifth decade, he was stocky and broad-shouldered, with a mop of thick black hair. His eyes were bright blue, trained keenly on Drew, while his hands remained folded over the pommel of an upright broadsword, the blade turned down to the floor. Drew rubbed his throat, massaging life back into his vocal chords.

'Seems like the tombwraiths took care of your master, thief,' said Carsten, stepping over Rook's body.

'I'm not . . . a thief!' gasped Drew.

'Lost your way did you, lad?' said Carsten. 'Happens all the time up here. A boy's just wandering around through the vales and grasslands, takes a wrong turn, ends up on top of Tor Raptor. Easy mistake to make.'

'I came here . . . with Baron Griffyn . . .'

Carsten gave Rook's body a kick, the corpse rolling over, black feathers fluttering around it.

'Rubbish!' sneered Red Rufus, clenching his taloned hands, ready to strike. 'Griffyn died years ago. You're one of the Crow's men.'

Red Rufus brought his hand back, fingers open, his big black eyes narrowing to slits.

'You're a dead man . . .'

'Wait!' shouted Carsten, causing Red Rufus to turn.

Another figure had descended the staircase. A tall, partly-changed Hawklord staggered down the steps. His wings were already retreating into his back, the beak grinding back into his jaw and skull, feathers disappearing beneath his skin. He was bald with a full black beard, a little taller than Carsten, but they had the look of family. In his arms he carried a body.

'Is that . . . ?' said Carsten, stepping closer.

'It's Griffyn,' said the newcomer, his head bowed, beard bristling as he grimaced. 'Dead: I found him below the cliffs.'

Carsten and Red Rufus looked back to Drew where he lay on the floor, his eyes darting between them all.

'I told you I came with him!'

'And yet you live while my lord lies dead?' said Carsten.

'Let me do 'im, Your Grace,' said Red Rufus, hopping from foot to foot now, keen to be on with the business of killing.

'Who is this?' asked the bald, bearded Hawklord.

'My name's Drew. Drew Ferran.'

Red Rufus was about to strike when Carsten snatched him by the forearm, causing the red-feathered bird to squawk at his liege.

'*You're* Drew Ferran?' he said in disbelief, ignoring Red Rufus. 'Half of Lyssia is searching for a boy by that name.'

'This is Wergar's son?' asked the bearded falconthrope.

'Just words, Baum,' replied Carsten. 'I still think he's an agent of this dead Crow, sent here thieving. He'll say anything to live . . .'

'How *does* he live though, brother?' said Baum. 'The Screaming Peak and the tombwraiths: *only the Heirs and the Honest may enter*? This Crow lies dead but the boy survives.'

Carsten cocked his head to one side, aspects of the hawk never far away. He crouched on his haunches in front of Drew while Red Rufus paced anxiously behind him.

'Good question, Baum. Boy, how *do* you live while the Crow lies dead?'

Drew reached behind his back, his torn cloak falling to one side to reveal the sword he'd found in the tomb.

Carsten and Baum both gasped, while Red Rufus stuck his avian neck over his lord's shoulder, his eyes running along the length of the blade. Carsten moved from his crouch, dropping on to one knee, while his brother gently placed Griffyn's body on to the floor and did the same.

'What is it?' said Red Rufus, agitated by his falconthrope cousins' show of reverence.

'The sword,' whispered Baum, recognizing the blade straightaway.

'He's Wergar's son, all right,' said Carsten, taking hold of Red Rufus and drawing the old bird to the ground into a bow. 'He's the rightful king of Westland.'

Drew staggered to his feet, looking down on the three Hawklords who knelt before him. They reminded him of the tombwraiths he'd encountered that night, striking the same poses that the phantoms had when they'd seen the sword.

'I don't . . . please, I don't understand. And for Brenn's sake, my lords, don't kneel before me!'

The three rose, Red Rufus a little quicker than the other two, stalking to the rear of the tomb.

'The runes beyond this crypt are a warning,' Baum said.

'None may enter the Screaming Peak but the Heirs and the Honest: this law the tombwraiths honour.'

Only the just and rightful lord may enter: that's what Baron Griffyn had told Drew about the tomb.

'How did the tombwraiths know I wasn't a thief, come here to steal the sword? They tore Rook to pieces!'

'That sword,' Carsten said, pointing to the grey, metal blade, 'was the weapon of Wergar the Wolf: *Moonbrand*, forged for his ancestors in Icegarden by Sturmland's greatest smiths centuries ago. The wraiths wouldn't have allowed you to pass if you weren't truly Wergar's heir. Did it glow, lad?'

'It was already glowing, but when I picked it up it shone with a white light.'

'The Sturmish enchanted the weapons of the Werelords,' said Baum. 'The steel glows like a torch under moonlight.'

'And the rest,' muttered Red Rufus, cryptically.

'But what's it doing here?' Drew asked, trying to piece together the jigsaw.

'It would appear our dear, departed Griffyn brought it here for safe-keeping after Leopold took the throne. Who could have known that one day Wergar's child would climb Tor Raptor and reclaim it as his own?'

Drew thought back to Griffyn's words once more: *I brought it here: I kept it safe.*

Drew had heard the sword's name before. Queen Amelie had mentioned it in Highcliff. *My father's sword.*

'My lords,' said Drew, sliding Moonbrand into his battered weapon belt. It was his turn to kneel now, Baum and Carsten looking to one another in surprise while Red Rufus watched distrustfully. 'I was here with Baron Griffyn's blessing. We came to the Screaming Peak because we needed to call you back. The war that has taken hold of Lyssia, we, the army that stands before the Catlords of Bast, are in dire need.'

'In need of what, son of Wergar?' asked Carsten, his blue eyes shining like ice.

'We need the Hawklords.'

PART VII

Death from Above

I
The Guest

The first rays of sunlight illuminated Windfell Keep as a trio of servants stood in the lord's chamber, watching their master frantically rifle through his desk. Each held a casket, lid open, half-filled with coins, gems and artefacts. The Falcon-lord tugged loose a drawer, tipped its contents on to the table and sifted through them with feverish fingers.

'It must be here somewhere,' murmured Baron Skeer, clawing through bound scrolls and checking the seals of each.

The doors to his study were wide open, the booted sound of guards' feet echoing through the corridor beyond.

'What the devil's going on?'

The question came from the doorway, Skeer glancing up to find his guest, craning his head around the corner.

'I'm leaving,' said Skeer briskly. 'Ah, there you are!'

His eyes lit up as he snatched a scroll with a red wax seal: the Lionshead, King Leopold.

'Leaving? Are you insane, Skeer?'

'You'd leave too if you knew what was best.'

The old Falcon checked the seal, making sure it remained unopened.

'What's the scroll?' said the visitor, striding into the room, looking back as another group of soldiers raced by in the corridor. They may have worn the brown, feather-trimmed cloaks of the Hawkguard, but each man was there on secondment, a soldier of the Lion. Windfell had been Leopold's foothold in the Barebones for fifteen years, in which time the soldiers had seen little by way of combat, growing careless and out of condition. Suddenly, conflict was approaching, and the Hawkguard's fear was palpable.

Skeer stashed the scroll in the belt of his robes.

'A decree made by the old king.'

'That states what?' asked the Falcon's guest, trailing his hands over one of the open caskets that the servants held.

'That my position here as baron is lawful. Leopold asked me to rule here for the good of the Seven Realms.'

His guest laughed, a rasping cackle that rattled in his chest.

'For the good of the Seven Realms? For the good of *you*, Skeer, and no one else!'

The guest slammed the casket lid shut, causing the Falconlord to jump. The baron scooped up a further handful of trinkets and barged past his visitor, dumping them into another box.

'Why the concern over your position, old friend? Why the

activity within the halls and corridors of Windfell? Why so fearful for your life all of a sudden, Skeer: explain what's happening!'

Skeer stepped closer to his fellow Werelord, who was a good foot taller than the old bird. The baron stared up into the squinting off-centre eyes of the crooked count.

'My cousins, Kesslar,' said the Falcon. 'The Hawklords return!'

'What do you *mean* they're returning?' shouted Kesslar as he marched after Skeer, the baron's servants getting under his feet as he tried to catch up. He shoved one out of the way, the young man crashing into the corridor wall and spilling half the contents of the casket on the floor.

'Pick those up!' squawked Skeer as his servant snatched up the jewels.

'How can the Hawklords return?' repeated Kesslar. 'They're all dead, aren't they?'

'Not dead,' corrected the Falcon. 'Banished. Forbidden from ever returning.'

'Yet you say that's happening? How can you know?'

Skeer's eyes were frantic as he peered through one of the tall arches that looked out over the mountains beyond. He strode to the stone sill, ducking his head from side to side, searching the sky fearfully. Beside the towering keep of Windfell, the Steppen Falls crashed down through the Barebones, working their way to the Longridings far below. A line of bridges spanned the falls, carrying a road from the city down to the grasslands.

'Did you not *hear* it?'

'Hear what, Skeer? The waterfall? Of course I do: you sound like a mad man!'

'No! The Screaming Peak! It's calling them home. They're returning to Windfell.' He turned towards a set of double doors guarded by soldiers.

'I thought only the Lord of Windfell could enter the crypt of your ancestors?'

Skeer looked back at Kesslar briefly, as the Hawkguard opened the great doors.

'Griffyn?' asked Kesslar. 'That old buzzard's behind this? I left him behind in Scoria – I'd be amazed if he got out of that hellhole alive!'

'Well, he's out,' grumbled Skeer, the soldiers following out of the doors and down a flight of steps into the huge, circular courtyard within the keep. Curving granite walls rose high around them, stone ledges lining them on every level, the ancient seats of the Council of Hawklords. A carriage waited, horses kicking their hooves impatiently, alongside a platoon of Skeer's personal guard.

Kesslar was thinking fast as he stumbled down the steps behind the Falconlord.

'If Griffyn escaped Scoria . . .' he muttered. *Who else escaped the island of the Lizardlords? Surely few of them could have survived? If they find me here . . .*

Skeer spun, raising his voice.

'He *is* returning, and he brings the banished Hawklords with him!' he cried. 'I don't give a flying spit about the where or why that helped him get here, but these are my *enemies*. They won't forget the part I played in this city's downfall. I was there when they chopped Griffyn's wings off, for Brenn's sake! If he's returning, do you think he'll be in forgiving mood?'

Kesslar watched the baron storm across the courtyard towards his waiting soldiers. He counted thirty of them and they struck the Goatlord as an uninspiring bunch. Their armour and uniforms were pitted and shabby. A couple of the men glanced up at the skies nervously.

This is what happens when you're posted to a ghost town in the peaks of the Barebones.

'Why not stand and fight?' shouted Kesslar. 'There may only be Griffyn returning.'

'True,' replied Skeer. 'Then again, what if they all return?'

'Wave your precious scroll at them!'

'I'm not a fool, Kesslar: that scroll will provide me with protection throughout Lyssia, but in the eyes of the brethren whom I turned against? That's a risk I'm not prepared to take!'

'Where will you go?'

'You ask too many questions, old friend!' yelled Skeer as his men loaded his chests and personal belongings into the carriage. 'If you hurry, there's a seat here for you! Make haste!'

Kesslar turned on his heel and ran, passing more soldiers who were hurriedly evacuating the keep. Following the curving corridors and sweeping staircases, the Goatlord crashed into the room he'd been occupying, dashing straight to the side of his bed. He reached under, gnarled hands catching hold of the five-foot trunk that was stowed beneath. With a heave it slid out. Kesslar took a key from his pocket and unlocked it.

The true fortune of Scoria lay inside: gems and jewels that had been captured from every continent. Rubies the size of fists; ingots of enchanted Sturmish steel; diamonds as big as apples; coins, crowns and coronets; regal rings and magisters' rods. Kesslar allowed himself a momentary smile. That fool Ignus and his inbred brothers thought they'd get the better of him. Kesslar had already been plotting his heist, long before the Wolf boy and his allies decided to spoil the Lizards' party in the Furnace. If anything, their escape and the ensuing chaos helped Kesslar make his getaway.

He locked the trunk shut once more, heaved it across his back, and set off through the door. Kesslar shook his head as he ran, cursing his luck. With Haggard lost to him and his bridges with Scoria utterly burned, Windfell had been his last hope of a place to recuperate and reform his plans. He and Skeer had always looked out for one another. Long ago the old Falcon had even sold Griffyn to him, along with his daughter, Shah. Their business relationship was about the longest standing friendship the Goat had ever known, Skeer being possibly the only therian he could ever truly trust.

His stay in Windfell should have been a quiet, relaxed affair. Let the rest of Lyssia crash and burn; he and Skeer would remain in the Barebones, looking down on the chaos below, ready to join the fray once the victor was decided. Or, failing that, remain hidden away while all their foes slayed one another – it made little difference to Kesslar. Instead, the old wretch Griffyn had somehow sprouted a new pair of wings and flown back to Lyssia, even making it as far as the tomb on Tor Raptor. Kesslar couldn't hear the *screaming* as Skeer had described it, but he didn't doubt his friend for one moment. Something was coming.

The corridors were near deserted by the time Kesslar bounded down towards the double doors that led into the courtyard. He was too busy grunting, the box on his back heavy with treasure, to pay attention to what lay ahead. At the last moment he looked up, stumbling to a halt as his knees buckled beneath him.

In the brief time it had taken him to grab his trunk, the yard had been transformed into a scene of battle. The Hawkguard were trapped within the circular court, screaming and shouting as they defended themselves from aerial attack. Their spears jabbed skywards, swords slashing at the air, as they desperately sought shelter from their enemy. Many lay dead on the ground, and the unmistakable figure of Skeer could be seen with his back to the carriage while the chaos exploded around him, the horses bucking to break loose. He looked up, face stricken by terror.

A dozen therians rode the wind around the courtyard, great raptor wings keeping them aloft as they rained death down on the soldiers. Some wore breastplates, others were barechested; some carried axes and swords, others fired bows or threw javelins. While they favoured different armour and weapons, they were inextricably linked as kinfolk; each was unmistakably a Hawklord, legendary warriors thought to be lost from Lyssia.

Their wings, with feathers of different shades of brown, red and grey, rose majestically from their backs. Their muscular arms were still human in appearance, while their legs were those of birds of prey, wide splayed feet that ended in deadly talons. Most fearsome of all were their heads, hooked yellow beaks screeching with fury, dealing death in the blinking of a big, black eye. They swooped through the Hawkguard, tearing them to shreds, ripping them apart, tossing their warm corpses into the air.

Skeer saw Kesslar and made a break towards his old friend. He darted through the screaming guards, deceptively agile, as dismembered bodies fell across the courtyard. The Hawklords were enjoying this moment, meting out long-awaited justice upon those who had pillaged Windfell. Even Kesslar, a man used to violence, blanched at the Werehawks' grisly work.

Skeer was close now, leaping up the steps towards the Goatlord. 'Kesslar!' he wailed as he neared him, hands reaching out in desperation, a shadow passing overhead.

With a bone-shattering *crunch*, an Eaglelord landed on top of Skeer, knuckled yellow feet crushing the baron's body beneath him. He held a broadsword, but that wasn't the weapon he'd used on the turncoat Falcon. Dark talons clenched together, the hooked blades digging into the skin of Skeer's back, catching on his ribs and spine as they ground flesh and bone together on the stone steps. The Falcon cried out in horror, screaming Kesslar's name from his traitorous lips. The Eagle turned his head to stare at Kesslar, blinking briefly, before tearing Skeer apart with his feet.

Kesslar raced back inside, dropped the trunk and slammed the doors shut, dropping the locking bars into place with a clang. His heart felt like it might explode, his hands shaking as he caught hold of the trunk handle again, dragging it away from the doors and the battle in the courtyard. He heaved the box over to the windows from where Skeer had, only moments earlier, stared out over the mountains. With few alternatives, Kesslar craned his neck out and looked down the keep's curved granite wall. There was a twenty-foot drop from the window to rough rock below. Windfell perched upon a sheer cliff-face, protecting it from attack, the bridge road over the falls being the only way to reach it on foot. The cliffs were sharp and jagged, impassable to humankind, and therians for that matter. *Most* therians.

He let the beast take over quickly, every moment's delay making his death more likely as the Hawklords hammered on the double doors. His chest expanded with three great cracks, ribs bursting to take on the Weregoat's mightier physique. He tore the robes from his back as wiry, grey hair raced over his body. His legs transformed swiftly, huge, muscular thighs supported by powerful black hooves. His eyes shifted further around his skull, long black pupils dissecting globs of molten gold. The horns emerged from his brow, thick as tree trunks, coiling round upon themselves – the devil incarnate.

Snatching up the trunk in one grotesque hand, the Weregoat clambered out of the window and jumped. Kesslar's hooves hit the rocks and somehow managed to take hold, his free hand grasping the wall for further support. To anyone other than the Goatlord such a feat would have proved deadly. Unperturbed, Kesslar shuffled and jumped his way around the keep's base, making his way round, past the outer walls that surrounded the city, towards the road ahead. Above, he heard the cries of Skeer's soldiers as they were chased through the palace, butchered where they were found.

Finally he approached the cliff road, a yawning chasm his only obstacle to freedom. The gap was fifteen feet, from a standing jump, but once more, Kesslar's faith in his therian ability and his own survival instinct provided all the impetus he needed. Shifting the trunk to his other arm, he crouched low and leaped, propelling himself forward as if his legs were spring-loaded. The Goat sailed through the air, landing safely on the road with some feet to spare.

Kesslar grinned triumphantly, glancing back at Windfell just the once.

'Goodbye, old friend,' he said, before turning and sprinting towards the first bridge on his powerful, therian legs.

The first bridge was the tallest and longest of all those that spanned the Steppen Falls, the white stone road riding the elegant arches that held it over the mighty torrent of water. Misty clouds from the waterfall shrouded the centre of the bridge from view, the promise of freedom awaiting him beyond the veil. Kesslar kept his pace up, jogging away from the city, black hooves striking the white granite underfoot as he ran into the spray. He was unsure of where he was headed, but an opportunity would arise soon enough. Something would surprise him, sooner or later.

As it happened, he was surprised far sooner than he could have imagined. His hooves skittered to a halt on the wet road as the beating of wings caused the mists to part. A large shape loomed into view overhead, the spray swirling through the backdraft. With dread, Kesslar saw the Hawklord drop something from above, the dark mass landing on the bridge, barring his path. The figure rose to its full height, stepping forward, slowly materializing through the mist before Kesslar's bulging eyes.

'It cannot be!' gasped the Goatlord, staggering backwards in disbelief.

Drew Ferran growled. The last of the Grey Wolves paced forward, Moonbrand raised and vengeance in his heart.

'Kesslar!' Drew shouted over the roar of the Steppen Falls. 'Your past has caught up with you, and you must face our rage!'

2

The Steppen Falls

The Goatlord looked back the way he'd come, the cries of battle echoing from Windfell. He tugged a long, black knife free from his belt, holding it up defensively.

'Stop running, Kesslar,' growled Drew. 'Surrender now and I'll spare your life.'

'You believe my life is *yours* to spare?'

'Drop the knife,' said the Werewolf, his teeth bared as he stepped closer to the Ram.

'You think you can intimidate me, child?' shouted the Goat, but there was a tremble to his voice. 'Your father was the same! Bullied his way across Lyssia, and what good did it ultimately do him? His own friends turned against him!'

Kesslar laughed, backing nervously through the mists, losing all sense of direction. Drew kept his eyes locked on the Goat, ready to leap upon him at a moment's notice.

'They'll turn on you too, Wolf! All those you hold dear! History repeats itself, boy: you're your father's son!'

'Drop the dagger,' said Drew. 'You've nowhere to run.'

Kesslar's hooves backed up to the edge, sending chalky pebbles scuttling off the bridge.

'Your weapon, Kesslar.'

The noise of the waterfall was all around them, a constant, tumbling cymbal clash. Kesslar looked behind at the deadly drop, and then squinted at the dagger in his hand. The Wolf towered before him.

'I've had a good life, haven't I?' chuckled Kesslar, his laughter false and grim. 'Spent so long putting people in cages: maybe it's time I tried the view from the inside out? Perhaps the change will do me good?'

'The knife.'

The Goatlord tossed it across the bridge, metal clanging against stone as it skittered to a halt. Kesslar put his long box down in front of him and dropped to one knee, his head sagging forward. Drew, trying to remain calm, felt dizzy with triumph, having forced the Weregoat to surrender without even drawing blood. *There's always another way*, he reasoned silently to himself.

'You've done the right thing, Kesslar. I'm no monster. I'm taking you back to Windfell, let the Hawklords judge you. See what they –'

The sentence was cut short as the large wooden trunk was propelled forward by the Goat, shoved along the floor in front of him. Drew had no option but to jump into the air to avoid being hit. By the time he was returning to earth, Kesslar had already leaped, springing forward from his crouched position, his powerful horned head catching the Wolf square in the chest.

The Werewolf sailed through the mist, landing on his back with a crunch. Stars flashed as the world spun. His vision blurred as he tried to right himself. The hammering of hooves on the road approached rapidly. Drew raised Moonbrand up, his hold on the sword flimsy. A powerful kick from the Goatlord's hoof almost broke Drew's arm, the precious sword flying from his grasp.

With a wheeze he rolled over, the fingers of his hand scrabbling over the white stone as he searched in vain. Another kick to his guts sent him rolling, over and over, before he shuddered to a halt by the bridge's edge. Grunting, he pulled himself on to all fours, wincing as his bruised ribs grated, nerves firing with pain. He caught the sound of hooves through the mist once more. He raised his left arm up, the stump deflecting the blow at the last second and slamming Kesslar on to the floor.

Drew dived for the Goatlord, but his movement was clumsy, the youth still stunned from the injuries he'd been dealt. Kesslar snatched at the Wolf's throat, throttling Drew as the lycanthrope's jaws snapped towards his face. The Wolf's claws came up next, his right hand tearing at Kesslar's chest, arms and wrists, trying to shake the Goat loose. The golden eyes bulged, the Weregoat snorting with exertion as he put all his strength into the chokehold.

Drew tried to bring his legs round, tried to grapple with the lower half of the Goatlord, but Kesslar's powerful legs kicked him clear. Drew felt his stamina faltering, his limbs growing weak as the fight began to slip away. He focused his energies into his throat, straining against the Goat's grip, concentrating solely on not letting the beast snap his neck. *A little longer*, he prayed. *Just a little longer . . .*

Kesslar rolled him over, first straddling him and then standing. Drew's hand and stump fell away as the Goatlord choked the life from him.

'This is how you die, Wolf,' grunted Kesslar. 'At my hands. Alone.'

'Not . . .' spluttered Drew, the Werewolf's mouth wide now, tongue lolling. The veins and muscles bulged around his shoulders and throat, a last stand against suffocation. Kesslar shook him, coaxing the final words from the dying lycanthrope.

'Speak, Wolf!'

'Not . . .' croaked Drew. 'Alone . . .'

He lifted his weak hand, a clawed finger pointing through the mist. Kesslar looked up and saw three figures appear through the mist. Their features were unreadable through the spray, but their outlines were instantly recognizable. The giant figure in the middle carried an enormous mallet in his hand, a hammer that would take the strength of two regular humans to lift it over their heads. The prowling woman, stalking forward, her spear raised, ready for attack. Last of all came the heavy-set warrior carrying the spiked mace, swinging his deadly club menacingly.

'No!' shouted Kesslar, as the Werewolf threw his arm out.

The clawed hand tore at Kesslar's hamstring, the mighty leg buckling instantly, loosening the Goatlord's grip. Drew collapsed as the Goat staggered back, bringing his hand to his throat as the Wolf vanished, his therian energies exhausted. He lay on the floor as the Goatlord screamed, clutching his bloodied leg. Kesslar tried to back away, but it was no good. His enemies surrounded him in the mist, shadows that would have their revenge.

With a furious roar the Weretiger dashed forward, lightning fast, her claws tearing across Kesslar's chest. Then he was flying in the other direction as Taboo caught him with another claw, this time across his throat. Then she was gone, returned to the mists.

'Turn on me, would you?' choked Kesslar, trying to staunch the wound at his neck. 'They chanted your name in Scoria, Taboo! I turned you into a goddess! This is how you repay me?'

The snorting sound from behind was the only warning the Wererhino gave him. Krieg's huge horn punched into Kesslar's back, launching him into the air. Drew watched as the battered Weregoat sailed over him. He landed beside the trunk, his clawed hands fumbling over the wood as he struggled to rise, his back broken, leg snapped and throat torn. The Goat still managed to pick up his precious box, holding his treasure close to his chest as the last therian gladiator advanced.

'Whatever he's paying you,' spat Kesslar, his mouth frothing with bloody bubbles. 'I'll triple it! I have here the treasure of Scoria. I'll share it with you. What do you say?'

The Behemoth brought his huge mallet back, his body shifting, doubling in size as his shadow filled the bridge. His broad head, tusks and trunk rose through the air as he put all his weight behind the final blow. Drew looked away at the last, the Weremammoth's hammer flying, the stone block crashing through Kesslar's box, shattering the timber as if it wasn't there. The mallet shattered the Goatlord's ribcage as Kesslar's body took flight, disappearing off the bridge into the white spray, leaving a trail of blood, gems and jewels raining through the air in its wake.

The Behemoth let the mallet fall to his side.

'Take it with you.'

Krieg was at Drew's side, the horn slowly receding, the broad neck thinning once more as he cradled the young Wolflord in his arms.

'My throat . . .' whispered Drew, his voice hoarse.

'You'll live, Wolf,' said the Rhino, as the Behemoth joined him.

'Thank you,' Drew croaked.

'Thank your Hawklord friends,' said Krieg as he helped the Wolflord to his feet.

Taboo slinked towards them, Moonbrand in her hand. For a moment, she examined the blade, checking its balance, giving it a few swipes through the air. Drew was momentarily transported back to Scoria and the wild, arrogant felinthrope he'd first met. That Taboo would have taken the sword for herself. She flipped the blade around, holding the round, white metal handle out towards Drew.

'The king dropped his sword,' she said, smiling, as the Steppen Falls thundered around them.

3

The Ratlord's Skull

The torchlight sent shadows racing down the spiral staircase ahead of them, flickering phantoms that danced out of sight. Each curving step down the narrow stairs took them deeper into the belly of the citadel of Vermire, closer to the tomb of the Ratlords. Vanmorten led the way, the Lord Chancellor's long black robes dragging over the wet stone steps, threatening to trip up the magister following. Hector stayed close behind the Ratlord, grateful for the illumination, fearful he might stumble and fall at any moment.

'Mind your step, Lord Magister. I wouldn't want you breaking your neck.'

We can't have that happening, dear brother. Not when we're so near to our prize.

Hector's Boarguard, increased in number, had accompanied him on the two-day ride north. There were now eight, Ringlin and Ibal complemented by the six Ugri warriors who had been the bodyguard to Slotha. Hector had been unaware of the Tuskun tradition that dictated that a defeated lord or lady's vassals would immediately swear allegiance to the victor. As such he now had six of the mightiest warriors from the frozen wastes at his disposal. The thought was comforting to Hector, especially considering their destination.

Vanmorten and a platoon of the Lionguard had travelled also, escorting the Lord Magister up Grimm's Lane. Word must have been sent ahead that Hector was on his way, for the Vermirian army awaited them in number at the top of Grimm's Lane. Armoured pikemen, mounted bowmen, filthy foot-soldiers and black-cowled scouts; the escort grew as they neared the city of the Rat King, all wanting to catch sight of the magister who had once been Vankaskan's apprentice. Hector kept the Boarguard close at all times. He knew that Vanmorten despised him, the very act of escorting the young Boar to Vermire repulsing the Rat. His business was unfinished with the Lord Chancellor, just as it was with his dead brother.

Two other members of the Rat King, Vorhaas and Vex, remained upstairs in the Citadel, watching over the Boarguard, while the eldest sibling led Hector into the tomb. War Marshal Vorjavik was away campaigning, leading the Lyssian army through the Dalelands alongside Onyx's Bastian force. His twin brother, Inquisitor Vorhaas, had remained behind in Vermire, looking after the Rat King's homeland. He'd shown surprise at the decision to allow the magister into their family crypt, but had held his tongue after a glare from Vanmorten. The youngest brother, Vex, had looked on from a distance, apparently studying the Boarlord's every move. Hector no longer spooked very easily, but Vex set his nerves on edge.

You'll have to watch that one, brother, Vincent had hissed.

Arriving at the base of the staircase, Vanmorten strode across to an unlit torch that hung from a bracket. Lighting it, he walked on to a rusted iron gate, feet slapping through the puddles. The stench of damp and stagnant water was overwhelming, while the constant sound of dripping echoed around the catacomb. Vanmorten reached a scarred, skeletal hand into his robes and withdrew a key, unlocking the metal door. It swung open with an ominous creak. Hector followed him through.

Stone coffins lined every wall of the room, some recessed within the crudely carved ore-stained rock. The scurrying of rats replaced the dripping noise, as Vanmorten's distant diminutive cousins fled from the torchlight. A black marble box, less than two feet square , stood on a pedestal in the centre of the low-ceilinged chamber, yet to be moved into the walls like those of the Rat King's ancestors.

'Here he is,' muttered Vanmorten unenthusiastically. Hector had known from his years in Vankaskan's service that the brothers disliked one another.

'This is it?' asked Hector, surprised to be faced with a small box and not a coffin.

'What part of "*only his skull remaining*" did you not understand, boy?' snarled Vanmorten.

'If you could leave me alone,' said Hector, smiling politely.

'That's not going to happen, little pig. You may have fooled Opal and the prince, but I won't be tricked so easily. You've had your fun. Say your piece to his box and let's be on our way. I won't dance to your tune a moment longer.'

'With respect, Lord Chancellor, my business with your brother is a sacred and magisterial matter. The Guild of Magisters' secrets go back to the Great Feast. To have you present while I bless his remains would be blasphemous.'

Vanmorten sneered within his hood. Hector got a whiff of the decayed, burned flesh within the cowl as the Ratlord grated his teeth in annoyance.

'You can find your own way back up, piglet,' said the Wererat, tossing him the key. 'Lock up when you're done. And leave *everything* as you find it. I shall know if you've disturbed anything. Understand?'

Hector nodded, smiling. Vanmorten stormed from the chamber, disappearing up the spiral staircase. Hector followed to check he was gone, before closing the door as quietly as its rusted hinges would allow. He locked it, checking it was firmly shut. Then he turned, walking back to the black box. Hector removed the lid and placed it gently on the floor, before reaching into the box and lifting the grotesque bleached white skull of Vankaskan.

Oh, dear brother, gasped the Vincent-vile. *He's beautiful!*

'Now, my old master,' he whispered, marvelling at the partially transformed skull.

'To work.'

The chanting was fast and breathless, ancient words of magick known only to the few. The black candle burned brightly in Hector's right hand, oily black smoke billowing from the flame and gathering under the ceiling above. He tipped the candle over his open left hand, the molten wax pooling in his blackened hand, pouring between his fingers, searing the flesh and racing down his arm. All the while the chanting continued as the Boarlord sat, cross-legged.

The box had been removed from its plinth, the skull of the dead Ratlord now gracing the stone pedestal alone. A circle of brimstone was carefully laid out around it on the ground. Hector's words rattled from his mouth rapid-fire, unintelligible to anyone other than a magister. He stopped chanting suddenly, clenched his fist and slammed it down on to the stone floor once, twice, three times. The skull shuddered on the plinth.

'Rise, creature, and answer your master's bidding!'

Hector felt the cold rush into the room. The candle flame sputtered, fighting the breeze, clinging to the wick and refusing to die. While the candle remained lit, the rest of the crypt darkened as the shadows crept in all round, the blackness all-consuming. The coffins and walls were swallowed by the darkness, the gate that led to the stairs vanished. Even the torch at the foot of the stairwell spluttered out, leaving the candlelight as the only illumination in the chilling chamber.

A low chuckle bloomed slowly in the centre of the circle of brimstone, the yellow powder shifting as if caught by a breeze. The laughter rose, rasping like a blade on a file, causing the skin on Hector's arms to bristle.

Well this is a surprise, hissed the spirit of Vankaskan, tied to the dead Ratlord's skull in the form of a vile.

Hector listened for Vincent, but heard nothing, his brother

silent in the presence of a spirit as powerful and steeped in magick as Vankaskan.

'I've surprised myself, my lord,' said Hector. 'I wasn't sure your spirit would still be here. I thought you might have moved on.'

Alas no, sighed Vankaskan. *My time in the mortal world isn't over by a long chalk. One cannot be surrounded and immersed in magick one's whole life and not be affected by it in death. Once one crosses over, the bridge remains, and as easy as it is for one to pass along it . . . things . . . can always come the other way. But then, you'll know that already, won't you, Hector?*

The young magister shivered at the mention of communing; the dead Ratlord was clearly already aware of Hector's dabbling in the dark arts.

'I'm in control, my lord,' blustered Hector. 'I know what I'm doing.'

Do you? You've raised my spirit, awoken me from my slumber, bottled my soul in the form of a vile. You know what you're doing? Can you imagine how angry *you've just made me, calling me to you like some kind of plaything?*

Hector leaned back from the edge of the brimstone circle, as he felt the cold breath of Vankaskan's vile wash over him. He saw its shape now, a smoky black cloud of malevolence that paced the yellow line like a caged beast.

You think this sulphurous dust can stop me, Hector? You think I won't find a way out of this little prison you've constructed for me? Why did you summon me, Hector? Did you hope to get answers from me? An apology perhaps for the path I set you upon?

Vankaskan's words came thick and fast, loaded with hatred

for the young Boarlord. Hector recoiled, turning his face as if the vile's spittle might spatter his cheek.

I will find you, Hector, hissed Vankaskan. *I'll come looking for you, once I'm free of this crypt. You've woken me now, Boarlord! I shall not sleep! I shall not return to the darkness!*

Hector turned towards the skull on the pedestal. Slowly, very deliberately, he reached out with his wax-covered, blackened hand and placed it within the circle. The Vankaskan-vile gasped as Hector drew his hand back, clearing away the yellow powder. He lifted his hand, the brimstone mixing with the cooling wax that was setting over his fist and forearm.

'I'm right here,' said Hector.

Are you mad? gasped the Vankaskan-vile. *Is this suicide?*

'No,' answered the young magister, rising to his feet and stepping into the broken circle. He felt the dead magister's vile now, enveloping him, its claws moving around his throat, trying to prise open his mouth and see his insides. Hector ignored the spirit, picking up the skull in his right hand. He opened his left and clicked his fingers, the wax cracking and tumbling to the flagged floor.

'I'm here for everything, Vankaskan.'

The Vincent-vile was on to the Ratlord's vile in an instant, tearing it off his brother

What is this? What's going on?

'You don't understand, Vankaskan. There are more powerful creatures of magick than you out there. I met one; it shared its secrets with me.'

The Ratlord's vile screamed as the Vincent-vile tore into it, biting and clawing at the shadowy form.

Release your hound, Hector!

'Every ounce of knowledge your rotten skull has held on to, every scrap and cantrip of magick lore, I'm going to take from you, Vankaskan.'

Hector ran his scarred hand over his throat where the wound from his encounter on the White Isle still remained. Vankaskan's spirit continued to wail as the Vincent-vile devoured it, bite after bite, smoky black morsels of pure magick torn from the air. Hector's heart and head pulsed as the vile feasted on the dead Rat's secrets. He stared at the skull in his hands, Vankaskan's power rushing through his body, filling every corner of his dark and dangerous soul.

'You took your time, Lord Magister,' said Vanmorten as Hector arrived at the top of the staircase.

Behind the Ratlord, Vorhaas and Vex huddled, deep in conversation, looking every inch like a pair of villains plotting treason. Ringlin and Ibal rose from where they sat with their Ugri companions. The soldiers of the Rats had formed a circle around the eight Browncloaks, watching the Boarguard all the while.

'Well, you will bury your dead beneath the pits of hell, Lord Chancellor,' replied Hector, a note of derision in his voice.

Vanmorten covered the distance between them in a swift stride, his long robes swirling around him, dark as night. The Boarguard moved for their weapons, but the Vermirians' swords and halberds were already poised to strike.

'How dare you come here, thinking you can speak to *me* in such a way! What makes you think I won't . . .'

Vanmorten's speech was cut short as Hector raised his ungloved left hand to his face, placing his forefinger to his lips. 'Hush.'

The hand was unrecognizable, the flesh withered and clinging to the bones as if drained of all fluid. Fingers, palm and forearm were all black, as if burned by a raging fire, giving the limb a skeletal appearance. The necrotic flesh remained taut as the knuckles clicked against one another.

'Your hand . . .' said Vanmorten, shocked by the appearance of Hector's mummified limb. The Ratlord lifted his own disfigured fingers to his throat, running them over the scarred flesh of his neck.

Hector opened his palm and examined it, as if noticing the changed appearance for the first time. He turned it one way and then the other, as though it belonged to another person, alien to the rest of his body. The skin of his face was the opposite, drained of blood, white as a skull. A sickly sheen of sweat glistened across his features as he smiled at the stunned Ratlord.

Blackhand, whispered the Vincent-vile.

'My hand?' repeated Hector. 'Oh, my hand is strong, Lord Chancellor. I have your brother to thank for that.'

4
Crossroads

A crowd had gathered in Windfell's great hall, returning Hawklords from the length and breadth of Lyssia and beyond. Each stared at the rough stone wall behind the carved wooden throne, their faces etched with sorrow. Drew stood among them, watching with grim wonder. A pair of threadbare, tattered wings hung staked to the brickwork, metal spikes having held them in place for many miserable years. The skeletal frames now resembled a moth-eaten spiderweb of thin, white bones, the odd remaining feather still clinging to the rotten remains.

'Take them down,' said a choked Count Carsten.

One of the still-transformed Hawklords moved quickly, flying towards Baron Griffyn's severed wings. Reverently, he lifted the torn bones and feathers from the spikes, gently folding them close to his chest as he returned to the ground.

Thirty Falconthropes filled the hall, each one ready for battle. More were sure to follow. Drew had expected them all to look similar to one another, but he couldn't have been more wrong. The Hawklords came in all shapes and sizes, as different as Krieg, Taboo and the Behemoth were from each other: tall and rangy, short and wiry, heavy-set, slight, young, old, fit and out of shape. The tombwraiths had soared across the continent, seeking out the Hawklords wherever they hid, carrying Tor Raptor's screams to the four corners of Lyssia. Each had heard the call and answered.

As Griffyn's wings were taken away, the assembled Werelords looked to their most senior noblemen, Count Carsten and Baron Baum, the Eagles. Neither therian was as tall as Krieg or the Mammoth, but they were as imposing in their way, their muscular chests rippling beneath banded mail breastplates. The black-haired Carsten's broadsword remained sheathed in its scabbard, while the bald and bearded Baum leaned on his spear, the weapon fashioned from a deep red wood, filed and burned to a terrible point. Drew wondered if the spear was naturally that colour or whether it remained stained from the recent battle.

'Take the throne!' called one of the Hawklords from the rear of the hall. A chorus of cheers broke out as the Werelords raised weapon and voice in support.

'The brothers!'

'Our new Lords of Windfell!'

Carsten raised his hands to quieten the crowd while his brother smiled and shook his head.

'Our enemies might have taken Griffyn from us, before we

could be reunited, but the baron's bloodline lives on,' said Carsten.

'This throne is not ours to take,' added Baum, his voice deep and rich. He lifted his spear and pointed it over his shoulder symbolically.

'Lady Shah is in the custody of King Faisal in Azra. *She* is the rightful Lady of Windfell and it's our duty to return her to her father's throne.'

Nods and murmured agreements rumbled around the room, each Hawklord accepting the Eagles' words without question.

'How soon do we fly to her aid?' asked Red Rufus, his scrawny neck bobbing as he spoke. The scar that had been visible from the top of his head right down to his throat as a Werehawk was all the more livid in human form as it gouged through the left side of his face. He cut quite a different figure now from the fellow who'd wanted to kill Drew in the Tomb of the Hawklords.

Red Rufus continued. 'How long has the Jackal held her prisoner? Wergar should have killed him when we had the chance. The only good Omiri's a dead one.'

'It's not as simple as that, Red Rufus, as well you know,' said Carsten, turning and holding his hand towards Drew.

The Wolflord looked surprised when Carsten beckoned him, painfully aware he was a stranger among these people – they didn't know him from the next man. The doubts had returned. What did Drew really know? What could he say that might convince them to aid him? Baum nodded, encouraging Drew to approach. Krieg's firm hand pushed him forward, through the crowd, the Hawklords parting as he walked towards the dais. He climbed the steps, standing between the two Eagles and turning to face the assembled room.

Humans had joined therians in the chamber, those hardy souls who still lived in the Barebones having returned after the sight of the Hawklords coming home to roost. Drew looked over to his companions. Krieg nodded encouragingly while the Behemoth looked on impassively. Taboo bared her teeth, somewhere between a snarl and a smile.

'Faisal isn't the enemy,' Drew said at last turning to the assembled throng. 'Azra's surrounded by the Jackal's foes: Doglords to the north and Hayfa to the south. Between them they'll overrun Azra.'

'I fail to see why we should care about the demise of Faisal,' said Red Rufus. It was clear to Drew that the old falconthrope still distrusted him.

'Aye,' agreed another. 'Leave the Hounds and Hyenas to tear one another apart. They're savages.'

'The Azrans *aren't* savages. They're a proud people, not unlike yourselves.'

Red Rufus scoffed, but Drew continued.

'Baron Griffyn's last wish was that his people should fly to Faisal's aid. That's why Shah remains there, already lending her wits and wisdom to the Jackal's cause. I understand the ill feeling you have for one another – the war you fought on Wergar's behalf has left wounds that have festered over the years. But a new enemy's at the gate. The world is changed.'

'It's not so different,' said Red Rufus. 'I see we're still expected to follow a Wolf.'

Drew winced. The old Hawklord's attitude was belligerent but well-founded. *Away from their homes for fifteen years and my first request is that they join me in battle? I'd feel the same.*

'This is *everyone's* fight. The threat won't go away. You can't stay out of a battle that rages around you – the Catlords will come knocking. We *need* you. I was told the Hawklords were the bravest warriors to fight by the Wolf's side, and loyal to the last.'

'Loyal to old Wergar, young cub,' said a voice from the rear of the group.

Another voice chimed in. 'You expect us to swear fealty on account of the love we had for the dead Wolf?'

'We should fetch Shah!' cried a third Hawk. 'Get her out of the desert. Leave the Omiri to butcher themselves.'

Carsten and Baum watched and listened in silence, leaving the debating entirely to Drew.

It's my task to convince these men that they should join me, thought Drew. 'It's not as simple as leaving them to fight it out,' he said aloud. 'The Catlords are behind the civil war in Omir. Canan's Doglords aided the Bastians' attack on Highcliff, and now Prince Lucas returns the favour. The young Lion sits on the throne, his counsel coming from the Rat King and the Werepanthers, Onyx and Opal. So long as Lucas and his cronies rule, nobody is safe. They mean to take *everything*, to crush the uprising of the free people of the Seven Realms. The fighting in Westland and the Barebones, the battles in Omir – it's all one and the same. This is a war for Lyssia, and one that Bast is winning.'

Drew felt his chest rising as he spoke, his words honest and true. His blood was up and his self-belief was solid. Although Red Rufus was the voice of doubt among the Hawklords, many of the old therian's brothers seemed unconcerned by him. They nodded as Drew spoke, jaws set, eyes glinting with steely resolve as they saw the fight that lay ahead. If Drew had doubted the cause previously, that reservation had been vanquished.

'Believe me, the Jackal's our ally. The Cats are the constant throughout. The Dogs, the Hyenas, the Crows, the Rats are just adding their muscle and might to these enemies of the free people of Lyssia. Lucas might reign in Highcliff, but he's a puppet, a mouthpiece. It's his friends from across the sea who seek control over the Seven Realms. Onyx and Opal are the power behind the throne. If we help defend Azra, break the back of this assault from Canan and Hayfa, then we have Faisal's army behind us. Each battle we win, we shall gain fresh allies. It starts with Azra. First we drive them out of Omir, then the Barebones and Westland. We chase them back across the Lyssian Straits, all the way back to Bast.'

His voice had deepened now, his words coming out loud and heavy, bouncing off the walls of Windfell's great hall. Every man and therian watched intently, caught up in the Wolflord's passion.

'There are three other therians in this chamber who have joined me in the fight. None are Lyssian – each hails from a land far away. They fought me in the Scorian arena, and now they fight by my side: free therians, united against a common enemy. I trust each with my life.'

He looked at his three friends from the Furnace. Each of

them bowed back, as the assembled Hawklords stared reverently at them.

'These Werelords have travelled to a foreign land where they can expect little more than suspicious looks of fear and distrust. Their homelands have already been seized by the Catlords. They've seen first hand what Onyx is capable of. I would return with them to Bast, once the fight here is won, lend my life to their cause in return for their sacrifice. They've put their faith in me, and Brenn be my witness I won't let them down.'

Drew glanced at the skin of his curled fist, the flesh now grey as the Wolf fought to emerge. His eyes had yellowed over, and he could see the Hawklords nodding as one. Falconthropes clapped one another on the shoulder, punched their chests and raised their weapons.

'Join me,' growled Drew. 'Let's take the fight to the Beast of Bast.'

The great hall of Windfell, silent for so many years, thundered with the sound of swords beating against shields and falconthropes cheering.

The Hawklords had returned.

Two hours had passed since Drew's passionate speech in the great hall, and that time hadn't been wasted. Windfell's circular courtyard was a hive of activity as the Werehawks prepared for battle. Drew, Taboo, Krieg and the Behemoth had equipped themselves, replacing their battered gear and torn clothing with kit from the Hawklords' armoury. Drew had found a studded black leather breastplate, fashioned in the style of the Sturmish smiths, with buckles and clasps that allowed the armour to change shape as a therianthrope shifted. While there were steel breastplates and chain shirts that might provide stiffer defence against blade or bow, the leather felt right for Drew, more lightweight and less cumbersome. Besides which, the wide-eyed youth in Drew found himself grinning: it looked fabulously fearsome. He even found a woodland cloak that wasn't a million miles from the tattered old Greencloak he'd been gifted by Bergan and, snatching it up, he was ready to depart.

The Hawklords looked resplendent, armed and armoured, gathered and ready to take flight. News had spread quickly. The population of Windfell continued to swell with humans returning to the city. While the majority who'd left might never return, some had made new lives in nearby hamlets and settlements on the Barebones' slopes. With the sudden activity in the city above, they'd rushed home as if they'd heard Tor Raptor's screams themselves. Many now hurried around the halls of the mountain keep, helping their former lords make preparation for war.

In all, thirty-three Hawklords had returned, and thirty of them would fly to Omir. It wasn't the hundred Drew and the late Baron Griffyn had hoped for, but thirty falconthropes flying into battle was still a tremendous coup for the Wolf and his allies. Three would remain in the mountain city to prepare the people for what lay ahead; ensuring the last reminders of Skeer's reign were tossed from the parapets and Windfell was returned to its former glory.

The first 'wing' of Hawklords had already taken flight, ten

of them taking to the skies in the dim light of dusk. The second wing was now leaping skywards from the courtyard as they pursued their brethren into the clouds. Drew was the last of the therians from the Furnace to depart, Krieg, Taboo and the Behemoth having been taken off in the first two wings. Two Hawklords had been needed to carry the Weremammoth, each holding an arm as they lifted the giant aloft.

Drew stood apart from the remaining Hawklords, lost in his own thoughts while they made the final adjustments to their armour ahead of the journey. He unsheathed Moonbrand and stared at the dark leather that spiralled about the handle, the wrappings centuries old yet unfaded by time. The white stone pommel was polished smooth, its likeness to the moon it was named after unmissable. In the warm light of day, the blade was steel grey, unremarkable.

'What tales you could tell,' he whispered, imagining his ancestors' battles. An unending stream of questions ran through his head. *Will this sword help reunite me with my friends? With Hector, Whitley and Gretchen? How many lives have been taken by this blade? How many wars won? Can one good soul really make a difference? Just a shepherd boy from the Cold Coast?*

'If ever a fight was just,' he murmured.

The flapping of the Hawklords indicated that the final wing was taking flight. He slid Moonbrand back into its scabbard, before returning to the remaining falconthropes. Only three remained, and as he approached two of them suddenly took to the heavens.

And then there was one, thought Drew, striding up to the Hawklord who would fly him into the heart of Omir.

'Hang loose like a bag o' bones, you hear me?' said Red Rufus, running his thumbs around the collar of his golden breastplate. 'Limp as a dead man. That's what I need you to be.'

The old therian was shifting as he spoke, rusty-coloured feathers sprouting from his face as the yellow beak emerged. He straightened his bent frame as great red wings emerged through flaps of leather that ran down his armour's back. As old as Red Rufus was, he was in remarkable shape when in therian form, his legs transforming into those of a powerful, deadly raptor. The skin of his calves hardened, reminding Drew of the reptilian limbs of Ignus and Drake, while his feet split into four immense, long toes, ending in curling black talons. The big predator's eyes blinked as Rufus towered over the spellbound Wolflord.

'I'm carrying a precious cargo. I'd like to get you to the Jackal in one piece. Understand, boy?'

Drew nodded as Red Rufus shook his wings, ruffling the feathers. A shortbow hung from one hip and a quiver swung from the other.

'Ready, Wolf?'

Drew was about to answer when the clattering of a horse's hooves beyond the walls distracted him. It was swiftly followed by shouts from the men who remained in the keep. Drew made for the commotion as he saw a crowd gathering outside the gate.

'Where are you going? We need to be away – the last wing has already departed!' warned Red Rufus.

'A moment!' cried Drew, rushing off before the cantankerous old Hawklord could object further.

Directly outside the keep, the townsfolk had gathered around a horse, its rider slumped in the saddle. As Drew approached the man tumbled into the arms of the surrounding men and women. Some cried out when they noticed his cloak was dark with blood, broken arrow shafts protruding from his back.

Although he wore battered military clothes beneath the cloak, Drew reckoned he was much younger than himself. The youngster's face was ashen – a sheen of sweat glistening as his eyes fluttered. Drew counted four broken arrows in all, peppering his back and pinning his Greycloak to his torso. Recognizing the uniform instantly, Drew snatched his own waterskin from his hip. He bit the stopper off and held it to the boy's mouth. The boy drank greedily, spluttering on the liquid.

'Steady,' said Drew.

'I'm a healer, my lord. I can tend to those wounds,' said an old woman at Drew's shoulder, looking on with grave concern, but the Wolflord ignored her for the moment, pressing the injured Greycloak for answers.

'You're from Stormdale? A little young to be one of Manfred's men, aren't you?'

'His son,' said the boy, a bout of coughing racking his chest.

'What news?' asked one of the men nearby.

'I have family in Stormdale,' said another.

Drew raised his hand, calling for silence.

'Highwater's fallen. Stormdale's next. Villagers and farmers, women and children: surrounded,' spluttered the boy, his voice fading. 'No mercy. Crows and Rats. Kill us all . . .'

The crowd at Drew's back parted as Rufus stepped forward, flexing his wings and casting shadows over the townsfolk.

'Come, Wolf. You delay us. We need to go. We need to leave now.'

Drew looked at the young Stag, the boy's eyes closed, his head lolling heavy to one side. Drew lifted him carefully, cradling him, feeling the fever-heat rolling off him. He turned to the old woman.

'Lead the way,' he said, holding the boy close.

Rufus grabbed Drew by the shoulder, holding him fast. 'You're not listening, Wolf!'

Drew tugged himself free from Rufus's grip, glaring at him. 'We're not going to Omir.'

'Have you lost your mind, pup?'

'Not at all, old bird,' said Drew, his patience worn thin by the grumbling Hawklord. 'You and I fly to Stormdale.'

Epilogue
Man and Boy

No sooner had the lightning flashed than the thunder followed, tearing the sky apart above Moga. Ten ships blockaded the harbour, the Catlords' navy having chosen the Sturmish port as their base in the far north. Flags from Bast, Highcliff and the Cluster Isles flapped in the fierce wind, the rain threatening to tear them from the masts. The fleet had arrived straight after the *Maelstrom*'s departure, on the hunt for the remainder of the Wolf's Council. While others had followed the pirate ship, the remaining force had taken Moga for their own.

Three men crept along the harbour road, hugging the walls and rushing between buildings. Passage was slow on account of the size of one of them, the man twice as big as his two companions. To be found on the streets after the ninth bell had tolled was punishable by death: fully two dozen Sturmish pirates swung from the gallows that had been set up in the crowded marketplace, two or three hanging from each of the scaffolds. Arriving at the ruined warehouse on the northernmost end of the docks, the two smaller men took up lookout positions in the shadows that shrouded the splintered building, while the enormous one squeezed through the broken doorway. The storm crashed overhead as the rain hammered down, the inside of the building exposed to the elements through the ramshackle roof. The big man shook the water from his heavy black cloak, the jewellery that adorned his hands and wrists jangling as he advanced into the heart of the warehouse. Another man emerged from the shadows, a weaselly looking fellow with a tatty black beard and a cutlass in his hand.

'My lord,' he said, nodding humbly in the presence of the newcomer. The noble dismissed him with the wave of a fat, gem-laden hand.

'No time for pleasantries, Quigg. Where are they?'

The bearded pirate turned, leading the huge man deeper into the building. The floorboards groaned under the fat one's weight, threatening to splinter and carry them both into the harbour water below. The spluttering coughs of the young boy drew them through the shadows. The child sat on a barrel, a filthy old coat wrapped around him for warmth. He looked up as the two approached.

'Baron Bosa,' said the boy, jumping down from the barrel to bow dramatically before the fat man. Bosa rolled his eyes at the lad's show of etiquette, considering the dire circumstances.

'You know me, child?'

'I've heard plenty about you, your lordship, from my shipmates and my captain.'

'And where's your ship now?'

'Dunno, sir; she sailed off without us. They done him in, sir. Least they tried to.'

'How is it you didn't drown, boy? The Sturmish Sea could kill any man, yet you live?'

The boy shrugged.

'And you claim to have saved your captain's life?'

The boy supplied no answer, simply staring at Bosa with big brown eyes. The Whale of Moga turned to Quigg.

'Where is he?'

The black-bearded pirate pointed beyond the boy towards the dark recesses of the warehouse. The fat Whalelord strode past them, searching the shadows for his brother therianthrope. He found the man lying within a grounded rowboat, a tarpaulin laid across him as a makeshift blanket. His face was white, eyes red-rimmed as he stared up at Bosa. The Whale reached down and pulled the tarpaulin to one side, revealing the injured man's torso; the usually pristine white shirt was stained dark.

'I see you have visitors in Moga,' whispered the wounded sea captain, trying to smile through bloodied teeth. 'How long have they been lodging with you?'

'My dear, sweet Vega,' sighed the Whale, his voice thick with concern. 'What have they done to you?'

Acknowledgements

I need to say a few words of thanks to the elite team of guys and gals at Puffin HQ who have not only supported me while I wrote the Wereworld series, but also got the books into readers' hands. Clever birds, these Puffins.

Much gratitude to Francesca Dow, MD extraordinaire, and to publishing director Sarah Hughes – I should probably restrict thanks to 140 characters as she's fluent in Twitspeak! #cheekynorthernblighter

Huge thanks to Jayde Lynch, Julia Teece and Vanessa Godden who've had to endure my company – and obsession with Full Englishes – while we've toured schools and festivals the length and breadth of Britain.

Cheers to Samantha Mackintosh, Julia Bruce and Mary-Jane Wilkins in editing, for polishing my dirty lumps of coal into something that sparkled.

Thanks to Zosia Knopp and her amazing rights team, including Jessica Hargreaves, Camilla Borthwick, Joanna Lawrie, Susanne Evans and Jessica Adams. Thanking yous to Winsey Samuels in production, Brigid Nelson and the children's division sales team, Carl Rolfe and the Penguin sales reps, and *merci* to Rebecca Cooney in international sales.

Thank you to Kendra Levin, my US editor, for all her hard work and enthusiasm.

And they say you should never judge a book by its cover. While there's a great deal of truth to that adage, I have to say that a spiffy cover really does bring a book to life. Thanks to fab designer Patrick Knowles and ace artist Andrew Farley for helping to make Wereworld turn folks' heads. A special word of thanks has to go to Jacqui McDonough, Puffin's art director and the first person I ever reached out to many, many years ago when I was trying to get into publishing as an illustrator. When I say 'reached out', a more accurate description would be 'pestered for two years'. Whodathunk we'd finally get to work together after all that time, missus?

Last two thanks go to my left and right hands: my editor, Shannon Park, for believing in Wereworld from the get-go, and my wife, Emma, for spotting my shoddy grammar and enlightening me in the process. Cheers, m'dears!

Thank you all.

It all started with a Scarecrow.

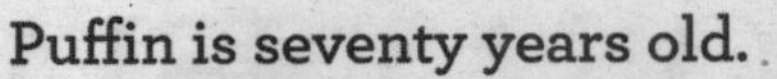

Puffin is seventy years old.

Sounds ancient, doesn't it? But Puffin has never been so lively. We're always on the lookout for the next big idea, which is how it began all those years ago.

Penguin Books was a big idea from the mind of a man called Allen Lane, who in 1935 invented the quality paperback and changed the world. **And from great Penguins, great Puffins grew, changing the face of children's books forever.**

The first four Puffin Picture Books were hatched in 1940 and the first Puffin story book featured a man with broomstick arms called Worzel Gummidge. In 1967 Kaye Webb, Puffin Editor, started the Puffin Club, promising to **'make children into readers'**. She kept that promise and over 200,000 children became devoted Puffineers through their quarterly instalments of *Puffin Post*, which is now back for a new generation.

Many years from now, we hope you'll look back and remember Puffin with a smile. **No matter what your age or what you're into, there's a Puffin for everyone.** The possibilities are endless, but one thing is for sure: whether it's a picture book or a paperback, a sticker book or a hardback, **if it's got that little Puffin on it – it's bound to be good.**

LESLEY THOMSON

The Detective's Secret

First published in the UK in 2015 by Head of Zeus Ltd.

This paperback edition first published in the UK in 2015 by Head of Zeus Ltd.

9 7 5 3 1 2 4 6 8

A catalogue record for this book is available from the British Library.

Paperback ISBN 9781781857717
Ebook ISBN 9781781857694

Printed in the UK by Clays Ltd, St Ives Plc

MIX
Paper from responsible sources
FSC® C018072

Head of Zeus Ltd
Clerkenwell House
45-47 Clerkenwell Green
London EC1R 0HT

WWW.HEADOFZEUS.COM

grew u[illegible] el, *A Kind of Vanish*[illegible] Prize in 2010. Her se[illegible] *Daughter,* was publis[illegible] 300,000 copies.

The Detective's Secret

'Lesley Thomson is a class above.'

IAN RANKIN

'A terrific crime novel. You are left with a feeling of utter satisfaction.'

ELLY GRIFFITHS

'This book has a clever mystery plot – but its excellence is in the characters, all credible and memorable, and in its setting in a real West London street, exactly described.'

LITERARY REVIEW

'A gripping, haunting novel about loss and reconciliation.'

SUNDAY TIMES

'This emotionally charged thriller grips from the first paragraph, and a nail-biting level of [illegible]'

Also

Seven

A Ki

The D

T

The De

The Runaway (A Detective's Daughter Short S

Stare. It is the way to educate your eye, and more.

Stare, pry, listen, eavesdrop. Die knowing something. You are not here long.

From *Walker Evans at Work*, with an essay by Jerry L. Thompson

413 The Thames is a tunnel.

414 The river is a tunnel, it's civil infrastructure.

415 The river is a tunnel with an uncountable number of entrances.

416 When you go into the river you discover a new entrance – and in yourself you uncover an exit, an unseen exit, your exit. (You brought it with you.)

From *Another Water: The River Thames for Example*
by Roni Horn

For the Nelson sisters who have had a profound influence on my life: May Walker, June Goodwin and Agnes Wheeler.

And for Mel with my love.

Reckitt Road
Quick Road
Fraser Street
Devonshire Road
Wood Street
Wilton Avenue
Ashbourne Grove
Balfern Grove
Cornwall Grove
Chiswick Lane
Bennett Street
Hogarth Lane
Short Rd
Paxton Road
Netheravon Road S
Chiswick Mall
Chiswick Eyot
Church Street
Palmyra Tower
The Garden of the Dead
Unit HQ
Chiswick House Grounds
Burlington Lane
Corney Road Cemetery
Jackie & Graham's house
Nicola's house
Grantham Road
Lonsdale Road
B350
Ravenscourt Park
Hamlet Gardens
Stamford Brook
King Street
A315
Cleveland Avenue
Chiswick High Road
Lucie's house
Justin's house
St Peter's Grove
Theresa Road
St Peter's Road
Black Lion Lane
St Peter's Church
A4
Upper Mall
The Ram
The Bell Steps
River Thames
Netheravon Road
British Grove
St Peter's Square
Beverley Road
Netheravon Road S
Chiswick Mall
Chiswick Eyot

Prologue

October 1987

Clouds streamed across the sky. Street lights obliterated the stars; the moon wouldn't rise until midnight, four hours away. A fierce wind rattled reed beds on Chiswick Eyot and tore through the undergrowth. Cross-currents on the river made rib-cage patterns; patches of stillness in the black water resembled corpses.

The Thames was rising, a deadly confluence of tide and turbulence. Miniature waves broke across Chiswick Mall; water welled in gutters, covering kerbstones and lapping at the steps of St Nicholas' church. A storm was gathering force.

At night Chiswick Mall was outside time. Misty yellow light surrounding iron lamp standards might be gas lit, cars were carriages on cobblestones. On the foreshore of the Thames, the clank-clank of a barge's mooring chain against the embankment wall beat the passing of no time at all.

A shape reflected in the river was dashed by a squall; it resolved into a tower. Utilitarian, a cylindrical tank supported by stanchions, the water tower was built in the Second World War to protect riverside wharfs and factories from fires. Long in disuse, the wharfs demolished, the tank was empty, the pipes stripped out. Fifty metres high, it stood taller than the brewery and the church spire and dominated the west London skyline. Against streaming clouds and tossed boughs, the tower, designed to withstand bombs and tensile stresses, seemed as if forever falling.

A cage attached to one supporting column housed five

stairways connected by a platform; the last arrived at a narrow metal walkway that gave access to the tower. Violent gusts harassed the grille, testing steel rivets.

A man hurried through the church gates, skirting the water; he ducked into an alley between the brewery buildings and struggled up the staircases into the tower, head bowed against the wind. Minutes later, a woman emerged from the subway by the Hogarth roundabout and went into the alley. Checking about her, she pulled on the cage door and, both hands on the guard rail, began an awkward ascent.

'I hate this place.' Her voice rang in the concrete tank.

He watched as she zipped up her slacks, smacking at dirt although there was none; he kept it clean. Grimacing, she eased on brown leather faux-Victorian boots, doing up the laces with slick-snapping efficiency.

'You wanted secrecy.' The man pulled on underpants, his nakedness absurd as their intimacy of the afternoon ebbed. Her boots had heels. He had advised flat shoes for safety, but was glad she had ignored him. She was his fantasy woman.

He had put himself out to get the key from the engineer. The man had kept it after the developers went bust – as ineffectual revenge for non-payment – but there was no point in telling her of this effort: it would not convince her to leave her husband.

'Come and be with me.'

She had insisted that they leave no spending trail. No hotels, no meals out. No risk of meeting anyone they knew or being remembered by strangers. She had admitted that nylon sleeping bags on the tank floor, drinking wine from the bottle and feeding each other wedges of Brie on bite-size water biscuits spiced up the sex. Strangely there was no handle on the inside: he propped open the thick metal door with a brick and, once she was inside, he locked what he called the 'front door' after her. She'd surprised him by saying that the danger of being locked in made her feel alive.

'You'd feel alive all the time with me.'

She knew that, she had told him.

'The apartment has a view of the sea.' He had told her he would take a year's lease. Things had changed, she'd said as soon as she arrived. It had spoiled his performance.

'Another bloody excuse!' He shouldn't have said that.

He buttoned his shirt, saw he'd missed a button and started again. She was pouting and air-kissing into her compact mirror. Already she had 'gone', planning the kids' meal, back to her life that was death. The knickers he had bought her lay discarded beside the used condom – just the one this time. Last time she had agreed to leave; today she said her family needed her.

'I need you.'

'The flat does sound beautiful.' She appeased him, shrugging into her coat.

'Then leave!' He always tried to be everything her husband was not. Mr Perfect. He'd once let her know the other girls didn't need persuading. She knew there were no other girls.

She smoothed her skirt over her stomach and he was aroused all over again.

'You look lovely.'

'That wind nearly blew me off my feet,' she said again as if she hadn't heard him. 'There's a storm getting up.'

'It's not all that's "getting up"!'

She came over, put a hand on his crotch and whispered, 'Next week.' She didn't usually do this when she was about to go; he dared to hope it meant something good.

'I can't hear any wind,' he said. 'It's nothing.'

'You told me this place is soundproofed!' She looked about her as if she'd just arrived. 'It's like a prison cell.'

'Sea view versus a mauso-bloody-leum!' he snarled. Usually he toned down his accent.

'In my heart I'm yours, you know that.' An off-the-shelf response.

It frightened him that he could hate her. He saw why people killed their lovers. If she were dead, she would stay.

He tensed his jaw. 'Do you have sex with him?'

She was rootling in her handbag. She squirted perfume on her wrists – not for him, but to expunge him.

'You promised to leave.'

'You'd be horrified if I turned up with two kids in tow!'

He tortured himself with a vision of her with a leg over the blubbery husband, letting him pump away inside her. In his dreams there were no kids in tow.

'Bring the girl. Let him have the boy.' Unlike the husband, he played fair.

She laughed and looped her bag over her chest as he advised, for safety.

'I'm leaving on Saturday.' His palms tingled at the decision made there and then.

'You said we had a month.' As he had hoped, she was upset.

'I'll be at the station at three on Saturday. If you're not there, I'm going.'

'It's too soon.' She kicked the brick aside and stepped on to the spiral staircase.

'It's always "too soon".' In her heels he wanted her again.

'I can't just leave.'

Not a 'no'. His venom evaporated. 'Be careful in those boots, that wind is strong.' Too late he recalled he'd underplayed the wind.

'I climb mountains in these.'

Not with me.

He followed her down the staircase and stopped her in the lobby by the front door.

'Promise me you'll give it some thought,' he said, but really he wanted her to give it *no* thought, just to leave. 'I'll be there next Saturday at Stamford Brook. At three. You won't regret it!'

'Darling, don't—'

He cut across her: 'You owe it to yourself. We only have one life – let's make the most of it! When we're settled, we can get the kid. One step at a time. Your life now is like living in a coffin, you said so yourself!'

He went towards her, but she blew a kiss and turned away. The bottom door shrieked when she opened it. He watched until she reached the caged staircase, and then he returned to their room.

Without her the magic had gone; it was a just cold concrete tank. He stuffed everything into the holdall, anxious to follow her, to see her when she wasn't with him. She had left him the Brie, not out of generosity, but because she wouldn't want to explain how come she had it.

Footsteps. She was coming back. He grew excited and regretted packing up the sleeping bags. 'Hon, you came back. I knew you would!'

There was a deafening report.

The tank door had shut, he stared disbelieving at the grey metal. Beware the jokes of those with no sense of humour. The lack of handle wasn't sexy now. She was on the other side of the double cladding, daring him to lose his nerve.

'Good game!' His temples thudded from the alcohol and he needed a pee. This was her revenge for his ultimatum. 'Joke over!'

Wind fluted through vents near the ceiling – she was right about the storm. Daylight no longer drifted in; the street lights didn't reach so high. Bloody stupid to have said leave the boy, he liked him. The walls emanated chill.

'He's a good kid, I'll treat him like my own son.' His voice bounced off the concrete.

There was a distant vibration – the bottom door slamming. There was no keyhole this side; his key was useless.

'Maddie!'

In the dark, the man wondered if, after all, it was not a joke.

One

Monday, 16 September 2013

Forty-three minutes past eleven. Dead on time, Jack brought his train to a stop at Ealing Broadway Underground station. Late-night passengers decanted and straggled up the stairs to the street. As usual he had seven minutes and thirty seconds before his journey to Barking. He would stable the train at the Earl's Court depot and then the night was his.

Ealing Broadway was the end of the line. On autopilot, Jack strolled up the platform to what, with the 'turn around', was the front of the train, glancing into the carriages. There was one woman in the second car. She was leafing through a *Metro* and looked up as he came alongside her. He thought he saw a flicker of fear pass across her face and quickened his pace. At this time of night a woman travelling alone might feel vulnerable; Jack hoped she would see his uniform and know he was a driver and not a passenger who could threaten her.

He opened the front cab door. Being a driver he swapped between different, but identical cabs at each end of the train during the course of a day or night. Travelling up and down the District line, he was never in one place for long: he thrived on the mix of stability and change. As the proprietor of a cleaning company, Stella restored stability in different locations. Pleased by this tenuous link between their working lives, Jack considered texting her. He put his hand in the fleece pocket of his uniform for his phone. But Stella called a spade a spade. His whimsy frustrated her and at this time of night would worry her. When Stella worried about Jack, she allocated him cleaning jobs – he worked part-time for her cleaning company, Clean Slate. Thinking of Stella made him wistful because since her mother had gone on holiday to Australia, she hadn't been herself. The change was fractional: a pause before she replied, an arrangement misremembered, a minute late to meet him because she'd walked the dog. Stella cared about her mum more than she let on.

Her father too. Two years after his death she still cleaned his house, ate supper there and did her emails at his computer with no sign of selling the place. Jack had once asked her if she was maintaining it for her father's ghost. She had retorted that she was waiting for the housing market to pick up. But prices were rising and even next to the Great West Road, the end of terrace in Hammersmith would fetch a small fortune. He dismissed the lurking notion that it was not a ghost Stella was waiting for, but a real live man. When Stella ended a relationship – eventually she always did – the dumped partner ceased to exist. Except her last man, the one who she thought a David Bowie lookalike, had left her with a dog; undeniable proof he had existed for her once.

He felt something in his pocket and fumbling under his phone pulled out a folded slip of paper.

To Let.

Apartment in Water Tower.

A cosy home with detailed views.

If you crave silence and a bird's eye view – Jack squinted at the type in the watery lamplight – *then Palmyra Tower is your home. Guardian wanted for Grade 1 listed Water Tower. You will sign a year-long contract with no breaks and be available to take up residence as soon as your application is accepted.*

It was the flier he had found lying on the doormat when he left the house that morning. He had shoved it in his jacket pocket and, intent on getting to work, had thought no more about it. Reading it now, Jack was intrigued by the imperative *you will.* He touched his face to stop an involuntary twitch and, shivering, zipped up his fleece. The cheap pink paper didn't compete with Clean Slate's glossy brochure.

The style was a marketing ploy that Stella would reject as too obvious an attempt to be different. However the paper did carry an unnerving air of authority, so in that sense it had worked.

Beneath the text was a fuzzy photograph of the tower. It was functional, effectively a tank on stilts; a caged fire escape-like structure attached to one column gave access to it. It stood metres from Chiswick Eyot, an island in the Thames. As a boy, Jack had once tried to climb it, but couldn't open the cage. The steep aluminium staircases and narrow treads were not for the vertiginous.

There was no phone number on the flier. At last he found an email address in tiny lettering: *info@palmyra-tower.co.uk*. Regardless of the amateur appearance, Jack guessed there would be a deluge of responses. For many, the tower would be the dream home. He scrunched up the flier and stuffed it back in his pocket. Leaning back on the cab door, Jack gazed up at the sky.

This section of the District line was above ground. The moon was a waning crescent in the sign of Leo. Stella was a Leo, as his mother had been. Two women with attitude, courageous and strong-willed. Jack's mother had died when he was a boy so what he didn't know about her he made up; this meant she was his particular brand of perfection.

A plane cut below the moon on its descent into Heathrow, the rumble of its engine carrying on the night breeze. Jack thought of the moon as his friend; it accompanied him on his walks. Or it had until he promised Stella to 'stop all that', although he doubted she understood what 'all that' was. The second hand on his watch ticked towards three minutes to twelve.

As soon as he stepped into the cab, Jack had a premonition of what would happen when he turned the key – it had happened here before. The motor whirred, but didn't start. His train was going nowhere.

He reported the train out of service, activated the door at the rear of his cab and went down the aisle of the cars ushering passengers off: seven altogether. Vaguely he noticed that the woman he had seen earlier wasn't among them. Back on the platform Jack felt a pricking at his temples: like last time, this breakdown was a sign. Like all signs, its meaning had yet to reveal itself.

The coffee stand was shut; a metal box covered with stars, it might be a magic trick about to emit a cloud of doves and many wished-for things. The moon had gone behind a cloud and the temperature had dropped. Jack picked up an empty coffee cup from the platform and tossed it into a litter bin two metres away. *Bull's eye.* The tracks hummed. He returned to the top end of the platform and, as the train approached, tipped a hand to the driver. His greeting wasn't returned. When the train was stationary, he peered into the empty cab at the rear.

With no train, he had no set number. Set numbers were the means of identifying a train and allocating it to a driver, but to Jack the set number was a sign. This train's number was 126. The last time this happened, his set number was 236 and led him to Stella.

Jack was tempted to rush from the station to evade whatever fate 126 decreed.

Running away is no escape if you don't know which direction is 'away'.

Jack rubbed his temples to eradicate the voice. Recently it came unbidden, like the voices of a high fever, and uttered dictums like a seer. It didn't feel his own. He looked up and saw the driver walking the length of the train towards him.

'All right?' Jack nodded.

'You're Jack.' The man had acne and looked no more than sixteen. 'They said you'd be here.' He offered no clue as to what he thought about this.

'Yes.' Jack agreed.

'I wanted you as my trainer, but you were fully booked,' the driver continued in a querulous tone.

'Ah.' Jack smiled. 'No matter, we're all the same.' Not true. He knew he was the best trainer, as he knew, although Stella never told him, that he was her best cleaner. Fact. Jack climbed into the cab after the driver. The doors swished shut.

The driver gripped the handle, his every nerve directed to his task. This wasn't the first time Jack had witnessed the terror of a novice driver. For him, responsibility for hundreds of passengers had come naturally when he had settled into the seat for the first time. It had felt right. But Jack wasn't like others.

Hands resting on thighs, Jack gazed out at bunched cables and silver rails converging and parting as the train left the station and increased speed.

On Google Street View, Jack could travel with the roll and click of a mouse. As if operating it now, he zoomed in on Stamford Brook station and focused on the strip of platform a hundred metres away. Yet again he was reminded of the toy station he had bought as a boy. Grey and brown plastic with a detachable ticket office and a couple of sweet-vending machines, added for free because the toyshop man had felt sorry for him.

Jack's train slowed as it entered Stamford Brook station. There was one man on the westbound platform: he would have a wait: the information board was blank. Trains would be diverted to Richmond because of his dead train at Ealing Broadway. He felt a flash of poignancy that he had abandoned it to be shunted without him to the Acton depot. His concern for inanimate things frustrated Stella.

Jack's attention was taken by the headlights of a Heathrow-bound Piccadilly train lighting up the rails ahead. After Hammersmith, it wouldn't stop until Turnham Green.

Nervous of overshooting the platform, his driver was applying the brake too soon. The last time Jack's train had broken down at Ealing Broadway, he had been sitting in the cab of a novice driver. Everything about this man was the same as the other; both moved their lips as if silently talking. The Piccadilly train was nearly on them – its headlights flooded the cab. He braced himself for the slipstream after it passed his train.

Jack glanced again at the platform for Richmond: still no train on the board. No need to hurry, but the man on the platform *was* hurrying. The wheels of the oncoming Piccadilly line train clackety-clacked closer. A tinny announcement came through the platform speakers: 'Stand well away from the edge of platform two. The next train is not scheduled to stop at this station.'

Five metres to go until the end of their platform. Jack's sense of déjà vu was oppressive, as if the last time had been a rehearsal for tonight.

'Take it right up,' he said softly, using the same phrase as last time. 'Get your passengers off. We don't want them pitching on to the line.' The man shoved the handle forward. Jack smelled his fear. 'Keep connection with the lever, coax it. The engine is you and you are the engine.' Something was wrong.

All stories are the same.

Jack banished the unwanted voice and saw the man on the platform lit by the headlamps of the Piccadilly train. The man gave a backward glance and abruptly broke into a run along the platform. Did he think the Piccadilly line train would stop? He was looking at Jack – not a glance, a proper look as if trying to express something. Jack had seen the expression before. Then the man was in mid-air above the tracks, caught in the glare of light as the Piccadilly line train thundered into the station. The man's body hit the windscreen and rolled under the cab. All was over in a second. Carriages jolted along and blocked Jack's view. Both trains halted. Jack looked at his watch. Six minutes past twelve: *126*.

A haunting wail carried across the station. The Piccadilly driver was sounding the whistle for staff to assist trackside. The bleak marking of a life extinguished.

Jack's driver was a waxwork, his hand frozen over the controls. He had berthed their train perfectly, seemingly unaware of what was happening metres to his right.

Later, at the inquest, Jack found that his driver had indeed seen nothing. Only Jack and the Piccadilly line driver, a man called Darryl Clark, had witnessed the incident. The few District line passengers had been asleep or plugged into headphones in a private world and although the other train was packed, it was impossible for anyone to have seen the man go under the front of the cab.

'What's your name?' Jack touched the man's arm, intending to ground him.

'Alfred Peter Butler,' he replied as if reporting for duty.

'You did well, Alfred. We'll stop here, you need a break and I think they might need some help here.' Accompanying Alfred Peter Butler through the carriages, for the second time in an hour, Jack informed passengers that a train was out of service.

Like Stella, Jack was comfortable with emergencies, everyone acting according to their role. While the tannoy announced delays, he and his driver checked seats and gangways for abandoned possessions. In the past he had found wallets, handbags, a tatty London street atlas that he had been allowed to keep, even a Springer spaniel lashed to a pole by its lead.

Alfred Peter Butler escorted their little troop down the stairs and across the station concourse, Jack bringing up the rear. To their right, Piccadilly line passengers were streaming down the westbound staircase, there was the buzz of muted exchange, word had got around.

It was a 'One Under'.

Jack Harmon dubbed himself a *flâneur*; he walked the night-time streets of London, observing others unobserved. Unlike a *flâneur* he cared about those he watched. Courting mortality, feeling the imminence of death, he hunted out those with darkness in their souls and minds like his own. Jack entered the homes of what he dubbed his 'True Hosts', those who had killed or would kill if he didn't stop them.

Jack was quite aware that he sought a re-enactment of the day his mother had died, a day that for him, as for many, was when his world stopped. As when a film is watched again and again in the vain hope that the next time the victim won't die. He drove in the tunnels of the London Underground to find his way back to *before*.

Affecting nonchalance, Jack strolled across the station, singing softly:

'Humpty Dumpty sat on a wall,
Humpty Dumpty had a great fall.'

His hair blown back from his face by a cold night breeze, Jack guided passengers through the gap in the concertinaed gate to the street. Even though it was after midnight, traffic on Goldhawk Road was nose to tail, slowing for those filing over the zebra crossing. Someone was watching Jack from the top deck of a 237 bus; he supposed it was a man – a baseball cap was pulled low over the eyes. The bus moved towards King Street and the reflection of the blue station fascia wiped the figure out.

In ten years of driving a train, Jack hadn't had a suicide. Some drivers had it twice, while others went their whole working lives without a person jumping in front of their cab. Jack could not shake the conviction that tonight's incident was the culmination of many signs.

The station office reeked of sour sweat. Alfred Peter Butler was huddled in a corner nursing a mug of tea, staring at his feet. The other driver was texting on a BlackBerry, thumbs skimming the tiny keys. Someone on the phone confirmed that the 'customer' was dead. Jack refused tea. He kept to himself that he felt nothing. He told himself that since his mum died, he had nothing left to feel. Jack fastened the grille and ran up the stairs.

There was no one on the platform where the man had been. Lights from the train cast bleak stripes of light across the tarmac. Jack could feel the dead man's presence in the deserted station.

Staff had rigged up lighting gear for the paramedics, due any minute. Confident that the train driver had dropped circuit breakers to cut the electricity, Jack vaulted on to the rails and crunched over the ballast. Sharp stones jabbing him, he peered beneath the train's underbelly.

A splash of red. A hand curled over the live rail. The man wore a wedding ring; the thick gold band spoke of status, hopefully of love.

'Wake up,' Jack had said to his mummy.

He leant in and touched the man's ring finger. It was warmer than his own and still pliant.

'I will save you,' he had told his mummy.

Blood was soaking the front of the man's shirt. Globules of blood seeped into the ballast. Jack trembled; his teeth began to chatter. The man's eyes – hazel flecked with green, the pupils dilated – fixed Jack with the impassive gaze of the dead.

Eyes are like fingerprints, they don't alter with age.

'I knew that!' Jack found himself retorting out loud. He clambered out from under the train and hauled himself on to the platform. A woman in paramedic green was fumbling with a body bag. He stayed to see the man zipped into the bag and laid on to the stretcher. He accompanied the crew back down to the ambulance.

'Go well.' Jack formed the words silently, touching his cheek to stay a tic that happened at certain times. He watched the ambulance turn on to King Street, heading for Charing Cross Hospital's mortuary. No blue light required.

In his statement about the incident, Jack didn't put that, before he died, the man with the ring had looked at him. It wasn't pertinent.

His shift declared over, he strolled down to King Street and into St Peter's Square as the church clock struck a quarter to one.

The set number was 126. The man died at six minutes past twelve. From the moment he had stopped at Ealing Broadway, his every action and interchange was a sign. For Jack, death was a beginning, it was a sign that something else would happen.

Eyes are like fingerprints, they don't alter with age. The voice got there first. Jack had seen the man before.

With no True Host to watch, tonight Jack went back to his own house. The building was dark; he never left a light on. A wind had got up – forecasters warned of a hurricane-force storm coming

– it battered the panes and shook casements swollen from the rain.

His door knocker was a short-eared owl fashioned from brass tarnished with age. Her burnished feathers flickered when she puffed up in greeting. Jack sang:

'All the king's horses,
And all the king's men,
Couldn't put Humpty together again.'

Two

Saturday, 19 October 2013

'He left me!'

Stella was rubbing at an oily stain on a hearth tile with a dash of detergent on a damp cloth. The stain was lifting. The voice startled her; she thought her client had gone out.

'No warning.' Mrs Carr put her palms to her cheeks in a pose of desperation.

Jackie had briefed Stella that Mr Carr had walked out on his wife in September, but from how she was behaving now, Stella thought that it was as if he had abandoned her that day.

'I'm sorry.' Stella avoided commenting on clients' lives. Many would lay out their problems as if she could wipe them away as she could any stain. Jackie counselled that listening was integral to the job, but Stella was unwilling to put this in the staff manual: it invariably led to leaving a job not completed, which triggered a complaint. Jack had the right balance; he provided emotional support and did the cleaning within the allotted time. But Jack wasn't like other people.

'You don't expect someone you love to lie. You miss tiny signs. Hesitation when you suggest meeting, and when you arrive they end a call without saying "goodbye" and pass it off as a sales call or wrong number.' She did a smoothing motion with her hands as if rubbing in moisturizer. 'Blood is thicker than water, he said, then he tells lies about my family.'

'Ah.' Stella wanted to get on with scrubbing the tiles and washing the skirting. Jack was always seeing signs, tiny or not. The best advice she had about relationships was to avoid them. Blood was thicker than water and she was tempted to suggest it was best to start on a stain with water rather than use hydrogen peroxide, which could bleach the colour out of a carpet.

When she gave Stella the job sheet, Jackie had warned, 'It's a complete tip, dirty and neglected.' Often such scenarios were prompted by a friend or relative calling Clean Slate to halt the slide into chaos. But Mrs Carr herself had rung, which, Jackie and Stella agreed, hinted she would be co-operative, likely to pay promptly and let them get on with the job. Wrong, it seemed. However, she had been keen to get the job done, which included working on Saturday mornings.

Stella liked 'cleaning sites' where she could make a radical difference, but because of the estranged husband, she had judged this was one for Jack.

'He'll need to use the Planet vacuum. He'll like that, he thinks it's like a steam engine.' Jack was like a magpie around the polished chrome casing of the cleaner.

'He got himself one for Christmas – isn't that typical of our Jack!' Jackie had laughed.

As it turned out, Jack was doing day shifts for the Underground, so it was Stella who, fifteen minutes earlier, had parked her van in Perrers Road, a modest street of flat-fronted terraced houses close to Hammersmith Broadway. The little house was less dirty than Mrs Carr had described. It smelled of long-ago-cooked meals and fusty upholstery, but the Planet vacuum wouldn't be needed. Stella applied their basic cleaning package. The biggest issue was mess.

'I trusted him!' Mrs Carr sagged on to a sofa arm, the only clear surface. Piles of clothes, CDs and DVDs, shoes and electrical gadgets, an iPod, a couple of phone chargers, portable disc drives and a tangle of cables were scattered on the furniture, on the floor.

'It might help to move?'

'Why should I? There's no such thing as love. Water under the bridge now. I can't turn the clock back.'

Mrs Carr spoke as if she had physically tried to. Stella's gaze wandered to a clock on the wall, a replica of an old-fashioned train-station clock. When she left here she had to walk Stanley before going to her mum's flat and watering her plants. Over the last weeks she had got into the habit of dropping in on her way to Terry's. This would be the last time; her mum was due back tonight.

'He said we need "space" and bolted.'

Jackie said Stella did the leaving to avoid finding out what it was like to be left. Stella resisted pointing out that David being detained at Her Majesty's pleasure, where pet dogs were not allowed, was hardly her leaving him. It was difficult to miss that Mrs Carr, pale with aquiline features and dark brown eyes, was beautiful. Stella had liked David because he wanted deep cleaning and looked like David Bowie.

'Please take all this away.' Mrs Carr wagged a finger at Stella. 'Your company promises a fresh start. I want one of those.' She did a grand sweep with her hand and left the room. Stella heard the front door shut.

She went to the window. Mrs Carr was heading off down the street, shrugging into a padded jacket.

Happy to be finally alone, Stella filled six bin bags with all the stuff in the sitting room. This took longer than she expected because she opted to separate heaps of junk mail, newspapers and sweet wrappers from the clothes and electrical equipment which it seemed a shame to throw out. She wouldn't take her at her word. Jilted clients were apt to change their minds later and accuse Clean Slate staff of stealing.

Stella didn't consider it her business to tidy, unless restoring objects to places and positions designated by the client. She did arrange gilt silver candlesticks symmetrically on the mantelpiece and position a framed photograph of a man and a woman she guessed were Mrs Carr's parents – the woman looked like Mrs Carr – at one end, which, she hoped, would form a point of tidiness for Mrs Carr to model elsewhere in the room.

Mr Carr must have an extensive wardrobe because the clothes he had left would constitute many a man's entire wardrobe. He had favoured military-style clothes: camouflage jackets and trousers – for the desert as well as dense woodland. Sturdy walking boots, Dr Martens shoes. She rolled up a canvas belt with compartments for bullets. Into another bag went a pair of chinos, a selection of lambswool sweaters branded with the Stromberg logo and some polo shirts. Stella counselled against judging clients but, folding Ben Sherman shirts and Calvin Klein jeans into the bag, could not help constructing an identikit of the unfaithful husband. He was chisel-cheeked, cleft-chinned, with an army-style short back and sides, his looks less remarkable than Mrs Carr's. Several of Stella's clients were former soldiers; she worked contentedly alongside them, keeping their 'billets' tidy. No, none of them would leave their kit behind.

Not her business.

She hefted the bags of newspapers out to the van and lined up the bags of clothes in the hall to await Mrs Carr's final decision.

Someone was watching her. After Terry Darnell's death Stella had got the impression that her father was there when she was in his house. This had faded after she and Jack solved the Blue Folder case. Jack said they had laid his ghost. Stella said that it was because probate was completed. Terry couldn't be haunting her here.

She turned to the front door and stifled a yell. Mrs Carr stood perfectly still, staring not at Stella, but through her. She was so white that had Stella believed in ghosts she would have thought she was seeing one.

'I didn't hear you come back,' Stella said pointlessly.

'I asked you to take all that away.'

'I wondered, as it's all in good condition, whether you meant to give it back to your husband, if he could collect it, or perhaps a charity, a hospice or...' She trailed off. *Do what the client asks. Don't question anything.* This was why she allocated these jobs to Jack.

'I asked you to take it away,' Mrs Carr repeated.

Stella stowed everything in the van, pushing on the back door to close it. She returned to the house to confirm that the next shift was wanted as arranged, guessing it unlikely. Mrs Carr wasn't downstairs. Stella called up: 'See you on Monday, Mrs Carr.' The use of 'Mrs' seemed tactless, but she didn't know her first name and, besides, they weren't on those terms.

No reply. Stella ventured up three stairs and called again. Nothing. She gave up and banged the front door shut to signal her exit. She would warn Jackie to expect an email cancelling the contract.

In the van, she lingered over the job sheet to give the woman a chance to sack her in person. The upstairs blinds were down. The house gave no sign of life.

Passing Hammersmith's Metropolitan station, Stella pressed the button on her steering wheel. An electronic voice boomed through the car:

'*Name please.*'

'Jack Mob.'

'*Dialling.*'

'This is Jack, who are you? Tell me after the beep.'

Stella cut the line. The day could only get better.

Three

May 1985

The high garden wall cast a shadow over the single-storey prefab, a crude addition to the Victorian estate. The kitchens were built to cater for increased demand when pupil numbers reached their optimum in the 1950s. Tresses of ivy disguised much of the shingle cladding and were an aesthetic link to the mansion featured on the school brochure. Steam drifted from open window flaps and misted panes; the cooks inside might have been phantoms but for clattering dishes and pans and raucous chat. The afternoon air hung heavy with the smell of institutional meals, past and present: boiled vegetables, suet and sallow meat.

A diminutive boy, pale and thin, lingered at the corner of the building, gripping the drainpipe as if he would float away should he let go.

Simon had expected to find Justin sitting on the steps surrounded by the cooks in their white caps. The fierce lady who had told Simon to eat his cabbage would be mussing Justin's hair – they fussed over him like a prized pet. The kitchens were out of bounds. But Justin was not there. Simon had lost him again.

In the last months, one event had cheered Simon. Justin had arrived at the school.

Simon had been told to 'show Justin the ropes'. Proud to initiate him into the routine, he was dismayed when the new boy refused to do what Simon told him to. Simon had understood that abiding by the rules and working hard would endear him to the teachers and the other boys. But whatever he did or did not do, Simon was disliked. In a culture where physical perfection and prowess were valued, the fact that the first two joints on the middle finger of his left hand were missing, that he was clumsy and that he was too clever for his teachers assured his unpopularity. When Miss Thoroughgood had told him to look after the new boy, Simon had been happy. At last he had a friend all of his own.

A burst of laughter came from beyond the fogged glass. Illogically, because he couldn't have been spotted, Simon believed they were ridiculing him. Keeping low, arms hanging loose like a monkey's, he pattered past the building.

The path came to a dead end by a group of tall bins. Simon skidded on a scattering of potato peelings and turned his ankle. Tears pricked his eyes. Justin was missing, and it was Simon's fault.

There was a door in the wall opposite. Simon read the notice: 'Private'. Since the old man was found dead there on New Year's Day, the kitchen gardens were even more out of bounds. Simon had overheard Mr Wilson, the RE teacher, saying the 'gardener was lying dead as a doornail in the greenhouse'. He had written up this extraordinary piece of information in his notebook: 'dead as a doornail'. When he told Justin, the new boy had nodded as if dead gardeners were usual.

Simon should go back to the library and mug up on his Tutankhamun project for Mr Wilson, whom he liked, but then he thought: *Enter enemy territory and retrieve missing personnel. Evade capture.* It was his duty to rescue Justin.

A cloud hid the sun. The wall, spiked with flints as sharp as stone-age knives, overshadowed the boy. He stood at the cross-ways of three gravelled paths. Left, right and ahead, they separated raised beds in which tall weeds and nettles flourished. The gravel was blotched with moss, endive and rhubarb cloches made of clay peeped between cow parsley and thistle. Snails and slugs consumed bolted lettuces and once-prized dahlias. Fearsome fennel, gossamer foliage browning, towered over the herb bed, the geometric definition of which was lost to wooded branches of rosemary and clusters of sage. Garlic and thyme ran riot.

Simon marshalled facts. *Quarry last seen going to kitchens, doing his stupid hopscotch walk, like a girl.* Simon tripped on a bramble meandering across the path. He should report Justin to Mr Wilson. He liked Mr Wilson. His first name was 'Nat', not spelled with a 'G', but still the boys called him the Stick Insect because of it and because he was thin. The air was cooling. Simon had left his jumper on his chair in the library to make it look as if he was there. Mr Wilson would be cross that Simon had let Justin out of his sight.

He saw a greenhouse, beyond a rusting lawn roller. A crack. Simon dived behind the roller. Above his head a gull cried, derisive like the white capped cooks. The dead gardener groped at his leg. He shouted and scrabbled free. A cat, black with a white bib, was weaving about him. Simon liked the cat – although as Mice Monitor it had been his job to keep it away from the classroom. He put out his bad hand and stroked it; instantly it arched in appreciation, then it gave a start and darted away. Simon peeped around the roller.

The door to the greenhouse was open. The metal frame had buckled; slats of glass were missing. Shelves were filled with flower pots and seed boxes. No one was there, dead or alive.

He ventured further along the path, the weeds so high it was like a tunnel. Justin liked tunnels; he said he was going to be an engineer when he grew up. Simon had asked if an engineer drove engines and Justin had laughed and said he was stupid. Simon turned a corner and saw Justin sitting on the ground in the middle of a patch of sunlight.

'You're trespassing!' Relieved to find him, Simon grabbed Justin by the shoulders. He was surprised by the feeling of sharp bones.

'Let go!' Justin wrenched free. He was pouring water into a hole in the side of a pile of earth. The pool shrank as water soaked into the ground.

'I need to get more.' Justin spoke as if to himself.

'What are you doing?' Simon expected that Justin would be sorry and accompany him to the library where they were meant to be.

'This reservoir has to feed two towns. There's no need for a pump or a water tower, it's higher than the settlements, I'm using gravity.' Justin waved a hand. The ground had been cleared of weeds, earth flattened and marked with stones like a railway track. A gutter had been cut into the raised earth through which a tunnel ran. Justin had constructed it with lolly sticks and mud. Simon poked at the mound with his bad hand.

'Careful!' Justin grabbed Simon's wrist. 'It could collapse. I had to measure the sides, make sure the rolling stock can pass through.' Justin's father was an engineer. Simon's father worked with mad people and never smiled. Simon didn't want to be mad when he was grown up.

'Get off me, Stumpy!' Justin glared at him. 'Go away.'

'Your mummy's dead.' Simon said and was immediately horrified. He hadn't meant to say it.

'She's not. And anyway your mummy doesn't love you. That's worse. Mine loves me very much.'

Simon felt his eyes sting. Dashing at his face with his sleeve, he pulled out of the tunnel a red locomotive attached to three carriages.

'What's in here?'

The carriages uncoupled and crashed on to the tracks. He picked them up and peered in through the windows of one of them.

'Gosh, it's a dining car!' he exclaimed. 'Look, that's you and me having our lunch. Let's pretend we met there. I've got steak and French fries like the man in *Strangers on a Train*. Have you read it? It's my mum's favourite book. It's really for grown-ups. What are you eating?'

'I don't know what you're talking about,' Justin replied as if he didn't care either.

'Two men meet and become friends.' Simon chattered on happily, his mood recovering as he warmed to his idea. His mum had been impressed that he had read the book from beginning to end. 'Do you like tomato ketchup?' He imagined shooting it all over his chips like the man in the story.

'I am about to drive my train through the tunnel,' Justin said.

'I'll do it.' Brought rudely back to the present, Simon was terribly sorry to have made a mess, but this was all against the rules. He reattached the carriages and, lifting the engine, ran the wheels over his palm, making them spin. He pushed it on the impacted soil, wheels whirring, and watched with satisfaction as it sped into the tunnel. It shot out of the other side, carriages twisted and buckled, and veering off the tracks smashed into the watering can.

'You went too fast.' Justin rubbed his hand on his shorts.

Simon was horrified; he had wanted to help. He pulled on his bad finger and pretended he was a racing driver who didn't care about going fast.

'Can I have a turn?' Perhaps Justin had forgotten it was his own train.

'Unfortunately you cannot. I need to perform more test runs.' Simon pressed too hard on the locomotive and it sank into the earth. 'Stop doing that with your mouth,' he ordered.

Justin twitched his face on purpose to frighten him. 'I wasn't.'

'You were. I don't want to have to get cross with you.' The engine was stuck; soil clogged the axle and front wheels. 'There's nowhere for the passengers to get out.' Simon's palms were damp. Who had killed the gardener? *The enemy can smell fear.*

'I will kill you and bury your body so that no one will ever find you and then your flesh will be eaten and your bones will crumble.' Simon stuck his bad hand inside Justin's shorts and pinched him. 'I'll say you escaped again. Message understood?'

Simon tore the pin from the hand grenade and hurled it into the tunnel. He dragged Justin away as a blast tore into the mountain, pelting the enemy with clods of earth.

'You're mean.'

Simon pretended he hadn't heard Justin. He imagined radioing back to base. *Enemy camp destroyed. Mission accomplished.* He imagined being an entirely different person, someone who could make people do what he wanted. This idea faded before it had taken shape. Flushed with shame, Simon stared at his bad hand as if it were his enemy.

The boy hurried along the low vaulted passage, past the reception. Outside the cloakroom toilets he bumped into nice Mr Wilson.

'Hey, kiddo!' The teacher had a funny accent because he wasn't English. 'Have you seen your mate, Justin the Dreamer?'

Simon stopped, clutching at his bad hand.

Mr Wilson waited.

'He's in the library.'

'OK, Simon, can you make it your job to get him into dinner on time? We don't want him being late again.' Mr Wilson was smiling down at him.

'Yes I will, sir.'

Simon had lied for Justin. That meant he would like him.

Careful not to run – it was against the rules – Simon continued to the library.

Four

Saturday, 19 October 2013

Stella slotted the van behind a dented blue Toyota Yaris. It had been a long week, she could spend the evening on her own, catching up on emails. Jackie's street, tree-lined and spacious, was quiet considering it was close to a busy main road. Beyond the railings was a cemetery and, not for the first time, Stella considered she wouldn't like to live opposite dead people.

Her dad had owned a blue Yaris. This one's rear panel was a mismatch of replaced panels. Terry's car had been ten years old, but he had kept it immaculate. She could remember his car, but she couldn't conjure up his face.

A bus went by; its back draught rocked the van and light from the windows raked the interior, breaking her thoughts. There was a bleat. It came from the dog strapped into the jump seat behind her on the passenger side. She had installed the seat especially, because if he travelled beside her in the front, he risked being killed by the airbag. In the dim light the little beige poodle, the size of a cat, could be a ghost dog, a blurred shape with dark brown eyes. Stella had forgotten about Stanley. She wasn't cut out to own a dog. Just as well that she would be giving him back soon.

'We're here,' she remarked as she unclipped him. He climbed on to her shoulder and she manoeuvred them both out of the van.

On the way from her mother's flat in Barons Court, unsettled by the silent empty rooms, Stella had wished she could go to Terry's and empty her inbox over a microwaved shepherd's pie. Nothing personal, Jackie was a friend and Stella liked her husband Graham and their two sons, but she didn't fancy company.

However, the Makepeace family wouldn't require her to join in; they did the talking, leaving her free to eat, and then Jackie would let her wash up. Jackie was minding Stanley for the night while Stella went to fetch her mum from the airport.

'You like it here,' she said as the dog jerked the lead taut and snouted towards Jackie's gate. Stanley was left over from a relationship of the sort her mum called a 'wrong turning'. Stella had wanted to refuse, dogs were liable to cause mess, but months into minding the dog, she decided that relationships caused more mess.

The house next door to Jackie's was up for sale. Jackie was worried about this. The man living there now had been there since he was a boy and, Jackie said, he was a 'sweetie', kind and gentle; she hoped the new owners would be as nice. Stella thought again how living in a flat at the end of a corridor meant that, apart from the rare times she met anyone in the lift, she could avoid knowing her neighbours.

Clutching white wine, plucked from the chiller cabinet in Dariusz Adomek's mini-mart beneath her office, Stella took the dog over to a sycamore tree by Jackie's gate to lift his leg. The tree trunk was thinner than the others in the street. Jackie had told her the tree replaced one that came down in the 1987 hurricane and crushed their car.

She rummaged in her pocket and gave Stanley a biscuit as reward for peeing outside, to reinforce his toilet training as she had been told at his obedience class. Something fluttered to the ground. It was the paper she had found under a cushion at her mum's flat. Jack had cleaned the flat many times during her mum's six-week absence, but the paper was caught under the back of the sofa. The dog had been whining and when she gave in and pulled away the cushions, he had truffled out a bone-shaped biscuit. The paper was next to it. The writing was her mum's: 'Dale Heffernan, 38 Fisher Ave, Vaucluse. Likes sailing and B. Springsteen. Dislikes having time on his hands!'

During the first week her mum was away, Stella slept with her phone under her pillow expecting the call informing her Suzie was clinging to life. She had even looked up St Vincent's Hospital in Sydney. There had been no call. No call at all. Passing up Skype or email, Suzie sent two postcards to the office which Beverly, the admin assistant, stuck on the pinboard reserved for staff holiday messages. The sun was hot and there was a possum in her friend's attic. 'Love to Stanley.' In the second card she had wasted space with advice about the client database she had built, but had sent love to Stella.

Stella had told Jackie she didn't miss her mother. However, she found the comparative quiet at work uncomfortable; she missed the daily task list and the weekend calls informing her that Stanley wanted a walk in Richmond Park (as if her mum and the dog had conferred). Before Terry's death Stella might have welcomed the break from her mum's grumblings and demands. Now she wanted everything to be back to normal.

She stuffed the paper back in her pocket. Dale Heffernan was probably an ex-client.

Jackie and Graham Makepeace had lived in the 1920s semi for thirty years. Graham had made their gate; their initials, 'J' and 'G' intertwined, were carved into the beech struts. Jackie and Graham were still in love. Stella saw falling in love, like falling trees, to be fraught with the danger of crushed hopes and rearranged schedules.

'Heel.' She marched up to the front door, the dog trotting beside her.

Had Stella not met Jackie, the immaculate front door, gleaming window sashes and weed-free shingle path bordered by box hedging would have assured her she would like her. Jackie's mix of house-proud care and easy homeliness was apparent in the twisting branches of a laburnum, bracketed to protect brickwork, around the porch and the recycling bins corralled behind a trellis draped with honeysuckle.

The door flew open. The wine bottle slipped from her grasp; trying to stop its fall she kicked it on to the hedge.

'Hey, Stell!' A young man in a boxy leather jacket and hipster jeans was squatting at her feet submitting to a busy washing from the dog. 'Mum said you were coming. Sorry to miss you, I'm off out. They're all waiting for you.'

Gathering herself, Stella couldn't think of his name. She retrieved the bottle from the hedge. 'All?' she echoed.

Jackie's older son lived up north. Steve. Leeds. Teacher. This was Nick the dancer.

'Some guy Mum's got round.' Nick spun on his heel and leapt over the gate.

Stella froze. 'Is he staying to eat?'

'Sure he is – and there's candles!' Nick Makepeace grinned. 'He's your type!'

'On your way, Nicholas. Text if you're not coming home, so I can lock up.' Jackie pulled off an apron and popped a biscuit, magically produced, into the dog's mouth. She shook her head. 'Ignore him. In you come!'

Stella's last visits had met Jackie's promise of freshly cooked vegetables. Stella had forgotten there was sometimes another motive. Six months after one of Stella's 'wrong turnings', Jackie often launched a campaign to find Stella's Mr Right. It was six months since Stella had finished with David.

Always welcoming, the Makepeaces' kitchen, rich with the smell of roasting lamb, wine glasses glinting in candlelight, was tonight no exception. Graham Makepeace, mindful that Stella disliked kissing – for fear of germs – fussed Stanley instead.

A man stepped into the pool of candlelight and grasped Stella's hand, shaking it vigorously. 'William Frost, so pleased to meet you.'

Stella didn't need an introduction. An inch shorter than her six feet, in a dark suit and tie, this was Jackie's latest Mr Right.

Five

Saturday, 19 October 2013

'There is no step-free access at Hammersmith station until late November. Customers requiring step-free access should change at Earl's Court and use local bus services.' Jack shut off the public address channel and, as he drove out of West Brompton station, he sang under his breath:

'Little Jack Horner
Sat in the corner…'

Fulham Broadway, Parsons Green. At Putney Bridge station, about to close the doors, Jack consulted the driver's monitor and saw something on top of it. Someone had left a toy for the owner to reclaim; it must have been a driver because passengers weren't allowed beyond the gate. He leaned towards it.

It was a red steam engine. He felt a prickling at the back of his neck. It looked identical to the engine he had lost when he was little. Jack rose from his seat; he would hand it in at Earl's Court after stabling his train. Then he saw the time: he was running thirty seconds late. He sat down and checked the monitors again. A man was standing at the other end of the platform. Jack paused to give him time to board the train, but he didn't move so Jack shut the doors. He pulled on the lever and eased the train forward. Heading for East Putney station, he forgot about the man.

Jack was covering for a colleague on the Wimbledon line who did day shifts. Used to doing the Dead Late shifts, he missed the darkness. Only in the brick-lined tunnels, amid the dust, lit by the headlamps, like motes of gold, did he feel truly alive.

He resumed singing under his breath so that the passengers beyond his cab door wouldn't hear:

'Eating a Christmas pie;
He put in his thumb...'

His engine had been heavy, a grand thing to hold. The word 'Triang' was emblazoned on its boiler with the name, 'Puff-Puff'. Jack had taken it to the river, although his mummy had asked him not to.

'And pulled out a plum,
And said, "What a good boy am I!"'

Jack believed that what is lost will one day return. A circularity with no beginning or end. Even so, he was doubtful that the toy engine he had just seen was the same as the one he had lost in the water thirty years ago.

Distracted, Jack was midway through the West Hill tunnel before he recalled his self-imposed task. The tunnel ran beneath West Hill between East Putney and Southfields stations. Dictated by whimsy and coincidence – 'signs' – Jack was ever in search of hidden facts that would reveal profound truths. The length of the tunnel was one such fact. His colleagues didn't know and he hadn't found the answer on the internet.

Each time he entered the tunnel, something made him forget to collect the 'data': the time it took to travel from one end to the other. He only had a few more chances: his colleague would be back soon.

'And said, "What a good boy am I, am I
And said—"'

He stopped singing. The steam engine was a sign.

Jack stood in the dark hall and absorbed the silence of spectres. He went to the foot of the staircase and peered up. The banister wound into darkness and shadows of the spindles striped across the wall – like in a Hollywood film, someone had once said, perhaps his mother.

Every object, every shadow and splash of light had meaning or intent. When Jack was in his dead parents' house, he too was a ghost. Once, looking in the hall mirror to see his reflection and reassure himself he was alive, he had seen his mother's face through the blossoms of silver, a trickle of blood on her forehead. He had removed the mirror. An oval stain marked where it had been.

Tonight the house was not his friend. The owl knocker, as cold as brass, hadn't greeted him. He considered going to Rose Gardens North to see Stella, but remembered she was at Jackie's and then off to Heathrow to fetch her mother. Stella had rung him that morning, but not left a message. He wouldn't interrupt her at Jackie's.

In the dining room, printed music, discoloured to parchment yellow, lay open on the piano, the pages wrinkled with damp. Jack couldn't play the piano, it had been his mother's, but he knew the music by heart. The house was a tomb in which he glided wraith-like, catching snatches of conversation and glimpses of action in the low-wattage gloom. The threads of people's lives and deaths, the hidden facts. In the past he had craved their company. Tonight he wanted peace from his ghosts.

Another flier lay on the doormat. It would be an estate agent telling him someone wanted to buy his house, or maybe a pizza-delivery service.

It was none of these. One of his Tarot cards had blown off the hall table. Jack bent down and picked it up. He turned it over and stared at the image. A tower stood on the edge of a roiling sea, waves smashed against the sheer walls, the sky was dark and riven with a jagged thunderbolt. Out of the waves rose Poseidon clasping a trident, the representation of the crescent moon that connected the God to the night and to the instincts. In Tarot, the Tower augured the breaking down of old structures, the stripping away of the false self to reveal truth and integrity. Jack had turned up the card in the spread he laid out for himself on his birthday earlier in the year. He had not had it in a spread since.

His book of tides lay on the hall table. His mother had hit her head on the corner of the marble, a sharp corner, it had broken the skin. Jack shut his mind to the memory and snatching up the tide tables book, he flipped through the pages. He had promised Stella not to go on journeys in London at night, the time he liked best. The promise didn't include the eyot. The tide turned at two sixteen. If he got there in twenty minutes, he had hours before the river filled.

This time the owl fluffed her feathers. He assured her he wasn't breaking his promise to Stella – the owl was big on loyalty. Like the lions perched on plinths around the Square and the eagle preparing for take-off from the pediment above his head, the owl watched over Jack. Stella would despair if she knew that symbols on cards, creatures on door knockers, weather-worn gargoyles, even garden ornaments gave him direction and protection. He lifted the owl's tail feathers and lowered her; she tapped the strike plate. Time to go.

Eighteen and a half minutes later Jack was hopping and jumping across the exposed causeway to Chiswick Eyot. Fog blotting out rooftops on Chiswick Mall thinned briefly to reveal the tower. Then it vanished. Jack did a final sweep of the mall, and decided he was alone. He reached the eyot and climbed the bank, tracing a faint track into the undergrowth.

When he stepped into the silence of his Garden of the Dead, it occurred to Jack that it was strange that the Tarot card had fallen to the floor because he had secured the pack with an elastic band.

Had Jack waited, he might have seen that the pole by the embankment was not a pole. A man stood in the shadow of the moored barge. Jack's keen ear would have caught a sound and he would not have mistaken it for the rhythmic wash of the tide.

Across the mud flats he would have heard a lilting song:

'He put in his thumb,
And pulled out a plum,
And said, "What a good boy am I!"'

Six

Saturday, 19 October 2013

Jackie was in the passage when Stella came out of the downstairs toilet. 'Stell, any chance you could drop William at the station? He'd like a private word.'

'I'm going to the airport,' Stella objected.

'Gunnersbury station is pretty much on your way,' Jackie cajoled. 'I said you might be able to help him.'

'Is it cleaning?'

'Not exactly. Best he explains.'

'OK.' She would say no if he asked her out. Simple.

All evening the man had seemed more interested in Stanley the dog. For some women, his tactic would have worked, but the way to Stella's heart was not through her dog. Mr Right had got it wrong and she would tell him so. It was better to be straight with people.

'Does the name Dale Heffernan mean anything to you?' she asked Jackie.

'No, should it?'

Stella shook her head. Her mother often confided in Jackie; if she didn't know the name, there was nothing to know. Meanwhile she had another man to deal with.

'Can I drop you at the station?' she asked from the doorway.

'Great!' He jumped up and his paper napkin floated to the floor. He was too pleased.

She waited in the van while Mr Right – she had forgotten his actual name – was no doubt thanking Jackie for setting up the evening. The dog was perched in Jackie's arms. Stella glared at him as if he too was in on the scheme.

When she came to collect him tomorrow she would insist that these blind dates stopped. She preferred being single.

Idly she watched a dark shape flit between the graves, the shadow of a branch moving in the wind. She looked back at the house. Now Mr Right – or whoever – was petting Stanley. She tapped her foot, although she had plenty of time. The shape in the cemetery was not a shadow. It was a man in a long black coat.

Only one person looked like that. Stella craned over the passenger seat and looked out of the side window. Jack. He must have seen she had called, but he hadn't rung her to see why. He would say he assumed her initial call was a mistake if she asked him. Giving a huff – Jack had a reason for all his seemingly unreasonable behaviour – Stella climbed out of the van. She was about to cross the road – somehow she couldn't bring herself to shout over to him – but he had gone.

Stella got back in the van in time to see a fox lope along the verge inside the cemetery and vanish among the graves.

It wasn't the dead she minded; decay disposed of bodies, but at night the sprawling space offered opportunity for anyone to spy on the houses on Corney Road. What better place to bury a body than in a graveyard? Stella frowned. Her mum had said she was like Terry, seeing crime around every corner. The blue Toyota had gone.

The man couldn't have been Jack, she concluded; he had promised her not to go walking late at night.

By the time Mr Right joined her, she was grateful for the company.

'Gunnersbury station.' She started the engine.

The journey would take five minutes, but a lot could happen in five minutes. It took two minutes to get out of Jackie's street; Burlington Lane was busy with late commuting traffic heading west. Another minute to Chiswick Roundabout.

'I've not been up front,' Mr Right blurted out. 'I wanted to meet you.'

Stella knew London like a cabbie. Mentally she mapped out a short cut, but all the streets led back to the Great West Road.

'Jackie has got the wrong end—' A horn blared as a car cut up a van.

Mr Right was speaking, his words lost in the sound. On Chiswick High Road, she braked at red traffic lights. She could smell his aftershave; she traced the woody scent to Burberry.

The lights went green, thirty seconds to go. Bolstered by this, Stella asked, 'Sorry, what did you say?' She made herself concentrate.

'I wanted to see you because Jackie told me that, apart from cleaning, you solve murders.'

Involuntarily Stella lifted her foot off the clutch and, with a judder, the van stalled.

Seven

May 1985

Justin was taking ages to lace up his shoes. Twice he got it wrong and undid them. Simon suppressed anxiety; they would be late.

'Shall I do it for you?' he asked politely.

'I can do it on my own.' Justin pulled at the lace and snapped it.

This was the first time they had been alone since Simon had found Justin's secret place in the kitchen garden. He had been told off for leaving the library by the librarian, whom some boys called 'the Oyster'; his jumper over the chair hadn't fooled her. But the Oyster hadn't noticed Justin was missing.

'Would you like my lace?' Simon offered, already loosening it.

Justin made a knot with the short length. Without looking at Simon, he stood up and jogged out of the room.

Simon folded Justin's clothes into a proper pile, as neat as his own. Everyone had to be kind to Justin because his mother had died. Simon sometimes wished his dad was dead. That would mean two good things: he could share being half an orphan with Justin and wouldn't have to see his father in the holidays. If his own mother died, he'd want to die too. Justin's mother couldn't have been as nice as Simon's mummy or Justin might have tried to die when she did. Baffled by the complexity of this, Simon raced after Justin on to the field.

'You're late. Next time it's detention!' Mr Lambert the games master roared at him. He shoved him to the other end of the line of boys to Justin. The last time they had done cross-country, Justin had got lost and come in late. Mr Lambert had been nice to him, but in case it happened again, Simon resolved to stick close to him. Running was the one sport that Simon was good at. He anticipated obstacles: protruding roots, puddles, dips and jutting stones; he conserved energy, paced himself. He kept a steady speed regardless of gradient.

Today it was like in his dreams: Justin was shadowing him. Simon felt a burst of joy; they would represent the school, get in the Olympics, go for gold. He ran blindly on, tactics abandoned; he had boundless energy. Bramble branches ripped his shirt; drops of water from overhanging trees wet his cheeks. Justin was his friend; he would ask him to be his blood brother. On they ran, heel for heel.

Ahead of them was the line of trees; they were coming to the woods with minutes on anyone else. Simon must warn him to increase speed before the woods because the level ground allowed even weaker boys to gain. With a tip of the hand he signalled for Justin to pick up pace.

Justin wasn't there. Simon faltered and, stopping, he turned right around. There was no one there. Fifty metres back came a straggling line of boys. They were gaining on him. The bright red of their shirts stood out against the browns and greens, the sweep of the Downs. Justin couldn't have overtaken him. Ahead, the woods were a fringe of dark green and, skirting them, Simon saw Justin. He had cut up around the base of the hill. He had left the designated track. He was entering the woods by the pheasant run.

Plunging after him, Simon smashed through bracken, crushing saplings, slipping and sliding, all tactics abandoned. He ran between the tree trunks, fast and nimble; he couldn't call out, he would give them both away. At last he stumbled out of the canopy of trees on to a track rutted with tyre tracks and hoof prints.

Two metres away, in sunlight, Justin was sitting on a steep grassy bank. Simon staggered towards him, his lungs bursting. Justin was sucking on an orange quarter and chatting with Mr Lambert. Simon saw he had emerged beyond the finishing line. It was too late to hide: Mr Lambert had seen him.

The sports master handed Simon two hours' detention for cutting out some of the route, which was cheating. The boy didn't say that he had been trying to help his friend. Busy with his orange, Justin couldn't have seen him.

Eight

Saturday, 19 October 2013

'Who's been murdered?' Stella stopped outside Gunnersbury station.

'My brother.' Frost unclipped his seat belt and turned in his seat to face her. His bulk seemed to shrink the van's interior.

'Thing is, I run a cleaning agency.' Stella wouldn't be rude, but it didn't do to lead people on.

'Jackie said you are a detective.' Frost gripped the dashboard with his left hand, his other hand around the back of the seat. 'She said you were good.'

Stella was on the brink of explaining that her previous cases had been her father's unfinished business, they didn't count, but then she heard her mum advising that she scope a job before refusing it. A real live murder case, unconnected with Terry, was as good as deep cleaning.

'How did your brother die? And when?'

'A month ago. He supposedly jumped in front of an Underground train, near here at Stamford Brook.'

'Supposedly?' Stella felt a stirring of anticipation. Stella hadn't expected to miss her mum, but had found that her absence revealed how integral to her routine Suzie had become. Stella missed the advice on potential new business and new cleaning operatives. No one else shared Stella's excitement about the latest equipment to further increase standards of hygiene. With Suzie gone, Stella needed something else to challenge her. Now she saw that what she needed was a case. Jackie, as ever second-guessing Stella, had sent her one.

'I want you to find his killer.' He kept glancing out of the window as if the killer might be out there.

'Murder is a job for the police.' A year ago, the police had been her enemy. Her mum said that being a detective had taken her father away from his family. Stella hadn't thought of it like that, but fell in with her mum's take on it. By the time she was grown up, she saw her dad a handful of times a year and found little to say to him. After his death two years ago, memories of their time together from her childhood had returned so that she no longer felt antagonistic to the police – in particular Martin Cashman, a man a little older than her who had worked with her dad.

'They're not interested. Superintendent Cashman said there was no one else on the station platform and the only two witnesses, both drivers, confirmed Rick ran in front of the train. He was "satisfied" with the suicide verdict.'

'You don't agree?' Stella didn't want to go up against Cashman. He would suggest she stuck to cleaning and he would be right. 'Your brother's death sounds straightforward.' Wrong word. Jack was better at this stuff. She cast about for the name Jackie had said when she introduced him.

'Jackie warned me you'd be circumspect. All I ask is you hear me out.'

'Why do you think it wasn't suicide?'

'Killing himself isn't Rick's style. He sticks at things.' He looked away as if overwhelmed by his grief.

'Did he leave a note?' He spoke of his brother in the present tense. Perhaps he couldn't accept the man's death; in any case, she found his way of putting it unsettling. Odd to be in denial. Jumping in front of a train left little room for doubt that it was suicide. If Jackie hadn't referred him to her, Stella would give him no time.

'In the unlikely event that it was suicide, Rick would leave a note. He's hot on admin.'

'Was he— Had he had a drink?' Stella was careful. Not a good start to suggest the man's brother was a drinker.

'The post-mortem found whisky in his stomach.' He raked a hand through his hair. 'I know how it sounds.'

It sounded like the man had drunk enough to muster up courage to step in front of a train. She would let him down lightly.

'I have to go.' If her dad had died under a train she too would have doubted it: he wasn't that sort. Terry's post-mortem had been irrefutable. Yet he hadn't had a day off sick in his life, so his being dead had made no sense. It still didn't.

'Do you have siblings?' he asked.

'No.' She hoped he wasn't about to go down the 'you can't possibly understand' route.

'I hardly knew my brother. I'd say the guy was a fantasist. When we were boys, he was always playing soldiers. Not with me, I'm three years older. He had a gang, a couple of kids in his thrall. But he rang me an hour before he died. I had no signal so didn't hear the voicemail until after the police knocked on the door. I failed him once. I won't fail him again.'

'It's not failing.' Stella saw the time; she had to leave. 'What do you think happened?' Terry would have asked this first.

'Something – or someone – had frightened him. He sounded strange in the message. I hardly recognized him. I think he was murdered.'

Jack teased convoluted meaning from obscure signs; it frustrated her, but he did get results. Terry had followed hunches. Stella preferred the tangible.

'Can I hear his message please?'

'No. I deleted it after I heard it. Stupid, I know. The police clearly thought so.'

Stella's cleaning process was methodical. Stain by stain. She used the same process for detection. Clue by clue. However, this only worked if there was a stain – a clue – to start with. The only clue was the evidence. The man had jumped off a platform: end of, in all senses.

'I'm sorry Mr Righ— um, I don't see that we can help.' She turned on the engine. 'I have to get to the airport.'

'I'll come with you.' He clipped in his seat belt.

Nine

May 1985

He executed the plan perfectly. Every strut, every load-bearing beam, every cross fitted. He picked up the last girder – iron slats from a bench he had found behind the greenhouse – and, holding his breath, slotted it in. It held. Balanced on his haunches, he patted down the soil at the base of the stanchions.

Simon was in the kitchen garden. He had found a book on Isambard Kingdom Brunel in the library and he had made copious notes from engineering textbooks: a legacy of the owner of the house before it was a school. At first Simon borrowed books he'd seen Justin read, but soon he was on a path of his own. This afternoon he was constructing a box girder bridge. A present for Justin.

'It's the longest bridge in the country,' he would tell him. 'I made the arches and the central spans off-site, and erected the segments with a gantry crane.' He particularly liked the word 'gantry'. 'A gantry is a framework of bars, usually steel. It rests on two supports and is used for holding up road signs over motorways or for carrying electrical cables,' he told the garden. The bit about using a gantry crane wasn't true, but Justin wouldn't mind.

Mr Wilson had been thrilled to get a post at a boy's boarding school in the UK. It would go down well on his CV back home. Full of ambition and passion, he was determined to be the teacher the boys remembered when they were men playing their part in the world. He would be cited in articles, eulogized in biographies; through teaching he would be immortal.

It hadn't worked out that way. The boys mocked his accent. He had come into the classroom one morning to find 'Convict' daubed on the blackboard. It seemed that the English assumed every Australian had been deported from the UK. The fact that his great-great-grandfather *had* set off a spark of fury. Intent on flushing out the little tyke that had written it, he chose Simon as the 'fall guy' and accused him of the crime. He'd been sure that this would prompt the actual culprit to confess. He had been wrong. It seemed the boys were happy that Simon take the rap. He couldn't withdraw the accusation or he would look weak. The thing was a bloody mess.

Simon was the one boy who did what he was told. Out of all of them, in later life, he was most likely to cite Wilson as a key influence. The kid pored over leather-bound tomes; he wanted to be an engineer, not a boring banker or a Board Director or, buoyed by a trust fund, nothing at all.

While most of the boys mindlessly parroted answers learnt by rote or, like the kid whose mother had died, daydreamed, Simon was his star pupil. He read around subjects, told Wilson stuff he didn't know and made oblique connections. But soon the boy's adherence to rules got under Wilson's skin and bit by bit the man's objective shifted. A mild-mannered man, Wilson had become infuriated by Simon. He saw himself in the seven-year-old, a meek snap of a thing with no friends. Instead of encouraging Simon to find joy in new knowledge, he started to try to catch him out. He vented his annoyance at Simon's obsequious manner by gratuitously punishing him. He found justification in making an example of an innocent boy: it would bring the others into line.

The afternoon Wilson saw Simon leave the playground and sneak around the back of the kitchens was a gift. He went after him.

Simon walked his fingers over the boarding – he had taken the balsa wood from the workshop – and pressed hard. It creaked, but didn't break; the pressure was the equivalent of a ton. The spans had give and would withstand strong winds. Justin had explained that to him; he would remind him of that.

The boy was astonished at his achievement. Now he knew how to do it, they could build another bridge, or a tunnel – whatever Justin liked. Ideas raced fast and furious; hands together as if praying, Simon contemplated the breadth of possibility. It would be their secret.

He smiled at the distant thud of the garden door closing. Justin hadn't learnt his skill of stealthy tracking. Simon would teach him this. He scrambled to his feet, imagining Justin's face when he saw the bridge. Justin never smiled. Simon supposed it was because his mother was dead. He wanted to make him smile.

'You shouldn't be here.' Justin did a high singing voice. 'It's out of bounds.'

'I made it.' Simon realized Justin was imitating him. Unaccountably he felt afraid and fluffed his speech. 'I did the spans like Hammersmith Bridge.'

Hands on hips, Justin surveyed the bridge. 'The stresses are in the wrong places, it won't take a significant load.'

'I tested it,' Simon protested, his eyes swimming with sudden tears. 'It does.' Mentally he scanned his drawing for possible error. An engineer's mistake couldn't be hidden. Sir Stephen Lockett, the sanitary-ware millionaire who had wanted to be an engineer, whose house they lived in, had trusted the Tay bridge. It had collapsed. Sir Stephen's body was never recovered from the river Tay beneath. Forever restless, his ghost was said to roam the library at night.

Simon had imagined Hammersmith Bridge, the looping spans mirrored in the Thames. All he had achieved was a cluster of wood, stuck with glue. He saw it as Justin saw it and pulled on his bad finger. 'I did it for you.'

Justin's shoe caught a strip of wood. It broke off and fell into the 'river'.

'That's OK,' Simon said as if Justin had apologized.

Justin stepped on the bridge and crushed it.

'See? It can't take a decent load.' Justin kicked up a shower of gravel and, turning on his heel, strolled away up the path between the tall weeds.

Simon couldn't comprehend the devastation. He rubbed his palms on the back of his trousers.

'What are you playing at?'

Simon wheeled around. Mr Wilson was standing with his hands on his hips as Justin had.

'I built him a bridge,' Simon said and then corrected himself. 'I built a bridge.'

'You did, did you?!' Wilson folded his arms, wondering if the boy had whacked his head. He couldn't see a bridge in the mess of sticks and mud at his feet. 'Look at the state of you.'

'I tested it. My sums were right.'

He was dishevelled and pathetic. Wilson's triumph ebbed; he felt sorry for him and sick with himself.

'Simon, mate, you shouldn't be here,' he said gently. The kid was doing the thing with his finger, twisting and tugging it as if the injury was recent. No one knew how he came to lose his finger. Wilson would have a chat with Madeleine next time she visited the school. It would do him no harm for her to see him showing concern for her son. So many of the teachers here actually disliked children. If the boys knew why, they might stop teasing him. He'd even had it in mind to come up with a hero story in which the kid had saved lives and lost his finger in the process, but couldn't see how that would work, so had given it up.

'Come with me.' He ushered him up the path.

Intent on getting Simon away before another master saw him and insisted he get detention, Nathan Wilson didn't see the other boy crouched in the greenhouse.

Ten

Christmas Eve 1986

At the junction of Goldhawk Road and Chiswick High Road, traffic was nose to tail. Christmas Eve shoppers, weighed down with bags and packages, wove between the stationary vehicles. When the door of the off-licence on the corner opened, a burst of John Lennon's 'Happy Xmas (War is Over)' swelled above the idling engines.

None of this last-minute bustle reached St Peter's Square where tall Georgian houses, stucco dappled with lamplight, formed a stately contrast to the seasonal mayhem. The square, its park in darkness, was of the past more than the present. Frost sparkling between shadows of branches might be the footprints of ghosts.

Anyone watching from a window of a house on the west side, indulging in this fancy, might decide that the boy hopscotch jumping between the cracks in between the flags by the park railings was one such phantom. Nothing betrayed him as a child of the 1980s, when loads of money didn't so much talk as shout. He had stepped out of a Narnian wardrobe in polished brogues, his gabardine mac collar down despite the biting wind, hair in a precise side parting.

Many downstairs windows were a showcase for Christmas. Splendid trees were festooned with lights and quaint decorations in reds, gold and silver. Lanterns burned on sills; candles flickered on mantelpieces; darts of light bounced off glasses of red wine and port. Indeed, quintessentially Dickensian, the boy, suitably diminutive and pale, observed the tableaux through misted glass, quaking in the icy cold.

He arrived at a house on the south side. The curtains were closed. Perhaps the residents were away or perhaps they eschewed the festivities; the unruly box hedge and fractured plaster on Doric columns supporting the porch hinted at indifference.

An eagle was poised on the porch, wings spread. Timidly, his shoulders hunched, Simon regarded it as if it might devour him as easy prey. He scurried up the steps to the front door.

Simon had had no doubt that Justin would be pleased to see him. He would tell him he had left his boarding school too, that he lived near to him. They could see each other every day. He bent down and raised the letterbox flap. Inside was a fusty smell like the room under the school library. A black cloth had been pinned to the door, blocking his view.

'It's me,' he whispered. 'Your friend.'

Eleven

Saturday, 19 October 2013

'Thank you.' Stella took the ticket from the machine and stuck it between her teeth. Talking to machines was more Jack's thing. Luckily William Frost – as she had finally remembered he was called – hadn't heard.

She found a space on the car park's third level. In the lift to the Arrivals hall, she questioned her wisdom in letting Frost come with her. Suzie wouldn't approve; she was unhappy about Stella 'playing detective', like her father. Nothing William had said on the journey to the airport – or his long brooding silences – gave her confidence that he would win Suzie over with charm as Jack had.

'What do you think we could find that the police haven't?' They were alone in the lift.

'The truth. You finding the killer will be worth the money.'

Stella hadn't considered charging a fee. Their last two investigations – the Rokesmith and Blue Folder cases (not counting a missing cat Jack found in an empty house he was cleaning) – had been Terry's cold cases. No money had changed hands.

Frost was expecting to pay for a service Stella probably couldn't fulfil. She had built a successful business by avoiding risks, expanding only when there was the capital and demand. She had not taken on bigger offices or rewarded herself with a higher wage. She paid her operatives properly and invested in the best equipment. She had stuck to what she knew. She was not a detective.

'If the police couldn't find proof that your brother was murdered, I can't see how we can.'

'You clean for Hammersmith Police Station, don't you?'

Jackie would not have told him.

'I saw you in the compound.' He stopped beneath the Arrivals board. 'You wouldn't have that job if your firm wasn't thorough. Jackie assured me you leave no corner unclean. My brother was murdered. I know you will prove it and solve the case.'

'Perhaps it was a cry for help that went wrong,' Stella persisted, feeling every inch the pretend detective.

'A cry for help is taking tablets then texting someone. It's not jumping off a platform in front of a fast train.'

'He did call you.' She had to say it.

'He asked to see me, if he meant to kill himself, why do that?' Frost was adamant. Jackie had given him airtime, Stella reminded herself. She refrained from saying it was possible to survive a fall on to the rails: a client of hers had slipped off a platform when he was drunk and got away with a gash in his arm. Still, she supposed living to tell the tale – he told it whenever she cleaned for him – was unusual.

'You didn't get the call. Maybe that tipped him—' Stella stopped herself crashing into the unfortunate pun and, turning away, scanned the Arrival's indicator. 'The question surely is, did your brother have a reason to kill himself?'

'Baggage hall' was listed beside her mother's plane. She took up position at the mouth of the gate.

The first passengers – identifiable by suntans and summer clothes – straggled out, battling with trolleys bulky with cases, bags, surf boards, giant stuffed kangaroos. Many were hailed – cries and whoops – by people waiting by the ribbon. Stella edged around a man with a square of cardboard against his chest for a clear view of the exit.

'He did.'

'Who did what?' She kept her eyes on the passengers.

'About a month before he died, Rick remarked that long ago he made a mistake that had come back to haunt him.'

'Doesn't that make suicide more likely?'

'He isn't the type.' Frost was a stuck record. 'He said it in passing, I ignored him, felt like saying his whole life was a mistake, now I see he was trying to tell me something.'

Stella risked a glance at the man. In the stark airport light, his complexion was grey, eyes red-rimmed. She felt rather sorry for him.

Passengers were streaming by, jostling with trolleys, heaving bags, rolling cases into each other's paths. Jack wouldn't need proof: he would follow instinct, pay attention to his precious signs; he got results. She should have called him when she saw him in the cemetery. What was he doing there?

'Could someone have pushed him? Did they see anyone on the CCTV?' Her mum would be last off the plane; unused to travel, she would have mislaid her passport or got stuck in her seat belt.

'They saw no one on the film, but not all the station is covered. Whoever did this would know that.' Frost was animated. 'He has a car. I found it parked a couple of streets from his house. Why didn't he drive to see me? Obvious, because he didn't want to be seen leaving.'

'Who might have been watching?' Stella wondered why taking the Underground made it less likely he would be seen leaving, but felt it rude to pick Frost up on every point. She would never question a client's cleaning requirements.

'Is that your mother waving?'

A woman in a wide-brimmed straw hat that hid her face was sailing along wearing one of those billowing coats with bat-wing shoulders Stella associated with Australia. Suzie. Her trolley was heaped with makeshift bags. She was going so quickly other passengers had to veer out of her path. Stella couldn't see the suitcase Suzie had taken with her, and she had three times the luggage she'd set out with. She was waving, not just at Stella, but at everyone waiting. Stella leant out to get her attention. Her mother snatched off her hat and flung it on to her tower of bags.

The woman's face was scored by lines; her tan suggested she never saw the inside of a house. She wasn't her mother. Stella's relief was brief, for behind the woman was an expanse of floor.

There were no more passengers. Her phone buzzed. Distracted by Frost, she had missed Suzie. Stella read the text.

Staying in Sydney for two weeks. Feed plants. Mum x.

'She's not coming.' When she finally spoke, Stella's voice was gruff. 'I should have seen this coming.' She turned on her heel. 'She's had an accident – or worse.' What was worse? Her thoughts were racing.

'People often act out of character and surprise us,' William Frost said.

'Like killing themselves.' She stopped. 'Sorry, I didn't mean that.'

'Fair point. Rick took the train when he had a car and he shouldn't have been at Stamford Brook. I live on the Goldhawk Road, near Shepherd's Bush Green – he was out of his way. He asked to see me, then he went in front of a train. It doesn't add up.'

'Went out of his way?' Illogical behaviour generally had an explanation. They took the lift back to the car park. Stella forced herself to concentrate. Despite her text, she was on the lookout for her mother.

'His nearest Tube was Hammersmith, he should have got a train to Goldhawk Road station. I'm three minutes from there.'

'We need to pay.' Stella nodded at a bank of ticket machines.

'Let me.' Frost began feeding coins into the slot in the nearest machine.

'You needn't.' Everything was slipping away from her.

'I've taken your time, let me recompense you.'

Jackie had 'sent' William Frost to her. Stella trusted her judgement; Jackie wouldn't set Stella up for a fall. Watching him pick out the right change from a pile of coins in his palm, she deemed the man calm and practical, perhaps not the sort to get stuff out of proportion.

'I'll talk to Jack, my partner, and let you know our decision,' Stella said.

'Do you want a deposit now, and an advance on expenses?'

'That's not a "yes". If we do agree, it's "no win no fee".' Jackie wouldn't like that, but Stella would explain it was a trial. She wouldn't say that she balked at charging anything for detection.

'Who is this Jack? Are you together?' Frost startled her. 'Sorry, that's not my business.'

'Jack's a colleague.' Stella said sharply. 'He has a lot of experience.' She didn't say that he had been lurking in the cemetery earlier; there was much Frost didn't need to know about Jack. There was much she didn't know about Jack. Her mood dropped further. Jack had broken his promise.

'Will he agree?' William sounded anxious. 'I'd be happy with you if he doesn't.'

'We are a team.' Technically, Jack being in the cemetery wasn't breaking his promise. A graveyard wasn't a street.

On the roundabout Stella came up with a horrible idea. Dale Heffernan, the man who liked Bruce Springsteen, was Suzie's Mr Right. That was why she had flown to Sydney at the drop of a hat. Stella overshot the London exit and, circling it again, she told herself this could not be. Mr Right did not exist.

Twelve

September 1987

On a chill Saturday afternoon in London, an insidious fog made wraiths of the lamp-posts and telephone poles in Corney Road, a suburban street near Chiswick House grounds. It wiped out wires slung between the poles and lent the gates into the grounds a ghostly aspect. Emerging out of the grey, traffic on Burlington Lane was a procession of indistinct smudges of yellow.

Built in the 1930s, Corney Road was one line of terraced houses. Even with the tiled roofs and gables wreathed in fog, the houses retained the comforting appearance of a hot-chocolate advert. Threads of smoke wending from chimneys hinted at a crackling grate and leaping flames. Clipped hedges and shingled paths suggested domestic stability. Twenty minutes' walk from the nearest Underground station, the houses fell within the buying reach of lower-grade professionals: teachers, middle-ranking police officers and council workers such as planning officers and auditors.

The homely atmosphere didn't extend to the other side of the street where wrought-iron railings bounded Chiswick Cemetery. Angels with broken fingers and chipped wings gazed heavenwards; sublime Madonnas overlooked headstones. A breeze pushed at yew trees and set a chain looped around the gate into a Newton's cradle motion. Rhythmically it chinked against the post, the lightly pitched sound spelling doom in the quiet.

From Burlington Lane two black shapes clarified to a woman with a pushchair and a boy, belted into a gabardine mac, hurrying along. The boy had one hand on the bar of the pushchair, revealing that much of his middle finger on his left hand was missing. They were talking and joking, lending cheer to the damp and gloomy afternoon. The child in the pushchair, a girl of about two, was asleep, her head lolled to one side, her thumb slipping from her mouth.

They stopped at a house outside which was parked a lemon-yellow Triumph sports car. The front door opened and a man in a black wool suit hugging a battered leather briefcase came out. Strands of over-combed hair were lifted by the breeze. His sallow, gaunt features and stooping posture might look more at home processing coffins into open graves across the road than behind the wheel of a shiny TR7.

'Off to the funny farm for me!' The joke was perfunctory. He loaded his briefcase into the boot.

'Drive safely, doctor,' his wife replied without humour.

Blowing her a kiss and nodding to his son, the man folded himself into the front seat and drove off towards Corney Reach. When the throaty exhaust faded to nothing, she hugged her son to her.

'Just you and me, darling, let's have a cosy "lap" supper!'

'What larks!' Simon gave a skip.

'Ever the best of friends; ain't us, Pip!' She completed the ritual exchange and, stroking back his hair from his face, handed him the key to the front door.

Simon's throat was constricted with joy. His father was away; his sister didn't count. It was a year since he had left his boarding school and was living at home all the time. Since his first visit on Christmas Eve last year, he had knocked on Justin's door in the tall house with dark windows every week, but got no answer. He refused to give up hope. Justin had to answer one day.

Tonight his mum had talked to him in their special secret way. It was a sign. For the rest of the evening Simon didn't let her out of his sight.

Thirteen

Monday, 21 October 2013

'Dale Heffernan, 38 Fisher Ave, Vaucluse. Likes sailing and B. Springsteen. Dislikes having time on his hands!'

Stella reread her mum's scrawled note for the umpteenth time while she waited for Mrs Carr to answer the door. This was her second visit. She could hear footsteps scurrying about inside and guessed her client was tidying up, as some of Stella's clients did when she was expected. But given the mess on Saturday, she was surely not bothered what Stella thought.

She was no nearer to discovering who Dale Heffernan was. Her mum had replied to her text asking if she was 'OK' with 'yes'. The name made her think of Engelbert Humperdinck. Her mum often said 'Please Release Me' might have been written for her. Maybe Heffernan was a pop singer from the sixties that her mum had Googled. Unlikely.

Vaucluse sounded French. She had put Heffernan into Google and got a restaurant. She had tried Vaucluse. Unsurprisingly there was one in France. Scrolling down, she had found one in Sydney, Australia, and her dread crystallized into pricking dismay. Her fear escalated. Dale Heffernan would empty her mum's bank account and there was nothing Stella could do to stop him.

'I'm on to him!' Mrs Carr flung open the door. Stella pushed the paper back into her pocket, picked up her equipment bag and struggled inside. Her client was perkier than on Saturday. She seemed to have forgotten her displeasure with Stella for not following her instructions. Stella had long ago decided that some clients were enlivened by disaster. Their homes were a battlefield; it was her job to clean up for the next skirmish.

'Where should I start?' Stella laid her bag at the foot of the stairs. Last time Mrs Carr had taken up half the shift complaining about the unfaithful husband.

'I've found out where he was when he texted he was working late and couldn't see me.'

Stella gave in. 'How?' Why did working late mean her husband couldn't see her? Best not to ask that.

'It's clever. You can see where someone is by their texts. Don't switch your location on if you're leading a double life, I will find you!' Mrs Carr breezed into the sitting room.

Reluctantly Stella followed. With an imperious motion of her hand, Mrs Carr indicated for her to join her on the sofa where, with the clothes and clutter gone, there was now room.

'Look.' Mrs Carr was waving a phone. 'You press this key symbol and up comes a map with a blue dot pinpointing his exact location.' She jabbed at the screen. '*Voilà!*'

Stella knew it was possible to track a user's whereabouts; she had done it during the Blue Folder case.

'He was here, look.' Mrs Carr enlarged the map.

'On Chiswick Eyot?' Stella knew the scrub of land. She had ridden her bike there as a child.

'Of course not! Chiswick Mall. It isn't far from here and, I tell you, it's not for the faint-walleted. Whoever she is, she's got money. I can't match that.' Mrs Carr slumped back, apparently deflated.

'He could have been walking along it.'

'You don't pass through Chiswick Mall, it's out of your way unless that's where you're going.' She glared at Stella, seeming a hair's breadth from blaming her for her husband's betrayal.

'He told me he didn't see her anymore.'

Stella tried deflection. 'Where does he work?'

This seemed to perplex Mrs Carr. She hesitated and then, as if repeating something by rote, said, 'Wherever people want CCTV fitted and all the other surveillance paraphernalia.' She shook her head as if the question was superfluous.

'He could have been visiting a client then.' Stella wondered at herself for finding innocent explanations for Mr Carr, who had undeniably left his wife. She had cleaned in houses on Chiswick Mall; Mrs Carr was right, no houses there would give change from a million pounds. Odd, since he was in security, that Carr had gone to so much trouble to hide from his wife and made such a basic mistake.

'So you'll help.' Mrs Carr placed her hands on her knees as if a deal had been struck.

'With what?' Distracted, Stella hadn't heard her.

'You'll find out the truth.'

'We don't...' Finding estranged spouses might be the bread and butter of most private detectives, but it would not be the route for Clean Slate. Stella must leave; Jackie could parry any fallout.

'You will sort it, you're a cleaner!'

Stella was as certain as she could be that Mrs Carr was mad.

'I have more of these, so don't run away.' Stella undid the dog's lead, holding his collar, and gave him a biscuit from the pouch dangling from her belt. 'Re-lease!'

The poodle sped away over the grass and just as she thought he wouldn't stop he tumbled to a halt and faced her.

A gust of wind smacked her fringe across her face. She dragged her hood up and another blast smacked it down again. She had no hat. Stanley had upset her routine; she had to take him out come rain or shine. Jackie had suggested she employ a dog walker, but Stella had promised to mind Stanley; she had to do it herself.

'Stanley, come.' She spread her arms. The dog raced back and, full tilt, crashed against her leg, finishing in a sketch of a sitting position. Stella gave him a biscuit.

The afternoon was gloomy, strata of greys in the sky; there were darker clouds over the turrets of Wormwood Scrubs prison. Stella had wandered far on to the common; Braybrook Street was in the distance. She knew the area. Jack and she had interviewed a suspect in the Rokesmith case who lived in the street. Her dad had grown up around the corner in Primula Street and been a policeman in Hammersmith most of his life. She had seen a newspaper photo of Terry with other officers on his hands and knees doing a finger search on the grass where she stood.

Another gust of wind. Jack would say Terry was giving her a sign. She zipped her anorak up to her chin.

She remembered the buzz of that interview, the thrill of a solid lead. They had planned the questions and their approach. Good guy – her; bad guy – Jack. Like a real detective, she had written up the details afterwards and filed them. It seemed easy, looking back: they had boxes of paperwork to go on, salient information to pull out. With William Frost's case, all they had to go on was his conviction that his brother had been murdered. Suzie would say they shouldn't touch it and she'd be right. Or she would if she were here. Stella frowned. In reply to her message to him the day before, Jack had texted saying he was driving all day. She didn't want to talk to Jackie while she was in the office, or indeed when she was at home, as she would be telling Jackie there was nothing she could do for Frost.

Stanley had met another dog. Stella headed towards them. She had learnt that dog owners' etiquette required humans as well as their dogs to interact.

'How old is he?' An elderly man in a baggy rainproof jacket, a hand-knitted scarf knotted around his neck, was regarding the dogs as they sniffed each other's behinds. In the dog world, this was apparently polite.

'About two.' Stella wanted to explain that he wasn't her dog and that she wouldn't have him much longer, but that was giving too much away.

'Molly's submitting for a change! What's his name?'

Stella blinked, resisting the temptation to say she didn't know, which would appear ridiculous. 'Stanley.'

The man exclaimed: 'Same as me!'

'Ah.' For a wild moment, Stella wondered if he was David's father, Stanley's namesake. 'What's – um – what's yours called?'

'Molly.'

'That's nice.' He had already said. Stella scuffed her boots on the grass.

'Good to have met you, lad.' The man addressed Stanley; another thing dog owners did was channel conversation through their animals. Stella approved of this. She preferred being at one remove. The man melted into the shadows, his dog with him.

Her phone buzzed.

Can we speak?

Stella deleted the text, the second in a week. No need to speak; David wanted the dog back. Fine. She would ask Jackie to sort it. A drop of water stung her cheek. The dark clouds were now overhead; she heard a rumble of thunder. She whipped Stanley's lead from around her neck and cast about for him.

He was cavorting towards her with the skittish leaps that she had understood meant he was up to something. Front legs up then hind legs, like a rocking horse. What might look enchanting to others filled Stella with foreboding. She spied two dainty paws poking out of one side of his whiskery mouth, a long rubbery tail dangling from the other.

A Londoner, Stella had grown up with the adage that she was never more than six feet from a rat. Right now it was a lot closer than that.

While Stella was becoming accustomed to the dog's unquestioning presence, regarding hygiene they were poles apart.

'Drop!' she hissed, although there was no one to see. His capering accelerated into joyous leaps. The rat was hardly smaller than the dog. It must have been dead when he got hold of it.

She headed off towards Braybrook Street without a backward glance, a newly acquired ruse which worked. Frustrated by the loss of her attention, he abandoned the rat and, tail down, disconsolate, fell in by her side. Inwardly congratulating herself, Stella clipped on the lead and joined the pavement by the memorial to the three murdered policemen.

'Here fell...'

She could recite the names and date carved in the marble. The date the police officers were killed in Braybrook Street – 12 August 1966 – was the day she was born.

When she was eight, Terry had brought her to the remembrance ceremony held by the Metropolitan Police on each anniversary of the shooting. Her mum said it was typical he should think it a treat. In fact Stella had appreciated listening to the speeches and being solemn. Someone had said she was lucky to have a daddy, not like the children of the three policemen whose lives they were commemorating. The voice, Stella didn't remember now who had said it, had also said that 'life had better mean life.' Stella had liked Terry holding her hand as if, like Stanley, she might scamper off. For no obvious reason, Stanley barked sharply. Jack believed dogs could detect ghosts. If Terry were to haunt anywhere, this was a likely spot.

Another buzz of a text.

Where shall we meet? Jack.

Ram. 7.30? New case. That should whet his appetite. Seconds later she was proved right.

I'll be there! Jx

Perhaps thinking of Mrs Carr's check on her husband, Stella pressed the symbol beside Jack's text. She was taken aback. Jack was in the same place as the elusive Mr Carr, on Chiswick Mall near the eyot. Jack said there was no such thing as coincidence. She shut her phone, vaguely ashamed to have looked.

The dog was sitting at her feet. She rewarded him, thinking absently how she would be handing back a well-trained animal.

'Heel.' Stella and Stanley headed along Braybrook Street to the van, away from the memorial and its ghosts.

Fourteen

September 1987

'Ready for hunting and gathering!'

'Ready and willing!' Simon stood to attention. It was his job to forage for items on his mother's shopping list. They were in Marks and Spencer's on Chiswick High Road.

'We leave the trolley here and bring stuff to it.' His reiteration of the instructions was part of their ritual; his method was quicker than pushing the trolley through the shop. He had parked it in a recess beside the dairy cabinet and the back entrance.

'I'll be back in record time.' Everything was back to normal. Last week his mum had gone shopping without telling him. She had said she would take less time on her own, and he had been dismayed. Today was about proving her wrong. He peered at the list she was holding and memorized the first three items. 'A packet of water biscuits and eight ounces of brie. Daddy's off cheese.'

'It's not for Daddy,' she snapped.

'You don't eat cheese.'

'It's for guests.' She ruffled his hair and the boy allowed himself to breathe.

'Are there going to be guests?' Simon hung over the trolley handle. He hoped it was the woman who had just moved in next door.

'See how many you can get in, say, ten minutes.' His mother gave him the entire list.

'I shan't need that long,' Simon asserted. Although he relished the challenge, the change in operation worried him.

'Do it properly.'

'Synchronize watches.' He consulted his watch with luminous hands and markings for seeing on night expeditions, or in bed. Mr Wilson and Justin both had Timex watches.

She was looking over at the door to the car park and not listening. The boy sped off to the frozen section where, rootling around for crinkle-cut chips, it struck him that without the list she couldn't hunt for anything.

Simon minimized journeys to the trolley by collecting armfuls of food. He dropped a bag of lentils reaching up for cornflakes. This was awkward, but lots of short trips took longer. He would explain this; she loved his theories.

With four minutes to go, she still wasn't by the trolley. Simon unburdened himself, mindful not to crush the lettuce, tomatoes, eggs and butter with cans and bags of vegetables as instructed.

The automatic doors to the car park swooshed aside and Simon was hit by a draught of cold air. A woman with a girl about the same age as his sister perched at the front of her trolley entered. His mother was in the car park. The door shut and he saw sense. It wasn't her. He fetched six cartons of milk from the cabinet, the last items, and trotted along each aisle in search of her.

The list finished in twelve minutes and thirty-five seconds, he returned to base camp. It wouldn't have occurred to Simon to pretend he had done it in the allotted time. He and his mother told each other the truth; they had no secrets. Justin would be impressed because the ten minutes was meant to include his mum doing some too. Simon recorded each feat so that when he met him again, he could tell Justin.

Gingerly Simon went over to the back exit. The door opened when he stood too close to it. He looked out. The woman was his mother and she wasn't alone.

'Could you either go out or come away from the door? You're letting in all the cold,' an old man clutching a wire basket rasped at him.

Taken by surprise, Simon went outside.

His mother had parked their car by the entrance; there was no need for her to be by the pavement. Simon inched around the car, reassured by its solid familiarity, and crept along the gap between the cars and the wall. He got as close as he dared, but couldn't hear what she was saying. Blindly he turned and ran back into the shop.

He drifted mechanically along an aisle, supported by the trolley. He joined a queue, imagining he could pay, pack the shopping in the boot and drive away. He bottled sudden rage that being nine he could do none of these things. Simon felt as he had when Justin had left the school and Simon was no one.

'I've been looking everywhere for you!' She wrapped her arms around him, cutting out the light. He inhaled her perfume and another smell – smoke. She didn't smoke.

'I was here,' he replied numbly.

'You were meant to stay by the trolley.'

'Ten minutes is over.' He was by the trolley, but he didn't say that.

'Not by my watch.' She briskly rearranged cartons and tins, although she didn't need to.

'I got everything in twelve minutes and thirty-five seconds. That was without you helping.'

'Did you get grapes?' She was consulting the list.

'No.' He scrutinized the trolley. Grapes should be on top with the eggs. He looked at the list. Grapes were not there.

'I'll get them.' He worried that if she went, she would vanish again. The store whizzed by, shoppers pushed him, trolleys dug into his legs, he was jabbed in the ribs with a wire basket. Red or white grapes? They never ate grapes. Red.

'Come on.' She was about to pay for the shopping. 'Didn't they have white?'

'No.' The cashier raised one eyebrow; he knew he was lying. Simon felt himself grow hot.

She took the bags off him without saying, *You're my rock, I can't do without you.*

'You'll never guess who I met!' They were driving into their street.

'Who?'

'Mr Wilson, your religious education teacher from Marchant Manor. He left soon after you did, he's been living in London all this time!'

Simon pulled on his half-finger, the habit formed when he was a much littler boy and had still harboured hope it would grow back.

'Did he come to see me?'

'Of course not!' She laughed. 'He said "Hello".'

'Is he coming to teach at my new school?' Mr Wilson had said he was his friend.

'Stop being silly, Simon.' She never called him silly.

Simon sank into the seat and decided not to ask why Mr Wilson had been holding his mummy's hand.

Fifteen

Monday, 21 October 2013

Jack knew the sounds in the house. The owl's thud resonated up to the top floor and, regardless of who was knocking, she lightened his spirit. This sound was sharper. It was the letterbox flap. He glanced at his watch: ten to seven.

He peered out of the sitting-room window. He was meeting Stella, he couldn't be delayed. It would be a charity or Jehovah's Witnesses. It wouldn't be Stella, she always texted first.

A man in a black coat, a baseball cap pulled low, was going down the path. He didn't look up at the house as Jack would have done, certain that someone would be there. He was walking past Isabel Ramsay's house without dropping in a leaflet. Stella had advised Jack to put up a 'No Junk Mail' notice, but he liked to know what people were up to. He couldn't say this, nor could he point out that Clean Slate did leaflet drops. Stella wouldn't consider them junk.

When his father was alive – his mother too, he supposed – post was left on the hall table. Nothing there now. Nor was there post on the doormat. Downstairs Jack did up his coat, pleased to be seeing Stella and excited by a new case. He considered following the man, but it would contravene his promise to Stella and he'd be late. Something was under the marble table. There was a leaflet after all.

To Let. A5 and pink: another leaflet about the tower. The owners obviously hadn't found a tenant.

Rereading it, Jack considered that the word 'cosy' wasn't usual estate agent vocabulary. Stella would have no truck with 'craving silence'.

... crave silence and a bird's eye view, then Palmyra Tower is your home. Guardian wanted for Grade 1 listed Water Tower. You will sign a year-long contract with no breaks and be available to take up residence as soon as your application is accepted.

The phrase 'detailed views' was peculiar. From high up, the view couldn't be detailed; it would be better to emphasize the breadth of the panorama. Whatever, by now the owners would have found a tenant.

You will.

His eye lit upon the pack of Tarot cards on the hall table. Since finding the card on the mat he hadn't looked at them. At some point, though, he must have replaced the Tower card, it was face up on the top of the pile, tightly bound by the elastic band. A sign.

Jack smoothed out the flier on the marble top and scanned the text. At the bottom of the flier he found an email address. *info@palmyra-tower.co.uk*. He opened his phone and tapped out a message: *To whom it concerns, if it's vacant, please may I rent the flat in Palmyra Tower? Yours, J Harmon.*

On the doorstep he stroked the owl's tucked-in wing with a finger. 'You don't need a tower to see the world,' he whispered to her.

In the subway, Jack's voice was insistent and sibilant.

'Oh that I were where I would be,
Then would I be where I am not;'

He left the tunnel and hurried up the ramp on to Black Lion Lane.

Another voice completed the verse in the bleakly tiled tunnel long after Jack had gone.

'But where I am there I must be,
And where I would be I can not.'

Sixteen

September 1987

After dark, the gate to the cemetery on Corney Road was closed, so Simon used a hole beside a side entrance in the church passage. Inside, he scampered along between the mounds, alert for intruders. The good thing about living full-time in London was that he could go to his den more often. Another good thing was that no one at the Chiswick school called him 'Stumpy'.

It was two years since he had seen Justin, but he could picture him and hear his voice. Sometimes, in front of the bathroom mirror, Simon imitated his sniff and the jerk of his head. In two years, Simon's sister had learnt to jump and could manage a few words. Time and wishful thinking had rendered Justin a loyal confidant; he was Simon's best friend.

The boy cut along the boundary wall, out of sight of the houses that had replaced wharfs and factories by the Thames. The stench of the river deadened the air. His belted mac was damp from the pall of mist that was suspended above the squat stone tombs and mausoleums. Flaking and worn, the headstones had been erected in the early nineteenth century and their graves were sunken and smothered with browning weeds.

Simon looked across the cemetery and saw, far off, that the lit upstairs windows in his street were just a string of lights. He couldn't see his house. His dad wouldn't know he was out because Simon had pushed a pillow under his duvet. His mum said she was seeing a friend and Simon preferred to believe her.

The ground was crisp with fallen leaves etched with frost; his footsteps crunched in the chill quiet. Once he missed his footing and stubbed his shoe on broken masonry.

Simon reached a brick hut under spreading conifer branches. Originally used for storing tools which the maintenance crew had transferred to an aluminium shed by the Corney Road gate, one wall was lined with ancient plaques, scrolls and shields of blackened granite or slate, many stained the lurid green of carbonized brass. Traces of inscription – 'left us', 'dead', 'fell asleep' – were ghost messages.

Simon had noted all this on his first visit; they were signs to tell Justin about. That Justin lived so close to him in London was another sign.

He had stumbled upon the building two weeks earlier when he had rushed out after his mother, who had gone shopping without him. He had cut across the cemetery, intending to catch her at the Hogarth roundabout lights, but he was too late. Giving up, he had found the hut on his way back and made it his den.

A pile of leaves and branches was heaped by the side of the hut. He approached the door gingerly and, reaching up, tapped on the hut door. The rotting wood was spongy and crumbling and his knocking made little sound.

All clear. Inside it was pitch black. Simon's nostrils pricked with the smell of damp earth. He switched on his torch and found a broken flower pot by his granddad's old deckchair. First the mound of leaves, now this. He had an intruder.

He held the torch low to avoid light escaping out of the half-moon window. The table wasn't where he had put it; the wooden crates and the deckchair were set around it. Simon shone the torch into the supplies cupboard and saw his bottles of Coca-Cola were still there. He was pleased with himself for remembering the opener, although now that he was here, he wasn't thirsty.

He put his torch on end on the table and lowered himself into the deckchair. Now it faced the door, which was better. Who had been here? Practised at surveillance, Simon made sure no one followed him.

It was colder inside the hut than out and Simon wished he'd brought a jumper, but he was an explorer, so he mustn't mind.

The door burst open.

'Get out!' The command sliced the air. Hands pulled him out of the chair and pushed him across the table, pressing his face to the splintered wood.

'We've got a fugitive,' the voice shouted.

'Stop it!' Another voice – a girl, Simon thought. He couldn't move.

'I think you mean trespasser.' He mumbled politely, and decided not to say he couldn't leave because he was being pinned down.

'Name and rank?' The hand yanked his hair, forcing him up.

'Don't do that,' the girl said.

The hand let go. Simon fell to the ground and scooted over the damp earth to the wall. Peering up from behind a packing case, he saw a skeleton by the table. It had dark sockets for eyes. He melted with fear and the room dipped.

'Who are you?' The skeleton had a gun.

The room was dipping because the skeleton had picked up his torch and was waving it at him.

'Don't do that, you're blinding him.' The girl directed her own torch at the skeleton and Simon saw he was actually a boy with short hair and jutting cheekbones. Perhaps hearing the girl, he lowered the torch.

'I know him!' the girl said suddenly. 'He's at our school.'

'Shut up, Nicky, don't give away our identity.' As the spots of light cleared, Simon saw that the boy was dressed in army clothes, a jacket with epaulettes and lots of pockets that was too big for him.

'What regiment are you?' he rapped at Simon.

Simon knew the boy. He had seen him in a corner of the playground where no one went. He had been crawling along the grass below a wall, so at first Simon hadn't noticed him. He had stayed watching him; then, sensing danger, he had retreated before the boy realized he was there. No way out now: the boy was barring the exit and he had a gun.

'Answer!'

'Sorry, I—'

'What regiment?'

'I don't— There isn't a name.' Simon had no idea what he was talking about, but did know his life depended on giving the right answer.

'Who are you spying for?'

'No one.' If Justin were here he would kill the boy, Simon thought. 'I'm by myself.' He was lying, because in his mind Justin was with him.

'How do we know that? What are you doing here?'

'I was checking everything was in order. I was keeping watch.' Simon got to his feet, his mind busy. The girl placed her torch on the table and took Simon's torch off the boy in the army jacket. She laid it on its side. The beam bounced off the bricks and sent a dim glow around the hut. To Simon it looked like a cave.

The girl wore a duffel coat and her hair was pushed back with an Alice band, which made her look fierce. Simon knew her too. She had sat with him at lunch on his first day and asked about his last school. She hadn't been fierce then. She had got him seconds of sponge with hundreds and thousands and custard that he hadn't wanted because he was homesick, but made himself eat to please her. Best of all, she hadn't asked about his finger. He had since seen her in the playground and she had waved. Apart from his little sister, Simon didn't know any girls personally.

'You will follow my orders.' The boy's voice made him start.

'Yes.' Simon stood up straight and involuntarily clicked his heels together.

'Yes what?'

'I don't know what you mean,' Simon admitted.

'Yes, *sir*, I'm the Captain!' the Captain said. 'You are our prisoner. A trespasser,' he added.

Simon panicked. If they locked him in the hut, he would never be found. 'I have to get back or my—'

'He could join the unit. You keep saying we need to train up new recruits,' Nicky said.

There was silence while the Captain appeared to be giving this some thought.

'This is my lieutenant. She's our Official Codebreaker. Every undercover unit has one. If I were to let you in, you'd be a private and do as we say.' The Captain went to Simon's supplies cupboard. The torchlight glinted on Simon's bottles of Coke. The Captain took one out.

A flash of silver. Nicky raised her hand; she had a knife. Quaking, Simon flattened himself against the wall.

'You do it,' the Captain said to the girl and Simon saw it wasn't a knife, it was a bottle opener. He felt no relief.

The Captain sat down in the deckchair. This meant he had his back to Simon, but Simon knew there was no point in attacking him – he would get shot before he reached the door. Wrenching off the cap, the Captain stretched out long legs.

'You may not be fit for this unit.' He frowned at the bottle.

'Give me a chance,' Simon pleaded. If he were in a unit, Justin would be his friend. A unit changed everything. He could break codes too.

'Before you can join, you must prove yourself worthy.' The Captain tipped the bottle to his lips.

'How?' Simon felt despair. With his bad finger he would never be able to prove himself.

'Nothing and no one comes before the unit.' The Captain was rubbing at some mark on his trousered knee. 'You are trespassing in our headquarters, that's a capital crime.'

'He was here first,' Nicky said. From that moment Simon loved her. 'He must be brave. It's nearly eight o'clock now and he's out here on his own in the dark.' She added: 'We never come here by ourselves.'

'I do.' The Captain took a swig of Simon's Coke.

The girl looked at him and shook her head the way Simon's mum did at Simon's dad. 'I vote we set him free and recruit him. He could be useful,' she said.

Simon had never thought of having a friend who was a girl, although she had a boy's name.

'We have a Code of Honour. In this unit we look after each other. You have to swear allegiance and do your duty to me.'

'To the God and to Queen,' Nicky the Codebreaker said.

'To *me*,' the Captain repeated. 'Standing orders, you have to address me and the Lieutenant correctly and wear your uniform unless instructed by your commanding officer. That's me. You have to do as I say all the time or you will be court-martialled and shot.'

'*We look after each other.*' Simon had said that to Justin when he came to the school. He had found a unit that would look after him. Privately he swore allegiance there and then. Emboldened he said, 'I was thinking that your headquarters have been penetrated. It's contaminated.' He was pleased with 'contaminated'.

'What?'

The boy got out of the deckchair and leant over the table, knocking over the other torch. The shadows of the three children leapt and vanished as the torch rolled to a stop.

'There's leaves and stuff outside. They weren't there before.'

'It doesn't mean anything.'

'It means someone has been here. This flower pot wasn't here either.' Simon guessed that the Captain mustn't be contradicted.

The Captain snapped into action. 'The enemy is on the move.' He slammed the bottle on to the table.

'You're always saying that,' Nicky remarked wearily.

With a stab of perception that would get sharper as he grew older, Simon saw that the Captain was making it all up and that the girl had had enough of his stories. He saw a chink in the armour. Simon also saw that this didn't make the boy less dangerous.

Simon saw his chance. 'I saw someone so I came to investigate.' White lies were OK.

'I said he was courageous,' Nicky murmured, which seemed to anger the Captain. He chucked his empty bottle on to the ground, hitting soft earth. It didn't break. He faced Simon.

'Private, two tasks for you. In the next twenty-four hours you will find a new HQ and you will steal something valuable from your mother to prove your loyalty. If you fail, we will shoot you.'

‘That’s not fair,’ Nicky protested. ‘We didn’t have to do anything to join.’

‘We knew we could trust each other! He might have put those leaves there himself. Come on!’ The Captain stomped out of the hut.

The mist had lifted; the headstones were luminescent in the pallid moonlight. A keen breeze sent leaves and twigs through the open door into the hut. Simon started to clear them, but as they were decamping, there was no point.

He was slotting the key into the lock of his parents’ house when it hit him. The Captain had given him impossible tasks so that he would fail. Simon believed that if he stole from his mother he would die.

The boy looked back at the cemetery. Chiswick Tower loomed behind the yew trees. From high up there he could spy on the enemy.

Simon let himself breathe. He had found their new HQ.

Seventeen

Monday, 21 October 2013

St Peter's Church clock struck seven as Stella came out of the subway. She was deliberately early. The Ram had been her dad's local and she had suggested they meet there because it was close to Terry's. Since texting Jack, she had decided to refuse to take on William Frost's case. It was of the open and firmly shut variety. They wouldn't linger; she would return to Terry's and do a survey of industrial carpet cleaners, a task Stella viewed as a treat.

In the nineteenth century Black Lion Lane South had been a rural lane of workers' cottages fronted by hedgerows and surrounded by fields and orchards. The lane survived the urban creep of London until the 1950s when the extension of the Great West Road spliced it in two. Pedestrians reached the river from St Peter's church by a tiled tunnel. On the south side, a row of cottages opposite the Ram maintained a hint of country. The pub, once frequented by ostlers, street sellers and the costermongers and those who made a living from the reeds growing along the bank and on Chiswick Eyot, was now the hostelry of choice for professionals, bankers, actors and retired police detectives.

Stella pushed through the crowd and found Jack at a table out of the way, but with a view of the door. Still in his coat, reading glasses resting on the tip of his nose, he was deep in his *A–Z* guide to London. He jumped when her dog snuffled at his leg and pushed a glass of orange juice across to her. He wasn't drinking, not even his usual hot milk. To Stella's surprise, he had got a bowl of water for the dog.

'Did Suzie enjoy her trip *down under*?' He put on an Australian accent.

'I've no idea.' Stella hung her anorak over her chair and showed the dog the bowl, who bypassed it for a stray crisp. Tilting her glass at Jack in a vague toast, she sipped the orange juice.

'What do you mean?'

'I haven't seen her.' Stella got her Filofax out of her rucksack.

'Oh, I see.' Jack pursed his lips.

He would be thinking she'd not checked on Suzie since her return. For a man without a mother, he had plenty of advice on the subject.

'You *don't* see.' Stella flicked to the notes she had taken after talking to William Frost. 'She's staying in Sydney.'

'Forever?' Jack exclaimed. He looked stricken. Taken up with her own worry about it, Stella had forgotten how close he was to her mum.

'I'm to go on watering her plants. A clue that she plans to return. Or maybe not. Would you keep cleaning her flat, please.'

'Has she fallen in love?' Jack's eyes were brown liquid pools. Stella thought he looked upset.

'No!' she snapped because Jack had hit the nail right on the head. 'Mum says Terry was her wrong turning and that she's done with relationships.' Stella tried to remember when Suzie had last said that.

'Look, Stell, chill! Suzie is too astute to be fooled.' Jack fanned the pages of his *A–Z*, looking far from chilled himself.

Stella considered that she had taken more wrong turnings than her mum – some in this very pub. She should have suggested meeting Jack somewhere else.

'About this case, I have pretty much refused it. But Jackie suggested us to him and so I said I'd talk to you, not that there's much to say.'

'Talk to me.' Jack folded his arms and leant forward.

'In a nutshell, a man died and the verdict was suicide. His brother says he was murdered.' With repetition it sounded even more flimsy.

'What do the police say?'

'He spoke to Martin Cashman at Hammersmith. Reading between the lines, Cashman sent him packing.'

'What did he do? Hang himself, jump off Beachy Head?'

'Actually it was in your territory.' Stella realized she had been putting off saying how the man died. Jack was sensitive. When she first knew him, the colour green made him feel ill. She had cured him of that, but with Jack you still had to tread carefully. There was no way round this one. 'He was waiting for a District line—'

'Which station?' Jack interrupted.

'Stamford Brook.'

'When?'

'About a month ago.'

Stella got it. 'Was it your train?'

'No.' He shook his head. 'It was on the Piccadilly line.'

'But you know about it?' When Jack was upset he went a whiter shade of his usual pale. He looked like a ghost.

'I was there. His name was Frost – like the poet.'

'What poet?'

'Robert Frost.'

Stella consulted her notes. 'Frost wasn't a poet, he was in surveillance.'

'No, I meant— Never mind. I saw Frost go off the platform. Stamford Brook is one of the stations the Piccadilly line trains pass through at high speed. It's a good place for suicide, not that "good" is the right word.'

'So, it's cut and dried.' Jack's having been there gave them honourable grounds for turning down the case. It would be doing William a favour; he could let go and mourn his brother. Jackie was always saying you shouldn't bottle up grief. But Stella was disappointed. She wanted to work on another case with Jack.

'Why does the brother think it was murder?' Jack asked.

'Rick Frost, as he was called, told William he was being threatened and was on his way to tell him more when he died.'

'Feeling threatened sounds a good reason to kill himself.'

'You could say, but he's adamant Rick wasn't the sort. It's like Mum going to Sydney.'

'Delicious food, rich culture, sunshine and sea – how is that like jumping in front of a train?'

'It's out of character.' Stella checked her phone. It was breakfast time in Sydney.

'I'm telling him it's "no",' she decided.

'He'll be extremely upset.' Jack erred on the side of catastrophe. 'If Frost *was* murdered, it was a "perfect murder".' Jack opened his *A–Z* at the first page, as if preparing to read and said, 'the police checked the CCTV footage. He wasn't pushed – there was no one on the platform to push him.'

The dog growled. Stella was about to 'ssh' him when the growling erupted into a shrill cry, making heads turn. Jack was waving at the door.

'I remember him from the inquest.'

The dog was on his hind legs boxing the air, apparently full of joy at William Frost's arrival. Busy reining him in, Stella was too late to stop Jack agreeing to Frost's offer of drinks.

'Here's how!' William raised his glass and clinked theirs. Jack had asked for tap water.

Frost was dressed in the same preppy gear as when she'd first met him. Chinos, a lambswool jumper with a windcheater. When he took the jacket off, Stella saw one wing of his shirt collar was caught inside the jumper. This irritated her. If it had been Jack, she might have corrected it; as it was, she tried not to look.

'Jackie said I was in good hands.'

For a man who had lost his brother recently, Stella thought him too cheerful. 'I'm afraid we—' she began.

'Tell us about your brother.' Jack settled in to listen. Stella tried to catch his eye.

'I'm three years older than Rick, but it felt like a lifetime. We disliked each other from the off.'

'The spirit of the dead grows alongside the living. When you think of him in twenty years' time, he'll still be three years younger,' Jack opined.

Stella groaned inwardly. 'I should stop you, because the thing is—' she tried again.

'They live on through us,' Jack finished.

William Frost spread his hands on the table. Stella got the frightful notion he was going to suggest a séance. Jack would be keen on it.

'Rick was a fantasist. He tried to join the army, but he got turned down. He was prone to indigestion. He was rejected by the reserves too.'

'Makes sense. Soldiers have to be fit to fight.' Stella had intended to say nothing, keep it short.

'Rick should not have been in charge of a gun.'

'Why not?' Jack asked.

'He would have been trigger-happy, shoot you as soon as look at you. When he was a kid, he went around in full army gear, camouflage, the lot. Harmless stuff, but when most boys get interested in music or sport, Rick was still dressing up. I seriously thought he might blow us all up or become one of those weirdos who shoot their classmates.'

'Weird how?' Jack was leafing through the pages of his *A–Z*. He treated it like a bible, saying it helped him make decisions. Stella guessed that Jack had been fairly weird himself as a boy.

'As I told Stella, Rick was a surveillance consultant. Not MI5, more intruder alarms, CCTV. Suited his fantasy of pitting himself against the world. I pitied his wife. When he told me about the threat, frankly I ignored him.' He finished his beer and pushed the glass away.

'Was he in debt?' Stella asked.

'He was tight with money, but it's worth checking out his business. I know he hasn't left his wife sitting on a gold mine. Worth talking to her too. It wasn't all hunky dory in that particular garden.'

William hadn't told her this on the airport run. Jack had a knack of getting clients to open up.

'What about friends?' Jack was asking the right questions.

'None. At the funeral, it was just me and his wife.'

'What's her name?'

Any minute surely Jack would say he had seen Rick Frost jump off the platform. All these questions was him letting Frost down gently.

'Tallulah.' Frost frowned. Stella nearly pointed out that he would have to accept personal questions if they agreed to take the case. She avoided commenting on the name, partly suspecting him of making it up.

'You don't know what or who was threatening him?' Jack finished his water.

'No, but as I say, it's worth checking out his clients.' He wiped a hand down his face. 'I hardly ever saw Rick. I meant to say last time that it's my fault I didn't get that last call from him. If I had, think I would have put him off. I was on an all-nighter to finish a job – I'm a graphic designer, we have tight deadlines. If I'd not had my phone on silent maybe he'd be alive.'

'If he was murdered, it didn't matter,' Stella said, less to reassure than to be precise.

'Then I had a couple of constables at my door asking me to come and see Tallulah. I did try ringing him, even though they told me they believed it was his body at the station. Idiotic. Got his voicemail and assumed the police had his phone – in those situations they don't answer – but later I found out it was missing. Another reason why I think he was murdered. He was dead, how could he get rid of his phone?'

'What did the police say?' Stella asked.

'They thought it had been stolen by kids. Then when it hit the news that it had belonged to a dead man, they dumped it. Station staff found it a couple of weeks later, under the platform at Ealing Broadway.'

'Sounds likely.' Stella felt bound to defend Cashman and his team, who seemed in fact to have it sewn up. 'Who has it now?'

'Me. The police kept it, but it's been wiped so they found nothing on it so gave it to me. Odd, don't you think?' He laid a black iPhone down on the table. Its silver case looked to Stella as if it was bullet-proof.

Stella was grateful that Frost had brought them something tangible.

'Odd and not odd,' Jack murmured serenely. He was looking at his street atlas.

Stella was impatient. Jack didn't need the *A–Z* to tell Frost that he had been at the station, that he had seen his brother die and knew it was suicide. It was time to end this charade. She caught the words Chiswick Mall on the page; Chiswick Mall was the street where Mrs Carr's husband had texted her from.

'I'm guessing you've decided against taking this case?' Frost folded his arms. 'Jackie said you'd hear me out, so thanks.' He nodded to Stella.

'We'll take it,' Jack said. He reached out and, picking up Rick Frost's phone, put it in his coat pocket.

'Will we?' Stella was aghast. She was tempted to snatch back the phone and slam it down on the table.

'We will need to talk to his friends and relations, starting with his wife.' Jack jumped up, indicating the meeting over. Stella got up too.

'I can give you my sister-in-law's details, but she won't meet you. She's refusing to see me. Guess I remind her of Rick.'

Jack beamed at him. 'We can find ways in.'

Stella didn't think she would like Jack's 'ways'.

William Frost pulled on his jacket. 'I have an idea for getting into her house. Go undercover as a cleaning company and ask questions incognito. Clean Slate *is* a cleaning company so you have carte blanche to do a search and gather clues.' He was animated.

'Not a bad idea.' Jack was watching the dog nosing at his feet. 'However, we don't just turn up on doorsteps with our brooms, we have to be invited.'

'Cold call her.'

'For domestic jobs we post leaflets. We only call businesses after we've sent an email,' Stella intervened. They hadn't made cold calls since her mum had gone to Australia.

'Post her a leaflet.' Frost had an answer for everything.

The atmosphere had cooled.

'It's unethical,' Stella insisted. 'We don't clean under false pretences. As Jack said, we'll find another way to speak to Mrs Frost.'

'You're making it harder for yourselves. What if she's my brother's killer?'

'You are welcome to find another investigation agency.'

'I admire your approach.' Frost's face was stiff as a mask. He made a show of getting out his own phone and consulting it as if about to call a competitor in front of them.

'Do you think she is?' Jack looked away from the dog.

'Sorry?' Frost put away his phone.

'Mrs Frost – Tallulah – do you think she murdered your brother? It would save time if you told us your suspicions,' Jack said.

'She's not the killer.' He folded his arms. Jack said it was a sign of defensiveness, but, big and broad, William Frost would win any fight.

'Is she a beneficiary of his estate, life insurance, the house, death-in-service pension?'

'Yes, but why make a murder look like suicide? She won't get his life insurance.' Frost shrugged his shoulders. 'You have to fight fire with fire. You need to get into his house and knocking on the door all nice and polite won't do it.'

'It's possible she would get his life insurance.' Stella dredged up an unasked-for lecture from a client who was a lawyer, while cleaning his bathroom grout. 'Providing the policy was taken out a significant period before death and your brother disclosed any mental health issues.'

'Exactly!' Frost exclaimed, as if Stella were corroborating his point.

'Did he have enemies?' Jack wasn't giving up. Although the question cropped up in crime dramas, Stella found it unconvincing. She could number her friends on one hand – two fingers – but she didn't think in terms of how many enemies she had. Clean Slate's operatives, including Stella herself, had upset clients – cobwebs missed, bleach used instead of tea tree oil, rival companies hunting for tips that mystery-shopped their service – yet they couldn't be described as enemies. Or could they?

'Rick installed recording devices in air-freshener dispensers and alarm clock radios. He fitted those intruder alarms that collect stats on staff entry and exit. They lead to sackings, divorce, shattered reputations. Lots of reasons for revenge.'

'Would that be aimed at your brother's clients rather than him?' Jack queried.

'Who do you suspect?' Stella was pleased by the question. It would tell them as much about Frost as who might have killed his brother.

He pursed his lips. 'I don't point fingers.'

'It would help if you did?' Jack said. They were being a team.

'Look into his business. As I say, I bet he had a lot of enemies. He certainly had no friends. I'm sure the reason the army refused him was he had "psycho" stamped on his forehead.' He hadn't answered the question.

'Who do you—'

'If anything occurs to you let us know.' To Stella's surprise Jack got a Clean Slate card from his coat and scribbled a number on the back with the stub of a pencil.

When Stella shook William's hand, she was surprised that it was without grip.

After he had gone, she asked Jack, 'Why did you say we'd take it?'

'If it's not suicide, like I said, it's the perfect murder. His idea about going in undercover was good. Please tell me you were pretending when you said we wouldn't do it?'

'We're not compromising Clean Slate. People need to trust their cleaners.'

'Still, I'd like to know why Mrs F. isn't speaking to William. That stuff about looking like his brother is nonsense. I saw the picture at the inquest, I thought then how they didn't look like they were brothers,' Jack mused. 'We only have his word that he was at home all night.'

'The police went round.'

'Hours after his brother died.'

'Why would William ask us to solve a murder he had committed himself?'

'A clever murderer flirts with capture. He or she can't help themselves; they want to test their brilliance and stave off boredom. Behind his charm, Frost is ruthless. He didn't like your refusing his idea one bit.'

'And who is called *Tallulah*?' Stella groaned.

'Tallulah Bankhead, the actress,' Jack replied promptly. 'She laid a foundation stone in St Peter's Square when they built the Commodore Concert Hall. You must have seen it.'

Stella despaired of having an ordinary conversation with Jack. Although the name was familiar, so perhaps she had seen it. Terry had taken a photograph of the Commodore on fire when it was being demolished: she did remember that.

Stella reproached herself for her impatience. Jack had seen a man die; she should cut him some slack. If he believed this was a case, she would go along with it. But despite William Frost coming via Jackie, Stella did not trust him.

'If Tallulah was alive she'd be a hundred now.' Jack glanced at his watch. 'Goodness, I'm on the Underground in one hour, forty-three minutes and fifty seconds. Come on!' He stuffed the street atlas in his coat and jumped up.

'Where to?'

'Stamford Brook station. I'll show you where Rick Frost died.'

Eighteen

October 1987

The quarry moved along Burlington Lane. He kept a distance of ten metres, already composing his report for the unit. A woman in a black coat and high-heeled boots and a black handbag is walking fast along…

Simon's mother was visiting Mrs Henderson, the lady with the fishpond and a hundred knitted animals. She always gave him cake when he went too, but his mum said he was to stay at home with his sister because when he was working, his father forgot she was there.

'She usually comes with us.'

'No she doesn't.' She squirted perfume on her wrists. This lie had made it easy to steal her wedding ring from the lacquered box with the tiger's face. As soon as she had gone, Simon grabbed his mac from the rack and rushed after her.

She was crossing at the lights, the wrong way for Mrs Henderson's.

He could catch up and demand to know where she was going, but she would lie. Simon admitted to himself that she had been lying to him since he left Marchant Manor and was back living at home.

Traffic on the Great West Road slowed to a stop; a girl was staring at him from the back seat of a car. Simon smiled at her. She poked out her tongue and ducked out of sight. Simon stopped. Then the lights changed and the car moved off. When he looked again, the pavement was empty. He had lost his mother.

The tide was out. Disconsolate and unwilling to go home,

Simon crossed the causeway to the eyot and, scrambling up the bank, slumped against the trunk of a weeping willow. He looked back at Chiswick Mall through the reeds. There was no one about. Stuffing his hands in his mac pockets to keep warm, Simon felt something. Her ring. Since stealing it, guilty and ashamed, Simon had put it out of his mind. He held it to the sky: there were letters engraved on the inside, 'Vita Nuova'. This didn't make sense. His mother was called Madeleine not Vita.

Obscurely, this unfamiliar name convinced Simon that he had been tracking the wrong woman. His real mother would be eating cake with Mrs Henderson. If the ring belonged to someone called Vita, why was it in her drawer?

At his feet was a white stone, smooth as if polished by water. Inchoate with emotion, the boy snatched it up and, stepping across the clearing to a gap in the reeds, he hurled it as hard as he could into the river.

The front door was opened as he scratched his key at the lock.

'Where have you been?' She was wearing the National Trust apron he had bought her for her birthday.

'I went to see Mrs Henderson.' A master stroke. He stared at her, unblinking.

A clock ticked in the living room; somewhere his sister was laughing.

'What do you mean?' She wasn't looking at him.

'I had banana cake.' *Tell me I can't have. You were there, you didn't see me. Say it!*

'Simon, we agreed you'd stay here. I left Mrs Henderson early and went shopping.' She was walking away from him. 'Sweet of you to go, but tell me next time. I do love her banana cake!'

'Actually it wasn't banana, it was a Victoria sponge.' Demons urged him on.

'We're eating in five minutes,' she said as if to no one.

In the bathroom, Simon ran the gold ring over the fingers of his bad hand, his special trick. It was lighter than a coin. He told himself that his mum had been at Mrs Henderson's and then gone shopping. Next time he would give her ring to the Captain and say his mother's name was Vita. Next time he would lead the unit to the tower.

Nineteen

Monday, 21 October 2013

> *'There was a man of double deed,*
> *Who sowed his garden full of seed;*
> *When the seed began to grow,*
> *'Twas like a garden full of snow.'*

Jack's voice was amplified under the railway bridge. The wind had got up since they'd been in the Ram; it funnelled under the bridge, smacking Stella's hair across her face and flattening the dog's ears to his head. A train clattered above, wheels clunking on the tracks. Stella tugged the dog's lead to chivvy him, for the grey-encrusted pavements implied that, prompted by the racket, pigeons roosting on the girders might shit on them. It would not be a sign of luck.

Jack skipped out of the way as a straggle of late commuters came out of Stamford Brook station. Stella's acute sense of smell identified a mixture of scents and body odours and she hurried after Jack into the ticket hall.

'Single to Barons Court. Please.'

Stella was nine when she had made her first solo journey on the Underground. Terry had been called to a job, so she had to return by herself to the flat her mum had rented since their separation. Terry had folded a ten-shilling note into her purse with the lion motif and, crouching, patted her down and stroked her cheek with his thumb as if she was crying. She must *not* talk to strangers, she must be polite to anyone in uniform, even if they were strangers, and she must keep away from the edge of the platform.

'It will be an adventure!' He had tucked a strand of hair behind her ear.

'I wish you were coming.'

'Next time, Stell. We'll go to Upminster and back!'

Perhaps to sweeten the dull misery of access weekends, Terry told his daughter he would grant her three wishes – proper wishes, not things like wanting to fly or live with him and her mum like 'before'. Since these were her greatest wishes, Stella generally plumped for an ice-cream sundae at the Wimpy Bar or feeding ducks in the park, which was really for babies. The last time she had seen Terry alive, he asked if she remembered the wishes. She hadn't. The station brought them back. Too late. Terry was dead. No amount of wishes changed that.

Art deco glass lampshades hanging from the ceiling cast a washed-out light over the ticket hall. In 1975 it had been dingy and grim, and bristled with the possibility of bad people that her dad worked long hours to put away.

She heard a popping; Stanley jerked the lead. It came from a photo booth by the entrance. The curtains were shut; she couldn't see legs beneath. It was an odd time to get your photo taken, she thought. Stanley growled.

'Ssssh!' In here a bark would be deafening. She snatched him up and stroked him to distract him. Jack had started his chanting again:

'When the snow began to melt,
'Twas like a ship without a belt;
When the ship began to sail,
'Twas like a bird without a tail.'

He flourished his pass and swiped them through the barriers. 'This way!'

'I must pay,' Stella protested.

'We're not going anywhere.' Jack was running up a wide staircase. 'It happened at six minutes past twelve, later than tonight,'

Jack said when she joined him on the platform. 'There're three more trains after that. He used his Oyster card, he didn't buy a ticket.'

'Why bother, if he wasn't going anywhere.' Stella frowned at her quip. If an inspector asked to see her ticket, she didn't want to explain she was looking at where a man had killed himself.

Jack broke into her thoughts. 'A single or return ticket might have indicated his state of mind.'

Suicide wasn't an option, but if it were, Stella would approach it like cleaning. Clear the decks, identify materials and equipment, allow for the unexpected – damp, cockroaches or cancelled trains. An Oyster card saved money; even if there was to be no future to save it for, she would factor it in.

'An Oyster card says business as usual. It might mean he didn't expect to die.' Stella looked across to the eastbound platform where that afternoon she had waited as a child, avoiding the gaze of strangers. It was deserted now. Then she had been fearful of forgetting to get off at the right station or sitting next to a stranger. Most of all she had fretted that her mum would be cross that Terry had let her travel alone. That came true; Suzie still referred to how he had 'abandoned his daughter'.

The announcement board above their heads was blank and dark as Jack said it had been the night Frost died. It was a risk to let a child travel alone on the Underground. Terry had trusted her and she had justified that trust.

Trains still went from Stamford Brook to Barons Court, but her mum was on the other side of the world and Terry was dead. Stella pulled herself together.

'You said Frost was standing still, then he ran. Sounds like a snap decision. Sit!' Stanley was straining towards the end of the station, an area of darkness beyond the staircase balustrade. Dogs weren't like children, she couldn't warn Stanley about live rails or strangers.

'He's sensed Frost's ghost,' Jack observed.

'Or he's smelled a food wrapper.' The case was thin enough

without Jack introducing the supernatural. She could smell aftershave, no doubt lingering in the air from a passenger; there was no one but themselves on the platform. 'Besides, didn't you say he died up there?' She pointed in the opposite direction.

'He broke into a run, then swerved off.' Jack walked along the platform. 'Right here.' He crossed to the outer side, perilously close to the edge.

'Jack!' The dog was still pulling on the lead. Dogs were meant to make the owner feel protected. His behaviour was freaking her out.

'Before he jumped, he looked at me.' Jack was on his haunches. He continued to recite:

'When the bird began to fly,
'Twas like an eagle in the sky;
When the sky began to roar,
'Twas like a lion at the door.'

In the empty station his voice was different. Stella wished he wouldn't do this.

'A person about to jump looks at the train. Frost looked at me.'

'Perhaps he changed his mind'

At last Jack moved away from the track. 'I heard a man on the radio who survived jumping off a bridge and straight away regretted it. Water is like concrete if you hit it at speed, and the impact sucks you under. Water is incredible,' he marvelled. 'It comes from the river and it returns to the river.'

'Did you tell the coroner?' Stella pulled him back to the present.

'They want facts, not impressions.'

Stella was tempted to suggest impressions weren't useful at any time, but Jack's impressions had played a role in solving their last two cases. He seemed able to place himself in the mind of a murderer.

'Why did he run along the District line side then cross to the Piccadilly?' Jack pushed his fringe off his forehead and scanned the deserted platform. In the dim light Stella couldn't see his face; his eyes were lost in their sockets. She looked down the platform; the wooden seating booths were empty, the announcement boards remained dark and the tracks were silent. She felt uneasy. It wasn't just that a man had died here. She zipped her anorak up to her chin.

'We should go,' she said.

'Plenty of time,' Jack replied. 'It was as if he changed his mind.'

'Frost was out of sight of the driver? Had he seen Frost, he would have braked,' Stella hazarded.

'Good point. At the inquest the driver's statement said Frost came out of nowhere and he had no time to brake. On the other hand he didn't need to run, why not simply step off?'

Jack's reflection in the partition glass of the nearest booth was warped and strange. Stella thought again how, if she didn't know him, she would be unnerved by meeting him at night. She *was* unnerved anyway.

As if to underline her thought, Jack walked on and resumed his rhyme:

'When the door began to crack,
'Twas like a stick across my back.'

Like this he was impossible. Stella let him go. She watched him until he stepped out of the last pool of light into the shadows and, giving into the dog's straining, she walked back up the platform towards the stairs.

'They never do what they're told, do they!'

Stella stifled a shout.

'Sorry. I didn't mean to surprise you.' A man was by the wall. She couldn't see his face, although he reminded her of someone – she couldn't think who.

'You didn't.' She kept her voice level, although surely he must hear her heart smashing against her ribcage. Besides, he would know he had surprised her.

'They have finely tuned senses,' he remarked. 'Lovely dog.'

Stella was impressed that he put the back of his hand towards Stanley rather than tried to pat his head. He must know about dogs. Stanley licked his fingers. So much for protection. Jack was at the other end of the station; he could do nothing.

She looked up the line. Behind the brick building, they were only visible to the driver of a westbound train, but there was no train at Ravenscourt Park station, a dot in the distance. Any driver would see two people chatting. Which was all it was. *Come on, Jack!*

'He's not mine,' she said. 'I'm giving him back soon.' The man would be surveying the track. Better to do it at night with fewer trains, she supposed.

'He's pretty.' The man took his hand away and surreptitiously wiped it on his coat.

'Thank you,' she said, as if the compliment were for her. 'I'd better go, my friend's waiting.' *Be polite to strangers.* She let him know she wasn't alone.

The Piccadilly tracks were humming. Whoosh! Lights strobed, making her blink; doors and windows flashed a hair's breadth from her. The clunkety-clunk then faded to nothing. Stella swept Stanley into her arms and ran down the platform looking for Jack.

'I thought I'd lost you!' He was in the last shelter, legs crossed, tucked into the corner as if resting after a Sunday-afternoon stroll. He was facing the Piccadilly line track. She collapsed next to him, too agitated to care when he continued to recite his rhyme. Jackie believed that reciting rhymes helped Jack to think.

'When my back began to smart,
'Twas like a penknife in my heart;
And when my heart began to bleed,
'Twas death, and death, and death indeed.'

'He wasn't running towards the track.' Jack linked his arm through hers and drew her closer.

'What?' She would put up with this from no one else. It was freezing, although the glass gave shelter from the wind.

'What's the matter with him?' Jack was looking at the dog. Stanley had begun straining on the lead again.

'He must want to go back up there. Sit!' Stella rewarded the dog's obedience with a fishy treat from the pouch strapped to her waist.

With Jack sitting so close, Stella began to warm up. There was a flicker and she saw that a Richmond train had been flashed up on the board.

'Fear. It wasn't the calm expression of a man acting on a decision. The look on his face was fear.' Jack let go of her arm and set off back up the platform. He continued talking. 'William Frost said his brother was frightened of someone.'

Stella caught up with Jack at the top of the staircase. 'Suppose he was where that inspector is? You wouldn't have seen him, after all. If not for the dog, I could have missed him there. It is probably out of the CCTV's line of sight.'

'What inspector?'

'A man surveying the line.' The dog wasn't pulling any more, so she let the lead slacken. 'Except Frost wouldn't have seen him either.'

'Where is he?' Jack demanded, seeming suddenly alert.

'Who?'

'The inspector.'

Stella lowered her voice. 'Behind that building at the end of the platform.'

Jack strode along the platform and around the brick building at the end of the station.

Stella started after him but, contrary to his behaviour since they had arrived at the station, Stanley now refused to move. She was still urging him to 'heel' when Jack returned.

'No one there. What did the man say he was doing?'

'He didn't say. I presumed he was inspecting the line.' Now that she thought about it, the man had no torch, no notebook and was all in black, unwise for working on the track. 'I suppose he was waiting for a train. Odd to leave when it's due.'

'Oh no!' Jack exclaimed.

'What?'

'Frost wanted me to see who was behind him. It was a sign. But of course I kept watching him.'

'Meaning?' Stella started walking down the stairs.

'Meaning you were right – there *was* another person on the platform that night.' Jack took her arm again, feet in step they returned to the ticket hall. 'I need to go or I'll be late for my pick-up at Earl's Court.' He let go of her arm and made for the eastbound platform staircase.

'I could give you a lift.' Stella was unwilling suddenly to let him go.

'Thanks, but there's a train in three minutes and thirty seconds. Are you OK going to the van by yourself?' Jack hesitated as if he'd picked up on her unease.

'Of course!' Stella shook her head at the idea she would not be.

'Oh, here, I almost forgot. take this.'

Stella saw a flash of silver. It was Rick Frost's phone.

'What can I do with it? You're the techno whizz.'

'It's been wiped, remember? You may as well have it for safe-keeping. For your files.' He nodded as if to emphasize his words. They were detectives, they would have case files.

Stella watched Jack until he vanished at the turn of the stairs. She was standing where Terry had that afternoon; she had turned at the top of the stairs and looked back to see him still there watching her. Jack didn't look back.

A square of white lay inside the photo booth: a set of rejects carelessly dropped. Stella batted aside the curtain and retrieved it: flipping it over she stared unbelieving. In each of the four shots was a man. He was facing the wrong way; the photographs were all of the back of his head. No one did that by accident. Not seeing a bin, Stella slipped the sheet into her anorak pocket.

Goldhawk Road was quiet – no traffic, no sign of the inspector or of the man who had used the photograph booth. On the bridge, the Richmond train slid to a stop, the windows yellow squares against the sky.

Hurrying Stanley beneath the bridge before the train moved off, Stella got an incoming text. It was Jack.

Frost wasn't running towards the train, he was running away from someone.

Twenty

October 1987

By half past four the last of the light gave way to dusk. A pewter-grey sky dulled the waters of the Thames, and conflicting currents between Chiswick Mall and the eyot, fast flowing and dangerous, plaited the surface.

The scrawl of traffic on the Great West Road was muffled by the brewery, a bulwark for the gale that smacked against the embankment wall and harassed mooring chains. On the far bank, spindly larches along the towpath bent against the force. An undulating moan resembled a wail of regret, ever more insistent. A storm was brewing; some talked of a hurricane.

On Chiswick Eyot, beneath the hiss of the wind, the river rose with the wash and hush of the turning tide and a constant trickling. Where once the Thames had dredged up oyster shells and fragments of clay beer mugs, now it offered up more vivid London detritus to the ragged shoreline. Plastic bottles, rubber gloves – blue, yellow, red – tangles of nylon rope, a fractured storage crate.

Three children scampered out from the church porch and, battling against the gale, made it to railings overlooking the beach. Abruptly one broke away and pointed with a half-finger. 'Follow me,' he cried.

Simon sounded more confident than he felt. Aided by the wind he marched along the pavement, careful not to check that the others were behind him, for fear of betraying doubt that they would be.

He ducked down a cobbled passageway, the stones slick and black. Someone stepped on his heel. Simon switched on his torch. It was Nicky. The Captain was there too. They had obeyed him.

'Where are we going?' the Captain demanded.

'Can't you guess?' Simon shone the torch into his face. He ran along the alley and halted by the cage door. He shone the torch upwards. In open-mouthed awe, as if watching a spaceship land, the children gazed up at the tower.

'What is that?' The Captain's voice quavered. He rattled the cage. The hum of vibrating metal rang in their ears after he let go. 'We shouldn't be here,' he said to Nicky.

Simon pulled on his half-finger. If the Captain ordered her to leave, Nicky would go and it would be over. In the last hours Simon had formed two ambitions: one, he would impress Nicky so much she would be his friend; two, he would become the Captain. Lying in bed late the previous night, the boy had worked out that either of these ambitions would lead to the other. Somehow this would lead him to Justin.

'We shouldn't be *anywhere*,' Simon said. 'The unit works undercover. We "slide under the wire of rules and regulations".' He had mugged up on spies. He saw Nicky smile and turn her head away to avoid the Captain seeing. It was going well.

Simon turned the handle in the grille. The door opened with a terrible groan.

'Anyone could get in. It's not secure,' the Captain objected. 'Let's go.'

Simon was thunderstruck. In a flash of a second he understood the situation. The Captain was scared. In all his planning and imaginings, Simon had supposed the Captain invincible, a formidable opponent. But he had an Achilles heel. With a steady hand, Simon shone the torch into the other boy's face and, deathly calm, said, 'We could get a padlock, but it would give us away.'

'How did you know about this place?' the Captain whispered.

'I found it on reconnaissance.' Simon was airy. 'It's the ideal HQ. It's fortified with full sight of the surrounding territory.'

'It must belong to someone,' the Captain persisted.

'It belongs to me.' In the dark Simon smiled. The future was unfolding: the water tower *was* his; he was the host and they would be his guests. He would be the Captain.

'We should come in the day,' Nicky said.

'It is the day,' the Captain snapped at her.

'I meant with more light,' Nicky said. She darted a look at Simon and he felt his nerve falter. As if it had been orchestrated, they were hit by a gust of wind. The metal vibrated and jangled.

'I'm Captain, I'm going first.' The Captain fell into Simon's trap.

'This is illegal. We can't go in, it's not ours,' Nicky said.

'We can if we want, we're allowed,' the Captain replied coldly.

Simon jammed his hands in his mac pockets. Used to exclusion, he was at home with the 'divide and rule' tactic.

'Don't be stupid, your mum would—'

'Shut up, Nicky.' The Captain rounded on her, yelling above the rising howl as the gusts became more frequent.

Simon took a risk. 'Perhaps we should wait for the light.' He addressed the Captain, careful not to look at Nicky, but hoping to indicate that he was with her. Living with warring parents, Simon had learnt how to be on two sides at once.

'Nicky is scared.' The Captain peered up through the criss-cross of silver lines.

'*You* hate heights and this is high!' Intending kindness, the girl unknowingly sealed both her own and the Captain's fate. The Captain was afraid of heights. That was his Achilles heel. Simon saw that Nicky was trying to protect him. That the Captain should need protection implied he was weak.

The Captain pushed past them into the cage and began to climb. The grille shook as he ascended, the high-pitched thrum mingled with the wind.

'You're mean.' Nicky's breath was hot on Simon's ear.

Simon felt that the giant columns stretching high above might crumble and crush him. He turned in time to see a shadow on the glistening brickwork in the passage. Nicky had gone.

The wind intensified to a howl. Stung by her accusation, he set off up the staircase.

A curving walkway was fixed to the base of the tank with rivets and protected by a thin metal rail. Simon tried to grab it, missed and fell on to his knees. The pain winded him. Grasping the rail, he shuffled forward. The Captain stood with his back to the tower wall as if at gunpoint.

'You're mean!'

Long ago Justin had said the same words. Simon flushed with shame. What had happened with Justin's tunnel in the kitchen garden wasn't mean. Justin was his friend; he'd tried to save him. He wouldn't save the Captain. He let go of the rail and, avoiding looking down, he strolled along the walkway towards him.

The Captain didn't move, obviously fearful that even a twitch would send him plummeting down.

Simon found a handle set into the steel; he pulled it and the door opened with a shriek.

'What is this place?' The Captain spoke like a ventriloquist, head stiff, mouth like a letterbox.

'It's a water tower, it stores water and redistributes it.' Justin had told him the basic principle; since then Simon had looked them up.

'If it's full of water, it's impractical.'

'It's empty, it was "mothballed".' If only Justin could hear him. 'This is a panopticon! We will spy on the enemy; they won't know we are here. If there's hundreds of enemies, they won't know there's only the three of us. Wherever they go we will track them. We have three-hundred-and-sixty-degree vision. The tower gives us supremacy!' Abandoning grammar Simon spread his arms like Tutankhamen, the Boy King.

'We can't spy all the time, there's school.' The Captain began a slow sideways shuffle towards the door. Once inside the tower he leant over, hands on knees, panting as if he had run a marathon.

'The enemy won't know when we're not here.' Simon cast back to his notes taken in Chiswick library. 'They won't know when to attack, so they won't attack.' Belatedly, he properly grasped the brilliance of the idea.

Before Simon could stop him, the Captain shut the tower door. The clang ricocheted around the walls like a series of explosions. His mum told him never to shut doors in unfamiliar places, like the chest freezer in the basement. Simon tried the handle and hid his relief that the door opened. He pushed it to, carefully. Justin said you had to respect buildings.

Light drifted in from a porthole high above. When Simon turned on his torch he saw they were standing by a twisting spiral staircase. Up and up it went.

There was a door to the left. The Captain kicked it open and went inside. They were in a huge circular room with rough cement walls. Simon kept the door ajar. With no windows there was no sense of how high up they were: this seemed to make the Captain braver. Simon's authority depended on the Captain's fear. He fiddled with his half-finger.

'There's loads of space for when we – *you* – recruit. And it's dry.' Simon didn't know why he was whispering.

'We can't see out? How do we see the enemy?' The Captain paced the perimeter.

'We go on to the roof. And there are those slits in the walls. They don't know we can't see through them. Anyway it's not what we see, it's what the enemy *thinks* we can see.'

'How do we get upstairs?'

Simon was saved from admitting he didn't know by a dreadful screech. Then an insidious hum like singing, accompanied by metallic tapping. The boys froze. Someone was coming down the corkscrew staircase.

'You idiot! The enemy are in occupation.' The Captain pushed Simon against the wall. 'Lure them off,' he hissed. 'When it's all clear I'll go for reinforcements.'

'He might be armed.' Simon realized that 'lure them off' meant 'let them kill you'. This was what the Captain meant by loyalty.

Simon was furious with himself for leaving the door ajar. His adherence to safety might now cost him his life. At least the Captain had shut the big entrance door, so the enemy wouldn't immediately suspect an intruder. As he thought this, a howling gale rushed into the lobby and he realized the entrance door had been opened. The powerful draught pushed their door open further. Simon tried to back away from the gap, but the Captain stopped him.

'Go out there,' he hissed.

Simon shook his head vehemently. 'I won't until they know we are here.'

The staircase was humming again. There was someone else there.

'Promise me you'll—' a man said.

Simon shuddered. The man was so close, that if Simon reached out he would be able to touch him, but the wind and his own terror stopped him hearing all the words.

He couldn't hear the other person.

' —next Saturday at Stam—. You won't regret—'

A mumbled reply. Simon shut his eyes, but could only hear the first man.

'You owe it to yourself. We only have— life— make— of it. When we're settled we— the kid. One step— time— like living in a coffin, you said so—!'

Simon crept to the opening and, peeping out, saw two people. In the thin light from the porthole they looked like Hosts. Simon's word for murderers, he had told Justin.

One was the man. His head was bald on top like a monk and he was bent over the other person. He was kissing them. Simon was repulsed and wished he was at home with his mum, but she was out with a friend. He didn't care about being captain, he just wanted to be on the sofa watching a film with her – the best of friends – the two of them.

The man moved towards the gap. Simon retreated, but again the Captain stopped him. The other person was a woman. Dark hair, blue coat. His mother's hands. There was the big red stone on her wedding ring. Her real wedding ring; it wasn't the one in his pocket. He could make no sense of what he was seeing. *It was his mother.* Instinctively he moved towards her and then was jerked backwards and manhandled to the floor. The Captain was on top of him, his hand clamped over his mouth.

The clanging began again. Then silence.

The Captain was by the door.

'She's gone.' He clasped his hands, bending forward as if in agony. 'That was a real live prostitute!' He snuffled with stifled giggles. 'Did you see?' He dipped about the tank, clutching his stomach.

A prostitute.

Simon kicked out at the Captain, but he was on the other side of the concrete room and out of his reach. He scrambled to his feet and launched at him.

'She is not a pros—' he spluttered.

'What else would she be?' The Captain grabbed him and spun him around. His height and age played against Simon; in seconds the Captain had him in a tight grip like a straitjacket. He shoved him up against the wall and hissed, 'Shut up! The man is still up there.'

Gradually it dawned on Simon that the Captain had never seen his mother.

It was not his mother. By now she would be making the tea at home, giving his sister a bath; he must leave.

'You're scared of her,' the Captain jeered.

'I'm not.' Simon edged towards the door, but the Captain was blocking him.

'Prove it.'

'How?' Now the Captain was being mean, but Nicky wasn't there to hear.

'Go up that staircase and come down again. Only after I've counted to twenty. Then you can be in the unit!'

'What if he comes out while I'm there?'

'That's how you prove your loyalty. If you don't do that, I'll have you court-martialled and shot.'

'I stole my mum's wedding ring, like you said.' Simon fumbled for the ring, but couldn't find it.

'You what?' The Captain grabbed Simon by the shoulders again and shook him, making his teeth clack together.

'Like you wanted, I stole it off my mother.'

'I didn't say steal her wedding ring! She'll call the police and expose us!'

'She won't.' Simon was suddenly sure. The ring had been in a box hidden at the back of her dressing table; his mother didn't want anyone to know it was there. She wouldn't call the police when she saw it was missing.

'You failed one mission, you'd better succeed at this one.' The Captain's voice was kind. He might simply be concerned.

'To twenty?' Simon confirmed.

The Captain gave a terse nod. 'Twenty seconds.'

Simon crept out into the little space at the foot of the stairs. He put his bad hand on the rail and stared up at the twisting staircase. The tower door was beside him; if he made a dash for it, the Captain would be too frightened to chase him. But he would never see Nicky again, he would never be captain and he could never recruit Justin to the unit. He would be a *no one*.

He climbed very slowly to avoid making a noise, but even so the staircase began to hum. The constant turns disorientated him. Halfway up there was another door, made of metal and very thick. It was open a few centimetres.

'Hon, you came back. I knew you would!' The man was inside.

One. Two. Three.

Simon looked over the platform rail. The Captain was a few steps below. Simon hadn't heard him climb the staircase.

Seven. Eight. Nine.

The Captain was on the platform, behind the open door, his eyes blazing. Hazel flecked with green, they didn't blink. He was smiling as if he liked Simon.

A resounding crash echoed around the tower. Heedless of falling, Simon hurtled down the staircase and plunged out of the main door.

On the narrow walkway a violent gust flung him against the

guard rail. He teetered over the edge of the yawning darkness and dropped to the floor, his knees grazed by the cold metal. Fingers groping for the holes in the grille surface, he crawled along it to the staircase and flew down the stairs, his feet hardly touching the metal.

On Chiswick Mall, he stopped and looked up. The massive tank housing loomed above him, a crouching demon against the darkening sky. There was no sign of the Captain, but through the vents in the tank Simon believed the man with the bald patch was watching.

Simon cut through the churchyard; tripping and stumbling between the graves, he aimed for the string of pinprick lights of his street.

On Corney Road, a stitch in his side and with bloodied grazes on his knees, Simon slowed to a walk and limped along to his gate. His home was the only house with the curtains open, the lights blazing. His mum was sitting on the sofa. She glanced out of the window. Simon told himself that she had been there all the time. That it was him she was looking out for.

Twenty-One

Tuesday, 22 October 2013

'Mary, Mary, quite contrary
How does your garden grow?'

A scream. Balanced on his haunches, Jack grabbed at a willow frond. A gull was perched on the tide marker. As he watched, it opened its beak and let out another anguished cry.

The sun had gone behind a cloud; soon it would be dark. Absorbed in weeding his Garden of the Dead, Jack had not considered he could be stranded on the eyot. Usually alive to alteration in the rippling water, this evening, mulling on Rick Frost's mysterious death, he had lost sense of time.

'With silver bells and cockle shells
And pretty maids all in a row.'

Jack snipped the last of the reeds and grasses in the bed. The wild flowers – London rocket, wild garlic, poppies and flixweed – that, over the last year, he had planted in honour of the dead attracted bees and butterflies in the spring and died back in the winter. They surrounded a circle of white stones that represented the souls of his dead. At the centre was his mother.

He fetched his coat from beneath the willow and a paper flew out of the pocket. Jack snatched it up. Besides his planting and the stones, he left no trace of his visits to the eyot. Only once, when he was young, had he met others in his garden.

To Let.
Apartment in Water Tower.
A cosy home with detailed views.

It was the flier for the tower. He thought he had filed it with the scant paperwork involved for his moving. It must be the first one he had received. Through the curtain of willow fronds Jack saw the water was rising. He stuffed the leaflet back in his pocket and wended his way beneath a canopy of brambles and briar to the western end of the island. His direction was counter-intuitive: the shortest route to Chiswick Mall was the other way, but the river had already submerged the end of the causeway by the eyot. Jack knew it was easy to slip off the causeway and be pulled under by the Thames's unforgiving currents.

The scene altered with every turn of the tide, but blocks of stone and brick remained embedded in the mud. He knew which would sink under his weight and to side-step slicks of slime that hid mud as deep as quicksand.

Two people were on the beach by Chiswick Mall, a woman and a boy of about three. The child ran about, his legs kicking. Arms flailing, he lacked economy of movement. At the edge of the spreading pool, he hurled a stone into the water, which plopped into the shallows. Jack would throw like that, letting go too late, curtailing momentum. When Stella threw a ball for Stanley, it could pierce the sky.

Jack paused when he reached the steps below Chiswick Mall. In the diminishing light the tower was menacing. According to the flier, it was no longer called Chiswick Tower, but had been renamed Palmyra Tower. He recalled that his father had been commissioned to build a bridge in Palmyra, a suburb of Perth in Western Australia. Seemingly insensitive to the fact that the boy had lost his mother, he had sent him a postcard of Fremantle Cemetery and told him about an unmarked grave for Martha Rendell who was hanged in 1909 for murdering her stepchildren. Jack kept it in his box of treasures. Substituting the name of the tower for one of a foreign city 'dis-located' it from its history and surroundings. It was, Jack felt, a betrayal.

None of the windows in the tower were lit, but still Jack had the crazy notion someone was up there watching him.

'Let's get home, have tea and then bath and bed.' The woman's voice carried across the beach. 'Leave those stones, you've got enough.'

The boy had gathered a bundle of rope, stones and wood. 'Can I have it like soldiers?' he piped.

'They're not soldiers, they're fingers. Yes, if we go now.'

Jack caught a reflection in the water of wings outspread. The gull he had seen earlier was floating on a thermal. Jack had once had a 'cosy home'.

'They're not soldiers, they're fingers.'

He leant on the railing overlooking the river. The road would flood in twenty-three minutes. The woman and her little boy hadn't passed him; he would have seen them. They must have seen the tide coming in, but even so he should have warned them. There was no one on the pavements; no car was driving away. Even the gull had flown away.

The boy and his mummy were the streaks of grey in the darkening sky, the snatches of light on the water. Jack understood why they left no footprints in the mud.

A glow lit up the wool weave of his coat.

'Hey!' He was hearty: Stella didn't believe in ghosts.

'My mum has faxed Jackie, she'll be back tomorrow evening. I'm to clean the spare bedroom and change the sheets. We know what that means.'

'Do we?'

'She's met a man!' Stella's cry was like the gull's.

'What did the fax say?'

'What I said about the sheets.'

'So she mightn't have met a man. If she has, is that such a—'

'My mum is a bad judge of men,' Stella huffed down the line.

'Not so bad. She chose Terry.'

'She walked out on him!'

'It could be the friend she's been staying with.' He wouldn't mention Stella's own shaky judgement of men. She didn't rush headlong into relationships, she made her mistakes after much consideration.

'It's not.' Stella was trenchant.

'She's asked you to make up the bed in your room, not her own bed. That sounds like a friend.'

'Mum would never share her bedroom.' Stella was arch. 'I'm to collect her – *them* – from the airport. I can't meet you, I have to get over to her flat now.'

'That's a good sign.'

'What is?'

'She wants you to meet this person, instead of springing him or her on you.'

'She *is* springing him on me.'

Above the brewery, the tower was a palpable presence.

'Shall I go with you?' Stella kept his ghosts at bay.

'Thanks, but no need. I've started putting together a plan of action. We need to know Frost's friends, his likes and dislikes, his routines. I'll send it. I've tried to describe the man I saw at the station. Meanwhile Frost's wife is our prime suspect and no, I haven't changed my mind, we'll find another way to talk to her.' She rang off.

Jack knew that Stella's objection to the man – if the mystery guest was a man – would be out of concern for Suzie. He suspected that were he in Stella's shoes, he would be concerned at having a stranger taking over his bedroom. He would mind his mother calling his bedroom 'spare'; it would make him feel as though he didn't exist. He hoped that if Suzie Darnell had met a man, he would like him.

Ghosts. Spare bedrooms. Hot toast and honey. The falling away of old structures. The revelation of the true self. *A cosy home.* His home. Jack recognized the signs. In the light of the lamp-post he saw he had an email. It was from– *info@palmyra-tower.co.uk* and headed without apparent irony: –

Your tower awaits you.

Twenty-Two

October 1987

The carriage clock in the sitting room struck two.

'I have to go out.' His mother was rinsing a mug under the tap.

'Where?' He had begun to hope she was staying in the house with him. He could tell her what she planned to do, but that would make it true and it wasn't true.

'Shopping.' She put the mug on the draining rack. It fell on to its side, but she didn't notice. 'For apple crumble, your favourite!'

He wanted to say he hated apples, but he couldn't lie to her. Her wedding ring – her real ring – was on the shelf behind the taps.

'You'll lose your ring if you leave it there,' he said instead.

'If I leave it there, it won't get lost.' She tipped water out of the washing-up bowl.

'I'll "forage" for apples.' He was suddenly happy. She really was going shopping.

'You've got homework.'

'I haven't got homework, I just have to write what I did at the weekend.'

'That's homework.' She still had her back to him. 'Simon, if you want to be helpful, go and get your sister.' She snapped off her rubber gloves.

'Is she going too?' That made no sense: his sister was too little. 'She can't "hunt and gather".' He had a thought. 'The weekend hasn't happened yet.' Justin would like that argument.

'Now!'

His sister was sitting on the sitting-room floor, walled in by big coloured bricks.

'You're going shopping, Beeswax!' His name for her because with her blonde pigtails and stripy jumper she resembled a bumblebee. It didn't occur to Simon to take out on her his resentment that she was going when he wasn't allowed. He made the expedition to Marks and Spencer's sound as exciting as he actually thought it was.

One by one he lifted away the bricks, sorry to dismantle her construction, then reached down and hauled her up. Staggering, he nearly dropped her. This highly entertained her and she let out a raucous chortle.

In the hall he cajoled her into her anorak and then fixed her into her buggy. He fetched plastic bags from the cupboard with the vacuum cleaner and jammed them into the buggy's carrier. When she craned around to watch him, he did a monster face and made a scary noise. She chortled again.

'Sah. Sah!' Her attempt at his name. She could say words like Mama, mat, bottle.

Heartened by her delight in him, Simon kissed her on the forehead. She smelled of talc and shampoo.

'Bees, your job is to spy and report back to me, OK?' he whispered.

If his mother thought she could keep secrets, she was wrong. When his sister said 'mat', she didn't mean the thing you wipe your feet on. She hadn't got to grips with 'n', she was trying to pronounce 'Nat'. Mr Wilson's name was Nat. The boys at Marchant Manor spelled it 'Gnat' and called him a stick insect behind his back. Simon didn't call him this because he had thought Mr Wilson was his friend. His mother wasn't going shopping, she was meeting Mr Wilson.

'I'm off, Simmy.' She used her name for him and fluffed his hair and, pleased, he considered he might be wrong about Mr Wilson and it was shopping after all. She took her coat from the hooks and opened the front door.

He scrunched up his nose. 'You smell funny.'

'Don't be horrid, darling, it's perfume as you well know. Start your diary. We've had most of today, haven't we, and when you've written it, read it to Dad.'

Today my mummy went away with Mr Gnat Wilson the Stick Insect. The Captain said she was a prosit... a pros—

His sister was tootling like a train, their sign; he shot her a smile and choo-choo sounds of an engine.

'I could write about the shopping.' Simon looked down. Her shoes were pointy and shiny with spiky heels. He had never seen them before.

'Sah. Sah!'

The buggy clunked over the brass threshold and the front door shut. His mother had left the scarf he had bought her with his pocket money on the hook. *Pocket money.*

Simon rushed upstairs and into his bedroom. He wrenched off the lid of his money tin. Inside were seven fifty-pence pieces. He dropped them into a pocket in his trousers.

He pulled on his mac and ran out of the house. Outside he saw her green Citroën 2CV. His mother had abandoned her pretence of shopping at the gate.

The water tower blocked out the sun. Simon waited until his mother appeared on the other side of the subway and then ran down the ramp, through the tunnel and up the other side. Chiswick Lane was a problem, a straight road with the park on one side and houses on the other so that there was nowhere to hide. Luckily she never looked behind.

By the time he got to the radio repair shop at the top of Chiswick Lane, she was metres from him on Chiswick High Road, walking fast.

He fell into pace with a woman holding hands with two girls, younger than him. If she glanced back, she would assume he belonged in their family.

The family peeled away, leaving him exposed. His surveillance skills were unnecessary: she didn't look anywhere but where she was going. He could have walked alongside her and she wouldn't have seen him.

They were nearing Marks and Spencer's – she might after all be shopping; she didn't need much so that was why she didn't want him to come. It was why she had left the car.

He dashed across the zebra crossing without waiting for the traffic to stop. A blaring horn, a slant of red as a bus missed him by centimetres. Someone shouted.

He hurried after her under the bridge, now so close he could hear the rattle of the buggy wheels. Outside Turnham Green station, he used a newspaper vendor as a shield. She was at the gateway to the platform when he entered the station. He asked for a return to Upminster, the end of the line; he could go either way with it if she was going to Richmond or Ealing Broadway. He had no idea of the cost of a train fare, so he pushed all of his fifty pences under the glass.

He shovelled up change into his bad hand and went up the stairs. There was a train in the station; he got on as the doors were closing.

Simon grabbed a central pole and looked up the carriage. She might not be on the train. He tried to see if she was on the platform, but the train was already out on the open tracks. She might have gone the other way. He was sick with himself for his stupidity.

He made his way up the aisle to the end, grabbing at poles, and peered through the glass doors. She was standing up, wheeling the buggy back and forth as if to lull his sister to sleep, but she was carrying her – the buggy was empty. As Simon noticed this, his sister looked at him and put out a hand, fingers splayed as if to catch him. He retreated and trod on something.

'Watch it!' A man in jeans, his woolly jumper tucked in, legs sticking out in the gangway, glared at him.

'Sorry.'

The jumper was striped, but red and gold, not yellow and black like his sister's.

'What you staring at?' the man said.

'Sorry.' Simon hugged a pole and risked another look through the carriages. His sister was chattering to his mother, she would be telling her she had seen him. 'Sah, Sah!' He hoped his mum wouldn't believe her.

At Stamford Brook station, his mother turned the buggy around and backed off the train. A man helped her lift the buggy out on to the platform. Simon jumped down and saw instantly that his sister was looking for him. His mother glanced in Simon's direction. He didn't have time to move, but she was looking right through him as if he was invisible.

He waited until she disappeared down the staircase, then chased after her, holding his trouser pocket to stop the change jangling. Outside the entrance on Goldhawk Road, she pushed the buggy over to one side and stopped. It was precisely three o'clock. All of sudden he understood what was happening. He had caught only a fragment of their conversation at the tower, but he knew his mother did things by the clock – in that she was like his father. She was leaving home with Mr Wilson. Properly leaving, not going shopping or going to the tower. She lived in a coffin and now she was escaping. Why hadn't she asked him to come with her? Simon pulled on his half-finger. Why was she taking his sister? She was meeting Mr Wilson on the dot of three. She was on time.

His head filled with questions, the boy drifted out of the ticket hall into plain sight of his mother. She had her back to him and was looking up and down Goldhawk Road, her handbag hanging from her shoulder, the flap open.

Simon realized he was exposed and shrank back behind a closed newspaper stand. The headline on the vendor's box read *Lester Piggott Jailed*. He didn't know what to do. Justin would know. He saw that one of his sister's arms had flopped over the side of the buggy. She had fallen asleep. He wanted to lift it up and lay it on her lap. *There, there, Beeswax, sleep tight and make lots of honey*. Their private joke.

The minute hand on his watch went around five times. He risked leaving his post and wandered back into the station. One strategy was to tell his dad everything and let him deal with it. He dealt with disturbed people all the time. He could 'section' Gnat Wilson, a thing his father did that Simon assumed meant cutting people up into pieces.

Simon looked at the station clock. It was a quarter past three. Mr Wilson was fifteen minutes late.

The man with the jeans and the stripy jumper from his train was running towards him from the road. Fleetingly Simon supposed he had got off at the wrong station. He tried to move out of the man's way, but was stopped by the photo booth. Stepping away from it, he lost his balance and his leg slid out from under him; he tried to get his balance and felt a boot catch his calf. There was a thump. Mr Wilson! He grabbed at the man and kicked at his leg.

It wasn't Mr Wilson. It was the man from the train. Simon was shoved aside by a man in station uniform who grabbed the man and pushed one of his arms behind his back.

Something flew across the ground. Instinctively Simon caught it. Black leather with a flap that was open. It was his mum's handbag.

'Police!'

'Thief!'

'Get him.'

Stamford Brook station teemed with people: passers-by, station staff, passengers from an Upminster train pulling out of the station. There was the whoop-whoop of a siren and a Ford Focus with chequered strips and flashing lights tore up to the zebra crossing. Two police officers pushed through the gathering crowd. It took a few moments for someone to see a small boy in grey school trousers and a jumper with a tear in the sleeve, sitting slumped against the photo booth clutching a woman's handbag. A few more moments for the people who dragged him to his feet to understand that he wasn't the accomplice of the culprit but the son of the woman whose bag had been snatched.

Simon was taken outside to where his mother was talking to a woman police officer. His sister reached up a hand and he squeezed it.

'You and me against the world, Beewax,' he whispered to her. 'I'll protect you. Always.'

'Bzzzzz!' she replied confidentially.

'Kid's a hero,' a man in London Transport uniform told the police officer. 'Tackled the guy – piled in there. Fearless. That boy loves his mum!'

Simon didn't take his eyes off his mother. Unblinking he stared, and when she looked away he spoke quietly so that no one else would hear: 'Since he's not come, we can go hunting and gathering.'

Twenty-Three

Wednesday, 23 October 2013

Stella waited while Stanley sniffed at a lamp-post. She swapped hands on the lead as he pottered around the post to prevent him becoming wrapped around it. They were outside the house on Primula Street in Hammersmith where her dad had been born and lived until he moved with Suzie to Rose Gardens North. Terry had swapped the hum of the A40 for the Great West Road. Stella had a photograph, presumably taken by Suzie, of Terry leaning in the doorway, with her nana and herself, aged four, on the doorstep of the house she was outside now.

Terry's father had died of a heart attack when he was fifteen.

'I was at school, I rushed out of the biology lab, dodged across roads, I didn't care. I stood on the path outside our house and yelled, "Not my dad! Not my dad!"'

When Terry himself had died of a heart attack, Stella had resented the disruption to her work.

Not my dad!

The semi-detached red-brick house looked smaller than she remembered. A wheelchair ramp had replaced the step. Her nana would disapprove of the double mattress slumped against the wall and the television dumped on balding turf. Gone were the marigold borders and window boxes in the photograph. A plastic urn, faded and cracked, flourished with dandelions by the ramp.

Her nana's ashes were scattered at Golders Green Crematorium. Terry used to visit the memorial book on the anniversary of her death. Terry was cremated at Mortlake. It hadn't occurred to Stella to put an entry in the memorial book for him. Suzie hadn't let

Terry's death get in the way of expressing her dissatisfactions about him. Recently, Stella realized, her mum had been quieter on the subject. She had someone else on her mind. *Dale Heffernan.*

Her phone was ringing. Jackie.

'William Frost wants to get hold of Jack.'

'Did he say why?'

'No. You OK with working with him?' They hadn't yet spoken about Jackie referring the case.

'Yes, although I'm not sure we can help,' Stella said. She saw a face at the upstairs window and for a second assumed it was her nana. 'He said he knew you when he was a boy.'

'Hardly. William's brother Rick used to play with our neighbours' kids. We'd just moved in, all our cash was soaked up by the mortgage, we were on rations, no sofa or table. There were two children next door, a sweet boy as thin as a rail and his cute sister, think her name was Lulu, something like that. Their parents' marriage was on the rocks, the dad was a psychiatrist with a fancy car, chap never passed up a chance to be sarcastic about his wife – talk about airing dirty linen! The boy was playing substitute husband, protective little mite. I made Graham promise that those parents wouldn't be us one day. I think we've succeeded! The boy – or man – moved out years ago, he rented the house out and is only selling it now. We're holding our breath as to who buys it. Good neighbours are gold.'

Stella drifted along the street, content to listen to Jackie's chat about her home life.

'Anyway, William got Jack's answer machine. I said to call you. I'm guessing that with Jack's new venture, he can't spare the time.'

'He's not driving every day.' Stella assumed Jackie meant the day shifts Jack was doing for a colleague whose partner was unwell.

'I'm thinking of his move. It's today, isn't it? He's already in a state about that owl! I told him, "Take it with you." He won't, he said it's like taking the fireplace or half the garden. She – he says it's a "she" – belongs with the house. Jack gets attached to things. I said to Graham, "That owl is a constant in his life. The lad's not got many, poor lamb!"'

'Not many owls?'

'Things, people, places. A legacy of losing his mother young means that he's slow to trust others, you know that. I do hope this is a good decision. He could get lonely up there.'

Jack hadn't said he was moving. His working for Stella wasn't a pass to his private life, but Stella had supposed they were friends. Jack didn't have a pet, certainly not an owl. He wasn't interested in her dog, not that Stanley was her dog.

Jack was leaving Clean Slate.

A man was walking towards her. Stella moved to let him pass. He moved too.

'There you are!' William Frost was barring her way.

'Jackie, I'll have to go.' She rounded on him. 'How come you knew I was here?'

'My brother designed this app, it shows me where any of my contacts are at any time. I'm testing it for him.' He shrugged. 'I *was* testing it. I found you in minutes.'

'What do you want?' Stella did not like being 'found'.

'I tried Jack. What a dark horse he is!' He seemed oblivious to her annoyance.

'He's moving house,' Stella retorted. She didn't have Jack's new address. Unwilling to admit that he hadn't told her what it was, she hadn't asked Jackie for it.

'You and me then!' Frost said. 'Let me buy you lunch.'

The pub was crammed with sleekly dressed lunchtime office workers. Bulky in her wellingtons and anorak with a small poodle on her shoulder – in case he trod mud into the carpet – and wind-tossed hair, Stella felt out of kilter. She went for cheesy chips and a ginger beer and, while William threaded his way through the crowd to order food and drink from the bar, she retreated to a table at the back. It was next to a cleaning cupboard and immediately the whiff of polish calmed her. She gave the dog water in his collapsible bowl. He drank greedily and then flopped against her leg, his sodden muzzle soaking her trousers. Once this would have horrified her, now she barely noticed. She flipped to a clean page in her Filofax, clicked on her Clean Slate ballpoint and wrote today's date at the top, underscoring it for good measure. Glancing up, she caught sight of Jack by the door. Dropping her pen, she half rose.

'Food's on its way.' William slid into the seat opposite and handed her a frosted tumbler of ginger beer. 'This is nice!' He clinked a large glass of red wine against hers. 'Here's how!'

'Cheers.' Stella sat down and drank her ginger beer. She gave a spluttering cough – she had forgotten she hated fizzy drinks. Bubbles bursting in her gullet, she looked for Jack, but couldn't see him.

'Two seconds.' She got up and, unleashing the dog from the table leg, pushed through the throng to the door. The pub faced Wormwood Scrubs common, an expanse of green. There was no one there. No sign of Jack. She was about to text him, but saw she had no signal. Reluctantly – she could do with Jack with her – Stella returned to the table.

'Let's start with your brother.' She spoke with a confidence she didn't feel. Jack was moving; perhaps he'd come into the pub to get a sandwich.

'As I said, it's his wife you should be talking to.' William raised his glass as if in another toast. 'Being his brother didn't mean we were close.'

'It's a start.' Not having a brother, Stella couldn't argue, but she found his unwillingness odd. Why had he gone to such trouble to find her? 'Let's start with his likes and dislikes.'

'How will this help find his killer?'

Stella tapped her pen on her lips. She didn't know how it would help or why she'd asked. She glanced at her phone, hoping, despite the lack of signal, that Jack had texted. 'If this is a pre-meditated murder, his personality and his routines might have contributed to his death. Obviously if it was a random killing, it won't help at all.' Faintly pleased with herself, Stella wrote 'Likes' and 'Dislikes' divided by a line.

'Liked the army, disliked me, liked spying on people, disliked heights.' William gave a satisfied huff as if giving the correct answer in a pub quiz and sat back for a young man to put a plate heaped with a slab of steak and a mountain of chips in front of him.

Stella's chips came on a large platter nestling beside a jungle of salad that was way beyond a garnish.

'What was he like as a boy?' Stella untangled a chip from threads of molten cheese.

'I was three years older, a big age gap when you're small.' William drained his glass. 'We didn't share friends.' He was devouring his steak with the urgency of someone refuelling before whizzing off to do something dangerous and pointless, a quality Stella grudgingly admired.

'Who were his friends?' she asked.

'That's overstating it. He didn't have friends as such; he had a gang who did what he told them. They had a hideout in a graveyard near our house.' Frost looked around him as if expecting to see Tallulah Frost in the pub. Stella looked too, still hoping to see Jack. It couldn't have been Jack, she decided.

'Rick was the sort of boy who pulls legs off spiders. One of them ended up marrying him.' William dropped his voice as if they might be overheard.

'One of the children in his gang?' He couldn't mean spiders.

'Total surprise. Rick wasn't interested in relationships, gay or straight, he was in love with the army. Can't say there was much love lost between them.' He frowned. 'And hey, the army don't want soldiers chewing on Gaviscon double action before going into battle!' He tossed his balled napkin on to his empty plate, the edges soaked red with bloodied juices. 'Me, they'd have had like a shot, as it were!'

Stella could imagine William Frost leading a platoon in the army, striding forth without hesitation. She doubted he suffered from indigestion.

'He designed that tracking app. If he didn't know anyone, why did he care where anyone was?'

'I didn't say he knew no one, just that he didn't have friends. No point in tracking someone you trust.'

'Can anyone use that app?' Stella examined her fingers, an idea forming.

'Give me a name and bingo!' He snatched up his phone. 'The one drawback is that the person can tell you're "watching". A pair of eyes pops up at the top of their screen. You have to hope they don't notice – and few people would. Rick would have sorted that if he'd not—'

'In general' – Stella waved her hand – 'does it keep a history of people you've followed? If we knew your brother's movements, we might find out who he thought was a threat.'

'The software must be at his house.' His reply was pointed.

Stella got the hint. She was not dressing up as a cleaner. Their plates had been taken away without her noticing. She berated herself; she was too easily distracted to be a detective.

Jack had been doing day shifts on the Underground – for a friend, he'd said. She had thought that, apart from herself and Jackie, he had no friends. She didn't count Lucille May, the flighty journalist they had consulted for the Blue Folder case who, like lots of older women, had a soft spot for Jack.

'Do you want a coffee?' William was on his feet. Again he glanced about him.

'White no sugar, thanks.' So far in this interview she had netted nothing. They had said their prime suspect was Rick Frost's wife. Perhaps Jack's idea that William Frost had executed the perfect murder and couldn't resist boasting was correct. He seemed intent on saying how he was better than his brother and something was making him jumpy. She felt a wave of unease and was grateful to be in a packed pub and, although he was fast asleep at her feet, to have the dog with her.

While he was at the bar Stella scribbled down a list of questions. Jack would angle them to encourage William to talk laterally, to ramble on and give himself away. Stella wanted to cut to the chase and instil shock value. *Did you murder your brother?* If Frost could commit a perfect murder, he would lie as convincingly. She needed Jack to scrutinize body language while she asked the questions. Jack was on her mind; that was why she thought she had seen him. Where was he moving to?

William had left his phone on the table. Stella could see him at the bar giving their order to a woman. She snatched up his phone and brought it to life. Nearly passing out that he hadn't protected it with a password, she tossed the handset back on to the table.

The woman was pouring coffee into cups on the counter. Stanley must have sensed something was wrong because he was on his hind legs, front paws on her thigh. 'Ssshh!' she admonished him, although he had made no sound.

William was leaning on the counter in conversation. The woman had stopped what she was doing. Ignoring Stanley, Stella retrieved Frost's phone.

She had no idea what the app was called and swiped screens back and forth looking for it. She found an icon of a magnifying glass. *Stalker Boy*. She shivered and glanced up; the woman was putting saucers under the cups. The dawdling would be annoying in another circumstance, but now every second counted. Stella willed Frost to keep up the banter as her fingers, damp with perspiration, dabbed on the icon and opened the software.

It worked intuitively, like Google Maps. She keyed in Jack's number and pressed a button unreassuringly labelled *Seek and destroy*. An explosion motif spread across the picture to the sound of glass shattering. It must have reverberated around the pub and she looked to see if William had heard, but he was still chatting. The phone emitted the sound of footsteps, slow and measured, then louder and faster. *Come on!* She cursed Rick Frost's sense of humour – or drama. William was holding the cups; he was moving away from the bar, still talking.

A crosshair symbol targeted *Chiswick Lane South*. Stella grabbed the handset and guided the cursor to it. The *Seek and destroy* legend changed to *Shoot*. She 'fired'; the image did a kaleidoscope swirl and up came a shot of a concrete cooling tower. So much for the accuracy of the app. She had no time to check that she had put in the right telephone number because William was coming across the carpet towards her. She dropped the phone; it slid over the table and landed on William's chair.

'Sorry about that, the barmaid was telling me her life story.' William put the cups down and noticed his phone. The backlight was on. Stella nearly fainted as he handed her a coffee. Stella took it, her hand trembling.

'My mother's arriving home tonight.' She dared not look at him. Taking a sugar sachet from a bowl on the table, she ripped it open with her teeth.

'My app will tell you if she's in flight this time!' William picked up his phone, seemingly unsurprised that it was open, the icons ready. Stella went ice cold. 'What's her flight number?'

Her mouth dry, Stella read it from her diary, the numbers and letters swimming before her eyes. Frost was playing her; he was letting her know he had seen her with his phone.

He had said it stored previous searches. Stella hadn't erased her search. She went into a flop sweat and it was all she could do not to fling her coffee at the phone.

Seek and destroy!

'Last sighting was at Sydney Airport. She'll have turned her phone off. I think you can be confident she's coming this time!' He laid the phone down in front of her as if it were a gun.

'Thanks.' Something was escaping from the folder in her Filofax. It was the sheet of pictures from the photo booth at Stamford Brook station. On an impulse she pulled it out and laid it on the table.

'Do you recognize the person in this picture? I realize it may be difficult.'

She had forgotten to tell Jack about the pictures. Looking at them now, even upside down, Stella was surprised to see the back of the man's head bore a resemblance to Jack. Was that what he was doing when she was talking to the man on the platform? It was horribly likely.

'Is this a joke?' Frost's friendly manner had evaporated.

'It's a bit of a punt. I found it where your brother died.' She didn't say where. Terry would say, 'Keep something back.'

'He's facing the wrong way. How could I?' William pushed the sheet back to Stella and pocketed his phone.

'Did you enjoy your brother's company?' *What did you enjoy about your brother's company?* might elicit more. She was sickened. By searching for Jack on *Stalker Boy* she had revealed to William – and to herself – that she didn't trust Jack. She had exposed them.

'Not one bit.' William's eyes were like pebbles.

Twenty-Four

Wednesday, 23 October 2013

Jack closed the door and the quiet was instant and profound.

His desk and chair were bathed in sharp sunshine; a rectangle of light shone on his bed. Through the north-facing window he could see only sky. It was so high up, nothing interrupted the view. The kelim from his parents' hall lay beside the bed. He had never noticed that it matched the bedspread; his parents had probably bought them at the same time. There was so much he didn't know. His cupboard was set between the flat door and the north window.

The removers not only worked to a short lead time – it was a mere two days since he had answered the advert – they had had an acute sense of space – it was a prerequisite for transporting furniture in confined areas – but this was different, they had put everything where he would have put it himself. Someone had a mind like his own.

He crossed to the south-west window. From there he could see all of Chiswick Eyot. He could also just see his meandering path into the centre of the eyot, but was relieved that his garden was hidden. He could follow the Thames in both directions: towards Barnes and past Hammersmith Bridge.

The window sill was the thickness of the tower wall, over a foot in depth. Jack settled into the alcove. As the leaflet said, the views were detailed.

He hadn't visited the tower before signing a six-month lease with Palmyra Associates. As well as being able to move in so quickly, Jack had been astonished to get a reply within the hour accepting his request. He had offered references, Stella as his employer and Lucie May, his journalist friend, for character. The second was foolhardy; Lucie wouldn't know if he was trustworthy and nor would she care. Isabel Ramsay had known him from when he was a baby, but she had been dead two years. The email said references were not necessary. Jack had never rented a property. After his parents died, he inherited their house and when he stayed with Hosts he did so in secret.

The lease had arrived that morning. When he posted back the signed copy to Palmyra Associates, he'd noticed that the PO Box on the 'return' envelope had a West London postcode. Their website was a holding page which, considering Palmyra Associates only operated online, was surprising. But then, he had found the tower through a flier so maybe they didn't need one.

They had forgotten his stuff. Jack leapt off the sill. The removers had not brought his photograph albums, newspaper cuttings, Host notebooks, journals mapping his train journeys: the record of his life. At some stage he would have to put his mother's clothes, paintings and papers into storage. Jackie had sourced him a self-storage unit on the Great West Road. Time enough for that. Stella – who was being tardy in selling her dad's house – would at least understand that.

Stella didn't understand that he believed inanimate objects – like clothes, books, furniture, even his owl door knocker – had feelings. He was in no hurry to pack up his house. He couldn't bear to think of the suitcases, his mother's clothes and pictures locked in a cell with no light or sound, abandoned. Jackie said he would have a key and could visit any time. She had assured him he could rent a unit with an ambient atmosphere, free of damp and insects. It might be rather better than everything remaining in his unlived-in and unheated house, she had carefully suggested. Jackie was the Queen of Tact. If she was here now, she would retrieve all his things with no fuss or bother.

Jack ran around the partition. The table from his playroom and two of the kitchen chairs were under the south-east window. The logical place for these was against the partition, leaving a route to the bathroom. Jack would also have put them by the window so that he could watch. He looked out through the reinforced glass. He could see the detail on the turrets of Hammersmith Bridge; over in Kensington, a cluster of green would be the trees in Holland Park. Far off, the North Downs morphed into a bank of pink-grey clouds like a snowy mountain range. It would be too late to fetch his things tonight.

Jack slid aside a panel and revealed a large space, the quarter of the circle. Were he not upset, he'd be excited by the shower. Tiny nozzles in the ceiling would send out powerful jets of water. In an old water tower, there would be ample pressure.

Jack had chosen the removers recommended by Palmyra Associates because they knew the tower. Few firms would be willing to negotiate the stairways outside, even less the spiral stairs to the flat. Clean Slate offered attic clearance and Stella wouldn't balk at a tower, but he had been keen to do the move alone. Although Stella would have arranged the furniture according to logic rather than spirit, at least his stuff would be here.

Jack plodded back to the main living area and sat on the end of the bed, nursing an ache in his chest. It was a kind of homesickness, although he had only briefly known a home to be sick for when he was very little. The door to his cupboard was ajar so he got up to shut it.

Every shelf was full. Cardboard wallets, file boxes, bundles of letters, notebooks in a row, spine out. At the top, exactly where he would have stowed it, was his biscuit tin of particular treasures. Beside the cupboard by the north window to the right of the door was the clay bust of his mother set on its square plinth. How had he missed it?

So quick to panic, he had missed his laptop, his street atlas, his green-glass lawyer's lamp. The removers had stocked the kitchen cupboards with his pans and the hot milk mug Stella had given him. In a drawer they had stowed his parents' cutlery. On a shelf above they had arranged the blue enamel tins labelled 'Tea', 'Coffee' and 'Sugar' that Isabel Ramsay's daughter had given him after the house clearance. They had left a litre of fresh milk in the fridge, semi-skimmed as he liked it, and thought to leave out his pot of organic runny honey beside the cooking knives.

Jack stifled any disquiet that strangers had handled his personal things and read his mind and set about heating some milk. After years of searching he had found a home.

He sat in the kitchen, sipped his milk and watched a man walking his dog along the towpath on the south side of the river. On Hammersmith Broadway, cars moved with more order than was perceptible at ground level. Before him was the city in miniature; he was floating above London as if on a magic carpet.

His elbow jogged a leather case tucked into the corner of the sill. It wasn't his. He prised open the lid and inside found the most beautiful, elegant pair of binoculars he had ever seen. Chrome and black, substantial but not heavy, with a soft leather strap. He had planned to buy a pair, but it seemed that they came with the tower. Palmyra Associates had thought of everything. He put the strap around his neck and raised the binoculars.

Jack trained the glasses on the river, inching it over the eyot, along the mall to the Ram pub. Tilting the sights a fraction to the right, he hovered at the bottom of the Bell Steps. In the dwindling light, Hammersmith Bridge was a watercolour sketch, lights reflected in the water. Rush hour had started: headlights and brake lights on the Great West Road, the Hogarth roundabout and the flyover were broad sweeps of a paintbrush, red and white streaks. Holding the binoculars steady, Jack surveyed London. He saw without being seen. He had found his panopticon.

He swung back to the bridge and focused on a double-decker bus creeping south. On the top deck, two women sat on the front seat. One was laughing as she glanced at her reflection in the window and adjusted her hair. Her companion faced ahead. Behind them, a lad in his teens was wearing the neutral stare of disinterest typical of passengers travelling alone. Headphones on, he chewed gum mechanically. Jack felt the engine's vibration and heard the laughter and the tinkly chatter of music escaping from the headphones as if he were there too.

Jack's scrutiny was diverted to the footpath on the bridge. There was someone leaning on the railing. He craned forward, thinking that if it was someone contemplating suicide, there was nothing that he could do to prevent them. He could call the police, but they wouldn't get there in time.

The man was wearing a baseball cap pulled low over his brow. Abruptly the man stepped back from the balustrade and, looking towards the tower, he shifted his cap as if in greeting. Jack was in an unlit room a quarter of a mile from him, yet the man was looking at him.

The binoculars hit the table with a crash. Jack tried to apply Stella's logic. Without binoculars he couldn't see the bus, so the man couldn't see him. Stella would say guilt that he was spying had convinced him that the man was looking at him. She wouldn't like him secretly watching people. This was the second time a man had been drawn to his gaze. There had been the man on the bus outside Stamford Brook station the night Rick Frost had died. He too had worn a baseball cap. Plenty of people did.

The binoculars were undamaged, but had dented his table. He looked again at the bridge and adjusted the focus. It was hard to keep a steady sight on a target or track a moving one because with the slightest twitch of the wrist he travelled hundreds of metres. The bus had gone. Jack felt no guilt that he was watching unseen. The tower gave him 360-degree surveillance.

Jack returned the binoculars to their case, relishing the musky scent of the leather. It was dark, so he felt his way around the partition to the main room and found the light switch. A gentle glow revealed dips and grooves in the concrete wall.

Under his desk he spotted four blue lights: a Wi-Fi router. There had been no mention of Wi-Fi connection in the leaflet or the contract, and Jack had been content to do without it.

He fired up his laptop and was presented with a choice of two routers. This high he hadn't expected to pick up other connections. 'CBruno'. Unwise of the owner to use their name; it gave easy advantage to True Hosts, murderers or would-be murderers who stopped at nothing to catch their prey. His own router identifier was a mix of letters and numerals. Jack typed in his password and seconds later saw he had an email.

It welcomed him to the tower. They had sent a workaday list of instructions: where to find the fuse box, spare light bulbs and window locks, how to work the boiler and the thermostat and when it was bin day. It wished him well in his new home and was signed 'on behalf of Palmyra Associates'. The company might be large, or perhaps, given the lack of website, was small posing as large. Jack didn't care. Typing a 'thank you', he reflected that the tower was perfect and he had the perfect landlord.

He was preparing for bed when he heard a glug from the sink in the kitchen as if liquid was being poured down it. He tiptoed to the doorway. Of course there was no one there: it was one of the sounds of his new home.

His phone was glowing.

Need to see you. Where are you? Stella D.

Unlike Stella to write so late and to put the 'D'. There was only one Stella.

He texted the address of his tower and went to the kitchen. Palmyra Associates had left him a packet of Brooke Bond tea, Stella's favourite.

Twenty-Five

Wednesday, 23 October 2013

Stella found a space in the short-stay car park by a column marked '3D'. Jack would like that. She regretted refusing his offer to come with her to the airport; why had she thought she should meet Suzie's new man on her own? She told herself that Stanley, a good judge of character, would sniff out this Dale bloke. With the dog trotting at her heel, she crossed to the lift lobby.

'Excuse me.' A stocky man in a hi-vis jacket cut her off at the lift. 'No dogs allowed in the airport.'

'I wasn't thinking.' Rattled by William Frost, Stella had completely forgotten to leave Stanley with Jackie. She gave a tight smile and, 'tssking' at Stanley as if he was there without permission, she returned to the van and, with the dog on her lap, paws resting on the steering wheel, texted Suzie: *In car park with Stanley. 3D.*

The airport's website told her the plane had landed half an hour ago. Stella told herself that Jackie had a point; it would be good for Suzie to have someone special. Maybe she'd stop complaining about Terry as if he were still alive.

She turned her attention to the case. They had three suspects, not counting anyone Rick Frost may have exposed through his surveillance techniques. Tallulah Frost, William Frost himself and thirdly whoever had been at the station when Frost died. Being stringent she should include the man she had met when she and Jack were there. Although there was no reason to suspect him. He might have been doing exactly what she had assumed he was doing, inspecting the line. She dubbed him the inspector. Finally William himself. He had been strangely unwilling to help since bringing them the case and at lunch had seemed oddly nervy. He wasn't all he seemed. Stella put aside her antipathy towards him for using his brother's app to find her and returned to the question about Frost. Why commit murder, disguise it as suicide – and then persuade them it *was* murder? Jack thought it was warped vanity, Frost wanting credit for his cleverness. It was less gratifying to clean houses for sale after a death with no client to appreciate dazzling surfaces and germ-free crevices. The wife stood to gain the most by Rick Frost's death even if his specific policy didn't pay up for a suicide. They needed to meet Mrs Frost and see the house she had shared with her husband. Try as she might, Stella could think of no honest way to do this.

Stanley scrambled off her lap on to the steering wheel. He stood on the horn; his furious barking was drowned out by its deafening blare.

Stella saw Suzie weaving between the vehicles towards her, gesticulating with great sweeps of her arm. She wore her old macintosh, with the red scarf Jackie had given her for Christmas wound around her neck. Nothing indicated she had returned from an Australian summer – she didn't even have a sun tan. Stella got out of the van. Stanley was straining towards her mum, choking with the effort.

Her mum wasn't beckoning to her. At the end of a line of concrete supports (3A, 3B, 3C), a man was wrestling with a wayward trolley, mountainous with luggage. As if tacking a sailing boat, he leant out and slewed the trolley full circle. He pushed it into a pool of bleak lamplight.

It was Terry.

Suzanne Darnell took the man's hand and, grabbing Stella's, she pushed them together. 'Stella, Dale. Dale, Stella!'

Twenty-Six

October 1987

Before he went into the cage, Simon checked the alley behind him. There was no one. On his way through the cemetery he had hatched a plan. He would form his own unit, and the tower would be HQ. He wasn't scared. He would recruit Justin and Nicky. His little sister could be the mascot. He would let Justin be captain. The old Captain would be the enemy. After what happened the last time they were in the tower, Simon considered the Captain as good as dead.

It was a week since Simon's picture had been in the newspaper, together with an article about the brave little boy who had saved his mother from a mugger. Nicky had been impressed, although she hadn't said anything at their last meeting back in the old HQ. The Captain hadn't said anything either.

Simon forced himself on to the semi-circular walkway at the top of the staircase. He had forgotten how high it was; the ground far below tugged at him, urging him to leap – it was like walking the plank. The wind was much stronger up here; it, too, goaded him. He held on to the guard rail tightly, his woolly gloves slipping on the metal. Justin warned against leaving fingerprints. Not true – Justin had said, leave no trace. With no suspicion, there would be no reason to look for fingerprints. Simon heard the other boy's voice as if he was beside him now. Simon didn't trust himself to leave no trace. He let go of the guard rail and, hands and back flat to the concrete, shuffled to the door and crept inside the tower.

He swept his torch beam around. Its light bounced off the triangular metal stairs. This time, regardless of safety, Simon shut the tower door. He listened: Justin advised entrance to a property only after all sounds had been identified. The rumble of traffic and the harsh wind couldn't penetrate the thick walls. Simon believed he was alone. The door to the chamber where he had hidden with the Captain was set into a recess behind the staircase. It was closed.

His torch picked out something on the floor. Two black leather gloves. Simon's gloves had been knitted by Mrs Henderson to match his sister's mittens, but these gloves were for grown-ups. He didn't need to read the name in the lining. He guessed that the Captain had dropped his gloves when he'd run away and left Simon to die. He had complained they had been stolen; he would be too scared to come back for them.

Simon put them into his coat. When he placed a foot on the spiral staircase, he wanted to poo and had to clench his bottom until the cramps subsided. His heart smashing against his ribs, he began to climb.

This time the door was shut. He crept over the landing and put his ear to the metal. His bowels stirred again. Silence wasn't good, Justin said, better to hear the enemy and locate them. He craned over the rail; the steps wound off into the dark. No one knew he was in the tower. He could go. He went down four steps, spiralling this way meant he was facing the door, his nose at floor level. He ran up the stairs again and before he could change his mind, twisted on the ring handle. The door opened with a groan.

The boy was hit by a terrible stench of lavatories, potties and nappies, and thought that after all he had messed his pants. He felt himself. No, his trousers were dry. He took a step inside.

Dark streaks, dried and crusted, were smeared on the concrete floor. Simon went further into the room and saw that, after all, he wasn't alone.

Twenty-Seven

Thursday, 24 October 2013

A figure was on the metal walkway, tall against the London skyline. Fleetingly it occurred to Jack that, with no security camera, he could have no idea who was outside until he opened the door.

'He's my brother!' The voice was muffled within her hood; but for the dog glaring malevolently at him from her shoulder, Jack wouldn't have known it was Stella.

'Who is?'

'Dale Heffernan is not my Mum's new man, he's my brother.'

'Sugar?' He pulled forward one of Mrs Ramsay's blue enamel tins and lifted the lid. It was empty. They were in the kitchen. Stella sat with her back to the south-east window. The binoculars were behind her on the window ledge. Jack didn't know why he'd rather she didn't notice them.

'I don't take sugar.' He knew that.

He sloshed milk into his mug. The carton was light; he would need to buy more. Shopping involved a long descent, then a climb back up – a tiny price for living in a panopticon.

'Are you sure?' He handed Stella a mug of milky tea. 'Suzie had two relationships with Terry? Like Elizabeth Taylor and Richard Burton.'

'Yes.' Stella smiled wryly as she took the tea. At her feet Stanley emitted a guttural growl. Jack had forgotten about the protective force field the dog erected around his mistress. Stella didn't need protecting, and if she did, an animal the size of a tea towel couldn't do it. He led her through to the main room. Indicating she have the chair by his desk, he retreated to his bed a distance from the dog.

'They went out with each other for six months and split up. Eighteen months later Mum went back to him. She calls Terry her "wrong turning". Seems she took it twice.'

'That would put her back where she started.' Jack traced the journey in the air with a finger. 'Actually, no, if you turn right instead of left, then you would—'

'Jack! It's complicated enough.' Stella was still in her anorak, despite the effective heating. Jack hadn't worked out how to turn it off. 'Her parents didn't want her to marry a police constable. I never knew my grandparents, but she says they were snobby and interfering. When she found she was having Terry's baby, they made her give him up for adoption. She's regretted it ever since. The way Mum told it tonight, you'd think Terry was the love of her life.' Stella sipped her tea and shot him a look of gratitude: he'd got it right. 'They met the first time when Terry pulled her over one night for speeding in her Mini Traveller on Holland Park Avenue. He said he wouldn't charge her if she went out on a date with him.'

'I told you that.' Jack had found that out during the Blue Folder case. Stella hadn't believed him. Now he felt petty and was relieved that she hadn't heard. She had insisted that her mother had met Terry Darnell, then a spruced-up Mod in two-tone suit and winklepickers, at the Hammersmith Palais. Jack couldn't help himself, 'So they didn't meet while dancing?'

'Yes, the second time around. Terry taught her to do the bossa nova and she claims she never looked back.'

Stanley was sniffing along the wall by the door, pattering back and forth across the floor, his claws tapping on the wooden boards. Jack wished Stella would stick him back on his lead, he didn't trust him.

'Are you sure this Dale is Terry's son?' Nor did he trust Dale Heffernan. He recognized he was disappointed that Suzie hadn't confided in him. Had he known, he could have warned Stella. Except Suzie would have told him in confidence so it would have been another secret to keep from Stella. Better she had not told him.

'Are you listening?' Stella seemed jumpy. She clasped her mug of tea as if to warm herself, although she must be sweltering. 'Yes, I *am* sure!'

'I was thinking, Suzie can be impressionable. You hear stories of parents reunited with lost children and it turns out it's not them. People believe what they want to.'

'He's the spitting image of Terry, he must be his son,' Stella mused into her mug.

Jack didn't know how to help her. 'Shall we ring Jackie?'

'What for? Dale's not a client and it's past midnight.' Stella looked up abruptly. 'How come you've moved?' she asked. The words 'without telling me' hung there.

'It was a snap decision.' Stella didn't take action without meticulous planning, backed up by contingency plans. 'It was time for a change.' He couldn't say he was escaping his ghosts or that the tower was perfect for finding True Hosts.

'Are you leaving Clean Slate?' Stella addressed the question to the dog, who was still sniffing about by the door.

Lucie May would call her question self-serving, Jack knew it was as close as Stella could get to asking if they would no longer be friends. He sought to reassure her. 'A change of where I live, not of whom I know.'

Stanley began to bark, the volume increasing with each one.

'Sssh!' Stella put a finger to her lips. 'Good guard dog.'

The barking subsided to rumbling. Jack followed the animal's steely gaze to the door. There could be no one outside; he had made sure he'd shut the door downstairs.

'He doesn't need to guard. We're at the top of a tower.'

'He hears stuff we can't.' Stella looked about her. 'Who owns this place?'

'A company.' Jack didn't know anything about the owners. 'Their email said I am their first tenant. It used to be a water tower. We're in the tank.' He jumped up. 'Would you like a tour?'

Stella signalled for Stanley to 'heel'. Jack didn't want the dog prowling about his new home. The dog was recriminatory: his bark told Jack he should have asked Stella to help him move in; she was at her best when being practical. Yet she wouldn't have arranged everything as perfectly as Palmyra Associates. Stella cleaned houses; she didn't create homes.

The kitchen sink made the glugging noise of earlier. He leapt on an opportunity to get Stella's advice. 'It keeps doing this. Should I call the landlord?'

Stella turned on the tap. With the rush of water, the glugging stopped. Stanley tottered on his hind legs, reaching up, front paws skittering along the edge of the cutlery drawer trying to see. He was like a toddler, constantly wanting to be involved, grouchy if attention wasn't on him. Jack just prevented himself from saying, 'Shoo!'

'It's an air lock. Happens when water is drained from two sinks, or a bath and sink, at the same time. It's caught in the reservoir of one sink and when you drain one, air gets pushed up the pipe of the other one.' Stella visibly cheered up.

'I see.' Jack clasped his hands together. The world was uncertain and mostly he dealt with it – he was unafraid of darkness, literal or in the soul of a True Host – but sometimes nothing but the warm bright glare of Stella's practical attitude would do.

The tour took less than five minutes. Stanley barked when Jack slid aside the partition between the kitchen and the shower room. He was a nervy creature, more like himself than Stella, Jack observed. Stella noted the lack of frosted glass in the window and the toilet right beside it. He reminded her that no one could see in. She appeared to approve of the functional chrome lavatory with water-saving cistern on the criss-cross metal flooring, commenting only, 'You prefer baths.' She was still tetchy. He did like a soak in a bath, to the light of one candle, where he floated free and unfettered. Lucie May said he was trying to return to the womb and she was right. He couldn't explain that to live in a panopticon, he could forgo a bath.

'They can't risk flooding from this height,' he said.

'It's a water tower, a bath is a fraction of what this structure must have supported.' Stella wandered back to the main room, the dog at her heel.

The contract said no dogs or cats; Jack hoped this excluded visiting animals. Stella was inseparable from the dog. He wondered what she would do when she had to hand him back.

As if illustrating this attachment, Stella tipped out her rucksack on to his desk. A collection of dogs' toys and poo bags landed by his laptop. Out of this she extracted a stuffed meerkat in a Father Christmas robe and waved it at the dog, who, back snuffling by the skirting, ignored her.

'Did Terry know about his— this Dale?' Jack wouldn't grant him the status of 'son'. It must be hard for Stella.

'No.' Stella took her empty mug through to the kitchen. He heard the tap run, no glugging sound this time. When she returned, she was carrying the binoculars. She went to the north window and, lifting them, peered out into the blackness. 'If Dad had known, he would have included Dale in his will.' She adjusted the focus like a pro. 'He would have told me.'

Jack knew that Stella's father hadn't made a will, another of Suzie's complaints. *'He thought he was immortal.'* Stella had inherited all of Terry Darnell's estate – a house, no savings – because she was his sole surviving child. Or so Terry had thought.

'This One Under case is tough.' Stella held the binoculars steady.

'I've had an idea about how we might meet his wife.' Jack went with the change of subject. Stella didn't dwell on personal stuff.

'I can see the house of one of my clients from here,' Stella exclaimed. 'These are so powerful I can make out cracks on the pavement outside the door.'

This was the reason Jack was living in the tower, but Stella wouldn't be pleased to hear that.

'Someone's coming out. Well, that's odd. If I wasn't here, I'd think—' She darted forward and the instrument banged against the glass. 'Ouch!' She rubbed the bridge of her nose. 'I should go. Mum's bringing Dale to the office tomorrow – today, rather.'

Stella kept calling him Dale as if they were already best buddies.

She turned to him, still looking through the glasses. Jack wanted to shield his face as if she could see right into his head. She wouldn't like what she saw there. Often he didn't either.

'By the way, I bumped into William Frost today. We had a bit of lunch. I went through our questions with him.'

'We were going to do that together,' Jack protested. First Dale Heffernan, now William Frost. 'I was going to watch to see if he lied.'

'What with moving, I guessed you'd be tied up.' She lowered the binoculars, looking at Stanley.

Stalemate.

Yesterday Jackie had suggested he tell Stella about his move. He should have done. Stella hated surprises, so why had he given her one? He nearly told her about the steam engine on the monitor at the station, how finding the toy placed on top had stirred up disturbing memories long buried. But Stella would guess he was doing it to appease her and she wouldn't welcome hearing about it with her own past having come back to haunt her. Besides, it was probably not important.

'Why is your mum taking him to Clean Slate?' Suzie and Jackie would fuss over this Terry lookalike.

'Dale wanted to see where I work. He wants to watch me clean.'

'That's nice.' Surely the man had seen a woman use a vacuum before. Jack tried to believe it was straightforward: Heffernan had found a younger sister, he was keen to get to know her. He was not a bounty hunter intending to fleece his new family of their money. Stella lived frugally, but Clean Slate was doing well, and with Terry's legacy she was not on the breadline.

'He wrote to Mum via the adoption agency. He's upset he didn't pluck up the courage to do it while Terry was alive. He had assumed we'd resent him turning up. I told him Dad didn't like surprises, maybe this was for the best.'

So Stella had confirmed to Dale that Terry would not have welcomed him. Full of the best intentions, she could be clumsy around feelings.

'Why's he here now?' Jack had realized that Terry Darnell had doted on his daughter. Not something he understood: his own father Hugh had found having a son a challenge, as if he were a rival. Jack had never tried to rival anyone. *Not true.* Long ago there had been someone. He dismissed this thought.

'Mum is overjoyed to be reunited with her "long-lost boy"!' Stella rolled her eyes.

'So she lied about staying with a friend.' Jack was chastened by his barb.

Stella frowned, the idea clearly new. 'Not exactly.'

Stanley erupted into shouty barks and crouched low, facing the door, legs braced, tail flailing. Each bark jerked him off his feet. He began to dig, front paws blurred with the effort.

'What's the matter with him?' Jack didn't want the dog to scratch the wood – Stanley was demented. *No animals or children.*

'He's picked up a scent, a dead mouse or food dropped by the people here before.'

'No one was here before me.' Despite the busy rate of his paws, Jack saw he was doing no damage.

'Stanley!' Stella had an instant effect. She whisked over and, clipping on the lead, brought the dog to the desk and commanded he sit. He stared at the door, pupils dilated, eyes a smouldering brown.

'He's seen a ghost.' Jack went to where the dog had been digging. Of course it was colder on this side of the room, which was closer to the staircase.

'I'm guessing he doesn't like heights.' Stella shook Stanley's flapping paw as she gave him a morsel of chicken. 'What ghosts? You just said you're the first person to live here.'

Jack felt dread. The dog had come into the flat, tail up, full of curiosity. If he didn't like heights he would have objected on the way up. He touched the bars of a tubular radiator by the door. It had cooled; his indiscriminate twiddling of knobs earlier had worked. It must explain the drop in temperature. The dog continued to stare at the floor where he was standing. He looked down. There was nothing there.

'I'll take him away or the neighbours will object.'

'We're in a tower, there are no neighbours.' Jack should have been pleased by this. He suddenly missed the short-eared owl. Perhaps he should have brought her.

'Better go anyway, I'm seeing Dale in a few hours.'

'I'll see you out.' Jack quelled peevishness that she was leaving him to see 'Dale'.

'"Seeing me out" is not a simple matter.' Stella opened the flat door. 'Will you be OK with all these stairs? What about when you need to buy milk?'

'I'll stock up.'

When he opened the door, Jack expected it to be colder, but the landing was warm.

Stella craned up the spiral staircase. 'Have you been on the roof?' Her voice rang in the metallic vault.

'I don't have a key.' He must take this up with Palmyra Associates. It was autumn; they probably thought he wouldn't want access. Stella followed him down the stairs, the dog lolling on her shoulder, now calm. Above them the stairs wended out of sight. Jack opened the tower door and was hit by a blast of cold air. He reeled back and trod on Stella's boot. Steel-capped, she wouldn't have felt it, but he saw his clumsiness as a sign of how badly her visit had gone, as if they were strangers. As Stella said to him, they were supposed to be a team.

When she put him down, the dog pulled his lead free and shot off along the walkway, too close to the edge. Jack dived after him and stamped on the flailing lead.

'You saved him!' Stella shouted into the wind.

Jack watched in horror as the dog lifted its leg against a metal strut and peed over the side into mid-air. Stella brightened.

'*That* was why he was barking. He's really pretty easy to read. So, what was your idea about us meeting Rick Frost's wife?'

'Do a stakeout, park near her house in the back of the van. It's legal, it's what detectives do,' he added for good measure.

'We've got nothing to lose, I suppose.' Stella spoke over her shoulder as she went down the outer staircases, boots clattering, the grille humming with her tread.

Jack stayed on the narrow metal walkway after Stella had gone as the humming died to nothing. London was a cluster of lights like a circuit board. He went back into the tower and shut the door.

He was outside his flat when he remembered what Stella had asked about the roof. He didn't actually know if he could get up there – he hadn't tried. He crossed the little metal platform and continued up the spiral stairs. At the top he found a large roof light, showing only the night sky. It was a black rectangle. He shot aside two bolts and pushed it upwards. It was stuck fast. He took off his coat and, rolling up his sleeves, wiped his palms on his trousers and tried again. This time he lifted it a few centimetres. He climbed to the top step and, using his body as a lever, succeeded in opening it. Lacking a hydraulic hinge, it had nothing to keep it open beyond gravity. He would find some kind of prop.

He was at the edge of a vast circular area of decking surrounded by a wall. Pushing back the roof cover – he hadn't brought his phone, and did not want to be stuck up here – he clambered out and went over to the wall. It reached to his waist. Not high enough; again he was filled with the temptation he always had with heights, to chuck everything he was holding off and then to follow. He retreated from the wall and took in the vast panorama before him. The river was a stretch of darkness flecked with minute lights. He smelled the air: a mix of sulphur, mud, exhaust fumes and wood smoke. He raised his arms towards the sky and felt the wind blow his hair from his face. At last he had his very own tower. He was truly alive.

Bizarrely, right in the centre of the decking, was a garden shed. Jack supposed that was there to save him lugging tools up for tending plants. There were no plants, however; the space was bare. The shed doors were fixed with a padlock. He would ask the landlords for the key. It would be nice to have some pots up here; he could grow tough hardy grasses able to withstand cold air and the wind. A Garden in the Sky. It would be the antithesis to his Garden of the Dead.

He went back down the staircase to his flat. The heating had gone off, and the spot on the floor where Stanley had been digging was no colder than the rest of the room. Perhaps the fluctuation in temperature was to do with circular walls. His father would have known.

Stella had been his first visitor. That was a good sign. Jack looked across at his chair, which faced outwards as Stella had left it. He had suggested the stakeout to appease her. It wasn't sufficient. He should have said that the reason they worked well together was because she stuck to the rules and he worked in between the lines and beneath the surface.

Despite Stella's visit, he couldn't shake off the homesick ache. Before his promise to Stella not to walk the streets late at night, Jack would have taken a journey across the city to assuage the dull pain. He fetched the field glasses from the window sill, relieved that Stella hadn't asked about them. If she had, he would have had to tell the truth. He disliked lying to Stella.

He went to the window Stella had been watching from and trained the glasses on the Hogarth roundabout. He was rewarded by the sight of a white van, ghostly in the sodium lighting, waiting to join the Great West Road. Stella drove a van without the Clean Slate livery – Jack guessed it was because she preferred anonymity – nevertheless he was sure it was her white van he was watching. Moments later his conviction was proved right. He could see her clearly as she accelerated, keeping within the speed limit, towards the rise of Hammersmith flyover. She wasn't going to her flat. His heart sank. She had said she was seeing Dale in the morning, but it seemed she was going to Suzie's flat now. Without telling him.

One by one he studied the little streets that lay between the A40 and Chiswick High Road. Stella had seen a client's house from this window. He was looking from this window because in an oblique way it made him feel closer to Stella.

After a night journey, Jack used to 'retrace' his steps on Google Street View and take screenshots of houses, doors, windows and the blurred pedestrians and then store them in a file. Now, as he travelled along the streets, magnified through his lenses, he had to rely on his photographic mind to log the detailed views.

Jack rolled on to his back. He couldn't work out where he was. Gradually shapes resolved into his cupboard, the bust of his mother, the two rectangles of mauve-blue light were the south-west and north windows. He listened for what had woken him.

Tap. Tap. Tap.

He flew out of bed and around the partition into the kitchen. The mixer tap was dripping; water was collecting in the spout and dripping into the sink.

He turned on the tap, grabbed a beaker from the little draining board and filled it. He drank thirstily, refilled it and, tightening the handle, wiped his palm under the spout and cleared it of excess water.

Two thoughts bothered him. The dog didn't like him. That didn't matter, but it was affecting his relationship with Stella. She would have stayed longer if he hadn't been barking. What had bothered him was the look in the dog's eyes. Stanley had detected something he and Stella couldn't see, something Jack wasn't sure he wanted to see.

The other thing was Stella's brand-new Australian brother. Heffernan had dropped everything to return with Suzie to England. Why?

Jack knew he was apt to imagine the worst at three in the morning. He was at the mercy of treacly dark narratives that ended with him alone or being harried by strangers with no reason to care about him. If he made progress with the case, Stella would be pleased.

He reached for his phone. One person was awake at this hour.

'How're you fadging, poppet?' The corncrake laugh. 'Why aren't you here!'

'Are you free tomorrow, after my shift? I could be with you by ten to midnight. I'm driving a dead late.'

'Don't you mean thirteen and a half minutes to?' Lucie's idea of a joke. London Underground trains operated in split minutes; every second was counted. May descended into starter-motor mirth. 'Better than driving the Late Dead.' She began to cough violently. 'For you, sweetie, I'll cancel the moon! Although not tomorrow, I'm in Lincoln, meeting a ninety-nine-year-old twin who left Hammersmith at birth. The day after?'

After he had put the phone down, Jack settled under the covers. The tapping had stopped. He would become used to the tower.

His mind was caring for him: it conjured up music. From somewhere in his mind he conjured up the moody strains of the Smiths' 'How Soon Is Now?', his favourite. It mingled with Lucie May's clattering laughter. Jack fell into a deep sleep.

Twenty-Eight

January 1988

The three children walked in strict single file down to Chiswick Mall, the Captain in front. It was Sunday afternoon and Simon had reluctantly 'come out to play' as the Captain had put it to his mother in a smiley voice that Simon hadn't heard him use before. She had agreed on his behalf. 'Nicky is such a sensible girl.' Simon was dismayed; since last going to the tower, he had avoided the unit. The Captain had brought Nicky to convince his mum to let him out.

He had just persuaded his mum to go on a 'jaunt', her private name for their walks. They would stroll arm in arm around Chiswick House grounds – like an old married couple, she would say. She had told Simon she wished she'd married a lovely young man like him. One day he would make a girl very happy.

'I will marry you!' he had insisted.

'Darling, you can't, boys don't marry their mummies. But you are my favourite.'

'More than him?'

A shadow had passed across her face. *'More than Daddy.'*

'Not Daddy.' Before he could stop himself, but she hadn't heard.

They hadn't gone to the park for a long time, not since he had been to the tower and found— Simon had hoped after that everything would be normal again, but it wasn't. His mother behaved as if Simon were a ghost and, hardly eating, she looked like one herself.

'Left right, left right!'

Last in the line, Simon fell back into step with the other two. 'Where are we going?' he called out.

The Captain didn't reply.

Simon took consolation from the fact that Nicky had been invited, so he'd have a chance to show her he wasn't mean, to make her his friend again. On Chiswick Mall, the tower bore down on them, dark and menacing. Simon shuddered at what was up there.

The Captain pushed Simon against the railings on Chiswick Mall. He looked out over the beach to the eyot; it was shrouded in a bank of mist, losing definition. Water, slick as oil, was creeping across the stretch of mud. Simon was cross with his mother for agreeing when the Captain had asked her if 'Simon could come out to play?' He had stared and stared at her to make her say no, because they were going out to the park. But she had said yes straight away, without looking at him once. Then she had made it worse by kissing him goodbye, which ordinarily would have been nice.

'You murdered a man,' Simon said.

'No, I didn't,' the Captain fluted. Simon thought he looked guilty.

'He's dead up there.' The tower was above them. 'I saw him.'

'I left before you,' the Captain said, but with his cracked voice it sounded like a lie.

'You left me to die.' Simon believed this.

'You didn't die.'

'I saw you go up the corkscrew stairs into that room and I heard a fight.' Simon spoke clearly so that Nicky would hear every word.

'How do you know there is a room?' The Captain had him there.

'I went back and saw it.' Simon was quick. 'You dropped your glove on him. You told me you had defeated the enemy. The police will know it's your glove on the man's body. It has your name inside.'

The Captain was crying. Simon was amazed by the potency of his words. A plan took shape.

Nicky turned to him. 'Stop making up stories, Simon. If we're going to the island, we should go. It's getting dark and I have to get home.'

‘He’s a murderer,’ Simon asserted. The lure of his own home and the tea on the kitchen table was lessening as he drove home an unforeseen advantage.

‘No one’s murdered anyone. Both of you, stop it!’ Nicky sounded like his mother, Simon thought.

‘I have my gloves.’ The Captain bashed at his jacket, tugging out a handkerchief, a spray of bus tickets and sweet wrappers.

‘Let me make this easier.’ Simon was his dad talking to his mum, chatty and reasonable while Simon held his breath because his father made his mother cry and that always made his sister cry. He folded his arms and spoke reasonably: ‘This unit works for the good of the country. We don’t break the law. Murder is illegal. I am afraid to say that you’ll be flung in jail and killed.’ Simon’s breath was like smoke in the chill evening. The Captain had snot coming out of his nose.

Simon took a black leather glove out of his pocket and dangled it at the Captain.

The boy lunged towards him. Simon skipped out of the way.

‘The other glove is up there in the tower. It links directly to you. If you throw this one away, I shall say I saw you do it.’ He took the plunge. ‘And so will Nicky because she is here too.’

After the man in the tower was dead, Simon had thought it would go back to the way it was before, but it had not. His mother kept looking out of the window as if waiting for someone to come. *Him.*

‘What do you want?’ The Captain had meted out enough coercion himself to recognize it when it was applied to him.

‘I shall be captain.’ Simon folded the glove back into his mac pocket. ‘You and Nicky are privates. You follow my orders. If you stage a coup, I’ll tell the police you are a murderer.’ Simon had rehearsed this bit. ‘I shall recruit my deputy. He’s called Justin and he is my friend.’

‘Yes.’ The Captain agreed readily.

Had Simon been less intoxicated by the success of his cobbled-together ruse, he might have found this suspicious.

'Yes what?'

'Yes, Captain.'

It took him a second to realize the Captain was walking away. He stalked down the exposed slipway to the beach and was heading for the raised path that led to the eyot.

Nicky's voice startled Simon. 'I'm not going to be your "private", or his. This is a stupid game and it's gone far enough,' she told him. 'Give him his glove back and start being nice.'

'I am nice,' Simon said.

'You *were* nice.' Nicky went after the Captain; Simon had no choice but to follow. Stinking mud was all around him. Simon grimaced; his trousers had been clean on today. He slithered after the Captain and Nicky, hopping over jagged glass and jutting blocks of concrete.

Simon clutched the glove in his pocket and the leather, cool and limp, gave him faint hope. Gaining courage, he strode along the causeway to Chiswick Eyot. The glove was his talisman. He would win in the end.

He clambered up a fortification of concrete moulded as sandbags. Sprigs of groundsel and thistle thrusting between the gaps offered tenuous handholds. He plunged down a path that was covered by overarching branches that formed a dark tunnel. He caught a bramble; thorns scored a cut across the palm of his bad hand.

Super-sensitive – perhaps as a result of surviving in an unhappy household – Simon was alert to shifts in atmosphere. He had a sixth sense. As he made his way through, he felt a tingling at the back of his neck. Hardly daring to hope what it meant, he increased his pace.

Twenty-Nine

Thursday, 24 October 2013

'I know you say he didn't like surprises, but I wish I'd found my dad while he was alive.' Dale was helping Stella slide the bed in Mrs Carr's spare room back against the wall. 'I envy that you got to spend time with him, to grow up with him. I have a great adoptive dad, but once they told me, I was always wondering what my real parents were like. I wondered what I had missed.'

'Why didn't you contact them when you were younger?'

'Ah, you know, loads of reasons. I didn't want to hurt my parents' feelings, I was busy building the business, cowardice too maybe. What if they had told me to stuff it?'

Downstairs, the front door banged. Mrs Carr hadn't been there when they'd arrived. Stella had found a note pinned to the front door saying that the key was under the recycling bin and to put it back when she left. Horrified, Stella had done as instructed. Being dumped by her husband had made Mrs Carr careless.

Ultimately Stella had been relieved to find she wasn't there. It avoided the palaver of introducing Dale to her. This wasn't the ideal job for him to accompany her to, but when Suzie had suggested Hammersmith Police Station, Stella, keen to avoid the even greater complications of Dale asking questions about Terry's work that she couldn't answer, had suggested they come to Mrs Carr's. At least here he could be helpful.

That morning Stella had introduced Dale Heffernan to Jackie and Beverly and shown him around her office, which, being two rooms, was a quick affair. Now, kitted out in Clean Slate's uniform of a green polo shirt and blue trousers, he had already vacuumed the stairs and landing and shifted furniture in the spare room.

'He was by the river – Chiswick Mall again – where I saw him walking with *her*. I tried to follow him, but my car was on yellow lines. By the time I'd reparked, I'd lost him. No point in texting him, he would be furious if he knew I'd tracked him.' Mrs Carr stood at the end of the bed. 'Hello, who's this?' She stopped in her tracks.

'I hope you don't mind. This is my bro—' Stella corrected herself. 'This is my colleague. He's assisting me. I left you a message?'

'You did, but somehow I was expecting a girl!'

'I'm sorry to disappoint!' Dale was reattaching the headboard that had come loose when they moved the bed.

'Hardly!' She gave a laugh. 'Are you an Australian?'

'Got it! Dale. Good to meet you.' He arched his back and let out a sigh as if exhausted. Stella supposed there was no point in explaining he must always look 'ready and willing'.

'Are you sure it was your husband?' she said to distract Mrs Carr from asking Dale about himself and discovering who he was. That was a step too far.

'Of course I'm sure.' The animation that had made Stella suspect Mrs Carr wasn't entirely sane returned. 'Lulu to you.' She leant over and shook Dale's hand.

'Did you speak to him?' Stella asked. *'Lulu to you.'* Suzie had said Dale was a charmer. 'Mrs Carr?'

'And say what? He lied to me. What's to say? I'm tempted to tell my brother that I saw him.' She was batting the open door back and forth between her palms. 'Should I?' She was looking at Dale as if she had guessed his relationship to Stella and wanted his 'brother-take' on it.

'Ah, look, don't sweat it, that's what brothers are for!' Dale trod on the vacuum lever and the flex whizzed back into the cylinder, the plug flying about dangerously as in her staff manual Stella had warned it would.

Stella had texted Jack to join them and meet Dale; he had replied, saying he was doing a day shift. She was sure he hadn't mentioned this last night and caught herself wondering if it was true.

'My brother believes in loyalty.' Lulu Carr was talking to the door.

'Brothers are there through thick and thin, longer than husbands!' Dale offered.

Stella steered Lulu Carr back to the practical. 'Mrs Carr, your note said where to find the key. Anyone could have got in.'

'How else would you both have got in?' Lulu wandered out on to the landing. She nodded at Stella, 'And call me Lulu.'

'I could have come another day.' Stella had expected Mrs Carr – Lulu – to see her mistake.

Out on the landing she remembered they needed to empty the landing cupboard, and then she noticed Dale had missed patches on the stairs; she would have to do them again.

'You said you had the locks changed to prevent your husband returning. If he had come round, your effort and expense would have been wasted.' Stella hit on a key argument.

'If he was following me, he wouldn't have been here.' Lulu Carr went ahead down the stairs, leaning heavily on the banisters like a child trying to slide down them.

'Got you there, Stell!' Dale laughed. 'Mind you, that note would render your insurance void – it was clear instructions for the robbers.'

'You are right!' Lulu Carr reached the hall and stood watching Dale descend, clearly impressed with him.

Stella drove off along Perrers Road and paused at the end to join Dalling Road. In the off-side mirror, Stella saw that Lulu Carr was waving; she waved back. Dale had pushed the seat back and lay half prone, legs stretched out, eyes shut as if exhausted. He was only a couple of years older than she was, about to be fifty apparently. Surely a bit of vacuuming hadn't finished him. Stella, not one for going abroad – or taking holidays of any kind – did not factor in jet lag.

What she had said to Jack last night was true. Dale Heffernan was unquestionably her father's son. He had the same brown hair, although a trendier style, sticking up at the back and no doubt thickened with product; the parting was in the same place. On his forehead between the eyes was Terry's deep crease, deeper still as he got older and had carried some weight. With a shock, Stella saw that Dale had the same shaped hands as Terry, large with stubby fingers.

'We get clients like that, living a fantasy.' Dale settled further into the seat and, opening his eyes, folded his arms across his chest. 'Last summer one guy booked a table for two. No one else turned up. We were feeling sorry for him, guessed he'd been jilted. We see that a lot. Then he called over my old maître d', Barry, and complained at how long he'd been waiting to give his order. Barry was about to say that we were waiting for his friend when he realized the man had started talking to the chair opposite and he'd filled two wine glasses. He consulted with the chair, then ordered food for two. The whole evening he kept up a conversation with the chair. The food got eaten, but Barry and the waiting staff that night swore they never saw him touch the other plate. He'd created a *real* imaginary friend!'

'How is Lulu Carr like him?' Stella felt protective of her client. She shouldn't have confessed to Dale Heffernan her doubts about her sanity. It was a breach of confidentiality. She also thought that she didn't know her parents any better than Dale did, even though she'd grown up with them.

'The cheating husband? I'd bet my life that's total fiction. She strikes me as inauthentic.'

'What do you mean?' She felt unaccountably riled.

'Something about her doesn't add up. Mr Husband toddles off leaving a pile of clothes behind and lots of clobber. What man does that? He'll have to go shopping for a load more! It's like that English MP who faked his suicide. He left his clothes on the beach. My guess is our Lulu's made it all up, but why?'

'Whatever, it's not our business.' Stella was firm.

'You're right. Our job is to keep the lie intact. When the man left, Barry held the door open long enough for two people to walk out and he said goodnight twice. If any of my front-of-house staff had cracked a smile, they'd have been washing up for a week.'

Thrown by Dale's suggestion that Lulu Carr might not have told her the truth, Stella took a wrong turning at Hammersmith Broadway and drove on to the Great West Road. Ahead of her was Jack's tower. She had seen it many times, but, never having been asked to clean it, hadn't given it a thought.

Someone was on the roof. Jack had told her he didn't have access. Had he lied?

A car cut into her lane; she braked and flashed her lights. When she looked again, Jack wasn't there.

Thirty

January 1988

Chiswick Eyot was cut off from the mainland when the tide was in, but, Simon conceded to himself as he scurried along the path, the tingling sensation mounting, it would make a good HQ. At low tide, protected by thick, oozing mud, the advancing enemy would sink and die. It wasn't as good as the tower. But the tower was out of bounds now.

He arrived in a patch of scrub. At his feet was a circle of white stones with a patch of sunlight. They looked luminous. A small trowel and a fork lay in the soil beside the stones. Simon assumed they were the Captain's. The soil had been dug recently; lumps of fresh earth lay beside the stones.

Simon indicated the stones. 'This is brilliant.' His mouth was dry with mounting dread – the Captain must have a plan. He backed away.

'Stay where you are!' The Captain stood with his back to a screen of reeds.

'Don't speak to him like that,' Nicky said. Simon wanted to sing with joy: she still liked him. Despite Nicky being nice, Simon wished he were at the lake with his mum.

His mum had only agreed for him to come out with the unit because she wanted him out of the house. *She was going to look for the Stick Insect.* It gave him no satisfaction to know she wouldn't find him. Justin had told him that in America stick insects were called 'ghost insects'. A sign, but of what Simon had no idea.

'These mark where bodies are buried.' The Captain pointed at the stones.

The sun had gone in. The stones were still there, but now looked randomly scattered.

'You don't know that.' Nicky shook her head. '*Captain!*'

The reeds rattled in the wind, so tall they reached above the children's heads.

No one could see them from the shore. Simon's foreboding escalated to terror. The Captain hadn't brought him here to show him a new HQ. So taken up with his glove, Simon had been ambushed. He drifted closer to Nicky. She wouldn't let anything happen to him.

'My mum's expecting me. We're going out,' he blurted.

'*Mummy* said you could come out and play!' The Captain gave a short laugh. 'She likes me.'

'I should be getting—'

'I think they mark where there's buried treasure,' Nicky said brightly. 'The way they're arranged, it's like a clock.'

She was deciphering a code. Simon was impressed. When he was captain, he would keep her as Official Codebreaker.

'Anyway, Mummy's not there.' The Captain didn't seem to have heard.

'What do you mean?' Simon knew what he meant.

'Your *Mummy* left after us. Let's guess where she was going!'

'She's going to the park. I'm meant to be there too.' Simon pulled on his half-finger as if it might magic him away.

'Oh, I don't think so. Try again. It begins with a "T". Where do *prostitutes* go?' His tone could be mistaken for kind, but Simon, used to his dad talking to his mum, knew better. 'We understand why you knew all about the tower.'

'And we know what you did there!' Simon heard himself retort. The sound of the river rushing through the reeds hurt his ears.

'Stop it!' Nicky was looking at the Captain.

She didn't know what the Captain meant. Simon moved even closer to her, thinking to suggest they left. Before he could speak, he felt a thump on the back and was pushed to the ground. He was on his hands and knees, flailing at the reeds for purchase. The reeds cracked and snapped like gunshots.

The Captain had Simon by the collar of his mac and was dragging him over the earth. He shoved him through the gap in the reeds. Below was the river, fast flowing, grey and green. Simon heard the fabric of his mac tear; it was giving under his weight. Then everything went quiet and he clearly comprehended – a thought devoid of emotion – that he was going to die.

Flecks of foam were spinning on the water. He saw his own face, white and impassive, before it vanished in cloud of scum. Heat ripped across his scalp as the Captain yanked his head back by the hair.

'Leave him.'

Simon fell on to the ground and, gathering himself, looked across the clearing.

A boy stood in a ragged shape of light inside the ring of white stones. 'You are trespassing,' he said to the Captain.

For a split second Simon thought he was dreaming. So entrenched were his fantasies about his friendship with Justin that he had eliminated the two years in which he had not seen him. He discounted the numerous times he had called at the big house with the owl knocker and got no answer. In his mind the friendship had begun in the Pullman carriage of a train. He and Justin were like Guy and Charles in *Strangers on a Train*, his mother's favourite story. Justin was his friend.

'This is my land.' The Captain didn't sound very sure. 'We've occupied it.'

'You are trespassing.' Justin had grown taller since Simon had last seen him. He was taller than the Captain. He wore a black coat which reached to his ankles, the sleeves folded back. His hair was longer, long like a girl's.

'I knew you'd be here!' Simon exclaimed. 'This is who I meant!' he shouted to the Captain and gave an involuntary tug on his bad finger.

Justin didn't reply or look at him.

'Do you know him?' the Captain said to Simon.

'Yes.' Simon adjusted his belt and smoothed down his hair. 'He's my friend.'

'You are trespassing.' Justin addressed the Captain as if he hadn't noticed Simon or heard him.

'So you're friends with "Mummy's Boy"?' The Captain clearly hoped he had pounced on a weak link.

'I don't know him,' Justin replied calmly.

Above their heads a seagull screeched, long and drawn-out like a baby's cry.

'Justin, it's me, Simon, from that school with the garden. We made the tunnel there, remember? We, we had lunch in the Pullman carriage, steak and chips with ketchup.' Simon dashed at his eyes with the heels of his palms. 'Now I'm in a unit. You can be in it too. You can be captain – it will be brilliant!'

'He doesn't know you.' The Captain edged closer to the boy in the coat as if by diminishing the spatial distance between them he might forge an alliance.

'You are all trespassing!' Justin didn't raise his voice. 'The tide is turning. If you don't go now, you will be cut off from the mainland and drown.'

'You're lying,' the Captain said. But Simon saw that he believed Justin.

All the children heard a steady trickling and, through the reeds, Simon watched the river rise.

'Quick march!' the Captain shouted, and pushing Simon ahead of him, directed him back along the path. Away from Justin.

Simon looked out across the river. Properly dark now, he could just tell that the tide was coming in as Justin had said it would. The river lapped at the bottom of the slipway; the island was cut off. Justin could still be out there.

Simon had given the Captain the slip in the cemetery and had doubled back. He was by the railings on Chiswick Mall. The eyot was a dark crouching hulk, the trees and the land one black mass merging with the night sky.

'Justin,' he yelled across the water.

He flung off his mac and hung it on the railings; then he

struggled down the ramp and set off across the vanishing causeway of silted gravel to the eyot.

'Justin!' His cry, hollow like a seagull's and lost in gathering wind, went nowhere.

Simon was up to his knees in freezing water. From deep in the river, invisible hands tugged at his legs, trying to drag him off the causeway. There was no causeway: the finger of land was submerged.

The bells of St Nicholas' church struck five. When the wind blew from the east, the chimes could be heard in Corney Road. Simon's mother was assuring her husband she had been out for a walk by herself around the lake in Chiswick House grounds with their daughter.

'Why the fuck does she keep saying "mat"?' Simon's father demanded, infuriated by the little girl's insistently repeated sound.

His wife suddenly understood what the toddler was trying to say. Panicked, she explained how she was leaving the upstairs curtains open for Simon, who was still out with his nice friends, to see the sitting-room lights. But her frequently snatched glances out of the bay window were not for her son.

Thirty-One

Friday, 25 October 2013

Jack watched Tallulah Frost's house. He preferred to visit Hosts at night, but he was on another day shift and later was meeting Stella. She had been busy with Dale yesterday. Stella and Suzie had invited him for a late afternoon tea to Richmond Park, but he had said he was busy sorting out his new home, although the flat in the tower, being small, needed little sorting. Jack was in no hurry to meet the Brand-new Brother.

He had cased her house with his binoculars from the north window of the tower and confirmed the topography on Street View. He had logged 'alerts': a repair to asphalt on the camber, cracks in the pavement – stepping on cracks was very bad luck.

That morning Jack had chased up William Frost for his sister-in-law's address. Frost was still keen they go in as cleaners. Although he privately agreed, something in the man's tone had made Jack uneasy. He had refrained from telling Frost that his method of entering people's houses required no disguise.

Leaning on the trunk of a plane tree in the sunlit street, rolling a cigarette, Jack told himself he was reconnoitring for his stakeout with Stella.

Clicking the cursor on Street View, he had swooped and darted around the street with the aerodynamic ease of a bird noting all points of vulnerability, street lamps, sightlines from upstairs windows, frequency of vehicles and pedestrians. There were points of advantage too: trees, parked cars and a wall all offered hiding places from which he could observe unobserved. Jack had established dimension and distance between kerbs, gates and trees. Like any good intruder, he had identified the means of egress. On Google Street View's fabulous new feature – a timeline bar – he compared the image of the road in 2008 to 2012 when the last shots were taken. In four years the front door had changed from racing green to royal blue. Not keen on green, Jack approved. The bush in the front area had grown; straggling branches poked through the railings, obscuring the downstairs window. A point of advantage – he would not be seen.

The door was opening. Jack sidled back behind the trunk, snapping his newly made cigarette into his case along with the rest. Mrs Frost might only be putting something in the bin. People popped out of their houses with rubbish, leaving their doors open, allowing Jack to slip inside. In Perrers Road the bins were in view of the street, and in broad daylight, it wouldn't work.

A woman shrouded in a quilted jacket, hood up, was wrestling with an umbrella. It wasn't raining, but she didn't seem to have noticed. She pointed it directly at Jack's tree, opened it and, ducking beneath, stooped to the doormat. Jack nearly shouted with triumph – it could not be. She was leaving a key beneath it. He had been tempted to follow her, but she stopped by a car parked ten or so metres up the street and unlocked it. He moved around the trunk as her car, a blue Renault Clio, swept past him.

Jack nonchanlantly strolled across the road, noting a Neighbourhood Watch sign fixed to the telegraph pole. He opened the gate without hesitation, intending that a neighbour would assume him a friend, and with a carefree spin on his heel confirmed that no one was on the street. He latched the gate after himself – a watching neighbour would disregard a man who took trouble. Jack pressed the bell.

Thirty more seconds went by. Jack noted that weeds thrusting up through the brick path in 2008 and in 2012 had gone. Somewhere a car door slammed. A blackbird chirruped. A dog gave an urgent bark, answered by another further away. Reminded of Stanley, Jack felt a twinge of guilt; Stella wouldn't approve of what he was doing.

Thirty seconds, then he rang the bell again. After another thirty seconds, he lifted the mat and retrieved the key. This wasn't breaking and entering, he imagined telling Stella, this was visiting.

He opened the door and replaced the key under the mat. Without looking behind him for fear of rousing suspicion, he stepped inside.

Had Jack looked at the plane tree where he had been standing moments earlier, he would have seen he was wrong in thinking that no one was watching him. Nor did he see a figure stroll across the street, with the same nonchalance as he had exhibited moments earlier and, lifting up the door mat, take the key from underneath it.

Thirty-Two

Friday, 25 October 2013

'Have a scone, Stell. See how an Aussie does them!'

Stella had agreed to morning coffee round at her mum's. Dale slid a plate heaped with bite-size scones dotted with plump sultanas across the coffee table to her. Stella wasn't hungry, but refusal wasn't an option. She smelled the warm aroma of cheese.

Dale settled beside her on the sofa and popped a scone in his mouth. He was wearing a chef's outfit: white shirt, chequered trousers. He had been happy to wear Clean Slate clothes when he cleaned yesterday. She hoped he wasn't going to get her cooking and expect her to dress up.

'Not as good as our mum's, you're thinking!' He was calling Suzie 'Mum'. His adoptive mum was dead. Dale had said he was sure that from above she approved.

Stella didn't say that Suzie hadn't baked after she left Terry. She moved the plate away from the edge of the table in case the dog was tempted to take one. With an explosion of crumbs, she tasted butter, fruit and cheese. It was, she had to admit, delicious. She took another and was contemplating a third when Suzie breezed in carrying a tray with three mugs of tea. Stella noticed how well her mother looked. Even without the expected suntan, Suzie glowed with health. She had put her hair up in a bun, which gave her an air of authority. Sydney – or maybe Dale – had transformed her.

'Dale wants to open another restaurant. We've got a proposal.' Suzie clapped her hands upwards as if releasing doves. Stella couldn't help glancing at the ceiling.

'No, he has *not*!' Dale shook his head, a hand in front of his mouth to catch crumbs. 'This is Mum's idea. Sure, expansion is on the cards, but not until I've accumulated capital. I will *not* borrow.'

'I'm not suggesting borrowing, or not like *that*,' Suzie continued undaunted. 'Not from a bank. Stell, if you sell Terry's house, you could invest in Dale's restaurant business.' Her hand hovered over the plate, then quickly, as if stealing, she took a scone from the furthest side and appeared to swallow it without chewing.

'What did I say this morning? Stella's known me for five minutes. Days ago she didn't know she had a brother. It's "no go", OK? I'm good as things are.' Dale reached for another scone.

Stella felt the usual mix of annoyance and respect for Suzie. She never let the grass grow under her feet. Although once unwilling to venture further west than Richmond Park or, until relatively recently, from her armchair, her mum dreamt up expansion plans for Clean Slate and a job for herself and her dreams came true. Not this dream. Dale Heffernan was right, she hardly knew him. Besides, she rarely ate out, knew nothing about the catering industry or his cooking. A few scones wouldn't have her putting the house on the market. Jack thought she was holding on to it for her dad, which was obviously nonsense since he was dead. She wasn't ready to sell the house. It needed cleaning.

'Show Stella your book.' Suzie lit upon another scone and tossed it into her mouth like a seal receiving a fish. 'You have a magic touch, Dale-kins,' she mumbled into her hand, hunching her shoulders in delight. Stella had only ever seen Suzie like this with Jack.

Dale-kins.

'What book?' Stella managed to ask. Recipes, she supposed. Suzie must know she wouldn't be interested. Stella didn't cook, she microwaved a variety of ready meals, among which shepherd's pies predominated. She took another scone. Stanley was dozing, his chin on her boot. She kept still so as not to disturb him.

'Stella's a busy woman.' Dale flapped a hand and flashed Stella what she had come to think of as one of his smiles.

'No, I'd like to see it.' Stella inhaled a cloud of crumbs and coughed. She slurped some tea and washed them down. The tea was hot. She had expected it to be tepid. Few people made it as she liked it. One of these was Jack. Again she found herself musing on how odd this was when he only drank hot milk.

'Consider it, Stella, it's a sound investment,' Suzie hissed in a stage whisper when Dale was out of the room. He was sleeping in Stella's bedroom. She had peeped in on her way down the passage. Apart from a sleek black suitcase, tucked under the desk, it looked no different. 'Keep it in the family!'

'*Enough.*' Dale was back, a fancy-looking photograph album under his arm. Patterned with silver and gold flowers, it put Stella in mind of a memorial book. A black ribbon tied in a bow reinforced this impression. 'The restaurant business is volatile, customers are fickle, food prices erratic. Barry left last month to work for a vineyard out in W. A. I put my sous-chef out front and a customer complained he had the eyes of a serial killer! Lost a lot of covers! I took out a loan so I could come back with Mum. If you get a kick out of pumping ten-dollar bills down a plughole, I'm your man!'

Suzie pulled faces at Stanley, still dozing at Stella's feet, implying this was nonsense. Stella steeled herself; her mother on a mission was unstoppable.

'Hey, if Clean Slate was up the road, I'd hire you! We need excellent cleaners, and you treat hygiene as top priority. Now *that* is a sound investment!' Dale pushed the empty scone plate aside and laid the album down. It took up most of the table. Stella's mind raced with excuses to get out of ploughing through Dale Heffernan's family snaps.

Stella stared at a logo on the inside cover. 'That's the same as—'

'Isn't it remarkable!' Suzie clapped her hands again, sending a spray of crumbs over the carpet Jack had cleaned. Stanley pounced on them and moments later they were gone. One good thing about a dog, Stella had noticed.

'Sixty-Four' was the street number of Dale's first restaurant in Sydney and was apparently the year he was born. Set within an oval, the logo was made up of a six and a four back to front – like on a police car, Stella thought vaguely. Stella wasn't great on design, what had got her attention was the colours. The light blue six was Pantone 277 and the four was a vivid green – Jack used to hate it – Pantone 375. Dale's logo exactly matched the colours of Clean Slate's branding.

'Weird, isn't it?' Dale murmured.

For a fleeting moment Stella wondered if it wasn't weird and he had deliberately chosen them. But then he said he had only just found out who his biological parents were. The logo was over thirty years old.

She was relieved that Dale didn't fawn over each picture. Not of his family – it was a compendium of reviews and photos of his cafés and restaurants, from the catering service he had operated out of a clapped-out combi in the 1980s to '64', now a restaurant frequented by celebrities and the wealthy in Rose Bay. Ignoring Suzie's cries to linger, Dale whizzed past five-star reviews, profiles cut from newspapers and glossy magazines, and the sumptuous illustrations of 'sensational' dishes. Stella found she was interested and wished he would slow down, but she was due at Lulu Carr's in half an hour.

'So, that's my "brilliant career"!' Dale shut the book and returned to his corner of the sofa. Suzie put out a fluttering hand and brushed his arm.

'It's great.' Dale had kept a record of every year of his business. It hadn't occurred to Stella to chart Clean Slate's history. There had been reviews in trade magazines, a few awards along the way; she cleaned for celebrities, but wouldn't dream of naming them. Stella hadn't considered her working life as a career – brilliant or otherwise – it was just a job.

Dale and Suzie went into the kitchen to prepare lunch. Listening to her mum's laughter, Stella was sure that Jack suspected that Dale had come to London with the intention of worming his way into Suzie's affections and claiming his share of the inheritance. Jack would never have actually come out and said this, but it wasn't like him to turn down tea with her mum in Richmond Park. If this was Dale's plan, he was on the way: Suzie was hooked. Yet he had been quick to slough off Suzie's idea. Jack must be wrong. The man had asked sensible questions about Clean Slate, he was a sharp businessman. He didn't want shareholders; like Stella he kept control of the reins. But what if it was an act? More than once Stella had paid the price for being fooled. Perhaps the album had been cobbled together for Suzie's benefit – a soft sell. If it was, she had bought it.

Stella glanced at the kitchen hatch. Unusually it was closed. Dale must have shut it – Suzie liked it open. She pulled the album towards her. On the first page was an article from a newspaper called the *Sydney Morning Herald* about Dale opening a café on 8 August 1988 in a suburb of Sydney called Redfern. He had chosen that day, he was quoted, '*...because the date, 8888, is auspicious. I hope it will bring me good luck.*' Just like Jack.

She had been operating Clean Slate from her bedroom that year, resisting Suzie's demands to lease an office and 'put a stake in the ground'. Stella felt the prickling of goose bumps. But for the Simon Le Bon hair, the twenty-something Dale, lounging against the door of the café, the proud owner, might be Terry. In the photograph of Terry outside her nana's house, he had leant on the door in just the same pose.

Dale wore an apron with the legend 'Dale's Place'. Her dad had hated fancy restaurants as much as she did. He would have been unnerved by a son who cooked food with French names. Stella rubbed her face. Terry would have been astonished to discover he had a son. He wouldn't have cared what he did.

People, probably friends rather than real punters, could be seen waving through the café window. Stella had had no official opening for Clean Slate. As she had later told Jackie, people don't fuss about cleaners. Some even give the impression they do the job themselves and for those Stella used her plain white van. Dale's Place had served hot food all day. Terry would have liked it there.

Her eye skimmed a shot of a young man and a woman below

Dale's picture. The woman looked vaguely familiar, but she had one of those finely boned faces to be found in every generation. Stella's attention drifted to the article above the image.

FEARS MOUNT FOR MISSING TEACHER

> Five years to the day since English teacher Nathan Wilson vanished, police say they have no clue to his whereabouts. The forty-year-old bachelor, on a sabbatical from Menzies High in exclusive Vaucluse, set off last October on a three-month walking tour of New Zealand to 'feed his soul' and never…

'You'll stay for lunch.' Suzie swept into the room, bearing a bundle of cutlery and a clutch of wine glasses.

'It's nearly eleven.' Stella shut the album. She would be late for Lulu Carr.

'Not now. It's moules marinières with lemongrass. There's fresh parsley!' As if parsley was a rarity. 'Dale's making fresh crusty bread for it and at the same time he's preparing sea bream with milk-braised leeks for tonight, with saffron and vanilla cream sauce.' Suzie picked up the album and held it with the tips of her fingers.

Stella was on the verge of retorting that it must be usual for Dale to cook several meals at once, but Suzie had decided he was extraordinary, so no point. She was secretly impressed. She could be floored by the calculation of timings for microwaving two shepherd's pies for her and Jack.

'I've too much on.' She wouldn't mention the case. 'Say goodbye to Dale.'

Suzie lifted the album. 'We'll do a copy for you.'

Stella snatched up Stanley and pecked Suzie on the cheek. She hesitated in the doorway. The smell from the kitchen was appetizing; she was hungry. Suzie was cradling Dale Heffernan's life-story album as if it were a baby.

Thirty-Three

Friday, 25 October 2013

'Mrs Frost?'

The fridge hummed; the boiler fired up. Silence. Checking the time out of habit – it was ten forty-five; he would stay no longer than an hour on this first visit – Jack glided along the passage on his rubber-soled shoes. He pushed at a door on his right with a finger, the way people do in public toilets to check if they're free. It swung open. He bent down and looked around the door. People look for intruders at eye level, and don't see a person crouching ready to pounce. He was the intruder. Jack didn't want to frighten anyone, not even a True Host who made it their business to frighten others before they snuffed them out. Senses acute, he could pick up a shift in the air, a change in atmosphere. He called out again.

'Yoo hoo? Mrs Frost? I'm a friend of William. He suggested I drop by.'

In the sitting room, a sofa, an armchair and a coffee table faced a fireplace inlaid with Delft tiles. Jack's eye was drawn to a flat-screen television on the wall above the mantelpiece. Rick Frost had been in security, he would have rated gadgets and electronic equipment higher than a Rothko or Matisse. The Frosts obviously didn't go in for fuss or sentimentality. Stella would like the stream-lined look: nothing to collect dust.

Stella was all set to do a meticulous internet search into the deceased's character, but they needed to know the stuff people kept to themselves. Interviews weren't enough and anyway Stella had gone ahead and interviewed William Frost without him.

Jack must work undercover, which was appropriate, since Rick Frost had made his business from selling surveillance equipment. Stella would be pleased with the results. No need to say how he came by them.

On the mantelpiece was a silver framed photograph of a man and a woman. The man wasn't Frost, Jack had seen him both dead and in a picture released for the press. The haircuts were 1980s, big shoulder pads, bouncy hair. They must be Tallulah Frost's parents; she'd be unlikely to keep up a picture of her in-laws after her husband's death. He thought them both faintly familiar, but as a train driver, he saw a lot of faces; it made everyone look like someone he had seen before.

Along from the picture was a silver Wee Willie Winkie candlestick holder with snuffer. A ball bearing lay in the base. Jack sent it rolling around the candle. His skin pricked with horror; he shouldn't touch or move anything. *Leave no fingerprints, no trace.*

In the kitchen he found the back-door key hanging by the back door. An odd breach of security for a surveillance expert. Jack opened the door and stepped out on to a gravelled patio of about three metres square. The gravel would warn of the enemy's approach. A log bin under the wall provided escape: one hop and he would be over. A way out and a way in. Jack returned to the kitchen, locked the door and, hesitating, replaced the key. There was plaster dust on the top of the light-switch plate suggesting that the hook had been fixed recently, no doubt since Frost's death. That explained it. Frost would have known how easy it was for an intruder to smash a pane in the door and reach in. Jack doubted that Rick Frost used to leave the front-door key under the mat. Perhaps, shattered by his death, his wife had grown careless. Generally, the bereaved were keen to keep up the deceased's routines. Stella cleaned Terry's house and maintained everything as it had been in his life. Tallulah Frost had transgressed, which made it easy for him. Jack was disappointed to have no tax on his skill or experience. It had been too easy – a bad sign.

On the staircase Jack saw what had been troubling him. The

Frost home was clean. Not a speck of dust. Everywhere sparkled. In the sitting room someone had smoothed the carpet pile after vacuuming, leaving no tracks. Tallulah Frost didn't need a cleaner.

Cleaning could be an antidote to grief; although she'd never admit it, Stella's shifts had increased when her dad died. Jack relished cleaning, ever hoping to recreate the home he had lost long ago. If Mrs Frost did her own cleaning, she must be very upset indeed. Either that or she had found a cleaner on a par with Clean Slate. Stella had competition.

Singing softly under his breath, he mounted the stairs. If anyone walked in now, he had nowhere to hide. Jack's fingertips tingled. This was how he liked it.

'Old Mother Goose,
When she wanted to wander...'

Invisibility wasn't all about keeping to the sides of stairs or to the ends of floorboards where there was least give. Jack dipped into rooms unseen and crouched in a strip of shadow when the Host was near. He wasn't like the enemy Rick Frost had sought to ward off with alarms and sensors, he joined the household and learnt its darkest secrets.

'... Would ride through air
On a very fine gander.'

On the landing he listened for breathing or for the silence of held breath. All clear.

No dirty grouting in the bathroom or limescale on the bath. The chrome plugholes shone. On the landing Jack opened a built-in cupboard. It contained Mrs Frost's summer clothes and, judging by a gap on the left-hand side, had once held her husband's too.

At the back of the house Jack opened a door by the bathroom.

'Hello, Rick.' This was Rick Frost's sanctum. He lingered in the doorway, picturing the man who had lain broken and bleeding on the sharp stones. Jack felt profound sadness. Death was expressed by the gaps in wardrobes and the silence of overly cleaned rooms.

'Please give up your secret,' he breathed but detected no ghost.

Rick Frost had run his business from this room. The walls were taken up with shelves crammed with books on coding and intruder monitoring. Jazzy-coloured boxes of security software were emblazoned with exclamatory titles: 'Duress!' 'Panic Stations!' 'Dispatcher!'

Three filing cabinets left space for the arm of an L-shaped desk with a *Mastermind* chair in the corner. The other arm of the 'L' would have had a view of the back patio, but for the frosted window. Dedicated to combating human transgressions, mostly inspired by the darkness of the soul, Frost hadn't required daylight. To beat the enemy, it was necessary to have the mind of the enemy.

Beside the desk was a dustbin-sized shredder where Jack guessed Frost destroyed every scrap of rubbish.

Jack fitted his Clean Slate pen through the desk-drawer handle and was surprised when it slid open. Inside was typical desk stuff: a stapler, staples and a staple remover, a cloth tape measure, a roll of sticky tape and some AA batteries. Shutting the drawer he heard a clunk as something rolled to the front. He opened it again and found a bullet. Not so typical. When William had said his brother took part in battle re-enactments, Jack had supposed this was jousting with shields, not using modern weaponry. At the back of the drawer he found a rolled-up canvas belt bristling with more bullets. He shivered. Although no ghosts, he felt a nasty energy in the room.

On the desk was a thin silver laptop with a printer. Jack sat down in the spacious chair, appreciating how comfortable it was. He turned on the laptop. The machine sprang to life and demanded a password.

He'd expected this; Frost was in security. Most people were unimaginative about passwords, choosing pets' names or whatever they saw when they glanced up from the monitor: Webster, Shakespeare. Stella had used 'hygiene' until he made her change it. Frost would have a strong password, alpha-numeric for starters.

A wireless mouse lay on a blank mouse mat. No company logo. Frost's was a clandestine business: he would rely on word of mouth for customers. They must find out who they were and what he had done for them. There was a shiny dip on the right of the space bar; otherwise there was an equal amount of wear on the keys. No way to establish the letters in the password, which, infrequently typed, wouldn't be evident.

The mouse was on the left of the laptop. At the inquest the pathologist had said Frost's left wrist was broken, as if, going under the wheels, he had instinctively tried to protect himself. Jack had forgotten. Frost *had* raised his hand, not to stop the train, but to Jack. He had been trying to point something out to him. Not something. *Someone.*

The prime suspect was Stella's 'inspector'. Was he returning to the scene of his crime? Or had he followed William Frost to the pub and overheard Jack suggest to Stella that they go to Stamford Brook station? Suddenly Jack was sure the man was not there simply waiting for a train.

Jack peered closer at the desk. There were scratches on the laminated top, so faint that, but for the strip of sunshine on the desk, he would have missed them. Someone had written something on paper with ballpoint, leaving the indentation on the desk. A single moment of carelessness, for there were no other marks on the laminate. The error suggested the action was untypical, perhaps in a moment of stress.

Jack patted the breast pocket in his coat for his notebook and pencil. Laying a sheet of paper over the scratches, he shaded it with the pencil, keeping his pressure consistent. Gradually he revealed a series of marks, white against the pencilled background. He held it up to make sense of them and saw the camera.

Fitted above the door, it was white like the walls. It moved fractionally and a red light blinked. It had been filming him since he entered the room.

Numb with horror at his stupidity, Jack didn't hear the diesel engine until it stopped. He strode out to the landing and opened the door of the room at the top of the stairs: Mrs Frost's bedroom. It was probably a delivery van. The driver would go away when he or she got no answer – or it might not be for this house. He tiptoed to the window and peeped out through slatted blinds.

Outside was a van, back doors open. Beneath it Jack could see legs encased in trousers and sturdy boots. He knew them instantly.

Jack Harmon could break into and live in a stranger's home with a steady pulse and cool nerve, but as Stella heaved her equipment bag on to her shoulder and headed to the front door, the dog at her heels, he nearly fainted.

He ran to the landing and blundered into the bathroom, then back to the landing. Stella had agreed to William Frost's plan, she was working undercover as a cleaner. It explained the hyper-clean rooms, the lack of vacuum tracks on the carpet, the precise positioning of ornaments and the ball bearing at 'six o'clock' in the well of the candle holder until, like a game of Russian roulette, he sent it spinning. It wasn't the work of a rival cleaning company or of a widow assuaging grief, it was Stella Darnell at her best.

Jack must help her in with her bag. He froze. Stella hadn't told him she had changed her mind. She didn't want him, or William Frost, to know. A detective's daughter, she would be uncomfortable about her decision. If Jack greeted her in the hall, aside from frightening her, he would cause her deep shame.

He spun around, hands wringing. It was worse. Stella would realize he had broken his promise. He had betrayed her.

Thirty-Four

Friday, 25 October 2013

With green lights all the way from her mum's flat, Stella made it to Lulu Carr's on time, but she hadn't been able to drop Stanley off at the office. She could have left him at Suzie's. Dale said he loved dogs, but he seemed to 'love' everything so she took that with a pinch of salt. She would explain to Lulu Carr that Stanley, being made of wool, wouldn't moult. If she had allergies – and Stella suspected she did – the dog would not set them off. She rehearsed her speech in her mind as she reversed into a space outside the house. If there were any accidents – there won't be, he's toilet-trained – or if he caused any damage – he knows not to touch anything – she would reimburse her. Stella pulled her equipment bag from the back of the van and slung it over her shoulder.

She was reaching for the doorbell when she heard a single chime from somewhere in her anorak. A text.

Had to see bro. Key under mat. Lulu. x.

Not again! If this cavalier attitude to security was Lulu Carr's revenge on her estranged husband, it was self-defeating. She wondered about the brother; if he was loyal, he was probably also protective. When a person slid into chaos, it was often the relatives who called in Clean Slate. Stella hoped he wasn't fuelling Lulu Carr's obsession with her husband. Having just acquired a brother herself, Stella had no idea what to expect. However, Lulu not being there did mean she needn't explain why she had Stanley in tow.

There was no key under the mat.

This hitch did at least give her a reason to leave and get on with the 'One Under' case. So far they had three suspects backed up by flimsy evidence. Her internet search on Rick Frost had resulted in one page of double-spaced text, including a photo that looked like a passport picture. The lack of available information on him might be apt for a surveillance expert – Frost had left the faintest of footprints – but it wasn't helpful for finding his killer. But 'stick to one job at a time' had been her motto since she started Clean Slate. Stella texted Lulu Carr, *No key. Will you be long?*

Lulu texted back immediately. *Another one above door. Don't be cross!*

Stella stepped back from the door and looked at the narrow lintel above the door. She caught a movement in one of the upstairs windows. She shaded her eyes against the morning sunshine and saw only a flash of light as the sun hit the glass. She wouldn't put it past Lulu to be in there, watching, testing her. Perhaps if she had left without texting, Lulu would have cancelled the contract. At this moment Stella doubted she would mind. She could see the key. Checking there was no one in the street, she took it down.

She unlocked the door, picked up the equipment bag and, with Stanley beside her, squeezed inside. Stella was pleased to see that Lulu was still keeping the house tidy; perhaps she was on the road to recovery. It was good too that she was seeing her brother and not scouring the streets for Mr Carr and his mistress.

Stella laid the towel she kept in the van to dry the dog off after walks down in the hallway and directed Stanley on to it. Obediently he flopped down and contemplated her with a doleful expression.

She lugged the bag into the living room and got out her 'light-clean kit'. The room was already spotless, but Stella was the first person to applaud the cleaning of a clean room.

Ten minutes later, as the clock on the mantelpiece struck eleven fifteen, Stella came out of the living room to fill a bucket with warm water from the kitchen and saw the towel on the hall floor. No Stanley.

She ran into the kitchen and tried the back door. Surprisingly, given Lulu's lax attitude to keys, it was locked. She knew he wasn't in the sitting room. She took the stairs three at a time to the landing.

Stanley was sitting on the crimson mat, bolt upright, staring at the cupboard built into the space behind the banister rail. He was making a hideous guttural growl. Stella realized she had heard the sound for some minutes but, engrossed in getting the windows spotless, hadn't taken it in.

When he saw her, Stanley began to bat at one of the doors. It was loosely fitting and made a resounding bang. The cupboard had stored many of the husband's clothes, jumpers and more combat gear, which Lulu had carted off to the dump. Stella had helped her put her own clothes in there. There was nothing that Stanley could want.

'Stanley!' David had told her that if Stanley was fixated with getting under a sofa or nosing behind a bookcase, there would be a good reason. Last week, giving in to his barking at a filing cabinet, Beverly and Jackie had eventually shifted it, a half-hour effort, to find his stuffed rat wedged behind it. There could be no toy in this cupboard.

'What are you doing up here?' She reached for a liver treat, but the pouch around her waist contained cleaning gear. She went closer and stopped.

Lulu's bedroom door was open. She *never* left it open.

There was one room in the house that Lulu didn't want her to clean: her bedroom. Stella had dreaded to think what state it was in, so, looking in, was surprised to find it immaculate. Dominating the room, beneath swathes of fabric suspended from the ceiling, was the biggest four-poster bed she had ever seen. More suited to a stately home than a modest house in Hammersmith. Soft linen and lace billowed from the ceiling, suspended there like clouds. Great dust collectors, she fleetingly thought.

Mirrors placed at strategic points reflected the bed into infinity. The bedspread twinkled with gold and silver threads; intertwining blossoms in blues, green and reds were lit by a sun motif in the centre. The sun was not as bright as the flowers. Floating on top of the silk was a pool of water, golden like the sun. The awful truth dawned.

Stanley had peed on the bed.

'No, no. *No!*' Stella scrubbed at her hair. She bundled up the counterpane. No point in reprimanding Stanley, the moment he had laid claim to Lulu Carr's territory would be lost in his past.

Something dropped to the floor. Stella reached down for it. It was Lulu's driving licence. There were bite marks in the plastic cover. Flushing with horror, Stella flipped it open, praying that Stanley hadn't rendered it invalid. The photograph wasn't Lulu; the face that stared out at her was the same as the one turned up in her internet research. It was Rick Frost.

'Stanley!' Stella closed the bedroom door. Holding the counterpane high to avoid tripping, she hurried down the stairs. She piled it into a large IKEA bag she kept in her equipment bag for emergencies such as this, got her phone from her anorak and called Jack.

Pick up!

Stanley cantered back up the stairs barking frantically. The phone clamped to her ear, Stella raced after him, worried she had forgotten to shut the bedroom door. He was back at the cupboard. She swished his lead from around her neck and clipped it on, but he wouldn't move.

She heard a buzzing. It sounded like a trapped insect. It must be what he could hear.

At that moment Jack's phone cut to answer machine.

Closing her phone, Stella went over to the cupboard. The buzzing had stopped. Holding on to Stanley's lead, she flung open one of the doors. A fragrant smell drifted out, aftershave mingled with fresh cotton. No trace of her beeswax polish, and there shouldn't be aftershave: she'd washed down the wood after removing the husband's clothes. Jilted clients hired her to eradicate all trace of their partners. She would have to clean the cupboard again.

'Nothing, see?'

Stanley backed away, tail down. There were smells he disliked: lavender oil, Jack's washing detergent. This reminded Stella that she needed to find Jack. She shut the cupboard door and carried the dog downstairs. Picking up the IKEA bag, she opened the front door, and formed the proper question: Why was Rick Frost's driving licence on Lulu Carr's bed?

Driving to her flat to wash the counterpane, more questions winged in. Was Lulu having an affair with Rick Frost? Had his wife found out and killed him? Was that why she wouldn't agree to meet? If Lulu was having an affair with Rick Frost, that might be why her husband had left, although it was blatantly unfair to blame him. Conversely, it made it likely that, torn in half by two women, Rick Frost had killed himself. Or had Frost refused to leave his wife? That gave Lulu Carr herself a motive for murder. Perhaps she had hired Stella to wipe away the evidence. But then, why leave her bedroom, where the most evidence might be, untouched?

Waiting at lights on the Hogarth roundabout, hunched over the wheel, Stella's head jangled with the chaos of possibilities and incongruities. She needed Jack to restore the order, even if it did involve signs and ghosts.

Checking on the dog, she saw something by his feet. She leant back to see properly. It was a glove. He must have taken it from Lulu Carr's bedroom. She started to reach behind to pick it up, but saw his eyes. He had taken possession of it. They would have to trade. She hoped he would resist destroying it before she got to the flat.

Stella saw Jack's tower. Yet again there was someone on the roof. She leant on the wheel and narrowed her eyes. Jack was holding something. Binoculars. He was looking at her.

She was brought to by a cacophony of sound. Furious faces in her rear mirror, fists and fingers raised, horns blaring: she had missed the lights. Stanley joined in, emitting short sharp barks. Miming apology, but unable to drive forward, Stella pressed 'dial' on her steering wheel.

'Name?'

'Jack Mob.' Stella was as monotone as the computer. The lights changed to green.

'This is Jack, who are you? Tell me after the beep.' She pulled away.

She wouldn't leave a message. Her 'Missed call' would be enough. On second thoughts: 'I just saw you. Please call!'

Thirty-Five

Friday, 25 October 2013

'I just saw you. Please call!'

Jack took his train out of Southfields station. As if to emphasize Stella's voicemail, there had been two little eyes at the top of the screen on his phone as if she were watching him. The flat light of a dull grey day filling the cab matched his low mood and reminded him why he liked the darkness of the Dead Late shift. Again, he had forgotten to measure the time it took to pass through the West Hill tunnel. He had been distracted. Last time it had been the red Triang engine on the monitor at Putney Bridge station, a sign he had yet to understand. Today, he had been shocked by how close he had been to Stella – or her dog – finding him in Tallulah Frost's cupboard.

He fretted about Stella's text. She had seen him. He went over the words in her text, analysing them like a political correspondent for meta-meaning. 'Just' – presently, in a minute, a minute ago, recently, how recently?

Stella had broken her code. She had gone into Tallulah Frost's house disguised as a cleaner. Jack felt cold fear at the prospect of seeing her; he dreaded her telling him she had done it. Or far worse, that she didn't tell him at all. She said she had seen him – maybe she would divert her guilt to him for trespassing? Jack toyed with pre-empting any of this by telling her himself. She might forgive him.

He acknowledged the driver of a train coming out of Wimbledon Park. The woman looked like Stella, shortish dark hair. He had Stella on his mind.

Stella didn't end relationships with grand announcements. There would be no special treatment for him as her friend. She would stop giving him cleaning shifts or inviting him to Terry's for shepherd's pie. No more detective cases. They would drift apart. From his tower, Jack would watch Stella leading her life and have no part in it.

Jack couldn't explain to Stella that what she liked in him – his knowledge of human nature, his interpretation of actions, above all his cleaning – depended on walking night-time streets and keeping vigil in the homes of True Hosts until they let their guard down. Telling Stella was not an option. She would never forgive him.

'I just saw you. Please call!'

At Wimbledon Park, he watched passengers get off and on. The red steam engine was there on the driver's monitor, exactly where it was last time. He stared at the number on the boiler: '26666'. It was the same number as the engine he had lost in the river when he was a child. Did they all have that number or was it the same engine?

Even as he reached for the engine, he expected it to disappear, a ghost engine, so was surprised by cold metal. Instantly he was taken back to being a tiny boy, crouched by the river's edge, pushing his engine down the slipway.

Jack got back into the cab and put the engine in his bag. He pressed a button and, with a collective swish, the carriage doors closed. He pulled the lever and eased the train forward.

As the monitor slid out of sight at the top right of its screen, Jack saw a figure at the far end of the station. The shape, the bearing, was familiar. He had seen the same figure in another monitor screen at another station. That man, like this one, Jack guessed, had made no attempt to get on the train.

On the return journey to Upminster, leaving Wimbledon, Jack made himself think of nothing but the West Hill tunnel. Leaving Southfields, he could see the mouth of the West Hill tunnel ahead. Jack checked his watch: thirteen thirty-three. He forced himself to concentrate.

The second hand hit the fourteenth minute past the twelve. He fixed on the tracks, his mind blank, and maintained forty miles per hour. The darkness enveloped him.

'I just saw you. Please call!'

Thirty-Six

Friday, 25 October 2013

A strong gust of wind buffeted her. A tower might sound exciting on paper, but in reality it was dangerous and scary. Especially in the middle of the night.

She should have rung before coming. Jack hadn't replied to her text and, unwilling to text him again, she decided to surprise him. He did it to her all the time.

There seemed more stairs than last time and they were steeper. She had left her gloves in the van, and her hands burned on the frozen metal rail. The wind was like in a horror film, a moan rising and subsiding. Stella told herself it was the sound of it blowing through the holes in the metal stairways, but couldn't shake the impression of a baby crying in the dead of night. It was late, past ten o'clock. She was letting her imagination get the better of her.

There was a click. Jack had come down to let her in. Stella called out, 'It's me.' Stanley tensed. Probably because he wasn't keen on Jack.

She stepped on to the walkway, which was narrower than she remembered. No sign of Jack. A flurry of wind slapped her against the tower wall. She held the dog tight, mindful of breaking his ribs. They would both break everything if they fell off the walkway.

There was no bell. Stella huddled in the door recess and, sheltering Stanley in the folds of her anorak, rang Jack again.

'This is Jack, who are you? Tell me after the beep.'

Jack was always advocating spontaneity, yet here was proof it didn't pay off. Stella dared not look down. She might be on the ledge of a cliff face, darkness all around. She had never felt more alone. There was one place she could go.

Stella parked up opposite the mansion block in Barons Court. Ahead was the station, its lit fascia like a beacon. She thought of the fish Suzie had said Dale was cooking for supper and wondered if there was any left over. Too late to visit: Suzie liked an early night and Dale, who her mum said had jet lag, would be asleep. Stella had never had jet lag. She wasn't sure how it worked. It didn't seem to affect her mum.

When Jack was driving, he turned off his mobile. That was it. The living-room lights were on in her mum's flat. She was still up. A shadow slanted across the ceiling – two shadows. Dale and Suzie came to the window and, like subjects in a framed photograph, looked out. Stella fumbled with her key and pulled away from the kerb.

She got through the lights at the Talgarth Road junction and was soon back on the flyover. What could Suzie and Dale find to talk about? Stella talked about work when she visited her mum. They couldn't be swapping recipes; Suzie would soon run out.

Stella slowed at the Hogarth roundabout lights, where that morning she had seen Jack on the roof of his tower. He wasn't there now.

Since Jack was doing day shifts for a driver friend, it must mean his nights were free.

A man was striding briskly along the pavement. He passed the pub, head down, walking with a bounce on the balls of his feet, like a teenager. He wore a long black coat and his hair hung in locks to his shoulders. He merged with the shadows, vanished and then reappeared. There was only one person it could be. Stella slowed as he reached the subway. She couldn't stop or turn around. She lowered the passenger window to shout, willing the lights to go red. They stayed green. She looked in her driver's mirror in time to see Jack go down into the subway. If she went around the roundabout she could catch him on the other side. No, there were too many cars, even at this time of night; she couldn't swap lanes.

Jack had been coming from the direction of the tower. He had been there all along. He had broken his promise to her – he was walking at night. Stella minded less that Jack had lied; she was worried for him. One day he would get himself killed.

On Kew Bridge her phone rang.

'Number unknown'. Not Jack.

'I've found her!'

'Found who?' Stella tried to place the voice.

'My husband's mistress.'

Lulu Carr. Stella pictured the bedspread airing in her study. The stain had come out. She had forgotten about the glove.

'I'm on my way there!' Lulu's voice boomed in surround sound and Stella adjusted the volume.

'Stay where you are.'

Lulu opened the door before she could knock. She was waving a piece of paper like a flag of victory.

'I was right, I was bloody right!' she exclaimed in a hoarse whisper guaranteed to wake the street. Stella hurried her through the house to the kitchen.

'I found this in the cupboard on the landing.' She slapped the paper down on the table.

'What is it?' The paper was covered with pencil shading like a child's scribbled-out drawing.

'Secret writing. It's a number, look!'

Hardly secret then. Stella could see some random marks. She tilted the note to the light. The marks did look like numbers.

'I know where he is.' Lulu was looking out into the garden as if that was where her husband was. Stella had to end the charade.

'Lulu, when I was here earlier—'

'Nicola Barwick's been dying to get her hands on my husband.' Lulu slumped down on a chair. She spoke as if reciting from a script.

'Who is Nicola Barwick?' Stella remembered what Dale had said about the man in his restaurant with an imaginary friend.

'The spectre at our wedding. She was the bad fairy. My brother made me invite her – he has a soft spot for her. So did my husband. She twists men around her little finger. She's been waiting to twist the knife.'

'Lulu, I found—'

'They mucked around as kids, skulking in the cemetery over the road from us. My mother worried about my brother, he took it so seriously. I heard her suggesting to my dad they take him to a doctor, but my dad was a psychiatrist and it wouldn't have done to have a bonkers son, so he did nothing.' She spoke in a whisper and kept glancing at the back door as if afraid of being overheard, reminding Stella of William Frost's behaviour in the pub. She looked too, but saw only their reflections in the glass.

'What are you saying?' She closed her fingers around the driving licence in her pocket. Where was Jack?

Suddenly it struck Stella that Lulu might not know Rick Frost was dead. Years ago, one of her clients had been having an affair with a man who fell off a ladder at his home and died. He didn't turn up at the arranged place. Her client had seen a memorial notice in a newspaper six months later; by then she'd destroyed everything he had ever given her, assuming he had dumped her. Exactly as Lulu had been doing.

Lulu was still talking.

'This is written in invisible ink. He could never do anything normally. If we arranged to meet in a station or a café, he got there early to watch me waiting for him. Sometimes he wasn't there, but I felt I was being watched all the same.'

'Are you talking about your husband?' Stella might point out the marks weren't written with invisible ink since they could see them and she had a distant memory that invisible ink was made with lemon juice.

'What?' Lulu looked oddly guilty.

'I cleaned that cupboard, I didn't see this.' Why had Stanley been so interested in the cupboard?

'Exactly! Don't you see, someone's been here. No prizes for guessing who. I'm going to wipe away her crocodile tears!'

‘Maybe wait until the morning.’ Stella saw the time on her watch: ten past eleven; it nearly *was* the morning. ‘Lulu, how do you know Rick Frost?’ Gentle and friendly, she imitated Jack asking contentious questions.

‘What do you mean?’ Lulu stiffened and shut her eyes tight like a little kid hiding.

‘I found this.’ Stella laid the driving licence on the table beside the note. There would be time later to explain about her dog. The paper and the licence looked like exhibits from a crime scene. Perhaps they were. ‘Were you having an affair with Rick Frost?’

Lulu opened her eyes. ‘No, I bloody well was not!’

‘Why have you got this?’ Stella was morphing from cleaner to detective in one job.

‘Why have I got any of his things?’

‘You tell me.’ Stella coaxed. *Take your time*, she nearly said.

Stella felt the sensation that Jack often claimed to feel, like an autocue: she saw Lulu’s answer before she spoke.

‘Rick Frost was my husband.’

Thirty-Seven

Friday, 25 October 2013

'How's Stella Darnell? Still cleaning for England or cleaning up England?' Cigarette smoke puffed from between Lucille May's lipsticked lips.

'She works hard,' Jack said levelly. At best Lucie and Stella were openly hostile towards each other.

'Sure I can't tempt you with a nippet? No milk, but a whole damn bottle of Tanqueray is cooling its heels!' Waving her glass of gin and tonic at him, Lucie shut an eye against the smoke and eyed him beadily with the other.

Jack shook his head. 'No, you're all right.' Lucie held a scary amount of drink without obvious impairment to her thinking or her memory. A 'nippet' – a triple gin with a splash of tonic – would fell him.

It was ten past ten. Jack had returned from his driving shift that day restless and dissatisfied. Shocked by Stella coming to Tallulah Frost's house that morning, he had failed – despite his determination to focus on it – to calculate the length of the West Hill tunnel. If he knew the mystery fact, it would unlock other hidden facts.

He hadn't yet faced examining the steam engine he had found on the monitor. It was a sign of something he had tried to forget.

Stella had texted, saying she had seen him. He was scared to see her and was appalled with himself. He had been called a coward in the past – it was true.

He was taking refuge with Lucie May. Unfettered by a moral code, Lucie pursued her stories with blind ambition. While this wasn't an attitude he admired, being with Lucie, her diminutive frame lost in a jumper – a relic of a husband divorced along the way – curled on her sofa, substituting smoke for air and consuming gin as if life, not death, depended on it, Jack felt a braver and better person. He nestled in his corner of the sofa. The coffee table was lost beneath piles of back copies of the *Chronicle*, on which Lucie May had been chief reporter for nearly forty years.

Lucie had just filed a story – 'Hush hush, Jackanory, it's embargoed until next week' – so was 'demob bloody jubilant!' She had once told him she never drank on the job, but he could see that alcohol was taking its toll. Her skilfully applied foundation didn't hide a pinkish complexion or the crazy bright of her eyes.

'You've decorated.' Stella would approve of the newly whitewashed walls. Although with Lucie's nicotine habit it would not be white for long.

Lucie had reinstated the numerous photos of herself with the great, the good and the royal (the Queen in 1970, Prince Edward in 1985).

'I've scared away the ghosts.' Lucie contemplated her glowing butt, fitted it between her lips and sucked on it before pinching it out in an ashtray shaped like a woman's upturned hand. Jack's own palms tingled.

Long ago, a woman had killed herself feet from where they sat. Lucie had bought the house intending to write a book about the case – her pension plan – but the ghosts had got to her first, so there would be no book. Jack doubted a lick of emulsion would scare them away.

'Certainly should,' he said nevertheless. Perhaps, after all, it was a good sign.

'So what can I do you for?' Lucie rasped. Swirling her glass, she sent ice whizzing around it, faster and faster. 'Or is this just a social call?'

He got to the point. 'What do you know about the Palmyra Tower?'

'Zilch. Should I?' Lucie drained her glass and mussed up her expensively dyed blonde hair. Her gestures and tics belonged to a long-ago younger self, but somehow she got away with it. She reached for her cigarette packet on the sofa arm, but then seemed to think better of it. 'Where is it, Italy? Going on holiday, darling? Can I come?' She gave a cackle and picked up the cigarette packet.

'Chiswick Mall.' Jack was disappointed; he had been relying on Lucie, a mine of information about West London, to shed light on his new home.

'Oh, you mean Chiswick Tower!' She flicked up a fresh cigarette, lit it, inhaled and puffed out a swirl of smoke. 'Talking of ghosts!' She shifted about happily. 'Dead Man's Tower! I knew it was finished. Luxury accommodation! They'll make a mint from some poor sod happy to climb that scaffold and live in a water tank!'

Jack's head jerked and he sniffed to cover the tic that rarely surfaced. 'That's me.'

'Say again?' Lucie's cigarette hand was above her shoulder, the smoke spiralling upwards.

'I'm living there.'

'Lordy-lou!' Lucie funnelled smoke up to her brilliant white ceiling. 'Even for you, that takes the biscuit!' she said eventually.

'Have you written something on it?'

'*Wind Drowns Out Terror Screams!*'

Like himself, Lucie had a photographic memory. She could recite from pieces she'd written decades ago, both the headlines and whole passages from the articles. She had facts at her fingertips that no amount of Tanqueray would blur or blot out. Jack felt a buzzing in his solar plexus: dread or excitement, he wasn't sure.

'Tell me.' Jack tucked his own feet up, shoes clear of the sofa – Lucie was house-proud – and prepared for a cracking story.

'Chiswick water tower was erected in 1940 to protect local industry, the brewery and a shipbuilder's on the wharf where Pages Yard is now. It was meant to put out fires caused by German bombing, but I don't think it ever did. Unlike the one on Ladbroke Grove – a bomb hit the cemetery nearby and sent a headstone smashing into the side of a gasometer. But for that tower, Shepherd's Bush would be a memory!'

Gone were Lucie's corncrake tones and her brash flirty style. The reporter was cool and authoritative, her mind a fount of fact and folklore. Jack got a glimpse of the professional, brimful of hope and principle, that Lucie had once been.

'It was decommissioned in the sixties and became a white elephant. One resident campaigned to have it demolished in the late seventies, but the whole community rose up and objected. It might be a concrete monstrosity, but it was their concrete – you get it!'

She went to the cabinet on the other side of the room and, with Faustian precision, put together another nippet.

'It was listed and in the eighties a company bought it to turn it into luxury apartments. But it was a bridge – or a tower – too far and they went bankrupt. It stayed empty for another couple of years, Chiswick's own Centre Point. A consortium bought it about five years ago and began redeveloping it. They wouldn't do interviews – the project was cloaked in secrecy. Even I couldn't get a sniff. If you ask me, that was the point, talk it up – or not talk – so I gave up. I won't play that game.' She dropped a lemon slice into her drink and sucked on another. 'I didn't think the place would ever get a tenant. Trust it to be you!'

'Why? It's got amazingly detailed views.' Jack accidentally echoed the leaflet. The sensation in his solar plexus clarified into dread.

Wandering to her French doors, Lucie sniffed her drink with anticipatory delight. 'Because a man had lain dead there for nearly a year. Sorry, darling.' She turned around and grimaced at him.

'There's no sign of him now.' Thinking of Stanley's furious digging and sniffing, Jack wasn't sure this was true.

'The police couldn't identify him. He had perfect teeth, no fillings, nothing, but no dentist had him on their books. Teeth was pretty much all that was left – the corpse was skeletal after all that time. He was discovered by a representative of the consortium. You sure about it? I sure as hell wouldn't like to live in a place where a person had died.'

Jack refrained from pointing out that Lucie was doing exactly this, or that most flats and houses over thirty years old had witnessed a death.

'Who was the man?'

'They never found out. I dubbed him "Glove Man" since that was pretty much all there was of him. The nationals ran with that, not that I got any credit.' She opened the French windows and seemed to Jack to float on to the patio into the darkness beyond. He got up and followed her.

'I'm sorting this too,' she was muttering, glass in hand, as she leant down desultorily and wrenched up a weed, tossing it into next door's garden.

'Why did you call him Glove Man?' In the slant of light from the sitting room, Jack noticed that at long last Lucie had got rid of the rusted swing that had stood for decades in the middle of the lawn. He felt a twinge of regret. He fancied flying up into the night, but on a swing he would have to come down.

'They found a glove on the corpse's back. There was some argy-bargy at the inquest about whether he could have placed it there himself. Terry demonstrated it was just about possible, but the question remained, why would he? If he was going to kill himself and make it look like murder, then he should have framed someone. Obvious candidate was the owner of the glove, but that was never established. His fingernails showed signs that he had gone for the door and the walls, but being metal and concrete he had no purchase, nothing to grip, poor bloke. So he wasn't in a "framing frame of mind"!' Jack suspected she had made the pun more than once before.

'What was the verdict?' Was this another case of Terry's that had got away? That was the reality of being a detective. If you wanted to truly restore order, you should be a cleaner. He might say that to Stella. *Stella.*

'Open. The police thought he was homeless. He thinks: set up shop in the tower, but the door shuts. Effectively he's trapped in a giant toilet cistern! In the old days he'd have got out through the roof, but the builders had stripped out the pipework by then.'

'Why didn't you think he was homeless?'

'Apart from a sleeping bag, there was a champagne bottle in there, a high-class choice of tipple for a guy living on the street – or *above* the street. A used condom suggested he wasn't alone. They found more than one set of fingerprints, but nothing that figured on police records. Over the years enough people had been up there. I suggested to Terry it might have been a paedophile and his family were keeping *shtum*. What better way to disown him than his being locked in a tower? They might even have locked him in there!'

'Why did you think he was a paedophile?'

'The glove was too small for an adult. It wasn't his.'

'Could have been dropped by kids afterwards.'

'That was the official police line. But, as I said to Terry, even a kid knows better than to incriminate himself. Terry agreed, but without cogent evidence he couldn't raise a budget to take it further. Another mystery that haunted the poor guy.' She sipped at her drink. Despite her threadbare jumper, she didn't seem to feel the cold.

'Sounds like you had the answer. He drank too much, shut the door and was unable to escape.'

'There was no reason for the door to shut, it was at the top of a spiral staircase, as you know, so could only shut if someone deliberately pushed it. Ergo, someone who intended to lock him in. After so long the pathologist couldn't pinpoint time and date of death, but they narrowed it to late 1987. As I said, October was the month of the Great Storm, that hurricane that famously wasn't forecast. The wind was like a tempest – the lead flashings on our house rolled up like foil and we lost a load of roof tiles. It was deafening. No one would have heard Glove Man yelling for help. Even on a quiet night, I doubt the sound would have carried.'

She ground out her cigarette into the grass with the toe of her boot.

Jack was about nine in 1987; he had a hazy recollection of streets blocked by fallen tree trunks, pavements strewn with branches and smashed glass, cars abandoned. It gave him a bad feeling, the same feeling he got when he thought about the steam engine.

'Hundreds of feet up in a concrete vault, the man must have been stark staring petrified. It was likely he had heart disease, probably undiagnosed. Being a bag of bones they couldn't verify that. But it's likely the terror of being locked in a tank miles in the sky did it for him. Bam! His ticker packed up. Terry's lot did call-outs to surgeries, but drew a blank; no doctor had a missing patient with a dicky ticker. Poor Terry. A literal skeleton in the cupboard!' Lucie was gazing at the sky; she seemed to have forgotten Jack was there.

'I swapped notes with Terry. I had a bulging file because of the demolition protests. We kept each other's secrets.' She pinched up the lemon from her drink and threw it into the bushes. 'Stupid bugger, I said he needed exercise.'

'Who?'

'Terry.' She produced her cigarettes from the waistband of her trousers and stuck one between her lips. 'Stella see much of her mum?'

'Yes.' Jack knew the tactic. Lucie would appear to be asking after someone, but everything led somewhere. He wouldn't let his guard down.

'Mobile phones were a rarity then and they were the size of houses. So, end of Glove Man.' Lucie was with the story again.

The door in the tower was original. A man had battered on the galvanized metal before he collapsed with a coronary. The dog had tuned into the frequency of the man's terror and anguish; Jack, usually so alive to the presence of the dead, had sensed nothing. He had abandoned one set of ghosts – of his parents, of the self he preferred to forget – for a more potent phantom.

'How old was he?'

'Between twenty and forty, which gives lots to play with. One clue, he had a receipt in his trousers from the Fullers wine shop, as it was in 1987. That one on the corner of Goldhawk Road and King Street – your old neck of the woods, darling. No CCTV then and no one in the shop recalled the purchase. In that area, getting a bottle of bubbly is probably not a rare occurrence!' Lucie paused and contemplated the sky, where Jack could just make out faint stars.

'Stella's mum back from Oz yet?' she asked airily.

'Yes.' She was homing in. He steeled himself and tried to deflect her. 'I got a leaflet through the door about the tower.' If he was honest, Jack was thrilled to be living on a murder site. Another of Terry's unsolved cases: it was a sign. He would offer it to Stella as a recompense for his being in Tallulah Frost's landing cupboard. Except if he said Lucie had told him, it would make things worse. Stella wouldn't want to hear that Lucille May and her father had worked on a case together. It would be no recompense at all.

Stella and Lucie, chalk and cheese. Chalk and chalk as they weren't so different. Both of them had loved Terry Darnell. Jack wished they could get on.

'What's this Palmyra shit? What's wrong with plain old Chiswick Tower? Is that your name for it?'

'No, it was on the leaflet.' Jack pictured the pink sheet. Apart from Palmyra being an ancient Syrian city and a suburb in Western Australia, he had no idea what connection it had with the tower. With little sleep, his mind was a fog. He wondered again at his luck in getting the flat – not luck in Lucie's view. It had taken two mail-shots, so maybe she was right, potential tenants had found Lucie's articles about the dead man online and been put off.

He and Lucie were mavericks. Few would relish knowing someone had died a horrible death a couple of metres from the bottom of their bed.

'Palmyra rings a bell with me, but the older one gets, the more bells ring. Stay, young Jack, stay as you are!' Lucie touched his cheek with the back of her hand and meandered back to the sitting room. 'You should check out what your mystery guest looks like.' She pulled shut the French windows.

'Sorry?' Jack sat in his corner.

'Mispers!'

'Bless you.' It wasn't a sneeze, he realized.

'The Missing Persons' website. It lists the lost and unclaimed of Britain. Bodies found on commons, in alleyways, drowned in the Thames or hit by trains on railway lines. Glove Man hasn't got a photo, unfortunately, so nothing to see. They've done a sketch, so maybe one day someone might recognize him. I hope it's me.'

'I'll take a look.' Jack frowned to hide his excitement.

'Course you will, Rapunzel!' Lucie punched his arm. 'As soon as you're back in your tower!'

Jack drew his coat around him to hide that she was right.

Lucie May lit her cigarette and said in her Lucille Ball accent: 'Has Mrs Darnell brought a present back for her "one and only" offspring?' She smiled sweetly through a pall of smoke.

Ground Zero.

As if he hadn't heard, Jack asked, 'Does the name Rick Frost ring any of your bells?'

Thirty-Eight

Friday, 25 October 2013

Stella lived in a gated complex in Brentford, bought off-plan. She had opted for a corner flat on the fifth floor in the block – high enough for privacy (she was indifferent to the 'stunning views of the River Thames and across London'), but accessible should the lift break down. Had Stella been given to mulling on such matters, she might have thought it not dissimilar to Jack's tower. Silent and secure, with 'detailed views'.

For the first couple of years the building had been 80 per cent unoccupied. This had suited Stella; she didn't move to find a community in which to play an active part. She signed up to Neighbourhood Watch because keeping an eye out for intruders was what she did anyway. When the economy improved – for the income bracket that could afford Thames Heights – there had been an influx of new residents. Now only a handful of properties were empty. Despite this, Stella rarely met anyone going in or out.

Taught by Terry to be security-conscious, Stella appreciated the automatic gates that juddered open on to a drive winding between undulating lawns to garages and numbered bays. CCTV monitored the door of a fully glazed marble-clad foyer more in keeping with a multinational corporation HQ than a block of flats in Greater London.

With Stanley at her heels, Stella punched in the key code and slipped into the lobby. The door shut swiftly with a sigh, narrowly avoiding Stanley's back legs. Stella was gratified: her complaint about how long it took to close had been heeded. Most of her complaints – sporadic cleaning of the common parts and security lights that worked in the day but not at night – were ignored.

She was keen to get to bed: it had been a long and unsatisfactory day, culminating in the discovery that Lulu Carr was Tallulah Frost and her husband hadn't left her for another woman, he was dead.

At the end of the cavernous lobby – housing two lifts – a line of ceiling bulbs had blown, throwing it into gloom. Stella made for the lifts and was brought up short by the sudden hush of the lift doors opening in unison, a rare thing.

Two paths of bright light flooded the marble. Stella hung back to make way for passengers in both lifts. No one came out. She might have taken it in her stride, but Stanley began to quake, his tail between his legs. Tired and troubled about Jack's recent appearances in odd places – the roof of his tower, a cemetery and the pub – Stella was assailed by panic. To reach the staircase or the main door, she would have to cross the slants of light.

It was inconceivable that both lifts had descended empty at the same time. Someone had to have activated them. Stanley began to growl, giving her away. She snatched him up and, rushing across the marble floor, shouldered her way through to the stairwell. Behind her she heard the same hush. The lift doors were closing.

Up or down? Stella made a snap decision and ran up the stairs to her flat rather than down to the basement. Fifty steps versus ten. After twenty, her legs became leaden as if she were wading through water. Stanley had gone quiet, but with every step he got heavier. Her rucksack, weighed down with her laptop, bumped against her spine and her boots scraped on the concrete stairs, giving her away. All the time the lift must be travelling upwards, faster than she could run. Or it had gone down. She had no way of knowing.

Each floor was numbered, which was lucky because Stella soon lost count. She couldn't keep up her pace. Her lungs bursting, she had to stop. She stood for a moment, trying to get her breath, her chest heaving with hot pain. Hearing nothing, she edged to the banister. She looked up and then down, scared of seeing someone patiently waiting, looking out for her.

No one need do that. They would know exactly where she was.

Stella powered up the last flight and flung herself through the door at level five. She raced along the carpeted corridor, feeling for her key with her free hand. She hit the lock, missing it. She inserted it at the same moment as the lift doors were opening.

Stella tumbled into her hall and kicked shut the door behind her. Terry hadn't trusted CCTV or electronic locking devices; all you need is a power cut, he had said. As she turned the keys in the two extra five-lever mortice locks, she silently thanked him for advising she fit them, along with the London bar that made jemmying the door impossible.

Stanley leapt down and trundled off down the hall and into the living room, tail twirling like a flag. Slumped against the front door, her heart still pounding, Stella heard sloshing from the kitchen as he guzzled from his water bowl. Business as usual. She stumbled into her study, the 'second bedroom' opposite the living room, and took out her laptop. The lifts must both be faulty, she assured herself.

She began to close the blind and stopped, her hand on the cord.

A man stood on the path leading up from the gates. Only because she hadn't yet switched on the study light could she see him, because with no security lights it was dark outside. Tall in a long black coat, hands in his pockets. Jack. Full of relief, Stella reached for the window lock; she wouldn't bang on the glass and disturb the neighbours. The key was in the living room.

She waved. Jack didn't respond, although she was sure he could see her. He hadn't been there when she arrived – she would have seen him and he would have called to her. He had a key to the basement, so he could get inside. She got out her phone and texted him. Her fingers trembled and she made several mistakes before managing: *Are you ok?*

Nothing in his body language intimated he had received the text. No light glowing in his pocket. She dialled his number.

'This is Jack, who are you? Tell me after the beep.'

She would have to go down to get him.

Stella was about to open the front door when her phone lit up.

Fine. You? Jack didn't waste words.

Why are you here?

She froze. There were two watching eyes at the top of the phone screen. It must be William – he *was* stalking her. She was startled by the ping of a text.

Why are any of us here? Jx.

Stella went back to the study and, neighbours or not, raised her hand to bang on the glass.

Jack had gone.

Thirty-Nine

Saturday, 26 October 2013

Gender	Male
Age range	20 to 40
Ethnicity	White European
Height (cm)	172
Build	Medium
Date found	30/9/1988
Estimated date of death	Late 1987 (possibly October)
Body or remains	Body – skeletal
Circumstances	A male body was found in Chiswick Tower in Chiswick Lane South
Possessions	Empty bottle of Veuve Clicquot champagne
Hair	Medium-length brown
Facial hair	N/A
Eye colour	Unknown
Distinguishing features	No tattoos
Clothing	Casual Millets anorak, zip-up front, size 44; beige cotton trousers size 32 (brand name Racing Green); braces – blue; kipper tie – blue; leather brogues, leather uppers, plastic soles – black (brand name Clarks); crew-neck jumper – turquoise (brand name Reiss)
Hose	Calvin Klein blue Y-fronts with red piping and waistband. White socks
Jewellery	Gold metal ring engraved with 'x' in centre of which tiny diamond. Gents Timex wind-up watch, no numerals, markings dabbed with luminous paint. Black leather strap with lighter stitching

On a trawl of the Missing Persons' Bureau website, Jack examined pictures of dead faces – reachable by surmounting several warnings to stop the unwitting stumbling upon one. 'Glove Man' had been submitted by the Metropolitan Police on 30 September 1988. No picture, as Lucie had said. Jack thought the pencil sketch familiar, it could have been any one of his male passengers – that parade of faces on platforms when he pulled into stations.

After a year in the empty water tank, the man was beyond recognition. Jack could imagine the skeleton, wrist bones poking from the 'casual Millets anorak', the fabric fusty and faded, nibbled by mites. Grey bones mapped with scraps of brown leathery skin, a skull tufted with 'medium-length brown hair' the consistency of dried grasses. A skull's bared-teeth grin, which always struck Jack as gleeful rather than sinister. The empty eye sockets would have gazed back sightless. The man had died alone and unheard, perhaps unloved. After decades it was unlikely he would be matched with a missing person. Missing, but not missed. Once upon a time, over fifty years ago, Jack hoped there had been a celebration of Glove Man's birth. His individuality, the man he had been in life, was distilled on a website database to his taste in champagne.

Jack leafed through Lucie's file. 'If you find out who he is, he's mine, darling.' Side-stepping credit suited Jack. Stella had been uncomfortable when he'd asked her to take the kudos for their work on the Rokesmith and Blue Folder cases. *The Detective's Daughter Does Dad Proud* had been one of Lucie's headlines. Stella had only agreed when he pointed out the merits of anonymity: he could work incognito.

An hour ago Stella had texted enquiring if he was *OK*. She might be feeling guilty at going behind his back and – a classic tactic – projecting her guilt on to him. Jack had hoped she would suggest he came over to see her; although it was the middle of the night he could do with one of her shepherd's pies. They had much to debrief. But she must be avoiding him.

The first article Lucie had written on the case was printed in the *Chronicle* the week after the corpse was found and was headed 'Who Is the Man in the Tower?' Jack sang under his breath:

'The man in the moon
Came down too soon...'

The man in the tower hadn't come down sooner or later. The file included torn leaves from Lucie's notebook. He read that 'the corpse's jumper was knotted around his neck, although anorak zipped up'. This wasn't on the website, probably because it wasn't relevant to identification. Lucie had got it from Terry. She had said that the knotted jumper suggested a jaunty, laconic mood far removed from screaming in a concrete chamber until the heart gave out. Jack agreed that it belonged with quaffing champagne, if it had been drunk and had not evaporated over the months. The man had put on his anorak without unknotting his jumper and putting it on first. Lucie said this showed he must have died soon after he knew he was imprisoned. The night of the hurricane would have been cold; crazy to have a sweater, she had said, and not wear it.

Jack had momentarily forgotten he was in the room where the man had died. Not a room then, a concrete tank that for a year had served as a tomb. The place on the floor where the body had been was in shadow. The glow from his laptop drew the curving walls closer. He thought of a cardboard tube rolled tighter and tighter until there was no room to breathe.

He went to the door and, getting down on his hands and knees, shuffled across the floor. Oak boards laid over the concrete base were warm. A heat-exchange system took water from the Thames to cool and heat the tower.

In 1987, little had been done to the 5,000-gallon tank. According to Lucie's notebook, slats beneath the ceiling, glazed with red-and-yellow-coloured panes of glass, were part of that first tranche of development and not in the original tank.

The tower's designer – given its function Jack presumed it was an engineer rather than an architect – would have dispensed with conceits like a cupola on the roof. Access to clean the tank would be through a hatch in its ceiling; there was no sign of it now. The ceiling was over a metre above Jack. He was tall and could easily get to a hatch using a stepladder, even a chair. In 1987 the man had only a champagne bottle. If there had been a hatch it would have been out of his reach.

Why was he there? In the second article covering the inquest, Lucie – keeping within legal bounds – speculated on suicide. As she had told him, the man had no identification, a typical suicide trait. He had bought the champagne either with the right money, or returned to his home after buying it and left his wallet there before going to the tower. Every so often there were stories of people lying dead in their homes for months, even years. Neighbours would claim that the person had kept themselves to themselves. The inoffensive, it seemed, were less missed than the argumentative, boundary-disputing ones. Neighbours had assumed they were on holiday or had moved without saying goodbye. Glove Man must own his home or the police were right and he had no home. Otherwise someone was chasing some serious rent arrears.

If he had been murdered, a careful killer would remove anything incriminating or that would hasten the identification of the victim. The body was the biggest clue in a murder. Lucie believed it was murder and eventually Terry had agreed.

Jack rubbed his eyes. It was ten past three and he was driving in a few hours. He reflected that cases were like number-nine buses, not like trains: you waited for hours, then two came along at once. A man in a tower and a man under a train.

Lucie was convinced that the killer was a woman, whoever had shared the champagne with the victim. She had conceded that the man might be gay, but attributed the tidy scene to the feminine touch. Terry had agreed. A tidy man himself, Jack didn't share this logic.

Why not take everything with her? Terry had countered. Lucie had thought of that. She said the imagination behind the killing was a woman's. Carefully, she had constructed a suicide scene for the police. The man climbed the tower once. At the top, he had opened the bottle and toasted himself and his shit life. He had swallowed a handful of tablets and drunk the contents of the bottle until he lost consciousness. But his attire suggested panache, respect for style and ritual, 'strolling out' rather than going out with a bang. The killer hadn't legislated for a heart attack brought on by terror or the grazed and bloodied fingers. Lucie's notes reached a definite conclusion: Glove Man was having an affair and was murdered by his lover. One day Lucie would write the book, she said.

Jack saw there might be something raw and romantic about drinking champagne and making love in an abandoned water tower high above the city. The lack of windows would put him off, but there would be no need to give false names at a hotel or make up some story that the staff clearly did not believe. It was also possible that their relationship was legitimate: sex in a tower to spice up a stale marriage.

For the past few hours he had been dwelling on a case that wasn't just cold, it was cryogenically so. Apart from hiding in a cupboard from his co-detective in the house of a possible suspect, he hadn't progressed the Frost case for which they would be paid. All he had done was to betray the person he cared for most in the world. He could at least look at what he had found there.

He grabbed his coat from the bed and went through the pockets. The piece of paper with the marks on the desk was not in any of them. He flopped on to the bed, head in hands.

The sink's glugging brought him back to the present. He went into the kitchen. The tap wasn't dripping, although the bottom of the sink was wet. He hadn't run the tap since he came home. The last time was when he washed his Shreddies' bowl at 5 a.m. yesterday morning; it couldn't be damp from then. There must be a problem. He would have to contact the consortium about getting in a plumber. He hadn't the spirit to appreciate the humour of there being a leak in a water tower. To stop the glugging, he did as

Stella had and turned the tap on full and then turned it off. The pipes made a dull clunk. Stella had explained it was an airlock caused by two taps in a building being turned on at different times. At the time he had accepted her explanation about two sinks, but it didn't make sense: there was only him. His father would have understood how the tower worked. They had never had to call in a plumber or electrician when he was alive.

Jack returned to his laptop. He opened Outlook and addressed an email to Stella. Too late to text: she would be in bed.

Let's meet to take stock of what we have so far, he pecked at speed with two fingers, using one of Stella's phrases to reassure her. *Tomorrow. I'm on the Wimbledon line, finish late afternoon.* He was about to say he hoped the cleaning was going well, but she would think that odd. She cleaned somewhere most days.

I'm upset you didn't tell me you had changed your mind about pretending to be a cleaner— Jack stopped. He was about to say Stella was his lodestar and she had let him down. He pressed 'delete' and the cursor chewed up the last sentence. Better to say it in person. He sent it off and, returning to the Missing Persons' site, picked up Lucie's file.

There was nothing in any of her pieces or on the website about a used condom. 'On the right as you go in,' Lucie had told him, keen for Jack to match up his new home with the 'murder' scene. Terry's theory, she said, was that the man and his companion arrived and left separately, her first, leaving him to clear up. It explained the bottle and condom (only once, poor chap, Lucie had crowed): he had been about to stuff everything into the bag when the door shut. Later someone had taken the bag away. It had never been found. It would be at the bottom of the Thames, Lucie said.

She had said the door couldn't have blown shut in the hurricane and, looking at it now, Jack could verify that. It was at the top of the spiral staircase, out of the draught.

The prime suspect was an absence. Another kind of missing person. In the intervening decades no one had come forward to rule themselves out or hand themselves in. Perhaps the person had not intended to kill the man – he or she had expected him to get out. Or had planned to return but the hurricane had stopped them. People had died that night – perhaps the phantom companion had been one of them? Terry had conjectured that it might have been kids messing about and, finding the man dead, they had fled in panic, one of them dropping a glove. Lucie had decided that the glove was a 'red herring' left by kids who had nothing to do with the man being trapped. They had never claimed it for fear of being accused of murder.

The police had appealed to local sex workers, asking if anyone had had a client who had taken them to the tower. All had said no and that if asked they would refuse the job however high the pay. This made it unlikely that a woman had murdered her client.

The glove, black leather with a popper fastener and a crown motif indented on the cuff, came from Marks and Spencer and according to the label fitted boys aged between ten and fourteen. Terry had told Lucie it had lain along the man's spine, fingers pointing towards his head. The police withheld this information, as possible leverage with a suspect. Jack was surprised he had told Lucie. Being a journalist, she couldn't boast trustworthiness among her good points.

The police traced all the customers who had bought gloves in this range from the Marks and Spencer on Chiswick High Road with cheques, Access, Visa or American Express, but it yielded no leads. With such a wide time frame for culpability, alibis were meaningless. Nine of the 121 children for whom the gloves had been bought had lost one or both since purchase. Of these, three boys and a girl lived near the tower and of them, three – not the girl, Jack was gratified to read – were frightened of heights so incapable of making the precarious climb. The girl had lost her glove on a trip to the science museum. Lucie had added in the margin of her notes that Terry said her glove was later found.

Nearly thirty years later, he imagined Mr Glove Man still filed unidentified in a drawer at Hammersmith Mortuary.

Jack scribbled 'glove owners' list' on his pad to follow up. The man had been wearing a ring but no spouse had reported him missing. Perhaps they were separated or the woman had already died and he was a widower. Too many possibilities.

The website had a picture of the Timex watch and, as soon as he saw the simple dial, Jack recognized it. He shut his eyes and saw the 'TIMEX' written under the twelve. Like Glove Man's, this one had only a six and twelve with no date.

Jack's first watch had been a wind-up Timex. His father had had a Timex given to him by a German client, but it had a chequered band across the face. The trouble with having a photographic memory was that his mind was full of images most of which were of no consequence. In the eighties, there must have been lots of men, apart from himself, his father and the dead man, who wore Timex watches.

Jack gave a long-drawn-out yawn and his eyes watered. He looked again at the details on the database entry. No tattoos. For an organization seeking to identify corpses, the more marks or scars on a body the better. Tattoos, a moderately contentious form of expression in life, were a welcome clue in death. He had a scar on his thumb – so deep it must have scored the bone, Lucie said.

Jack looked to see if Stella had replied to his email, knowing she would not have. Although she frequently worked late, this was so late it was early. A thought occurred. She hadn't invited him over because she was with her Brand-new Brother. He would be making himself at home in his father's old house. Stella's house. He would be sizing up its worth.

His email to her was still in the Outbox. Jack was sure he had pressed 'Send'. He did so now. He received an email about money-saving tips, but the email to Stella remained unsent.

He confirmed there was a blue light on the router before remembering he had had incoming mail. There were five bars at the bottom of the screen depicting an 'excellent' signal.

His laptop wasn't connected to his router. It had jumped on to the one called CBruno that he had been offered when he first connected to the internet. The owner – C. Bruno presumably – was clearly not savvy about security. While he was using this connection, Jack's own account was not secure. He clicked to the dropdown list of routers – his and C. Bruno's – and as he did so, noticed the CBruno router script. WPA2-PSK. The code indicated a secure router, which meant he shouldn't have been able to access it without a password. Yet he had. Given this, why hadn't his email to Stella gone? He sent it now.

Jack heard a sound. If he hadn't worked it out from the silence, Lucie's information about the Glove Man told him that in the conversion the tower had been soundproofed. He could hear a buzzing, intermittent and insistent.

It was his phone. His imagining the Glove Man dying in panic and distress centimetres from his bed had upset him, his nerves were on edge. A blue subterranean light from his phone sent an insidious glow across the curving walls. He saw the room as the concrete tank it had been that night.

Open the door.

Jack dropped the phone before he had seen whom the message was from. He heard a distant boom: someone was banging on the flat door. He caught himself in the wardrobe mirror, a poster boy for a horror film, mouth and eyes wide open, hands clasping the sides of his face.

Far off, through the thick cladding, he heard his name being called. Without pausing to consider if it was safe, he flung the door open.

Stella was on the spiral staircase with Stanley in her arms. Never had Jack felt so warmly towards the dog, although from the fathomless brown eyes, it was unclear if the feeling was mutual.

'Lulu Carr is his wife!' Stella marched past him into the flat.

Forty

Saturday, 26 October 2013

'Stella I need to tell you—' Jack started as he shut the door.

'We've made a breakthrough!' Stella had intended to confront Jack about coming to her flat, but, reassured by his email saying that he wanted to 'take stock' – they were a team – she let it go. Jack would have had his reasons; best not to probe.

She dropped on to the chair by his desk and swivelled to face the room. Stanley sat at her feet, eyes on Jack. She didn't trust his mood and fished a liver treat from her anorak, popping it in his mouth. Jackie said Stanley got jealous of her giving Jack attention. Stella had disagreed. She and Jack were ships in the night – or day; she saw more of the dog so no problem. Besides, he was just a dog.

Jack went to the window, arms folded, his hands under his armpits. 'I wanted to explain why I was—'

'I'm cleaning Rick Frost's house. Lulu Carr is his widow!'

'We already know his wife is called Tallulah Frost.' Jack pushed off the window sill. Stanley got up, tail whirling.

'She's using her maiden name and a diminutive of her real name. Lulu is short for Tallulah. Tallulah Frost says she wants a fresh start, like we offer at Clean Slate,' Stella ploughed on.

'Is this your client whose husband left her?'

'He didn't leave. He's dead.'

'She lives in Perrers Road?'

'Yes!' It was late; Stella forgave Jack being slow to grasp the immensity of her discovery.

'So you were cleaning there already?' Jack asked. 'Before we got this case?'

'Yes! I've spent hours listening to Lulu – or Tallulah. I know more than I might if we'd interviewed her, except now I don't know what's true and what's made up. I told her we were working for her brother-in-law. She said he should mind his own business. He was right, no love lost there.'

'Stella, you are the best of Wonderhorses!' Jack spread his arms.

Stanley gave a shrill bark. Stella decided that Jackie was right about him getting possessive.

'It's a sign! Amongst the fabrication will be a kernel of truth. Her husband may have been having an affair. Strip away the narrative and we've got betrayal at the core of this case.'

Stella didn't quite see how Jack had arrived at this conclusion.

'Dying is like leaving. Suppose he was having an affair with this Nicola and then he died. Tallulah Frost or Lulu would feel rejected. OK, so now we have a suspect with a motive.' He put his phone and a plastic box of dental floss on the bedspread in front of him, presumably to represent suspect and motive. 'Lulu/Tallulah Frost finds out and chases him off the platform. She can't accept she's killed him so reframes it as being jilted which, as I said, is also true. I guess she's more comfortable being the victim than the persecutor.'

'She told her brother about the affair.' Stella felt exhausted. There were too many facts that might be fiction. Now she understood why Lulu's husband had left so much stuff. Where Lulu's husband had gone, he couldn't use an iPad.

'Speaking of Rick Frost, I had a word with—' Jack began.

'But she told me and Dale she saw him in the street the other day. Which obviously she couldn't have.' Stella felt a tightening under her ribs. She had been lied to. Lying was betrayal. She had been fooled.

'Probably believes she did. You often see a person you're grieving for out and about, on buses or waiting on the platform for a train. That sense that they've just left the room.' Jack was rolling a ball of rose quartz between his palms as if kneading dough. A birthday present from Jackie, it apparently signified love. Jack held store by lucky stones. Stella couldn't see how a lump of mineral signified anything. She had given Jack aftershave and had yet to smell it on him.

'So Dale was spot on!' Stella exclaimed.

'How come?'

'He said she was lying about something. He said she was "inauthentic". He got it straight away.'

Jack shook his head. 'Yes, well, it's easy to see stuff if you're not involved.'

'Lulu's not a murderer.' Stella didn't know why she had said that.

'Because?'

'She's not organized; her place was a mess. You've described this as a perfect murder. If Lulu planned to push her husband off a platform, we'd know exactly what happened.'

'It is possible to achieve perfection by accident. Like the beauty of light falling on the river because clouds part while you are standing there.'

Jack spoke to the rose quartz as if it were a crystal ball. Stella scanned the room for the aftershave. She had given him Armani Code Ice, not for the smell but the word 'code'. Maybe he kept it in the bathroom. She zipped up her anorak; right now Code Ice fitted the temperature of the tower.

'Let's do an audit of the suspects.' She brought Jack back to the matter in hand.

'William Frost.' Jack was prompt; he manoeuvred the dental floss to the centre of the bed. 'As we said, him having brought us the case doesn't absolve him of guilt. If he's so keen to solve this, why choose a cleaning company and not an established private detective? Or go back to the police.'

'He did go to the police and Martin Cashman wouldn't touch it. We came recommended by Jackie.' Stella would accept cleaning from a detective agency if Jackie vouched for them, but decided not to say this. She wanted Jack on point.

'Do we *know* the police aren't interested?' Jack narrowed his eyes. 'We only have his word he spoke to them.'

'You were at the inquest and you saw Rick Frost die. The verdict was suicide.'

'Nevertheless, it might be worth giving your mate Martin a call. Check out his thoughts, they might not tally with the official view.'

Stella was reluctant to waste Cashman's time. As her dad's old friend and colleague, he would give her plenty of it, but he would be humouring her. However, after her lunch with William she did wonder if he had been straight with her. He had definitely seemed nervous and wasn't happy when she made it clear she was going to investigate the case her way. Putting aside her growing guilt that she had used his app – with his permission and without – she didn't like that he had used it to find her. What else did he use it for?

'Lulu-Tallulah Carr-Frost is an obvious suspect and now we have a motive. She has the most to gain, as we've already said. Her lying to you puts her up at the top. I asked Lucille May about Rick Frost.' Jack slipped that in, knowing she wouldn't like it. 'She had already gone into his business. It seems that Frost only had one client, an engineering company. She couldn't remember the name: she's getting back to me. She thinks we're wasting our time and Frost's money.'

'Nice of her to worry.' Stella bridled, although she was beginning to think so too. She was peeved that Jack had gone to Lucille May without agreeing it with her. Some team. She hadn't meant to see William without him. She announced blithely, 'There's the mistress.'

'A mistress!' Jack had the right response this time.

'Lucille May didn't mention Nicola Barwick?' She felt bad for the smooth surprise. 'Well, according to Lulu, she was a wicked fairy and cast a bad spell at their wedding.'

'Did she?' Jack's natural belief in curses and bad fairies was greater than his capacity to be hurt. Stella was chagrined at her effort to put him on the back foot.

'Lulu was all for going to see her tonight. I had to stop her.'

'Why now?'

'As opposed to when?'

'Frost died six weeks ago – why is she tackling her now? What's changed?'

'She said she saw her in the street with her husband this week.'

'Which can't be true since he's dead.'

'Not if she's grieving.' Stella reminded Jack of his earlier point.

'That's different. Actually thinking you saw a dead person and acting on it by trying to see them is delusional.'

'So she's lying about that too?' Stella was losing patience with the woman who had called herself Lulu Carr.

'Maybe. Maybe not.' Jack tipped the rose quartz from one palm to the other. 'Something's nagging at me,' he said after a moment.

'What?'

'It's gone – probably means it's important. Go with her to see Nicola Barwick. Whether she's a mistress or not, she'll give us insight into Rick Frost's character.'

'It could be messy. What if Lulu attacks her?'

'Do you think she will?' Jack raised his eyebrows. 'You don't think Lulu capable of murder.'

'No, but—'

'Mess is what we need. Detectives stir the rubbish around and up comes an oyster!'

'Pearl.' Stella knew about searching through the rubbish: Suzie had gone through a phase of losing things in the pedal bin.

'What about the inspector?' Stella had the self-conscious impression she was playing at being a detective, deliberately calling innocent passers-by suspects to make it feel like a real case. She was no better than Lulu Carr. The man had been waiting for a train, he had been nice to her and to her dog, then he'd got on the Richmond train and gone on with his life. Were they twisting facts calling him a suspect?

'Describe him again?'

'It was dark. He was my height, so tall. I think he had brown hair, but there was no light so it might have been black. He was wearing a coat, I think. I didn't see his face.' Stella saw the hopelessness of the situation. They had no means of finding the inspector. He might as well have been one of Jack's ghosts.

Jack grinned. 'Sounds like me.'

'Not at all!' As soon as he said it, Stella realized that the reason why the man had seemed familiar was because he had reminded her of the side of Jack she preferred not to dwell on.

'Could it have been William Frost putting on a different voice?'

Stella was about to say no, but realized she couldn't. The man was tall, and so was Frost; his hair was dark, as was Frost's. Frost had a deep voice, but it would be easy to lighten it and the man at the station had said little.

'I don't know,' she said finally.

'William Frost, Lulu Carr, Nicola Barwick and the station inspector who may be Frost. Unless they all have alibis, that's three if not four suspects! Lovely!'

'How is that lovely?' It complicated an already complicated problem.

'The more suspects we have, the greater the chance we'll keep an open mind and ward off prejudices and preconceptions. Lulu and William will have alibis – the police no doubt checked them out, although, unless they're watertight, it doesn't rule them out. The other two are problematic. Pass me my phone – it's on the desk. I'll take minutes on the notebook app.'

Stella stopped herself rolling her eyes. Jack never took notes and certainly not minutes. Swivelling the chair around, she rootled amongst a sheaf of papers by Jack's laptop. Wistfully she recalled the wealth of material they had gathered for the Blue Folder case.

Dead Man in Tower, Screams Unheard.

'What is this?' She waved a photocopied sheet at Jack.

'Ah-hmm.' Jack cleared his throat. 'I was going to mention that.'

If Jack had been nervous about Stanley, it was nothing to how he looked now. His usual pallor was sheet-white.

'What dead man?' She read the byline: Lucille May. The journalist would be behind why Jack had moved to a desolate tower reachable only by a dangerous girder-type thing hardly wider than a pipe. She counted to five before she trusted herself to speak.

'*A man died after being trapped in a tower during the 1987 storm.* It was in *this* tower, over *there*!' Stella pointed to the floor by the door and uttered in a whisper. 'He literally died of fright all alone—'

'What is he doing?' Jack followed her finger.

Neither Jack nor Stella had noticed that Stanley had woken up. He was crawling very slowly along the floor, his stomach sliding over the boards, sniffing at the skirting by Jack's bed.

'That's why I went to see Lucie,' Jack whispered. 'The dog is never wrong, you told me that. He's sensed the ghost.'

'I meant about biscuits under the sofa, not a dead man in the living room!' She looked closer. 'What's he got in his mouth?'

Jack moved down the bed.

'Careful, he gets fierce when he's stolen something.'

'I can see fingers!' Jack breathed.

'Damn, it's Lulu's glove.'

It was the one that Stanley had been guarding on the seat in the van after leaving Lulu Carr. Preoccupied with the wet bedding and the driving licence, Stella had forgotten about it.

'Ignore him and he'll drop it. What ghost?' She heaved a sigh. This case and everything to do with it was out of control.

'Little happens in this part of London that Lucie hasn't delved into. She was working on a story about this tower until—' Jack stopped.

'Until what?'

'Until she stopped.' Jack kneaded the rose quartz between his palms.

'Why did she stop?' As she had with Lulu Carr, Stella knew what Jack was going to say.

'Terry died,' Jack finished.

'It was Dad's case? But this tower isn't in Hammersmith.'

'Terry wasn't working for Hammersmith. She said he was doing a stint in Chiswick.'

'How did he think the man died?' Terry would have got the

measure of Lucille May; he would know that any attention she paid him was for the sake of a story.

'He suspected murder, but had no evidence. He worked on it with Lucie in his spare time. The set of prints on the champagne bottle was most likely the dead man's, but being a skeleton they couldn't prove it. Terry's theory was that the murderer removed everything incriminating.'

'So you moved here to solve it?' Jack hadn't asked for her help.

'No. I've always wanted to live in a tower. I rang Lucie when Stanley alerted me to the ghost, and there've been noises.' He twirled a lock of his fringe around. Stella thought he was on edge.

'How did you know about it?' Stanley was back, his head resting on her foot.

'I got a leaflet through the door.'

'Who put it through?'

'A man. I didn't see his face. The consortium – my landlords – did a leaflet-drop.'

'What is this consortium?' Suzie had used the word when she suggested she buy Dale Heffernan's restaurant business. It was a posh term for too many cooks – or chefs.

'I don't know.' Jack shrugged. 'Not a consortium. I might be muddling it with the previous owners of the tower.'

Stella was exasperated. How could Jack rent a property without looking into who owned it? Anything could happen. Anything *had* happened.

The dog had dropped the glove. She got up and retrieved it from the floor by Jack's cupboard and returned to the desk. It was damp from Stanley's mauling, but undamaged. She turned it part inside out.

'It's got what looks like an "R" inside.' She laid the glove on the desk. 'Perhaps it's not Lulu's after all. Certainly not Rick Frost's, unless he had small hands.'

'He didn't. I saw them,' Jack replied.

'I can't see your phone.' Stella remembered her reason for looking amongst Jack's things. She needed to get to bed.

'It must be there.'

'It's not. Oh, but I almost forgot!' Stella spun the chair around and plunged her hand into her rucksack. 'Lulu found this in her landing cupboard. I'd already cleaned there, somehow I missed it.'

She showed Jack the scrap of paper, grubby with the shading of soft pencil. When Jack took it, she noticed his hand was shaking. She wasn't at all sure he'd done the right thing moving to a tower where a man had been murdered.

'Stella, I was—'

'It might be a phone number or a password, although it's too long for a phone number even with the country codes. Then I wondered if it was an IP address, but that's too long too.'

'I should have seen.' Jack knelt on the bed, the paper before him. 'These gaps are deliberate!'

'What gaps?' Jack made life decisions based on the set number allocated to his trains: all numbers were signs. However, like Stanley and his missing biscuits, Stella was learning to trust that he seldom got it wrong.

'These ones between the numbers. Frost must have been off guard because I got that almost immediately. Or he made it deliberately easy.

Jack scrambled over the bed and held the paper so Stella could see it.

'19 9 13 15 14   19 8 21 20   20 15 23 5 18   4 15 15 18.'

'It could be the serial number of the computer in his study,' Jack mused.

'Stupid if it's meant to be secret. You're always telling me to memorize passwords, not to write them down. He not only scratches it into his desk, but he takes a rubbing from the scratches and then drops it in a cupboard. So much for security!'

'The thing is, Stella, he didn't actually—'

'His wife has no sense of security. She left two keys outside the door.'

'If he did it in a hurry on the only available surface...'

It was nearly four o'clock. Far across the river, she saw faint lighter streaks of dawn. Jack seemed to have woken up while she was becoming as befuddled as the case – two cases now.

'I need to grab some sleep.' She got to her feet, rousing Stanley. At the door she stopped. 'I nearly forgot.' She told Jack about her mother's idea that she should invest in Dale Heffernan's business. She was quite aware that by telling him as she was leaving, she was making it seem unimportant because he would be bound to object. Jack was careful with money. So she was surprised when he merely nodded, but made no comment. She wondered suddenly if he was afraid. The place was very quiet. Creepy really.

'You OK staying here? You could come back with me.' Jack must have come to her flat earlier because he was afraid, and then, unable to admit it, had left. She would not embarrass him by bringing it up.

'I'm fine.' He pulled on his shoes, leaving the laces trailing. 'I'm doing a day shift tomorrow, it's easier to set off from here.'

Stella opened the door, noting the handle on the inside. At least Jack wouldn't be trapped in the tower.

'Yuk!' She clamped her hand over her nose. The smell on the landing was greasy and cloying. Like a decomposing body, but that was long ago.

'It's an olfactory hallucination.' Jack was behind her. 'A ghost smell.'

Setting off down the stairs, she heard the ping of a text and saw a series of numbers, no name.

Please can we meet? We need to talk.

'No we do not!' she retorted out loud.

'You all right?' Jack was behind her. Stella breathed in detergent, fresh cotton and clean wool. The smell in the cupboard at Lulu Carr's. Jack used the same detergent as Rick Frost.

'Yes.' She felt far from all right.

On the metal walkway, the wind was stronger. Reaching the staircase cage, she struggled down the first flight; then, looking up, she yelled over the howl of the wind, 'Lulu obviously hasn't told

William I am cleaning for her. Let's say nothing to him while he's a suspect. Agreed?'

'Yes.' Jack waved at her. 'Brilliant work, Stell!'

He craned over the gantry, hair streaming like a young king in a fairy tale. She was getting as fanciful as Jack.

'It was a coincidence. I had no idea it was Frost's house.' Stella made laborious progress down the vibrating metal stairs, eyes ahead because to look down would be fatal.

'No such thing as a coincidence!' came Jack's vanishing cry.

Stella had forgotten to show him the photographs from the station booth. It was too late to go back now, she felt dead on her feet.

Had Stella gone back when she thought about it, she would have seen that she wasn't Jack's only visitor that night.

Forty-One

Saturday, 26 October 2013

Jack didn't think he had slept, but the blue lit numbers on his alarm said four fifty and he couldn't account for his thoughts since he had gone to bed after Stella left. He had been hugely relieved that she hadn't lied. But he hadn't confessed to hiding in the cupboard, nor had he admitted that he had rubbed the numbers on to the paper. That he had confessed to visiting Lucie May netted him nothing; Stella wouldn't consider dishonesty up for barter.

Stella didn't claim to be flawless. She had transgressed in the past, but he had never thought she had lied to him. Why had he thought it this time? The answer was Dale Heffernan.

Four fifty-one. The digits on the clock floated on the inside of his eyes. He feared Stella would be influenced by the Brand-new Brother. Jack was certain the man had come for her money. He had passed up the chance to meet Heffernan, knowing that in a week he would be gone. A mistake: Stella never saw the enemy coming; Jack should judge Dale for her.

He rolled on to his back. He heard birdsong far below in the gardens of Chiswick Mall. He lay listening to it, and then was puzzled. He had shut the windows before he went to bed, wanting absolute silence. The tower was high above the trees, too high up for birdsong. It was another auditory hallucination. His mind was busy compensating for what he had lost.

The pale blue light of dawn outlined his binoculars on the north window sill. When Stella had looked through them on her first visit, she had said she could see one of her client's houses. Although she had many clients all over West London, he was sure the house she meant was Lulu Carr's. If Stella had pointed out the house to him, he would have recognized the address when William Frost gave it to him and the whole cupboard thing needn't have happened. If—

He shut his eyes. This case was different to the others because a client was paying them to solve it. It mustn't make them change how they operated. Jack met subterfuge with subterfuge; he looked for minds like his own and inhabited them. He read the signs. His eyes snapped open. He had a sign.

He reached over the side of the bed and pulled the steam engine from his bag. He switched on the bedside lamp. Post-office red with 'Golden Arrow' painted in yellow on the boiler. Below this were the emblems of the Union Jack and the French Tricolour. The engine was the same model as the one he had lost in the Thames as a boy.

Jack got out of bed and padded into the kitchenette. He placed the toy on the south-east window sill overlooking Hammersmith Bridge.

He returned to the main room and, opening his cupboard, fished out the biscuit tin in which he kept his treasures. He laid them out on the bed. Tokens from True Hosts; a teaspoon; a chip of green glass; three milk teeth (not his own); two postcards; a pure white butterfly pinned in a box; postcards from his dad's work trips abroad, including the one of Fremantle cemetery. He put aside the pack of passport photos held with an elastic band, faces he carried in his mind. Lastly, he found the lock of his mother's hair. A musty smell of damp dust, stale perfume and of all the homes he had stayed in drifted up from the open box.

The newspaper cutting lined the bottom of the tin. It was dated Thursday, 22 October 1998.

STUDENT MUGGED IN GRAVEYARD

By Lucille May

A woman walking her dog found what she thought at first was the body of a young man lying across a fallen headstone in Chiswick Cemetery just before 07.00 a.m. yesterday morning. However, when the police arrived at the scene, they detected a pulse and the man was rushed to Charing Cross Hospital.

The man, identified by a cheque book and later confirmed by his distraught father as Simon Carrington, aged 20, of Corney Road, Chiswick, is in a critical condition at Charing Cross Hospital with his family keeping vigil by his bedside.

Detective Inspector Terry Darnell of the Metropolitan Police is appealing for witnesses.

There it was in a small square of black and white. Leaving the cutting on his desk, Jack shut his box of treasures and returned it to the cupboard. Unbidden the words came into his mind. Dead people can't kill.

You are safe.

It was not what he thought, Jack told himself.

Returning to bed, he found he had a text. Lucie May.

Ring re RF inquest. LM.

In the dead of night, Lucie was on the job. As she had been when she worked with Terry. The police detective and the hard-nosed reporter swapping notes and information, both of them restless and stubborn, unable to let the mysteries lie. Jack shuffled further under the duvet. He hadn't told Stella his suspicion that exchanging information about an unsolved case was not all Terry Darnell and Lucie May had done into the small hours.

The sink made its glugging sound. Living up here had blurred the line between reality and dreams. As if to illustrate this, the Smiths' song 'How Soon is Now' drifted back into his mind.

Jack dreamt that Stella was there at the foot of his bed, holding her dog. 'I wanted to be your friend.' She had the voice of a boy.

'We still can be.'

'You denied you knew me. Three times.'

'No, that was Peter, the disciple.'

'I know your name.' It wasn't Stella, it was—

Jack was dully aware that he was dreaming and tried to wake.

He forced open his eyes, the lids heavy with exhaustion. There *was* someone at the bottom of his bed.

'*Stella?*'

He tried to speak but sank back into sleep. This time he didn't dream.

Forty-Two

Saturday, 26 October 2013

It was ten o'clock and the streets were quiet. Stella had insisted on fetching Lulu Carr; she wouldn't put it past her to go earlier than an agreed time and tackle Nicola Barwick before she arrived.

Barwick turned out to live around the corner from Jackie in Corney Road in Chiswick. Although Jackie had brought her the case, Stella didn't want to bump into her on the job. Jackie belonged to the bright world of cleaning and tidying, not to the mess of an adulterous separation and a wife confronting a possible mistress.

They parked opposite a modern terrace house in Pumping Station Road, a quiet street parallel to the Thames. According to Lucille May's article, the development of detached and semis had replaced the light industry and wharfs that had occupied the stretch on the north side of the river for over a century. Stella knew the terrace; one of her first clients had lived here.

'She killed him to keep him.' Lulu had said this several times on the journey from Hammersmith. She was regarding the house opposite with malevolence.

'You don't know that.' If Lulu had killed her husband, it made sense to point the finger at someone else. Stella was trying to resist prejudice or preconception about the suspects, but she rather liked Lulu and didn't want her to be guilty. This was not thinking like a detective.

'I need to hear her say, "I was sleeping with your husband."' Lulu batted at the dashboard pettishly.

'She won't say it if she wasn't.' Stella looked over at the house. A light glowed through diamond-patterned glazed glass in the front door. It briefly dimmed; someone was in the hall.

Stella remembered the client because the woman had called the police to report that she had seen Stella going into the DHSS on Shepherd's Bush Road. She accused Stella of claiming benefit while earning. Unknown to Stella at the time, Suzie had gone to the woman's house and 'frogmarched' – Suzie's word – her to Shepherd's Bush Road. The woman had mistaken the police station for the benefits office; Stella had been visiting her dad. Terry confirmed this. The woman withdrew her complaint, but never apologized or paid her bill. The latter was the point of the exercise, Suzie believed; she had taught Stella to be circumspect about customers: they were not 'kings or queens', they were humans and didn't have to be obeyed. The episode had resulted in Terry and Suzanne Darnell meeting in the foyer of Hammersmith Police Station, united in their determination to clear their daughter's name. It was the last time they saw each other.

Stella reached behind, unclipped Stanley and plonked him on her lap. She shouldn't have brought him, but Jackie was vetting new office spaces and Beverly was at the dentist.

'How could you have seen him with Nicola Barwick the other day? You knew Rick was dead, you went to his inquest,' Stella asked.

'Yes, how could I?' Lulu perked up, apparently enlivened by a mystery she herself had invented.

Stella nearly shouted with exasperation. Was this what Terry's life had been like? She expected people to give straight answers. She yearned to be applying a cleaning agent to a cornice or wiping dust from the slats of a Venetian blind, tasks both fiddly and satisfying. Being a detective was like looking for hens' teeth.

'Look at this!' Lulu pulled a ball of paper out of her pocket and smoothed it out on the dashboard. 'One of Rick's "surveillance reports". He followed me around Marks and Spencer's on King Street, then met me for coffee at the Lyric Theatre as if he'd been there all along. Typical.'

'Did he give it to you?' Stella tried not to judge clients, but what with William's descriptions of his brother, and now Lulu's, she wasn't warming to the man.

'I found it in his jacket. He had the handwriting of a twelve-year-old. The mind of one too.'

'Maybe he told Barwick he wouldn't leave you,' Stella was mindful of keeping Lulu calm for the confrontation with Nicola Barwick. 'After all, he didn't.'

'So she killed him. Better he's dead than with me.' Lulu patted Stanley on the head – a dangerous move for he was head-shy. 'You know when a person has fallen out of love. That warmth you've taken for granted vanishes. You're feeling low and he chivvies you to buck up instead of kissing you better. He points out food on your lip and orders you to wipe it off instead of doing it for you. You ask if he's OK and he intimates you're mad. You believe you *are* mad. That's what you think, isn't it? That I'm mad! You must have felt that cold breeze of dying love, the gritty sick sensation of betrayal!' She bashed the dashboard again. Stanley tensed.

Stella didn't know about 'dying love'. Jackie said she did the leaving to avoid being left and suggested she give people more time.

Stella had put last night's text out of her mind, but sooner or later she would have to agree to speak to David. She shifted Stanley out of reach of Lulu.

Stella did know the gritty feeling of betrayal. It had kept her arms stiffly by her side when her dad waved at her before he drove away from her mum's flat the day they separated. She hadn't let either parent carry the little pink case her dad had given her for 'going away' to the new flat in Barons Court. He hadn't remembered she hated pink. Stolidly she had lugged it up the steps into the cold lobby of the mansion block, clacking across the tiles all by herself.

She was startled by a text. It was Jack.

Ask Lulu C about the glove. Why did that matter?

'Lulu, do you know—'

Lulu was already out of the van. By the time Stella had

untangled herself from her belt and the dog's lead, Lulu had knocked on Nicola Barwick's front door and was stamping her feet on the step, against the cold or perhaps with lack of patience.

'I know you're in there!' Lulu smacked the flat of her hand on the glass pane.

The door opened.

'Where is Nicky?' Lulu demanded.

'I'm afraid she's not here. Can I help?'

'This is her house,' Lulu insisted.

'Lulu, let's go,' Stella murmured.

'I know she's here. I have seen her.'

'She's moved.' The woman looked genuinely regretful.

'I'm her friend,' Lulu asserted.

'I'm sorry, but—'

Stella knew what the woman was thinking. If Nicola Barwick had wanted a friend to know where she was, she would have told her.

'It's a mistake. I'm sorry,' Stella said to the woman, who turned to her.

'Stella Darnell!' She put out her hands. 'You haven't changed a bit!'

Stella backed against a holly bush by the door, hardly aware of the prickles. It was the client who had reported her to the police.

'I know she's here.' Before Stella could stop her, Lulu had barged into the hall. 'Nicky?'

'Really, she's not—' the woman protested.

Stella gathered her wits. The woman was the same age as the client had been; she would be in her seventies now.

'You have been quick! I just rang the office. I didn't expect you so soon. And not *you* – I imagined you far too grand – one of your staff. I was going to send my regards but I got the answering machine.'

Stella had learnt to admit it when she didn't recognize people: ex-clients often hailed her in the street or in the bank. When she had improvised, waiting for a clue to identity to emerge, it had led to a minefield of misunderstanding.

'Do I know—' she began.

'Liz Hunter! You never were good with faces, but you had the nose of a bloodhound!'

Stella had first met Liz in primary school before she moved to Barons Court. They had gone on to the 'big' school together. When Terry was leading a major case and was plastered over the newspapers and TV, Liz Hunter was the only child at Stella's comprehensive who hadn't tried to worm information out of her, or ask her for his autograph. Had the term 'From Hero to Zero' been in use then, someone would have applied it to her dad. In the days after the Rokesmith murder, everyone wanted to be Stella's friend, but over time, as the case dragged on and Terry was on screens asking for the public's patience, the fifteen-year-old became the failed detective's daughter. No more invitations to parties and illicit trips to the pub. She wasn't asked to join the group going to the Duran Duran concert at the Hammersmith Odeon. Simon Le Bon's autograph beat Terry's by a mile. In the midst of this Liz Hunter invited her home for tea.

Liz would wait beside the bus stop on Kensington High Street where Stella alighted from the number 28 each morning and walk with her up to the school. She materialized by the gym block gate during lunch where Stella went to get away from questions about Terry and shared her sandwiches with Stella. Stella didn't have to pretend interest in the photographs of the Hunter family cat that Liz took for a project on feline genetics. Liz never asked her about Terry's case. Stella began to look out for her at the bus stop. She found a textbook on genetics in Hammersmith library and photocopied a paper on the domestic cat for Liz. When Liz was off school with a bug, Stella went round to see her. From then on she was a regular visitor. Stella thought it would be nice to have a brother who was good at maths. Liz had two such brothers.

After school, they went different ways. Stella started cleaning and Liz studied French at a northern university. Stella couldn't have said why she didn't reply to Liz's letters. After a while they stopped coming.

At the end of the Blue Folder case and of whatever she had had with David, Jackie had urged Stella to find friends outside the business. If she wouldn't join a book group or a knitting group, why not look up old friends? Stella said there were none. She had briefly thought of Liz Hunter, but doubted she would reply if she contacted her.

'I want a cleaner. I went online to find a reputable firm and found an article about you solving that case of your dad's that happened when we were at school.' Aside from lines bracketing her mouth and one or two grey hairs in an auburn bob, Liz was the same. 'Of course I rang Clean Slate!' She stood aside. 'Come in. Let's find your friend and have a coffee!'

'She's not my friend.' Glancing back at the van, Stella froze. Jack was standing beside it, his back to her. He had said he was driving today.

'I know him,' she exclaimed

'Know who?' Liz Hunter stepped out on to the pavement.

Jack had gone. In the distance Stella saw his tower, tall and menacing in the grey morning light.

'No one.' Stella went inside.

Stella was assailed by colours: green skirtings, yellow walls, a rug of red and orange stripes. A low table was crowded with vases of blues and greens. A nightmare to clean, but whatever the cost Stella would give Liz Hunter a large discount.

On a chair beside a door to a Juliet balcony sat Lulu Carr. Stella felt distinctly uncomfortable. Lulu was too calm. Legs crossed, her alabaster-pale complexion paler against the garish décor, she was smiling as if butter wouldn't melt. She was up to something.

Forty-Three

Saturday, 26 October 2013

Jack had one more chance to time the tunnel. It was his last shift on the Wimbledon line before he was back full-time on the Dead Late shift.

He placed his watch on the sill and, his hand steady, adjusted the lever to a speed of forty kilometres per hour. In the sun the tracks sparkled bright silver; up ahead was the West Hill tunnel. Jack cleared his mind. Stella would wonder why it mattered that he knew the length of the tunnel. He couldn't explain that it would lead him to discover who had left a toy train on the station monitors. Although Jack believed in ghosts, he didn't believe that a ghost had left it there. He could not tell Stella that the answer to the calculation about the tunnel would help him learn the identity of Glove Man and know who had caused Rick Frost to die under a train at Stamford Brook.

He braced himself. Second hand at the one-minute mark before ten: three, two, one! He plunged into darkness.

Bricks flowed up and over his cab, lit by the yellow of the train's headlamps. Six seconds, eight, twelve. At exactly twenty-four seconds Jack brought the train out of the tunnel into blazing sunshine.

Time and speed. The two numbers, 'forty' and 'twenty-four' were stepping stones; he was closer to the truth.

The platform at East Putney was crowded with morning commuters. Jack could see a station attendant talking into her loudspeaker pack, announcing his train. He slid his eye over the waiting faces, registering every one. He clipped his watch back on and opened the train doors.

He consulted the driver's monitor to the left of his cab and his good mood drained away. There was something there. He got off his stool. On the lower quadrant of the split screen he could see the attendant waving 'all clear' with her paddle.

The 'something' was a toy railway carriage. Jack whirled around and scoured the platform. It must have just been left or another driver would have seen it. The attendant would have seen it. She was now the only person on the platform. She did a shrugging motion: was he all right? Jack gave her a 'thumbs up' and got back into the cab. He shut the doors and eased the train forward. In his mind he trawled through the faces he had seen on the platform on the way in. One of them had been familiar but, as if in a dream, the image had faded.

You denied you knew me. Three times.

The sun shone through the windows. The cab was warm, but Jack felt cold.

Who could know that as a boy he had owned the same toys? He had been dismayed when his father replaced his steam engine with an inferior one of plastic. It pulled three carriages like the engine now on his window sill in the tower. Jack didn't suppose his dead father had placed the toys on the monitors. Nor had— He could not bear even to think his name. A name that belonged to a past that was better buried.

But someone had put the engine there. Someone who knew about the engine he had had when he was little. The back of his neck tingled. The connecting door between the cab and the passengers was shut. Even so, Jack was convinced he was being watched.

Jack stopped on the balcony overlooking the District line platforms at Earl's Court station and took the carriage from his bag. His carriages had been full of tiny figures, moulded in beige plastic. When his tunnel collapsed, the passengers were thrown from their seats and choked by mud. The tragedy wouldn't have happened if he had been driving. Until now Jack had succeeded in blotting out that afternoon in the kitchen garden of his school when his train had crashed in the tunnel.

The toy carriage wasn't empty. A man sat near the front. He was looking at him.

Jack shuddered as if the passenger could see into his mind. Pieces of a train set had been placed on top of the monitors. By a person who played with codes and signs. Someone with a mind like his own. Jack's own mind was being monitored. He had to keep it shut. He knew how to do that. Shoving the carriage into his shoulder bag, he began his calculation. He didn't need a notepad; his photographic mind held the numbers as if lit in neon.

Forty kilometres per hour was two-thirds of sixty kilometres per hour. Sixty kilometres per hour was one kilometre or one thousand metres per minute. Travelling at forty kilometres per hour he covered 666.66 metres (recurring) per minute. He had taken twenty-four seconds to go through the tunnel, 66.66 (recurring) metres every six seconds. Jack leant on the balustrade; below him a Wimbledon train arrived at the far westbound platform. Two drivers were swapping over. The new driver climbed into the cab; the other began to climb the central staircase.

There are four sixes in twenty-four. Jack multiplied 66 metres by four. A peace descended on him. The length of the West Hill tunnel was 266.66 (recurring) metres. He drew his coat around him as a dusty breeze swept out from the tunnel below. His mind was a vast plain on which images and ideas ranged far and wide. This hidden fact would lead him to more. This was being a detective.

Jack wouldn't be back on the trains for a week. He had time.

Into his opened mind came a glove. A black leather glove was found on the body in his tower.

Black leather gloves were two a penny, but it was less common to have a crown motif on the cuff and a popper fastener as Lucie had described in her notes. The glove Stanley had in his mouth in the tower had a crown indented in the leather. Focused on the dog's white teeth and mistrustful glare, Jack had seen the crown indentation by his upper incisor. Stella said the dog had stolen it from Lulu Carr's house.

There was no such thing as a coincidence.

Jack turned on his phone. Stella would be at Nicola Barwick's house. He hoped she was all right. He shouldn't have let her go off with a suspect on her own. His thumbs flew over the keyboard: *Ask Lulu C about the glove.*

He continued along the footbridge towards the Exhibition Centre. The tunnel was 266.66 metres in length; the fact had opened his mind and given him the glove. One fact led to another.

There is madness in your method.

Jack pummelled at his forehead. The thought – although a fact – had come unbidden into his mind; it was not his own. He had the notion he was being watched and, turning around, heard someone speak:

'It's Jack Harmon, isn't it?'

Jack looked at a stocky man with backcombed thinning hair. He had rheumy eyes as if in the grip of an allergy. He recognized the driver who had got off the Wimbledon train a few minutes ago, but he didn't know him. Another face he couldn't place.

'Yes.'

'Darryl Clark. We met at the— I was driving that train that—'

'Of course!' Jack saved him from finishing the sentence. Darryl Clark was the Piccadilly line driver who had the One Under at Stamford Brook. 'I saw you get off a District line train just then.'

'I got a transfer. I can't face that track. Still the same line, but it's not the same. You doing all right?'

'Oh yes, but then I wasn't driving the train.' It occurred to Jack that he wasn't doing all right. With all that had happened – the move to the tower, the toys on the monitor and Stella's brother – he had been distracted from the actuality of the death on the track. Darryl Clark brought it back. Rick Frost's expression: now he thought it was of fear and perhaps some vain effort to make Jack understand what he was trying to convey.

'Have you got time for a quick drink?' the man asked.

'It's a bit early for me.' Jack wanted to see Stella.

'Me too!' The man gave a sudden laugh, a shout, the sound pushed with effort from the depths of his chest. 'I meant a coffee.'

'Yes of course.'

The two men returned along the footbridge to the staff canteen.

'What was your set number?' Jack asked conversationally as they descended the staircase

'My set number?' Clark looked at him.

'For that train you just handed over.' Jack picked up his pace. Clark was shorter than him, but he was walking fast.

'Two six six.'

The length of the West Hill tunnel: 266.66 metres.

The signs were working.

Forty-Four

Saturday, 26 October 2013

'Please could I use your loo?' Lulu Carr stood up when Liz Hunter returned with a tray of coffees.

'By the kitchen, door on the left.' Liz placed three white china mugs of coffee on the coffee table and pushed a plate of biscuits towards Stella. She sat in a chair matching Lulu's on the other side of the balcony door. 'Is your friend all right?'

'She's not my— She and Nicola Barwick have unfinished business.' Stella accepted a biscuit and nibbled at it, reminded of Dale's scones. The biscuits were not as nice. Aware of how odd Lulu's behaviour must appear, she was tempted to tell Liz Hunter everything, but however annoying Lulu was, she wouldn't betray her confidence.

'It's ridiculous that I can't give her Nicola's address. But she was adamant. I must tell *no one*!' Liz Hunter handed her a cup of coffee. 'I can pass on a message for her though.'

'I'm not sure that will—'

'But hey, it's so good that you turned up in person! Fancy you not realizing it was me when they told you at the office. Have to say, I've often wondered about you. I've missed you, Stella.'

Liz Hunter had always said what she felt. Stella hadn't missed her or she would have seen her. Stella thought that Jack would agree about it being more than a coincidence. Whatever it was, she felt distinctly uncomfortable. She would do Liz an estimate and leave. Lulu would have to make do with leaving her number for Nicola Barwick.

'I'm fine, thanks.' Although Liz hadn't asked how she was. 'What about you?' Stella enquired in a spray of crumbs.

'Life's been in turmoil. I'm coming out of a divorce.' Liz gave a laugh as if she had made a joke.

'So you haven't lived here long?' Stella took another nibble of the biscuit and bit the side of her cheek. She washed down the biscuit with lukewarm coffee. Where was Lulu?

'I came back from Paris when Dad died two years ago to be nearer Mum. My brothers are here, but they're worse than useless! Max never visits and although Rob manages the odd afternoon, he flops on the sofa and watches telly with her. At least he doesn't bring his washing any more. I was sorry to read about your dad – he was a kind man.'

Stella had never thought of Terry in those terms and was interested that Liz had noticed.

'Sorted!' Lulu Carr was in the doorway, beaming at them both. Stella would underplay a visit to the loo rather than treat it as an accomplishment.

'Tuck in.' Liz waved at the coffee and biscuits. Stella remembered that it was typical of Liz not to ask questions. Right from when she had rescued Stella from a cupboard in their infant school, Liz Hunter had taken any crisis or unusual situation in her stride.

'Actually I must dash,' Lulu said. 'I've had a text from my brother. He needs me!'

She blew them both kisses and was gone before Stella could gather herself and go with her. With growing unease she excused herself and went to the toilet.

Stella stood in the little cloakroom and considered the low-slung toilet. There was a tiny corner sink from which hung a diminutive towel. The cistern wasn't filling, but the tank was small; it had probably already done so.

The towel was soft and dry. A bar of lavender soap was wedged behind a squat mixer tap. Stella picked it up. It was tacky, not wet. Running water over her hands, she worked the soap to a lather. It slipped from her fingers and shot into the basin. She captured it and put it back behind the tap, then rinsed and dried her hands.

The soap was now flecked with suds, and the towel was damp. Lulu wouldn't go to the toilet without washing her hands. Whatever she was doing while she was out of the room, she hadn't been near the toilet.

Liz was in the kitchen, washing up the mugs. 'Another coffee? I'm having one.' She flicked the kettle switch.

'Yes, thanks.' Stella would do the estimate and allocate an operator for Liz. Wendy would be right for her. She settled into a chair at the end of a long wooden table that was large enough to sit ten.

A tall blue Smeg fridge matched eggshell-blue units. A set of shelves was stacked with assorted mugs and plates, many with chipped rims. A collection of glass Kilner jars was grouped together on the fridge. The vibration of the motor would shift them incrementally and eventually they would fall. Stella decided against pointing this out. The fridge door was papered with neat rows of notes, takeaway menus and cards for different trades clamped by large magnets in primary colours. Apart from the top one, they were arranged with five items per row; Stella liked this. During the estimate she would photograph their precise positions so that after cleaning they could be put back accurately. Her phone buzzed.

'Where are you?' Her mother's first question whenever she phoned Stella's mobile.

'At a friend's.' She doubted that her mother would remember Liz.

'A friend?' Her mother sounded disbelieving.

'A client,' Stella said to put Suzie off.

'I won't keep you. Dale and I are going to Richmond Park again, he's taking me in his lovely hire car.'

'That's nice.' A hired car would be more comfortable than her cleaning van, although Dale had said he thought it was 'cool'.

'Stella, just to say, make sure you're in tonight, he's got a surprise for you. Seven fifteen. I've left Terry's key with Jackie.'

'I'm not sure I can—' Suzie had gone. Her mum knew she didn't like surprises. Stella considered phoning back, but thought better of it; she would seem ungrateful and after all it could do no harm for Dale to go to Terry's house. Terry had been his dad too. Belatedly she wondered how Suzie knew Stella went there in the evening.

Liz interrupted this thought. 'How's your mum doing?

Stella had intended to say Suzie was fine, that working at Clean Slate got her out of the house. Instead she told Liz all about how Suzie still behaved as if Terry was alive and how she'd upped sticks and gone to Australia. That Stella had gone to the airport and her mother wasn't there, that she was still in Sydney. Finally Stella told her about Dale Heffernan. How he looked just liked Terry and that her mum hadn't complained about Terry being a 'wrong turning' since Dale had arrived. This bit hadn't occurred to Stella until she told Liz. She described how Dale had taken her mum on shopping trips to the West End, to posh restaurants and cooked for her. Suzie seemed to be having the time of her life. This too hadn't occurred to Stella before. Drawing breath, Stella realised she hadn't asked her mum where she was meant to be 'in tonight'. She spent her evenings at Terry's, but Suzie didn't know that. Liz was talking.

'Sounds like he's bonding with his biological mum – with you both – it doesn't always work out that way.' Liz was ripping up basil leaves and scattering them over fanned slices of avocado, tomato and mozzarella on a plate. She presented food on the plate with care like Dale did.

Stella had drunk the second cup of coffee and eaten all the biscuits without noticing.

'Rather strange for you, perhaps?' She looked at Stella with concern.

'I've hardly seen him. When he goes back to Australia, everything will get back to normal.' When Dale Heffernan had gone, her mum would return to her job at Clean Slate. They would resume their trips to Richmond Park every other Sunday with fish and chip suppers on Thursdays.

She heard a sploshing. Stanley was drinking out of a dog's bowl on a mat by the back door. Stella had forgotten about him. Liz had given him water. He caught her eye and, tail flapping, trotted over and put his paws on her knees. Stella stroked sodden fur back from his muzzle, drops of water dampening her trousers.

'He can lie on this while we eat.' Liz returned with a cushion from the front room and dropped it in the corner by the fridge. 'Lie down.' She invited him nicely.

Stanley approached the cushion, nosed it about, dragged it away from the fridge to the middle of the kitchen and climbed onto it. He flumped down and, heaving a sigh, went instantly to sleep.

Stella had assumed the food was for Liz and was about to say it was too early to eat, but her watch said it was five to one. They had been talking for three hours.

'You've trained him well!' Liz laid out tubs of olives and hummus, a plate of hot pitta bread and another of sliced meats. 'Stanley! Lovely name.'

'I'm minding him for a friend. Stanley was his father.' Liz had told her about her husband and his affairs, how she had had it with the 'sting of betrayal'. If she had stayed, Lulu could have joined in. Stella wasn't ready to swap stories about the Mr Rights who went wrong. David had not been Mr Right. That morning she had ignored another text. She wondered how she could give Stanley back without meeting him or involving a third party.

'Tuck in, Stell.' Liz took two bottles of mineral water from the fridge, one still and one sparkling. No one but Jack and Jackie called her 'Stell'. Liz had been the first to do so.

'Thanks.' Stella picked up her knife and fork and unfolded one of the triangles of kitchen towel that did for napkins, relieved there was no fuss and formality.

'He's going to miss you. Any chance your friend might let you keep him?'

'No chance. Stanley is attached to him.'

'He's attached to you, he's fixed on your every move!'

Stanley wasn't asleep. He was watching her. Without a dog to walk or think about, she would get more done, Stella reminded herself.

Stella scooted a helping of avocado salad onto her plate. She had first tasted avocado at the Hunter house. Liz's mother had coaxed her. *'Just a smidgin, love, you can't dislike what you've never tried.'*

Liz's family didn't call her dad a failed detective. Liz's dad had said he wished all the police were like Terry, a 'people-person'.

On the few occasions Stella had eaten avocado as an adult – generally at Jackie's – she would think of Liz and wonder where she was.

Liz poured mineral water from the still bottle into Stella's glass, a green tumbler dotted with air bubbles. Jack said imperfection was a sign of perfection. Liz hadn't offered the sparkling bottle. She must have remembered that Stella hated fizzy drinks.

'I'm sorry I wasn't able to help your friend.' Liz was tipping the leftovers into plastic boxes and stowed them in the fridge. Stella had completely forgotten about Lulu Carr, neither of them had referred to why Stella was there in the first place.

It was an hour and a half later and Stella was washing up the lunch things.

'I did try to tell her.' Stella didn't say again that Lulu wasn't a friend. She would have to explain about the case and Liz would think she was trying to be a detective like her dad and feel sorry for her.

'I'll drop Nicola a line and let you know what she says.'

'Thanks.'

'To be honest, Stell, I was cautious because, when she left Nicola made me swear to tell no one where she was staying. Very cloak and dagger.'

'What do you mean?' Stella rinsed the last bowl and fitted it into the draining rack. She knew why. She should level with Liz. Nicola Barwick had been involved with Rick Frost and, when he died, she had guessed Lulu had found out or that Frost had told her. She knew Lulu would want to see her. Stella saw suddenly that the floaty, feminine manner was a front. Lulu worked like a steel trap.

'I don't know Nicola well, we worked together. When I needed somewhere to rent, she offered here. A friend had died and she needed a change of scene.'

'What did you mean by "cloak and dagger?"' A detective, she probed deeper.

'At work she was as cool as a cucumber, ahead of the game, but nice with it. One of the few you could trust. When I came to see the house, she was quite different – nervy, talking fast, she seemed hardly aware of me. She hustled me inside as if someone was out there watching her. When she gave me her forwarding address, she confessed that she was being hassled by an ex. I had to promise not to give it to anyone. I presumed her friends and relations knew. But then this man turned up asking for her and now you've come. Nicola doesn't seem to have told anyone but me.'

'What friend?' Stella asked sharply. Stanley sat up.

'A guy she's known since they were kids – not the scary ex, I soon established that. He said they were only friends. He asked for Nicola's address – so difficult when you have to refuse someone nice. He told me she had asked him to check I was OK and that he would handle anything I needed. He was the only person in touch with her. I've found out since that he was testing me to make sure I didn't give away her address. I passed! To be honest I couldn't have given it to him because at that point I'd managed to lose it!' She dried the plates and put them back on the shelf. 'He warned me not to trust anyone – even murderers are charming!'

'He said that?' Stella pulled off the rubber gloves, finger by finger. She wondered at the comparison.

'He's rather put me on alert.' Liz laughed. 'Little traffic goes down this road and, except at weekends, hardly anyone walks by, so I catch every footstep. At night, it's as quiet as the graves over the road! My mum used to say I had a vivid imagination, you remember!'

'Has this man been back?' Mrs Hunter had told Stella she kept Liz's feet on the ground. Stanley's chest was pigeon-puffed, head back, ears pert as if he had heard something. The relaxed mood of lunch had gone.

'Yes! I was coming to that.' Liz rocked on her heels. 'We're seeing each other! Nothing serious. Justin – that's his name – understands that after Gary I can't rush into anything. Although between you and me, this time I don't mind if I do! I'd joined one of those dating websites and what happens? I meet a guy without leaving the house!'

'That's great. What does he do?' Stella's mind raced. Was Nicola Barwick frightened of the same person as Rick Frost?

'You sound like Dad, he used to quiz me about boyfriends!' Liz was girlish. Not the girl Stella remembered, who had been cool-headed about boys, but more like the sort of girl Liz had little time for at school, who lost interest in talking to other girls when a boy she liked came over.

'Justin's an engineer, he's passionate about his work. Gary was down on everything so it's refreshing.'

'How do you know he's a friend of Nicola Barwick's? Despite what he told you, he could be the ex.' Detectives had to take risks, even if it meant losing the friend she had only just found. If Lulu was right and Nicola Barwick had killed Frost, she had gone to some effort to cover her tracks.

'If you met him you'd understand. I trust Justin.' Liz filled the kettle and flicked down the lever; it began to hiss. 'He and Nicola were close, he says.'

Stella wasn't sure she trusted anyone. Not even Jack, it seemed.

'Were?' she echoed.

'*Are!*' A shadow passed across her face. 'Justin talks as if he'll never see her again.' Liz put the bottles of mineral water back in the fridge.

'I thought you said he did see her.'

'He says she's stopped answering his calls. He's upset she doesn't trust him – as I say, he thought they were close.'

'Is he sure she's OK? Suppose this man has found her?' Stella said.

'She told him not to contact her again. She says it's a risk.'

'What's the name of this ex?' Stella mentally put him at the top of their list of suspects.

'Nicola didn't say.'

'Doesn't your guy know? Justin.'

'He says she never introduced her men to him. I can imagine that; Nicola never talked about her private life to me either.'

'Do you have a number for her?'

'She only left a postal address. She told me to take any repair bills off the rent. I had a problem with the boiler, but Justin sorted that. He doesn't just build bridges and tunnels, he can turn his hand to anything!' Liz was fiddling with the fridge magnets. She straightened two and closed the gap in the top row that had irked Stella, who had forgotten that they had shared a liking for order.

'That's odd.' Liz held up a bright red magnet.

'What is?'

'Nicola's address isn't here.'

'Are you sure?' Stella might suggest that leaving the address on the fridge for all to see was unwise, but then Jack said that the best place to conceal something was in plain sight.

'Yes.' Liz got down on the floor. Sensing a game, Stanley beetled over and snuffled around her. 'It can only just have fallen off, I found it last week and finally posted off a letter that's been sitting here for weeks, making me feel guilty.'

'You said this man – Justin – has it. Couldn't you have asked him?'

'I couldn't admit I'd lost it; he's adamant that we must tell no one. Now I've lost it again!' she wailed.

'It must have fallen off.' Stella doubted this as soon as she said it.

'Maybe it's losing strength.' Liz examined the magnet as if she could tell by looking.

'Magnets last forever if you keep them away from power lines and don't expose them to high temperatures. It must be here.' Stella dragged the chairs away from the table. In the snugly fitted kitchen there were no crevices or cavities. The truth dawned.

Lulu had not received a text from her brother. She had gone looking for a clue to where Nicola Barwick might be and she had found it on the fridge. She knew where to look: she hid keys in plain sight. She hadn't been near the toilet. She had got Nicola Barwick's address and would be on her way there now.

'Liz, there's something I need to tell you.' Stella took the plunge and told Liz who Lulu was and how she suspected Nicola Barwick of having an affair with her husband. She left out the bit about Lulu accusing Nicola Barwick of murdering Frost – no need to make Liz feel worse than she did.

'Where did you forward the letter to?' she asked Liz.

'I can't remember.' Liz clamped the magnet back on the fridge.

'We need to warn her!'

'I've only sent on one letter.' She was staring at the magnets.

'Try to think, was it in this country?' Stella must not hurry her; Liz had always thought before she spoke, a trait Stella respected.

'It made me think of drawing,' Liz said eventually.

'What?' This was like being with Jack.

'The word was something you use for a… charcoal, that was it!'

'Is it a place?' Stella pulled out her phone; she would call Lulu Carr and hold her off.

'It's not the name, it's what I associated with it.'

Stella got Lulu's answer machine.

'I'm in mourning, I can't talk. Please don't leave a message after the beep, I shan't call back.'

Stella prevented herself letting out a wild scream.

'Charbury!'

Stella dabbed Charbury into Google Maps. There was one near Chipping Norton in Oxfordshire and one in East Sussex.

'What was the county?' She forced herself not to shout.

'East something.'

East Sussex then. Stella knew the name. Two years ago, Isabel Ramsay, her favourite client, had been buried in the churchyard at Charbury. The Ramsay family had invited Stella to the funeral but, unable to face another funeral so soon after her dad's, Stella had done a cleaning job instead. Jack had gone alone. For a mad second Stella believed that if she had gone, she wouldn't be facing this problem now. She should leave the magical thinking to Jack. The length of the journey to Charbury – one and a half hours each way – had been her excuse for not going. Lulu had been gone over five hours, ample time to find Nicola Barwick.

Forty-Five

Saturday, 26 October 2013

Jack laid the tray on the wood veneer table. Tea for Darryl Clark and hot milk for him. The canteen wasn't large, about twenty-six metres by ten, and today there was only one other person there, a middle-aged black man in a blue driver's polo shirt reading an *Evening Standard* by the serving hatch.

The staff canteen at Earl's Court was a bland combination of pinkish quartz screed flooring and salmon walls, with faux wood tables and red plastic chairs. Fluorescent lights chequered a tiled drop-ceiling, casting an even light and ensuring that drivers relaxed, yet remained alert.

A used tea bag lay soaking into a napkin on the table, a plastic stirrer placed beside it – like items of evidence in a crime, Jack found himself thinking. Pulling himself together, he gathered up the tea bag and tossed it into a flip bin by the food hatch. He caught an item on the noticeboard. Three flats for rent in West London, all apparently within easy distance of the District line. Nothing matched the Palmyra Tower; he had been lucky.

The driver by the servery lounged with his chair tipped back, arms folded, seemingly unaware of Jack. Nevertheless, to avoid their conversation being overheard, Jack moved closer to Darryl Clark.

Clark sat like an obedient child, hands on his lap, the shadow of a smile on his face as if determined to be cheerful. Jack recognized a man suffering from trauma. Clark unloaded the tray and propped it against the table leg, but made no move to drink his tea. Instead, he picked up his stirrer and with trembling hands swirled it back and forth in his tea, although he hadn't sugared it. He stopped abruptly.

'How are you doing?' Jack asked softly.

'OK now.' Darryl lifted the mug with both hands and drank in gulps. 'I started back on the Piccadilly, but coming out of Hammersmith, I felt like shit. That was with a co-driver doing the driving. At Stamford Brook, I swear I felt the train go over a bump where he fell. I kept quiet about that, didn't want them thinking I'm mad. Bloody feels like it.' He blew too hard on his tea and, without noticing, slopped it over the side. 'They fast-tracked the transfer to the Wimbledon line.'

'You're not mad.' Jack swept away the spill with his napkin.

'You OK? Were you off work too?' Clark's eyes flicked from side to side.

'No, but it's different for the driver.'

The man cleared his throat. 'Have you had one before?'

Jack understood Clark's need to ask a question that only a driver who had had a One Under could ask another.

'No.'

'It's my second. About twenty years ago.' Clark snapped his stirrer in two. 'A young woman. Joanna Hayward, she lived in Barking. She "got off" at Earl's Court.' He had a stolid expression. 'Turned out it was her third attempt. She was alive when she went down. They often are. I shouted down to her to keep away from the rail, the juice was still on. She never took her eyes off me as she put out a hand and grabbed it. Just like that.' He snapped the stirrer into smaller pieces. 'In those days, as I remember, they had you back on the trains sharpish.'

'Tough,' Jack agreed.

'Yes and no. I was young, I was pissed off with her for choosing my train!' Clark shook his head. 'It's like cooking with a knife and then slitting your wrists with it. Or, well, maybe not—' He picked up Jack's stirrer and broke it in half.

Jack was reluctant to join in, unsure it would help Clark to discuss the pros and cons of suicide.

Shaking his head, Darryl picked up the remaining sachet of sugar and poured it into his tea. The man was on autopilot.

Jack remembered Clark had sought him out. 'How are you now?'

'It hits me at night, like a film going on in my head. You get that?'

Jack didn't say he had a song replaying every night when he went to sleep, or mention the hum on the spiral staircase, the mythical birdsong and the glugging sink. Clark wouldn't want to know about his ghosts. He looked over at the hatch: he might get an apple muffin to take to the tower. Two even.

'It was harder for you. You were with him,' Clark remarked.

'What do you mean?'

'All that time waiting for the train and then he jumps. Did you see anything odd about him? I had him for a split second, so in my statement for the inquest I couldn't even say what he looked like. You were waiting on the platform with him.' He looked hostile, as if Jack had been remiss.

Jack felt a change in the air. He glanced again at the hatch. It was shut. The other driver had gone. The only witnesses to the death had been himself and Darryl Clark. The novice driver in whose cab he had travelled hadn't seen a thing. Still, he had been affected; he had since handed in his resignation.

'I wasn't on the platform.' He was careful not to embarrass Clark by pointing out his mistake. 'I was in the District line train.'

'I saw you.' Darryl was implacable. He snapped Jack's stirrer into splinters.

'You saw me afterwards. I was in the office.'

'You were on the platform, at the Hammersmith end. I didn't know you were with the Underground until I saw you clearing the station.'

'I was on the other train,' Jack repeated gently. He put down his mug. 'Are you saying there was someone else on the platform other than Rick Frost?'

'Was that his name?' Darryl Clark's drink was midway to his mouth. 'I tried not to hear.'

'Yes.'

'He's nobody to me. I don't want to know why he did it, or anything about him.' Clark's voice grated.

'But are you saying you saw someone else on the platform with him?' Jack had seen this before: drivers who didn't want to know that the person who had been killed by their train was human, with a name, a home and a family.

'He was looking at the dead man, before he died, I mean.' Clark gave a mirthless laugh and rounded up the snaps of plastic.

'Did you tell the police or the station staff?' There had been nothing in Clark's statement about another man.

'I assumed you'd tell them it was you.'

'It wasn't me,' Jack said again, more to himself.

'Nowadays I'm checking every bloody passenger for a sign they might top themselves.' Clark wiped a hand down his face and took a shaky sip of tea.

Clark hadn't been at the inquest; his manager had read out his statement. He had described the 'deceased' as 'flying out of nowhere'. He had followed protocol to the letter. He had left his cab, turned off the electricity and escorted his passengers off his train.

In the deserted canteen, Jack heard again the squeal of brakes and the piercing whistle Clark had sounded to alert station staff. Since moving to the tower, his mind was full of new, unfamiliar sounds. Maybe the recurring Smiths' 'How Soon Is Now?' was his brain's way of blotting out the soundscape of Frost jumping in front of a train.

'Another drink? A muffin maybe?' He had forgotten the server was shut.

'Food sticks in the craw. My wife's got me on Complan! The counsellor says it's a long haul.' He flashed Jack a smile.

A bad death would be hard: ghosts were the restless dead unable to make peace with themselves. Jack wondered if, like many drivers, Clark believed in ghosts. He saw all sorts of phantoms, wraith-like figures flitting about the platforms of the ghost stations.

'I keep thinking, could I have dropped the handle sooner, hit the brake quicker?' Darryl Clark leant over the table and Jack caught a tang of hair product; Stella would identify it instantly, he thought irrelevantly.

'I've killed a man. My kids' dad is a murderer. I repeat that every morning in the mirror.'

'You didn't kill him.' Every time they climbed into the cab of a train they risked a One Under. The incidents were rare, but it could always happen and they knew it. In that sense Darryl *had* killed Rick Frost.

'It's on the cards every time I'm in that cab.' Darryl had read his mind. Jack felt queasy; since living in the tower his mind wasn't his own.

'It was suicide, not your fault,' Jack insisted. No need to muddy matters with his suspicions of murder. 'What did this other man look like?'

'Like you, since I thought he was you.' Clark's patience was clearly wearing thin.

This had to be Stella's inspector, the man dressed in black she had met at the end of the platform. Jack wanted to text Stella, but with Clark there, it would seem insensitive.

'That bit of track after Hammersmith used to be my best bit of the journey,' Clark said ruefully.

Drivers didn't usually refer to their shift as a 'journey', that was Jack's word. Jack warmed to him.

'You were at the inquest.' Clark sat back in his chair. 'What did he say?'

'He wasn't there.' Whoever was on the platform hadn't come forward. He and Stella had established that the area where she had met the man was a blind spot, out of camera range. Jack tried to recapture the faces of the passengers he had ushered out of the station. None fitted Stella's description; no one had looked like himself.

There had been a man on the top deck of the bus that stopped at the zebra crossing on Goldhawk Road that night. Jack had been unable to see his face; he had a cap pulled low over his eyes. With no evidence, no proof or reason, Jack was quite sure that it was the man he called Stella's 'inspector'.

The Piccadilly train had come down the line from Hammersmith. Clark had seen a man step out from behind the staircase housing. Looking behind him, Rick Frost had seen him too and had started to run. The last person he had looked at, with his hazel eyes flecked with green, was Jack.

'You didn't murder him,' Jack said again to Darryl Clark. He wished he knew who had.

Forty-Six

Saturday, 26 October 2013

Stella drove around the corner into Corney Road and pulled in by the cemetery when she remembered it was a one-way street and she was going the wrong way. She was about to turn the van around when she saw she was outside Jackie's house. She had a sudden longing to knock on the door and invite herself in. But it was nearly four o'clock and Jackie would be at the office. Instead, she must drive to a village fifty miles away in pursuit of a woman who misguidedly wanted vengeance on her husband's mistress. Liz had urged her to call the police, but Stella wanted to hold off. She didn't think Lulu capable of violence: she was all theatre and bluster.

She had turned down Liz's offer that she come too; she had also refused to leave Stanley behind. Hazily she supposed that having a dog with her would be a good thing in a remote village in the countryside. Her recollection of Mrs Ramsay's description of Charbury was that it was in the middle of nowhere.

She did want Jack. If Lulu Carr had found Nicola Barwick, he'd know what to do. She tapped out his number on her phone on the dashboard. At the same moment a woman's voice reverberated around the van.

'It's me.'

There was a huff from the jump seat: Stanley was preparing to bark. 'Sssh.' Stella put a finger to her lips. She had answered an incoming call.

'What?' It was Lulu Carr.

'You took the address!' Stella snatched the phone from the cradle and clamped it to her ear.

'You would have done the same. She was being jobsworthy not giving to me.'

'That doesn't mean— Oh never mind.' Lulu was unrepentant, but Stella should have bargained for this. Lulu operated on a different plane, one where her own needs dominated all others. Perhaps a good detective couldn't afford to put honesty and respect for privacy before the case. Jack would agree.

'Did you find Nicola Barwick?' Stella pictured blood, mess, flashing blue lights. She should have called the police.

'Stella? I can't hear you! You've gone dead!'

The oldest trick in the book was to pretend the line was bad if asked an awkward question. Stella's mum did it all the time.

'Stella, hello?'

Stella took the phone from her ear to give Lulu a moment to decide to play it straight and saw she had pressed the phone too close to her ear and activated the mute button. She sighed and switched the call to the van's speaker system. 'Yes, I'm here.'

'Thank God. I thought you'd been attacked.' Lulu sounded as if she was inside a metal box.

'Did you find Nicola Barwick?'

'She escaped minutes before I arrived.'

'Escaped? You mean she had gone?' Stella tried to keep it real.

'Liz Thing tipped her off.'

Stanley made a stuttering noise in his throat. Stella looked around; he was staring at her, his pupils dilated. A spooked dog was all she needed. 'Good boy,' she mouthed.

'She wouldn't do that, and anyway, she didn't have her number.' Stella shook her head as if Lulu could see her. 'I was with her the whole time,' she added as a sliver of doubt inserted itself. Liz could have warned Nicola Barwick... but no, Liz wouldn't have lied to her.

There was a light on in Jackie's sitting room. Perhaps the dancing son was at home?

'Do you actually have a brother?' she heard herself say.

'Yes! I texted to say I had her address and he texted saying "You won't rest until you've been there." He watches out for me.'

'Would he have gone there?'

'I didn't exactly give him the address. I want to fight my own battles.' Lulu's voice quavered. Perhaps she recognized that texting her big brother didn't fit with her new-found independence from him.

'What does "exactly" mean?' Stella felt she was clutching at straws. Terry had said, pay attention to the words people use, just one word can give them away.

'I said it was Charbury. I said I'd used Google Street View, Rick was always on that. I said the house was next to the village stores. He wasn't interested. My brother's a busy man.'

Lulu Carr spoke as if Stella might dispute this. Stella had enough to deal with, with her own newly acquired brother, so she wasn't about to tackle someone else's.

Stanley began to sing, an insistent mewing that was almost human. He had been on a cushion in Liz Hunter's kitchen for hours. Stella was cross with herself; he needed to pee. She reached around and unfastened him. He plunged through the seats and landed on her lap.

'When did Nicola Barwick leave?'

'A neighbour said about an hour before I got there. Serves me right for stopping off for some lunch. I posted my number through the letterbox to ask the owner to ring me. Doubt they will. I said there'd been a death in the family, which is true!' Her voice was sibilant, and the consonants popped like small arms fire. Stella adjusted the volume on the dashboard. 'Nicola guessed I was on to her.'

Stella opened the door and Stanley scrambled on to the pavement. He pulled her across the road to the cemetery. With a balletic sweep of the back leg, he hopped along the verge, spraying the railings as he went. The droplets of pee glistened in the lamplight.

'Lulu, to stop you barking up the wrong tree, Nicola Barwick told Liz she was being stalked by a bloke who can't accept their relationship's over. Was Rick like that?' Not unless her stalker is a ghost, she nearly added.

'He was exactly like that. I told you. He had me on twenty-four-hour surveillance.'

'But he's dead. If it was him, it means that Nicola could come back to London,' Stella said. Not, however, if the man was someone else entirely. Or, indeed, with Lulu in her present mood. Up until now Stella had thought of Nicola Barwick only in relation to Frost's death. Liz had described her as nervy, and someone had driven her to leave her home and go into hiding. Now she had moved on. Liz was right; they should ring the police. Stanley was straining on his lead.

'I spend a fortune on a taxi haring down to some godforsaken place in Sussex on a wild-goose chase and you tease out the answer over a lunch. Stella, you are a great detective!' It was impossible to tell over the phone if Lulu was being ironic. Stella was inclined to think not – it wasn't her style. It was the second time in twenty-four hours she had been praised for doing pretty much nothing. Jack had been ridiculously happy that she had found out about Lulu being Mrs Frost. Then, as now, Stella didn't have the energy to disagree. She ended the call with a promise to see her on her next cleaning shift.

Stanley pulled her through the gates of the cemetery. Stella was surprised it was still open: it was hardly practical to tend the grave of a loved one in the dusk. Her mind on Nicola Barwick, she let Stanley lead her off the path towards a wall that she realized was the one opposite Liz's house. She would have been tempted to go back, but as she was leaving Liz had received a text from her new man so she wouldn't be there. Stanley lifted his leg by a danger sign that warned of open or sunken graves, unstable memorials and uneven ground.

In the distance was the church. High above the spire Stella made out Jack's tower. Splashes of sodium-orange light illuminated a track winding between the graves. It was not sensible to be alone in a cemetery after dark. Stella promised herself they would have a quick walk, then return to the van and she would ring Jack. She increased her pace.

Women were murdered by stalkers. Stella had heard of a case on the news recently. The police had ignored more minor bullying until the day the man had smashed his way into the woman's flat and strangled her. Nicola Barwick could be in danger. She stopped by a Madonna and got out her phone. The signal was down to one bar, but she got a connection.

'Cashman speaking.'

'Martin, it's me, Stella Darnell.'

'There's only one Stella! I hoped you'd ring, I just heard about your brother.' His voice reverberated: he was on speakerphone. 'About time he turned up! Be good to meet him.'

'My brother?' Stella was momentarily blank.

'Darren, David—?'

'Dale. How did—' No need to ask. Suzie, so hot on privacy she disliked coffee shops recalling she liked a double espresso, had been telling the world that her son made 'soufflé as light as gossamer'.

'Shot me back twenty years to when I first met Terry.' There was a click as he took the receiver off speakerphone. Sounding more intimate, he continued, 'Fancy a drink? I told Terry I'd be there for you if stuff ever came to light and Terry was… hmm… wasn't here.'

'Thanks, it's fine.' Stella was about to ask what Martin meant when Stanley tugged hard at his lead. Concerned that he might drag her into a sunken grave or an unstable monument, she unclipped him. Why did Martin think she needed to talk about it? Dale was here and then he would go.

Terry had been Martin Cashman's boss and his best friend. After Terry died, Martin had made it clear he was 'there' for Terry's daughter. At the time Stella had rebuffed his help; later she had asked him a favour and he had turned her down. Now she was circumspect: Martin had been Terry's friend; he owed her nothing. Since Terry hadn't known he had a son, by 'stuff' Terry couldn't have meant a situation like this.

'Brothers! Mine borrowed my Lexus last week, to impress some new woman he's conned into dating him, and he pranged it on a post box!'

Jackie had said it was a shame Cashman was married with kids – a chip off Terry's old block, he would be perfect for Stella. Solid and practical, he would take no nonsense. Stella didn't believe in 'perfect' and didn't ask what 'nonsense' from her it was that Cashman wouldn't take.

She was buffeted by a gust of wind.

'Blimey, where are you?' Cashman exclaimed.

'I'm by a grave – on a path – I'm outside,' Stella said. She told him about Nicola Barwick, leaving out that Lulu Carr suspected she had killed her husband. Terry's daughter or not, and despite her track record in solving cases, Martin wouldn't like her turning detective. 'Leave it to us,' he had said.

Tapping on his keyboard, he breathed loudly into the receiver, as loud as the wind. 'Nothing on the system – she hasn't put in a complaint. I can check with Sussex, though there's not much we can do if she hasn't come forward and with no hard facts…'

'She can't come forward if she's missing.' A patch of white that she had thought was Stanley was a headstone. Hearing herself, Stella added, 'But I see what you mean.' Were it not for Liz Hunter, Stella might doubt that Barwick even existed.

'The neighbour told your friend that Nicola Barwick said she was going away.'

'Something must have happened to make her leave,' Stella said.

'Trouble is, unless she tells us, or fails to turn up where she is expected, our hands are tied. My guess is that she'll ring your mate when she knows her new location. When she does, encourage her to give us a call. We can slap an order on this bloke – he may already have a record. Get me some information and I'll see what I can do.'

Stella thanked him. About to end the call, she was hit by another squall and staggered into a dip in the ground.

'Stella?'

'Yes.'

'Up for that drink anytime, OK?'

Right now she could do with sitting in a pub with Martin Cashman, swapping information about the latest cleaning products with 'stop and search' stats.

'OK,' she agreed. 'Martin, what do you know about that man, Rick—'

A busy man, Cashman had gone.

Stella wandered deeper into the cemetery, peering into the spangled darkness in search of Stanley. The street lamps on Corney Road were dots. The pale shapes of headstones mingled with shadows of trees, created Stanleys everywhere. She heard a scuffling and blundered off the track, furious with herself for letting the dog off his lead.

'Stanley!' She was loath to shout, though there was no one alive to mind.

She tripped on tussocks and clods of earth and, at last coming upon a path, found the source of the noise. A plastic bag caught on a bramble was not Stanley.

'Stanley!' Stella dared raise her voice. Wind smacked at the plastic bag and whooshed through the branches. No dog.

Flitting blobs of beige danced and goaded her amidst darker shapes. She was fooled by finger-pointing angels, more Madonnas, and laughing cupids with dimpled cheeks. Row upon row of headstones, half hidden by grass and brambles where light didn't penetrate: none were Stanley.

Stella fumbled inside her anorak for the whistle. Sickened, she pictured it in the glove box with the spare poo bags.

A stick cracked, a scurry of footsteps. Stella plunged on, keeping the wall on her right as rough navigation. Her ears attuned, she shouted 'Biscuit' and 'Chicken': anything to lure him to her. Twice she tripped on sunken masonry, heedless now of falling into a coffin-sized hole. The ground dipped and she fell on to one knee and made herself listen.

Nothing. Her mouth dry, she put her fingers to her mouth and gave a long low whistle. Her heart lurched when the sound was repeated. She did it again. Again there was a whistle, long and low, longer than hers had been. It wasn't an echo. Someone had whistled back. Stella fought the impulse to run. Jack said running gave the enemy your location. What enemy?

Trees outlined in the gloom swayed as one, leaning eastward as blusters ripped at the last of their leaves and tore at their branches. In gaps between gusts, Stella heard rustling. It came from the darkest section of the cemetery. She walked purposefully towards it, skidding on loose stones, her boots crunching on the hard, but even surface, giving away her location.

Stanley was running towards her. It really was him. His movements were jerky, back legs flinging up and then down. Stella remembered the dead rat; he had something forbidden – anything he found here was forbidden. Ecstatic at his transgression, he wouldn't let her put his lead on and would refuse treats and ignore commands. They would be here for hours.

Stanley cavorted away in the direction of Corney Road, pausing every so often to confirm she was coming. The trick was to go the other way. Stella had no choice but to go further into the cemetery because, lacking traffic sense, if she pursued him to the road, Stanley would see a car and give chase.

Stella walked towards the boundary wall, not looking to see if he was coming or he would race away. Poodles possessed a lethal combination of intelligence and tenacity; she must keep her wits about her.

In front of her was a brick building. In the light of street lamps beyond the wall, she made out graffiti tags sprayed on the brickwork. A silver stencil of a skull and crossbones gleamed in the thin light. A grille was fitted over the doorway, another covered a half-moon window.

Intent on ignoring Stanley, Stella pulled on the grille and it swung open. Something pushed against her calves and she nearly shouted with fright. Stanley dropped whatever was in his mouth and nosed through the gap.

Got you! Stella swiped up the discarded bunch of dead flowers and tossed them into the bushes. She remembered that Jackie had put a torch app on her phone. Switching it on, she went in after him.

The air was chill and dank. High up in the wall a semi-circular window let in pinkish light. Even without a door, the hut offered shelter from the wind, which was now a distant moan.

She clipped on Stanley's lead and shone the light about her. In one corner was a warped and dirt-encrusted cupboard. Through mesh doors she saw two cans of Coca-Cola and a bag of crisps. A flea-bitten deckchair and three broken packing cases were grouped around a table. There were no leaves or rubbish on the floor, no tell-tale cigarette butts: it was as if someone had swept it recently. Probably a kids' den – house-proud kids. Stella approved, although a cemetery wouldn't be her choice.

She heard the whistle again. Stanley growled.

'It's the wind.' Hearing her voice, feeble and hollow in the crypt-like hut, Stella was less sure. Surely it was late to be putting flowers on a grave. She scooped Stanley up and, tripping on the deckchair, hurried to the doorway.

Two things happened. Her torch went out and the grille shut with an ear-splitting clang.

Forty-Seven

Saturday, 26 October 2013

'Sorry, wrong house.'

It wasn't the wrong house, it was the wrong year. The man regarding Jack with an enquiring smile was Terry Darnell. Not the Terry Jack had met briefly, but a middle-aged Terry with life still to lead. A ghost.

'You all right? You look like the driven bloody snow!' The timbre of the voice was Terry with the West London accent swapped for North Shore Sydney. In a minute Jack would pinpoint the suburb. It wasn't Terry Darnell, it was the Brand-new Brother.

'You wanting Stella?' *Stellah*. The man lounged against the door jamb, a tea towel on one shoulder, as if he had all day. Jack, who did not have all day or night, considered barging past him.

'She's expecting me.' He was terse. 'I texted.'

'Sure. Come on in. I've just got the central heating working – place was cold as a tomb!' He stood aside to let Jack in.

'Crows' Nest, zip code NSW 2065,' Jack murmured, looking up the stairs and into the living room, expecting Stella.

'Bang on, Professor Higgins! Stella tell you?' Dale banged shut the front door. The man was noisy.

'I worked it out from your accent.' Jack frowned to hide his pride. No one had called him Professor Higgins before.

Dale continued, 'You know Sydney?' He whipped the tea towel off his shoulder and began flexing it between his hands as if exercising his pectorals. Jack guessed he was one of those men who need always to be testing themselves and, more annoyingly, testing others.

'Yes.' He stared into the sitting room. The table lamps and side lights were on. He caught lavender oil. Stella preferred plug-in deodorizers; essential oils were liable to stain. He went on down the passage to the kitchen where, it being exactly eight, Stella would be microwaving her shepherd's pie. A cloud of garlicky steam billowed out when he pushed open the door. It made him aware he was hungry. Stella would heat up a ready meal for him too, but it had never smelled so good as it did tonight.

'She's due any time now.' The Brand-new Brother trod on his heel. While aware it was an absurd notion, Jack had hoped he had gone. Why was he here?

'Is she expecting *you*?' Jack nearly voiced the question.

'The more the merrier, unless you're a veggie?' Dale was clattering at the stove. 'If so, I can rustle up the finest omelette this side of – where are we? – *Ham*-mer-*smith*!' He flapped his towel as if his pronunciation were a linguistic triumph. 'Place of my birth!'

'Sometimes I'm vegetarian,' Jack said haughtily, ignoring the last comment. Did Dale think being born in the same borough as Stella gave him carte blanche to her house?

A large pan was bubbling on the back ring of the stove. Light drifted through the glass panel in the oven door. Jack pinpointed background whirring to the oven fan. He perched on the edge of a chair and fished his phone from his coat. No text from Stella. Last night she hadn't said the Brand-new Brother would be here. No reason she should, yet he was put out. Stella couldn't have known.

'Is today a meat-eating day? We've got lamb stew with baked potatoes. Big surprise for my little sister. Her favourite, Suzanne says. It's my old man's recipe and goes down a bomb at our pop-up café on a winter's night! Too rough and ready for my restaurant crowd!' He let out a guffaw. He must have seen Jack's face because he said, 'The dad I knew as my dad, not my biological dad. The dad that dealt with the daily shit and footed the bill!' He gave another hooting laugh and, diving forward, sipped on a spoon of stew and smacked his lips. He picked up a clean spoon, dipped it in the mixture and passed it to Jack. 'Catch the cumin – hope you like raisins!'

Jack couldn't come up with an excuse to refuse. He took the spoon and blew on it, then put his lips to the bowl of the spoon. It was the most delicious food he had ever tasted. Garlic, cumin, lemon with coriander as an aftertaste. Each herb and spice had kept its separate taste while blending to create perfection.

''S nice,' he admitted.

'Oh, wait on, I never introduced myself! Guess you know all about me from Stell.' Dale thrust his hand out to Jack. 'Dale Bardia Heffernan. And you are the train driver?' He gave a toot-toot. Presumably this was a joke.

'Jack.' Jack shook the outstretched hand, mindful to clasp tight. For a moment the two men were in a contest, each gripping the other's hand as if their lives depended on it. Jack let go first because he felt silly.

'Bardia?' He arched his eyebrows, disliking himself for asking the question that had begged to be asked.

'Yeah, don't hold back, everyone has a view! Dad was a bit of a hero in the Second World War. The guy was forty-three when I was born – I've got three older sisters. Dale Senior was part of Operation Compass; he took part in the liberation of the port of Bardia in 1941. My sister has it as a middle name, but when the longed-for boy came along, they dusted it off and gave it to me too! My party quip is: Thank God he wasn't at Dunkirk!'

Jack refrained from asking why that name would be worse. He noticed it would be easy to miss that Heffernan had been adopted: he spoke of his Australian family as 'real'. Jack wondered if he spoke this way with Stella and her mother.

'Stella generally heats up a ready meal. She hates fuss,' Jack pronounced, arms folded.

'I'm on that. The coriander garnish is optional, but I recommend it. I had a tussle with the garlic, then went for it. D'you think she'll hack it?'

'I don't know.' Jack was honest. Stella liked honesty. Dale

appeared concerned to please Stella, but if he wanted a share of her legacy – the man was a bounty hunter – he was wrong to think cooking a slap-up meal and heating up the house was the way to her purse.

In the two years since she'd inherited the house, as far as Jack knew, Stella had never turned on the heating or the oven. She maintained Terry Darnell's synchronized lighting, on timers to fool burglars. She had changed nothing. For a time, at the end of the Blue Folder case, he had thought she would sell up, but then she slipped back to the old routine of being custodian, as if keeping it clean for the day when Terry returned. Or so Jack believed.

After Dale's cooking spree, Stella would have to air the house to chase out the stale stew odour or it would hang about for days. In Terry's house her adherence to rituals – cloths and sponges laid out in readiness for cleaning – was votive. All the signs of Terry that she had worked to preserve had been erased. His cereal bowl, spoon and coffee mug that she kept on the draining board had been tidied away. In one evening the Brand-new Brother had obliterated everything.

Jack felt grim satisfaction that Dale and his lamb stew would get short shrift from Stella. She would be stunned by the warmth, the mood lighting and the smell. Jack dreaded the hurt that would flit across her face and her stilted efforts to hide them. He couldn't bear to witness her struggle to make sense of the transformation. He considered leaving, but that would be the act of a coward.

Despite seeing Heffernan's true motive, Jack did feel rather sorry for the fellow. No one was going to enjoy the next few minutes.

'Fancy a drink while we wait?' Dale held up a bottle of De Bortoli, a New South Wales Merlot, and a glass. Jack's stomach did a flip; Heffernan's smile was Stella's when she was relaxed. He was about to refuse, he wanted to keep a clear head, but if he was to help Stella he must be more relaxed than he felt. He nodded.

'Jack, help me out here. I'm wondering…' Dale held the bottle at the base, a hand behind his back like a waiter.

'What?' Jack signalled for Dale to stop pouring.

'Stella is like me.'

Jack bristled. 'How?'

'Reliable, does what says she'll do. She was meant to be here at seven fifteen. What'd she tell you?'

Jack shrugged. Stella wasn't expecting him. Terry had kept the wall clock three minutes fast, but even so that made it ten past eight. She was late.

'Are you worried the food will spoil?' he sniped.

'Hell no! It's a stew, the longer it mulches the better. I'm bothered by Stella being late. Suza— my mother told her about tonight. She agreed to be here.'

'Here or at her flat?'

'Jackie said to come here; Suzanne asked her to give me a key. Stella's not the type of girl to bail out, is she? You know her well.'

'I don't.' But he did. Stella fulfilled agreements, she saw contracts through, however difficult. She never 'bailed out'. A trawling dread overtook Jack's trepidation about Stella's reaction to home cooking and a functioning central-heating system. He grabbed his phone.

'This is Stella Darnell, please leave me a—'

He felt a wash of shame that, overtaken by his own feelings, he hadn't considered Stella's safety. She was never late. Not unless something had happened—

'I don't want to ask Suzanne, that'll worry her. Jackie's not at the office any more,' Dale said as he turned off the heat on the hob and the oven.

Stella had gone to see Nicola Barwick that morning. Although it was hot and steamy in the kitchen, Jack shivered. Stella hadn't been in touch with him since – why had he only just noticed?

A loud rap on the door startled both men. A shadow filled the glass in the door, silhouetted in the porch light. Obliquely Jack observed there was a porch light. He had the crazy notion that this time it really was Terry's ghost.

Dale got there first. He flung open the front door. 'Hey, sis!' With a flourish of his tea towel he welcomed her inside.

Jack found he couldn't move.

'Sorry, I couldn't find my key. That lamb stew smells brilliant.' Stella stopped rummaging in her rucksack and came in, Stanley at her heels.

'It was meant to be a surprise!' Dale crowed with mock disappointment.

'Stella has an acute sense of smell. She could tell you all the ingredients,' Jack said, but no one heard.

Stella looped her rucksack over the newel post and nodded to Jack with an expression he couldn't fathom. With Stanley pattering at her heels, she went after Dale down the passage to the kitchen. Jack trailed after them.

'It's my favourite.' Stella was sluicing her hands under the tap. 'I'm very hungry.'

Stella was never hungry. She ate when she was empty or because it was on the schedule; she regarded food as a nuisance. Tonight Jack was inclined to agree that it was.

'Hey, little feller!' Dale swept the dog up and held him on the other shoulder to the tea towel. He fired up the ring on the hob.

'He will bite – he doesn't like being held. It's best to warn him...' Jack subsided into silence. The dog was systematically licking Heffernan's face.

He stood in the doorway. Brother and sister were chatting and joking, moving around the room, getting out plates, knives and forks, filling wine glasses as if they had known each other forever, rather than three days. Jack was the odd one out, the stranger.

He was opening the front door when Stella called to him. He would walk and walk and never stop. This was worse than if she had found him in Lulu Carr's cupboard.

He nearly didn't answer. 'What?'

'There's a litre of milk in my rucksack. Bring it through. We'll need it for your hot drink in our meeting after supper.'

Jack shut the door and, fending off an impulse to cry, lifted the bag off the post. He sat on the bottom step, the bag between his knees. The milk was cold; Stella must have just bought it. Was that why she was late? The bag tipped open; he clamped his legs together and caught something in his lap.

Even if Dale had not switched on all the lights, Jack would have recognized what he held in his hands. The Pullman carriage belonged to a train exactly like the one he had owned when he was little.

Forty-Eight

Saturday, 26 October 2013

'You never lose track of time.' Jack waited until Dale had shut the front door behind him and they were alone.

'I lost track of Stanley.' After her account of her visit to Nicola Barwick's house and the discovery of a long-lost school friend, Stella described an escalating ordeal in Chiswick Cemetery. It had finished with being stuck in a shed, the gate having jammed shut in the wind.

'Stanley dragged me in. On the way out, a noticeboard said they don't allow dogs in at any time!' She seemed rather excited by her inadvertent transgression, Jack thought.

Stella tossed a treat into the dog's basket – the only addition to the house since Terry's death. The dog caught it mid-air, snapped it in his jaws and curled into a ball. If she hadn't had the dog, Stella wouldn't have gone into the cemetery, Jack thought. Owning dogs was dangerous. Cemeteries and dark unpopulated stretches of ground in a city were short cuts or choices of murder sites for his True Hosts. Bodies were often found by dog walkers, he knew that.

'I saw that toy carriage in your bag.' He was stirring honey into his hot milk. He had briefly entertained the fancy that it was a present for him, but Stella wouldn't buy him a toy, she thought toys were for children. Jack shuddered. The carriage had given him a bad feeling.

'I found it in the shed when I was looking for another way out.' She placed the carriage on the table. 'I panicked and must have shoved it in my pocket. I'll take it back tomorrow.'

'Don't go back!' Jack said.

'It was a kids' den, it'll belong to them. I've stolen it.'

Stella rolled the carriage about on the table, stopping by the mugs as if they were stations. Jack was anxious to have a go.

'I'll do it for you.' He peered in through the carriage windows. Unlike the carriage he had found earlier that day, this one was full of passengers sitting at the tables on which were glued plates, cups and minute cutlery. Delicately, Jack prised open a door and revealed a steward balancing a tray with a glass of brandy and a cigar. A man sat alone; his table had no food on it – presumably the order was his. Although the dining car must be heated, the figure wore a coat and what looked like a baseball cap. Everyone else was eating or in conversation with fellow diners, while the man looked out of his window, but not with the ruminative expression of a lone traveller: he was looking at Jack. Although moulded in beige plastic, Jack was certain the figure was a model of the man standing in the middle of Hammersmith Bridge he had seen through the binoculars the night he moved into the tower. The same man had watched Jack from the bus on Goldhawk Road just after Rick Frost died.

'It's a sign,' he breathed.

'A sign?' Stella echoed. 'Of what?'

Jack was back in the school kitchen garden. He saw a flash of broken crockery, smashed glasses, stricken faces pressed against jammed windows, lobster thermidor, pâté de foie gras mixed with mud and spliced with the lolly sticks he had used for tunnel struts. The sound of the Smiths couldn't drown out the screams and cries for help that would never come. In the silence of the aftermath of the crash, he had heard a chinking, like a timorous call for attention and, finding himself alone, he had left the smashed-up tunnel and followed the sound. He had come across a gate leading out beyond the school kitchen garden. It was out of bounds. A dog lead dangled from a post. In the zephyr-like breeze the catch clinked against the wood. Even then he had known it was a sign.

Jack put his mug down. Fingers steepled, he whispered, 'There's stuff – I haven't said.'

He told Stella about the other carriage and the engine on the monitors in the stations. He told her about the length of the tunnel and that the answer, 266.66, was repeated on the engine. His finger trembling, he showed her that it was the same as the number on the side of the Pullman carriage: 26666. He got out the carriage he had found that morning. Another 26666. He coupled it to the Pullman and sent it around the table, stopping at Stella's mug stations. Stella didn't interrupt or tell him it was nonsense or that he was imagining things.

St Peter's church bells chimed midnight. Jack and Stella had been awake most of the last twenty-four hours.

Finally he told her about the boy called Simon who had wanted to be his friend at school. The boy was dead. Jack said he had made himself forget that time long ago. Until the toy train brought it back. Suffused with shame, he found the words to tell her that at his boarding school he was for a time a bully. He had been bullied too, he said, wondering suddenly if that bit was true. Was what Simon did to him actually bullying? Huddled in his coat, his milk gone cold, Jack told Stella all about Simon.

When he'd finished, she took the carriage on another round of the table, stopping at his mug, then at hers, berthing it at the honey pot. She said, 'School can be a tough place for kids. Jackie says it was hard on you being sent away after your mum—' She set the carriage off on another circuit of the condiments. 'Are you saying you think this boy – man – called Simon killed Frost and left you these bits of train? He'd surely have got over you having a go at him by now. Could he be the inspector I met on the station?'

'No, Simon's dead. He's been dead for years.' Jack put his hands to his ears. He heard the pounding of the sea crashing on some far-off shore. More and more he felt his mind wasn't his own.

'How did he die?' Stella was examining the wheels of the carriage; Jack could tell she was trying to be tactful.

'He was mugged. Actually in that cemetery you were in tonight.' He used 'actually' to imply it was a coincidence, so as not to worry her. 'He died later in hospital.'

'So these toys were left by a ghost?' She betrayed no sarcasm.

'No.' *Yes*. 'Simon was only trying to help me.' Simon had wanted to be his friend. Jack had never let himself think this before. He had punished him for liking him – perhaps because he didn't like himself.

'Anyone could have found the carriages or the engine. It wasn't your usual route, you drive the Richmond to Upminster line, and I certainly didn't plan on going into the cemetery.'

'Someone could have followed you and left the carriage where you'd find it.' Jack spoke as his thoughts unfolded. 'Did you hear anyone while you were there?'

He could see from Stella's expression that she had.

'I thought it was the wind,' she admitted. 'How would anyone know I would go in or that I'd find the hut?'

'He – or she – could have lured Stanley away from you. Did you happen upon the hut by accident or did Stanley lead you there? The most potent of plans are plotted in chunks and put into action as situations occur. This person didn't lure you to the cemetery, but if they were watching you, they'd have seen you go in. Cue to set the plan in motion. If you had gone after Lulu Carr to Charbury, they would have left the carriage on Isabel Ramsay's grave.'

'I was following Lulu, I mightn't have visited the grave. How would they even think I might?'

'Wouldn't you?' Jack said levelly. Mrs Ramsay had been Stella's favourite client.

Stella reddened. 'Yes, I would.'

'Such a person will do their homework. They enter someone's mind and alter the course of their actions. When the time comes, they end their life. We are dealing with a merciless professional.'

Stella grabbed a brush from the corner of the kitchen and began sweeping the floor. 'Have we now got three cases to solve?' She didn't sound fazed by the prospect.

Jack stroked his chin. 'Not necessarily.'

'Could this Simon from your school have a relative he told about you?' Stella scooted a minute scrap of onion skin and a stale dog biscuit into a dustpan, and banged it into the swing bin. She gripped the brush handle like a spear. 'Is someone out to get revenge?'

'There was a sister.' He was impressed at Stella's lateral thinking – detective thinking.

'What was her name?'

'No idea, although I'm sure he told me. I tried to block him out.' He had tried to disappear Simon. *Simple Simon*. 'He made us prick our thumbs and press them together so we'd be blood brothers.'

'That's silly nonsense – it didn't make you brothers. What did you do exactly? Why was it such a big deal?' Stella leant on the brush handle.

The distance that divided them was a metre of lino. It might be a yawning chasm.

'I said I didn't know him.'

'Was that all?'

He didn't want Stella to understand. He wanted to keep her opinion of him intact.

'If someone was out for revenge, and quite honestly I doubt they are, then this is a weird way to go about it. Anyone who knows you would see that a train is the perfect present.'

'True.' Pleased by Stella's observation – she knew him – Jack resumed his drink, although it had cooled. 'Their intention would be to unsettle me. In fact – well, I have to say it's working.' He didn't look at Stella.

'OK, so this is what we do. I'll return this carriage to the cemetery; you can hand in the ones you found to Lost Property. We'll show him or her that we don't care. We've got bigger fish to fry.'

Stella washed her mug, scrubbing vigorously inside it with a scouring pad. She put it on the draining board. The cereal bowl and spoon were back. She had cleaned and put away the empty stew pan after supper. Jack was faintly reassured: Terry's kitchen was restored; it was as if Dale had never been there.

'That wouldn't work.' Jack couldn't say that though Simon was dead, he lived on in his head. Getting rid of the train wouldn't expunge him. Stella's straightforward and honest solution belonged to a cleaner, sunlit world. 'You shouldn't go back to the cemetery on your own. I'll do that.'

'Why would that be better? At my primary school a girl stuffed me in the cleaning cupboard. I got Ajax powder in my hair. I haven't been minded to drop expensive toys around London for her nor can I see anyone doing it on my behalf.' She looked at Jack. 'She worked for Clean Slate a few years ago. I gave her the top clients; she got into corners and sanitized stainless steel sinks to a sparkle.' Stella seemed cheered by this recollection. 'My friend Liz rescued me from the cupboard.'

'Was that why you launched Clean Slate?' Jack wanted to steer Stella off cupboards.

'No.' Stella cast him a look. She flipped open her Filofax and wrote 'Rick Frost' on a blank page and put today's date. Subject closed. Case meeting open. 'That text you sent me about asking Lulu Carr about the glove Stanley took?' She clicked on her ballpoint. 'What with the drama of Barwick's disappearance, I forgot. What's the significance?'

Jack couldn't say his calculation of the West Hill tunnel had led him to make connections that were intuitive with no basis at all in everyday reality. Stella had been patient when he explained how working out the length had opened up his mind; he wouldn't tax her patience further.

'It's tenuous. Lucie May said that the dead man in my tower was found face down with a black glove placed on his back.'

'You think it's the same glove?' Stella was doing her very best to go with him.

'I know, it's tenuous, but because of the 26666...'

Stella would consider herself honour bound to contradict any information given by Lucie May. Now was not the time to say that Terry had told Lucie about the glove. As she so often did, Stella surprised him.

'Tenuous is us. Black gloves are common, but not ones with crowns on them.' She wrote 'black glove with crown motif' in her Filofax and looked at him. 'Are you thinking the cases are linked?'

'One connection is Terry, but since he was a police officer, no surprise there.' Jack silently blessed Stella for the open mind she must have resolved to keep.

'Jack, if you seriously think there is someone out there looking for you, come and stay in my flat, just till we gauge the lie of the land. There's CCTV, a London bar and three mortice locks.'

'I live in a tower, how much safer could I be!'

Jack squinted in through the Pullman carriage windows and gave a yelp.

The dog leapt from his basket and bounded about the kitchen barking, head thrown back. It was the same sound he had made in the tower, and it struck a note of dread in Jack's chest. Dogs sensed more than humans.

Stella had dropped her pen. 'What's the matter?'

'The man has gone.'

'What man?'

'The man who was waiting for his brandy, the one looking—' Jack gesticulated at the empty table in the carriage window.

'Oh for goodness— He – *it* – must have fallen out. Shake the carriage.' Stella puffed out her cheeks. She shooed the dog back to his basket and fed him another treat. She retrieved her pen from the floor.

'Found him.' She handed Jack the plastic man. 'That glove is for a child, but Lulu does have small hands. I'll confirm it with her. OK, so back to our suspects. Lulu, William Frost, the inspector, Nicola and Nicola's stalking ex. I really do think we can rule out Lulu Carr. The woman's impetuous, but I don't see her harming anyone.'

'What if she had found Nicola Barwick and is pretending she didn't?'

'She's not that wily. I'm not even sure she believes they were having an affair. I wonder if she's made it up. She strikes me as inauthentic.' Stella folded her arms as if pleased with her idea. 'Mind you, I do think she's hiding something. She did lie to me about her husband leaving her, but even so I don't think that makes her a murderer.'

'And William Frost?' Jack asked.

'I don't trust him. Ever since he brought the case to us, he's been evasive and unhelpful.' Stella added William Frost to her task list.

'What about this man your friend Liz is seeing? He claims to be a close friend of Nicola Barwick's, but she never told him about moving from Charbury. Nor did she give him her Charbury address in the first place. Now he's involved with her lodger. Fishy, don't you think?'

'People can't help who they like,' Stella said. 'Liz wouldn't do anything stupid.'

'Whom,' Jack said before he could stop himself.

'Sorry?'

'People who make mistakes rarely think they are making them.' Too late Jack realized that Stella would think he was referring to her past; in fact he was thinking of Dale. 'What's his name?' he asked hurriedly.

'I've forgotten.' Stella looked annoyed with herself. 'I'll ask her more about him.' She noted 'Liz Hunter's man' down on her list.

'What about this brother of Lulu Carr's? If Frost was cheating on her, the brother might be unhappy – that's a motive.'

'It's a big step from being unhappy to killing a man.'

'That's the kind of thing brothers do. Goodness knows what Dale Heffernan would do on your behalf.' Jack was being sarcastic. Immediately ashamed, he wished the words unsaid.

'Dale isn't my real brother,' Stella said in a small voice.

'Yes he is.'

'I know *you* better than I do him. Blood isn't everything.'

Jack hid his pleasure. He opened the carriage door and slotted the little figure through and tipped up the carriage until he was back at his table awaiting his drink. He took the carriages around the 'stations' again.

'Lulu Carr says he's protective,' she said. 'That means he might do anything.'

'What's his name?' Jack heard himself repeating the question. 'The inspector, the brother, the boyfriend: we need names and faces for these people.'

‘Is he a suspect?’ Stella was arch, although he hadn’t meant it as a dig.

‘Until we cross him off.’

‘Lulu didn’t say. I might ask William rather than make her curious.’ Stella noted this down and sat back contemplating the growing list with evident satisfaction.

‘After what Darryl Clark – the driver of the train that hit Frost – said, we need to focus attention on your inspector at the station,’ Jack said.

‘I keep forgetting to show you.’ Stella fiddled in the pocket in her Filofax and brought out a square sheet. ‘What do you make of this? I found it in the photo booth the night we went to Stamford Brook. Someone must just have left the booth before we came down from the platform. You’d gone to get your train.’

Jack stared at the four images. They were of the back of a man’s head. His hair, thick and brown, fell just below his collar. He was wearing a white shirt. He looked at all four pictures although they were repeats of the same shot.

‘His back is to the camera,’ he said at last.

‘Er, yes!’ Stella was impatient. ‘Who does that? I wondered if it was the inspector-man I met? I heard the machine going just as we were going up to the platform. I thought then it was an odd time to get your picture done. The timings would fit. He probably dived into the photo booth to avoid us seeing him.’

The corpse in the tower had been face down. When Simon had come to say sorry about the things he said in the room below the library, Jack had turned his face to the wall.

You denied you knew me. Three times.

Stella was still talking. ‘—I thought at the time it was a funny mistake to make. I’ve had duds in those machines when the flash goes before you’re ready but I always face the right way! It does look a bit like him.’ She held up the pictures.

‘I thought you said you didn’t see the man’s face.’

‘I didn’t, but as we’re keeping an open mind—’

‘I didn’t see him at all.’ Jack pushed the pictures back. ‘We need to see him from behind.' He was thinking out loud now. 'There's an Agatha Christie story in which the murderer is seen from the back, in fact it's on a train—'

'Jack.' Stella's patience had run out. 'Would you go back to Lucie May and ask her what else Terry told her?' She called Stanley out of his bed and fastened on his lead.

Another of Stella's surprises. While he'd been worried about upsetting her, she was concentrating on the case. He was sure she didn't know there had been anything serious between Lucie and her father. She was able to put aside personal feelings for the bigger picture. He could only dream of being like her. Inchoate with emotion, Jack could only nod.

'What shall we do about the toys, since you don't want to hand them into Lost Property?' Stella asked. 'You shouldn't go back to the cemetery on your own.'

'Let me check a few things.' Jack wasn't ready to share the idea he was forming. He wasn't ready to take it on himself. He jumped up and rattled at the handle of the back door. 'Where's the key?'

'Same place as usual, with the forks in the cutlery drawer.' Stella slung on her rucksack. She knew him well enough not to ask why he was going out the back way.

'Lock up after me.'

On the patio an icy blast stung his cheeks. Stella stood by the door, the dog at her side. Behind her the kitchen looked cosy; an aroma of stew lingered. Hauling himself up onto the wall at the back of the garden, Jack imagined going back with her to her flat and drinking hot milk on her spotless cream sofa.

'Be careful.' But his words were flung away by a powerful gust. Balanced on the garden wall, he turned to wave. The kitchen was dark.

He caught the distant slam of the van door, the engine firing, the sound drowned by the howling wind.

Forty-Nine

Sunday, 27 October 2013

The south-east window in Palmyra Tower looked out on to the looping spans of Hammersmith Bridge. On the sill were sticks and coils of twine that Jack had collected from the riverbank as a child. These were shored up by flint and limestone washed smooth by the Thames. On top of the 'embankment', Jack had laid the steam engine.

He took out the two carriages from his workbag and coupled the new rolling stock to the engine. He repositioned everything on the ballast. He had a train. He contemplated his tableau.

He heard the sneeze of the funnel and shaded his eyes from the smoke. The hot furnace made his skin smart and his arms ached from heaving shovelfuls of coal. At full pelt, pistons racing, the engine could do fifty-four miles per hour.

The sink glugged. He went over, ran the hot tap and chased out the airlock. Yet again the water was cold – he must email the consortium – but then it went warm again, and the issue lost its urgency. He returned to his train and became aware of the buzzing he heard intermittently and had vaguely attributed to a trapped fly or wasp. A red light winked on the burglar alarm sensor above the window. The instrument should be pointing to the front door to catch an intruder at the only possible point of entry. It was pointing at him.

Jack was about to reposition it, but it was delicate, he could break it. It would be there for insurance purposes. As he had told Stella, the tower was safer than anywhere. Elbow resting on the table, chin on his cupped hand, he imagined tucking into Dale Heffernan's lamb stew in the Pullman car.

This fantasy was shattered by the memory of earth and stones raining down. The tunnel had caved in on the train. Jack had blamed himself for the miscalculation of width and roof strength. But he never made stupid errors.

He fetched his binoculars from the north window sill. He trained them on the beach by Black Lion Lane where he had gathered the flotsam and jetsam. No one there. He swung the glasses away and tracked the towpath along through Furnival Gardens to the bridge. A lone car was making its way across to the Barnes side.

Jack lowered the instrument. He picked out a cotton bud from a pot on the table and dipped it in a pot lid filled with steam oil. He loved the delicate smell of the oil. Holding the engine steady, he travelled the bud along the coupling rods and over the crosshead and sidebars. In a hoarse voice he spoke to Glove Man's ghost: 'Dust is the enemy of wind-up clocks and steam engines. It must be kept out of the mechanism. Oil enables smooth working, but the paradox is that it also attracts dust.'

His memory of that afternoon in the kitchen garden was visceral. He could see every step of his construction. The roof struts had been strong; he had designed the width of the tunnel to allow for wide rolling stock. He had made no error in tension or loading. Simon had hijacked the engine and driven it too fast into the tunnel.

Few had known Jack had lost his red steam engine. One of them was Simon. He had made the mistake of confiding in him: he had hoped that if he told Simon a secret it would get him off his back. But Simon was dead; he *was* off his back. Jack had tried not to be relieved when his father showed him the newspaper cutting, but he had hoped that his bad memories would die too.

As if to reassure himself, Jack went to his desk for the cutting. He shifted his laptop, moved aside his *A–Z* and the lamp. No cutting. He looked underneath the desk, widening his search to the floor and under the bed. No cutting. He emptied out his treasure box on to the bed, but the cutting wasn't there, nor had he expected it to be. He remembered leaving it on the desk. Stanley must have taken it. Jack tried to remember if Stella's dog had visited since he had taken the cutting from his box, but his sense of time since moving to the tower was unreliable. Yesterday seemed years ago. Years ago uncomfortably close.

Jack scratched day-old stubble on his cheek. He didn't need the cutting to know that Simon was dead. For a long time he had relegated him to a dark unvisited place in his mind. Someone else must know about his red steam engine.

You denied you knew me. Three times.

His mind was not his own.

The Smiths 'How Soon Is Now?' drifted into his head. Jack stuck his fingers in his ears, not expecting it to work since it was inside his head, but it did lessen the sound.

Jack found his phone. 'Lucie, it's me.'

'Of course it is,' Lucie May crooned. It might be three in the morning, but Lucie was, as he expected, wide awake.

'Please would you search your files for a mugging in 1998?'

'Honey, there's been a few of those!' She guffawed. 'Drill down for me, would you?'

'A teenager called Simon was found dying in Chiswick Cemetery that year.'

'Why didn't you say? "*Body Found in Graveyard!*" Come!'

The line went dead. Jack left the tower.

Fifty

Sunday, 27 October 2013

'It was mistaken identity.' Lucie May was eating a carrot, still with a flourish of leaves attached to the end, as she leafed through a bulging file.

A fire burned in the grate, drawn curtains shut out the damp gusty night. Jack sipped the mug of hot milk and honey she had presented him with on arrival and nestled into his corner of her sofa.

'Proof, if we need it, that life is stranger than fiction.' She handed Jack a photocopied sheet on which she had scrawled, '*The Sun*, Saturday 24th 1998.' She took a bite of the carrot. 'I played a blinder with that story, straight into Fleet Street, it paid for a new boiler. Called myself Lucille to please my mother! God rest her.'

DEAD MAN WALKING

By Lucille May

Two sons. Two futures. One life. Madeleine and Harry Carrington kept vigil for hours by the bedside of the young man they believed was their 20-year-old son Simon until he died.

Found badly beaten in Chiswick Cemetery on 20 October by a woman walking her dog, the man never regained consciousness. The dog owner, Joan Evans, told us she assumed he was a tramp until she saw his 'nice shoes'. Her neighbours' son wore an identical pair. His face hugely swollen, he was identified by Harry Carrington for his shoes and light blond hair. Blinded by tears, he signed permission for his only son to have emergency surgery on his internal organs.

The young man battled for his life. His 13-year-old sister read him messages from pals, family and our readers. His mum read articles about bridges and tunnels – Simon was to be a civil engineer after graduating from the University of Sussex. The family played his favourite song, the Smiths' 'How Soon Is Now?' and told Simon they loved him until his heart stopped.

When the pathologist, Dr Peter Singer, was preparing to conduct the post-mortem he noted the medical records. Simon Carrington's eyes were brown, and he was six feet one inch tall. The body on Singer's slab had blue eyes and was five foot ten. Simon was missing half a finger on his left hand. The dead man's fingers were intact.

That night 20-year-old Simon walked through the door, toting his dirty washing, asking, 'What time's supper, I'm famished!'

Detective Superintendent Terry Darnell told a crowded press conference, 'We are overjoyed that Simon is alive. However, someone's son has been murdered. We must establish his identity so his family can grieve. We will work to bring his killer to justice.' Asked if the police had any leads, he declined to comment. Darnell dismissed any connection between the man found dying in Chiswick Cemetery and the decomposing body of a man discovered a stone's throw away, locked in Chiswick Tower, ten years ago almost to the day, in October 1988. That man has never been identified.

'So how come you missed this?' Lucie sounded as if she was astounded Jack had not read all her articles.

'I wasn't living in the UK,' Jack said.

'Fancy.' Lucie May gave a shrug of mild disapproval.

In 1998, Jack, like Simon, had been twenty years old. Simon wasn't dead. Jack was supposed to feel relief. He did not. He had told himself that the idea of his mind being invaded was absurd. It was a symptom of tiredness or, as Stella might have said, 'his overworked imagination'. Simon wasn't dead. He had never been dead.

Jack marshalled himself. 'The attack was in Chiswick Cemetery, so why was Terry involved?' Chiswick Cemetery was opposite Jackie's house. Stella had been wandering around it a few hours ago. So had someone else.

'The young man died in Charing Cross Hospital, and the two police divisions cooperated on the case with Terry in charge.'

'Did they ever identify him or catch his attacker?' The print swam. Jack put down the article. *Simon was alive.*

'A damp squib of a story! The police had the dead kid's fingerprints on file. He was eighteen. They hadn't checked because of the kid's father identifying him as his son. Fancy not remembering your boy had lost a finger! None of the family spotted it. Sounds like my family. I could have sat down to supper with an arm missing and my dad wouldn't have batted an eye.' She nibbled the carrot down to the leaves and tossed the clumsy bouquet on to the table. She went on, 'Shock, he said. His wife looked embarrassed. Unhappy pair. Anyone could see she wished it was him on the slab instead. The dead boy was Ryan Morrison, unemployed, no qualifications, an incompetent petty thief. His prints were all over two houses in Corney Road. The owner of the other house had caught up with Morrison and chased him into the cemetery. He reclaimed his transistor radio and a toaster and smashed Morrison to a pulp. Job done, didn't think to let the police know!'

Lucie scrambled off the sofa, walked on tiptoe to her drinks cupboard, did a pirouette in her stockinged feet and returned. She was on another of her wagons, Jack concluded.

'He got a suspended sentence for a disproportionate response. We had sacks of letters in his defence, many saying "good riddance" to Morrison. There are some lovely people out there!' She gave a corncrake laugh.

Simon hadn't been interested in tunnels and bridges at school.

Jack remembered Simon rolling coins over his fingers, the stump moving like a lever. The coin flashed and danced before his eyes.

If Simon was alive in 1998, it didn't mean he was alive now. Jack banished the thought. You only got so many wishes that another person was dead before you had to die yourself.

'So, I hear Terry Darnell's boy's been found?' Lucie May switched on an e-cigarette and regarded it happily.

'Who told you?' Jack snapped.

'Who didn't! It's all over Hammersmith Police Station. The Dowager Darnell is swinging from the rooftops, crowing that she's got her baby back. I was thinking, maybe she'd do an exclusive for the paper. It's a great story!'

'It's private.' Stella would be horrified. Lucie gave short shrift to Suzie, the love of Terry Darnell's life, at least according to Jackie.

'If only Terry had lived to see him.' Lucie was fleetingly pensive. 'Anyway, darling, what's your interest in Carrington?' She puffed on her e-cigarette, eyes bright with news-hound fervour.

Jack told her about the steam engine and the carriages, and about the boy who had tried to be his friend when he was seven.

'You're saying this steam engine means that this bloke is telling you he *still* wants to be your friend twenty-eight years on?'

'He's the only one alive who knows what the engine means to me.' Lucie, like Stella, didn't have time for semiotics or portents; neither woman would change plans because of a squashed lump of chewing gum shaped like a shark on a pavement. 'I don't think he wants to be my friend any more.'

'Your steam engine was in the papers.' Lucie scowled as she vaped on the e-cigarette. 'You had a tantrum in the street cos your dad wouldn't buy you one. Hardly top secret.'

'Most people won't remember. But Simon won't have forgotten. You've put here that he was training to be an engineer: when we were at school he wanted to be an astronaut.'

'A typical little boy's ambition. Like wanting to be a train driver, it's not real. Or not usually.' She blew steam at him.

Jack didn't say that when they were boys Simon had shadowed

him, copied his gestures, taken out books when he returned them to the library. Had he copied his ambition and made it his own?

'How would he know where you are and why would he care enough about Stella Darnell to be creeping among graves after her? If the guy's an engineer, presumably he's got some engineering to do.' Lucie puffed out another cloud of steam.

'If he's following me, he would know Stella is my friend.' Jack went cold. Simon had been following Stella. Jack needn't wonder how he'd found her; the Simon he remembered would have found a way.

'Here's my take on this, Jackdaw. Some kid left the engine at the station. A bloke – any woman would have handed it in – is rushing for his train and he dumps it where a driver – you, honeykins – will see it. The parents will have reported it lost if it's worth a bob or two. Mystery solved!'

'Passengers aren't allowed beyond the gate where the monitors are.'

'Oh and this Simon character would let that bother him?' Lucie widened her eyes.

Despite him telling Stella they were dealing with the meticulous planning of a ruthless professional, Jack couldn't see how Simon could know about his shifts: he agreed them at short notice. Simon would have needed access to his rota. A shadow of unease passed over him; again he reassured himself that at least in the tower he was safe.

Lucie batted his arm. 'Listen up! After you left the other day, I dug out my file on your "One Under". I texted you, remember?'

'Oh yes.'

Ring re RF inquest. LM. Some detective, he had forgotten about it.

'After the inquest, the widow was at it hammer and tongs with Rick Frost's brother in a side street. You know me, never off the clock. I hid behind a van and watched it all.'

'They were having sex?'

'No! Arguing. I couldn't hear them, but they looked fit to kill. Suddenly they start kissing like two bloody turtle doves, not breaking, but making up. They saw me and sprang apart. I added in a para about them comforting each other and left the rest to the imaginations of our gifted readers. Even so, my soiled nappy of an editor said we couldn't use it.'

Which brother was Lulu Carr upset about? Another lie. Like Stella, Lucie liked hard evidence. He had hard evidence. Jack gave her the glove Stanley had stolen from Lulu Carr's house and left in his tower. Handing it to Lucie, his fingers tingled. His intuitions were never wrong.

'This glove was found in Rick Frost's house. Did Terry tell you the names of the children whom the police interviewed about their lost gloves? This one has the letter "F" inside the lining. That might be a "W" or maybe a "V", but it's smudged.'

'Now you're talking!' Lucie flung down her e-cigarette and, scrambling off the sofa, ran out of the room. He heard her taking the stairs at a faster pace than he imagined her capable of. She returned with another manila file and another carrot. He wouldn't dampen her resolution with a warning about excess consumption of beta-carotene.

Lucie licked a forefinger and, flicking through the file, drew out a page of lined foolscap covered with what looked like crazed hieroglyphics. Her shorthand was faster than most people's speech.

'Terry told me this in confidence – pillow talk! I keep a secret by forgetting I know. If I'm ever hypnotized, governments will fall. Luckily I wrote this down. This is just for you, Jack.'

Jack wasn't fooled. Lucie claimed to adore him, but she worked alone or, it seemed, with Terry. Anything she shared would be chalked up as a favour to him that one day she would call in. He felt a coil of unease, less about the prospective favour, than because he saw he was right about Lucie's relationship with Stella's father. Stella must never find out; it would break her heart.

'So here's the list. Alphabetical and look who's at the top!'

Jack tried to take the sheet of paper from her, but she held on to it and jabbed at it with her carrot. He leant over and read the name she was pointing at. 'William Frost!'

The first step in a case was to assemble the jigsaw pieces. Only then could you begin to fit them together. They had a lot of pieces.

'There's more!' Lucie was clearly enjoying herself. 'Not long after Glove Man was found, a boy came into Hammersmith Police Station and reported seeing a man and a woman going up there the year before. The timing fitted, but when a detective went to get his statement, the kiddy did an about-turn and claimed he'd got the location wrong, he'd meant Chiswick House grounds and he couldn't describe the pair. The policewoman ticked him off for wasting their time. Terry reckoned that the first story was true, so he went to see the boy, who was adamant it was Chiswick House grounds. The parents got antsy, said he had only been trying to help. Terry's hunch was that the boy had been warned off by someone, but with the mum and dad standing guard, he couldn't pursue it. So that was that.' She whacked the sheet of paper with her carrot, her e-cigarette bobbing between her lips. 'Brace yourself, Jackanory!'

Jack didn't need to brace himself: his nerves were taut piano wires. Like Lucie's secrets, he had tried to erase Simon from his mind, but he was alive. Simon was inside his mind.

'In 1988 the boy was ten. He'd be thirty-five now.' She clamped a hand on Jack's leg.

'Guess what?'

'What?' Jack obliged.

'The boy's name was Richard Frost!'

'Otherwise known as Rick Frost,' Jack exclaimed. 'Yes!'

Fifty-One

October 1988

'What did you say?'

Simon eased forward in the deckchair; then, feeling undignified, he struggled out of it and went to the supplies cupboard in the corner of the hut. He propped a foot on one of the packing cases that served as seats for foot soldiers. With Simon's promotion, there was only one foot soldier: the Captain who was now the Private.

The Private lingered in the doorway, his body angled as if he might turn and run, yet the dull lustreless look in his eyes belied this. His angular body was framed by the grey mausoleums, headstones and a manicured yew tree in the cemetery beyond.

'Come in, *Richard*!'

The boy flinched as if hearing his real name spoken had hurt. He stepped inside and, in a belated attempt at attention, clicked his heels together.

A shadow fell across the doorway.

'Who's there?' Simon shouted.

'It's me, Captain.' Nicky came in and, giving a sharp salute, fell in beside the boy.

These days it was a proper unit, Simon thought. Justin had never answered the note Simon had put through his door.

Why didn't you say I was your friend when he asked?

The question presented itself as it had repeatedly over the last year, since they had found Justin by the river.

Letting the others stand there, Simon inwardly reviewed the facts to himself. Justin and Nicky had been his friends and they had betrayed him. Mr Wilson had betrayed him, but he had been punished and, until two weeks ago, Simon had almost forgotten about him.

Simon could find no proper punishment for betrayal. Yet no one could get away with such a terrible crime. His mummy had betrayed him. Simon blinked away this thought.

'You must be punished,' he informed them.

'I did exactly as you told me.' The boy was pulling at his middle finger the way he used to do when he was imitating Simon. He was frightened, but Simon supposed he was mimicking him and it fuelled the inchoate fury that these days was always gnawing his insides. A sense of injustice was corrosive.

'I went to the police and told them that when I said I saw a man I had made a mistake.'

'He did. I went with him,' Nicky suddenly said.

'Did I say you could?'

She shook her head, whether in agreement that he hadn't said she could or because she found him too much, Simon couldn't be sure. He wanted to trust Nicky. He tried to explain to her, 'We are an undercover unit. We never show ourselves. Especially not to the police. You shouldn't have gone too. Neither of you should.'

'You ordered *me* to go.' The boy was distressed.

'I told you to go and undo the bad you did. You shouldn't have gone to the police in the first place. This unit stands together. You tried to get me put in jail. You are a traitor!' Simon fought to stay calm. 'You must be punished.'

'How?' The Captain was perhaps anxious to get the torture over with. 'I did what you said and I've been demoted.' He looked down at his chest as if to show there was nothing left of him.

'What would you do if it was me?' Simon hit on a method that would stay with him all his life: to punish people with their own demons.

'I d-don't...' the boy stammered.

'You'd have me court-martialled and shot.' Simon smiled, raising his eyebrows for confirmation. 'Remember?' He saw from her face that Nicky did. He saw her like him a tiny bit more.

'I didn't mean that.'

'I think you did and it's a good idea, don't you think, to set an example?'

Simon strolled past them to the door and cast a look across the cemetery. Dusk was falling. At this time of evening, the shadows shifted and it seemed that the statues moved. Simon wasn't afraid. Not any more.

He had brought the hut back into service as their HQ. The tower had been out of commission and now had police swarming all over it. The eyot had been occupied by the enemy. Simon knew he went there. He left him little signs: he moved the stones, he planted some bulbs, but had no idea if Justin had seen. Simon didn't pretend that Justin was his friend. When he had seen him on the eyot, he had looked right through Simon as if he was no one. He had denied that he knew him. The final betrayal.

Mr Wilson had told Simon that the disciple Peter denied knowing Jesus. Three times, it said in the Bible. He had said that by doing so Peter hadn't just betrayed Jesus, he had betrayed himself. Simon now understood what he meant. Justin was lost to him as a friend, but he was lost to himself too. Only Simon could save him.

'I didn't say I saw your mum going into the tower that day. I lied and said the people I saw were in Chiswick House grounds and were not a man and a lady. My brother even told them he had lost the glove. I did everything like you said.' Richard hiccoughed.

'You didn't lie. You never saw my mother,' Simon said. 'Why did you go to the police at all? You thought you were cleverer than me. If you go there again, I will tell them the truth. That you are a murderer and that your brother lied for you.'

'They told me off for wasting their time.' The boy scuffed his boot with the soft earth at his feet.

'You are not fit for this unit.' Simon echoed the Captain's own words.

'Give him his glove back, Simon. It's not even his, it's his brother's, so he's already been punished by him for taking it and getting him involved with the police. We all know Richard is innocent. This is a silly game. Let's stop.'

'Please let me go.' The boy made the mistake of nodding his thanks to Nicky.

'Please what?'

'Please, *Captain*.' The boy rubbed his nose on the sleeve of his windcheater. Simon had forbidden him to wear his Captain's jacket: he had seen that if he stripped him of the trappings of authority – uniform and rank – he could sap him of his strength, his identity. He could make him nothing.

Taking a bottle of Coca-Cola from the supplies cupboard, Simon put out a hand. Nicky tried to hand him the bottle opener, but Simon indicated the campaign table. Slowly she laid it down there as if giving up a gun. Simon snatched it up and, applying it to the bottle, prised off the cap. He didn't toss the cap away, as the Captain had done at their first meeting, he placed it with the opener on the table like the spoils of war.

'You see, the thing is, if either of you were to tell the police, or anyone about anything, you'd be put in prison. Your glove is evidence.' Simon was perfecting an imitation of his father: reasonable, always careful to explain a situation. His father, a psychiatrist, would be able to see right into their heads. Simon had convinced the unit that he could too.

'It's his brother's glove,' Nicky reminded him. She looked very pale, as if she had begun to guess there was more to the boys' exchange, that it was not a game.

'Have you told him?' Simon didn't address the question to her.

'No.'

'No what?'

'No, Captain.'

'See, if you did, I'd have to tell them you called my mother bad names. You lied to them – I'd have to tell them that too. I'd have to tell them everything that happened.'

The boy started nodding and didn't stop.

Simon had envisaged Nicky as official codebreaker, his

right-hand man. 'Did he tell you what he said about my mum?' he asked her.

'Ye-es.' She reddened. 'He shouldn't have, Simon, he knows that. It was mean.'

'Can I have my glove?'

The boy had no sense of timing or nuance. Of this, Simon, better able to read minds than his father, was openly scornful. 'You can go now,' he told Nicky.

'What are you going to do?' She was obviously frightened, but her sense of justice got the better of her. Perhaps the girl sensed that the time when Simon no longer valued her had not yet arrived.

'We are going to have a chat. You can go. Be back here tomorrow and we'll form a plan of action. We have much work to do. The police will be on the watch, so we have to resort to deep cover.' Simon was cheered by this prospect.

Nicky hesitated, looking at the Private. Then, with obvious reluctance, she retreated out of the door. Once outside she darted between the graves to the path. Simon waited until she had become another shifting shape in the cemetery, a trick of the light.

'What's going to happen?' The boy was quaking, his eyes – hazel flecked with green – never left Simon.

Simon let a silence fall before he answered, 'One day I'll come for you.' He addressed the Coke bottle. 'The thing is, you won't know what day that is until it comes.'

Outside, Simon kicked at a pile of leaves by the door that hadn't been there yesterday and, reaching in, shut the door. Zigzagging across the cemetery, he avoided uneven ground and toppled headstones, on the lookout for Nicky, whom he wanted to trust. Until it was shrouded in gloom, he saw with satisfaction that the door was still closed. The Captain had done as he had commanded.

At the gate, in a pool of lamplight, Simon consulted his Timex watch. He noted that it was teatime: toast with honey and a mug of hot milk. As she always did these days, his mummy sat in the sitting-room window, watching for him. Or so he told himself.

Simon had noticed that since the day when he had tracked his mother to Stamford Brook station, she had reverted to how she used to be with him.

From now on, he decided, he would stop being nice. Everyone would have to be nicer to him.

Fifty-Two

Sunday, 27 October 2013

Jack shut his flat door. His clock said half past five. He had been with Lucie May for an hour. Walking there and back didn't count: he hadn't broken his promise to Stella, he imagined telling her.

Moonlight slanting in through the north window etched in silver his few bits of furniture – the bed, the cupboard, his desk and chair – like a photographic negative. Outside the beam of light everything was in deep shadow. Soon it would be dawn.

He flicked on the green lawyer's lamp on his desk and everything shrank to prosaic normality. He went into the kitchenette.

The twine, pebbles, sticks worn by the tides and bleached by the sun, and the flattened ballast were bathed in moonlight. The steam engine and the two carriages had gone.

Jack tore around the circular space, shoving aside books, papers, jumpers, shirts; he shook the duvet until the futility of his search caught up with him, a wolf snapping at his heels. He came back to the window and sat at the table. The binoculars lay where he had left them before going out to see Lucie. He snatched them up as if they might vanish too and looked out through the window.

Two lorries were on Hammersmith Bridge, heading into town. A centimetre adjustment took him several metres north. There was something by one of the buttresses. He twiddled with the focus although it was already sharp. It was only the barrier for buses. He combed the towpath either side of the river and arrived at the eyot. An area of pitch dark. He became accustomed to the lack of light and distinguished the swell of the tide and the gradual emergence of the causeway. He couldn't see anyone on

Chiswick Mall, or beneath the stone porch of the church, but he sensed a shift in atmosphere. Someone was there. Someone was watching him.

The same someone who had found their way into his tower and stolen his train.

Simon knew where he lived.

He ran to the window in the bathroom. He had told Stella there was no need to have frosted glass so high up.

The narrow walkway outside was well below the level of the windows. Only a high-wire artist would consider launching a ladder from it.

Yet Simon had got inside.

Jack could write to the landlords, ask for extra locks. He could have Stella's London bar and her many mortices. Jack stormed back to the main room. He pulled up the lid of his laptop and typed in his password. He changed his password every week. He chose set numbers from his timetable on random dates picked from his diary with his eyes shut to ensure they really were random.

If Simon could get into his mind, he could break the code.

Jack's fingers raced over the keys. He told Palmyra Associates there had been an intruder but that nothing was stolen. Strictly speaking, this was true: the train wasn't his. He said they must have been disturbed, but that he expected them to return. As he wrote this, he realized how upset he was. He had believed the tower to be impregnable, but it was not. He asked them to treat his request as urgent and pressed 'Send'. The message remained in his Outbox. He tried again and saw the problem.

CBruno. The other router had kicked in again.

He clicked on the drop-down list, but CBruno was the only router offered. He dived under the desk. His router was off. He clasped it in both hands and, clumsy and impatient, he indiscriminately pressed every button. At last it flashed with a series of lights that steadied to the required blue. Getting up, he heard the sink glug.

'No you don't!'

Frantically Jack ran to the sink and turned on the tap. Water thundered around the sink, splashing his chest, his face and the draining board. He turned it off and reached for a towel to mop his face. He glanced at the floor beneath the window.

The train was on the floor. The engine must have tumbled off the ballast and pulled the carriages after it. The stones had given way under the equivalent of a weight of over a hundred long tons. Jack had put artistic interpretation above accurate engineering. His father would never have done that.

He was relieved that, thanks to C. Bruno's router, he hadn't managed to send the email. Simon had not after all got into his tower. He was crediting him with too much power. Stella and Lucie had agreed on one thing: after all these years, Simon would have forgotten him.

Out of sight, out of mind.

Before going to bed, Jack confirmed that the outer door was secure. He went up to the top of the spiral staircase and confirmed that the skylight to the roof was locked and that the bolts were secure.

Inside the flat, he turned the mortice key and left it at an angle so that it couldn't be pushed out of the keyhole from the other side and then teased beneath the door, a trick he had used himself. The door fitted exactly within the aperture, so that not even gas could escape, but in the past Jack had achieved the impossible: he took no chances.

In bed, he was reluctant to turn out the light and lay looking at his books ranged on a shelf above the cupboard. His roving gaze halted at the purple-spined copy of *Strangers on a Train* by Patricia Highsmith. He jumped out of bed and pulled it out from the others.

> When Guy Haines meets Charles Bruno on a train he cannot know that his life will change forever. Charles Bruno proposes a sinister deal – each will murder for the other – Guy assumes he's joking until Bruno calls and says he's kept his part of the 'bargain'. Now it's Guy's turn…

Charles Bruno. *CBruno.*

A search on Google Images netted at least five Charles Brunos: two black, three white; all but one were smiling. None looked mad. Or bad. Charles Bruno was just a name. Jack reconnected to his own router, deleted his email to Palmyra Associates and logged out. The C. Bruno who owned the router – Colin, Christopher perhaps – had doubtless never heard of *Strangers on a Train*. Stella would say he was over-complicating things. She would say none of it was to do with Jack's past; they were investigating a murder and the murderer was out there somewhere, trying to stop them.

Jack returned to bed and turned out the light. He heard creaks and cracks as heat ebbed from the cladding and floorboards settled. The Smiths' 'How Soon Is Now' began, increasing in volume, as his mind took over. Entering a dream, Jack told a sheeted figure that the words, the chords, the melody – such as it was – were embedded in the walls, in the body of the tower.

How Soon Is Now? was a message from the dead man.

Fifty-Three

Monday, 28 October 2013

'It's the letter I forwarded to Nicola earlier this month, it's been returned, I guess by the owner of the house. It seems she's moved.' Liz regarded an envelope lying between Stella's latte and her Americano with hot milk on the side. 'I didn't like to open it.'

They were seated in a coffee shop on Hammersmith Broadway. Liz had rung Stella when she was cleaning Terry's old office at Hammersmith Police Station and asked to see her 'as soon as possible'. Stella had opted for the only place she knew that was both close to the police station and allowed dogs. Stanley lay under the table, his head resting between his paws.

'So what do you think?' Liz asked.

'About—'

'Shall we open it?'

Two years after his death, a letter occasionally came for Terry. Stella disliked having to open them. But this letter might solve the case. Lucille May would have no compunction about ripping it open. Jack neither. Would Terry open it?

Nicola's London address was printed in capitals, small and neat. Stella had seen the handwriting before; Lulu had scoffed that her husband wrote like a twelve-year-old. 'This is from Rick Frost,' she exclaimed.

'I forwarded it last week, that doesn't make sense—'

'This is postmarked the sixteenth of September, the day he died.' All they had to do was open it. She had tried to take Jack in hand for not opening his post as soon as it arrived. Between his work at London Underground and Clean Slate, she was sure he earned well, so it couldn't be the worry of bills that put him off. As with so many things to do with Jack, Stella found she couldn't ask him why. 'If your friend Nicola is coming back, we can give it to her.' Stella found a solution.

'And if she doesn't?' Liz added milk to her coffee, holding the jug high so that it came out in a long thin stream. 'Isn't this the evidence your dad's policeman friend wanted?'

'Martin can't open mail on our say so – we might have stolen it. It's probably "interfering with the mail, intending to act to a person's detriment without reasonable excuse", or some such. And that neighbour down in Charbury saw Nicola, so she's not "missing".'

'We don't know where she is now,' Liz pointed out.

'We don't know where she was planning to go, so we can't say she didn't arrive,' Stella echoed Martin Cashman's line. She took out her phone. 'I'll call Lulu and ask exactly what the neighbour said.'

The phone rang and rang; Stella mouthed an apology to Liz. She was about to give up when Lulu answered. Stella asked for a blow-by-blow account. She was annoyed with herself for not asking for it the first time they spoke. Terry would have done.

'I was about to ring,' Lulu yelled. 'Nicky's landlady called!'

'What did she say?' Stella was ready with her Filofax.

'Her name's Chris Howland – for Christine, I suppose. Honestly, the things people mind, she was quite tetchy that Nicky went without saying goodbye.' A blast of air roared down the earpiece; Lulu bellowed over it, sounding as if she was at sea in a storm.

'Can you talk now? You sound as if you're outside,' Stella asked. She wrote down the name 'Christine' and underlined it and nodded to Liz, but Liz was looking at her phone and didn't see.

'Yes. Chiswick Cemetery. I'm weeding Mum's grave. It's her anniversary,' Lulu shouted.

There must be some moral code about talking on a mobile phone in the presence of the dead, Stella thought, and looking up saw scraps of rubbish flying across the Broadway like crazed birds. A newspaper had caught against the railings outside the Underground, held there by the force of the gale. Commuters scurried past the plate-glass windows, pushed and buffeted by the wind. When the café door opened, a strong gust blew napkins off the tables and scattered sugar sachets. The storm that forecasters were warning of was building.

'Christine was upset Nicky had typed the note!' Lulu bellowed.

'What's wrong with typing it?'

'She said it was too official. I told her: Nicky doesn't do "friends", if we don't count trying to steal my husband. And no, I didn't say that to her. I promised to call her if Nicky turns up – she wants to hand back some excess cash; Nicky had paid in advance – if she lets the house before the lease expires. I told her to think of it as compensation for the typing! The woman's a forensic specialist!' Lulu spoke as if this explained everything.

'You have Christine Howland's number?' *Detection wasn't just about asking questions – it was asking the right questions.* Lulu, scatty though she seemed, had been more thorough than Stella gave her credit for. Stella felt as if a fog had settled above her head, stopping her thinking straight. This came of having so little sleep over the last few days.

When she ended the call, Stella apologized again to Liz.

'Don't mind me. Justin's just texted, suggesting I visit him at home, that's a step forward!' Liz looked radiant.

Stella rang the number Lulu had given her.

'Chris Howland?' A woman answered with the preoccupied tone of someone too busy to talk.

'Stella Darnell here, I'm looking after Nicola Barwick's house in London.' Embarrassed by her fib, she flashed a look at Liz, but she was texting on her phone. 'You returned Nicola's letter.' She paused. Nothing. 'Nicola didn't mention leaving Charbury so, like you, we're surprised.' She went for a point of commonality.

'I should have kept it. She's coming back.'

'She called you?'

'No. I was doing a last tidy – incredibly I've got a new tenant

– and I found her purse and her passport in the kitchen bin of all places. She'll be back, she can't get far without her passport!'

After the call, Stella turned to Liz. 'Something isn't right. Why would Nicola throw her passport and money in the bin?' But Liz wasn't listening.

'Stella, could I just use your phone? I was in the middle of replying to Justin and my battery has gone. It would be simpler to ring him.'

Stella watched Liz weave her way through the café to the street. Her coat billowed out when she stepped on to the Broadway. Whoever this Justin was, he was making her smile. Jackie said that was her definition of 'Mr Right'.

'He sounds nice,' Stella remarked when Liz returned. 'What's his second name?' She felt suddenly duplicitous; Liz might not be inclined to answer if she knew the true reason for her interest.

'It's rather Mills and Boon. Venus. Justin Venus. Lovely, don't you think?'

'Yes.' And familiar. But with so many clients, most names struck a chord. Although Stella did think she might remember someone named after a planet.

'Confession, Stell! I've done that thing we did when we were girls – I practised writing Elizabeth Venus!' Liz gave a harsh laugh. 'It's not like I want to marry him and if I did, I'd keep my name. Don't say a thing!'

Stella didn't have a memory of doing this at school or whose name it had been if she had. She came to a decision. 'Hold on to the letter. If you see Nicola, tell her Christine Howland's got her purse and passport. If she doesn't turn up in the next twenty-four hours, I'll tell Martin Cashman.'

Outside the café, Stella texted Jackie to say she was running late for their catch-up meeting. Afterwards, she watched Liz crossing the Broadway at the pedestrian lights, her light eager walk unchanged since they were sixteen. Liz had always been optimistic. To her, good things had happened before, and they would again. Liz would put Justin Venus in this bracket. Stella should feel happy for her, yet she didn't.

Had Stella watched her old friend a moment longer, she might have noticed a man in a long dark coat with pale features step from the shadows of the arcade and follow Liz into Hammersmith Underground station.

When Stella returned to the police station compound where she had left her van, she received two texts. Jackie wanted to shift their meeting to later in the week and Suzie wanted her to come to her flat as soon as she got the text. With no meeting, Stella now had time.

Ten minutes later she parked outside her mother's flat. Her phone rang, but she didn't recognize the number on the screen.

'I've lost my phone. I'm in a call box.' It was Jack.

'Can you remember where you last had it?' The sort of annoying question Suzie would ask; if Stella had lost something she never knew where or when.

'My flat. This morning at eight thirteen.'

'Have you given it a thorough search?' Suzie again. Stella glanced up to the top floor of the mansion block, almost expecting to see Suzie and Dale framed there. There was no one at the window. 'I'm sure you have. It'll turn up, it's a small space.' She was conciliatory.

'I'm not so sure, it's like I'm living in a vortex. I've lost that paper with the numbers on it too.'

Stella was surprised, despite his floaty way of being, Jack was always good with actual objects, he never lost things. He sounded distressed, but it was usually she who assumed the worst. It occurred to Stella that he was quite like Liz: he had faith that something good would happen, although his optimism couldn't be based on what had gone before.

'I'll get you to ring when I'm in the tower so I can trace it. That's if the battery hasn't drained.'

'What about that "Find my phone" app?' It was rare for Stella to offer Jack technical advice.

'Never thought I'd need it; I've never lost it before.' He did sound upset.

Stella told him about her conversation with Chris Howland and her decision about the letter. He said nothing about the letter; she knew he would have opened it there and then. She guessed he'd have no trouble opening other people's post if required.

'Is he a relation of Alice?' he asked.

'Who?'

'A girl in Charbury went missing in the sixties. Big case at the time. Lucie May did a follow-up on it. He *must* be related to the girl. Things come full circle; in the end there's only one story, although we always hope for a different ending.'

'Chris Howland is a "she". She's a forensic scientist,' Stella added for no good reason. Lucie May filled Jack's head with unpleasant stories; Stella brought him back to the present. 'It means Nicola Barwick's alive. It also means she's still a suspect for murdering Rick Frost.'

'She's in trouble.' Jack was grave.

There was a series of beeps.

'Jack?' Stella looked at the phone screen. The call was still live.

'Here I am. I've fed in more coins.'

'I'll call you.' Stella swept the glove box for loose change before realizing how absurd she was being; it wasn't her that needed the coins. Lack of sleep did not agree with her.

'No need, I've got plenty.'

'How do you make out she's in trouble? Doesn't this imply Nicola Barwick has something to hide?'

'Chris Howland didn't actually speak to Nicola. She's right – a typed note is official. It's easier to trot out a message with a ball-point on the back of a circular. Howland thought they had a rapport so the typing jarred.'

'Suzie types faster than she writes – her handwriting is unreadable. I wish she would type the lists she leaves for me.' Suzie hadn't left one of her lists since she went to Sydney.

'A typed note might be written by anyone.'

'She signed it. Odd, though, when I did the cleaning estimate for Liz, I saw a laptop on the desk in Nicola Barwick's study. Liz said it was Barwick's, so what did she use to type it on?'

'She could have had a tablet. But did she have a printer? I vote we get that letter and steam it open. Please can I be the one who does it? I love doing that. Or I think I would,' he added quickly.

Stella raised her eyebrows. Jack would steam open his own post – if he could bring himself to open it.

'No, it's illegal. I've told Liz we'll wait for Nicola Barwick to call her. Why would she throw her purse and passport into the bin? It's like the man who sat the wrong way in the photo booth. How could she do that by accident?'

'Accidents don't happen. She wanted Howland to find them. She *hid* them in the bin. The note was intended to make us think Nicola Barwick had gone abroad. The passport and purse are signs that she hasn't.'

'Are you saying she's been kidnapped?'

'Maybe not bundled unconscious into a car boot. She probably walked out of the cottage, but found a pretext to go back into the house and that's when she dropped them in the bin. Clever.'

'A risk. Christine Howland mightn't have seen them.'

'She had to act quickly. You said Howland is in forensics; Barwick guessed she'd check the bin. I'd know you'd check through the contents of my rubbish bin.'

'I'll call Martin. He said to if we had proof.' Jack knew how she would behave. Stella liked that.

'The note isn't' "proof" – the opposite in fact – so he won't be impressed.'

Stella could imagine Martin telling her that it added up to sweet nothing. When he had promised Terry to be there for his daughter, he hadn't bargained on nuisance calls from her.

'Where are you?' Jack asked suddenly.

'I've just got to my mum's. She wants to talk about me. It'll be about investing in Dale's business.' Strange question, Jack never asked where she was.

'Are you going to invest in it?' He sounded far away.

'The guy can cook, it might work.'

'Stella, those photos you found in that passport booth at Stamford—'

Jack's voice was drowned out by more beeping. Stella waited for him to drop in some coins. When the beeps stopped, she remembered. 'Does Justin Venus mean anything to you?'

Her question fell into phone silence.

Fifty-Four

Monday, 28 October 2013

Please may we meet? We need to discuss Stanley.

Stella reread the text. David had softened his request by implying he would negotiate. When he had asked her to look after his dog, she had refused, relenting only when the alternative was kennels. A dog required endless walks and tireless games with tuggy rope spiders and squeaky toys. Months on, she had built into her routine the blowy strides on Wormwood Scrubs common or Richmond Park with Suzie, and now with Dale too. Her mum had advised training classes: Stanley needed discipline. After weeks of these, it baffled Stella that he would 'sit' and 'stay' at her command and come when she called. She began to take care of his toys, restoring Mr Ratty – the stuffed rat he took to bed with him – to his original cream colour with sluice washes.

Stella had brought Stanley for their afternoon outing to Wormwood Scrubs common. Dale hadn't been at Suzie's that morning. Stella wondered if he was in on Suzie's proposal, typed and bound, 'ready for the bank'. The document was in her rucksack. Suzie seemed to have forgotten that she had advised Stella to stick to the core activity of cleaning and not risk ruin.

In her old bedroom, Stella had seen an album like the one displaying the history of Dale's business. She guessed that Suzie had bought it for volume two of his life story. No doubt she was going to put herself and Terry – his lost parents – in it.

Some women might have been upset by their mother's obsession with a long-lost son. Stella, ever practical and expecting little, took it in her stride. She hoped, though, that her mum would at some point return to her job at Clean Slate.

Stanley was bounding around on the grass with a stick three times his size, desperate to impress her. She pressed the 'rapid shutter' button on her phone and took pictures – although she wondered if she would want to look at them after she had handed him over.

Stella realized she didn't want to give Stanley back. Then she revisited her earlier observation; despite David's text, there was no room for negotiation.

S will be at the police memorial in Braybrook Street on Friday @ 2pm. She pressed 'Send' before she could cancel the text. It was two o'clock now, she had four days to pack Stanley's things. Tonight she would wash Mr Ratty.

The text had dented her good mood. An hour ago Jack had emailed an account of his findings. Although heartened that he had laid out all the information gathered so far, Stella was worried too: a typed report wasn't Jack's method. She had some sympathy with Christine Howland's response to Nicola Barwick's typing. Maybe talking about his school friend and finding the toy train had shaken Jack up more than he had let on. Jack had been about to say something about the photo-booth pictures when he was cut off, but had put nothing about them in his report. She opened it again. He had used the Courier font as if he'd written it on a typewriter.

```
Update Report for Clean Slate Investigative
Agency (CSIA)
Jack Harmon (agent) 28/10/13
```

- A boy called Richard Frost reported a man and woman entering the tower on the night of the 1987 hurricane. When police followed up, he said it was two men in Chiswick House grounds. (Source: Lucie May – Terry thought first story true.)

- A boy, William Frost, was interviewed about missing glove. Glove Stanley took has crown motif like first one. Police failed to connect WF to RF – see first bullet point. (Source: Lucie again.)
- After Rick Frost's inquest William and Lulu rowed in street then kissed. Proper kissing. (Source: Lucie.)
- Darryl Clark – Piccadilly line driver of train that hit Rick Frost thought I was on platform. (Link: Station inspector and Simon Carrington.)
- Meant to say that the den where you found 2nd carriage was used by Frost's gang in the eighties. (Lucie told me.)
- To do:
- Ask William Frost about his relationship with Lulu C. It changes everything.
- Ask William Frost about Rick F's childhood gang. Who was in it? Ask him for advance on expenses. (Jackie said about expenses. I've just thought about gang.)
- Ask Liz Hunter the name of Nicola's friend.
- Check out Rick Frost's study at his home – ask Lulu Carr (Frost-whatever)for access to his computer.

Jack x

Stella pictured Jack in rolled shirt sleeves, glasses on the end of his nose, pecking the keyboard with two fingers like a private investigator, around him a semi-circle of screwed-up balls of earlier drafts. A good image, although he could touch-type and didn't have a printer in his tower. Without having been to his house, Jack assumed that Rick Frost had an office in his home; he thought like a detective, she thought. On the other hand, it was a safe assumption that a man involved in surveillance had a computer.

Stella looked up. A man was under the trees. Stanley was heading towards him. She blew on her whistle. Stanley hesitated and then trotted with renewed purpose towards the man. The man didn't have a dog with him. Not everyone liked dogs. Since minding Stanley, Stella had become suspicious of anyone walking on commons or in parks without a dog. She whipped the lead from around her neck and hurried over the grass.

'Stanley!'

In the failing light of the impending storm, Stella saw the man was wearing a black coat. It was Jack. Jackie must have told him where she was.

Stanley halted and crouched low on the grass. Stella felt a twinge of guilt that he made his distrust of Jack obvious. She blew her whistle again and the recall training paid off; abandoning the stick, Stanley belted back to her. She rewarded him with a morsel of chicken and, straightening, splayed out an arm in semaphore greeting to Jack. There was no one there.

It was dangerous to shelter under the trees in a storm; surely Jack knew that. Stella set off at a pace across the grass towards where he had been. The wind was back in force and the sky threatened rain. Stanley trotted in front, stopping to make sure she was behind him.

Far off she heard the rumble of thunder and looked around. She was alone on the common.

She reached the trees and it was as if dusk had fallen. The mesh of branches above cut out what little light there was.

'Jack?' She felt awkward calling out his name. It might be like the other night, when he hadn't got together the courage to admit he was nervous of the tower. Her boots loudly crunched over a bed of beech-nut shells.

She took out her phone to see if he had texted. Nothing. She was about to put it away when she saw a symbol at the top of her screen. She peered at it. It was a pair of staring eyes.

Stalker Boy. The logo of Rick Frost's app. William Frost again.

'Stell-ah!'

Confused by the wind, Stella had no idea where the voice came from. She retreated deeper into the trees. She had to find Jack.

Over the two years she had known him, Stella had learnt to put up with Jack's odd behaviour. His sudden departures out of the back door, a propensity to sing nursery rhymes and recite poetry, and above all his night-time searches for his 'True Hosts', those with a mind like his own, intent on eliminating those who got in their way. She had made him promise to stop walking the streets at night. Yet Jackie advised it was best not to try to change people, to let them be.

'Stella!'

Stella crept around a tree trunk and looked out across the common to Braybrook Street. There was someone by her van. She took a few steps over the grass. It was William Frost.

'You've been stalking me!' she exploded at him. Walking past him, she fired her key at the van.

'I wouldn't go as far as calling it that, though I confess my brother's app got me here.' As if the app had transported him to her against his will. It explained the watching eyes on her screen. Stella felt her heart rate slow down.

Tempted to tell him where to go, she thought of Jack's report and said, 'We need to talk.'

'That's why I'm here.'

She strapped Stanley into his seat, thinking fleetingly that after she had given him back there would be no use for the seat; she would get it removed. She climbed in the driver's side.

'I've got questions.' This wasn't how Terry did it: no tape machine, no plain-walled room and no second interviewer. No Jack. In fact she did have a tape recorder. 'Are you OK if I record this?' She showed him her phone.

'Am I under caution, Detective Darnell?'

She fitted the phone into the cradle on the dashboard and, preventing herself from saying 'For the benefit of the tape', flipped to her notes in her Filofax.

'The police interviewed you in the eighties about a lost black glove. Where did you lose it?'

'I didn't lose it.'

'You told the police you had.'

'My brother stole both my gloves; he lost them. A glove was found on some man who died in that tower by the river. I told the police that I'd lost my gloves in the park. Christ knows why I covered for him, but Rick was scared stiff of heights, he couldn't climb a stepladder, certainly not a tower, so it was a harmless fib.'

Stella fumbled in her pocket. 'Is this your glove?' She thrust it at him, hoping Jack's hunch was right.

William took it off her and turned back the cuff. 'There's a "W" inside, the "F" has worn away. My mum and her labels! But where did you get this?'

'Do you know Nicola Barwick?' She heard Terry in her head: *You ask the questions. Don't give away what you know.*

'She was a friend of my brother's. Did she have this glove? Nicky wouldn't have killed him, if that's your theory. She was a kind girl.'

'Why "was"?'

'*Is* then. What is this, am I under the spotlight now?'

'Do you know where Nicola is now?' *Don't be led by the interviewee.*

'Not at this moment.'

'What were you arguing about with Lulu – with Tallulah Frost – in the street after your brother's inquest?' *Surprise them with your questions, give them no chance to anticipate or rehearse.*

Stella clicked her ballpoint on and off to agitate him, then remembered the microphone and stopped.

'I told her I thought that Rick had been murdered. She refused to believe me.'

Safety first: avoid being trapped with a person you suspect of murder. Don't ask questions likely to inflame. The houses in Braybrook Street were dark; if she shouted for help, no one would hear.

'Why didn't you tell us you were having an affair with Tallulah?' *Avoid open questions and tackling a point head on.*

'Because I'm not. Any more,' William said after too long a pause.

'You didn't think it pertinent to tell us this?' *Know when to be silent.*

He loosened his shirt collar, although the top two buttons were undone. 'It's over.'

'Why is it over?'

'Tallulah – or Lulu as she'd restyled herself – promised she'd leave my brother, but kept putting it off. When Rick was killed, I ended it, the whole thing had got out of hand. I couldn't live with the guilt. I had betrayed my brother. I was having a relationship with his wife and when he asked for help, I wasn't right there. I missed his call. But listen, I didn't want this to divert you. I didn't kill my brother and nor did Lulu, or at least—'

'You hinted we should talk to her. Was that out of revenge? Did you plan to frame her?'

'No! It was me that ended it, so it would be stupid to take revenge on her.'

Stella momentarily lost the thread of her argument. Was this what it was like for Terry? *Stain by stain.*

'You said you ended it because she wouldn't leave. Presumably if she had left her husband, then you'd still be with her.'

'I don't know. I thought I knew her, but I'm not so sure.'

'Meaning?'

'I have a feeling that someone's following me.'

'Like your feeling that your brother was murdered?'

'If you like, yes.'

'Why do you think it's Lulu?'

'She has the most to gain from Rick not being around. Simple.' He gave a shrug.

'Are you sure it was her?' Stella remembered Lulu arriving back, excitedly telling her and Dale that she had seen her husband in the street with his mistress. Had the 'husband' been William, not Rick? William had left her.

'With this app I can check where someone is. It was definitely her following me.'

'You were with Nicola Barwick.' Stella was gratified by his look of surprise. Like a boxer she must concentrate on one area and then suddenly go for another part of the body – mix it up.

'That's why I was coming to see you. I think that whoever was threatening my brother is after me.'

Rain pattered on the roof of the van. Black clouds made a false dusk that merged with the trees where Jack had stood. Stella hoped he wasn't still out there.

'Where were you the night your brother died?' *Stick to the basics.*

'I already told the police, I was at home alone, working, so yes, no alibi, it could have been me.'

He turned sideways in his seat to look at her as he had done the night she had taken him to Gunnersbury station. Then she had supposed he was one of Jackie's Mr Rights. How simple that problem seemed now.

'But it wasn't me.' He leant forward and touched her arm. 'Stella, you have to believe me.'

Stella's phone buzzed with a text. Excusing herself, she turned off the recorder.

Can't see you tonight. Driving. Jack had found his phone.

If Jack was out there, he could see her with William. She dialled his number.

'This is Jack, who are you? Tell me after the beep.' Her patience evaporated.

'Could I use your brother's app?'

'I should have told you sooner.'

'Your app?'

'Tallulah or Lulu's at home, if that's who you want, I checked.'

'It isn't.

Stella submitted to William's instructions – she couldn't say she had used the app before. When she put in Jack's number, up came the *Seek and destroy* icon. The cross hairs zeroed and found the target. Her heart thumped. Jack was on Du Cane Road, passing Wormwood Scrubs prison; if she went now she might catch up with him.

'I have to go.'

'Stella, I—'

'Now!'

She leant over and pushed open the door for William to get out. 'I'll call you,' she shouted back to him as she drove down Braybrook Street.

Fifty-Five

Monday, 28 October 2013

'Where's Jackie?' Stella burst into the office.

'Gone home. She got a text from Jack. She's put me in charge!' Beverly was Jackie's assistant. She was in her mid twenties, dressed immaculately in a short black dress with precise make-up, a precision that didn't extend to her work. Kneeling amidst piles of papers on the floor, Beverly tackled the filing as if searching for something. 'Shall I make you a cup of tea or coffee?' Beverly made perfect tea.

'No thanks.' Stella had the urge to say 'yes', to sit at her desk and plan next week's rota, scrutinize application forms, fix visits with prospective clients and prepare quotes. She could not. She had a case to solve.

'What did Jack want?'

'He told Jackie he was passing her house and noticed a window open. She's gone home to close it. When she got there, she found it was closed! She thinks Jack got the wrong house.'

'When was this?'

'An hour ago. She asked me to lock up. I've done it before.'

Stella couldn't absorb the detail. By the time she had got to Du Cane Road, there was no sign of Jack. The wind was blowing and it had been raining hard and in his dark coat he was as good as invisible. How had he got to Corney Road so quickly?

'I was going to drop Stanley off with Jackie, but, um—'

'She said to say I can look after him,' Beverly said.

'Are you any good with dogs?' Stella only trusted Jackie with Stanley.

'My mum breeds poodles, and I help out.'

'OK then.'

'We're old friends. Actually, I was about to say, I think he needs a drink.'

When she looked back through the wired glass in the office door, Beverly was putting a document into a drawer in one of the filing cabinets. Stanley was snoozing in his bed by her desk. He was more at home in the office than she was.

'You didn't tell me about William Frost?' Stella said as soon as Lulu Carr opened her front door.

'Sorry, is that your business?' Lulu eyed Stella coldly, no longer the scatty woman who Stella had assured Jack wasn't capable of murder.

Establish who has the most to gain by a person's death: usually the spouse, partner or close relative. 'Gain' doesn't have to be financial.

'I'm investigating your husband's death, so yes, it is my business.' Stella stepped into the hall and, closing the door, leant on it. This wasn't how she talked to her cleaning clients. 'I think it's time you started telling me the truth.'

'You weren't truthful. You pretended to be a cleaner when all the time you were spying on me.'

'I didn't know who you were until I found your husband's driving licence.' To Stella's surprise – she had expected her to brazen it out – Lulu appeared to accept this.

'My husband killed himself. They said so at the inquest, but William said it was murder, that Rick would never kill himself. William was just looking for a way to dump me. He behaved as if *I* killed him. Well, I've proved him wrong!'

'How?'

'Come with me.'

Lulu went up the stairs, so Stella had to follow her. On the way up, she tried Jack again.

'This is Jack, who are—'

'I've found out who killed my husband.' Lulu went into Rick Frost's study. She sat down in the black swivel chair and scooted the mouse about. The computer screen awoke.

Stella was looking at the picture of a room, taken from above. It showed a black chair, a desk and filing cabinets. It was the room they were standing in. There was a man sitting in the chair. With a shock, Stella realized she had seen the back of his head before. She looked behind her. Above the door, a camera was fitted to the wall. A red light blinked. It was on.

'I cracked Rick's password. My brother suggested I try his company registration number and he was right. This is who Rick told William was a threat.' She jabbed at the screen. 'He killed my husband.'

Lulu moved the cursor and the man on the screen came to life.

He opened a drawer in the desk, shut it and opened it again. He took something out. Stella moved closer. It was a belt with bullets in it. As she saw this, Lulu opened the same drawer in the desk and pulled out the same belt. She put it back and shut the drawer. The man put the belt back.

He sat so still that Stella thought the film had stopped. Then he leant forward and seemed to be peering at the desk. He took something from his jacket and scribbled on it as if crossing something out. Then, as if startled, he got up and went to the door. Stella saw his face. It was Jack.

She grabbed the mouse off Lulu and paused the film. She read the date and time at the bottom of the screen. It was the day she'd found the driving licence. The time was eleven minutes past eleven. The time when Stanley had barked outside the landing cupboard. Now she knew why. Jack had been in there.

'This man didn't kill your husband,' Stella said firmly.

She bent forward and looked along the desk, as Jack had done in the film. She ran her finger over faint indentations in the veneer.

'Is this the password?'

'No, his password isn't that long!'

'I wonder if it's the serial number for his phone.' She rummaged in her anorak pocket and pulled out the plastic bag with Rick Frost's phone that Jack had given her on Stamford Brook station, the night they visited it together. She pulled off the silver cover and squinted at the tiny lettering on the back. There wasn't a serial number.

'Whose phone is that?' Lulu Carr asked impatiently.

'Your husband's.' Too late Stella realized that the police would have given the phone to Rick Frost's next of kin, his wife, not his brother. William must have taken it from Lulu without her knowing.

She shook her head. 'No, it's not.'

'What do you mean?' Lulu never said what Stella expected her to. In that respect she was rather like Jack.

'He scratched his initials on the back of his phone. So worried about people stealing it. That doesn't have any scratches on it.'

'Are you sure?' Stella looked at the smooth shiny black surface. Not a scratch in sight. The phone in fact looked brand new.

'Of course I'm sure. The man was obsessed with holding on to his stuff. That's not his phone.'

'So who has his phone then?' Stella asked. And, she thought to herself, who left a brand new phone with no data on it where the police would find it?

'Good question. I suggest we start with the man in this film. What's he looking at?'

Stella crouched down and examined the numbers on the surface of the desk. Jack had left the paper with the numbers on in his flat and it had disappeared. She drew open the desk and found the bullet belt that was on the film. She also found a block of sticky notes and a bundle of Bic ballpoints bound with an elastic band. Typical of Jack to take a pencil rubbing when he could have written them down. Then Stella remembered Jack's dictum about leaving no trace and inwardly apologized. Except Jack had left a trace: he had left a film of himself.

She began scribbling down the numbers on a sticky note and then stopped. Jack did nothing for effect or as part of some fantasy. He honed his skills. He had taken a rubbing because he wanted not only to reproduce the numbers, but to see how they were written.

She looked again at the laminated surface of the desk. Jack had noticed that the distance between the numbers varied. He had guessed Frost – it was safe to assume the numbers were carved there by Rick Frost – had been in a hurry.

'19 9 13 15 14   19 8 21 20   20 15 23 5 18   4 15 15 18'.

When she had looked at the numbers on the paper with Jack, before he said he lost the rubbing, he had suggested it was a serial number of a computer. She had thought it was the IP address of a computer, although the latter didn't fit. Now she saw that the gaps between the numbers were irregular. Some greater than others. They were regularly irregular.

'Lulu, I wonder if Rick left this as a message for you,' she said slowly.

'He was always leaving me messages. Stuck them all over the house. Cryptic notes letting me know he knew I'd seen my brother, or where I'd been. The man was mad.' Lulu began to cry.

Stella ripped open a handy pack of tissues from her rucksack and passed Lulu one.

'I think it might be a warning.' Stella was feeling her way; the thought had come from nowhere. 'If these gaps are to distinguish the numbers, then the first five are nineteen, nine, thirteen, fifteen and fourteen. Do they mean anything to you?'

'No, they do not!' Lulu flapped at the air with her tissue.

'If it's not a serial number, it might be a code.' Stella heard herself sounding like Jack. 'Did you have a code, you know, a secret thing between you both?' A question she had never asked a client. Thinking of Jack, she must tell him about Rick's phone. She dialled him again and got his answer machine. When they were looking at the pencilled rubbing, Jack had commented that Rick Frost only had one computer in his study. She had supposed he had special detective powers so she hadn't asked how he knew. He knew because he had been here. Jack had lied to her. Stella made herself concentrate on Lulu.

'We had nothing between us. Unless you count a wall when he slept in here.' Lulu gave a hooting snort into the tissue.

'If it was a code, it'd have to be something you'd easily get.' Stella found a tactful way to say that Rick Frost would allow for Lulu not being used to codes and computer languages.

'Rick lived in a fantasy world. I should have listened to Simon, he warned me that "the Captain will betray you",' Lulu wailed.

'The Captain? Do you mean William?' Stella folded the sticky note into her anorak pocket. No point in pushing Lulu once she was upset.

'Rick. Simon called him the Captain because of their idiotic army games. It was bad enough when they were kids, but Rick never grew up.' Lulu's eyes swam with tears. 'My brother says Rick only married me to spite him; he used to bully my brother when they were boys. I wonder sometimes if Simon has ever forgiven me for marrying Rick.'

'Why would Rick have wanted to hurt your brother?' Stella didn't like the sound of the brother. At least Dale wasn't like that.

'Rick hated my brother and I think Simon was right, he hated me too. Rick watched me from this computer. There are cameras all over the house, haven't you noticed?'

Stella had noticed. She had thought they were burglar alarms.

'Rick wrote "Activity Reports" detailing where I had been, what I had been doing and who with. I found them all on the computer. Whom, I mean,' Lulu added.

'Whom.'

'Sorry?' Stella roused herself.

'Grammar. My brother's always correcting me, a horrid habit that I've caught off him.'

Stella wasn't listening. She ran her finger over the marks on the desk. Perhaps they hadn't been scratched directly on to the laminate, but were indentations from pressing too hard on paper with a ballpoint. Frost hadn't written them for Lulu; if he had, he would have taken a less subtle approach and left her notes all over the house. He had written the numbers down and sent them somewhere, but whom had he sent them to?

'If he watched you constantly, then Rick must have known

about William.' Stella didn't know whom to believe, Lulu or William. Neither. She got a feeling in her solar plexus. It was one of Terry's hunches. 'Lulu, don't take this the wrong way, but do you think your brother could have had anything to do with Rick's death?'

'You've been talking to William! No I do *not*. My brother looks out for me. When I told him about the Captain and Nicky, he reminded me that he'd promised to protect me. William's only jealous; he says I don't need protecting. All those boys think Nicky is Miss Perfect.' She dabbed at her nose with the tissue. 'This code-thingy was probably for her, she was Enigma Woman!'

'She was what?' Stella fought to keep bafflement at bay.

'In their unit, Nicky-Perfect was the Official Codebreaker. I can't imagine there were many codes to break for a bunch of kids sneaking about a graveyard wearing flower pots and shooting insects!' She balled up her tissue and tossed it at the scratches on the desk.

'Who was Nicola Barwick with when you saw her in Chiswick Mall that time? It can't have been Rick, as you told me then – he was dead.' Stella tried to keep on track.

'My brother,' Lulu muttered. 'He said he'd stopped seeing her, that I was right not to trust her. He had her by her arm, holding her tight, all over her like a rash. He lied to me!'

Stella examined the numbers she had copied on to the sticky note. The most obvious code was to swap out numbers for letters, but that was too easy. Then again, while Rick Frost had been hot on surveillance, it seemed he was a kid at heart. He mightn't have been a genius with codes. The one and the nine were together – so nineteen – then a gap followed by a nine and another gap, then thirteen, fifteen and fourteen and a bigger gap. She calculated out loud, 'The nineteenth letter in the alphabet is "S" and the ninth is "I". The thirteen is "M" and—'

'Simon,' Lulu whispered.

'Simon what?'

'Carrington.'

'Isn't your maiden name Carr?' Stella quelled frustration.

'My father wasn't my real dad. Mum had an affair and I'm the result. I don't know my real father's name so I shortened Carrington to Carr. Like I said, I wanted a "fresh start".'

Stella doubted that lopping off a bit of your surname amounted to a fresh start. 'If we assume the numbers closer together are one word, then this could be a message. Four words starting with Simon.' Stella put a line between each word. 'This next one has four letters. Another "S" and eight is—'

'I told William that I guessed Rick had found out about us and he killed himself. It proved he loved me after all.' Lulu's words were blurred with sobs. She snatched up her tissue from the desk.

'It's an "H",' Stella exclaimed. 'The two and the one are close together so "twenty-one", which is "U", and then twenty. That's a "T". "Shut"! "Simon shut". What did he "shut"?'

'How should I know?' Lulu huffed. 'A case, his mouth, my mouth, a door—'

'A door! Yes, this last grouping has four numbers. The first is "four". A, B, C, D. "Simon shut something door". To make sense it should be "the", but there are five letters. We know twenty is a "T", then we've got fifteen and a twenty-three.' Stella counted out the letters on her fingers. She got lost and started again.

'Tower,' Lulu offered dully.

'"Simon shut tower door".' Stella folded her arms. 'What kind of sentence is that? Is it another code?'

Lulu had stopped crying.

'Lulu, where is your brother now?' Stella demanded.

'Simon was so sweet to me when I was small. When Dad was cross with me, he would say I wasn't his daughter. Simon would take me out for walks by the river and tell me not to listen to him. We went to his HQ in the cemetery where he was the Captain. He once gave me a bottle of Coca-Cola. It tasted of blood, but he told me it was a magic potion to keep me safe. He'd say, "It's you and me, Lulu, against the world." When we were first married, Rick hated me seeing Simon and told me not to trust him. William once said he loved me. No one had said that to me before, but after Rick died, William became like him and Simon. They were always checking up on me.' She tossed her hair back. 'My brother's got this thing on his phone; he can find me wherever I go. To protect me, he says.' She slumped back in the chair. 'So has William. Rick gave it to him.'

Stalker Boy. Stella said nothing.

'Does your brother protect you?' Lulu suddenly asked.

'I don't need protecting.' As she spoke, Stella wasn't so sure.

'Who's that man?' Lulu nodded at the picture frozen on the computer screen.

Stella had hoped Lulu had forgotten about Jack. 'My colleague, he works undercover,' she said. 'So, exactly when did you tell Simon Carrington – your brother – about your affair with William?' Was this how Terry felt when all the disparate bits of information, subtle nuances and apparently random events started making sense?

'I can't remember. I told you they hated each other,' Lulu muttered.

Stella's eye fell on two framed pictures beside the monitor. They weren't in the paused film; Lulu must have put them there very recently. The photograph of Lulu's parents had been on the sitting-room mantelpiece downstairs.

The other one showed two people in their late twenties. Stella recognized Lulu and guessed that the man was her brother, he looked like the man in the picture with Lulu's mother, who it seemed was not her actual father.

Cleaners shouldn't have opinions about their clients' homes, while detectives should. Simon Carrington had delicate features framed by locks of dark hair. In black and white, she couldn't tell the colour of his eyes; they were light, almost ghostly. He was looking at the camera with such intensity that she felt he could see into her head. His gaze was empty, his face without expression. Stella considered again that Lulu didn't take after her mother. However, were it not for the stubble on his chin and lack of make-up, Simon Carrington might be his mother's double.

He looked like Jack.

Stella opened her phone and, fingers clumsy, swiped through her camera roll to the picture she had taken of Stanley dancing with his stick on the common. She tweaked it and enlarged the screen until it filled with the trees in the background. She manipulated the image until she found the man under the trees. He was out of focus, but his face was just about distinguishable.

Simon shut tower door.

'Is this your brother Simon?' Stella held up her phone to Lulu. Jack lived in a tower. She had to stop herself shouting at Lulu. 'Take a look.'

'How can I... Ye-es, I think so.' Lulu sniffed into the tissue. 'That doesn't mean anything. He goes for walks.'

But it did. Stella had seen the man before. He was the man standing on the lawn outside her flat. It wasn't Jack. He was the inspector at Stamford Brook station. *Stalker Boy.*

'Lulu, where is your brother now? Where is Simon?'

There was a creak on the stair. Both women shrank from the door. There was nowhere to hide. A faint buzz. Stella caught the camera lens tracking them. A red light was blinking.

'You left the front door open.' Warm and friendly.

Lulu pushed past Stella.

Stella stared at the man in the doorway.

'I was trying to tell you all this when you rushed off.' Holding Lulu close to his coat, he stroked her hair. William Frost looked over her head to Stella.

'Tell me what?' Thoughts, pictures, impressions. Stella tried to arrange them. *Stain by stain.* All the stains had joined up.

'When you asked me about the glove. I remembered that Rick had said it was to do with the glove. I ignored him. He was always coming out with stuff like that – the guy was paranoid, I know that. He had to control everything. But it got me thinking. After I told the police I had lost the glove in the park, Rick was nice to me, far nicer than necessary. Made me wonder, had I covered for him without intending to?'

'This isn't Rick's phone.' Stella waved the phone at William. 'Someone took his phone, swapped the case and left it for the police to find. You said Rick had the stalking app on his phone, didn't you?'

'Yes—'

'So whoever has his phone can find out where anyone they want is and stalk them?'

'If they have their number, yes.'

'Where is Simon now?' Stella shouted at Lulu. Simon was the name of the boy Jack said he had known at school. Jack said there was no such thing as coincidence.

'I don't know.'

'Where does he live? You must know!'

'I don't.' Lulu sobbed, waving her hands in front of her face as if clearing away cobwebs. 'He's very private. He takes me out for meals. I don't go to where he lives. His father left the house in trust to my mother – he cut me out of his will because I wasn't his. Simon gave me half the value of the house. He's a fair man, you see. The other day I walked past the house and saw it's up for sale.'

'They used to live next door to Jackie, in Corney Road,' William said quietly.

'Why didn't you say?' Stella demanded

'Why would I? I didn't think it was anything to do with who killed Rick.'

'There were two children next door, a sweet boy as thin as a rail and his cute sister, think her name was Lulu, something like that. Their parents' marriage was on the rocks, the dad was a psychiatrist with a fancy car, chap never passed up a chance to be sarcastic about his wife – talk about airing dirty linen! The boy was playing substitute husband, protective little mite. I made Graham promise that those parents wouldn't be us one day. I think we've succeeded! The boy – or man – moved out years ago, he rented the house out and is only selling it now. We're holding our breath as to who buys it. Good neighbours are gold.'

Stella remembered Jackie's words. She let the information fall into place.

'Stay here! Lock the windows, don't answer the door to anyone! If he has Rick's phone, he'll be using his app and will know you're both here. He knows we're all here.' She looked at her phone. There was a pair of staring eyes at the top of the screen. 'Turn off your phones!'

Stella snatched up the framed photographs and, shoving them into her rucksack, ran down the stairs and out of the house. Despite her instruction, she didn't think to turn off her own phone.

Fifty-Six

Monday, 28 October 2013

The wind whistled down Chiswick Mall, its screams and whines punctuated by bangs and smashes as flower pots, garden ornaments and benches were dislodged from window ledges and hurled on to the ground.

Shrouded in a billowing cagoule, hooded and shapeless, Liz Hunter could have been mistaken for being drunk or a passenger on the deck of a ship tossed and rolling in high waves. She swayed and staggered, to the left, to the right, into the gutter, stopped and set off again, quickening her pace. She kept close to garden walls and hedges. She paused every now and then and consulted her phone to reassure herself she was following Justin's directions. She looked up and saw the tower. She was here.

She checked her phone again; Stella hadn't replied to her text.

'Let's see the letter?'

She jumped. A man stepped out of an alley. It was Justin. She nearly hugged him, but he didn't like being hugged. He looked annoyed.

'Can we get out of this wind?' Liz shouldn't have texted Justin and told him about the returned letter. She had hoped he would have advice, but he seemed cross. Maybe he minded after all that she hadn't told him Nicola's address. She had been so pleased with herself for demonstrating to him she could be trusted to say nothing. She should have waited for Stella. She should have done what they agreed and waited to see if Nicola would come for it.

Although she had been looking forward to this, their first meeting in his home, Liz was suddenly sure she shouldn't have come.

'No need to worry about the letter. Indeed, from now on there's no need to worry at all,' Justin remarked pleasantly. His crossness apparently gone, he took her hand.

'That's marvellous!' She laughed, although she didn't feel in the least like laughing.

'This way.' He led them down a narrow passage that smelt of rotten leaves and urine. The bricks glistened in the lamp-lit dark.

'I feel bad, Justin. You see, I decided to open it. It's from the man who died at Stamford Brook station whom Nicola knew when she was little. It's a list of numbers. Twenty-seven altogether. Justin, are you any good at deciphering codes?'

'As you say, let's get out of the storm. I've brought us a bottle of champagne and cheese and biscuits. I hope you like brie. Come up to my tower!'

'This is *your* tower! How amazing!'

Fleetingly, Liz Hunter considered whether it was wise to have told no one where she was going. Then Justin drew her close and she breathed him in.

Fifty-Seven

Monday, 28 October 2013

A strong gust of wind buffeted the van. Forecasters were warning people to stay inside unless their journeys were strictly necessary. A storm called St Jude was going to hit southern Britain tonight. It was strictly necessary to find Jack.

Stella saw she had a text. Jack always contacted her in the end. It was from Liz. *Call me.*

Liz would have to wait.

In the dark, headlamps in her rear mirror dazzled her. She couldn't tell if she was being followed.

There was no point going to Jack's tower, he had told her he was driving. He didn't answer his phone when he was on the trains. She drove around Hammersmith Broadway twice to try to lose Carrington if he was out there, and then pulled off into Sussex Place. Immediately she saw her mistake: it was a dead end. She flung the van around and headed back towards the Apollo on the Broadway. She slowed down and checked her mirror again, although Carrington couldn't be behind her. She'd stopped in a parking bay opposite a mansion block, and confirmed the doors were locked. Just in case, she kept the engine running.

Stella forced herself to think rationally. If she called Martin Cashman, he would remind her he required evidence that Nicola Barwick was missing, that Rick Frost had been killed by Simon Carrington. If he had, Lulu Carr and William Frost would be unreliable witnesses at a trial. William had lied about his glove and not been honest about his relationship with Lulu. Even if the glove was matched to the one on the dead man, it wasn't a link to Simon.

Lulu didn't know truth from reality. The Piccadilly line driver might identify the photo of Simon, but his testimony wouldn't stand up in court because he had initially thought the man on the platform was Jack. Simon Carrington had been clever; he featured nowhere.

Simon. Stella's heart was palpitating. This was like a game of Patience: the cards were falling into place, with one card blocking a suit.

She reached into her bag and lifted out the pictures. In the light of the street lamp, Simon looked nothing like Jack. His mother was smiling off camera at someone to her left. Stella could see a snippet of shoulder. Someone had been cropped from the image.

Out of the blue, Stella smelled Dale's scones. She trusted her olfactory sense. She had seen the woman's face before. The sight of her mother holding Dale's album flashed up. Stella realized where she had seen the woman. She texted Suzie: *Send photo of first page of D's life story.*

There was one person who would help her get evidence for the police. Stella drummed on the steering wheel, dismissing the idea. The van was hit by a vicious squall, it lurched and she dropped her phone. She scrabbled for it in the passenger footwell.

She had run out of options. She brought up her contacts list and found the number. Against any better judgement Stella had ever had, she pressed 'Dial'.

'Stella Darnell here. Are you free?' She waited. Then: 'I'm on my way,' she said.

Fifty-Eight

Monday, 28 October 2013

There were no rattling casements or creaking joists. Jack couldn't hear loose tiles crashing off roofs or recycling bins and bottles clattering along empty streets, hurtling and twisting. The only sign of the storm were murky grey clouds that streamed across the sky, joining and re-forming, and flurries and blusters tearing at the surface of the Thames.

Jack sat in the Hammersmith Bridge window, resting his binoculars on the heel of his palms. A coil of steam rose from his mug of hot milk. The domestic scene belied his mood: he was full of foreboding.

He had been positive that he had lost his phone in the tower. But he had looked everywhere and not found it. He had tried to email Stella, but the storm must have caused his internet connection to break. He had decided to find a phone box and ring her, but when he stepped out on to the walkway, he was blown over to the rail by the force of the wind and admitted defeat.

Though Jack knew he was safe in the tower – if he couldn't get down, no one could come up, yet he didn't feel safe. When Stella had shown him the passport photo of the back of the man's head, he had said he didn't recognize him. He recalled the image. It wasn't so much the head, but the back of neck, above the shirt collar. It might be nearly thirty years, but Jack knew who it was. His senses attuned to the slightest sound or movement, he trained the binoculars on Chiswick Eyot.

Somewhere out there, Simon Carrington was alive and he was watching.

Fifty-Nine

Monday, 28 October 2013

'It's the Detective's Daughter!' An electronic cigarette cocked above her shoulder, Lucille May exhaled a cloud of vapour. Stella caught a whiff of peach.

Stella had expected this. Lucille May relied on sex appeal, she didn't relish female competition. Least of all from the daughter of the man who, Stella suspected, was the love of her life. Stella had convinced herself that Lucille May wasn't Terry's type, but she didn't know what his type was.

'Come in, since you're here.' Lucille waved the cigarette in vague invitation and sashayed on pink leather pumps to her sofa.

'Tea, coffee, water? If you're still off the booze.' Lucille twisted the top off a bottle of mineral water, gulped from it and flopped back, apparently exhausted, lending little weight to her offer.

'No thanks.' Stella ignored the jibe that was prompted by her refusing triple gin and tonics on previous visits. The water and the electronic cigarette suggested that Lucille May was on a health drive. Stella caught the buzz of a text. 'Excuse me.' She opened her messages.

'Social networking is vital these days. Not for me, of course, I'm established.' Lucille blew a peach-scented cloud towards Stella.

Suzie had photographed the whole newspaper cutting from Dale's album. Laboriously, moving the text into view on the small screen, Stella read:

FEARS MOUNT FOR MISSING TEACHER

Five years to the day since English teacher Nathan Wilson vanished, police say they have no clue to his whereabouts.

The forty-year-old bachelor, on a sabbatical from Menzies High in exclusive Vaucluse, set off last October on a three-month walking tour of New Zealand to 'feed his soul' and never came back.

Apart from a possible sighting in the NZ town of Wangherie and another on Manley's Shelley Beach early one morning, no one has seen or heard from Wilson, described by colleagues as a loner with no living relatives. Neighbour Byron Carter, who lived in the same apartment block in Cremorne, said Wilson introduced him to his fiancée (pictured left). 'The girl was quick to say he was "jumping the gun, they were just friends". Nat looked pretty crook, bloke was smitten.'

Inspector Todd Mangen of the NSW Police Force told a packed press conference at the Local Area Command on Pacific Highway this morning that Wilson's bank account has remained inactive and the mystery 'fiancée' has not come forward. They have no reason to suspect foul play, but with no contact from Wilson, they fear for his safety and welfare.

'We are in the dark,' Mangen said. 'It's as if Nathan stepped off the planet.' He appealed to anyone with information or who recognizes the woman to contact Harbourside LAC.

In the photo, the woman was resting her head on Wilson's shoulder. Some friend, Stella observed. Wilson was ducking to ensure he was in the frame.

'Don't mind me.' Lucille May regarded her nails.

'Read this.' Stella handed her the phone.

Amid a plume of steam, Lucie May languorously scrolled down the screen.

After what seemed to Stella a frustratingly long time, Lucille waved the phone, 'Jack said you knew, so why come to me?'

'Sorry?' Jack wasn't there when she was looking at Dale's album.

'The Prodigal Son! Doesn't Darnell Junior look like Simon Le

Bon. What a dish!' She fanned herself with a hand. 'Get you, Miss Marple. First you solve Terry's biggest unsolved case and now you've found his long-lost son.'

'What do you mean?' Stella's windpipe constricted.

'Terry went to his grave without finding his boy. I pulled strings like a crazed puppeteer, but nothing – and Mr By-the-Book wouldn't bend police rules. He dies and the Cleaner flies in on her magic broomstick and conjures up the lovely Dale!'

'Dad knew about Dale?' The words battered Stella's skull like brick bats.

'Mrs Darnell says to Terry, "Here's your new daughter, oh and by the way I gave away our son!"' She swigged some water. 'Sorry, I know it's your ma!'

'I meant the article next to it.' *Stick to the basics*. 'The one about the missing teacher.' Her dad didn't come to see his newborn baby daughter in the hospital for three days. He had always said it was because he was called up to hunt for the killer of the three police officers in Braybrook Street. Was it because Suzie had told him he already had a son?

Lucille May scrabbled under a cushion, retrieved a pair of black-framed glasses and jammed them on her face with one hand. Gone was the flaky manner; she studied the article with a frown, e-cigarette held aloft.

Terry had known about Dale. Stella looked about the room and made herself do a cleaning estimate, although there would be nothing to do. Lucille cleaned like a pro. Was that why Terry liked coming here? Was it in this room that he told her he had a son and swore her to secrecy because his daughter didn't know?

'She killed him.' Lucille May whipped off her glasses. 'Country as big as Australia, she could bury him in the outback and get on with her life.' She puffed on an arm of her spectacles, scowled and swapped it for the cigarette. 'So, you and Jackanory ride again!'

'He didn't die in Australia.' She gave May Lulu's photograph. 'This is Madeleine Carrington. Her daughter was married to Rick Frost, the man who died under that train in September. You covered the inquest.' She had to trust the journalist, even if it wasn't two-way.

Lucille May narrowed one eye and exhaled a plume of steam. She regarded the picture as if weighing up whether or not to believe Stella.

'It's the same photo as in the Australian article.' Stella pointed at the phone. 'You can see that the man cut out from the picture is the missing teacher, Nathan Wilson.'

'You're saying he did a John Stonehouse and faked his death?'

'Who?' Stella asked.

'Before your time, kiddo.'

'He covered his tracks. He wanted to start again. A fresh start.' Stella thought of the Clean Slate strapline.

'Some fresh start, he rotted in a tower!' May spoke with some relish. 'Let me get this straight, Madeleine Carrington killed her son-in-law, is that your theory?' Lucille asked.

'The framer's details are on the back; it's dated this September. Madeleine Carrington died a year ago. The date on the back is a week or so after Frost died under the train. Looks like someone else other than Madeleine cut Wilson from the picture.'

'Madeleine Carrington also went under a train at Stamford Brook. I wanted the headline "Station of Death" when Rick Frost died there too. My wimp of an editor vetoed it. She did it in front of her son. Riddled with cancer, she'd obviously had enough, but selfish all the same.' Lucille replaced the cartridge in her cigarette. 'I should have spotted the connection!'

'What if her son murdered her?' It was falling into place. Stella outlined the points to Lucille May. Simon Carrington had promised his sister it was her and him against the world. He hadn't forgiven her for countermanding his advice and marrying his sworn enemy; it was the last straw when he found out she was having an affair with the Captain's brother. To deflect him while not really understanding the level of threat she was deflecting, Lulu had suggested her husband was also having an affair with Nicola, the woman Simon had loved since he was a boy.

And then there was Jack.

'That's a hell of a leap!' Lucille pulled a face at her pun.

'Simon and Lulu's mother had an affair with Nathan Wilson. The date on that Australian article is in the eighties. Carrington was married with a son by then.'

'So when shy "boy next door" Nathan Wilson was crowing to his neighbour in Sydney about his fiancée, she was leading a double life.'

Lucille May finished her bottle of mineral water, rammed the bottle down until the neck met the base and screwed the top on. She tossed the crushed plastic at a waste bin on the other side of the room. It glanced against the rim and rolled away. Scrunched paper and wrappers around the bin testified to earlier misses.

'Time to take stock.' Lucille clambered over the top of the sofa. 'Grab an end.' She dragged a whiteboard out from the back of the sofa. 'Lean it against the fireplace.' She produced a pen from a packet under a sofa cushion, yanked the lid off with her teeth and knelt by the board.

'We'll start with Madeleine Carrington.' She wrote the name on the board. 'At some point she went to Australia either to see Wilson or she met him out there. Easy to verify and it doesn't matter for now. She is connected to Rick Frost, how?'

'He married her daughter Tallulah, now called Lulu.'

Lucille wrote 'Lulu' and drew a line between the names.

'Madeleine has a son.' Stella liked whiteboards and was at her best with flow charts.

'Name?' Lucille tapped the board.

'Simon. He is now our prime suspect.' Stella felt mildly silly using the phrase, but Lucille dashed down 'Prime Suspect' and underlined it.

'Does he know you suspect him?'

'Not as such…' Stella began.

'Meaning?'

'I spoke to a man I assumed was surveying on Stamford Brook station last week. I think now he was Simon Carrington.'

'What makes you think he wasn't a surveyor?'

'It was dark and he had no equipment.'

'Now you're talking like a 'tec!' Lucille drew a box around Simon's name.

'Jack went to school with a boy called Simon—'

'I thought I knew the name!' Lucille May flung down the pen and began to rifle through a heap of files on the coffee table. She detached a fat manila folder. 'Here we are. I found this after Jack had gone. Simon Carrington's the name of the CEO of the company that redeveloped the water tower. He's an engineer. I tried to interview him, but he never replied to my emails.'

'Simon is the only person who knows Jack liked trains when he was a boy. Jack thought he was dead.'

'So did his family. Another missed connection: I should have seen that. Carrington was the boy who didn't die at Charing Cross Hospital. I need a database.' She underlined 'Prime Suspect'.

Stella reached down to stroke Stanley; her hand swept the air. She had forgotten he was with Beverly. By now she would have taken him to Jackie's as arranged. When he was away from her, she had no means of communicating with him, rather like Jack. At the end of the week Stanley would be gone and she would never see him again. Jackie hadn't texted to say he was there. Stella forced herself to concentrate. Her head ached as if there were cogs turning slowly. 'As you told Jack, Rick Frost was the name of the boy who reported the couple near the tower. It must have been Madeleine Carrington and Nathan Wilson. My guess is he recognized Simon's mother and went to the police, and then Simon forced him to withdraw his statement.'

'There's a motive.' Lucille scribbled. 'Motive: tell police about Mum' next to 'Prime Suspect'. She tossed down the pen and clambered back on to the sofa, thumping a cushion for Stella to join her. Unearthing a Windows tablet from under the files, she opened it and, swiping at the screen, brought up Google.

'Teacher's name?' she barked.

'Nathan Wilson.'

'Nath-an Wil-son.' Lucille May typed with two fingers as Stella had imagined Jack doing for his report.

There were many Nathan Wilsons. Lucille skipped the offers to link in with Nat Wilson or be Facebook friends with Nathan of Idaho or of Bermondsey. She put in 'missing', 'teacher' and 'Australia'. Up came the Australian Federal Police website for missing people.

'Here we go.' She switched off her e-cigarette and handed it to Stella. She read out the wording on the masthead. '*One person goes missing every fifteen minutes.* That's two since you arrived here.' She shot a look at Stella as if she was responsible, angling the screen so Stella could read it.

According to the profile for *Wilson, Nathan Bertram*, he was last seen on Saturday, 22 November 1986, the year of his birth was 1947, his gender male. His complexion was described as pale, his hair and eyes were brown and build slim. Under *Circumstances* she read that Nathan Wilson was last seen at Vaucluse High School, Vaucluse, Sydney, NSW. He had told colleagues he was flying to Auckland the next day. It said: *The above photograph was taken in 1986. Police reported his passport missing from his Cremorne apartment. He never flew to Auckland. Grave fears are held for his safety and welfare.*

The man in the picture looked like Lulu Carr.

Lucille May scrolled through a gallery of photographs of missing people. Some were grainy or out of focus, others cropped from a group pose like in Wilson's picture, with disembodied hands on shoulders; the missing ranged from teenagers to older people. Jack believed there was a finite number of faces. If you lived long enough, you saw them all. Vaucluse was where Dale lived. Sometimes there had to be coincidences.

The types of photographs differed too. Some, Stella guessed, were scrambled out of a shoebox by a distraught relative. Passport-booth portraits, one black-and-white shot of a man not seen since 1966, the year Stella was born. Holiday snaps, a man in strong sunlight with a background of blue sea who had gone out to buy breakfast and never returned. Stella vaguely expected the pictures to betray some sign that the person was about to slip through the net of life. A faraway look in their eyes, a troubled expression, but none gave a hint of what lay ahead. They might have been her clients.

A banner on the website announced that 96 per cent of people are found within a week. Cashman had expected Nicola Barwick to return. She roused herself: 'Go to the UK Missing Persons' site.'

'Shut your eyes if you're squeamish,' Lucille warned. 'This is a gallery of dead people.' Deftly she resized the two missing person websites, the UK and Australian, on to a split screen.

'Bingo!' Lucille said under her breath. On the screen was Wilson's Australian profile, with the UK entry that Stella recognized as the one Jack had shown her.

Stella reread the list of clothes and items found with the body. The bottle of champagne and the child's glove. When she had looked at it with Jack, she had dismissed the sketch of the dead man. With only brown hair and a bone structure to go on, it couldn't be realistic. Comparing it to the photograph of missing teacher Nathan Bertram Wilson, she saw it was a good likeness. In the picture, Wilson was wearing a light blue jumper. A turquoise crew-neck jumper was listed among the clothes found on the body in the tower.

'Stella, you have matched a name to a face, or a skull!' Lucille was enveloped in a peachy fug. 'Nathan Wilson is Glove Man!' She handed Stella the tablet and returned to the whiteboard. 'So, when Simon was a boy, he locked Wilson in Chiswick Tower. The guy died. Carrington went back and planted Rick Frost's glove on the corpse, presumably to frame him. Is it possible he still held it over Frost when he was an adult? Surely Frost could have gone to the police and explained? Wait a minute.'

Lucille May scooted over to the coffee table on her knees and shuffled the files around until she found a file labelled 'One Unders'. Stella was grateful Jack wasn't there to see.

'Yes! I checked out the clients Rick Frost's company had. Only one by the end. Guess what they were called. Palmyra Associates!'

'So?' Stella was losing it. Again she tried to stroke Stanley. Jackie had promised to text when Beverly brought him. That was hours ago.

'Palmyra Associates are civil engineers. They do most of their work abroad. No website, but I looked at their listing at Companies

House and, wait for it! The most recent UK project is Palmyra Tower and, winding back, who is the CEO?'

'Simon Carrington.' Stella could not hide her own triumph.

'Right! Looks like Simon C. had Frost by the short and whatsits!'

'Rick Frost bullied Carrington when they were boys, his sister told me.' She didn't say that Jack had said he had been unkind to Carrington.

'This is one cool story!' Lucille May waved her e-cigarette like a conductor's baton. 'One less missing person for the Australian police and one identified Misper for our guys. Shame Terry isn't here to celebrate.' She took a long vape and, it seemed to Stella, a shadow passed over her face. 'I owe you, Officer Darnell.'

A true reporter, Lucille was interested only in her story. Stella didn't share her excitement. Stella remembered Jack's expression when he told her about Simon. He had been afraid.

'Here we are.' Lucille pulled out another manila folder from the stack on the coffee table. She sat down next to Stella on the sofa and spread a huge sheet of paper across their laps.

Stella's phone rang. Jackie.

'Don't want to alarm you, Stella.'

Stella became alarmed.

'Beverly gave Stanley to a man who came to the office. He said he was Jack's brother and that I'd sent him. Foolish, and she knows it, but apparently he was the spitting image of Jack, so she had no doubts. She did take up his suggestion she call Jack to confirm it, but he didn't answer his phone. If only she'd called me.'

'Jack doesn't have a brother.' Stella was numb.

'I know that. Beverly does too, now. She's distraught. I said it wasn't her fault. I did wonder if it was David?'

When Stella rang off, she couldn't think or speak.

'Read this.' Lucille May tapped the sheet with her e-cigarette.

Stella tried to make sense of tiny printed text within a vast diagram.

Discrete entrances ensure that tenants in either residence rarely meet. Each has the experience of being a sole occupant. An internal staircase utilizes the pre-existing pipe cavity in the central shaft, giving both dwellings access to the roof. There was a signature at the bottom next to a printed name. It was Jack's father's name.

'What is this?' she demanded.

'It's a plan of Palmyra Tower.'

'Jack never said his father was the architect!' Stella couldn't hide a sense of betrayal. She stared at the technical rendition of spiralling staircases, steel supports and intricate pipework.

'Hold your horses! He doesn't know.' Lucille rattled the sheet. 'The first developers were faithful to the original use of the building as a water tower. They hired an engineer – Jack's dad – rather than an architect. He incorporated the pipe cavities into the new design, but when they went bust, he wasn't paid. The poor guy was shafted, he should have known better, but after his wife died I suspect he took what he could get.'

'My dog has been stolen—' Stella stopped, a stolen dog was not a 'cool' story. David hadn't trusted her to hand Stanley back on Friday, he had gone to the office and taken him. Stella let herself breathe. David wouldn't hurt Stanley. 'But Jack's flat is the only one in the tower,' she said instead.

'Oh no, it isn't! No guesses as to who lives downstairs. Call Jack!' Lucille May leapt to her feet, sending the engineering drawing flying up.

'Jack's lost it.' The fluttering in Stella's stomach became a frantic beating of wings.

'He can still talk on the phone.'

'He's lost his phone. I thought he'd found it, but I think—' What did she think? David looked like David Bowie; he was nothing like Jack. Jackie had left the office because she had got a text from Jack saying the window was open. He had not got the wrong house – he hadn't sent the text.

'Simon Carrington's got Jack's phone,' Stella shouted.

'Come on!' Lucille was already in the hall.

'Where are we going?'

'To find your dog and to save Jack!'

Sixty

Tuesday, 29 October 2013

'Come out, come out, wherever you are,' Jack whispered with false bravado.

On the eyot something was moving amongst the bushes and stunted trees. The tide was out, the beach between the eyot and the shore was discernible only by an absence of light. It was like a great chasm.

Jack trained the lens on the brushwood and reed clumps and saw he hadn't been mistaken. Nosing along what, at high tide, was the perimeter of the eyot, he saw a creature. A fox.

Jack slumped back in his chair, his face slick with perspiration. It was past midnight and the wind was strong. It didn't only disrupt humans, it blew birds off course and, stunning them, caused them to 'crash'. Guillemots who lived by the sea would tomorrow be found dead on the streets of London. He raised his binoculars and scoured the beach with them. The creature lacked the prowling fluidity of a fox, it was trotting about with no awareness of a predator. It was Stanley.

Where was Stella? Jack dropped the binoculars, flung on his coat and rushed out of the flat. He leapt recklessly down the spiral staircase and heaved open the lower door.

On the walkway, he was again blasted by the wind: it lashed at him and pushed him centimetres shy of the edge. He inched along, paying the slender rail through his hands like a rope, his skin burned by the ice-cold metal. At last he reached the cage. Wind harassed the grille, shaking it violently.

'Stella!'

His shout was whipped up and away. As he struggled down the stairways, Jack was bounced against the sides of the cage. Stella had come to the tower, but with no means of telling him she was outside, she must have gone away. She had gone to his Garden of the Dead. She had missed her footing and been washed out into the river. A vicious current had pulled her down. Stanley was searching for her. This dreadful narrative could not be true, Jack told himself.

'Stella!'

On Chiswick Mall the wind roared about his ears; it scooped tiny stones and flung them at him. Head down, he slithered down the steps and on to the foreshore. His shoes sank into the mud. He raced along to stop it pulling him down, using rubbish strewn at his feet as crude stepping stones. He knew the terrain; forcing himself to calm down, he found the causeway.

He reached the steep bank of concrete-moulded sandbags and pulled himself up to the path. Without his phone he had no torch. He felt his way over the land, touching the branches, the reeds. At last he arrived at the place where he had seen Stella's pet. The dog wasn't there.

'Stanley? Here, boy.' Stella said that dogs sensed uncertainty; it made them less likely to respond. He lowered his voice and commanded, 'Here, Stanley.'

In his hurry, Jack hadn't brought any food. He had nothing with which to entice the dog. He was overtaken by tingling panic. *Where was Stella?* The river was oily black; he could see nothing.

'Stanley?' The sound was parcelled away by the wind. The St Jude storm had arrived.

He reached the place where Rick Frost had tried to throw Simon Carrington into the river. He had stopped him. Did Simon remember that Jack had saved his life? Jack clambered up the bank into his garden.

The line of white stones had light of their own. To him, disorientated by the storm, the place was strange. The rush of reeds and the scrape and rasp of leafless trees, their branches lashed by the storm, were not the sounds of his garden.

Jack tripped and fell. A remorseless squall tore at his shirt.

'Stella!' he sobbed, kneeling in his Garden of the Dead as if in prayer.

Something pushed at his pocket, and then tugged. He felt a cold snout and, peering down, found Stanley beside him. The dog nuzzled up to him and licked his cheek with a warm tongue.

Jack grasped the dog around the waist. Struggling to his feet, he grabbed at flailing branches. He couldn't go back the same way, he might fall into the river. He risked the inner path where he might meet Simon. He inched forward, feeling for compacted ground that defined the path. He pushed through reeds and brambles and emerged opposite Chiswick Mall. The street lamps were out – there was a power cut. He couldn't see his tower.

The dog was quaking, his woolly coat sodden. He had been in the river. Had Stella tried to save him? Jack lowered the little dog to the ground.

'Go find Stella!' he whispered. Like his mistress, Stanley had a powerful sense of smell. He would lead Jack to her.

Stanley stood at his feet shivering, unclear what Jack wanted from him.

'Go find!' Jack shouted.

A gust of wind hit the dog and he tottered against Jack's legs. He hadn't sniffed a scent. Jack picked him up and the dog burrowed into his neck. Stella couldn't be out there. Jack began a perilous journey across the mud.

Had anyone looked out from a window in one of the houses, their eyes accustomed to the dark, they might have made out two figures, tall and of similar build, wending their way over the mud. An onlooker might have assumed them to be of one party, for their pace was synchronized as if their walk was choreographed. When the man in front paused to locate a stepping stone, the other, twenty yards behind, paused. He moved only when the first man resumed his journey to the shore.

No one was watching.

*

The storm was deafening, wind whistled about his ears, the banging and crashing of loosened casements was underpinned by the relentless thud of a barge smashing against its mooring.

Jack regained the camber and, slipping and sliding over debris chucked up by the river, the wind swirling around him, struggled past St Nicholas' church. A clanging jangled in his head, like discordant bells, although the actual bells were silent. He ducked into the alley and saw he had left the cage door open. It swung back and forth, the clanking resounding in his ears.

In the dark Jack couldn't see his feet. Numb with cold, he was in a dream where limbs are lead and air is water. He chose his moment between the furious slamming of the gate and pushed into the cage, clutching the dog.

On the third stairway, Stanley cocked his head. Jack made it to the platform and looked down. A shadow moved. It was his imagination. There were shifting shapes and shadows everywhere. Nevertheless: 'Who's there?' He couldn't bring himself to say the name, to admit his existence.

You denied you knew me. Three times.

A splitting tore the air. One of the rivets on the cage sheared. The structure was adrift from the wall. Jack ran up the last two stairways and flung himself on to the metal walkway.

Time telescoped twenty-six years to the night in 1987 when the man had been trapped in this tower. Scared and alone, his voice drowned by the roar of the wind. Jack imagined that the wind he heard now was a scream of terror. He pressed his back to the cold concrete as the walkway lurched like the deck of a ship pitching on stormy waters.

London was chaotic. The storm battered trees and tore up fences, tossing them like kindling. On King Street, a 27 bus rocked and tilted against a shop front, wheels a metre from the road, a ship on a reef. On Hammersmith Broadway, a lorry slewed into a railing and coarse sand spilled over the road. Cars and houses were crushed by branches and blocks of masonry. No planes flew in the sky; no trains travelled along tracks engulfed by soil when embankments gave way. Drains blocked and roads flooded. Power lines came down.

Jack saw there was no point in turning the clock back. Wherever it stopped, someone would die.

You denied you knew me. Three times.

His tower had survived over seventy years; it would withstand the storm. He pushed his way inside the little lobby. Simon couldn't reach him here. He held tight to Stanley and navigated the spiral stairs. He whispered to the trembling animal:

'This is the house that Jack built.
This is the malt
That lay in the house that Jack built.'

Jack placed Stanley on his bed. The dog's saturated fur soaked into the duvet and a damp patch spread around him. Streaks of mud flattened his whiskers and plastered down his chest. He was a scrap of a thing, his button-brown eyes wide with fear. Intermittently he was gripped by an immense shiver; like a Mexican wave it travelled from his head to his toes. Stella said it was threatening to stare at dogs so, affecting nonchalance, Jack sauntered into the kitchen and filled his cereal bowl with water.

He studied the meagre contents of his fridge for something Stanley might like. There was a lump of stale cheddar on the top shelf. Jack felt shame he had so little to offer. Stella would want him to feed Stanley. His throat caught: he was thinking as if she would never come back. He pulled himself together and pared off the hard rind and the top of the cheese and cut it up. Cupping the cubes in his palm, he returned to the front room.

'Here you are, Stan—'

Stanley was beside the bed, sitting bolt upright. Jack chucked him a bit of cheese and resumed his rhyme.

'This is the rat,
That ate the malt
That lay in the house that Jack built.'

Stanley didn't move.

'Yeah, good boy, no reason you should trust me.' Jack tried a bright tone. The dog was circumspect. Like his mistress.

'This is the cat,
That killed the rat,
That ate the malt
That lay in the house that Jack built.'

He tossed a cube of cheese a little closer to the dog. Stanley looked at the cheese and then at the partition wall as if choosing between them. Jack threw another cube, further away from him this time. The dog looked at the wall. The dead man had been found on the other side of the room, by the door. Why was Stanley here?

The dog began to dig furiously at the partition wall as he had on the boards where the body was found. The animal was distressed; he was missing Stella. Confounded by the wind, he had confused the wall with the door. Jack couldn't make it better – he too missed Stella. He should not have come up here; he should have gone to the police.

Jack squatted down to see what Stanley was fixated by. A line had been drawn, straight as if with a ruler, but it was so faint that, if it weren't for the dog's fuss, he wouldn't have seen it. It did a right-angle turn and went vertically up the wall and stopped centimetres above his head. It continued horizontally a metre and came down again. It was the outline of a doorway.

Jack strode around the partition wall to the kitchenette. The wall came out in a 'v', about sixty centimetres at its widest point. Diverted by the curving walls, Jack hadn't noticed that the wall was on a slant.

Jack had always wanted to live in a panopticon like Jeremy Bentham's nineteenth-century concept: a tower that observed prisoners from behind slatted windows. The prisoner could never be sure how many officers were up there. There need be none.

Thinking they were being observed, the prisoners, Bentham believed, would behave.

When pipes hissed or the sink glugged or his internet connection switched to a router labelled CBruno, Jack had found explanations for the anomalies. 'How Soon Is Now?' was only his mind soothing him, as his mother used to do. Simon had sent him signs, clues and messages, but, intent on keeping watch on the city, Jack had dismissed them.

Simon didn't want to be his friend any more. Of all the places Jack could be, the tower felt the least safe.

Stanley shrank away from the wall. Jack picked him up. Cold air drifted into the room. The line was a crack. The crack was widening. Jack heard a whisper:

'This is the dog,
That worried the cat,
That killed the rat,
That ate the malt
That lay in the house that Jack built.'

Sixty-One

Tuesday, 29 October 2013

'Come on, Stella.' Lucie May was wrestling into a red woolly coat that covered her like a tent. She wound a yellow scarf around her face, muffling her voice. 'Would you mind doing the driving? I never learnt.' She asked as if Stella had an option.

Outside the storm was wild. Wind hit the windows and roared about their ears. As soon as Lucie was in the van, Stella accelerated away from the kerb. The passenger door swung out.

'Steady on, Officer Darnell. If we are the cavalry, can we at least stay on our damned horse!'

Neither woman spoke as, keeping to the speed limit, Stella drove through deserted streets, littered with smashed fascias, glass, sheets of roof felting, tiles and branches. The wind rocked the van as if it was being attacked by an angry crowd.

On King Street, Stella swerved to avoid a car's exhaust pipe and slammed into a recycling bin, dragging it several metres under her fender. Jack was in the tower believing he was safe from Simon, but instead he was a lamb to the slaughter. Simon had taken Stanley.

Overwhelmed by a hopelessness that was unfamiliar to her, Stella drove under Hammersmith flyover and on to the Great West Road. Her phone lit up with a text.

'What does it say?' she shouted at Lucie.

Lucie fished her glasses out from a voluminous leather handbag, taking a maddeningly long time to extract them from the case and fit them on to her face. She extracted the phone from the dash-board cradle and frowned at the screen.

'It's from Jack!'

‘What does it say?’ Stella yelled, her foot squeezed the accelerator pedal.

‘*The cock has crowed*. Oh Lordy-lou, that boy!’

‘What does that mean?’ For once Stella was inclined to agree with Lucie about Jack.

‘No idea. Does he have a pet hen?’

‘He has an owl – no, that’s a door knocker.’

‘You’re worrying me, darling.’

‘Is it in the Bible?’ Stella didn’t know where her question had come from.

‘Damn right! It’s the Last Supper. Jesus says that Peter will disown him three times, before or after the cock crowed, can’t remember. Anyway, Peter’s adamant he won’t betray Jesus, but he does. Three times!’

‘Jack wouldn’t betray anyone.’

‘Jack refused to be Carrington’s friend. I think in this scenario, Carrington is Jesus.’ Lucie May pulled her scarf away from her mouth. ‘We’re dealing with a madman!’

‘Simon sent this text. He’s got Jack’s phone!’ She smacked the dashboard. It occurred to her that Jack put a kiss after a message and this one had no kiss. She berated herself for dwelling on irrelevant detail while missing the key issue. Simon Carrington had Jack’s phone. What would he do next?

She signalled left into Church Street, bumping the van over debris strewn over the road from bin bags and chucked up from the riverbed, and braked opposite the passage to the tower. She tried to open the van door. It was stuck.

‘It’s the force of the storm.’ Lucie made no move to get out. ‘Do a three-point turn so we’re facing the other way.’

‘That’s ridiculous!’ Stella pushed harder and opened the door five centimetres, then stuck her arm into the gap to stop it closing. Excruciating pain took her breath away. She was caught in a giant vice. She pushed with all her might and managed to release her arm.

Lucie was puffing placidly on her e-cigarette. Giving in, Stella started the engine and did what amounted to a ten-point turn, revving the engine and stamping on the brake.

With the wind blowing against the back of the van, the door was snatched from Stella's grasp when she opened it. They both clambered out of the van easily, sheltered from the gale by the bonnet. Only then did Stella notice Lucie's shoes. Slip-on pink high heels.

'You can't wear those, you'll fall,' she shouted against the wind.

Lucie delved into the huge handbag and produced a pair of pink Hunters. Leaning on Stella's arm, she hopped about on each foot and swapped her high heels for the boots.

Stella pulled her phone out of her pocket, looking in vain for a text – any sign – from Jack. All she saw was a pair of staring eyes at the top of the screen.

Stalker Boy.

Who was watching her?

Stella stepped out of the shelter of the van, and a powerful rush of wind felt as if it would rip her hair from her scalp. She reached up to pull up her hood and saw the tower.

Someone was on the roof.

'JACK!' she yelled. She tried to point him out to Lucie, but the journalist had crossed the road and was stomping off down the passage.

The cage door crashed open and then shut, harassed by the wind. Above the clamour of the storm, Stella heard a high-pitched humming as if some choir was singing. It was the wind whistling through the grille. She wrenched open the door. Her little finger bent back; distantly she registered that it might be broken. She hustled Lucie into the cage and on to the first stairway. As they climbed, the frame shook, the force of the wind increasing with each step. Fixed on Lucie a few steps above her, Stella had no sense of making headway.

Lucie staggered on to the walkway and leant recklessly on the flimsy guard rail. All that stood between her and a plummet of several hundred metres was a length of rusting iron. Stella waved at her to come away, but Lucie was shouting and gesturing. Stella turned and saw what she was pointing at. In a freak lull in the storm, she heard Lucie: 'Rivets. Gone! If rest go, it's curtains!' Her telegrammatic words rang out above the wind.

As if to illustrate this, the frame swayed out from the wall: another rivet had snapped. The walkway shook. Stella took Lucie's hand and lunged at the door. Already open, it gave way and they fell inside, stumbling at the foot of the spiral staircase. Lucie shut the door.

In the sudden quiet, Stella heard music. She recognized the Smiths.

'I never could bear that band. Enough to send you back to take a jump.' Lucie stuffed her cigarette in her coat pocket and clutched her handbag.

'It's Jack's favourite,' Stella said.

'Get away!'

'It's a sign.' Stella clattered up the staircase, shouting, 'Jack, it's me, Stella!' Her words reverberated against the concrete wall. 'And Lucie.'

Jack's flat door was closed.

'He's on the roof.' Stella continued up the staircase.

'We're coming!' Lucie's tone implied she was playing hide and seek.

At the top of the spiral staircase was a flat ceiling in which was a glass hatch of a metre square. Stella stretched up to slide the bolts. It was open. Of course it was – Jack was up there – but why shut the skylight?

Stella slammed her hands against the glass, but it didn't shift. She pushed harder but it made no difference – she lacked the strength to lift it; the glass alone must weigh thirty kilos.

Stella went up to the penultimate step, until she was so close to the skylight that she had to crouch. She flattened herself against the curving glass, her feet either side of the stair, grasped the handrails and, pushing, manoeuvred herself to half standing. The hatch didn't shift.

'Wait!' Lucie inserted herself into the gap between the top step and the skylight above Stella. She raised her hands above her head and splayed her fingers on the section of glass beside Stella's back. 'Say "when"!' she gasped.

'One, two, three. Push!'

Stella and Lucie began to straighten their bodies, the action like two levers. There was the crack as the rubber seals parted and the frame lifted a centimetre, three, five centimetres. It stopped.

'Keep going!' Stella spoke through clenched teeth.

'I'm a bloody short arse, that's my lot,' Lucie gasped. She was standing up, her arms were extended to their limit. 'It's down to you, Officer.'

Stella felt the weight increase as the frame went beyond Lucie's reach. A blinding pain shot down her back. She stood on tiptoe and gained a fraction more height; the weight was on the back of her head – her neck must break. She had stopped the lid closing, but lacked the height to raise it further.

She dared not move.

'Move over,' Lucie whispered. Keeping the frame in place, Stella shuffled along. Lucie's pink high heels appeared on the step above her. Forcing herself to ignore the agony, Stella concentrated on them: patent leather, pointy toes, stiletto heels. This was not the time to dress up. Lucie fitted them on and Stella thought of Cinderella, her thought cut off by a bolt of pain like a flame travelling from her head down her spine. The lid was closing.

'Stay with it, Officer,' Lucie spluttered as she eased her foot into the second shoe.

Stella stopped breathing. If she let it drop, she would not be able to lift it again.

'One, two, three!' Lucie raised herself up, standing taller in her shoes, the narrow heels wobbling on the metal tread. Stella gave one last push.

The skylight tipped as the angle activated the pneumatic hinge. The lid stopped when it was vertical. Stella crawled out of the aperture on to the roof. Ahead of her was a garden shed. She blinked, sure she was seeing things.

The wind howled. Across London the air was frantic with a cacophony of alarms: house alarms, car alarms; emergency service sirens whooped. She struggled around the shed. No one was there.

The roof was empty.

Stella strained out over the parapet.

Jack!

Sixty-Two

Tuesday, 29 October 2013

'Stanley!'

An echo – from above or below – in the dark. Jack's perception was skewed.

'Stanley,' he whispered again.

Stanley!

The dog's claws skittered on the iron treads. He was close by. Jack let himself breathe. The air was dank and chill like a tomb. His nerves screamed at him to go back to the safety of his flat. Nowhere was safe.

He put out a hand and felt concrete, cold and crumbling. He shuffled down another step, tip-tapping his shoe, testing for the next one. He was on a spiral staircase. The treads were narrow and steep and the angle of the rail told him it spiralled like a corkscrew.

Humpty Dumpty sat on the wall,
Humpty Dumpty had a great fall.

Simon was inside his mind. The dog had slipped behind him. Even without light, Jack sensed that the animal was hanging back; he too was scared. Jack had no choice but to go on. He must face Simon. He could not deny him again.

The central column in the tower wasn't a key supporting stanchion. It was a shaft, built to carry pipes and give access to the roof. Lucie's article had said Simon studied engineering at university. Simon had outwitted him.

With each step the metal vibrated, accumulating to an insidious thrum. It was the sound he had attributed to the Glove Man's ghost.

Simon had waited until he was asleep and then he'd crept up the shaft, opened the wall beside Jack's bed and entered his flat. The tower was no refuge. Like Icarus, Jack would pay for his hubris.

Faint light spilled through slits in the concrete. Inside his flat there were slits high up in the partition wall and in the kitchen. Jack had believed that they provided a free flow of air between the two rooms but there was no door between the spaces, so air could flow without vents. Drunk with the power of living in the watch tower commanding a view of London, he had made basic engineering errors. He had ignored Simon's signs. His wings were aflame.

The meagre light increased with each step. Nerves electric, Jack paused. Should he go up or down?

You choose!

He detected a change in the atmosphere. The walls whispered, 'Truly I say to you, this very night, before the cock crows, you will deny me three times.'

The dog wasn't behind him. Jack clattered down the steps and found him bunched in the corner of a cramped space, eyes black in light that leaked in from a porthole. Jack gathered the little animal up and folded him into his waistcoat.

The Smiths track filled his head.

Jack had seen the porthole from the outside. It was beyond the reach of the walkway that circled half of the tower. Stupidly he hadn't considered where it was inside the tower. He returned to the staircase.

Running away is no escape if you don't know which direction is 'away'.

He swept his hand over the concrete wall, the rough patina grazing his fingertips, and found a door.

'Good boy.' He whispered Stella's mantra to soothe the dog. 'It's all right,' he breathed into Stanley's ear. A warm tongue slathered his cheek, soothing him instead.

With a click the door swung inwards. The music swelled.

'Hello, Justin. Here I am.'

Sixty-Three

Tuesday, 29 October 2013

Dazed, Jack shifted Stanley on to his shoulder and walked into a semi-circular space. Shapes resolved into a bed, a cupboard, a desk with a chair. It was identical to his flat above.

'I'll tell you a story
About Jack-a-Nory,
And now my story's begun;
I'll tell you another of Jack and his brother,
And now my story is done.'

Jack couldn't see the source of the voice.

'Welcome!' Low laughter.

'You'll frighten the dog.' Jack shouldn't have drawn attention to Stanley.

'Why did you save me from drowning if you wouldn't be my friend?' No laughter now.

'Where is Stella?' Jack demanded. The voice was coming from the corner of the room, which was in shadow. It had broken since he last heard it, but, like eyes, voices don't alter.

'Don't disappoint me with silly questions.'

Outside, the St Jude storm was raging, but in here, but for the Smiths music, it was quiet.

You are trespassing. This is out of bounds.

Jack clasped his forehead with his free hand as a faint throbbing in his temples increased to hammer blows. The words were inside and outside his head.

The light in the room was increasing incrementally, like a sunrise. Shadows dwindled as ambient light washed over the curving concrete walls. There were no windows.

A quarter of a century had passed since Jack had seen Simon. He was wearing a long black coat with a baseball cap low over his eyes. He snatched it off and flung it on the bed. His face was smooth as if experience hadn't touched him. But for this, Jack was looking at a version of himself. Simon flicked his fringe from his forehead in the manner of Jack.

'I've called the police. They'll be here soon,' Jack said.

He distinguished pictures on the partition wall behind the bed. As the light brightened, he made out close-ups of men and women. Their faces were different, varying hairstyles and ages, black, Asian, white, but each had the impassive expression Jack knew from those waiting on platforms when he pulled into stations. Their unregistering gaze, like that of the dead, would slide over him as he brought his train to a stop. The faces on the wall were his passengers. There was the man with large ears and wispy hair, and the jittery woman in her forties who he suspected was a drinker. She stood on the same spot at Ravenscourt Park station every evening. The young woman so like his mother that Jack could believe she had returned from the dead. And the woman at Ealing Broadway station the night his train broke down.

The end photograph was not a face. Silver tracks glinted in the headlamps of an approaching train. Just visible, insubstantial as a ghost, was the driver. Jack recognized himself.

'Silly Justin.' With a half-finger, Simon waved something at him. Thinking it was a weapon, Jack stepped back against the wall. The door had shut. There was no handle. Simon didn't have a gun. He was holding Jack's mobile phone.

'The Cleaner is here. Redoubtable, isn't she! We did have a nice chat on the station while she did her best to hide her fear. Yes, I was the "inspector" at Stamford Brook station. I'm disappointed it took you so long to work that out.'

'What were you doing there?'

'Another silly question. Where you go, I go. *Justin*. Thanks to the handy little "stalker" app on Rick Frost's phone. He was quite clever, all said and done, you know!' He tugged on his half finger and continued.

'But for the soundproofing, you'd hear the Cleaner and the Reporter blundering about on the roof. They think you've jumped. Poor Justin, his past caught up with him and, unable to bear the shame, he jumped. The Reporter will relish writing that.'

'They won't think that. There's no body.'

'By the time they ask themselves that question, it will be too late. They'll find your body soon enough.'

Jack had never been alone in his tower. Simon had been there. Simon was the man on the bus outside Stamford Brook station; he was the man on Hammersmith Bridge. Simon had delivered the fliers about the tower through his door. He was the man in the crowd.

Jack had been Simon's Host. He hadn't read the signs.

'More disappointment, I thought you'd read them sooner.' Simon spoke soothingly, as if he could follow his thoughts.

Into Jack's mind came the thought that if his own mother had lived, he might have wanted Simon as his friend. But had she lived, he wouldn't have been sent away to school and he wouldn't have met Simon.

'You betrayed me.' Simon spoke in a kindly tone. 'More than three times, you denied you knew me. What did Mr Wilson teach us? There was a man who didn't practise what he preached. By now the Cleaner and the Reporter will have worked it out, but I hoped you'd get there before them. You recognized his Timex watch. I supposed it would be plain sailing for you after that.'

'Mr Wilson was the man trapped in the tower.' Jack nodded as he got it. He had recognized the Timex watch. Stanley tensed; he stroked him. 'You were the one who shut the door on him.'

'At last!' Simon tossed Jack's phone back and forth between his hands. 'Mr Wilson was the only person who bothered with me. He found me in the basement after you locked me in that last time at school.'

'So why kill him?'

'He betrayed me, like everyone else. Like you did, Justin.'

'You killed him because he betrayed you?'

'Do you consider betrayal a minor transgression? Your Cleaner puts a high price on loyalty. That was one thing in her favour. You and she are haphazard detectives, but you get there in the end! Shame for you it is the end.'

'So why Mr Wilson?' Jack asked again.

'My mother, the lovely Madeleine, met Wilson when she was on a business trip to Australia. She left me for a month to go to a banking conference in Sydney. She was at the conference all right but, as my dad in one of his rather cruder moods once shouted at her, she did less banking than bonking!' Simon raised his eyebrows. 'She met Wilson in a bar. He did his disappearing act and followed her over here. That man took my mother away from me.' He smiled brightly. 'Mr Wilson had to pay for his sins.'

'So you killed him?' Jack repeated.

'Call it the wrath of God. A week after the hurricane, I went back to the tower to warn him to stay away from her, intending that he'd have learnt his lesson. He was on the floor by the door, stiff and cold and dead.'

'The post-mortem thought it likely that Wilson had a heart attack.' Jack had thought the sketch of Glove Man on the Missing Persons' site was familiar. He had assumed it was because he saw so many faces, some of which were on the wall before him. The main reason he had dismissed it was because he had blotted out that time at school. He had blotted out Simon.

'Your mother may be dead, Justin, but it's no excuse for cruelty. Simon tried to care for you. He only wanted to be your friend. Now you have no friends.' The man tapped the Bible. 'One day you'll understand what you have done. God watches over us all.'

'I shut the door on him.' Simon tapped his lips with Jack's phone. 'I killed him just as that train driver you bought coffee for the other day killed the Captain. It should have been me standing him a cup of coffee. I have much to thank him for. He was my amanuensis. The Captain knew his day had come.'

Jack had sensed a presence on the balcony overlooking Earl's Court station. He should have trusted his instinct that he was being watched. Simon had been there.

'Mr Wilson thought my mother was joking. When he realized he was trapped in the tower, he called her names, he shouted unforgivable things about her and about me. When I got outside, the hurricane was raging. I had to go – it was dangerous to be out.'

'Where is Nicola Barwick?' Jack interrupted him.

'In good time, Justin.' Simon ran a coin over his fingers, tumbling it over the top of his hand, his half-finger bobbing. At school, Simon had done it to impress him; Jack knew he was doing it now to mark time.

'Tell me my nickname at school?' Simon said.

'Stumpy.' Jack had made it up.

Simon flicked the pen into the air, caught it and continued his trick. His hand resembled a giant insect. The boys had called the teacher a stick insect. Jack's past was flooding back.

Stanley struggled to be let down. Jack lowered him to the ground and he ran across to the bed, leapt upon it and settled down. So much for dogs sensing danger. Perhaps that was exactly what Stanley had done: he had gone to Simon, the little boy who had only tried to help and was lonely.

'You have known what it's like to be shunned. To see people's eyes glaze over, that flash of disappointment, even panic, when they hear you're on their football team. They tell you a chair is taken when you try to sit down – all the empty chairs in the class are taken. You were my blood brother, but you did nothing. You told me my mother didn't love me.'

'I was unhappy. No one wanted to talk to a boy touched by death.' Jack had had blackness in his soul. Mr Wilson had intoned:

'*And then if anyone says to you, "Look, here is the Christ!" or, "Look there he is!" do not believe it. False Christs and false prophets will arise and show signs and wonders, to lead astray, if possible, the elect.'*

'I don't have friends,' Jack said. Stella and Jackie invited him to their houses. Clean Slate's cleaning team and Beverly in the office had bought a cake in the shape of an engine on his birthday. Dariusz in the mini-mart beneath the office and Cheryl in the dry cleaner's checked he had eaten recently. There was Lucie May and, before Dale turned up, there had been Suzie. Isabel Ramsay was commemorated in his Garden of the Dead. He did have friends.

> *Then Jesus said to the chief priests and captains of the temple and elders, who had come out against him, 'Have you come out as against a robber, with swords and clubs? When I was with you day after day in the temple, you did not lay hands on me. But this is your hour, and the power of darkness.'*

Jack rubbed at his forehead to stop the voice.

'Quite a contact list for a man with no friends!' Simon was looking at Jack's phone. 'Hmm, I don't see myself here.'

'I didn't want a friend. I wanted my mum and my toys. I wanted my bedroom and the tree in our garden. I wanted to make tunnels and bridges like my dad. I wanted to go home. I didn't want a friend!' Jack's voice reverberated off the concrete.

'You told the Captain you didn't know me. The cooks called me greedy when I asked for seconds, but you got thirds because your mummy was dead.'

Abruptly the music stopped.

'I am the engineer, not you.' Simon raised his voice. 'It's me that builds bridges and tunnels. You only drive in them and wonder about how long they are. This is my tower, not yours. As you know, the best way to vanquish your enemy is to become him. Look for the person with a mind like your own. All those True Hosts – and for what? Time and time again the Cleaner has to save you from yourself, but not this time.'

'How do you know about the Hosts?'

'Oh, Justin! You can do better than that. You and me, we know how to make ourselves invisible, how to garner facts about those we shadow. You taught me surveillance tactics. You told me that, unless they've done wrong, most people don't think they're being watched. I wanted you to see me, but even when you did, you looked through me and failed to read the signs. You promised the Cleaner to stay in at nights. She's made you soft!'

He tapped at the screen on Jack's phone with his stubby finger. 'Look, the Cleaner's sent you a text. *Stella mob*! Stella mop, perhaps!'

Beware the jokes of those with no sense of humour.

'*Simon is alive. Stay where you are, I'm coming.* She's ahead of you, Justin! So you're happy to be her friend, or would you like to be more than friends? Is that why you hate Dale, the Brand-new Brother? What shall we reply to her? *Too late, he's dead?* or *Leave or the dog dies!* Shall we tell her you have betrayed her? That you were hiding in the house when she was there? They say anger helps assuage grief. My sister should know, although it's guilt at her own betrayal she has to assuage, not grief. She's in with the Captain's brother. She lied to me. She is Wilson's daughter – betrayal's in the blood.'

'Wilson wasn't in a relationship. He was in love with your mother. Who did he betray?'

'Me.' Simon might have been a small boy, his face untouched by the years. 'Really, Justin, did Jesus really die for the likes of all of you?'

'I can't turn the clock back.' But Jack had tried to.

'I have looked for myself inside your head, but I'm not there, am I? I was dead to you.'

'I told you your mother was having an affair with Mr Wilson. I saw them in the car park at school.'

'You weren't being kind, if I remember. You laughed.'

'Yes, I did.' Jack had wanted someone else to have a reason to cry. He had felt a thrill of cruelty as he told the boy that his mummy had kissed the RE teacher.

'Knowledge is power,' Simon said. 'It did at least mean I was no longer in the dark.'

'I was jealous your mother was alive. I wanted you to think she loved Mr Wilson more than you so that you'd be alone like me.' Jack had blotted out this self of his.

'I overheard him asking my mother to come away with him. She went to meet him at Stamford Brook station. I followed her. When he didn't come, she would have assumed he had betrayed her. Until I found him dead in the tower, I did too. When they found him, she must have guessed that it was Wilson's body in the tower, but she kept it to herself. She let his family wonder where he was for all those years. His mother died not knowing what happened to him. My mother knew. Perhaps she kidded herself it wasn't his body up there because she never stopped looking out for him. She kept the living-room curtains open at night. She would follow men in the street and then see they were strangers. She knew I didn't believe her lies about where she was. She knew why I was at Stamford Brook that day. She may have suspected I shut that door. We became strangers. I waited for the right time and then I killed her. Just a little push. You see, betrayal is unforgivable.'

'She didn't betray you.' Jack spoke mechanically.

'Only because he didn't come to the station. It's intention that counts. She was going to take my sister because she was his child. She was going to leave me.'

'Did she take bags with her to the station?' Jack asked.

'No, that would have given her away.'

'So she didn't plan to leave you.' Jack snatched at a sliver of hope, but Simon wasn't listening. 'Simon—' Jack saw what he had done to Simon. Not just him – he recognized he was not solely to blame – but he had played his part in changing Simon. It was no excuse that he had been unhappy; he had destroyed Simon's faith in people. Jack wanted to plead, not for his life, but for forgiveness, but it had been too late a long time ago.

'The day I found Mr Wilson lying dead on the floor of the tower, I learnt that if you dislike someone, they don't have to live.'

Simon jumped up. 'Did you get all my signs? I'm Charles Bruno and you're Guy Haines. Like Bruno in *Strangers on a Train*, remember I told you? I see loyalty in reciprocity. I do your murder, you do mine.'

'They aren't real. It's a story.' Jack heard his mistake. He could neither placate nor argue with Simon.

'Fiction is a way of being alive. Or dead.' Simon looked about him. 'I wonder if my treacherous mother let her mind drift to those walls in your flat while she had sex with Mr Wilson. Is the concrete stained with her passion?' He faltered briefly.

'Where is Nicola Barwick?' Jack dreaded the answer.

'Nicky tried to be clever, but lucky for me, my sister, thinking only of her own feelings, told me what Nicky had done with her passport. That she had betrayed me. Up until then, I had still hoped she was my friend.'

'Where is she?' Jack pushed past Simon into a kitchen the same as the one in his own flat. A train was on the window sill, set on top of stones and strands of twine. A pair of binoculars sat on the table by the 'Hammersmith Bridge' window. Simon had replicated everything. He had known what Jack was thinking because he had a mind like his own. He could follow him in all senses of the word.

Simon slid back the partition panel to the shower room and went inside. Gingerly, sensing a trap, Jack stayed in the doorway.

'Nicola Barwick, this is John Justin Harmon.'

A woman was seated on a chair by the partition. Long hair straggling down her shoulders, she was dressed in a loose-fitting fleece jacket and jeans. She had the dull-eyed look of the passengers' faces in the other room. Jack could see no gag, no ropes restricting her, but she seemed unable to move.

'Are you alright?' He heard how lame his question was. He recognized her. 'You were on my train, the one that broke down at Ealing Broadway last month,' he said. 'You got off before I cleared it.' Her face was one of the pictures.

'I thought you were *him*.' She was matter of fact.

Jack stepped towards her.

'Don't come closer or he will kill us all.' She didn't move.

Jack saw that Nicola wasn't alone. A woman sat on a stool in the shower cubicle, as if entombed in a huge glass case. Unlike Barwick, she was dressed smartly in black bootleg trousers tucked into knee-high leather boots, with a wool jacket over an ironed shirt. She too wore no gag and wasn't visibly restricted. Simon entered people's minds; he had no need of physical fetters.

'She's right.' Simon paced about Nicola as he might an exhibit. 'Nicky only pretended to be my friend. She left her house without telling me where she was going. Friends don't do that.'

'My mother will call the police. I'm due there to cook her supper. My brothers will come looking.' The woman in the shower cubicle spoke with authority. Jack felt a frisson of reassurance that vanished as quickly as it had come. Her threats were impotent: Simon didn't care.

'I *was* your friend.' Nicola Barwick sounded weary as if she had repeated this many times. 'Until you made Richard climb up here. He was a cruel boy and he became an unkind man. But you have become worse. You took revenge on him and on all those around you. He even married your sister because he was frightened you would report him for murder. You took over his company and threatened to bankrupt him. He lived in fear of you. In the end he went to William for help, but you were there first.'

'Running away is no escape if you don't know which direction is "away".' Simon laughed. 'We know that, don't we, Justin! He married my sister because he thought it was the best way to hurt me. He wasn't frightened of me, he wanted to destroy me.'

'Are you Liz?' Jack asked the woman in the shower. She nodded.

'Liz was my friend too until she started talking to the Cleaner,' Simon explained. 'She broke her promise. She told her about me.'

'I only promised not to tell anyone about where Nicola was!' Liz's voice trembled, and Jack saw that, behind the bravura, she was frightened. There was nothing he could do; Simon had planned it meticulously. In a locked tower, there was no way out. Or in.

'Did you call him Justin?' Jack asked Liz, remembering something Stella had said. Another missed sign.

'He said his name was Justin Venus.' She spat out the words.

'That's my grandfather.' Jack exclaimed. Simon knew everything.

'Come on, Justin.' Simon beckoned with his half-finger. 'You two will be OK here, I've shut the windows to keep out the storm so you won't hear a thing.' He gave a low laugh. 'Nor will you be heard.'

'The police are on their way,' Jack said stoutly, but his tone lacked conviction.

'This is how it is.' Simon addressed them all. 'The Reporter and the Cleaner are here. The Cleaner spotted me on the roof so they have gone up there and now they can't get down. They will be shouting, but in this wind… it's a pity, but no one will hear them. Today, or rather yesterday, since it's after midnight, was St Jude's feast day, so the gods have named this storm after him. Mr Wilson told us that St Jude carried the image of Christ. Some think St Jude the brother of Christ. We were blood brothers, weren't we, Justin? Or shall I call you Jude!'

Jack heard the prattling small boy, eager to cheer him up, whom he had put out of his mind. Nicola Barwick had liked Simon. That boy had gone.

Returning to the front room, Simon lifted Stanley from the truckle bed. Jack expected him to attack Simon, but he nestled on his shoulder. There was a flash of silver; Simon had a knife. He opened the door. They were at the foot of the spiral staircase that led up to Jack's flat.

'Stella!' Jack yelled. This was his only chance.

The silence was profound. No Smiths, no sink noise, no storm. The soundproofing was effective.

'Effective soundproofing.' Simon pulled open the door and a powerful gust of wind hit them, bringing with it the cloying odour of river mud.

'After you, *Guy*!' Still holding Stanley, Simon stepped out on to the walkway and, his bad hand clasping the knife, he said, 'Come with me.'

For the first time in his life, Jack did as Simon said.

In sudden squalls, freezing rain hit them from every direction. Soon, despite his coat, Jack was soaked through. Simon was walking ahead of him over the causeway to the eyot. He never looked to see if Jack was behind him. He had slung Stanley over his shoulder and, in occasional gleams of light, Jack saw Stanley's eyes watching him; like Liz Hunter's they showed fear. The dog wasn't fickle, he was playing it safe; his gaze willed Jack to do the same.

The tide was out, but already, beneath the wailing and moaning of the wind, Jack heard the trickling of water filling miniature creeks and gullies in between debris on the beach. Pools were spreading and joining up.

Jack saw that Simon walked with no hesitation. Not once did he stumble; like Jack he must know every stone, every jutting slab of concrete embedded in the mud. Adroitly he avoided the viscous mud that, like shifting sands, threatened to pull them below the glistening surface.

Jack couldn't think of escaping because Simon would read his mind and stop him.

On the eyot, Simon stopped and, shining his torch into Jack's face, said, 'You're the Captain, you lead the way.'

Obediently Jack took them along his hidden path deeper into the undergrowth. Jack tried to keep his mind blank, to keep Simon out. He forced himself to think of the calculation of the West Hill Tunnel: 266.66 recurring. Recurring. *Recurring*.

Jack hoped Simon was taking him to Stella. He trod heavily, deliberately snapping branches and reeds to warn her of their approach.

'The Cleaner won't hear you,' Simon said.

They arrived in his Garden of the Dead, out of sight of Chiswick Mall and of the tower, and hidden by a screen of reeds and willow fronds from any boats on the Thames. Jack couldn't see Stella.

Simon's voice broke into his thoughts: 'I've done my murder. Now it's your turn.'

They were standing by the gap in the reeds where, nearly thirty years before, Jack had stopped Rick Frost – the Captain – from pushing Simon into the Thames. Below, the river raced on: oily, turbid, toxic; the rain shattered reflections to nothing. Were he to fall, within seconds the current would drag him down. Shocked by the icy cold, Jack knew he would not struggle. Simon would watch until the black water closed over him, then he would walk away.

Sixty-Four

Tuesday, 29 October 2013

The perimeter wall was chest-high with no footholds. Stella couldn't see directly down without clambering on to the edge. She peered into the darkness. The triumph of opening the skylight was long gone. Rapid crosswinds battered the trees and bushes on the eyot. A finger of stony ground leading out from Chiswick Mall was fractured as water rushed over the stones.

'There he is!' Lucie exclaimed.

Jack, hair wild and straggling, his coat billowing, was moving in a zigzag along the fringe of the island. He changed direction, changed again. Whipped up by the wind, the river was rife with conflicting currents, their strength measured by the speed at which wood, scum and rubbish, churned up from the river's bed, streamed past. Waves rolled and crashed, driven by the force of the storm. A sack floated past. Even in the dark and from high up, Stella could see it was a dog, lifeless and bloated.

'Jack!' She waved both arms, but he was too far away and the wind was too loud.

'He's trying to get back, the tide's turning!' Stella yelled to Lucie. Lucie, puffing on her e-cigarette, nodded.

From their vantage point, Stella could see that Jack was going the wrong way. He should continue to the western tip of the island where, although it was shrinking, a scrap of land offered a safer route to Chiswick Mall. He was taking the most obvious way, but already the river was rising.

Something hit Stella in the eye, as hard and sharp as a stone. She wheeled away and rubbed it with her palm. A raindrop. Water thundered down, drops coming from all directions as the wind battered them. In seconds she was soaked. The island was a blur. Hands over her face, she peeped through her fingers.

Jack was picking his way across the stony ridge, but already the end nearest Chiswick Mall was submerged. He could go no further.

'Go back!' Stella jumped up and down, flailing her arms. There was still a path, narrow and already broken, at the other end of the island. Water stung her eyes: she couldn't see him properly. She heard a clap of thunder.

Turning around, she saw that the skylight had slammed shut.

She heard a shout, faint about the roar of the wind. Lucie was scrabbling at the parapet wall.

Stella rushed over and, cupping her hands over her forehead to protect her eyes from the pounding rain, looked to where Lucie was pointing.

At last Jack was making for the far shore of the island. Already the eyot was officially an island, the path was disappearing as the stretch of water widened. Cold rain pelted her head like hail, but Stella didn't put up her hood. She fixed on Jack as he struggled across the ground, flailing at reeds to prevent himself slipping into the river. She could see he wouldn't get to the other path in time. He had left it too late.

'Jack!' Stella yelled. There was more water than land. 'We have to stop him!' she bellowed at Lucie, while aware that they could do nothing.

Jack reached where the beach had been and teetered on the edge of the water. Waves broke around his ankles. He stepped in and began to wade. At first he made good progress, but then he floundered; he held his arms above his head to keep them clear of the water and waded deeper in.

'He should wait,' Lucie bellowed in Stella's ear. 'He should stay where he is.'

Jack pulled his coat tight, the water now up to his waist. He gave into the water and pushed himself along in an awkward upright crawl. He slipped and went up to his neck, then regained his footing.

'Take off your coat!'

Although she guessed what Lucie had said, Stella only heard 'coat'. Jack's coat was like a second skin; he wouldn't take it off. Saturated, it would be hampering him. He went under, came up and, struggling against a current, went under again.

Through the rain, Stella stared at the river. Jack had told her once that he couldn't swim.

Sixty-Five

Tuesday, 29 October 2013

'We need to find some way out. We can't just sit here and do nothing.' Liz Hunter slid back the shower screen and stumbled out on to the metal floor.

'He's locked us in and, as he said, no one will hear us in here. I've been shouting and no one has come. You don't know Simon. He's thought of everything. There is nothing we can do.'

'We can't give up,' Liz protested. 'He's not thought of everything – he hasn't even bothered to tie us up.'

'That's because he knows we can't get out. He let a man die in here and blamed another boy for it. He murdered his brother-in-law and his mother. He's a cold-blooded killer.'

'I'm not prepared just to sit here and wait for him to come back and kill us. What is this hold he has over you, Nicola? Over everyone?' Liz glared at Nicola Barwick sitting stock still on the chair.

'He gets into every corner. Nowhere is safe. Even if we escape, he'll find us.'

'We have to try!' Liz dragged Nicola to her feet. 'That man just got in and it wasn't through the door. Come on, Justin – Simon – will be back any minute.'

They ran through the little kitchen to the main room. Ahead was a door of galvanized metal. Liz Hunter banged and kicked it, making only dull thuds. There was no handle.

Nicola pulled aside a cupboard and examined the wall behind. Nothing. She ran to the bed and, sitting on the floor, pushed it back with her legs. It shifted a few centimetres.

'Here, let me.' Liz joined her. Together, the women pushed the bed several metres out into the room and stared at the exposed partition wall. Liz saw the same hairline cracks that, unknown to her, Jack had seen in his own flat earlier. 'That's it!' She ran against it and fell back nursing her shoulder.

'It must have a secret mechanism.' Nicola got down on her knees and crawled along the skirting.

'Out of the way.' Liz lugged the black swivel chair over and prepared to use it as a battering ram.

'Simon is an engineer, he doesn't work with brute force.'

'He's a killer,' Liz retorted.

'He doesn't use violence, he relies on leverage and coercion. He deals in stress and load bearings.' Nicola had reached the end of the skirting.

'There's money on the floor.' Liz tried to pick up the ten-pence piece lying where the bed had been. 'It's stuck.'

'Try pushing instead of pulling!' Nicola was beside her.

Liz pressed on the coin with the flat of her thumb and, with a rumbling, the wall slid aside.

Two women stepped into the room. One of them, billowing in a bright red coat, had a gun.

'Don't move!' she shouted.

'Stella!' Liz exclaimed.

'Do you know them?' the woman in the huge red coat asked Stella. Water was pooling into the room from their clothes. Liz saw that they were soaking wet. The 'gun' was an electronic cigarette.

'Stella, this is Nicola Barwick,' Liz said.

'Where's Simon Carrington?' the woman in the red coat asked.

'He's gone with your friend, Jack. That was ages ago – he could be back any minute. Stella, I think he was going to—' She couldn't use the word 'kill'.

'This way!' The woman with the cigarette dipped back into the darkness beyond the wall. 'We've found the way out. A shed is not always a shed.'

Stella was stony and unresponsive. Liz knew it was because she had realized that her friend Jack would be dead.

Sixty-Six

Tuesday, 29 October 2013

The tea was warm and sweet, not how Stella liked it, but she didn't care. She pulled the foil blanket tighter around her. The liquid warmed her, but did nothing for the profound numbness that made her feel she was floating above her body. Hazily she hoped she would always feel this way.

Jack wouldn't feel the wind or the rain. He couldn't feel the cold. *Jack*.

If Jack had heard her ask him about Justin Venus from the pay phone before his money ran out, he could have told her it was his grandfather's name. She had seen the headstone herself. Lucie May had known instantly when Liz told her. But then Lucie May made it her business to remember names and faces. Stella was a cleaner.

Stella heard a ping and looked at her phone as if Jack might have texted. It was from Liz Hunter. She had texted an hour earlier, but everything was disrupted by the storm. Liz had opened Rick Frost's letter to Nicola Barwick. Attached was a picture of it: '19 9 13 15 14   19 8 21 20   20 15 23 5 18   4 15 15 18'. If I die, tell the police about Simon.' Unable to reach Stella, Liz had told the man calling himself Justin Venus. The very last person she should have told.

If they had read the letter in the café, Jack would be alive.

'Stella, I'm sorry.' Martin Cashman climbed into the ambulance and sat down on the bed beside her.

'It's OK,' she said because she couldn't say just how much it wasn't OK.

'Lucie May says you're the next of kin,' Cashman said.

Stella was grateful he was being businesslike. She didn't want sympathy. She didn't want to feel anything.

'We're not related.' Stella shook her head. 'Jack doesn't have any living relatives.'

'You can nominate a person who isn't a blood relative as next of kin. Lucie May says Jack Harmon nominated you.'

'How would she know?'

'What doesn't Lucie know!' He smiled briefly.

A cordon of police tape and cars had been set up along the mall. The plastic smacked in the wind. Through the rain, the flashing lights of emergency vehicles were like stars falling. Stella was thinking like Jack. No, she wasn't; no one thought like Jack. Through the open doors Stella could see her van. It was inside the cordon. She had parked it in another life, the one where Jack was alive.

Jack.

'Clean Slate for a fresh start!' Why did they offer that? She didn't want a fresh start. When someone dies, you want the old life back. You want everything to stay the same. A fresh start was like dying all over again.

'Jack.'

'Sorry?' Martin Cashman said.

'Nothing.'

Cashman extracted Stella's empty cup from between her hands.

'What about Jack. Have you found him?' Stella hadn't meant to ask.

'We think so.'

'What do you mean?'

'Stella, I need you to—' He got up, putting his arms out as if she might fall. 'We have found a male, white Cauca—' He stopped, evidently remembering who he was talking to. 'I asked Lucie May, but she says she can't face it. I've seen her at dozens of PMs, but I guess this is different. It's different for you too, but—'

'I'll do it.' Stella got off the bed and jumped down out of the ambulance, the blanket around her like a cape.

Chiswick Mall was impassable: the river covered the camber. Waves, lashed up by the wind, pushed it up the street.

'Where is he?' she asked.

'This way.'

A group of people were huddled on the slipway. In slick black rainwear they looked like crows picking at carrion. Stella was thinking like Jack. He would know the word for a collection of crows.

Jack.

A long black roll of carpet lay at their feet. A body bag, sleek and black and zipped up, looked like rubbish in the storm-littered street.

The first dead person Stella had ever seen was Terry. The strain gone from his face, he had looked better than when she had given him his Christmas aftershave weeks earlier. The next two bodies she saw involved blood. After the third one, Stella had believed herself inured to the sight of death.

Jack.

If she saw him dead, it would be true.

She walked away. The wind roared about her ears. She reached her van and flung open the passenger door.

Lucie May nearly fell out on to the pavement. She kept hold of her tablet, the screen casting a glow over the wet flags.

'You have to come with me!'

Lucie struggled upright.

'I can't do it by myself,' Stella said.

'I told Cashman, I've got to file the story. It's an exclusive with the *Mirror*!'

'Now!' Stella leant in and switched off Lucie's tablet.

'I look a fright, but I suppose he won't...' Lucie patted at her hair.

'Jack won't know!' Stella said.

'No, of course.' Lucie took Stella's arm.

Something grabbed her leg. She lashed out, dislodging it. It happened again; she shook it off and kicked harder.

Lucie was gesticulating. Stella wheeled around, fists ready. A creature cowered by the slipway. Stella stared unbelieving. Then it was rushing to her and swarming around her legs. Stanley was alive and she had nearly killed him.

Stella snatched him up and buried her face in his chest. His coat was damp and matted with mud. He smelled of the river, of dank undergrowth. She sniffed again. Shampoo, washing powder – biological – honey soap… Stanley smelled of Jack.

Martin Cashman escorted them down the slipway. Someone stepped into the lamplight.

'Martin, I'll do it,' Jackie said. 'Jack Harmon was like another son to me.'

'Thank you.' Martin began to lead her to the 'roll of carpet'.

Jack had been there for her dad's funeral. He had stopped her from driving away before it began. If it were Stella in a zip-up bag on a wet pavement in the dead of night, he would see she came to no harm. Jack would insist that if someone had to identify her – to see her dead – it should be him.

'Let me.' Stanley on her shoulder, Stella strode down the ramp. A man introduced himself. She heard 'pathologist'.

'Ready?' he asked.

'Yes.' No.

A crumpling of plastic, a zip buzzed. Someone shone a torch above the exposed face, keeping it clear of the body to soften the light.

Stella forced herself to look down. The eyes were shut, the lips so pale the skin hardly showed. A straggle of hair smeared across the forehead. Although effort had been made to clean his face, there were streaks of mud on his cheeks. The bag had been opened to his chest, the hands folded. Stella found she couldn't speak.

'This man has been pronounced dead before, so let's get it right this time, folks!' Lucie May was by her side, around her an aura of steam. 'This is the man who owns that tower over there. He refused to give me an interview.' She nodded at the pale hands. 'That's Simon Carrington. Distinguishing mark? The man has two joints missing on his left middle finger. There's a sister: she can do the formal thing; but one thing I can say, this is *not* Jack Harmon!'

There was a shout from the direction of the river. The rain had abated, but the wind was stronger. There were no lights on the opposite bank. The Thames was in darkness.

A movement. A light moving towards them over the water. The chugging of a motor. Stella made out a boat with two figures hunched at the stern. As it got closer, she saw it was a police launch. Carrying Stanley, she walked down the slipway. She started to run.

The blood pounded in her ears and the dog felt lighter as he moved with her. She waded into the river oblivious to the ice-cold water up to her calves and fell against the boat. Hands pulled at the sides and dragged it up the cobbles.

People were all around her, police and paramedics. Jackie was by her side, Stanley tucked into her neck. The paramedics were lifting something out of the boat. Against the wind, Stella heard Lucie: 'This is Jack Harmon. His middle name is Justin. John Justin Harmon.'

Stella felt her legs go from under her and was supported from each side. Jackie and Martin Cashman held her up.

A shout.

Scrambling, footsteps, an engine revved. Stella was dazzled by headlights from the slipway. She was steered out of the way of two women with a stretcher. Stanley began to bark. Shrill and informative.

John Justin Harmon.

In the glare of the ambulance lights, Stella was aware of Lucie May coming away from the river, talking into her phone. She took Stella's hand and shook it up and down as, speaking into the mouthpiece, she yelled, 'He's breathing!'

Sixty-Seven

Tuesday, 29 October 2013

'So when did Terry find out he had a son?' Stella fixed on the flickering television screen in the 'Relatives' Room'. An old episode of *Dad's Army* was showing; she watched the platoon pass the camera one by one. The volume was down, but – whether it was not quite off or she was imagining it – she could hear the theme tune in her head. The men stumbling across some common made her think of Simon and the Captain, Captain Mainwarings both.

Lucie and Stella had been sitting on the plastic bucket chairs in Charing Cross Hospital for two hours while Jack – who had been in the river, clinging to a clump of reeds and fighting against the current – was treated for hypothermia and a strained arm.

Two hours gave ample time for Lucie May to spill every bean on Terry that she had.

'On the day he came to see you in Hammersmith Hospital, three days after you were born, he'd been on that search for Harry Roberts who killed the policemen.' Lucie sucked on her cigarette even though it was switched off. Her tablet was on her lap. She had been in busy email contact with more than one newspaper, but in the last half an hour there had been a respite. It was then that Stella asked her about Terry. Lucie was the one person she could rely on for the unvarnished truth. Lucie wouldn't restrain herself with concern for Stella's feelings and for this Stella was grateful.

'How did he find out?' Stella didn't need to ask.

'Suzanne told him. He reckoned she was fed up that he had put an armed man before a newborn daughter. To be honest, I'm inclined to agree. He was working around the clock, but all it took was two minutes. Terry wasn't great on multi-tasking unless he'd had a drink and we—'

Stella put up a hand: the unvarnished truth had limits. 'He never told me,' she said.

'He thought you'd be jealous, that if you knew you had a brother you'd assume he loved him more. Terry was always scared you wouldn't love him. Cock-eyed thinking, if you ask me, and I said as much. Dale became the skeleton in your family's cupboard.'

Stella had had enough of skeletons, and cupboards for that matter.

On the television screen, the titles for Hitchcock's *Strangers on a Train* were showing. This reminded Stella of Simon Carrington's train, left at Underground stations and in the cemetery for Jack and her to find. Jack had a copy of the novel on his shelf; it was one of the few he had brought with him to the tower.

Looking at the television, Stella asked, 'Did you love Terry?'

Puffing on her dead cigarette, Lucie concentrated on the screen. 'This is Jack's favourite film.' She reached for the remote and turned up the volume.

'Did you?' Stella repeated.

'Yes, stupid mare that I am, I did.'

Sixty-Eight

Friday, 1 November 2013

Dale and Suzie were on the step when Jack opened the door of Terry's house. Beside them on the path were two enormous suitcases. Dale was holding a picnic hamper. Jack was tempted to find a reason to flee back to the tower, but since Stella had come and collected him from his overnight stay in Charing Cross Hospital she hadn't let him out of her sight. Jackie and Stella had made up a bed for him in what had been Terry's bedroom. Dale had sent over a vat of soup that Jack had to admit was an elixir, its effects instantly curative, not that he'd let it cloud his judgement about the Bounty-hunting Brother.

He'd promised Stella to take her to the airport and mind Stanley while Stella and Suzie went with Dale to the departure gate. Later that day Stella was handing Stanley back to his owner. She hadn't said, but Jack guessed she wanted the dog with her up until the last moment.

Stella also wanted Jack to help with Suzie after Dale had gone and Suzie lost her son for a second time.

'I've brought us a Heffernan starter-pack!' Dale grinned.

Jack caught the smell of freshly baked bread. Stella had told him that while he was staying with Suzie, Dale had treated them both to bagels, dark rye toast and honey, flatbreads with hummus, fruit loaves with sultanas and currants and lashings of butter. Jack could have told Dale that, apart from a cheese sandwich from the mini-mart beneath the office that she forgot to eat, Stella barely touched bread. In a few hours Heffernan was flying home to Sydney, then there would be no more cooking.

The house was as warm and bright as it had been on the evening that Dale had made lamb stew. Jack had filled the cafetière, and a rich smell of dark-roast coffee wafted down the hall. Stella had asked him to lay the table. Now Jack felt a wash of alarm. Heffernan's deadly weapon was his skill in whipping up delicious concoctions – potions – to gain Stella's trust. Against all odds, it had worked.

'Welcome back to the land of the living, Jack. Tuck in!' Heffernan ushered him into his usual seat, facing the kitchen door. 'When I did the cleaning with Stella, I thought that Lulu was weird about the man she'd seen in the street. I couldn't work out if she meant her brother or her husband was with the other woman. Beware of brothers!' Dale handed Jack a plate on which grilled bacon, tomatoes with scrambled egg, garnished with parsley, were tastefully arranged.

Jack had to be alert to protect Stella from her brother's underhand intentions. Australia might be the other side of the world, but the internet wiped out the distance. Money could be wired from London to Sydney in seconds.

'So, Jack, we're lucky to have you, mate! Your old school friend tried to drown you. How come that wasn't in the paper?' Dale asked.

Stella came to the rescue. 'We want Jack working undercover.'

In her syndicated article for the *Mirror*, Lucie May had described Simon's campaign of revenge on his mother's lover, Nathan Wilson, his RE teacher at school. The boy had believed the Australian had only wormed his way into his confidence to reach his beloved mother. As Jack considered this, he thought of Dale and was struck with the idea that history was repeating itself.

As a stand-in for an unloving husband, Simon's role was usurped by the teacher. Over thirty years he had planned careful vengeance on his betrayers. His brother-in-law, Rick Frost, whom Simon still called the Captain, was a long-standing enemy. His sister Tallulah was the love child of his mother and Wilson, but Simon cared for her and protected her. When she began an illicit affair with William, she truly betrayed him. He could convince himself that Rick had married her out of spite and she was 'innocent', but when he found out she was in love with William, he was appalled and could find no refuge. He saw it as a final betrayal: it was tantamount to nullifying him. Nicola Barwick, the third member of the children's gang, sided with Rick Frost against Simon. Simon fell for his sister's unfounded suspicion that Barwick was having an affair with the Captain. From then on, she wasn't safe.

Lucie May hadn't told the story of Simon's obsession with a boy who refused to be his friend and how, growing up, he had adopted Justin's mannerisms and ambitions. How he had spied on him, tracked him through the streets and ultimately got inside his head.

Jack had told no one that Simon hadn't tried to drown him. He had wanted Jack to kill him. He had planned to turn Jack into a murderer like himself. A true blood brother. That would remain his secret.

'Here's a taste of "Sixty-Four" until you all make it there!' Dale's tactic was upfront. It had worked on Suzie; it was working on Stella. Even on Stanley, busy with his helping of scrambled egg.

'Tuck in, guys.' Heffernan handed Jack a mug of hot milk and slid a pot of manuka honey over to him. He gave him a look, a flick of the head, like a private signal. Jack wouldn't be drawn into some joke at the expense of Stella and her mum.

'I'm going to miss our cosy meals around the fire,' Dale said to Suzie.

'Me too.' Suzie was smiling bravely. Jack felt a pang of sorrow. Whatever else, Heffernan was Suzie's son. He couldn't imagine what it would be like to give a son away and then have him come back. Even if he planned to fleece you for all you were worth.

Stella finished and laid her cutlery together. 'I've considered Mum's proposal.' She got up and collected the plates.

Jack gripped the sides of his chair. Stella hadn't talked to him about it – not that it would have made any difference; when Stella decided on something, that was that.

'I can't invest in another business. Two is enough.' Stella carried the plates over to the sink.

Jack nearly shouted with joy.

'I don't want investment, we sorted that,' Dale protested.

'You run one business,' Suzie corrected Stella, her lips pursed.

'I run a cleaning company and…' Stella took a breath, '…a detective agency.'

Jack hadn't expected that. When Stella took a risk, she did it in style. He tried to catch her eye.

'Wow!' Dale broke the silence.

Jack took another croissant and slathered it with honey. Containing his triumph, he detected well-concealed disappointment in Heffernan; Dale would be a practised con man.

'We should be going soon,' Jack said, although they had another half an hour. No one answered. He finished the croissant.

'I've always advised sticking to your core activity,' Suzie reminded Stella.

'I know, but—'

'Detection is what you do.' Suzie folded her napkin. 'You find dirt and wipe it away – you clean up. Clean Slate is turning a healthy profit, but you must reinvest to grow. The company needs to develop. A static company is a shrinking company. It's right to diversify within your core activity.' She poured herself the rest of the coffee and raised her mug. 'To Clean Slate Detectives!'

Jack snatched up a roll and ate it. Suzie, like her daughter, could deal out surprises. Stella would have expected her to argue, to have sound reasons why the idea was a bad one, but she had supported her.

'So, Terry knew he had a son.' Stella nodded to her mother.

The mood in the room dropped.

Terry and Suzie had kept their secret from their daughter. Simon would call it betrayal. Jack smeared the last of the crumbs off his plate. Simon would be right.

Terry had compounded the betrayal by confiding in Lucie May. Apart from Terry, Suzie at least had told no one.

'Terry could have used his position in the police to find you, but he respected the law, so he didn't,' Stella said to Dale.

Dale rolled his shoulders. 'I never came looking for you guys.' Jack could see that his confidence had ebbed.

'Stella, he thought of you as his only child, that's why he left you everything,' said Suzie.

'No, Mum, he didn't think that.' Stella squeezed out detergent into the bowl and snapped on rubber gloves. 'Terry didn't make a will, so as his only surviving heir, in the eyes of the law, I inherited everything. This place has never felt mine. I didn't work to get it.' Stella rinsed the plates under the tap.

'Terry worked so you could have it,' Suzie said. Jack had never heard her speak in such a conciliatory way about Terry before. It must be the 'Dale effect'.

'Terry would have been there at the airport to meet you. I gather he considered a trip to Australia, but couldn't get insurance because of his heart,' Stella added. Jack guessed Lucie May had told her. It seemed she had told Stella a lot of things. He thought he was pleased.

Suzie threw down her napkin. 'Are you saying Terry knew about his heart?'

'Terry knew a lot of things he kept to himself.' Stella turned to Dale. 'Terry liked good plain food and after Mum left he lived on ready meals. He would have liked your lamb stew, providing you ditched the garlic.' She gave a quick smile and stacked the plates on the dish rack. Jack saw that Terry's bowl and spoon and cup had gone. 'If Terry had met you, he would have put you in his will,' she added.

'You don't know that, Stella.' Suzie was fierce.

'I do.' Stella repacked the hamper. Everyone sat back as she wiped the table. She turned to Dale. 'Half of this house is yours.'

For Jack, what happened next was a blur. There was a knock at the door. No one moved to answer it. Stanley started barking and ran down the passage. Jack went with him. There was a taxi at the gate and a man was on the path, already walking away. He turned around and Jack saw him like an identikit: pronounced cheek-bones, glittering eyes, an elegant green serge suit. He was a double of David Bowie.

He was Stella's ex and he had come to get his dog. Jack guessed this wouldn't have been the arrangement or Stella would have told them. The man must have broken their agreement. With these thoughts whizzing through his mind, Jack forgot about Stanley until the dog whisked through his legs and leapt at David Bowie.

'Good boy!' David – that was his actual name – crouched down and buried his face in the dog's coat. Jack conceded that the man had a right to the dog's enthusiastic greeting. Stanley was his dog.

He was distracted by another black cab pulling up behind the one that had brought 'David Bowie'.

'Fare for Heathrow?' the driver called through the cab's open window.

Jack spread his hands in apology. 'We don't need a taxi.' Who had called him?

'Please give Stella this letter.' The 'David Bowie' ex thrust Stanley into Jack's arms. 'Tell her she can keep him. He's hers now.'

'It's for me.' Dale was on the doorstep.

The man called David was in the first taxi and being driven away before Jack found he was holding an envelope as well as Stanley. He stuffed the envelope in his pocket and held on to Stanley tightly.

'Stella's taking you to the airport,' he reminded Dale. 'We all are.'

'Change of plan. I hate goodbyes, I get choked. Do me a favour, Jack, help me with this stuff.' Dale heaved two suitcases and a carrier bag out on to the path. He left the carrier bag on the path and struggled down to the taxi with the cases. The driver came to meet him.

Jack grabbed the bag and, still holding Stanley, went after him. Vaguely he noticed it was the bag Suzie had arrived with.

Dale climbed into the taxi. 'The girls think I'm in the bathroom.'

'I don't like goodbyes either,' Jack heard himself say.

'I thought you'd get it. I kept trying to catch your eye to let you in on it, but you were eating for all of us!'

'They'll be upset that you've gone.'

'Listen, Jack, I have a sister in Sydney and if some joker rocked up claiming to be her brother, I'd give him the evil eye. You are right to be wary of me.' He was seated in the back of the cab. 'I wanted to meet Stella, my biological sister, and see where I might have grown up. It's not great to know you were given away, even if you get the reason, but this way, I might get closure.' He clipped on his safety belt. 'My adoptive parents were happy and I had a great childhood, even though there was no spare cash and the Parramatta Road's not quite as salubrious as this bit of Hammersmith. If I'd stayed here, then I too would have been trundled between two homes like Stella – but at least there would have been two of us. I could have been there for Stella. I mind that.' He shuffled along the seat closer to the window. 'At least Stella's got you.'

'I'm not her brother.' Jack had got it wrong. While he had been thinking of himself, Dale had been thinking of Stella.

'No, mate, you are not!' Dale reached through the open window and grasped Jack's hand in his. 'Tell the world's best cleaner that Old Man Darnell's will must stand as it is. For obvious reasons, she'll listen to you.' He let go of Jack's hand.

'I'll support Stella with whatever she decides.' Jack stepped away from the car, holding tight to Stanley.

'Course you will, Jacko!' He grinned at him. 'Oh, and Jack?'

'What?' Jack heard himself sounding gruff and tried to smile.

'How come you knew exactly where in Sydney I grew up? You said Crows Nest when you met me. You were right on the mark. How could you know that? Did you check me out? Wouldn't blame you if you did.'

'I lived in Sydney once.' Jack looked up at the sky. Clear blue, the storm had gone. 'I moved there in 1988 and lived there for some years until my father got work back in the UK.' His father had worked on a bridge over the Hawksbury River outside Sydney that was never built – typical of most of his projects.

'Fair dinkum!' Dale ramped up his accent. 'What suburb?'

'Crows Nest, then Manly.'

'Good on you, you're an Aussie after all! Get yourself there again and I'll shout you more than a drink! Bring Stella.'

As Jack stepped away from the taxi, he heard the echo of Dale's earlier words. 'What did you mean, "for obvious reasons"?' he asked.

'Jack, for a smart guy, you are one dillbrain around women!' Dale leant forward and tapped on the glass partition. 'We're good,' he called to the driver. The car drew away from the kerb.

St Peter's church clock struck eight.

Jack watched it round the corner into St Peter's Square. *Bring Stella*. He thought again how close Simon had come to making Stella his fourth victim. She had shown him the picture of Simon under the trees at Wormwood Scrubs common. If William hadn't come when he did, Simon would have lured her further in. He had planned to hurt the woman who mattered to Jack more than anyone in the world. Or worse.

'For obvious reasons, she'll listen to you.'

The clock finished striking.

Dale was mistaken. There was no obvious reason why Stella would listen to him.

The first thing he saw when he went back into the house was Dale's album on the stairs. He must have put it by his suitcases and forgotten to pick it up. Jack grabbed it and flung open the front door, but the taxi had long gone.

'Did he get off all right?' Suzie asked. She and Stella were sitting at the table sipping freshly made coffee.

'You knew?' Jack exclaimed.

'I heard him booking it.' Suzie tore a scrap off Dale's last croissant. 'I think he wanted to spare me. I'd said I hated goodbyes.'

'I didn't know that.' Stella pushed a mug of hot milk towards Jack.

'Because it's not true. I *love* them, but when Dale confessed he needed diazepam to make it to his dad's funeral, I guessed that he wouldn't handle us waving him off to his plane! Me, I'm all for waving goodbye, doing a good tidy, then getting back to the old routine!'

'I'll have to go to the airport. He's left this.' Jack laid the album on the table.

'I asked him to hide it in the hall.' Suzie picked it up and, shifting her chair to make room for Stella, she asked her, 'Are you sitting comfortably?'

'I should get to the office.' Stella shot Jack a look; he could guess her thoughts. Dale Heffernan had not entirely gone; he had left them with episode two of his life story.

'Stella Darnell, this is your life!' Suzie handed the album to her daughter.

Stanley on his lap, Jack read the heading over her shoulder. 'Clean Slate: the Story so Far'.

Suzie had pasted the pages with testimonies from clients, before and after photographs of carpets and worktops, the changing logo over the decades. There was Stella in the late nineties, modelling the first uniform. A section headed 'Staff' featured group photos of cleaners, starting with Stella as the only one. Cuttings from trade magazines of Stella at gala ceremonies collecting awards: one for excellence in disaster restoration; several for excellent customer service and low staff turnover. An article by Lucie May described how Stella had built up a cleaning empire single-handed.

'Thanks, Mum.' Stella's voice was thick. 'How did you find all this?'

'I've been collecting it since the beginning. I never thought of making an album!' Suzie shut Dale's breakfast hamper and did up the straps. 'Shows you all that you've done. That's my daughter!' She ate the last bit of croissant.

Stella hefted the hamper out to the hall. Jack caught up with her by the front door.

'I forgot to say, that guy you went out with, who Stanley belongs to?' He heard himself imitating Dale's upward inflection.

'I'm handing him over at two p.m. this afternoon. Actually, Jack, I was going to—'

'He said you could keep him,' Jack finished.

'Until when?'

'Um, well, until he die— Forever. He said he doesn't want him back.'

Stella started to smile. Still smiling she returned to the kitchen. He heard her saying, 'Mum, I'm taking Stanley for a walk, do you fancy coming?'

It wasn't until Jack got out the key to unlock the tower that he found he still had the envelope 'David Bowie' had handed him. He was about to text Stella, but she would be walking Stanley. He was seeing her that evening. He would give it to her then.

Epilogue

Monday, 4 November 2013

Mist hung over the eyot. The tide had ebbed, exposing the causeway. The river flowed fast, the water murky and unforgiving. The beach was dotted with smashed glass, plastic and wood. Last Tuesday morning St Jude's storm had left in its wake a trail of devastation across southern Britain. Four people were dead.

On the eyot a snapped reed, a crushed leaf and one footprint were signs of the route he'd taken with Simon. He paused by the gap in the reeds where Simon had tried to make Jack kill him.

'Why did you save me that time if you wouldn't be my friend?'

'I would save anyone.'

'I'm not anyone.'

'No, you are not.'

'You won't save me this time, Jack. Justin. It's your turn to murder.'

He stared through the gap in the reeds at the rushing water below, thinking that the spangles of sunlight would join up and become Simon's face rising out of the blue-grey water. Right until the end, Jack had refused to do what Simon had wanted. It was his turn to murder and he had refused.

The white stones in his Garden of the Dead glowed in stippled sunlight. Jack took four more stones from his coat and, one by one, added them to the circle.

'Nathan Wilson. Madeleine Carrington. Rick Frost.'

He held the last stone in his palm.

'Simon Carrington,' he whispered as he laid the stone within the circle.

'As I walked by myself,
And I talked to myself,
Myself said unto me:
"Look to thyself,
Take care of thyself,
For nobody cares for thee."'

'What do you call a group of crows?'

'A murder.'

Stella seemed satisfied by his answer, although he doubted she believed him. She held up the front page of the *Chronicle*.

'*Detective's Daughter Does It Again!*'

'We didn't actually solve the case.' She was squatting on the floor in the main room of the tower, where his desk had been. The removers had taken everything back to his parents' house, leaving the space as bare as it was when Mr Wilson had come here with Simon's mother.

Stella spread the *Chronicle* on the floor. She had popped in on her way back from the office.

'We worked it out, but more by luck than ingenuity. We didn't realize it was Simon until he had captured you. We'll have to get better at this business if we're going to offer it as a service. We missed all sorts of clues. Dale saw that Lulu Frost wasn't what she said she was, but I ignored him. He texted Mum and me to say he'd landed safely.'

Jack saw a cloud briefly pass across her face. He suspected Stella of missing her brother.

'We did solve it. We discovered it was murder by suicide. We gave the police new evidence.' Jack was at the north window. He picked up the binoculars from the sill.

'I still don't see why Rick Frost ran when he saw Simon. It can't have been the first time – he was married to his sister after all,' Stella said.

'Remember what Nicola Barwick told us? She hid behind the hut one night when they were kids and overheard Simon telling

Richard Frost that one day he'd punish him. Richard would know when that day came. The boy was in Simon's grip: Simon had his glove and over time his threat gained potency. Rick knew Simon was closing in. Something impelled him to text William and go to see him. He saw Simon in the dark at the end of the platform and panicked. Simon didn't have to do anything. He simply had to be there. Over time he had become a potent threat to Rick, the embodiment of his darker side, the boy who had bullied and humiliated Simon.'

'Martin Cashman said we should have called him in earlier,' Stella said.

'You tried and he said he needed evidence.'

'He said Nicola putting her passport in the bin was evidence.'

'Maybe he should have listened to William Frost when he came to him in the first place. The main thing is we fulfilled William's brief and he's paid us. By hook and by crook we've done our first job. Your staff manual says do what the client wants and no more. We've closed Terry's "Glove Man" case too,' Jack reminded her.

'Clients don't ask us to clean and expect us to guess where.'

'Like we do with cleaning, we'll improve the more crimes we solve.' Jack trained the binoculars on one of the plane trees in St Peter's Square. The St Jude storm had denuded it of leaves. He added, 'Lucie's happy. She might never write that book, but she's done a spread for the *Observer* magazine and been read all over the world. She's back in the mainstream!'

'Lulu still loves Simon, even though he killed her real father and her mother. Simon never appreciated his sister's loyalty,' Stella said.

'Actually I think he did. His mother betrayed him, as did his teacher, and by refusing to be his friend, so did I. It poisoned his soul.' Jack couldn't bring himself to tell Stella the things he had said to Simon when they were boys.

'His mother having an affair wasn't betrayal, she was still his mother,' Stella said.

'She lied to her son. If you can't trust your parents to tell you the truth, whom can you trust?' Too late Jack thought of Terry and Suzie. They hadn't lied to Stella; they had avoided telling her truth.

'Parents don't have to tell their kids everything,' Stella replied.

Jack didn't say that having a brother *was* Stella's business. She had her own way of squaring things.

'Rick Frost looked at me before he jumped off the platform because he recognized me. We had met only once, when we were boys. I never forgot his eyes, hazel flecked with green, without a glimmer of warmth or life in them. That night on the station, they were full of fear. I did forget where I'd seen them before.' *You are trespassing.* He had erased the memory.

'He wasn't a nice man, but he didn't deserve to die.' Stella said. 'What was that about you denying him three times? Lucie said it's in the Bible. I didn't have you down as religious.'

'I learnt early that if you deny something or someone, you can wipe them away. I didn't want things to be the way they were. I didn't want to go away to school and I didn't want Simon to be my friend. By denying he was, I meant him to go away.'

'No reason you should have been Simon's friend. We choose who we like.' Stella was looking at the photographs in the *Chronicle*. Lucie's editor had printed the passport-booth pictures of Simon facing the wrong way. Jack had refused to look at them properly when she had tried to show him. Another sign he had passed up.

'Simon was an engineer. He calculated every stress point, every weakness; he covered every eventuality. When Nicola Barwick slipped through his net, he befriended Liz Hunter. He hadn't reckoned on William bringing us the case, but his plan was like water: regardless of obstacles, it found a path. He had watched me for decades, biding his time.' At walking pace, Jack shifted the binoculars out of the square and up to the church on the corner of Black Lion Lane.

'How could he know where you were?'

'From up here. Simon delivered those fliers; he knew I wouldn't be able to resist the chance to live in a tower, my own panopticon. He organised the removers, he made sure everything was exactly where I would have put it. He knew everything about me. Once I moved here, I became his True Host. Simon had stolen Rick's phone and replaced it with a decoy one for the police to find. William told me Rick had invented an app that tracks wherever you are. Simon stalked you and me. He knew where we were all the time. Chilling thought, isn't it?'

'Yes.'

Jack saw that the idea made Stella uncomfortable. He tried to reassure her. 'Not any more, though.'

He focused on St Peter's Church as the bells chimed five times. He had noticed that when he looked at places through the binoculars, even in the soundproofed tower, he heard the local sounds. He shifted to Terry's house on Rose Gardens North and gave a start.

'There's a massive white pantechnicon outside your dad's house!'

'You're not the only one moving.' Stella wandered out to the kitchen. She called back, 'I'm selling the flat and moving into Terry's. The garden will be good for Stanley.'

'That's great.' Jack was stunned. Stella was giving up her high-security flat with its three mortices and London bar for a house on a street with neighbours. He saw that it was fair that Stella give Dale half of the value of Terry's house, but hadn't expected her to take action so soon – and not this action. While he was retreating to his childhood house – returning to the ghosts – Stella was moving on. He murmured:

'I answered myself,
And said to myself
In the self-same repartee:
"Look to thyself,
Or not look to thyself,
The self-same thing will be."'

It wasn't all about ghosts. He had missed the short-eared owl knocker on his door and wondered if she had missed him.

'Can you see how they're doing?' Stella was back.

'They're going.' Jack put down the binoculars.

'I'll go down.' Stella was zipping up her anorak. 'Listen, I bought sparkling wine to celebrate the end of the case – cases – and that we're keeping Stanley.' She gave Stanley a fishy treat. 'Fancy coming over? I've taken Dale's stew out of the freezer. It just needs a flash in the microwave.'

'I'll do a last check and meet you at the van.' Jack hid his delight.

Stella was on the spiral staircase when he remembered the envelope David had given him.

'I'm sorry! I totally forgot – Dale going put it out of my mind!' Jack hung over the railing and handed the letter to Stella. 'I hope it doesn't matter that it's late.'

Stella took it from him. Seconds later, Jack heard the thud of the main door closing.

She had said '*We're* keeping Stanley'. He stopped himself doing a little skip.

Dear Stella,

When I asked you to mind Stanley, you weren't keen, but you do things properly. You will have cared for him and he will have become attached to you – and I think you to him too, so it is best if you keep him.

I'm going to live far away – somewhere where I won't see a Clean Slate van in the street and feel sad. I would like to say a proper goodbye. I know you hate them, but maybe just this once you might make an exception.

If you are willing, I'll be at Stamford Brook station tomorrow at 3 p.m. Please come without Stanley – I couldn't bear to see him. I'll wait fifteen minutes, then, if you don't come, I'll suppose you didn't want to see me. Here's to a Tabula Rasa!

Love,
David

PS You might want to change Stanley's name because you didn't choose it.

The letter was dated last Friday. By 'tomorrow' he had meant Saturday.

Leading Stanley across the road, Stella walked past her van on down to Chiswick Mall and leant against the railings overlooking the eyot. She folded up the letter and tucked it into her anorak pocket. Once again she reminded herself that 'Mr Right' didn't exist. Her phone beeped. *David.* She snatched it out of her pocket, registering that there were no staring eyes at the top of the screen.

Fancy a drink tonight? x. It was Liz.

When they were young, Liz had sent her letters to suggest they meet. She never rang Stella. She gave her space to decide. Stella had said she was cleaning or had left it a while before replying and then not replied at all. Liz knew what Stella was like. She didn't try to change her.

Can't tonight, tomorrow? You OK? Liz had liked 'Justin Venus'.

Nicola Barwick was moving back into her house in Chiswick. Liz was going to buy Stella's flat in Brentford. Stella had been reluctant to do a deal with a friend, but Liz had persuaded her. The flat was quiet with a view over the river and, with its locks and pass-codes, secure. Liz had said she trusted Stella. Stella's phone pinged again.

See you at the Ram on Black Lion Lane? Yes I am OK, thanks to you, 'tec! Lxx.

Stella shuddered to think what Simon Carrington might have done if he had not drowned before he could make it back to the tower where he had left Liz and Nicola Barwick. Nicola had said that Simon Carrington was once a nice little boy. Stella found that hard to believe.

Jack hadn't told Stella what had happened between him and Carrington on the eyot and she wouldn't ask him. There was a lot about Jack that she didn't know and didn't want to know. When he came down from his tower, she would say that she had been wrong to ask him to promise not to walk in London at night. Jack must walk where and when he liked.

Stella couldn't bring herself to admit to Jack that she had used

Rick Frost's stalking app to locate him. She couldn't bear that she hadn't trusted him.

If Jack asked her why she had changed her mind about him walking at night, she wouldn't be able to explain, except that if she had to make a promise not to clean, she would find it hard to keep.

'You will always be called Stanley,' she told the dog. 'It's who you are.'

Jack put the binoculars back in their case. He would keep them. Simon had given them to him as a present, he wouldn't reject them. He slotted them back into his bag alongside Simon's toy train.

He had lived with the darkness of own unkindness to Simon. Like Rick Frost, he had lived with threat, if vague and amorphous. Even though he had assumed Simon was dead. Simon's death did not lessen the feeling. Jack knew he would always live with the darkness.

Stella was the light. While she could be awkward and insensitive, she would never set out to cause hurt. If someone hurt her, she absorbed it and carried on. She never sought revenge. She hadn't held it against Suzie, or Terry, that they had kept so important a secret from her. She had accepted Dale into her life. Stella did what was right.

He listened. No glugging sink, no vibration on the spiral staircase and no music seeped from the curving grey concrete walls that had witnessed death and silence.

His mind was his own.

The Tower card had turned up in his Tarot reading on his birthday. It was a sign. He had ignored it. Simon had forced him to experience the chaos and destruction that the card might be said to herald. He had made him face the darkness in his soul. The tower – the card and the building itself – had made Jack see himself. To have posted it through his door, Simon must have been inside his house and taken the card from the pack on the hall table. He was a True Host in more ways than one.

Jack returned to the eyot window. Light sparkled on the Thames, the calm before the ebb tide. A plump seagull perched on the tide marker on the eyot. On the beach at the western tip of the island were two figures. A woman, hands on hips, was watching a little boy pushing what looked like a steam engine down a plank of wood into the water. A dart of sunlight dazzled Jack and he blinked. Thinking to get the binoculars, he looked again and saw that, but for the gull preening itself on the tide marker, the beach was deserted.

On Chiswick Mall, Stella and Stanley stood by the railings facing the river.

They were waiting for him.

Acknowledgements

In the course of researching and writing *The Detective's Secret*, many people have been generous with their knowledge, experiences and time.

The help of Frank Pacifico, Test Train Operator for the London Underground, has been invaluable. Although he's nothing like Jack in character, Frank has succeeded in imagining Jack's preoccupations and, as we travelled the District line, he offered me fitting 'driver' observations that enabled me to see through Jack's eyes. Any mistakes or errors regarding detail of the London Underground are mine.

Jack isn't a believer in coincidences, so I wonder what explanation he would have for my finding that the information from brothers of two childhood friends proved to be key to my research. My thanks to them both.

The designer Tom Dixon is the brother of my beloved old friend Vikasini. Tom kindly lent me his water tower and I spent one hot summer morning wandering through it. I looked out at London from the roof and imagined Jack's panopticon. In this novel I have taken the liberty of moving Tom's tower across London from North Kensington and relocating it beside the River Thames at Chiswick.

I grew up in Hammersmith, up the road from Tanya Bocking and her brother Nat. While trawling the internet, I landed on the Water Tower Appreciation Society's website and found that the writer and photographer Nat Bocking is its secretary. I am grateful to Nat for sending me links and a reading list, which included *Water Towers of Britain* by Barry Barton, a fascinating account of their use and construction.

As always, my thanks go to Detective Superintendent Stephen

Cassidy, retired from the Metropolitan Police. Again, any factual errors regarding the police are mine.

Thanks to: Emeritus Professor Jenny Bourne Taylor of the University of Sussex for her recommended reading from the nineteenth century – the spirit of this century haunts this story.

My partner, Melanie Lockett, listens to and gives discerning comments on my unfolding ideas. When words arrive on the page, she is my first reader. Thank you.

Stella's dog Stanley was 'trained' courtesy of Michelle Garvey at Essentially Paws. Any of Stanley's wayward behaviour is my responsibility.

Lisa Holloway, Creative Industries consultant and lecturer, has given me valuable advice.

Thanks to: Tasmin Barnett, Domenica de Rosa, Marianne Dixon (aka Vikasini), Juliet Eve, Hilary Fairclough, Christine Harris, Kay and Nigel Heather and Alysoun Tomkins, who, in varying ways, gave me encouragement along the way.

West Dean College in Chichester was accommodating and supportive during the writing of this novel; my thanks in particular to Rebecca Labram, Francine Norris and Martine McDonagh. Thank you to my agents, Capel and Land. My agent Philippa Brewster is exceptional. Much gratitude goes to Georgina Capel, Rachel Conway and Romily Withington.

Laura Palmer is the best of editors and a joy to work with. Big thanks to all at Head of Zeus, in particular Nic Cheetham, Kaz Harrison, Mathilda Imlah, Clémence Jacquinet, Madeleine O'Shea, Vicki Reed and Becci Sharpe. Once again, my thanks to Jane Robertson and Richenda Todd, who have given the text unremitting scrutiny, proofing and copy-editing respectively.

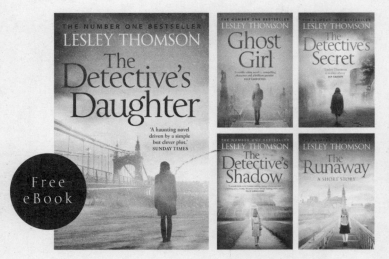